Applied

Mythology

by

Jody Lynn Nye

Meisha Merlin Publishing, Inc
Atlanta, GA

APPLIED MYTHOLOGY

An MM Publishing Book
Published by Meisha Merlin Publishing, Inc.
PO Box 7
Decatur, GA 30031

Editing & interior layout by Stephen Pagel
Copyediting & proofreading by Teddi Stransky

ISBN: Hard cover   1-892065-20-7
          Soft cover   1-892065-21-5

http://www.MeishaMerlin.com

First MM Publishing edition: September 2000
Printed in the United States of America
0 9 8 7 6 5 4 3 2 1

    Library of Congress Cataloging-in-Publication Data

Nye, Jody Lynn, 1957-
    Applied mythology / by Jody Lynn Nye.— 1st MM
    Pub. ed.
        p. cm.
    ISBN 1-892065-20-7 (alk. paper) — ISBN 1-892065-
21-5 (pbk. : alk. paper)
  1. Academic libraries—Fiction. 2. College students—Fiction. 3. Elves—Fiction. I. Title.
    PS3564.Y415 A88 2000
    813'.54—dc21

                                    00-009548

Table of Contents

Introduction	7
Mythology 101	9
Mythology Abroad	271
Higher Mythology	541
Jody Lynn Nye Biography	790
Jody Lynn Nye Bibliography	792
Don Maitz Biography	795

To Bill,
Who believes in me.

An introduction to Jody Lynn Nye

Whimsy is a delicate and dangerous kind of writing to attempt. It requires, not the wild and fancy-free turn of mind you might expect, but iron control and a sure ear for what will work. Those of us who attempt this particular brand of fantasy spend many hours trying to work out whether that next plot twist, that new character or bizarre circumstance you've invented, will break the slender cord suspending the reader's disbelief and dump both of you back into the real world again, bruised to the bone and determined not to let it happen again. To make it work takes a special kind of writer, one skilled at splicing the real world together with the new and unreal one seamlessly enough not to leave any telltale roughness around the interface. Some writers, surprisingly good ones, never get it right. But Jody Lynn Nye has mastered this difficult art, and succeeds in making it look easy, which is a lot more work than you'd suspect.

Jetlagged elves, diaphanous telepathic wind sprites and cranky subterranean-dwelling *bodachs* coexist in this world, or move cheek-by-jowl through it, alongside crooked and weaselly politicians, confused British secret service operatives, hot-air balloon freaks and various other mostly unsuspecting or basically clueless mortals, almost none of them willing to believe the evidence of their eyes when magic happens right in front of them. (But would *you*?...) Then add to this mix the engaging and (mostly) guileless Keith Doyle, a university student who stumbles on a bemusing fact—that there are fairies, not at the bottom of the garden, but living downstairs in the college library, illegal aliens with a difference—and helps them come to terms with the cultural barbed-wire tangle of modern North America, and the result is a leisurely and nonlethal explosive mixture that goes off, *bang*, in gales of laughter, when you least expect it. The good-hearted Keith manages to juggle his studies and interests with the never-ending business of helping his new friends solve the problems of being an elf in modern America (for example, your small-child size and pointed ears can cause you to routinely be mistaken for a Star Trek fan). He is not hypercompetent: sometimes, faced with the complexities of learning to handle as much magic as is good for one of the Big People, he drops the ball—which makes him all the more endearing. Through the course of the books, trips to Scotland and Ireland for the enchanted flowers which will indirectly allow the birth of the first native American elf, and efforts to stop unscrupulous local industries from polluting the elves' smallholding, combine to help not only Keith, but the Little People with whom he works, grow into more than any of them could have been without the others.

These books are a graceful and enjoyable romp through a world that looks like ours…but has some delightful differences. I hope you enjoy your sojourn there as much as I have.

Diane Duane
May 2000

Mythology 101

Chapter 1

"Are all now present?" the Master enquired, squinting over the top of his gold-rimmed spectacles. The light of two dozen burning lanterns hanging around the huge room flickered off the glass and metal frames. It glinted almost as brightly from the Master's coppery red beard and hair. Even his pointed ears had tufts of red hair sticking out of them.

On the benches around the wooden meeting table, the Folk shifted to position themselves comfortably. It wasn't often the whole Council attended a village meeting, so though the benches were long, the regulars had to suck in their sides to make room for their more occasional companions. It was a sign of the seriousness of the situation that there was no banter, no friendly arguments between the young Progressives and the older Conservatives.

"Gut. Then I declare that the meeting is open," the Master continued familiarly. "I recognize the Archivist." He nodded to Catra, a young female who wore her long brown hair in a severe braid.

Catra stood up and shook two sheets of paper at the assembly. "These I borrowed from the very desk of the Big Folk Chancellor himself. They detail a proposal to demolish our very home! They wish to build on this site a new library building of great height and size. It will have a new foundation made by filling in all the lower levels with concrete." She shuddered at the image of a wave of concrete rolling over their village and handed the document to the Master, who blew on the wick of a lantern to ignite it, and read the document through by its light. He nodded affirmation to the others.

"We're lost!" Keva shrieked. For all her hundred and seventy eight years, she had a voice that carried shrilly to the distant walls and echoed off them. Her fellow villagers looked around cautiously as if the Chancellor and his minions might hear her. "We must flee!" Her fellow Conservatives nodded solemnly.

"It's only a proposal at present," Aylmer said in a calm voice. He was a Conservative, too, but didn't approve of alarmism.

Holl, a chunky young fellow with thick blond hair, scratched thoughtfully at one tall pointed ear. "I think we should call in the help of the Big Ones who are our fellow students."

There was a general outcry. "No! You can't trust the Big Ones. They're too stupid." "They wouldn't help us. It's their own Chancellor and his Administrators who seek to put us out of our home." "Yes, ask them!" "Progressive! You want us to be annihilated; to have our culture swept away."

"The separation of aur folk fro' theirs must an' will continue," Curran, Holl's white-haired clan chief, told him severely.

"I think there are some that can be trusted not to do more than we ask," Holl insisted. "Ludmilla. No question of her, I hope. Fair Marcy, for example. And there's always Lee."

"Yes," agreed Enoch, a more somber-faced youth with black hair. "I know these well, and there are others, but I am not sure I would involve the young folk even if I trusted them."

"What about those peculiar walkings-about we keep hearing? Who's responsible for that? One of your trustworthy fellow students? You don't know either!" Curran snapped at Holl.

"I put it to a vote, then," the Master said, signaling for silence. "Those in favor uf asking for help vrom the Big Ones, raise your right hands." He counted. "Hands down, please. Those against, the left." There were no surprises. The Progressives voted in favor of Holl's suggestion. The Conservatives voted against the Progressives, whom they outnumbered two to one. He and Catra abstained. The Master felt that the Headman must remain neutral. Catra often declared that an Archivist could not take sides or it would ruin her objectivity. "Very vell. The motion is defeated at present. I adjure all uf you to put your minds to a solution, or ve may truly be homeless."

"I must return the document to the Chancellor's office before dawn," Catra reminded him.

"Qvite right. I must have a copy to study the details." The Master blew out his lantern. He picked up a sheet of handmade parchment slightly larger than both pieces of paper and laid it over the document. Stretching out both hands palm down above the parchment, the red-haired leader closed his eyes to concentrate. Under each of his hands, a shimmering blob of black print appeared and spread across to meet the other, then the joined mass rippled outward to perfectly straight squared margins. No one made a sound until he was finished. It was a difficult task for one of their kind to work from paper that had been printed with iron and steel.

"There," he said, examining the big sheet. "Vell enough. It vill do."

"Master," Catra chided him gently. "I could have used the xerox machine."

Chapter 2

"Mr. Doyle?" inquired Dr. Freleng, holding a thesis paper in the air with disgusted thumb and forefinger. The teacher's grey moustache lifted on one side as his lip curled. "This is Sociology 430. Don't you think this paper should better have been submitted to your Fiction Writing teacher instead?"

"Well, I'm not taking that course this semester," stammered Keith Doyle, scrambling to sit upright from his comfortable slouch behind the large frame of Mary Lou Carson. He met the teacher's eye and drooped back again. His narrow face turned red, only a few shades darker than his hair. "Um, no, sir. What's the matter with it, sir?"

"Or perhaps this is Introduction to Mythology? What is the matter? 'A Study of Human/Alien Interaction'? This paper was supposed to be on a documented facet of human behavior. Would you mind telling me when we made contact with extraterrestrials? I'm sure the government would be more than interested to know." Dr. Freleng opened his fingers and let the paper fall to Keith's desk, covering up the *Field Guide to the Little People,* which luckily the professor hadn't noticed. The other students snickered. Freleng dusted his fingertips together and eyed Keith with an air of doubt.

"It's a study based on theories I formed, speculations on the probable behavior of mankind when faced with alien cultures more technologically advanced than ourselves," Keith explained with patient resignation. "Older extraterrestrial cultures. I based it on my research into recent western contacts with older civilizations, such as the Chinese."

"Of which you seem most disparaging," Freleng said, gesturing at the paper, on which a circled red F adorned the title page. Keith stuck out his chin determinedly.

"I think nonwestern cultures suffer from the overeager come-on that they get from Western anthropologists. Think of the business of the desert tribe religion which believed in planets it couldn't see, just because those researchers asked 'em leading questions. Look," Keith said earnestly, "when zoologists are observing rare animals, they're so careful not to interfere with their natural behavior. It's almost like people don't get the same privilege. It's as if, well, because they're different they're told they have to change to conform."

Freleng turned away from Keith's indignant stare, fluttering a dismissive hand at him. "Preservationist poppycock. Field anthropologists act with more responsibility than that toward their subjects."

"Yeah, sometimes, but what about Peace Corps volunteers? Missionaries? We make change look too attractive, too imperative, playing down the importance of their own, diverse cultural facets," Keith went on, his voice loud with conviction, quoting phrases from the Sociology textbook, which Freleng ignored. It was one of the professor's own favorite tricks, and he hated to have students use it back to him. "They've done without Coca Cola for centuries. They don't need it now either, but we dictate to them, the times when we don't collapse at their feet and shout "teach me," instead. We impose our impressions of how they should be on them. Our opinion molds them."

"Yeah," added a girl with brown-black hair, seated two rows ahead to Keith's left. She had clear, pale skin with just a dusting of dark freckles across her nose and cheekbones, and Keith had been watching her avidly all semester. "Like little—I mean, short people. Tall ones tend to treat them just like children. They react to an unspoken assumption that if someone is smaller than you are, he must be younger, and not as mature. Or if they're obviously older, they must be senile, or something less than mentally competent."

Keith was amazed. Usually the majority of his fellow students sided with the teacher on how they felt about his peculiar essay topics. As a rule, they all thought he was crazy. He felt much encouraged by Marcy Collier's unsolicited support. Not only was she beautiful, but she was a fellow philosopher.

"Yes, Miss Collier, I have your paper here," Freleng turned on her. "You expressed your opinions on paper with *somewhat* more coherence than Mr. Doyle, though you failed to identify most of your research sources. I require clearer footnoting than that, as you are aware. It is worth fifteen percent of your grade on any paper." Her paper fluttered down, marked with a circled C.

"Um," Marcy Collier echoed Keith's discomfort of a few minutes past. The teacher's cold gaze made her writhe. Her eyes dropped, and she addressed her reply to her desk. "They were field study subjects. They asked me not to identify them by name."

"I see. In those cases, it is traditional to supply a pseudonym with the actual age, sex, profession and social condition, so that we can judge as much by the subject as by their statements. However interesting such statements may be, they offer only half of the data we use in our studies. Your essays each constitute ten per cent of your grade for this course. The final exam carries more weight, thirty per cent, but displayed application of skills learned in class is twenty per cent of your grade. Please bear that in mind."

"Yes, sir. I'll do that next time, sir." Red-cheeked, Marcy shoved the paper into her bookbag. Keith glimpsed lots of red ink through the back of the last page before it vanished. Old Freleng had taken her bibliography to pieces. Hah. His own paper probably looked like a Rorschach test. He felt sorry for her. He felt sorry for himself. He slumped back into obscurity behind Mary Lou. Her paper had an A on it, as usual.

At last, the bell rang. "That one was really dumb, Doyle," Burke Slater jabbed Keith with an elbow as he jostled past the others out of the classroom. "Real comic relief."

"I think you're wonderful to stick up for the primitive tribes," offered Abby Holt, a brown-haired girl in blue jeans who tended toward mystical topics herself.

Keith smiled and pushed past them into the hallway, running after Marcy as she maneuvered through the crowded corridor of Burke Hall. "Hey, wait! Marcy?"

"I've got a class in McInroe next period," she said curtly, her eyes narrowed at him. Keith thought she cleared tears out of her throat. She wasn't the type who usually got C's, he decided, and she was taking it hard. He pulled his own crumpled essay out of his nylon backpack.

"I got an F," he said, smiling at her winningly. "Wanna trade?"

She looked at his paper, and then met his eyes. The sullen mask broke. "Oh, God, what am I going to tell my parents?" Marcy wailed, tears dripping down her cheeks. "I've never gotten a C in my life. Dr. Freleng is a fiend. It's too late for me to drop the course now. I've had all A's all my life. My parents expect it. They just won't understand. I'm failing."

"I wouldn't call a C failure," Keith said, jumping forward to open the door for her and following her out into the brisk October air. Leaves swirled away from their feet as they dashed across the narrow streets toward McInroe Hall. "I'm a B man myself. I do get

A's but I don't expect 'em. If you're not in the front line you don't get shot at as often."

"Get what?" Marcy shouted, avoiding an ancient Volvo which screeched backward into a suddenly available parking space on the curb.

"Shot at!" Keith yelled. "Teachers love to pick on A-seekers. Besides, we're Freleng's favorite victims because we're not seniors or grad students. We're making it look like it's too easy to take his class. He considers it a put down. I can't blame him."

"I wish I'd never taken it," Marcy said miserably.

"It isn't a total loss," Keith soothed her. "It's your only C, remember? Would you like to join forces against the evils of Sociology? We can study together. Misery loves company, you know." He fished around in his pocket for a folded wad of tissues and wrapped her fingers around it.

"Well, I'm in a study group already…." Marcy dabbed at her eyes, but her voice had steadied again.

"Oh, come on. I know about Honors study groups. They sit around and compare Daddy's tax returns or talk about interesting atoms they have met."

"It's isn't an Honors group. This is a different kind. Hey," she said, changing the subject, "how'd you know I'm an Honor student?"

"It's written all over you. Places you can't see." Keith waggled his eyebrows wickedly. "Besides, I've been watching you. Haven't you noticed?"

Marcy shook her head. "I'd rather study alone. I get more done that way."

"Well, just Soc. then." Stairs, and then another door, opening into another echoing tiled hall full of hurrying figures. "Say, can I read your essay?" Keith asked, suddenly. "It sounded really interesting to me. You can read mine, but I guess you'd probably think it was fiction, too," he finished, suddenly sounding disgusted. "Nobody respects a scientist anymore."

"Sure you can," said Marcy, thrusting the paper into his hand. "Now I'm going to be late. Thanks for the Kleenex. See you."

"See you." Keith watched her dash away.

Level Fourteen of the Gillington Library stacks was quiet in the afternoon. Unlike the system most buildings used, the library stacks

were numbered top to bottom, so the uppermost of the eight half-
high floors above ground was Level One, and the lowest, in the
third sub-sub basement was Fourteen. The library itself was numbered normally, its four full height floors numbered from the bottom to the top. It confused a lot of freshmen the first week of
classes, but since there were separate elevators for the two sections,
students got used to the concept in a hurry. They put it down to
typical Administration baloney. One more thing to be ignored.

This level was devoted mainly to historical archives, a compre-
hensive collection of Americana of which the University was ap-
propriately proud. Rare books were stored down here until they
were called for in the usual way by users of the reading room upstairs. On occasion, masters' degree candidates could get a special
pass to peruse the shelves themselves, but they were rarely here during the afternoon. The archives librarian took advantage of the silence and pushed the book-cart through the rows of tiered shelves,
listening to the sounds of the building as it settled, replacing returned
books. She was a thin, pinched-faced woman who looked right
with her salt-and-pepper hair tied into a tight bun. Fallen books she
straightened up in their slots with a scolding expression as if they
should have known better than to tip over.

With her narrow hands, she deftly sorted through a sheaf of
old newspaper folios. The yellow-brown pages in their transparent
folders were crisp and fragile. As she stacked them gently into a
library box, she heard footsteps coming swiftly toward her, and
turned away from her task to see who was running. Probably students who had forced the stairwell lock with a plastic I.D. card.
"This level is restricted," she said sternly. "No one is to be here
without authorization. Did you hear me?"

No reply. She heard high-pitched giggles coming from that direction, shut the storage box with a snap, and started off to dispense
some discipline.

Suddenly, the librarian heard the same giggle from behind her.
She spun and ran back that way, her shoes flapping on the floor. No
one was visible at that end of the aisle. She stopped. Again heard
running footsteps, the soles of the shoes grating with a sandpapery
hiss on the concrete floor.

"Stop that!" she cried. "This is a library, not a racetrack. Who
are you? Show yourself. Leave this building at once." Her voice

rang in the hanging metal beams. "I will call Security if you do not leave NOW!"

The giggles erupted echoingly into the silence. She ran toward the dancing sound, but it dissolved into silence before she found the source. "Hello?" she called softly.

"Helloooo," came a whisper from behind her. She jumped and let out a small scream of frustration. The falsetto laughter bubbled up again as the footsteps ran away. This was not the first time she thought she had heard students chasing themselves around in the dark. Thought it was funny to flaunt their disobedience and startle her. They wanted to use her level in place of the back seats of their decrepit cars. "Horrible brats." In all her years, she'd never been able to catch the miscreants, or even see who was making the noise. Gremlins, that's what it was. Old places were said to have their own resident spirits. The echoes in here were positively uncanny. It might have been her own voice distorting into that insane laughter, but she wasn't sure. They needed better lighting in this library. That was certain.

Looking this way and that, the librarian walked back to her cart to resume her task. The cart refused to roll forward. She kicked at the brake on the left front wheel, but to her surprise, it was off. She leaned all her weight against it. The cart would not move.

She pulled on it from the front. It wouldn't come forward an inch. Neither would it move to either side. It was as if the cart was cemented to the floor. She stacked all of the books from it on the floor and tried to shake it loose. Nothing. The librarian was ready to sob with frustration. There was nothing physically wrong with the cart, no reason why it should not roll normally, but it was firmly rooted where it stood. She stacked the books back onto it, somewhat less neatly than before. Her hands were shaking.

Dealing the cart a final disgusted shove, she headed for the elevator to get the janitor. He would have to oil those wheels before she could continue. When she had turned around the head of the row, there was a loud creak and rumble. The woman scrambled back to see the cart rolling away by itself. For a moment, she thought about running after it, but a blast of mocking laughter sent her scurrying into the elevator instead, fleeing for the safety of the faculty lounge. Years ago the dark and dusty cubicle had been designated a Civil Defense fallout shelter, and that gave her twitching nerves a sense of security. No one would question her spending a few hours lying down on the couch. The old library was widely believed to be haunted. She would feel safer if she could finish up later, preferably with another librarian for company.

But when she did come back, the books would be on their shelves and the cart empty, and she knew it. It had all happened before.

"Well?" asked Pat Morgan, glancing unsympathetically at his roommate as Keith staggered across their dorm room and dropped with a melodramatic thud face first onto his bed. Pat went on watering houseplants. "So, tell Uncle Pat. What'd you get on the Sociology essay?"

"F," groaned the voice, muffled in a pile of laundry. "F for Freleng. He hates me."

"Fair enough. You hate him."

"How can a sociologist be so closed-minded?"

"Those who can't, teach." Pat was an English major, and loved one line cappers. He was tall and hollow-chested, and had a tendency to stoop over, so he seemed to be perpetually out of breath. His long, lank black hair made him look like a repertory company Richard III out of makeup.

"And what about those who can't teach?" Keith said, shaking the twisted sheaf of paper at him. Keith's looks tended to make people think he was jolly or bad-tempered, depending on one's predispositions about red hair. He was short, straight-backed, and thin. His eyes were hazel, and changed color with his mood. Right now, they were blue. He buried his head in the laundry again.

"Oh, hell, maybe you can fix it up and ask him to regrade it. Say you didn't understand the assignment. It's only the first paper. Here, give me that." Pat dropped the plant mister in the sink and snatched the essay out of Keith's hands. "That stuff's clean, by the way." He tilted his head toward the pile of clothes in which Keith was lying. "Your turn to fold. No creases this time or you'll eat 'em."

Keith rolled onto his back, broadcasting socks across the floor. "I can't tell him I didn't understand it. I made a big deal about its social importance right in the middle of class."

"You've got a death wish," Pat said without looking up. He detoured around their shared wooden coffee table and sat down at his desk. Unlike Keith's, which had fantastic towers of books and papers teetering around a central cleared workspace, Pat's was a uniform level of possessions about ten inches high on which the current books and assignments lay. "You know I read this once before. I still think there's nothing wrong with it. It's an interesting theoretical examination without any actual field study. He's probably insulted because you told him through this paper that you consider all the other sociological studies, like inner city and Appalachia, boring and not worth considering."

"Well, they are boring. Every other social scientist has studied them to death. I can't find anything new to say about one. Even the minor stuff I'd explore has been overdone by everybody else."

Pat considered for a moment. "True. But I think he gave you an F because you piss him off. Why don't you turn this one in to Mythology, the way he suggested?"

"Because Mrs. Beattie has heard it all before, too. Wait until he reads my next one, on leprechauns. I told you about Marcy, the girl in my class?"

"Oh, yeah? She noticed you yet?"

"No. Ah, unrequited love. But she's very shy. That's one of the things I love her for. She doesn't throw herself at me."

Pat blew a raspberry at him. Keith shrugged it off.

"Anyway, I think she's got a boyfriend, somewhere, one of those guys who's 'above reproach,' and all that garbage. The way she's been acting, I think she's afraid of him. What she really needs is someone charming and harmless, like me. I've got her paper here, from the same assignment. I want her research materials. I think I can use 'em."

"Harmless. Oh, God," Pat groaned, shaking his head. "And the good Lord forgive you the lie."

"Never mind that. I've got this terrific theory about why the little people only appear to drunks and other unreliables," Keith began, spinning a towel in the air and catching it so it folded in half neatly over his extended forefingers.

"That's because you are one, jerkface." Carl Mueller came in the door, warding off flying laundry with one hand. He wore his thick light brown hair in a modified crewcut which, with his typical sour expression and healthy muscular build, made him look like an angry Marine.

"A leprechaun?" asked Pat.

"Sure," added Keith. "Viewed only by drunks and other unreliables. That's why you can see me, Carlitos." He whirled a towel like a bullfighter's cape. Carl and Keith had a Spanish class together, which he hated and Keith loved. Anything that Keith loved, Carl hated.

"Don't call me that, asshole," Carl said, staring belligerently at Keith.

"I never call you that asshole. Donde esta la pluma de me tia? How's things in Track?" Keith innocently changed the subject, gauging that the last ounce of tolerance left in Carl had just evaporated. "Want a beer?

Carl grunted. "Okay. But cut the Carlitos shit. I'm dropping the class anyway."

"Too late," observed Pat, who always knew the course schedules. "Last day without penalty was Thursday."

Keith opened the little refrigerator under his desk and pawed through it, emerging with three beers and a box of vanilla wafer cookies. "Here, peace offering. See you later," he told Pat.

Keith took his snack, Marcy's essay, and the *Field Guide* out into the hallway. He hated to concede the territory to Carl; it was his room, after all; but there was no point in starting another argument. There were just some people that were automatically and irrevocably rubbed the wrong way, and Carl was one of the ones he'd so rubbed.

It was all a matter of attitude, Keith had decided a long time ago. Carl was too serious about life. He wanted so badly to do something important that it affected everything he did. He needed a cause. The guy was born to be a Senator or Albert Schweitzer. Keith felt sorry for him. Of course, that didn't help him where Carl was concerned, who still reacted to Keith as if he was a flea: hyperactive, bothersome, and just out of reach.

Keith shrugged and opened Marcy's paper.

In the library, Marcy waited between the tall rows of bookshelves until no one was in sight. It was late afternoon, so there were few people around, but she could never be sure she was unobserved. With infinite care, she eased open the door that led to the fire stairs. It creaked loudly. She winced, but the sound drew no one's attention. The building was old, and everyone was used to its assorted settling noises.

She descended flight after flight in the darkness, her whispering footsteps confident, intimately familiar with her surroundings. At the bottom of the last concrete step, she halted and drew the smooth steel door open just wide enough to permit her passage. It slid shut behind her, and Marcy felt rather than heard the boom as it closed.

Two more flights of steps, and another door, and she passed inside, crossed the floor, with hulking shadows of more shelves darker than the darkness. From her pocket, she took a key, which gleamed a brilliant green. With the aid of its light, Marcy found her way to the hidden keyhole, inserted the key, turned it, and pushed the door open.

Light flooded out upon her, throwing a long shadow back between the bookcases. She threw up a hand against the glare until her eyes adjusted, and spoke apologetically to the circle of Little Folk and the tall human students seated at desks in the low-ceilinged room. They regarded her expectantly.

"Vell?" asked the Master, laying his pointer down on the easel.

"We got a C," Marcy said.

"If you examine your stated principles as an objective observer," the Master stated, reviewing Marcy's essay, "you will see that you are relying upon your reader to furnish his own mental pictures of your subjects. In order for your reader to come to agree with your premises, you must provide accurate images from which he can draw his conclusions, which if you have been skillful, will agree with yours."

"I didn't want to say too much," Marcy said in a low voice, feeling ashamed. "I couldn't draw accurate pictures." She stared at her desktop. "I probably shouldn't have attempted the subject. But I did want to try."

Her fellow college students present exchanged sympathetic glances. The Little People favored her with friendly gazes, but said nothing, as usual.

"Mees Collier, there vas nothing wrong with your attempt of the subject," the Master said gently, setting the paper on her desk and looking up at her. "Nor with your conclusions. It is merely that your audience was not prepared for it."

Chapter 3

A dorm hallway was by no means the quietest of places to read. It smelled strongly of sweatsocks and mold, and the carpet was perpetually damp. There seemed to be an unwritten rule for residence halls that the areas with the most traffic should be the worst lit, so Keith was left trying to read by the feeble brownish glow of dying fluorescent ceiling lights. Nobody ever seemed to look down toward the dimly lit floor while they were walking. He was kicked a few times by passersby who didn't see him. One student fell over Keith's legs, spilling a heap of fresh laundry halfway down the hall. After apologizing and helping to re-fold it, Keith fled to his Resident Advisor's room for sanctuary.

He poked his head through the doorway into the R.A.'s suite. "Hi, Rick. Can I borrow a corner?"

Rick MacKenzie looked up from his desk. He had a black crewcut over lightning blue eyes and a lantern jaw which twisted around a grin. "Sure, Keith. C'mon in."

"Thanks. There's no room back at the inn."

The RA's eyes narrowed dangerously. "Rubber band on the knob?" That was the signal that female company was being entertained by the other room-mate, and disturbances would be unappreciated. Rick maintained an unspoken rule that no one was to band out their room-mates on week nights on his floor.

"Oh, no," Keith assured him, folding up like a grasshopper on Rick's ancient green tweed couch. "Just a friend of his who isn't a friend of mine. Our pal Carl."

"Uh huh. What've you got there?"

Keith handed over Marcy's paper. "I think I've got research material for my next essay in Sociology."

Rick thumbed through the pages. "You're going to rip off one of your friends?"

"Heck, no! I'll give her credit for it. Look, she analyzed the stresses brought to bear on people with a racial tendency toward dwarfism. The whole thing about being treated like children because they're small. But by the internal evidence, these people aren't circus midgets, or African pygmies, as you might normally assume. In fact, they seem to have come from a temperate climate, with almost Arctic winters. And their oral tradition comes from pretty far back, suggesting resistance to technology."

"Isolation?" asked Rick.

"Well, yeah. It would have to be. We don't have much of an oral tradition any more. Not since we learned to write and use movable type. What do you do when you want to remember something?"

"I write it down."

"Right. Now, our ancestors just recited their notes over and over again until they'd memorized it to keep. Once in, never out. And they could pass it on from generation to generation. That's why those family feuds lasted forever. Take the Hatfields and McCoys."

"So? That doesn't mean these people had the same kind of background, or even that they're from this hemisphere."

"But I think they did. Look, if it wasn't for the part about the racial dwarfism, I'd have said they were Irish, or at least from one of the great islands in the northwest of Europe. Naturally I have a preference for Ireland."

Rick threw the essay back with an expression of disgust. "Oh, I get it. You and your little people. You know, they lock up people with manias."

"Just consider it a need to know. The evidence suggests that I'm not the only one with a mania."

"Don't go reading something into that paper. Probably she came upon a village of short people in Scotland who got tired of hearing 'How's the weather down there?'"

"I want to talk to these people. They might have oral legends of little people that I can use. It's the legends and such I'm interested in. I've read all the fairy tales and junk. I want information that hasn't been through thirty publishers. I want evidence."

"Oh, come on. What makes you think she would believe your wild ideas, let alone pass you on to her subjects? That's the last thing they'd want to talk about with an outsider. They're ordinary people, and they want to live their lives in peace. They'll probably think you're another one of those 'look-at-all-the-funny-people' journalists. Or just a nut. Which you are."

"Hmm," said Keith, thinking deeply. "I don't want them to think I'm crazy. All I want is their recollections. Fairy tales. Local legends."

"What makes you think that just because they're short they have any more knowledge of legends than Joe Schmoe up the street?"

"Just a hunch," Keith shrugged. "Something about the way she states her facts. She's leaving something out, and I want to ask what it is. She's usually so quiet in class. Perhaps she'll be more talkative over dinner." He rose and scooped up the paper, and started for the door.

"Whoa!" The RA's voice halted his headlong departure. "Dinner? Aren't you coming to the Student Government meeting tonight, Doyle? You're one of our best speakers. I think this'll be the night we can get a deciding vote on the library issue. If you don't come I guarantee we will lose."

Keith bashed himself in the side of the head with Marcy's paper, further crumpling it. "I'm sorry, Rick," Keith apologized, instantly changing plans again. "Yeah, I'm coming. I'll just drop this in my room and be right back with my notes. We can discuss strategy."

If anyone had told Mrs. Howard, Keith's sixth-grade teacher, that one day he'd be the eloquent darling of Student Senate Council, she'd have laughed until she choked. Occasionally, Keith thought of writing her a letter and enclosing a tape of one of his terrific speeches that moved millions—well, dozens—to his side of an issue. On the other hand, just because he thought it was terrific didn't mean a picky Language Arts teacher of the old school would agree with him.

Of the forty-five official members of Senate representing the fifteen residence halls on campus, only a third or so usually attended the meetings held every two weeks in the Student Common. Keith had been elected to represent his dorm, C. V. Power Hall, on a nomination moved by Rick, who as the representative Resident Advisor from Power had to be present at meetings, and liked to have his friends around. Pat had seconded the nomination, since it was the most likely way to keep himself from being chosen. English majors were usually favored delegates. Keith, who hadn't been present at his election, was upset for about two weeks, until he discovered how much fun it was to make hay out of Robert's Rules of Order. Thanks to Keith's enthusiastic support, there was now a college regulation on the books forbidding walking your zebra on the streets after dark. The actual wording of the rule banned any animal not specifically domestic in nature, and its proven intention was to prevent attacks or escapes by those animals after nightfall, but the committee which had proposed it to the Dean's council called it the Zebra Crossing Ban.

The other delegate from Power Hall was clear across the room, chatting with one of the girls who lived in Bradkin. Carl never sat with Keith and the RA; he seemed to think it spoiled his dignity. He had actually volunteered to serve in student government, which made him the legitimate object of derision by those who had been shanghaied into office. For once, though, he had a legitimate excuse for separating himself from the rest of his dorm-mates. They were on opposing sides of an issue.

To Keith, issues weren't life-or-death matters. The girls from Edison were proposing another formal letter of complaint to ARA Suppliers, concerning the poor quality of dorm food. Senate sent at least three of those a semester, and they hadn't done any good yet. The food was still just barely edible. On the other hand, Carl took his role as the voice of student opinion very seriously, and offered his support to matters he believed in. He hadn't the same gift of gab Keith had, and was regularly out-debated whenever they disagreed. For that reason and very little else, Keith made sure he and Carl were opponents no matter how trivial the issue. If Carl supported it, Keith was out to undermine it.

"Quiet, please! Hey, can it!" yelled Lloyd Patterson, president of the Inter-Hall Council. "Let's get this going, huh? I've got an exam tomorrow. I don't want this to drag on. Venita, will you take the roll?"

Venita March, recording secretary and RA delegate, rose, tossing her head. Venita was a friend of Rick's from his class at high school, and she taught self-defense part time at the University Women's Center. Her hair, a tall, superbly styled natural decorated with a plume, swayed for a moment after she had stopped moving. Rick stifled a snicker and Keith elbowed him. "Shut up. She'll cream you."

"I know, but I can't help it. That style almost touches the roof." He sketched height over his head with a hand twitching with mirth.

"*If* we may have some order," Venita asked icily, a quelling glance aimed at Rick. He lowered his arm, smiling with mock innocence. She shook her head at him, slack-mouthed, tapping a long-suffering foot on the floor. Rick folded his hands studiously before him and sat up at attention. Raising one eyebrow at him, she read down the list.

"You can tell she likes you," Keith told Rick sardonically.

"Okay," Lloyd said, after Venita sat down, hairdo a-quiver. "Any old business to take care of?"

"Dean's Council has ruled on the matter of student parking," a girl clad casually in blue jeans and a leotard spoke up. "All spaces will be allotted first come first served to dorm students first, frats and apartment dwellers second, and night school gets what's left. The areas will be divided into three zones, and students are supposed to apply to the zone center closest to their residence. The center lot will still be set aside for medical plates and visitors. Anyone caught parking there who has a school sticker will have their car towed and privileges revoked, no refund." There was a chorus of groans from both sides of the room. "I'm *sorry!*" she snapped defensively. "That's the best I could get. At least the people who live in Barber won't have to park all the way over near the frat houses."

"That's something," Venita said, encouragingly. She lived in Barber.

"Okay. That'll help," Lloyd acknowledged, making notes. "Anything else?"

"Yessir," Keith said, springing to his feet. "Doyle, Power Hall. I want to bring up the subject of the proposed library renovation project." He smiled triumphantly at Carl, who was just raising his hand. There was a deal of movement in the room, as the student delegates, recognizing the signs of a debate, separated themselves into three rough groups, with the center delegates undecided. Several pushed their chairs over to Keith's side of the floor, the Pro-renovation side, and settled down. Dividing up depending on one's opinion on an issue was an idea Keith had found in the rules governing the British Parliament, where MPs entered through different doors if they were going to vote 'yea' or 'nay.' The Council's meeting room had only one door, so he came up with a suitable variation. The other members liked it because it showed visible support for the issues, let them know who else was actually interested, and gave them something to do at meetings.

"You have the floor."

"Thank you." Keith moved into the center of the room, and assumed an orator's pose. Rick sat back to watch with obvious pleasure. "There is a proposal before the Dean's Council for replacement of one major building on the Midwestern campus. Dean Rolands has cut the choices down to two: a new Phys Ed. building, or a new library. To me, the correct choice is obvious.

"My question to the assembled Senate is this: why did you come to college? To run laps? To cheer at Big Ten games? Well, you're at the wrong school to begin with." Some uneasy laughter; Midwestern had pretensions toward national college football, but the team simply wasn't good enough. Carl glowered, and Keith continued. "But since you are here, it's to learn, isn't that right? To pick up skills which will be of use to you after graduation. I for one can't think of anything I'll ever do that involves vaulting over the horse or hand-walking on parallel bars. Can you?"

"How about weight-lifting?" someone asked.

Keith gestured at his narrow frame. "What weight?"

More laughter. "What about physical well being?" Carl demanded. "That's real important, too. And how about leisure sports?"

"P.E. in high school or grade school is good for learning about things like that. You get a whole selection of different sports and exercises. Variety. At the University, physical education is too specialized, too competitive. It's great if you're interested in playing volleyball or aikido, but you can just take an exercise course to keep fit, and that doesn't need any special space, or specific environment."

"The hell it doesn't," one of the opposing delegates sneered.

Keith went on, ignoring the outburst. "In fact, if you insist, you could keep fit by exercising in your dorm room. Why not?" He pantomimed doing jumping jacks, athletically at first, then bowing over more and more in mock exhaustion. "Your roommate asks, 'What are you doing?', and you say, 'I'm doing my homework for Gym.'" Laughter exploded around the room.

"Now, except for the one gym course we're required to take to graduate, fewer than 40% of the students at Midwestern ever set foot in the P.E. building again, and most of those are specialists. On the other hand, over 90% use the library. Why, even a few of the jocks do." More laughter.

"It's crowded in there during mid-terms and finals," one of the girls on Keith's side complained. "There's never enough carrels, and they lock the classrooms."

One of Carl's backers, Maurice Paget, a tall black student, raised a hand. "Couldn't that be negotiated with Library Services? If there was more study space available in the present structure, they wouldn't need to build a bigger building."

"The trouble is that they use those classrooms all year round, especially during finals," Keith said. "At maximum capacity, the student need exceeds available space. And Library Services wants to bring more study aids in, but there's nowhere to put 'em. Audio/video aids, records and tapes, works of art—even," a forefinger was raised on high, "*National Geographic*. All of these things are to be available for study, to give you the, well, wisdom of the ages, to prepare you to be whatever it is you want to be when you leave Midwestern. But wisdom dictates two things cannot occupy the same space at the same time."

"That's physics," Rick put in.

"Whatever," said Keith. "Wise men discovered physics, right? The need for a better building to house books and study aids, and provide more room for their users, in my opinion, far outweighs the wishes of a few jocks for a fancier fieldhouse."

"Very alliterative," called Lloyd from the center section. He never took a side. There was some applause as Keith sat down. Rick grinned, and they both looked to the other side of the room. Carl rose to his feet.

"What about the kids that come here on athletic scholarships?" he demanded. "Don't they get a voice?"

"Don't they have to earn diplomas?" Keith asked, counterpointing his question. "Just like anyone on a Math scholarship, the idea was that by the one outstanding talent they displayed, they were awarded a sum of money to continue their education by being more deserving than anyone else with that talent. In the opinion of the judges, of course. Ask my mother how I missed out on the Rhodes Scholarship." There were jeers.

"But I see what you're asking, Carl," Keith put on a reasoning expression that particularly irritated the other and Keith knew it. "Don't they deserve to have a forum in which their particular talent can be brought to the attention of such people as football scouts?" He paused. "Well.... no, not really."

"What?" Carl sputtered, starting to speak. "Why not? It's..."

Keith neatly cut him off. "The job of the college is to educate students and fit them out to seek their fortunes afterward. Having them available for scrutiny by scouts is a side benefit. Too bad there isn't a place for kids who are not dumb, but not academically inclined, just to go and offer themselves for professional sports teams.

Like theater auditions. As it is, this is the way the system works. Why should the academically inclined, for whom this campus really exists, suffer for the ten or so who will go on to earn six-figure salaries in pro ball?"

Rick poked him sharply in the ribs from behind with his toe, and Keith clamped his jaw shut, remembering too late that Rick was a P.E. major, and had hopes of one of those big breaks. "What Mr. Wizard here means, of course," growled Rick, "is that the needs of the many outweigh the needs of the few. To coin a phrase."

"Where have I heard that before?" Carl asked, sarcastically. "What you're saying is that the athletes don't deserve a good place to practice their skills. I disagree with you! You do need a particular place to do gymnastics or play football. The gym is too small. The pools leak. The lights are bad, and there aren't enough of them. The old building needs to be replaced, and a modern one with good lights, good floors, good plumbing, has to be built."

"Aha," Keith crowed triumphantly, jumping up. "Old? You call a gymnasium only twelve years old, old? Gillington Library is a hundred and fourteen. It had a minor face lift in the forties, when there was a lot of new construction here, but not a thing since. Haven't you ever heard the floor creak when you were looking for a book in the stacks, and wondered if it was going to collapse under you? Those of you who've been in the stacks for books, that is. The rest of you won't care if the building moves," a michieviously deferential bow to Rick, who had mentioned a quiet corner he and his girlfriend frequented. Dodging a kick this time, he went on. "If they ever have to make emergency structural repairs to Gillington in the middle of mid-terms, you'll wish you had voted to renovate it. You can prevent that disaster by voting for the reconstruction now."

Recognizing the need to rally newly awakened support, Rick swallowed his pride and exclaimed, "Think about it. I'm studying business, for the years after I don't want to play soccer any more."

"Or can't," Carl put in.

"Watch it, Mueller," Rick snapped, becoming serious. Carl acceded sullenly to the warning, and fell silent.

"Where would the new library be built?" Francine Daubiner wanted to know. She was one of the undecided.

"The Dean says that it would be built on the foundations of the old one, just as the Sports Center would go up where the P.E.

building is now." Keith had all the facts handy in his notebook. "Neither one could cost more than three million dollars, nor less than one million. Dean Rolands insisted on a reasonable range for the project. The other structure would follow in three to six years, depending on need and availability of cash."

"Part of that money would go for several computer terminals," Venita said, after examining the list Keith had submitted to the secretary. "Sounds like they've got some other projects tucked in there."

"All part of information retrieval," Keith pointed out, cheerily. "So, why don't we make it offic…"

"Okay," Lloyd stood up, cutting him off. "We don't have enough people here for the vote, so it'll have to wait. In two weeks, we'll have a mandatory meeting, full Student Senate, and finalize what our recommendation to the Dean's Council will be, and who gets to take it there." Everyone groaned. "Now come on. Is there any other business? No? Well, then, I declare this meeting adjourned…."

"Seconded," Carl said, still glaring at Keith, but warily, because Rick was looming behind the skinny student. The gavel fell, and the room cleared quickly.

Chapter 4

Ludlow heard a banging sound coming from the little cluster of administrative offices at the head of the hall. His eyes narrowed and he stopped swabbing the floor to listen more closely. Yes, definitely the noise of metal on metal, like a sliding drawer in a file cabinet. There it was again. Maybe one of the old lady librarians working late. He could complain to her about not reporting the leak in the ceiling that was sending a dribble of rusty water down the pale tan tiles of the floor.

The sound repeated itself, this time more frenzied.

Ludlow crept closer to have a peek around the edge of the doors through the narrow pane of glass that ran the length of the knob side, carefully still mopping so it looked like he was working, not spying. No one in any of 'em, and the lights were all out. Then where—?

The banging ended with a frustrated rattle practically under his ear. It was coming from the supply room. An intruder, certainly a thief. He tried the solid wooden door, shaking it gently. It was locked. The deadbolt boomed ominously in the door jamb. As soon as whoever it was heard him, operations within the supply room ceased. He unreeled the heavy ring of keys from its retractable lead on his belt and shouldered open the door, leveling the mop handle like a shotgun.

With a gasp, the intruder whirled, opening wide green eyes on him. Ludlow was disgusted. It was a kid. A little kid, with a head full of wild red curls, wearing a short, shapeless dress and socks but no shoes. She had her hands full of xerox paper reams and felt tip pens, some of which cascaded to the floor in her surprise.

"What are you doing here?" he demanded. "How'd you get in here? Never mind. You're coming with me. I'm calling the police."

The child didn't speak. Instead, clutching her booty, she lunged under his arm toward the door. Ludlow blocked her exit easily with the mop handle and reached for her. She backed up, her solemn gaze remaining fixed on his face.

"Where do you think you're going?" Ludlow asked. He felt not unkindly toward the child. After all, he had five of his own at home.

But you had to teach 'em what was right and wrong. And why the hell was she stealing office supplies, of all things? Didn't look like the usual college thief. Was she one of the teacher's kids? They'd have to come and get her from the Campus Security office. He opened his mouth to ask.

Swiftly, the red-haired child darted around his other side. Ludlow flung the mop away and grabbed for her with both arms. Squealing, she twisted free of his grasp, danced a couple of paces away, and pointed a hand at him.

Ludlow started after her, but found he was restrained by his belt, which was attached to the retractable keyring. The supply room door key, on the end of its tether, was still inserted in the doorknob. He pulled at it, but it wouldn't come free. He shook the knob angrily. The little girl, watching cautiously, started to back away up the corridor, the boxes of pens and paper in her arms. He snatched at the buckle of his belt, seeking to undo it, but unaccountably, the buckle tongue seemed to adhere solidly to the frame. There was no way for him to unfasten it or wriggle out of it.

The child turned around and fled. Ludlow, giving up on the hope of catching up with her, twisted and pulled at the key. It wouldn't budge. In fact, now it wouldn't even turn. He attempted again to undo his belt. The buckle held itself fast.

With a groan, Ludlow sat down on the floor, and wondered whether it would be more humiliating to unfasten the hinges and drag the door with him until he could find a way to dislodge his key, or to sit there and wait for someone to come along with a pair of shears and cut him loose from his belt.

Chapter 5

When Keith returned to the dorm room later that evening, Pat was there alone. Crumpled wads of waxed paper and foil from the college deli were piled up on the coffee table next to a fat biology textbook. "Do you have a test, Pat?" he asked. "I would have brought dinner in for you if you'd have mentioned it. Or at least kept you company."

Pat grinned wryly and rubbed his eyes. "Thanks. I'd rather study by myself. It's quieter without you."

"Everyone says the same thing." Keith threw a pillow at him.

Pat caught it dexterously with one hand, and pitched it back, catching Keith in the middle of the chest. "How'd the meeting go?"

"I think Carl went away to bury his shame or something. I was a big success. The assembly was overwhelmed by the thought of all those poor, homeless books with no place to go, evicted by the evil football team. The jocks'll scream, but the other appointees will be on our side. Lloyd cut the meeting short before we could call for the vote. I suspect him of being a secret athletic supporter. I think the motion'll carry next time, when we do vote on it. Required attendance by all delegates."

"That'll be popular," Pat said, cynically. "You'd have to drag me there in chains. Well, anyway, here," he said, and tossed some papers in his direction. He gave Keith an apologetic glance. "I went over that Sociology paper of yours again, and unless you can convince him that your idea is a radical new theory based on existing data, I'm afraid you'll have to rewrite it completely with real facts. It's okay the way it is if he'd go for it, but he won't. That's just my opinion, of course."

"Terrific," said Keith, dropping his notebook on the bed. Then a memory struck him. "Hey, Pat, where's that paper I showed you earlier?"

"I just gave it to you."

"No, the other one. Marcy Collier's paper. Had a C on it, not an F. I thought I left it right here before the meeting," Keith pointed to his bed.

"Sorry," said Pat. "I haven't seen it. Are you sure you didn't take it with you?"

Keith struck the side of his head with the heel of his hand. "Right. That must be it. I left it in the meeting room. What a mind. If medical science could locate it...."

"Get it tomorrow, and shut up."

"Yes, my leader."

"I owe you an apology," Keith panted, catching up with Marcy the next day after Sociology class let out. "I have looked everywhere, but I can't find the essay you lent me. It isn't like me to lose things like that. I'm usually trustworthy, honest."

"Oh, no, don't worry about it," Marcy assured him. "I got it back. It's in my apartment somewhere."

Keith dashed a hand across his forehead melodramatically. "That's a relief. I think I must have left it in the Inter-hall Council. My brain is deteriorating in my old age. But you got it back, for sure? Some kind soul brought it back to you?"

"Uh huh. Thanks for caring. I always throw out essays when I finish with the course anyway. And I'm sure not going to want to keep that one."

"Yeah, I know what you mean. Would you like to study to-gether this evening?" Before she could refuse automatically, he rushed on. "How can I whisper sweet nothings in your ear if I never have it all to myself? Lend me an ear. This approach worked for Marc Antony. On the other hand, look what happened to him."

She giggled, no longer nervous. "Oh, all right. I think I have an extra ear around here someplace."

"No, I'm sorry," Marcy said, meeting his eyes seriously. They were studying at the kitchen table in the apartment Marcy shared with three other girls. "I can't give you any of their names or tell you where to find my subjects. I promised. Freleng asked me the same thing for my essay. I finally made something up. I'd rather sacrifice my grade than hurt my...friends. I don't want to do the same for you; you'd know I was lying."

Keith's shoulders collapsed in disappointment. "Well, look, maybe if I told you what I want to talk about, you'd arrange for me to meet one man or woman."

"Go on," said Marcy, opening a bottle of Coke steaming with frost. She shook droplets of water out of two glasses sitting in the yellow rubber dish drainer and filled them.

"I have a theory about legends, that they have a base in reality. One of the most interesting things about them is that...thanks...they're everywhere. And they have a uniformity that intrigues me. Before mass communication, something got into the storytelling around the world that has little or no variation wherever you go. Dragons, for instance. On whichever side of the planet you ask, dragons are big, intelligent lizards. Most of them can fly. They eat meat. They hoard treasure. Chinese dragons are like Celtic dragons, and so on." He took a long swallow of Coke.

Marcy giggled. "You want to ask my people about dragons?"

"Nope," said Keith, warming to an interested listener. His smile seemed to wrap most of the way around his thin face. "What was called "Second Man," in *Antiquary*, back in 1926. I read your paper pretty carefully. Your subjects aren't pygmies, are they?"

"No."

"Caucasian?"

Marcy thought for a minute, then decided that one piece of information wouldn't reveal anything extra. "Yes," she said.

"Terrific! I'm Irish, you know," Keith began.

She looked critically at his hazel eyes and red hair. "I would never have guessed." He certainly had the gift of gab. She found that there was something appealing about him, in a face that exclaimed 'egghead' instead of 'jock.' She probably wouldn't call him handsome. Handsome to her implied square jaws and athlete's muscles, not sinews and those slim, clever-looking hands. Maybe 'cute' was a better word. But he looked like he would be a lot of fun to have around. Not her type, but not not her type.

"Sarcasm will get you nowhere, ma petite," said Keith. The ruddy eyebrows bobbed up and down. "I want to know about the little people. The fair folk. I'm trying to figure out where they went when they disappeared. *If* they disappeared. Another legend says that all the Irish are related to the Fair Folk. You can say I'm just doing a genealogy of the Doyle family. No, don't say that. I want to know if they died out, or if they went underground, or what?" He drank deeply from his glass and set it down with a satisfied sigh. "Is there anything unusual about your subjects that you're not telling me?"

Marcy was taken aback. Did Keith really have that kind of perspicacity, or was he just guessing? "*I* don't think so," she said at last, fingertip drawing rings around a minute puddle of spilled Coke. "Please don't be offended, but I think they'd think your paper's frivolous."

"So does everyone else," Keith admitted without rancor. "But it's not just a paper to me. My R.A. says I've got a mania. Okay, so I'm very interested in writing a paper on it for Sociology class, but I don't have to. Your subjects have a strong genetic tendency toward being short, right? Is there mixed fairy blood, or just recessive genes with no place else to go? Who knows? You pay more attention to stories with a personal application, you know. Some people are proud of the idea that they might be related to the fair folk. Like myself, for example. If they'd just talk to me about legends, the things they heard while they were growing up…"

"I don't think they would," Marcy interrupted hastily.

"Well, answer me this: are they all from the same village, or county?" Keith persisted.

"Yes. Maybe. Their coloring's alike. It's like yours."

"Are they Irish?" Keith leaned forward.

"I think so, but…."

"Great! Please, please ask if I can talk to any of them. I care. I won't publish anything if they don't want me to. It's to satisfy my own curiosity," he finished earnestly. "If they say no, well, I'll respect their privacy. If they say yes, I'll respect their privacy. Either way. The fact that you haven't thrown me out yet or called me crazy encourages me."

"Okay," she said reluctantly. "I'll ask."

"Blessings on you. I owe you a soda or something else wholesome. How about tonight?" She turned her head shyly away from him. "Aw, come on," Keith coaxed. "Is it your boyfriend? I'm no threat. I'm just a friend."

"No, it isn't that," she insisted, louder than necessary. "I have to meet with my study group."

"Hey, you mentioned that yesterday. Tuesdays and Thursdays. Can I come, too? I'd like to study with you. Get to know you better."

She bounced out of the kitchen chair, as if spring-loaded, and started to rinse out their glasses at the sink. "It's a closed group."

"You said that before, too, but they have to get members from someplace. Is it a sorority club? Women only?"

"No. Are you kidding? I'd rather have real friends."

What brought that confession on? Keith wondered. He studied her face. No, she wouldn't fit in with sororities. She was the right kind of pretty and the right kind of smart, but her skin wasn't thick enough. All his predatory instincts had been knocked on the head once he'd started listening more carefully to her. She aroused all of his natural protectiveness. Keith felt himself to be more effective as a big brother than a boyfriend. Not that Marcy was falling all over herself for him. As much as he hated to concede the field to the virtuous unknown, whoever he was, Keith hoped the guy was worth it. But she was darned good at changing the subject. "I'll be your best friend," he volunteered.

"Oh, cut it out," she snapped, her back to him. "I don't need pity."

"I know; I'm sorry. Look, do you want to go for a walk, or to a movie, or get married, or something?" he asked in mock desperation. "I can't leave until you're not mad at me anymore."

She turned around to retort, and he clasped his hands under his chin in supplication. He rolled his eyes up. So did she. "Do you always offer to marry everyone who's mad at you?" Marcy giggled.

"Only the women," Keith answered, animated again, like a Jack-in-the-box. Marcy shook her head, and glanced at the clock. Keith felt hope returning. "It's not an Honors group," he said impulsively, "or a sorority group, so if you sponsored me, could I join you? Maybe just once. I'll even sponsor you to Student Council, although I'm not so sure that's a favor."

"Okay," she said. "I'll ask."

"Two sodas!" Keith exclaimed. "And a movie. They're showing *Attack of the Killer Tomatoes* tomorrow night. You'll love it." Now he noticed the flowered clock over the sink. "Oops, I'm late for my next F. See you in Flunking with Freleng tomorrow."

"Don't remind me."

Keith appeared at the apartment the next evening clutching a bunch of daisies before him. A tall blond girl in sweat pants let him in. She gave him a disinterested once over and left him on the threshold, and walked back into the hallway.

"Marcy!" she called, and Keith heard her go on in a lower voice through the thin wooden walls, "your nerd's here." He chuckled, noticed another girl, one with brown hair, watching him from the kitchen table, and favored her with a toothy Archie Andrews grin.

She clicked her tongue in disgust, and went back to reading her magazine. Keith flashed a wink in her direction, and surveyed the rest of the apartment.

There was a war of styles going on in here, and it looked like Modern Pop was going to win by accumulated clutter. Posters, mostly those of pop music groups, were taped over the dusty green walls everyplace but the light switches and windows. Boxes of records flanked a mighty stereo system and a VCR. One of the girls who lived here had money. By comparison, the basket of skeins of yarn, spinning wheel and embroidery frame in one corner, and the modest bookshelf under the windows, took up scarcely any space at all.

"Thanks a lot," came Marcy's voice, faintly.

Another mumble from the other girl, of which Keith could only discern, "trouble with…"

"Look," said Marcy's voice, growing louder as she came out of her room, "I don't care what he says." She emerged into the foyer checking the fit of her dark green sweater and pale green slacks in the hall mirror. "Hi."

"Hello, there," Keith said, appreciatively. "You look very nice."

The sweater was embroidered with roses and the slacks were very flattering to her figure. He gave her an encouraging grin. She looked down selfconsciously, as if the combination was accidental. "Oh. Thanks."

"Shall we go down to the Student Union first? *Attack of the Killer Tomatoes* starts at eight."

"As long as it isn't *Reefer Madness* and *The Groove Tube* again."

Keith held open the door, and they stepped out into the bitter cold of the night. "It all depends on the vagaries of the studio distributor. Don't you know that's their subtle little way of telling us that the feature didn't show up?"

When the film ended, which did after all turn out to be *Attack of the Killer Tomatoes,* they walked over to Frankie's, a little bar and grill on the corner not far from the auditorium that was heavily frequented by the student population of Midwestern. Keith was enjoying her company enormously. In spite of her shyness, Marcy made conversation easy. "Sorry I can't take you anywhere classier," Keith said apologetically. "My roommate borrowed my car. I agreed to let him have it before I remembered we were going out this evening."

Marcy flinched. "Don't call it 'going out,' okay?"

"Whatever you want. It doesn't mean anything," Keith was upset at her discomfort. "I'm just your friend. Say," he demanded, with a lightning change of subject, "is Marcy short for anything?"

"No," Marcy stopped, and hopped uncertainly onto the new train of thought. "It's my whole first name. I think it's out of one of those cutesy comic books my mother used to read when she was little. It was almost Barbara, or Barbie for short, except my aunt had a daughter three months before I was born, and they named *her* Barbara. Thank God."

"Sounds terrible. You were lucky. My full name's Keith Emerson Doyle, because my folks are big Emerson, Lake and Palmer fans. My dad was heartbroken when I didn't want to take piano lessons. Or guitar. Or drums."

"Did you take something?"

"Yup. Clarinet. For a year and a half I sounded like leaky plumbing, and then suddenly, I could make music. Dad forgave me, and started listening to more jazz."

Marcy giggled. "Do you play any more?"

"Just to annoy the neighbors." Keith said with satisfaction. The waiter, a graduate student, stood next to the table with pencil touching order pad. "Order anything you want. I pawned an old family heirloom for our…outing tonight."

They settled on Cokes, and bacon, lettuce, and tomato sandwiches. As soon as the waiter went to put in the order, Keith leaned across the table and whispered in a conspiratorial tone to Marcy, "Well?"

"Well, what?" she asked in surprise.

"Well, don't keep me in suspense. What did they say?"

"Oh!" Marcy turned red. "They said they'd think about it."

Keith made a face. "They have to think about it? It must be the most exclusive study group in the world."

"Oh, the study group. I thought you meant…"

"Yeah, your subjects. Well, let them think about it, too. I've got all the time in the world. As long as they didn't say no. So I can come to the study group? Great! When's your next meeting?"

"Tomorrow…but you can't come to that either," Marcy said, lamely.

Keith blinked. His non-existent whiskers twitched. To him that was a sure sign of something interesting going on here, though he didn't know what it could be. He rubbed his chin thoughtfully. There again was that fact she was keeping hidden. And the more she held back from him, the more curious he became. She was doodling with her nails in the condensation on the side of her glass, avoiding his eyes. "If it's in your boyfriend's dorm room, he might get suspicious as to why I'm there," he guessed slyly.

"No, it's in the li—" She bit off the word. The library, Keith deduced. He smiled, pretending not to notice her verbal slip.

"It's just my week to get blackballed," he said, cheerfully. "Don't fret about it. If anyone at all wants me around, you know where to find me." The sandwiches arrived then, to Marcy's evident relief, and Keith allowed the subject to drop entirely. "Food," he exclaimed, happily. "I have to go out to eat now and again, so that I don't start believing what they feed us in the dorm is really edible. It sure couldn't be nutritious." He chewed a toasted corner.

"It is pretty disgusting. That's why I moved out of the dorms. Only it turns out my roommates are terrible cooks, too." Marcy attacked her sandwich with zeal, grateful that he had the tact to let go of an uncomfortable topic. Keith was nice and nondemanding. She listened to him talk pleasant nonsense while she ate, saying little herself. It was too bad she couldn't tell him what he wanted to know, but it wasn't her secret to tell. If she could have, she would have. Keith seemed easy to trust. "Um, how's your paper coming?"

"Oh, my research? Fine. Maybe I'll write a book some day. For example, did you know that the places where belief in the supernatural has been holding on through modern times are mostly agrarian or third world nations? It looks like as soon as a country or civilization goes industrial, stops being so close to the earth, those beliefs disappear. There's something scary about machinery; you lose sight of the fact that it isn't sentient. The only 'little folk' you have left are the malign ones, like gremlins getting in and gumming up the works." Keith made a face. "A long way from the kind little guys who sneaked in and made shoes for you while you were asleep. Since man can make shoes for himself while he sleeps, with machines, what do you need the fairies for? I guess the need for 'em dwindles when what was once considered to be impossible to do yourself became possible with technology. Either that, or blame the iron in steel. Very few things of magic could bear the touch of cold iron."

Keith let himself prattle on, his conversation only occupying a small portion of his mind. He could tell Marcy had something to think over, but not what. She was uneasy about having him encroach on her private activities; that was obvious, and understandable. The library. Well, since she couldn't enlighten him further, the only gentlemanly thing to do would be to follow her there and see what was going on for himself. He took a last satisfied bite of sandwich.

On the way back to Marcy's apartment, they had to huddle together against the sharp winds, now blowing almost parallel to the ground. Marcy discovered that her thin coat had an unexpected cold spot where she guessed the worn-out lining had finally given way under the arm. Keith had on nothing but a windbreaker, and was cheerful despite the fact that he must be freezing. He clutched her around her cold side, steering her around puddles riming over with thin, crisp ice. She huddled gratefully into his arm.

A boy with a wool cap pulled down firmly over his ears marched out of the gloom toward them, aiming his path directly between them. They dodged him, but ended up parting to dive for opposite edges of the sidewalk to make way to avoid the enormous knobby shopping bag the boy was clutching to his chest. Marcy gasped as a freezing gust went up the legs of her pants. As the boy passed, he glared at both of them, as if to blame them for the bad weather. From under black brows, his dark-eyed stare met Marcy's, and she flinched. She knew him. It was Enoch, one of the Little Folk from the hidden room. He shouldered away from the two of them and went on, heading in toward the campus.

"Boy, what's his problem?" Keith asked, glancing over his shoulder. Marcy looked a little dazed, and he held out an arm to her. "Forget him. Probably sore because he had to go grocery shopping in the cold."

To Keith's surprise, Marcy waved away the arm. "Thanks. I'll be okay now." She huddled into her jacket, pulling the spare folds of cloth around to the torn side, and lowered her chin to protect her throat from the wind. The boy's glance had disturbed her. She leaned into the wind, ignoring the puzzled expression on Keith's face. "Come on. It's late."

"Right," Keith agreed, hurrying after her.

Chapter 6

It wasn't much warmer the next day. In the shelter of a brick gatepost across from Marcy's apartment, Keith was congratulating himself on remembering to wear two sweaters under his coat, but regretting that he'd left his hat behind. Other students brushed by, some glancing his way, but most of them ignoring him, not wanting to turn their necks in the cold wind. A girl gave him a sideways look, and he smiled. "Hi, there," he offered. She turned away quickly, dismissing him. He sighed. "Cold-shouldered again. Nice day for it, though."

Overhead, the heavy sky was turning slate and dark purple. The National Weather Service had suggested that the first flurries of snow might be on their way; if not now, then certainly before the end of the month. Keith shrugged, huddling his ears into his collar. There was no such thing as an easy midwestern winter. One just hoped the inevitable wouldn't be too early in coming.

Broken brown leaves swirled through the iron tines of the gate, and collected, rustling, in the shelter between Keith and the corner of the wall. The wind increased in velocity, whipping the students from a walk to a run between the class buildings. Keith felt his nose and ears growing frosty and numb, tried not to think about them.

White sheets of paper cartwheeled down the sidewalk, pursued by their owner, a honey-blonde-haired girl in a pink aviator's jacket, waving an empty folder and yelling over the howling chorus of the wind. A few of the pages swirled in behind him, and he managed to trap them against the wall without crumpling them too much. He stepped out of his hiding place to help her gather up the rest.

"Thanks," she gasped, brushing her hair out of her eyes. "It's my research paper." Keith held the portfolio open while she shuffled the fluttering pages together. From the depths of a pocket full of oddments, he found a large paper clip which he offered to the girl. She secured the paper to the folder, flipped it shut, and smiled up at him. Her eyes were blue-green and very pretty. "Thanks again."

"No problem. You know us Boy Scouts," Keith said, becoming interested in pursuing the conversation, then over her shoulder caught sight of Marcy emerging from her apartment. He had to make a rapid choice between duty and pleasure, and curiosity won. "'Scuse me. Duty calls." He dodged out of sight behind the gate, and waited until Marcy had passed, heading toward the library. The girl in pink gave him an odd look, and went away without further comment.

He stayed outside the library until he could see which direction she was going through the glass doors. The heavy bronze frames creaked as he hauled one of them outward into the wind. Two other students behind him caught the metal door's edge, which burned their fingers with cold, and together they pulled it open. The wind shook it in fierce protest as they struggled inside. The thick plate glass windows thundered.

Keith kept to the edges of the foyer until Marcy showed her pass and entered the library stacks. Curious, he found his own stack pass, and went in behind her.

He almost lost his quarry on the ground level, until he noticed the fire stairwell door hissing shut. No one was allowed to use those stairs except the librarians. The general use staircase was in a different place. With a quick glance around to make sure no one was watching him, he followed. Her footsteps sounded out below him, and he trotted down the stairs, taking care to stay a flight above her. Either this study group met down in one of the conference rooms in the stacks, or he was probably going to interrupt Marcy and her boyfriend, having a private "study session." Keith made a face. He decided he didn't want to think about the latter, and stifled the little whine of jealousy in his mind.

It was dim in the stairwell, and the echoes sounded about him. Even his faint footfalls threatened to drown out the distant clatter of Marcy's steps. He was descending into No-Man's-Land, the private realm of the librarians. Keith felt as if he was on a safari, passing into dangerous territory. Did the library staff know that Marcy's group was here? The very secretiveness of her group excited Keith's already sharp curiosity. But what would Marcy think if she caught him following her?

Another set of footsteps joined the echoes in the hall. Keith stopped, wondering if it was the boyfriend, or someone else from her group. No, they were too definite, too deliberate. Not another student sneaking up the stairs. Someone with authority. Keith straightened up and let his shoulders swing in a nonchalant attitude, pretending he belonged here.

"Young man!" A tall dignified woman with a coil of black hair on her head swam out of the gloom. "What are you doing here?"

"Um, going to level eleven, ma'am," Keith said, blanching. He started around her, but she clenched his upper arm in a powerful grip peculiar to librarians engaged in administering reproofs.

"This area is restricted from students' use except during emergencies," she said coldly. Her scrawny neck and full cheeks made her look like an angry turkey. "You are to use the north stair only." Keith nodded politely, and tried to catch the sound of Marcy's footsteps. They had disappeared. The librarian escorted him forcefully to the eleventh level and pushed him into a waiting elevator. "Your privileges will be restricted to the study rooms for tonight."

"But my project...?" There was no chance of catching Marcy now.

"Your project will have to wait. You students must learn that you cannot break rules without punishment." She flipped his stack card out of his fingers and brandished it at him. "You may reclaim this from my secretary tomorrow morning. I'm Mrs. Hansen, the head of Library Services." The elevator closed with a snap on his protests.

Keith wandered around the reading rooms, keeping an eye on the stack entrance, until the Teaching Assistant on duty there threw him out. After that, he sat in the lobby, wondering if he should try to get into the stacks another way. He dismissed the idea, realizing that he would probably miss Marcy if he left his watch-post. Nine o'clock closing came, and the other students drifted out of the stacks. Marcy was among them, and she was alone.

"Hi!" Keith hailed her as she appeared.

Marcy smiled at him curiously. "How long have you been here?"

"Just a little while," he assured her. "I had nothing else to do. Thought I'd just wait and find out what your study group had to say."

"How did you know...?" Marcy exclaimed.

"You almost said it last night," Keith said, apologetically. "*The li*— Sorry. It's the bloodhound in me. And the rest of my face isn't so good, either. How about it?"

"I...They still say they'll think about it. Please. I'm doing what I can. Don't rush me. They're kind of...funny about having people join."

"No problem," Keith said, stretching as he rose from the marble bench. "Want to go for some coffee?"

"Sure," Marcy said, relieved. "I'm glad you're being patient."

"That's me," Keith said, taking Marcy's arm. "Patience is my middle name. Right after Emerson."

The next Tuesday, Keith spotted Marcy walking alone across the common, and hurried his pace to catch up with her. His mouth was open to call out a greeting to her, when Carl Mueller appeared from between two concrete posts on the edge of the parking lot, and matched his stride to hers. She smiled shyly and tilted her head to one side, responding to something Carl was saying with a satisfied smirk on his face. Keith was too far away to hear what they were saying, but it was obvious from the body language what he was seeing: this was the above-reproach boyfriend in Marcy's life. Carl fell neatly into that sort of pigeonhole. He considered himself to be a cut or so better than most of the other students, and had somehow persuaded Marcy to agree with him. Poor kid.

Keith had an impulse to run up and start a conversation with her, which would infuriate Carl, but Marcy would probably get upset if he annoyed her boyfriend. He assumed that Carl must be in the mysterious study group, too. That would explain perfectly why Marcy was uncomfortable about having him, Keith, around. Not only was Carl a snob, but he was a jealous snob, too. The guy probably monogrammed the flowers he gave her. He wondered if Carl knew he knew Marcy.

He followed them down the street, trailing about a hundred feet behind, until they came to Gillington Library. Hanging back so they wouldn't see him, he paused at the top of the steps, squinting through the double glass doors, until he saw which way they turned. Ah. Left. The stacks.

Feeling like a private detective on the scent of an adulterous divorcee, he flashed his ID card at the librarian on duty at the entrance to the stacks. Marcy and Carl had disappeared, and Keith heard the bang and whirr of the elevator. He ambled down the aisle toward the double metal doors, idly fingering the spines of books, as if looking for just any old thing to read.

Out of the corner of his eye, he watched the indicator drop. Either this study group met in the basement of the stacks, or the lovebirds were just looking for somewhere dark to neck. Not Marcy!

he chided himself, right hand slapping his own left wrist. She wasn't that type. Campy, but true.

The librarian, a thin woman of middle age who looked like a failed actress, glanced at him oddly. "Black widow spider," he explained solemnly, holding up his wrist for her examination. "The bite is usually fatal."

"Oh," she nodded, and then looked away, her forehead pulled into a puzzled frown.

The indicator stopped on Level Fourteen, which was the lower half of the third sub-basement. The library stacks were half-high levels, eight above ground, and six below. As far as Keith knew, there was nothing official that went on in those underground levels. They were archives; locked floors to be entered by library personnel only.

Unless Carl and Marcy had keys, they must have exited the elevator before then. And yet, he hadn't noticed the indicator stopping before it showed the basement numbers. Something most definitely was going on here. Cursing himself for not paying attention, he found the stairs, and started down to search the floors one by one.

Weaving his way through the low-ceilinged, narrow aisles of the stack levels, Keith put on a show of bored nonchalance flavored with the attitude any harried student had toward trying to find an obscure book out of which some teacher threatened to construct the entire final exam for his course. The first four underground levels were a snap. The lighting was good, and no one paid him much attention. The heavy thrum of the heating system spread a blanket of white noise throughout each floor. Maybe ten students occupied each floor in various isolated carrels, cramming for one course or another, with heavy head full of knowledge cradled in supporting hands over a textbook. But his search was frustrated. None of the meeting rooms was occupied. Marcy was nowhere around.

He wondered if he had mistaken another number for Fourteen. No, he was sure he had seen the indicator change from a one and a round number, and he was certain it wasn't 10. Also, it would have been quicker to walk down the two short flights of stairs. Capturing the elevator, he held the door open with one hand and punched at the last two studs in the double column. They refused to light up, obviously waiting for the key to be turned in the locks below to activate them. The door surged under his hand, and from somewhere in the bowels of the mechanism, the elevator emitted an imperative *BEEPum BEEPum BEEPum.* Petulantly, Keith gave the door a sharp shove before letting it slide closed. It thrummed away, the beeping fading into the floors above.

Carl and Marcy weren't on any of the four floors. That left the two security floors. What was so special about this meeting that it had to be held down there? Of all the inconvenient locations! At this hour of the evening, ninety percent of the classrooms on campus were empty. Maybe he was about to stumble into a communist satrap, or a weird religious cult. He mentally scratched the latter option; he couldn't really see Carl dancing around in a pastel muslin robe.

How about a spy ring? he speculated, as he stood in the stairwell, prying at the locked door to level Thirteen. Keith loved a mystery, especially one he didn't have to take seriously. He could see through the edge of the door that it wasn't quite latched, but that there was no knob on this side. With the tips of his fingers, he dragged at the painted metal door, pulling it a quarter inch out from the jamb. The hinges groaned and scraped, echoing deafeningly in the dim hall. He scrabbled at the emerging edge with one hand, but it slipped back flush. It was simply too heavy for him to hold it open with just one set of fingers.

He needed to get something between the door and the frame to keep it from slamming shut until he could get his hands free. A pencil was the only thing he had on him that was light and strong enough. It went between his teeth, eraser end outward, and he pulled at the door again. The rubber eraser skipped across the paint, jabbing the point of the pencil into his tongue. "Aagh," he mumbled around it, and then winced at the sound.

Carefully, he maneuvered it into the tiny opening of the door. It took him four tries before he could pull the door wide enough for the pencil to go through. It occurred to him too late that the point would have helped him widen the opening. Never mind. He let go of the door when the pencil was in place. It snicked shut onto the wood, and Keith stepped back, spitting out graphite.

Dusting his tingling fingertips together, he levered the door open and let himself through. A crumpled candy wrapper pressed into the latch socket was what had prevented the door from locking automatically. Keith deduced in his best consulting detective method that someone else without keys wanted access to these floors. In the pitiful light of a wavering fluorescent bulb high up in the stairwell, nothing out of the ordinary would have been visible.

Level Thirteen was poorly lit. It was also neglected, Keith learned, as he prowled around the room, peering into alcoves. Checkout cards lay strewn on the floor with scuffed foot-prints and dust on them, and here and there the end of an internal shelf had slipped, letting the books on it fall sideways, as if they were reclining, bored to be here in the dark. Just as in the twelve levels above, carrels and study nooks occupied two walls, and the elevator descended down a shaft drilled straight through the middle of the level, visible over the metal bookshelves. The room was surprisingly cold. They must have all the heating ducts closed, since no one used this floor much. It didn't have to be fit for human habitation, or for librarians, either. Keith wasn't sure about librarians.

Children's librarians were a little different. They seemed to like people, and all the ones he knew enjoyed their jobs. He admired their patience. Maybe it was that they were actively involved in teaching, helping their young charges to learn skills they had never encountered before, while their co-workers in the adult sections were just caretakers for what they perceived to be an unappreciative and disinterested public. Too bad there were no children's librarians here at Midwestern. On the other hand, maybe not. Keith would never get away with half of his favorite bent rules if there were.

Nothing here, anywhere on this level. That left Fourteen.

Once beyond the security door, there were no more barriers. Keith trotted down the last set of stairs, listening to his footsteps reverberate in the hall like ping-pong balls bouncing. He thought for one breathless moment he could hear other feet on the stairs, but guessed that the echoes were playing tricks on his ears.

Fourteen was, if anything, more deserted than Thirteen. There were no emergency lights down here at all. He felt his way to the elevator, wishing he had brought a flashlight. Not that he was afraid of the dark, but what if something jumped out at him? The light switches were somewhere on the central pillar. There was a groaning hum under the floor that raised the hair on the back of his neck, but that was from the furnace blowers. It was nice and warm down here, but not inviting. He decided he had to be wrong about Marcy being down here somewhere. It was dead quiet. There was no one down here but himself.

He touched the wall, found his way to the switchplate. The slots were empty. They required the insertion of a switchkey, something impossible to duplicate without a screwdriver or a paperclip, and Keith had neither. He felt for the elevator call button. He wondered where Marcy and Carl had gone. This was an old building. Maybe there was a secret passage around here somewhere, and they lost him on Level Eleven, right under the librarians' noses. His imagination drew up pictures of a spy sect, something to do with the CIA or communism, melded with the weird religious cult that worshipped IC chips. Men and women wearing gray business suits under sackcloth robes and chanting from mystic flow charts. He'd be intruding on a bunch of mindless hulks who would beat him up, and spread his guts out across Anthropology through History in the name of electronics.

"C'mon, I'm scaring myself," Keith said chidingly. His throat was dry and tight.

A click sounded behind him, a heel scraping against the concrete floor. Keith spun, just as the blinding beam from a flashlight hit him square in the eyes. His heart pounded, threatening to jump out of his open mouth.

"What are you doing down here?" a man's voice boomed.

"Uh," cried Keith, goggling. His voice had abandoned him. The beam moved closer, dazzling him with the sun-bright circle of yellow light at the center of the white, and passed, brushing the wall until it came to the elevator indicator. The flashlight turned vertical, as the hand holding it shifted to punch the call button. The light turned horizontal again, and stayed on Keith's face until the elevator arrived. Keith shrank back against the cold, rough stucco wall, trying to avoid looking down the hot torch-beam. He felt like a rabbit caught trying to cross a road. The other hand appeared now, reached up and shoved him into the car.

"Don't come down here again without authorization," the voice grumbled. As the doors closed, Keith caught a glimpse of a bearded man in a security uniform, and the flashlight, as it turned back toward the floor. Something about the guard's proportions seemed wrong, but before he could be sure, the elevator doors closed. His heart slowed down gradually to its normal pace.

He posted himself in a study carrel on Level Eight handy to the elevator and the stairwell, and waited for Marcy to reappear. The scrawny librarian kept staring fiercely at him, willing him to sit still and study. Keith smiled sweetly, and went on jumping up every time the elevator stopped near him. After an eternity of false starts, the elevator doors opened, and Marcy and Carl emerged, chatting. Keith raised himself up, and waved over the carrel wall. Marcy noticed him, and involuntarily started toward him, shaking her head, signalling a frantic 'no.' Carl noticed him then, and glared hotly, pacing ahead of Marcy. If Carl had been Superman with heat vision, Keith would have been a little crispy smudge on the floor. He ignored Carl, and smiled brightly at Marcy. "Hi!"

"Uh, hi," Marcy said, barely audibly.

"Good to see you," Keith said. "Marcy's in my Sociology class," he explained.

"I know," Carl glowered. He tugged at Marcy's arm, and she turned away too quickly, banging her knee against an exposed I-beam. She gave a soft gasp and nearly dropped her books, but she kept moving. Carl didn't seem to notice that she had hurt herself, and virtually pulled her out of the stacks. The last Keith could see of her was an expression of wide-eyed appeal. Or desperation.

"I'll see you later," he called to her.

"Please, just leave me alone," she breathed, clutching her books tightly. Keith subsided into his chair, puzzled.

"Shhh!" hissed the librarian, triumphantly.

Chapter 7

Keith spent most of Monday night in the company of his RA and several other members of the Student Government, on an act which required the utmost secrecy. It was a mission of mercy on behalf of Dan Osborne. He was a member who was attending the University on an athletic scholarship, and had won the first place medal in the regional swimming competition for the 440-meter race. Danny was ecstatic over his victory, and had been seen all day walking as if on air. The other members decided that it was up to them to keep him from getting a big head over his success, and maybe walking right out of the atmosphere before he noticed. It was for this reason that they were engaged in transporting his Volkswagen Scirocco from the parking lot to the bottom of an empty swimming pool at one o'clock in the morning.

They decided it was worth it to help him out, since the chances that the administration would blame Student Government for such a prank were suitably small. Pat, shaking off his lethargy for once, decided to help out. He was a friend of Danny's, too.

One of the guys in on the joke was an Engineering major. With the help of an architecture student, Sharon Teitelbaum, they had constructed a pair of jointed ramps that hung over the edge of the pool like a set of badly broken skis. Mere Business and English majors, like Keith and Pat, were delegated to be pallbearers and help carry the car out of the lot.

Once in the loftily-named 'natatorium,' Rick sprang the door lock, and took off the emergency brake. With four men on either side, they eased the car down the ramps.

"There," said Rick, with satisfaction. "It'll take him hours to figure out how we did it."

"Let's leave the ramps in the office," Keith suggested, "so it won't be too hard to find them."

"That doesn't mean a thing," Pat sniffed. "People who are intelligent enough to understand machinery don't become gym teachers." Rick hit him solidly between the shoulder blades, and he choked.

"Knock it off, Shakespeare," Rick growled in mock ire, "or I'll put you through the goalposts."

"Spoken like a true snob," Keith accused Pat cheerfully.

"Of course," Pat answered, airily. "P.E. majors stand right ahead of us English majors on the unemployment line."

It was quiet and dark in the hallway of the dormitory. There were a few students still awake, but they had their doors closed to keep the noise from stereos, TV's, passionate discussions or other activities from annoying people who would rather sleep. This floor was nearly empty. The figure sneaking toward Keith's room had seen everyone leaving over an hour ago. There would probably be time enough left.

With a look over his shoulder to ensure there was no one watching, the figure set down his bag and bent over the doorknob. A quick gleam of metal flashed, reflecting the safety lights at the hall's T-intersection, and the door creaked gently open. The figure stepped inside the dark room.

When they tramped back to their dorm room, fortified from Rick's personal store with beer and potato chips, Keith popped open the door, flicked on the lights with a flourish, and stopped short on the threshold.

"Oh, Pat," he chided his roommate. "You didn't tell me you were going to redecorate."

"Huh? Oh, shit," Pat said, pushing in past Keith. Books were scattered all over the floor, and papers lay in a chaotic snowstorm on the bed, the desk and the dresser. A broad map of sticky, brown film spread on the wall had obviously issued from the empty bottle of Coke on the coffee table. But the carnage was limited to Keith's side of the room. There could almost have been a line drawn down the center. Not a scrap of paper or a drop was on Pat's side. "What happened?"

"Well, if it's Santa Claus, he's two months early. And I really woulda preferred coal in my stocking. It's a lot more subtle."

"My man, you've been pimped. Who have you ticked off lately?"

"I bet it's Carl. Why else would your stuff be left completely alone? I'm going to go talk to him."

"Enough," Pat commanded, blocking Keith from leaving. "It's after midnight. Carl thinks you're a royal pain but not worthy of the trouble. Believe me, I've heard it all from him at length."

"But who else?" insisted Keith. He eyed the mess. "I'd better clean it up now. I can't sleep with that Coke dripping off the wall onto me all night. I'd dream of Chinese torturers."

"You'd drive them nuts, too. I'll go tell Rick, then I'll come back and help," Pat offered.

"Thanks." Keith wrung out a washcloth and set to work, grumbling. Pat slipped out of the room. In the stillness, Keith could hear him knocking, and then the low hum of voices. In a moment, Rick appeared at the door.

"Honest to God, Doyle."

"In the immortal words of Han Solo, Rick, it's not my fault."

"It never is. I'll ask around. Come and talk to me after dinner, okay? I'll tell Jackson and they'll change your locks tomorrow. It's the best we can do."

"Yeah. Thanks." Keith went back to work on the wall. "'Night."

His nocturnal activities left Keith feeling worn out all Tuesday. Only anticipation of solving the mystery of Marcy's study group kept him from declaring a mental health day and cutting Sociology.

When he got to class, he wished that he had cut. Dr. Freleng, in full knowledge that a holiday break was coming, and that all the other teachers were loading the students up with work, issued instructions for a new term paper, worth the usual 10% of the grade. Keith walked out of the room reeling with exhaustion and irritation. Marcy smiled at him sympathetically as she left. "See you later," she called.

"Absolutely," Keith promised.

This time, Keith made certain that he was invisible. He had positioned himself in the stacks on Level Eight, thumbing through boxes of crumpled periodicals. Marcy appeared right on schedule, and stepped into the elevator. After a suitable interval, Keith shoved his handful of magazines back into the box, and slipped behind the fire door.

He crept down the stairs in almost total darkness and into the bottommost level of the library. His mother used to say that if there was justice in the world, he would have been born with cat whiskers as wide as his shoulders to prove that one day his own curiosity would kill him. He wished for those whiskers now, as his head rapped against several metal bookshelves which laughed hollowly at him in the gloom. Odors and fragrances familiar to him tickled his nose in the thick warm air: concrete dust, mouldering paper and library paste.

A humming white line of light grew down from the ceiling and stopped noisily at the floor. Steel doors clashed open, and Marcy appeared out of the book elevator clutching her green notebook. She felt around her head for the nearest bookshelf and started forward, guiding herself with her free hand. The elevator closed behind her, cutting off the light. The confident tap of her shoes on the concrete floor passed Keith and went on down the row. He prayed that he could follow her without bringing down Dewey decimal system numbers .3440 to .785 on top of himself on the way. He sank catlike to all fours. Maybe he could crawl after her. Maybe not. It always looked easier when babies did it. He struggled along the floor, trying not to make any noise.

There was a fair amount of dust on the floor his movements stirred up, which he promised his twitching nose he would sneeze at later. His knees informed him that he was too old for this manner of locomotion. His ears informed him that he was doing a pretty good job of shadowing without making noise or being noticed. Marcy was keeping a slow pace ahead of him. A sudden light gleamed in her hand. Keith's heart jumped. If she had a flashlight she wasn't using until the last moment, Keith was going to have to do some fancy explaining. Certainly he was at a disadvantage: what could he say? "Hi, doll. Of all the library stacks, in all the universities, she walks into mine. Oh, what am I doing on the floor? I dropped my next line."

She stopped. Keith could see at last that the light she held came from a key. It shone faintly green against the keyhole of a low door behind the last row of bookshelves. Probably one of those keylights. A miniature flashlight would be vital down here, but the sure way she had found the door spoke of long familiarity. The door opened inward, and Marcy disappeared into a sudden riot of light and noise. It boomed shut behind her.

"Nuts," he said to himself. "Now what do I do?"

On hands and knees, he crawled carefully over to the door and felt over its surface for the keyhole. He found a polished square with a slot and put his eye to it. He could see nothing. It was as black as the room he was in. They, whoever *they* were, must have blocked it to keep light from leaking out and betraying the presence of the room on the other side. And what was that room? Keith didn't know of any further excavation or construction in Gillington Library. The perimeter of the stacks stopped where he was standing, or rather, kneeling, right now. This must be really top secret.

He could feel the bass hum of conversation vibrating the door under his fingertips. Leaning close, he set his ear gently on the rough wood, and closed his eyes to concentrate. Several people were talking, though their words were no more distinguishable than if they had been speaking under water. One tenor voice, its tone proving its owner to be seething with irritation, overpowered the others, and then went on alone somewhat more calmly.

Definitely the faculty advisor, Keith decided. But for what subject? Or purpose? There was something about this situation which made his imaginary whiskers bristle out. Why meet in the sub-sub-basement of the library, when at this hour three-fourths of the classrooms on campus were empty? And what about that key Marcy had? Its green light was unlike that of either phosphorus or any LEDs he'd ever seen. Must be some really neat mechanism. He was intrigued. Something very interesting was going on here. His thin nose twitched with curiosity.

And dust, Keith discovered in a panic. He was going to sneeze. His eyes watered as he pinched his nose to hold back the explosion. He rocked back on his heels until the impulse passed, and then hunkered down once more against the door. The room on the other side of the wall had fallen silent. Keith blinked in the dark with surprise. No voices, not even the faculty advisor's. Had everybody left through some other door? he wondered, holding his breath and straining for any telltale sound. No, if that place had a second entrance, Marcy wouldn't have to come down through the stacks, risking the librarians' wrath. No, he reconsidered, it was probably all set up with the librarians. Maybe he could coax one into telling him all about it, later. He gently cuddled his ear closer into the rough wood, leaning his weight inward.

A second later, he was measuring his length on the concrete floor of a brightly lit room, shaking stars out of his head. Marcy was halfway to her feet, about fifteen feet away from him, fingertips over her mouth, staring at him in shock. Right now he felt as surprised as she looked at his unexpected appearance. Her books sat atop the kind of wood and metal desk Keith called an 'iron maiden,' for its deserved reputation of discomfort comparable to the medieval torture device. There were fifteen or so occupied iron maidens in the room. From his undignified vantage point, Keith also recognized Carl Mueller. Aha, you scum, he thought. There were other college students there, but most of the rest of the class were adolescent kids, and they were all gawking at him. If this was the "study group," what were *they* doing here? Were they what the mystery was all about? Was Marcy ashamed to admit that she talked about her homework with a bunch of genius midgets? Or was it something more sinister, like a government think-tank?

A figure introduced itself between Keith and the rest of the room. Keith's eye traveled upward—not too far—past a pair of short legs, a protuberant belly and a barrel of a chest, to a round face bethatched and bewhiskered with hair of bright carrot red going white over the ears. Pointed ears! Keith's jaw dropped open. He blinked and twisted his neck to change his angle of view. An optical illusion? No, they were pointed, all right, and about five inches high. That was impossible! They must be made of latex, like theatrical artists used. And then again, maybe not. He opened his mouth to say something, but the man stopped him with a curt gesture of his hand. A pair of goldrimmed spectacles sat on the bridge of a pugnaciously turned-up nose behind which iris blue eyes regarded him icily. By all that Keith knew or imagined, there was a living leprechaun standing there looking down at him. "Top o' the morning to ye," he cried, cheerily.

"Gut efening," said the leprechaun. He was the owner of the tenor voice he had heard through the door. "Vould you care to get up?"

Chapter 8

The Big Folk were surprised when Keith catapulted through the door. Holl and the other small folk were not. In fact, they were expecting him. Keith's footsteps had been audible for some time in the silence on the other side of the wall. He looked as surprised to be discovered as his classmates were to see him.

The Elf Master closed the heavy door with a thud, and turned to Marcy, whose face was beet red. Holl felt sorry for her. "Zo, Mees Collier, your friend has joined us. Not efen waiting for his infitation. Zit down zomevere, Meester Doyle." He crossed his arms patiently and stepped back to let Keith get to his feet. In control as usual, the Master was taking this blatant invasion of his domain nonchalantly, as if it was not the first time such a thing had occurred.

In fact it was not. Holl and Enoch sat back at their ease in the shabby maple-topped desks and watched with amused pleasure as the young man clambered up off the floor. His jaw was hanging agape. Though the others usually waited to be asked to join the group, one and all they started out disbelieving in their surroundings. Right now, Holl's classmates were regarding the intruder with sympathy. They all remembered what it was like to walk in. Sourpuss Carl was the only unfriendly face. He looked furious to see Keith, and his shoulders were bunched up around his ears, but he kept his seat. Soft-spoken Marcy had dropped her gaze to her books and was refusing to look up at anyone. Lee was tightening and loosing his fists. Holl glanced over at Enoch, who was obviously trying to judge Marcy's reaction to the intruder. It boded ill for Keith Doyle if he was Marcy's enemy.

The red-haired boy was trying to speak. Squeaky noises like unoiled door hinges in the wind issued from his throat, eliciting nervous giggles from the others in the room, so he stopped trying to talk and stared instead.

This boy had better recover soon, Holl realized. The Master's patience wouldn't last long. Holl snickered, watching Keith as the young man's eyes turned to him and Enoch. He smiled at them, and then started, like a shying horse.

"I know what he's thinking," Enoch whispered sullenly through his teeth. "The ears."

"They all do it," Holl murmured back good-humoredly.

Keith still stood in the center of the floor, apparently dumb-founded. The Master cleared his throat and regained Keith's attention. He pointed to the empty 'iron maiden' between Holl and Enoch. Obediently, the boy made his way over to the desk, still glancing over his shoulder again and again at the little red-haired man.

"He looks as if he thinks the Master's going to vanish if he takes his eyes off him," Marm commented, fingering his beard, leaning over toward Holl.

"He'll be wishing it before the semester's out," Holl confided.

With one hand on the back of the seat, Keith swung the desk under himself. Its legs screeched painfully across the concrete floor. He dropped into the chair, too fascinated by his surroundings to notice the noise. He smiled around at everyone, then subsided into a pose of attentive interest, fingertips drumming an excited tattoo on the battered maple desktop.

What was going on here? Who was the little guy? Was he a midget? Keith looked at him again, trying to work what he was seeing into some kind of reality.

Marcy wouldn't meet his eyes. Keith knew he had some explaining to do to her later, but he had hundreds of questions to ask. The teacher looked for all the world like Brian O'Connor, the Little People, legend of the Celts, the Irish—his own background. So how come he sounded like Bela Lugosi? And what were all these children doing here? With a start he realized they had pointed ears on, too, and two of the young faces wore beards. Were they in on the gag, or was there something here that was beyond his furthest expectations? Magic? Was there magic in this place? If so, there was no one so ready to appreciate it as Keith Emerson Doyle, scholar of legends.

"Hi, I'm Keith Doyle," he said to his two seatmates, and waited for a response. "Um, do you speak English?"

The black-haired boy cleared his throat with disgust and looked away. He had a fierce glower in his dark eyes that made Keith feel as though he'd been scrutinized by the genius kid brother of a girl he was dating for the first time. Keith had seen the light of blackmail on many a similar face in his time.

The blond lad was friendlier, and favored Keith with a real grin before going back to his carving. He had dishwater blond hair and the sort of chubby cheeks that one of Keith's aunts would have loved to pinch. The narrow, sharp-pointed knife dug in to the partially whittled stick, and a splinter of wood leapt away from the minute pattern.

He was good. His skill level was way above average for his age, which Keith judged to be eleven or twelve. Keith watched him work for a moment, then indulged himself in a good stare at the profile turned to him. The ears were pointed, all right, and just a bit outsized for the boy's face, but if they were fake, the guys in Hollywood would fall all over each other to meet the makeup artist. The whorls seemed exaggerated, and the tip swept backward, continuing perfectly the lines of cheekbone and eyebrow up and toward the back of the head. The elfin girl on the boy's other side spoke softly, and the boy brushed little wood shavings onto the floor and turned his whittling over in one hand. He scratched at the ear with his little finger, thinking. The skin reddened where the nails touched. The little girl caught his eye and smiled up at him over her friend's head. She had a thick ponytail of red-brown hair and shockingly green eyes, and looked about ten years old. Her own ears, poking coyly out of the ruddy mass, went rosy when she blushed at Keith's wink. He glanced around at the rest of the group, suddenly aware he was being stared at. Every face wore an expression of serious concern. What were they worried about?

Those ears were real. *They* were real. Keith's smile widened. There were several people with ears down here. It was one thing to want to have a dream come true, and completely something else to have it happen to him. Not one Little Person, but a whole group! The Little People were alive. Keith's heart raced with joy.

Carl looked ready to explode. This so-called study group was obviously something he had wanted to keep to himself and a few select friends. Keith wanted revenge. Carl knew how much Keith wanted to find something like this—whatever this was. He'd certainly been forced to listen to enough recitations of Keith's theses on the Fair Folk and assorted legends. How'd he like it if...? Keith let mischievous plots wander into his thoughts. Revenge: all his computerized report cards reduced to gibberish; Keith had friends...Toothpaste on the telephone receiver. Four o'clock in the morning phone calls. A pie in the face at Graduation. Make him look like a fool in front of the whole world. Subscribe him to every lewd ladies' unmentionables catalog in the country.

He was brought back to the present by the sound of a throat clearing imperiously. The red-haired teacher was gesturing at a slate perched on the bed of an easel. *My God,* thought Keith, *it really IS a study group.*

"May ve continue mit today's discussion? Mr. Mueller, you had made a fery good point regarding the exchange of ideas between different cultures. There is likely to be more interaction, more exchanges, including admiration, between peoples in positions of equal or mutual security. As your example, the British und the Americans."

Distracted from his study of Keith, Carl smiled smugly, and settled back in his chair, tapping the eraser end of a pencil on his desktop to suggest that the question had been a snap for him. He was at home here. Probably he had been coming down here a long time. Keith felt like exacting instant retribution, but King Brian O'Connor was way ahead of him. The teacher peered over the tops of his lenses at Carl, looking like a frog about to surprise a fly.

"Vould you suggest that the exchanges are permanent societal incorporations, or rely upon ephemeral trends? How are they accomplished?" Carl stopped tapping, and sat up a little straighter.

"Uh, what do you mean, sir?"

"Vhat makes one culture accept facets of another?"

Keith raised his hand. He was awed by his surroundings, envying the other Big People present their privilege, but the teacher's question inspired a reply. The little guy sure knew his business. Keith had to admit that he was also determined to one-up Carl, so he might as well participate rather that just sit admiring the scenery. "Sir?" The little teacher swung away from Carl.

"Our new addition, Mr. Doyle." He pointed a forefinger at Keith.

"I would suggest, uh, sir, that most permanent exchanges start with trends, and depending on its quality of positive acceptance or nonacceptance, and reassertion, say through channels of mass communication, they may get incorporated permanently."

One thick red eyebrow arched up, wrinkling the teacher's forehead. "Examples?" He pronounced it 'exahm-ples'.

"Umm. Hair styles. Slang expressions. They go both ways across the Atlantic."

"There is no need to prove your knowledge of geography." The other students tittered, including Marcy. Keith was relieved to see that she was relaxing. He must be doing all right. "Very vell, you have an opinion. That is gut. I vould like to see three to five pages from you on the subject, to see if you can support your thesis. Bring it mit you in five days."

"Yes, sir," said Keith, elated. He had been accepted! He was part of the mysterious group, associating with, well,...elves! Well, the old guy might be one. Otherwise this was some sort of weird group that met in costume. No, it felt right to him. He had made a legitimate discovery; he felt it to the roots of his hair. These other pointy-eared people were probably the old guy's kids. He counted them. Seven. Prolific old bugger, wasn't he?

On the other hand, they might not all be kids. None of the others besides the teacher had any lines on their faces. They could all have been under fourteen, just judging by size. But what about the ones with the beards? He'd find out; if not the next time he joined the group, the time after that. That one sexy girl across the room was a perfect miniature Marilyn Monroe, with waves of thick blond hair and a body to match. If it wasn't for the fact that her feet didn't touch the ground from the seat of the desk, he would have to swear he was looking at a fully grown woman. As it was, she seemed more on the order of a little girl playing dressup with mommy's clothes. Her face was round and perfectly smooth, no makeup.

She noticed him looking at her and raised an eyebrow coyly, the corner of her mouth smiling an obvious invitation. Real live jailbait. He grinned. The blonde grinned back. Keith blushed, and she giggled silently into her hand.

And then it dawned on him, that he had just been assigned to do a research paper, and that it was due on Monday. The smile melted off his face, and he groaned, settling his elbows on his desk with a thump. The blond boy on his right snickered. "You'll learn to keep your mouth closed," he told Keith in an undertone, watching the teacher's back cautiously. "He gives extra work to the *schmartkopfs*."

"Thanks too late," Keith muttered back, slouching over his elbows. "Teachers are all alike." Then he realized the boy had spoken to him. Funny, he didn't look German. Or sound German. Except for the one word, he could have been the kid next door. Well, well, well...

An hour later, the teacher rose from his stool and nodded to the class. Without a word, the group dispersed, the humans heading out the door through which Keith had made his spectacular entrance. There was no knob on this side, but the door seemed to adhere to the fingers of the first person to touch it, and stayed obediently open until everyone had passed through.

The little folk moved toward a lower wooden portal, which opened onto a hallway about four and a half feet high. The blond boy shot him a friendly glance, and scrambled out of the desk after his fellows. "I'll see you, widdy," he said. Keith watched after them for a moment, trying to decide whether or not to follow them, and then looked around for Marcy.

She was already gone. Keith dashed out into the library after her, but the elevator at the end of the dark aisle was already on its way up with a load of students. Behind him, the classroom door hissed shut, closing him out in the dark. The line of white light cast between the elevator doors shimmered upward and was swallowed by the invisible ceiling. At best, the library elevators could only hold four people comfortably. Three human students, all strangers, their shadows deepening as the light disappeared, waited in the dark for the car to return. Carl and Marcy were probably in it now. Even though it required a key to operate the elevator down here, he refused to doubt anything if the...if THEY were involved.

Casually, Keith sauntered over to the others and asked out loud, "So, how long have you been coming down here?" He tried hard to keep the excitement out of his voice, but he could tell he wasn't succeeding.

For a time, there was no reply. Then a female voice, which Keith guessed to be attached to the fashionably dressed girl with *sorority* written all over her, said uncomfortably, "Oh, a while."

"Who is the red-haired guy? What's his name?"

"He's just the school-master," she said. "I don't know what his name is. That's all I've ever heard him called, Master."

"And the kids?"

"Fellow students," one of the young men said shortly.

"What class is this?"

"Sociology," the other man said. His voice was thunderously deep.

"Sociology?" Keith shouted. The others shushed him. "Sociology," he repeated in a whisper. "I'm failing that now with a *real* teacher."

"No," said the girl firmly. "*He* is a real teacher." The others all murmured assent. There was no question as to who 'he' was. "Last year, he was teaching mathematics. I was failing calculus miserably, and my boyfriend took me down here. It was the one course I had to take for my major that I just couldn't pass on my own. I understood it after the Master explained it. He's teaching those kids anyway, and the more the merrier, I guess. The other teacher was just no good. I'm grateful."

"Me, too," said the first young man. "Before Math it was Greek."

"Where does that other passage lead?" Keith asked, thinking of the low door.

"We don't know."

"*What* are they?"

"We don't know."

"Elves?" the girl volunteered uncertainly. No one scoffed at her.

"Where do they come from? Why are they here?"

"We don't know."

"Aren't you curious?"

"Oh, sure," said the second young man. "But they don't answer any personal questions. They're good at ignoring 'em. After a while, you stop hitting your head against the wall and just do your assignments."

"Not me," said Keith. "I have a very hard head. By the way, I'm Keith Doyle."

The elevator's light reappeared in the ceiling and crept downward. He could see silhouettes now, as the two other young men stuck out their hands. "Lee Eisley," said the first, his cap of curly, black hair glinting in the light. "Barry Goodman," said the second. "Teri Knox." Keith shook hands with them all.

The elevator door opened, and disgorged a librarian with a cart. She stuck a key into a wall panel. Fluorescent lights flickered on over the aisles. Keith's eyes stung from the sudden brightness. The woman shrieked when she saw them waiting there, but recovered her composure quickly.

"What are you all doing down here?" she snapped suspiciously, in a voice like her cart's. "This is a restricted level."

"We, uh, came down the stairs. They were unlocked," Keith lied, waving vaguely behind him, thanking the unseen that it wasn't Mrs. Hansen. "We got lost." He gave her what he hoped was a melting smile.

She was unimpressed. "That is impossible. No one is allowed down here without a pass." Elbows out, she pushed the cart into their midst with typical librarian arrogance that they had better get out of the way or be run over. Its wheels squealed an earsplitting protest. Keith, with assiduous politeness, bowed her past him. Teri giggled.

The woman gave them a sour glance over her shoulder. "Stay off this level unless you get authorization from the Head of Library Services," she said firmly, and stalked off behind the squeaking cart.

"Yes, ma'am," Keith said, buoyed on his joy. "Uh, you need to oil your axles. That way you won't squeak so much."

Her back stiffened, and she turned to make a suitably quelling retort, but the elevator door slid closed on their grinning faces.

"By the way," Teri said, just before the elevator stopped on the ground level, "It's very important that you don't tell anyone about...the class. No one else knows it's there."

"How can the librarians miss that door?"

"Believe me, they just don't see it. Nothing's visible when the light is on," Lee said adamantly, his long curly hair bobbing as he talked. "I've tried, and you have to know what to look for."

"The Master doesn't want to be bothered by just anyone," Barry said, belligerently. "You're in on something special. Don't ruin it for the rest of us."

"Of course not," Keith assured him with all his heart. "I know how special it is. I'll keep it very quiet."

"Please," Teri begged. "He's already threatened once to exclude...big folk. I really value the class, and I don't want to stop going. It's like, well, touching a fairy tale. That sounds dumb, I know. But it's really helping me in my regular classes, too."

"I understand. Believe me. I promise," said Keith. It seemed to him the other three heaved a sigh of relief. He smiled placidly at nothing. Touching a fairy tale...He might have phrased it that way himself. Keith decided he was going to enjoy this class.

Keith was still determined to get the most pleasure that he could, but it was much harder work to enjoy it, now that he was a functioning member of the secret class. His paper had been dissected during the second session by the Master, and Keith was made to endure a grilling session on his facts and opinions that left him sweating.

To his surprise, no one laughed at him, even though he was fumbling over words. In fact, he noticed real sympathy on more than one face, both from Big People and Little People.

None of the Big People, now all friends of Keith's except for Carl, voiced what they thought was the origin of their fellow classmates. None of them dared to make a guess. Keith called them elves, for their empirical resemblance (awaiting more data, he would say), and the handle stuck, almost as if the students were thankful that someone had suggested one.

He wanted to ask Marcy what she thought, but she was still avoiding him. He felt a little guilty, realizing that he was avoiding her, too, but consoled himself that he had a lot of new information to assimilate, and she would understand. If she ever spoke to him again. He promised himself that he would apologize to her at the next earliest opportunity.

Keith watched his new classmates with fascination, a little taken aback by how natural and ordinary the Little Folk were. They seemed to be just short people with funny ears, though he felt there was more to them. He was also exasperated by the distance the two groups put between one another. He was held back from making his own overtures by the worry his own fellows exhibited that somehow he would spoil their special haven. More than ever, he was determined to make himself goodwill ambassador from the Humans to the Elves. After that, it should be easy for the others to follow his lead.

Marcy, after listening blankfaced to an impassioned, melodramatic apology on bended knees from Keith in the middle of the parking lot blacktop, unexpectedly broke up into hysterical laughter. "It's okay," she told him, clapping her palms over his mouth to halt the torrent of apologies. Keith regarded her over her folded hands with big, sad hazel eyes. "I forgive you. The Master was going to let you come in anyway. You just didn't know. I wish I could have told you, but you would probably have thought I was out of my mind. If I had trusted you, you might have understood, but sometimes you seem so crazy. So I guess I owe you an apology, too."

"Thanks," Keith said, and then paused. "I understand. I'm having a little trouble believing in it, too. But I'm working on it! Say, I didn't know you were going out with Carl."

"What business is it of yours?" she snapped suddenly, circling around him and walking away.

"None at all," Keith admitted cheerfully, getting up and following at her elbow. "I'm a business major. Professional curiosity, you know."

"I'm sorry," Marcy said, her anger dying away as swiftly as it rose. "It's just that we're fighting. Mostly about you, I'll have you know."

"Good," said Keith. "I've decided that what I want to do in life is be Carl Mueller's Nemesis. It would make my life complete if I could drive him bananas. To think he knew where I could get...*research material,* and was keeping it to himself. I mean, what was he saving it for? I had to believe in magic on sheer faith." He shrugged. "I'm sorry, too, if you really like him."

Marcy was silent for a long time, staring at the ground before her feet as she walked. "I'm not sure any more. He's nice enough to me, but he's so—he's so *ambitious,* I think. It isn't healthy."

"The man without a cause," intoned Keith, sounding like a television movie announcer.

"Yeah, exactly." Marcy's thoughts seemed to be carrying her far away, to a place she didn't seem to care much for.

"But he's an A student. What's he doing in the Elf Master's class?" They walked up the stoop in front of Marcy's apartment building, and he held her books while she searched for her keys. "It's for dopes like me, who need tutoring."

"You're not a dope, Keith. Teri brought him in," Marcy looked up from her purse at him. "Didn't she tell you?"

"Nope. Probably ashamed of herself."

"Oh, come on. He's not that bad."

"Maybe not," Keith admitted, changing the subject with admirable tact. He still felt he owed Carl a grudge. "Remember the paper I told you I was researching for my Mythology course? I got an A on it. Without using any...material from class."

"Congratulations," said Marcy, spilling her purse and books onto the kitchen table. "It sounded pretty good to me."

"Thanks. I've been wondering if I ought to check my theories out with some of our classmates."

"I don't think that's such a good idea," Marcy insisted, with a trace of her former reluctance.

"Why, just because they dodge 'personal questions'? Well, maybe I could take one of 'em out to dinner. I bet it's all peer pressure. If I can isolate one, maybe I can get him to talk. Or her," Keith said, thinking of the little blond girl. Then he noticed the look on Marcy's face. "Oh, no. You're not going to tell me no one's ever tried to socialize, are you? You are," he accused, before she could open her mouth. "I could see it in your face. And everybody else's, too. Why not? My god, Big People on this campus have been associating with them for how long now?"

"Five years," Marcy said in a cautious undertone, listening for her roommates.

"Five years, and they're still strangers. Some neighbor you are."

"Well, what about you? You're just curious," Marcy pointed out defensively.

"Downright weird, my roommate says," Keith added, unabashed. "But sure! Here you are with an incredible opportunity, to talk to legends, and you hold them at arm's length."

"It's not like that at all," Marcy said, getting excited. "They wouldn't like being called legends. And, it's more like, well, I'm too shy…."

"But not everyone is," Keith said, more gently. "I'm not. Wait and see. I'll get to know them better, and then I'll introduce you."

Marcy giggled. "But I know them already."

"No, you don't. But that's okay. You've already got a nodding acquaintance going. That's a good start."

Chapter 9

At the next class meeting, Keith decided to begin making friends. He sat down deliberately between the blond kid and an older, bearded elf that he hadn't seen before. The boy winked at him again before going back to his customary whittling. Keith watched for a while with close interest, and then noticed the other fellow was watching, too. When the Elf Master was called away to attend to something at the other end of the mysterious tunnel, Keith struck up a conversation.

"Good, isn't he?" he asked the bearded one, who seemed surprised to be addressed by a Big Person. He grunted.

"Needs practice. He's too showy. That pipestem'd break the first time it got a look at a set of teeth."

The boy lifted his head from his work. "Now, Marm, you know that's not so," he said, patiently, laying down the blade.

"It is so. You want strength in a bitty piece of work like that, you need a harder sort of wood, or work across the grain."

"Here," said the boy, thrusting the tiny thing past Keith, and into the other's hands. "Look for yourself. It's not wood. It's bone. I suppose your eyes are getting too old to tell the difference."

"Well," said Keith, "for bone, that looks pretty good. I think. His wood carvings are really fine, aren't they?" he added hopefully. The older elf grunted his approval.

Marm turned the little stick over in his hand. Keith could see that its length was covered with a pattern of interlocking broad-leaved vines. It was astonishing that anything that small should be so perfect. He couldn't tell what Marm was complaining about. Probably just jealous. "Yah, you're right. Must be a goat's bone, now that I see it closely. Yah, a goat's bone. Fine work, Maven."

"What did he call you?" Keith demanded of the young elf, astonished.

"Maven. The Maven. That's what everyone calls me. It's a Yiddish word, means 'expert.' My name is Holl. And by the by, thanks for the compliment."

"Sure. I meant it. Where on earth did you get a Yiddish nickname?" Keith asked, not to be diverted. Jewish elves? Holl started to answer, but stopped, and held up both hands to shush him. "Why..."

"Quiet, you widdy, can't you hear him?" He puffed out his ruddy cheeks and blew bone fragments off his desk, then sat up straight.

"No...." But in a moment, the clicking of a pair of heels on the tunnel's concrete floor floated up over the rest of the noise. The Elf Master was returning. In a moment, all the voices ceased, and everyone sat at polite attention.

"Quiet," the Master said wearily, though there was no noise. "Ve vill continue. Tay," he gestured at the second bearded elf, a pale blond with sharply tilted eyebrows, "has briefly outlined the development of modern agrarian society. Vhat, Mr. Eisler, vould you say were the primary social changes brought about by the Industrial Revolution in the agrarian countries of the vorld?"

Keith hung back when class ended, and tapped Holl on the shoulder when he got up to leave. He kept his voice low as the other students passed by him. "Listen, I think your work is really good. Do you think I could come over some time, and see other things you've carved?" Keith tossed his head toward the low doorway. "I couldn't do that stuff. I'd cut my fingers off."

Holl cocked an eyebrow, and peered at him a good long time before answering, knowing full well what Keith was asking, and giving it honest consideration. "You're a different one, Keith. I'll see. Maybe you can come for an evening meal. The older ones won't gripe so much about a visitor while they're eating. And I don't mind an audience for my work."

"Terrific!" said Keith. "In exchange, I hereby invite you to be my guest in the dining hall. Only you probably won't think it's much of a favor when you've tasted the food."

"A good guest never counts the dishes served, nor spits out the mouthful he's chewing."

"Right. Always eat every meal as though it was your last."

"Wait here. I'll ask now." Holl vanished down the echoing hallway. After a while, he returned. "You can come. Wait by the big sycamore outside the back of the library building in an hour and a half. I'll find you there. You'll need to be on your best behavior, boy."

"Yes, sir!" Keith saluted. His voice rang in the classroom, picked up tones from the concrete floor.

"Shush," said Holl, turning back into the tunnel. "You'll make them change their minds."

Keith held his jubilation until he reached the ground level of the library. When the elevator door slid open, he could contain himself no more. He danced out, and let go with a wild, "Yahoo!"

"Shhh!!" a librarian hissed sternly.

Following instructions, he waited, concealed behind the library building. About two hours had passed since the end of class, and Keith felt if he had to stuff in one more particle of excitement, he would explode in a shower of sparks. The Maven—boy, what a name—told him to keep out of sight of the path and sit tight. They would have to wait for the right moment to let him inside. Keith had no objections. If they had managed to keep themselves hidden for this long, he wasn't going to be the one to blow their cover. What would Marcy say if she knew where he was going? He did a little dance, which he quickly converted into jiggling around for warmth in the chilly evening air as a couple of students passed him. He smiled at them, and craned his head after them as they walked away.

He heard a grating noise from behind him, and spun around to see where it was coming from. A whole section of the stone wall four feet high, beginning an inch or two above the grass, had sunk back, leaving a deep, black opening. A hand extended through and beckoned to him. With a quick glance around, Keith dove for the hole and skittered to the side as the stone facade grated ominously back into place. He found himself standing in a passageway so narrow he had to press his shoulders together to turn around. He put out a hand to feel for the mechanism, but found nothing but the back of the stone wall. On his other side was rough brick.

"Keith Doyle," said a voice in the dark, sounding ominous. He jumped.

"Y—yup?" he affirmed.

"Welcome, then. You're just in time." A lantern flamed alight, and Holl was there looking up at him. "Follow me."

A short while later, Keith found himself sitting on a low bench, surrounded by a host of miniature humans; adults and children both. He kept his elbows very close to his sides, which meant he had to dip his head every time he wanted to take a bite from his miniature fork. Now I know how Gulliver felt, he thought, ignoring an itch along his ribs for fear of knocking over the tiny old lady on his left.

Gingerly, he extended a hand to pick up the jug of milk, and poured some into his wooden cup.

Holl sat across the long table from him, occasionally studying him with a humorous twinkle in his eyes. He was aware how ridiculous the big youth felt, but it was a lesson in humility to watch how well Keith handled himself in adverse conditions. He could also see that old Keva was wearing her pincushion on her belt, and it was undoubtedly sticking into Keith's side. To his credit, the big fellow wasn't complaining. She had probably left it there on purpose, spiteful old hen. Good for him. He was a fair guest.

The others of Holl's people were not demonstrating themselves to be hosts worthy of such a guest. More than once, Holl had heard an unfavorable comment, fortunately inaudible to Keith's less sensitive ears. "What's he want to come in here for? To gawk, I'll bet." "Dey neffer let us alone vonce dey know. How ve know he has any discretion?" And from the oldsters, "His kind've been faithless before, for sure, darlin'. What difference will only a few generations make?"

"Uh, you know," said Keith, "this pitcher looks just like the kind we used to have at my summer camp. They're really indestructible. I oughta know. I used to shoot off bottle rockets from one."

Keva stopped chewing with a shocked intake of breath. She stared at the human balefully.

"Oh," Keith continued, misinterpreting her ire. "No one was hurt. I did it out next to the lake."

"Are you after suggesting that we took this pitcher from your summer camp?" Keva demanded.

"Now, Keva," Holl chided her, but the old lady ignored him. The other diners fell silent, listening.

Keith regarded her with puzzlement, his narrative dying away to silence. "No, not at all. That's up near Chicago. They're mass produced. There must be thousands of them around the state. It just reminded me of camp. Sort of homey. I'm sorry if you thought I meant anything by it."

Keva nodded warily. "Well, all right then."

"If camp was something you enjoyed," Holl interjected, shushing Keva. "Otherwise, perhaps we should apologize to you for reminding you."

"I didn't mind camp," Keith acknowledged cheerfully. "I think my parents only lived for the day when they could send all five of us to camp at once."

There was another sursurrus of whispers around the room again. From Keith, there was no sign that he could understand or even hear any of it, but Holl's attenuated hearing translated them clearly. "Does he accuse us of stealing?" Hmmph, you old frauds, thought Holl, grinning to himself. And where did you think our things come from these long years? Do hens lay plates? Or curtains?

Keith looked around at the tables of elves, most of whom were glancing at him openly or covertly while they ate. He guessed there must be eighty or ninety of them. The little old lady had gone back to her own meal, pointedly turning her back to him as best she could in the limited space available. Keith made a mental note to apologize to her later. He sent a questioning glance to Holl, and received an amused gesture to go on eating and ignore the old lady. He figured that she must be the local equivalent of his great-aunt Martha, a woman who enjoyed bullying her relatives into believing that they had really offended her so she could demand apologies for the imaginary insults. He took another sip of milk and turned his attention to his surroundings.

The planked wooden tables were dark brown and polished smooth on top, but carved prettily around the sides. A few of the chairs at the ends were made to match, as were the benches, but a number of chairs were obvious refugees from a kindergarten. Keith had noticed one, occupied by an extremely dignified elf with silver-templed black hair, that had the alphabet and a teddy bear painted on the chair back. The dishes were mostly ceramic, hand-thrown with a great deal of skill. Blue, green and yellow were their favorite colors; the elves made their clothes in the same hues they painted their dishes.

At each long table sat a few elderly elves, others that he would term 'middle-aged,' and an assortment of younger ones that he guessed were up to twenty years old in Big People terms. By the common resemblances, each group represented one extended family. It was touching to see that little silvering-blond grandmother feed the tiny infant on her left to give the tired brunette on the child's other side a rest and a chance to feed herself. There weren't too many babies in the room. Each table had two or three, rarely more. The one behind Holl had four toddlers, all of which looked exactly alike, and each of whose little bottoms could comfortably fit on the palm of Keith's hand. His classmates were scattered among the clans, as he called them to himself, so they probably weren't all sisters and brothers.

The Elf Master occupied the head of a table to Keith's left. Next to him sat Enoch, the young elf with black hair. Enoch had met Keith's glance on his way in, and apart from that one glance, ignored him. Keith decided not to think about him, and just smiled at anyone else whose eyes he met. On Enoch's other side was the pretty, auburn haired elf girl whose name was Maura. She smiled sweetly back when he grinned at her, and looked down again at her plate.

The food was good, what there was of it. The servers, elves of both sexes, trundled over with big (to them) steaming crocks of stew, baskets of bread and bowls of vegetables, and then sat down to serve themselves and their families. Keith prayed his stomach wouldn't grumble as he filled his doll's-dish with stew from the crock and took a piece of bread. He promised it the pound cake he kept sealed in a tin under his dorm bed for emergency midnight snacks. He even promised it extra breakfast if it would keep quiet for now. In his excitement over the coming meeting of the study group that afternoon, he had forgotten to eat any lunch, and he was embarrassingly hungry now. He tried to eat slowly, but in a few small bites, the plate was empty.

The crock thumped to a halt in front of him. "There's plenty," Laniora, his pretty brown-haired classmate coaxed him, from two seats down to Holl's left. With a grateful smile, Keith dished himself another helping.

The bread was something special. It was soft and fresh-baked, with a crisp, thin brown crust. The aroma made him sigh and lift his eyes heavenward, which drew laughter from his tablemates.

"Dinna worship it," snapped Keva. "Eat it!"

Obediently, he ate it. It was delicious, and he said so. A moment later, an extra portion of bread plumped down next to his plate, and the sharp pain withdrew from his side. He had forgotten all about it until it disappeared. Holl grinned at him suddenly and Keith grinned back.

At the meal's end, Keva gave him a frosty little nod and smile, and walked away. Keith rose and bowed to her, scratching his side. Then he bowed to the elders clustered at the end of the table. The old man at the end inclined his head and went back to his own conversation. Since Holl showed no inclination to hurry away, Keith sat down again.

"You've flattered Keva," Holl told him. "It was her bread. She's the baker. It was her pin cushion in your ribs, too."

"Oh," said Keith. "She your aunt?"

"She's my sister. I'm the middle one of three. Right now three, that is," Holl said blithely. "That was my baby sister down there at the end of the table. Three is considered a big family with us. My folks are a progressive pair."

"Sister? Hmm, hah, uh, how old is she?" Keith asked, amazed. "Never mind that; how old are you?"

"Old enough, my lad. In terms of this world, forty years have passed since my birth."

"Forty? Of course you look about twelve. I should have guessed. Wow, I would have thought you were more my age. I'm nineteen."

"Let's shake," Holl extended a hand. "I'm considered a young adult to my folk, too. We'll call that common ground enough to build on."

Keith shook the hand, engulfing it in his own, and discovered they were nearly alone in the big room. "Where'd everyone go?"

"To the living quarters. Some call it the village, but that's a fanciful title. It's a big place like this one, only divided up to the clans. Come and see."

They walked through another low tunnel similar to the one that led from the schoolroom, though this one sloped down at a slight angle. The passage was dimly lit high along each side, though Keith couldn't see the fixtures from which the flickering light issued. "You don't get many...er, human...visitors down here, do you?"

"No, indeed not," said Holl. "You're the first in a long, long time."

"Then why me?" Keith asked, walking stooped over with a hand running along the ceiling checking for rafters and bumps. "Ouch. I feel like Quasimodo."

"The Hunchback of Notre Dame. Because you asked, Keith Doyle, and I trusted you, so you were allowed to come. I'm taking a chance on you. It's my nature to take chances. The others think I'm too progressive, but I call it a hereditary failing. My parents don't mind."

"You read a lot of classics?" Keith inquired, ducking to avoid an electrical conduit.

"What else is there to do in a library?"

"I guess I never thought what it was like to live in one." Keith had a sudden vision of the secret door in the wall opening, and thousands of elves pouring out into the library, pulling books out of the shelves, using the microfiche readers, calling up articles about leprechauns from PLATO, and stern little elf librarians hissing "Shhh!" He chuckled.

"Come on, then," the young elf called out, disappearing around a sharp bend in the hall. Keith hurried to catch up.

"When this building was built, back along, they made this floor to be a maintenance way, to take care of the pipes and the foundation," Holl said, stopping to point out the sheaves of conduit that ran along the ceiling here and there. "Only it was never used much. And the one below it *was* the foundation itself. You can see that no one your size could walk down here for long without giving himself a good backache. As long as nothing went wrong with the pipes, they had no reason to look for a way to get at them. And we make sure that nothing goes wrong with the pipes. They've forgotten about it, see, and the parts of the blueprints describing this level and this part of the steam tunnels were destroyed, all by accident. They kept them in this very same building," Holl said, innocently. "We had a friend who warned us to get rid of access ways and plans when we came here...but she's no business of yours." The elf's tone was a definite warning.

"A good friend," Keith said, tactfully not pushing for details. By the direction they were walking, he guessed that the rounded passage must run directly below the Student Common. He felt satisfied with the number of questions Holl *was* answering, and was content to let him talk. "How did you get here, Holl? And where did you come from?"

"Ireland, wasn't it?" Holl shot him a sideways glance full of mischief. Keith's theories were well known among his folk, and they considered them most entertaining.

"Yes, wasn't it?" Keith asked, not letting the jibe penetrate. "I heard your relatives talking up there. I've got cousins that really do look like you. Not the ears, but the rest of your features. The cast of them, as my grandmother would say."

The Maven shrugged. "Your legends may have some truth to them. I'm not saying how much. You don't think we get pleasure out of saying we're kin to the enemy, now do you? Simmer down, boy," for Keith was getting red-faced and waving his arms preparatory to a verbal explosion. Holl poked him in the midsection with a forefinger. "*You're* not an enemy yourself. At least I think not. But there'd be many more of us if there weren't so many of you. What normally becomes of highly interbred racial mutations under your typical intensive, impersonal scientific scrutiny?"

Keith's color faded slowly as he thought about it, and then he spoke. "Extinction."

"Uhuh. But fortunately among the characteristics we maintain are camouflage and silence. My kin have had much practice on their way across this continent. I can steal the eggs out of a duck's nest if she'll lean forward a mite."

"I can scare one silly and get the eggs that way," Keith volunteered. "I failed woodcraft in Boy Scouts."

"And can't I tell that? It's part of the quality of being obvious that makes me want to trust you. You were making quite a racket in the stacks that day. Any one of us could tell there was someone out there, though the rest of the Big Ones couldn't."

Keith opened his mouth.

Holl forestalled him. "And we heard you two days before that, when Bracey tossed you out. He's one of us, too."

Keith shut it again.

"This is where we live," Holl announced, stepping aside so Keith could stand up out of the low hallway. Rubbing his back tenderly, Keith squinted down the length of the room. "We lowered the dirt floor several feet. Used to be just a few feet high, but we like our head room. It makes for a far more congenial living space."

He certainly would never have suspected its existence. It covered an area the same size as the large library levels above but without partitions. The illusion of size was enhanced by the height of the ceiling, somewhat loftier than that of the dining hall one half level up, and the size of the structures within, which were perfect small scale models of the ones he was used to.

They were undeniably houses, though of a peasantish cottage type that he associated with woodcutters and Little Red Riding Hood. The roofs, solid, slanted, were, naturally, not needed under ground to keep off the weather, but they served to give the illusion that the village was in the upper air. Groups of cottages were scattered throughout the vast room. Neighborhoods, Keith realized with delight. They must be set up by clan. He could see his tablemates going about their business in the knot of houses nearest the passageway.

The same flickering light that illumined the passages lined the ceiling between bare rafters, though it was much brighter here, almost as bright as spring sunlight. It was as warm as springtime down here, too. The elves carried on life as usual with less noise than Keith would have thought possible for such a large number of human beings, but as Holl pointed out, he was probably mistaken about that, too.

A group of five or six children were playing tag around the corners of the small shelters, giggling as they managed to elude 'it.' It was a nice, quiet little village scene, but one that reminded Keith more of a Bronze age enclosure than something that could exist in the twentieth century, especially within a hundred feet, albeit straight down, of a modern university.

Before the cottage doors, here and there, a woman in a long skirt and blouse or the same straight legged pants the men wore, sewed, usually patching clothes, and humming to herself or chatting with a neighbor. The floor was packed earth, hoed up here and there to make way for tiny flower beds and herb gardens. Bunches of greenery hung in nearly every doorway, scenting the air, and adding to the springtime atmosphere. You'd never know it was October—a cold October, too—upstairs. And everywhere was the same ornamental woodwork, the sort of fine carving that Keith watched the Maven do during class for the last couple of weeks.

He fingered a small polished square panel set into the upper part of a wall, admiring the design of intertwining ivy leaves carved upon it. "Did you do this?" he asked.

"No," Holl smiled. "But you have a good eye for a pattern. My father's work, that one is. That panel keeps the house together."

"Oh?"

"Aye. Cohesiveness. Knits its bones. I learned my skill from him. Scrap wood's one thing that's available in plenty, so I never lack for practice pieces."

Keith leaned close to the wall, trying to see joins between the tightly fitted slabs of wood. No two pieces were exactly the same size, grain, shade, or quality. They looked as though they had been puzzle-cut together with a very sharp knife. Particle board clung to oak between bits of plywood, balsa, and pine. These elven builders could have given precision lessons to Pharaoh's architects. "So what's wrong with using nails?" Not that he could see any in the construction.

"They rust. They bend. Also, we tend to be a wee bit sensitive to having too much metal around."

"I heard that cold iron dispels magic," Keith said, teasingly. "Maybe that's why you don't use it."

"And maybe the effect is more like heavy metal poisoning, Keith Doyle. Call it an allergy. Don't look for foolish explanations unless no others suffice. There's plenty of common sense to go around. Even you could find some."

"I believe in magic," Keith said, softly.

"But do you know it when you see it?" Holl demanded.

"Probably not," Keith admitted, cheerfully. A fragrance of spices and baking tickled his nose, and he changed the subject. "How do you do your cooking here? I never smell anything out of the ordinary in the building."

"Oh, the chimneys over the fires are all vented together to the outside, toward the Student Common. We tried electric stoves once, but the cooks protested one and all that they couldn't control such an impersonal element, so that was the end of that experiment. They know where they are with wood-burning, and we left it at that. The steam tunnels run by here, and we make use of them. It's also from them that we get our heat. If you ever smelled any of the good cooking upstairs, you probably thought it was coming from the Delicatessen in the Common." Holl wrinkled his nose. "Or, if bad, from the Home Economics department. We don't eat fancy, as you see, so it's never anything unusual enough to bear investigation. Strong smells linger, so we're careful never to eat fish unless it's fresh, or any cooked cabbages at all."

Keith wandered between the shelters, nodding as nonchalantly as he could manage to any elf that met his eye, and most of them did, nodding back and smiling, trying to believe that he wasn't doing something unique and extraordinary in just being near them. But they preserved the illusion for him, and he allowed himself to make a full tourist's ramble of the big room.

He watched a handful of elves, male and female, folding sheets from a big wicker basket and gossiping over their work. Young ones played a complicated pretending game with toys on the ground. Keith saw a jointed toy horse clopping across the floor with an elfin toddler in pursuit.

"Electronic?" Keith asked Holl.

"No, it's all wood."

"Magic..." In delighted disbelief, he watched the horse look back over its shoulder and change direction just as the little one would have reached it. It was alive! The baby gave a crow of glee and turned to pursue his toy. Holl broke his reverie by tapping him on the shoulder.

"There's more," he said, beckoning him along.

"How's that work?" Keith asked, pointing at the horse, wanting to go back and investigate.

"Just a toy," Holl shrugged offhandedly, pulling Keith along. Keith took a quick look back before following around a corner. The child's mother had seized him up and was washing his face with a wet cloth. It was not a task the baby enjoyed, and he kicked and cried under her ministrations. She shot an apologetic look toward Keith, who smiled at her. The brown wooden horse stood at her feet and regarded its master with glass-eyed sympathy.

A thin pipe ran between the patterns of light on the ceiling, and divided into several smaller pipes, which descended along the wall and floor under the back of each house. Keith glanced over to Holl, eyebrows raised.

"Water," the elf explained. "We've run a tap pipe from the fire sprinklers. The pressure is kept constant, and again, no one notices."

"You think of everything." Keith looked around admiringly. "I wouldn't be able to work all this stuff out, even if my life depended on it. And yours do."

Holl looked pleased. "We've had time to work it all out. It wasn't so comfortable at first. But there's more. Did you know that there's a small river running under this building?"

"No," said Keith, astonished. "I've never seen any sign of anything like that. The nearest river is way down the road."

"Well, you're wrong; there is one. It's the way towns were always built. Underground rivers make a natural disposal system.
And we take water out of it upstream. Look here." He led the
young man to a broad patch of growing greenery. Tay, the blond-
bearded fellow from the Master's class, waved to them and went
back to pulling up carrots and tossing them into a slatted bin. The
bright orange vegetables were of unusually good size, and looked
amazingly alive in the artificial sunshine. Holl appropriated two
from under Tay's slapping hand, broke the greens off into a pail,
passed one to Keith, and snapped a crunchy bite out of his own.
"Hydroponics," he explained as he chewed. "These have their roots
dangling in the river. It's right under the concrete at this end of the
building."

Keith brushed the water from the carrot, and took a bite. It
was crisp, cold and sweet, and even tasted healthy. "Why would
they have built right over water? That's asking for trouble with the
foundation."

"Well, it didn't start out that way. The river has changed course
over the years. One more thing the University doesn't suspect is in its
basements. And it makes a perfectly viable hydroponic garden. The
water's always fresh. Waste goes in downstream."

"Wow." Keith didn't hide his interest. "How do you know so
much about a river no one's ever seen?"

"Oh, well, one of our folk has an earth-wise way about her. She
asked it, and she knows."

Keith nodded, trying to picture an elf-woman talking to a river.
It sounded plausible as far as he could tell. Though there was a quiet
buzz of conversation, and the occasional click-zizz! of a saw or tap-
tap of a hammer, the loudest single noise in the place was the sound
of his own shoes banging along on the concrete floor. Most of the
elves' footgear was a kind of soft-soled sock-shoe, sewn of suede
or leather, and pulled on without lacings. The children generally wore
a ribbon tied around each ankle to keep their shoes from falling off,
but a slower form of locomotion than running wouldn't dislodge
them. Holl was watching him wisely, noting Keith's study with silent
approval.

"It's peaceful here," Keith said at last.

Holl smiled. "It is that."

Nothing seemed ever to be wasted by the little people. Keith saw the same stiff flowered fabric used over and over again in different applications. Two little girls' dresses, several window curtains, an old woman's apron, and a gaudy young man's shirt had obviously all come from the same bolt. "And bed coverlets, too," Holl affirmed, after Keith mentioned it to him. "There are no looms in this place. That much wood we cannot spare, so textiles are some of the hardest things to come by. You'll see the same scrap of cloth recycled a dozen times before it's too badly worn to mend. It's a sure sign that fabric's on the way out when it becomes curtains. No wear to the body of the cloth, you see."

"Sure, I see," said Keith, musing. Now that he was aware of it, he saw that most of the fabrics here were well cared for, but old and worn, including his friend's clothes. Patches were skillfully blended on trouser-knees and jacket-elbows. Probably re-dyed, too, for camouflage. "Textiles, huh?"

"Huh. What we can't grow for ourselves, or make, or…er, find, we do without. Now, Lee Eisley, in the class, has a handy job as an assistant in the Food Services. He has been known to drop packages of meat in our way, and a few other feats of kindness, after…well, when we lost another source of supply."

"Don't you ever buy stuff you need?" Keith asked impetuously, and then wished he hadn't.

Holl gave him a pitying look. "How and with what, Keith Doyle? Shall I go out and get a job selling cookies? Or maybe helping out Santa Claus at a shopping mall?"

"Well, why not?" Keith had a sudden delighted vision of dainty point-eared elf helpers escorting hulking human children to Santa's throne. "No one would believe you were real, under the right circumstances. Nobody knows who Santa's helpers are."

"Why not?" Holl echoed. "Because these nameless workers have got backgrounds, backgrounds that your government knows about, and takes for granted. Maybe you don't know who they are, but they are known. It's a casual thing for you to have a job. It's your world. You've got a *social security number.* Everyone knows where you came from. An adult, especially one that looks like me, popping out of nowhere prompts questions, questions that we don't want answered in public, starting with 'where did you get them ears?'" His eyebrows drew together, and his voice took on the tone of a moronic teenager.

"I'm sorry. I feel awkward asking such dumb questions, but I don't how else to ask what I want to know."

Holl's face relaxed, and he slapped him companionably on the back, taking him solidly in the kidneys. Keith winced. "The trouble with you is that you have a basically honest heart. Haven't you heard it said to you by a thousand professors, Keith Doyle, that there are no dumb questions?"

"...Just dumb people," Keith finished, self-deprecatingly. The curious illumination in the ceiling was dimming, shading more toward a sunset finish: reds and oranges on one side, and already blue-black on the other. Some special effects. Whoever did the programming on that ceiling was good, Keith thought. It had been cloudy and rainy all day outside, and it was already long past dark up there, but here he was watching the sun go down in a perfectly clear sky. He envied the elves for being able to delay sunset as long as they wanted. They sure knew how to live. The little children were being called in by their parents. "Look, I'd better go," Keith insisted. "I've got some homework to finish tonight."

"Mm-hmm. Late for us, too. You're welcome here. I'll ask you to guest again some time. You've not met my family, yet."

"Yeah, I'd love to. Thanks for asking me! When would you like to come to dinner in the dorm? The food's not much to brag about, but there's lots of it."

A broad smile lit Holl's face. "I'll come with joy any time you like, if only to see how you explain me away to your friends, Keith Doyle."

"I'll think of something," Keith promised, smiling down at him.

"That's what I'm looking forward to."

Chapter 10

When Keith left the library complex, he ran all the way back to the dormitory and seized the phone. Pat was out, probably at play rehearsal. Keith felt if he didn't share his experience with someone, he would explode. He dialed Marcy's number and counted the rings impatiently until she answered.

"Hello?" She sounded irritated, probably interrupted in the middle of a good television program, or sleep, or something. Keith realized at that moment he had no idea what time it was.

"Hi," he sang, sounding heady even in his own ears. "It's Keith. I just had dinner with THEM. You know. Them."

"What?" Marcy demanded, sleepily. "Which them?"

"They, them. Holl and Tay and Maura and...I was right there, where they live. I *saw.* I just had to tell someone. You. I wanted to tell you. And, Marcy? Thanks for getting me in there. You don't know what it means to me. Well," all his breath came out in a rush on that one syllable, and he forced his tone to assume false casualness, "see you in class." He hung up the phone.

"Wait!" came a shriek out of the receiver. "Keith—?"

Keith threw himself around the room for the next few hours, unable to settle anywhere in his excitement. He waggled a finger chidingly at the Field Guide and the other books on legendary creatures stacked anyhow on his shelves, feeling pleased with himself that he now knew something none of them did. "I've got your numbers, guys." Real elves were more interesting than any of the pipe dreams and fictional illusions he'd ever read about. And how did those lights in the ceiling work? There were no wires or even *fixtures*...More unexplained data, and he had to know.

The ringing of the telephone disturbed him, so he took the receiver off the hook and threw the whole instrument under the bed.

The arrangement he had seen in the library basement amazed him. To do as the elves had done, to have created a viable living environment inside a dark concrete box without letting anyone ever see them, or know what they were doing, and to continue to exist—even prosper, to a certain extent—surpassed all means or vocabulary Keith had for expressing admiration. They were survivors. They ate, slept, cooked, made clothes and houses and tools, played, and raised children, all in a space the college had forgotten, and would have dismissed as unimportant and unusable if reminded of it. What were discards to his spoiled generation became raw materials in the hands of those concealed craftsmen. Look at what they did with scrap lumber and used curtains…

It troubled him that all their skill couldn't disguise the poverty of their situation. True, they could make beauty and function out of garbage, but it was still garbage. Now that he thought about it, there probably wasn't a whole two-by-four in the whole village. Then, too, there was the clothing. It was all of an old fashioned, loose, comfortable cut, intended to wear for a long time. None of it was way out of the ordinary, but remained far from fashionable. Just about every garment sported a patch, sometimes more than one. Keith thought guiltily of jeans he owned that had patches embroidered on them just for show. He would help supply his new friends with donations of fresh raw materials, anything they needed. He was good at finding things. What those elf seamstresses could do with pretty new fabrics—! It would take all his ingenuity to come up with a way to get what they needed; he certainly didn't have unlimited money. Keith scowled impatiently out his window at the night, wishing it wasn't too late an hour to start on his resolution. Textiles, food, lumber, kitchen utensils, tools…

The list was beginning to form in his head, when it occurred to him that he wasn't alone in his eagerness to help out the little folk. Lee Eisley was already doing it, though he had never let on when Keith grilled him about their classmates. He would have to find Lee and talk to him, and find out what needed doing most.

"Very vell," the Master said, leaning over the head of the table. "I declare that the Council of Elders is open, and all who need to speak vill be heard." He sat down and looked around, waiting for someone to speak.

The old folk around the table glanced at one another, but no one opened his mouth. With a rueful shake of her head, Catra got to her feet. "I would speak, Master."

"Gut. Vhat haf you to say?"

"You must already know, for I have not made a secret of my discovery." She turned to the others, holding up a small, neatly trimmed piece of newsprint in the lantern light. "As archivist, it is my duty. I found in a story one of the weekly newspapers that leads me to believe we are in grave danger of discovery." The room erupted into a hubbub of worried exclamations. "Now, wait. It doesn't go so far as to mention any of us by name. All it says is that folk answering our general description have been seen frequenting the streets of the Midwestern campus and town."

"Frequenting!" Curran exploded. "There's a bare few who go 'round and about, and no' often. Do we keep them from gaeng out, then?"

"No. Ve cannot keep them from their tasks. We need to do have them done."

"Huh!" Dierdre, Catra's clan leader, seated to her right, was glancing at the slip of paper. "'...as if Santa was setting up shop right here in the Midwest.' 'Tis an insult!"

"Stereotypes," Ligan agreed. "Too few stories for to choose from here." He was the eldest of the Master's clan, though it was the Master who spoke for the whole of the village.

"But who can have written this? Why now?"

"Is there no one new in the village class, now?" Ligan wanted to know.

"Just the vun, Keith Doyle," said the Master.

"You met him the other day at dinner," Catra reminded them, venturing a cautious opinion. "I don't think it could be he."

"And why not?" Curran demanded.

Catra shrugged her shoulders. "He doesn't seem the type."

"Ve must be more careful," the Elf Master said, peering at them all over the tops of his gold glasses. "Only at night shall the scavengers go forth, and hats worn. Approach no new Big Folk. If this is a security leak, ve shall stop it here and now." The others sadly nodded their approval. "Now, is there any more to bring to our attention?" None of the others raised a hand or stood up. The Master rose heavily to his feet. "Then the Council is closed."

Chapter 11

"Lee Eisley?" Keith inquired into a cloud of hot steam billowing out of the maw of an industrial dishwasher. A burly man dressed in a greasy white uniform levered his torso upright from the conveyor belt he was trying to fix, and peered at Keith.

"Nope," he boomed. "Back there." He gestured over one shoulder with a rubber-gloved hand, and went back to banging on the control box with a wrench. "Dammit."

Keith scurried past as the dishwasher belched out another blinding burst of steam. He shuffled by a column of white-enameled stoves and stainless steel work tables, where a dozen or so white-clad workers were making up huge batches of soups and salads. There was an incredible racket in the kitchens, the clanking and hissing from the dishwashers harmonizing with the growling mixing machines that were churning vast quantities of sweet-smelling dough. The yeast floating in the air made Keith sneeze on his way past them.

He found Lee, also dressed in white, beyond the next row of machines, loading fifty-pound sacks of flour and rice from a pallet into storage cabinets. He waited until Lee's hands were empty before attempting to attract his attention.

"Um, Lee?"

The older student started, obviously surprised to be addressed. He peered at Keith without recognizing him.

"It's me, Keith. From the class?"

"Yeah, hi." Grunting, Lee hoisted another sack to his shoulders and staggered it across the room. "What can I do for you?"

"If you have a minute, I wanted to ask you a couple of questions."

"Sure. Shoot."

"Um," Keith looked around. "It's about our mutual classmates."

"What?" The sack landed on its mates with a thud, and Lee spun, looking around for eavesdroppers, and seized a handful of Keith's shirt. "You crazy, asking me about that *here*? Get out, you jerk."

"They told me you've been, well, helping out." Keith went on, wondering if he was wise to have confronted Lee here.

"You heard wrong," Lee said, a little louder than necessary.

"Come on. I want to help, too." Keith said, persuasively. Lee's expression told him nothing. "I know you're helping. They told me. I'm sure there's things I can do, too. I've got some ideas. But there's stuff I need to know."

"I told you before. I don't know anything."

"But that was before. Before I knew you were taking supplies to them, out of Food Service stocks...." Keith lowered his voice to a confidential whisper.

Lee clamped a hand roughly over Keith's nose and mouth. "Shut up," he hissed. "All right, I have. So what? I still don't know anything."

"How long have you been doing...that?" Keith asked, more tactfully. His nose hurt. He rubbed it ruefully.

Lee went back for another sack. "I started doing it as a favor. I'm a grad student in journalism. I did my undergrad j-school work here, too. Five years. I took over when old Ludmilla asked me to help out her 'little ones.' Hell, I thought she meant feeding her cats." He scowled at Keith as if he resented his good deeds being found out.

Keith took a deep breath. "Who's Ludmilla?"

"She was a University cleaning lady. She retired four years ago. She still lives in town. If anyone knows about...them, she does."

"Do you know her address?" Keith held out a notebook and pen. Lee snatched them, and scribbled a few lines.

"There. Now beat it."

"Don't worry. I'm gone. Just your basic good Samaritan, doing my annual good deed. No point in intruding on other good deeds." Keith looked meaningfully at the food storage units. Lee seized a fifty-pound sack of rice threateningly, and Keith scurried away.

Chapter 12

Along one side of the campus ran rows of collapsible brownstone six-flats that were used mostly by students who preferred, and could afford, apartments to dorm rooms. The other tenants consisted of older people, couples just getting started, and people who worked at the University. The rent was cheap, so most didn't complain about the condition of the buildings. The address he was looking for was only two doors down from Marcy's place.

The crumbling concrete and brickwork were original issue, and in the dimly lit, redolent plaster hallways, Keith was sure he could trace some inscriptions hitherto found only in caves in prehistoric France. Heavy, varnished wooden doors hung at angles in their frames, letting triangular spears of light shoot out under them onto the worn runners. He could hear television soap operas blaring, muffled behind the thick walls, and distant footsteps, followed by doors slamming. Two giggling children, a sister and brother both aged five or so, heels slipping, dashed down the flight above him just as Keith rounded the landing. He moved himself out of their way against the banisters. "Hey, watch it," he complained.

"Sorry," the little girl called back, and broke into playful shrieks as her brother caught up and started tickling her. "Stop that! I'm telling! *Momma!*" Keith shook his head, grinning, and kept climbing.

On the fourth landing, Keith found the faded card that read "Hempert." He knocked.

A slender old woman with yellow-white hair opened the door. "Yes? How may I help you?"

Keith cleared his throat nervously. He was face to face with Ludmilla Hempert. Now how did he begin explaining what he wanted? "My name's Keith Doyle. I'm a…friend of friends of yours, Miss Hempert."

"Mrs. Hempert, but mein husband is these many years dead," Ludmilla told him, looking up at him with startlingly kind, flower-blue eyes. She wasn't much taller than the Elf Master, and she had the same kind of summing, patient expression. "Vich friends?"

"Your…the little ones."

"Ach!" She caught her breath, and gestured him to cross the threshold. With a cautious look over his shoulder, she shut the door. "Dey sent you?" she asked in a low tone. "Is someting der matter?"

"No," Keith hurried to reassure the old lady. She was already reaching for the limp wool coat hanging from the hook behind the door. "Really. Nothing's wrong. Truthfully, they don't even know I'm here. They're kind of...protective of you."

Ludmilla smiled, her cheeks lifting, and all the tired wrinkles disappeared from her face, making her look many years younger than the seventy or so she must be. Her hand fluttered down to her side, straightened her dress. "My kinder, like them they are. Zit down, please. Tea?" She darted ahead of him, hastening to dust off the top of a spotlessly clean, flowered sofa cushion.

"Um, sure. Thanks." Keith sank onto the couch, and found it so soft he was all but swallowed up in its embrace. Ludmilla rushed out of the room, and Keith could hear clinks and rattles coming from the kitchen. She returned in a moment, pushing a narrow, brass-bound tea wagon, on which was set a steaming pot, two cups and saucers, and a plate of sliced sponge cake. Keith sniffed appreciatively, accepted tea and a generous serving of cake.

"You know," said Ludmilla, sitting down opposite Keith in a deep upholstered armchair, "it is just today I am thinking of my little vuns. It is forty two years since first I met them."

"What?" Keith exclaimed, interrupting her unintentionally. "How long have they *been* here?"

"I am tellink you, young man."

Forty-two years ago, she began, I was working at night, cleaning the University buildings. My shift it was the least desirable, for which they paid me more money than was made by the staff during the day. We lived here. In those years, it was a family building, smelling of cooking, and everyone's doors stood open all day. I had three children, whom my husband and I were struggling to feed. Children are like young robins, always hungry. Food and clothes cost more than only one of us could earn. He worked in the daytime, and I at night, so that there would always be someone at home for them. I would not want my children to grow up thinking that they were not cared for.

The buildings were not so many in that time. The science center, which has grown so much, was then only the red brick structure onto which the others have been added. Connected it was to all the others by the steam tunnels. At first I found them frightening to walk through, for the switches of the lights lay far within, not close to the entrances. When I grew accustomed to them, taking five giant steps, often with my eyes closed against the darkness, my observation was that the lights were placed for the ease of workers, who made access by the hatchways and manholes. Between the Science building and the library was the longest passageway, fourteen lights long. The next longest, the Student Common to the Liberal Arts building, was but ten.

It was forbidden for anyone not authorized to make use of the tunnels. If you have never been in them—ah, but I see that you have, though I may guess you have not authorization. They run from place to place, always filled with warmth from the steam jets. The pipes along the ceiling, packed as they are in asbestos fibers, are like the veins in the back of a hand. The sound is like the beat of a heart, too: the source of my fear when first I walked down there. The lights hang infrequently, with pools of darkness lying between them.

I walk along the middle when I go through the tunnels, you see, where the skirts of light on the floor are almost touching, the least to be in the dark. When I am working, I place my things against the wall, in case there is someone else who walks through. That way they do not trip on my pail and mop, or tread in my lunch. The allowed time for my meal is one half hour, too short to go home to eat. I was careful to remember, for I did not wish to go hungry all night.

I heard scuttling in the depths of the buildings always. Rats lived there. They ate the insects: cockroaches, beetles; so they were pursued mostly when they were found on the levels used by the teachers and students. That was not my job. I do not like rats, and I killed as many as I could.

When I went, broomstick in hand, to investigate the sound, there came another clamor behind me, from the place where I had left my pail and my lunch. The rats again! They would not get my food if I could help it. Like the wind, I flew back there, ignoring the cold darkness. My broom handle I held like a spear. It was a miracle I did not break any of the hanging light bulbs.

There *was* something, a small, hulking shape crawling among my things. I swooped in upon it, striking it away from the bag. It slid across the rough floor, tumbling against the wall. If it was a rat, it was the largest of its breed I had ever seen in my life. A rat over two feet long! I raised the stick to crush its head, and it flung up its two paws, and cried out, "No!"

I was stopped by that. Never had I heard a rat to make such a humanlike noise. It sprang away quick as a wink when I let the stick down, but I was quicker. I thrust the bristle side of the broom in its way, and put down a hand to capture my prey. I grasped a handful of cloth.

My prisoner struggled and kicked, but I had it by the middle of its back, and it could not hurt me. It was so light that I hardly noticed its weight. Taking it into the light, I examined it. It was a black-haired child, clad in shirt and trousers, but what an amazing child! I thought immediately of the legends of my home, of the little house spirits, who would do good deeds or bad as it suited them. It could be that this little fellow was of the same type. What else but magic could account for its appearance? The eyes and cheekbones were sharp and wide, making it look like a little wild animal. And its ears were pointed, like a cat's laid back. But it was of human type, and it swung its tiny fists in the air, crying out in a language I do not know, trying to get loose from my grip. I stood as one frozen in place. Its face was dirty, and under the loose shirt which I clutched in my hand, its ribs were thin.

With a heart's wrench, I thought of my own children. This child, however strange it might appear to me, was but a child, and hungry. I made soothing noises to it, and it ceased struggling. Very slowly, I moved backward to where my lunch basket lay, and I lowered the little creature to the ground. It stood up, regarding me most warily. I opened my hand, let the broom lean against the wall, and stooped to my basket. Out of my eye's corner could I see that the child had already opened it, but I had surprised it before it could take any of the contents. In there I had apples, sandwiches, a pint bottle of milk, and a wrapped slice of cake. I am proud of my skill of bakery; my mother taught me, and she was much acclaimed in the village of my birth. Moving smoothly, with no haste, I laid the contents out in a line on the floor before the child. It was trembling where it stood, and I smiled at it to show I meant no harm. Small wonder it was frightened. Had I not just plucked the poor creature up, like a wild hawk hunting a rabbit?

Of a sudden, it gasped, and pointed open mouthed over my shoulder. I sprang up, spinning around, to see what had so alarmed it. Nothing was there. I turned back, just in time to see the little one dashing away, with all of my food in its arms. I laughed, for I had been fooled by an old trick, showing that my little one here had all of his wits about him, and I was sure, more than ever, that he was of the magical kind. I felt blessed for having seen it, and even more so for having done it a kindness. In our folk stories, it is important to do so. It brings no good to those who do them ill.

Only once did I ever tell my husband about seeing one of the Little People in the school building. He laughed, too, but in disbelief of me. Never to the end of his life did he credit my story. In his opinion, it was that the New Learning in the college would keep old superstitions away. But what, I argued, if it was not a superstition, but reality? He reasoned that if the Old Ones were real, then the New Learning would teach about them, too, and they did not. He had a firm opinion, but one of a closed mind. I think he was afraid to believe me. If one folk tale was true, a good one, he felt that the bad ones would have as much chance to be true, too. I loved and respected my husband, but I kept my own mind open.

At first he convinced me that I was imagining meeting the child, but I did see my little one again, and many times after that.

The next time I walked from the Science building to the library, far down the passageway, in the center of a pool of light, stood my milk bottle, on top of the folded napkin in which my sandwiches had been wrapped. Both were perfectly clean; the bottle gleamed as if it had been polished. I smiled. It was the little one's way of saying 'Danke.' I was much gratified, and when I passed through the tunnel, I left behind a quart bottle of milk, more apples, and a loaf of home-made egg bread flecked with bacon, an old recipe in my family. It was in my mind that the child must have parents, and if I would starve to let my own sons and daughters eat, in what pitiful state must this one's be?

It was many days before I saw any other sign of life in the course of my tasks. Every time, the bottle would be returned to me, left where it could not be missed. I know I was watched most carefully; others in the employ of the University passed along the steam tunnels, and yet they never saw or heard a thing. And my milk bottles never were found by anyone else.

You may ask how I could continue to provide food for people I never saw, when it might be I was pulling it away from my own family's mouths? There are those whose hearts Charity has never touched. I am not made that way. My mother always told me that hands open so they can give. Fruit was cheaply obtained. My sister's husband had a farm not far away, and we had often meat and produce from them. And I allow myself to be proud that I am a thrifty housekeeper. I could make but a little go far, so I was able to feed—three, I believed—extra mouths, without extra expense.

I was not the only one from whom food came, though I was the only one who gave it willingly. From my fellow workers came complaints that the rats were stealing their lunches, and that they were also to blame for the occasional disappearance of supplies from out of the dormitory kitchens. No one else reported seeing a strange child.

One night, I rushed through my tasks, and came last to the library passageway. I wanted to see if perhaps my husband was right, and I had been dreaming, or that I was, and had not. Out of my basket, I took milk and bread and fruit, and laid it in the light. But now, instead of leaving, I sat down beside my offering, and waited.

I believed that I could hear low conversation not far from me in the dark. My little ones were deciding whether or not to reveal themselves to their benefactress.

"Come out," I called. "I will not harm you." I held out my hands, empty of weapons, so that they could see them. More hurried conversation, though I could not distinguish of how many voices. At last, there was movement in the shadows. There stepped forward a figure. It was my little mannikin. Behind him came two others, a man and a woman, perhaps a foot taller than the child. Her hair was the same shiny black as the boy's, but the man's was orange-red. They were, as I had believed, much mended, and thin and hungry looking, but because of me, perhaps, less so than they must have been before.

I let my eyes devour my first glance in weeks of the child. It was good because I learned I was not mad, but also because my secret kindness had improved this child's lot. He was not as thin as before, and for a wonder, he was clean! His shirt was neat, and his face had been washed. I think that even before I knew myself, these little wise ones knew I would wait for them this night. His expression had not the hunted fear of our first meeting, nor the hard defiance, which so reminded me of my younger son. He had a formidable will, into which he would grow one day, with care. I felt a sympathy with the parents. There was more here to deal with than making their child stay presentable.

They next had my attention. I was made to think of refugees, clad in well-worn rags, whose war it was not, and who wanted only to be left alone. But from what war? Whence had they come?

"How do you do?" I asked slowly. At first it seemed they did not understand me. I repeated myself, both in English and German. Both were still uneasy, so I began to talk.

I said much about my own family, my children and my husband. I spoke of my own childhood, and how I came to America with my parents. How I grew up and went to school, how I began working, and when I met my husband. And how, when I was young, I heard stories in my village of people like themselves, the Wise Old Ones, the craftwise, who did good or evil as it pleased them; and when I had told one of the tales, the little man spoke slowly for the first time.

"Are there of them any left?" he asked me, with hope.

"I do not know," I admitted. "I never did see them myself."

I knew that he was disappointed. He did not pursue the subject; instead, asked me most seriously, "Why do you offer charity to us?"

So proud he was. Here there were secrets of his which I was keeping, and yet he was still challenging me. I pretended to be offended, and told him, "It is not charity to give gifts to new neighbors. I am a good neighbor." I kept my face solemn.

For the first time, he laughed. It made his face brighten. "Even so," he said, smiling. "But it must not be unreturned."

First they did give me this plate for my cakes and breads upon to sit. Never will any grow mouldy or stale while seated here. When I protested it was too much to give me for a little milk and meat, they only smiled.

They told me how it was that they had come to central Illinois, and how they found this place of shelter, which was warm, and yet not filled to brimming with people. They thought that here they could be safe. It had been many, many years since they crossed the ocean, but I know not how, nor where they lived until then. Of the Great War which was being fought, they knew little. Midwestern

University had its lowest enrollment and fewest teachers, as all had gone to fight in the War. I said that I would help them establish a home, and they took me to meet the others.

It was a leap in my mind to go from believing in one child, to a little family, but nearly a miracle it took for my poor mind to understand thirty or more poor beings, huddled together in the abandoned basement, fearful of discovery. Immediately, I thought of the newsreels, of the European horrors. Under cover of night they traveled, facing many dangers, avoiding cities, eating crops from the fields. But from where had they come, I asked? They never told me. But this place was here, in the heart of generous farmlands, and it seemed made for them, so they intended to stay.

"And so, it was my insistence that they closed off the lowest level of the library in which to live. The ceiling was too low for any classes to be held there. I think perhaps it was built by the government to use as a secret office, but it was too old; the government felt a closed door was enough, then. Tens of years had it been neglected. All that remained there were boxes of rotted wood, containing old books and other school property. The janitors were all old men, and they forgot that the place was there. Here I suspect magic, for one of these was Franklin Mackay, and Mr. Mackay had never forgotten one thing in his long life. I believe that after a time only I and my little ones knew there had ever been a lowest floor." Mrs. Hempert placed her tea-cup into the saucer with a resolute click.

"I sure didn't," Keith admitted. "How did Lee get involved?"

"The same way you have. A kind heart and a willingness to help. Since I retired, he has done all that which I used to do. He orders extra goods. No one notices the missing supplies, ever, for there is always so much wasted. But he was never closer to them than he is. He trades food for education. They were eager to exchange what they had in plenty, knowledge, for that which they needed. I helped to work that out. Their pride I could circle around, once I knew that. Lee was doing poorly, now he does very well. But he will soon graduate; then he will be gone. You will take his place. I am glad you are here."

"Me, too," Keith said, thinking deeply. "Tell me, where does their light come from? I mean, on the ceiling?"

Mrs. Hempert was amused. "I do not know. If I say magic, and you believe me, you do not know more than if I said nothing at all. Now tell me, how did you find your way into their home? I know it is well hidden. I watched as it disappeared."

"Well, there was a girl…"

The old woman smiled. "One whom you like a great deal?"

"Yes, as a matter of fact. She has another guy who is interested in her. Except that might not last too much longer. He's bullying her and she doesn't like it."

"A bully," she repeated thoughtfully. "No, that is not right. I shall have to speak about that. But I tell you I am glad you have found my little ones, and that you are friends."

"Why are you telling me all this, Mrs. Hempert?" Keith asked earnestly. "I'm really grateful to you, but…I'm a stranger. I could be a fraud, or a reporter who just happened to hear something. Why are you trusting me?"

"Are you not trusting me?" she asked, a twinkle lighting the blue of her eyes into sapphire. "If I went to a reporter and told him, 'I have seen elfs,' they vould tell me I am a crazy old voman, yes? And I trust you. At my age I have learned something about character. You are honest. I can tell. I can tell."

"Just one thing: what are they doing here?"

"Just living, like you, or like me."

Keith nodded, and got up to go. "Thanks for talking to me. Um, may I come back again?"

"Of course," she smiled, also rising. "And bring your young lady, too. We are in one another's confidence now. What will you do now with your new knowledge?"

"I'm not sure. Help out if I can. I won't tell anyone else." Keith stuck out a hand. Ludmilla put her right hand into his, and enfolded both of theirs with her other hand. She had a strong, warm clasp, and he realized that she had plenty of residual strength from years at her job. However fragile she may look, she was not feeble. "I'll tell 'em you said 'hi.' Hmm," he scowled, as he remembered Holl's warning. "Maybe I won't."

"If you can, you will. Good bye, Keith."

Catra continued paging through the weekly Midwestern gazette. Nothing new had caught her eye since the first article, though she had been especially vigilant. She was relieved. However time-consuming her task was, it was easier to bear than the fear of discovery once their presence was suspected there in the basement of this big building. Then, as she was passing up the advertisement pages for used cars, she found a two-inch column with the headline, "Circus Midget Colony?", that went on to describe 'miniature adults in a midwestern Illinois town.'

This article was still reasonably vague. Probably it was just an echo of the one from the time before; these little journals read one another's copy; it was clear from week to week where the sources were found. It had no detail, only rumor, but it would still worry the elders. With a deep sigh she marked it with a sharp fingernail and put the newspaper back into its folder. Later on, she could make a xerox copy of it, when the librarians had gone home for the night.

Chapter 13

Keith leaned conspiratorially over the secretary's desk at the office of the School of Nursing. "Hiya, Louise, baby," he purred, twitching one eyebrow, a la Humphrey Bogart. "We're goin' over the wall tonight. I need your help."

"What do you want?" Louise Fowler demanded, pushing Keith's hands off a pile of carbon paper. "Keep your paws off my desk. I'm going to search your pockets before you leave."

Keith bounced off, and dashed around the desk to kneel beside her. She deliberately cultivated a starched-stiff attitude in her duties as administrative assistant to the Nursing School, but Keith had a way of disarming her, and it usually meant trouble, either some he was planning, or some he was already in. He took her hand in his and said mournfully, "Such a lack of trust."

Louise pulled her hand back. "I don't have time for this. Do you want something?"

"Of course!"

"Well, what?"

"For a start, sheets. Gotta have something to tear up for rope ladders," he said, going over a list he had rehearsed in his head.

"Why? Haven't you ever heard of doors?"

"Whose jailbreak is this, anyway?" he insisted. "Maybe I'll use the surplus for my Hallowe'en costume."

"A ghost, right?"

Keith shook his head in mock dismay. "You're too quick for me, baby. I'll have to take you with me. Wanna be a moll?"

"Nope."

"Look, I'm serious. What happens to the medical center's old sheets and pillowcases when they get worn out?"

"Well, they go to the school, for nurses' training."

"And they come in like that whenever the med center gets new ones? Have they had any recent replacements?" Louise nodded. "Can I have some of them?"

"No!"

"Oh, come on. Please. It's to make some kids happy."

Louise stared at him suspiciously. "Are you serious?"

"Honest. May I never go to Mars if I'm not. It's a...Junior Achievement group," Keith announced, after a moment's pause.

"Okay," she sighed. "Come back this afternoon, and I'll see what I can find."

"May Allah bless you and all your children. And all the ones you don't know about, too." He departed, kissing his fingertips and bowing low to her as he backed out the door. Louise groaned and drew out her inventory card file.

"Sure I have fabric left over from earlier semesters," Mrs. Bondini said, accepting the can of cola from Keith. She slid the plate containing her tuna melt and french fries off the tray. Keith set down his own fries and a pair of turkey sandwiches, and put the plastic tray out of the way on an adjoining table. He had headed Mrs. Bondini off from the entrance to the Faculty lunchroom, pleading the need for a personal audience. Amused, she had accepted his invitation to eat with him in the University Deli. Evidently, she had memories of the course she had taught in three-dimensional sculpture in which he'd enrolled a couple of semesters back. "Why?"

"It's this Junior Achievement group I'm working with," Keith said, popping open his own can, and unwrapping a sandwich. "As I'm not too familiar with this kind of project, I thought I'd come to someone who is."

"And 'this kind of project' is...?"

"Um...Cabbage Patch Kids' clothes. All kinds of doll clothes. It'll be a big hit. They've something really different in mind. Costumes. Ethnic dress from other nations. That sort of thing." Keith smiled politely at her. After all, he was *almost* telling the truth.

"Well, aren't they supposed to sell shares and get their operating capital that way?"

"Well, first they need money to print the shares with. And I remembered you also taught the costuming course, so..."

"...So you figured I might be a soft touch," Mrs. Bondini finished cynically. "Remembering, of course, that the college owns those bolts of fabric."

"Mm-hmm," Keith agreed, innocently, tucking a quarter sandwich into his mouth. He tried to talk around it, struggled to swallow quickly. "And the thing is, I'm sure there's some, well...undesirable prints, or something, hanging around, that you might be willing to throw to me instead of the dumpster."

"Maybe." Mrs. Bondini rolled up the cellophane from her lunch and dusted her hands together. "Well, come with me, and we'll see what I might have for your future tycoons."

With an innocent smile, Keith followed her.

He had one more stop to make. In the History Department, he spent a little time going through the local archives. Everyone was away from their desks at lunch except a student aide, so he was able to root through the drawers undisturbed. Satisfied with his findings, he used the phone in one of the empty offices to put through a couple of calls, all the time looking around nervously to make sure no one was overhearing him.

Keith was in such a good mood that he didn't even flinch when Dr. Freleng handed out a new research assignment that threatened to cut into his dwindling free time. When the other students in the class shared their ideas for investigation he smiled vaguely and maddeningly. Even to Marcy who knew, or thought she knew, the reason for Keith's behavior, he seemed more ridiculous than ever.

"What is wrong with you?" she hissed in his ear as they left the classroom.

"Wait and see, my pet," he smirked.

That evening, he was late making his way to the class. The librarian on duty at the entrance to the stacks was not convinced when he told her that his two huge plastic-wrapped bales contained drop sheets for the painters that were coming in the morning. The bags were obviously heavy, and full of slippery bulks that showed a tendency to slump to one side.

"You can not bring those things in here! Absolutely not!" she insisted, so vigorously that her glasses slid off her nose. They dropped to the end of their tether, and bumped against her chest on every stressed syllable, especially the *nots*.

Keith sighed, trying to look patient and martyred, and wishing he could carry the bundles in through the elves' back door, though it would spoil the surprise. "I told you, Mrs. Hansen wants these on level ten. They won't be in anyone's way. I'll just put 'em where she told me to."

The librarian seemed taken aback by his evocation of a higher authority than herself. "Well, we'll see. I'll go ask Mrs. Hansen myself!"

Keith waited until she was out of sight, and then rushed himself and his two bundles into the stairwell.

It was far less harrowing, but no less clumsy an entrance than his first one into the hidden classroom. The bags wouldn't fit through the doorway at the same time, so he had to hold one in his arms and propel the other before him with a foot. The session had already begun. With a newly developed awareness of what to listen for, he could hear voices long before he ever got into the room. Carl Mueller was on his feet, red faced, with one hand in the air. Keith had most likely interrupted him in the middle of another deathless speech. He kicked the two bags into a corner and sat down. They sloshed against each other, and subsided.

Holl glanced over his shoulder, and looked curiously at Keith, who gestured to him to wait. The Elf Master favored him with the same expression, but Keith sat up attentively, hands folded, and displayed ingenuous interest in class proceedings. The Master was not distracted. He turned away from Carl and came to lean over Keith.

"Vhat haf ve here, Mr. Doyle?" he inquired, eyebrows raised.

"Um, nothing much," Keith answered, shrinking back in spite of himself.

"If it is nothing, then why is it so large?"

"Well, I *brought* them…"

"Obviously."

"…To see if you wanted them," Keith finished, his mouth dry. Suddenly his attack of generosity didn't seem like the good idea it had the night before.

The thick red eyebrows climbed nearly all the way into the hairline. "Vhich 'you' do you mean?"

Keith swallowed. This was not going at all the way he had wanted it to. He had hoped to bring the matter of the parcels up quietly at the end of class, when he could fade away without making a big fuss. And why was the old guy being so touchy? "Well, you all," he gestured, indicating the elves, then flipping the hand and shrugging uncomfortably, his carefully prepared speech deserting his memory. He had been positive the Master would be pleased. "Just some things I picked up here and there. Thought you could use."

He knew he was saying all the wrong things. After listening to Ludmilla explain to him how touchy they were about accepting favors, he had just spat out every buzz-word in the lexicon. The other students remained silent. The young elves were expressionless, but the humans looked positively irate. Lee had a bloodthirsty look in his eye that made Keith very nervous. He smiled hopefully at everyone. Whatever he had interrupted, it was a dilly. The others just watched him uncomfortably. Seeking to diffuse the tension, Holl got out of his seat, clearing his throat loudly, and dragged the bags into the center of the room. The young elves were around him in a moment, leaving the Elf Master pinning Keith to the back of his chair with a needle-sharp gaze of disapproval. There were exclamations of interest and approval from the Little Ones as they opened the bags. Holl made a great show of presenting the contents to the others.

"Look how useful these'd be," Holl said, championing Keith. He held up a white hospital sheet and tested its strength. "Still in best condition. The Big Ones are always tossing out things with life left in them."

"That's a truth," said Catra, tossing her long, taffy-colored braid out of the way. She rubbed the fabric between her thumb and forefinger. "Ah, percale. Nice fabrics. The one thing I've been wishing for. I'll have that. My mother will be able to do much with a sheet that big."

Her sister, the little blond elf, reached for the sheet's edge, a sour look on her face. Holl reached into the bag, and found it was full of sheets. He put another into her hands. "Candlepat, here's one for you." She beamed, tucking the bundle under one arm.

"Ahh." The others were sorting through the plastic sacks. The sheets were counted and divided up. Candlepat and Catra unfolded bolts of fabric and tried them together for style. Most of them were Christmas materials, red stars on white background, white stars on red, blue and white stripes, green and white, red and green. When they came to the green fabric decorated with small white stars, it looked like the two sisters might come to blows.

"I want that," Candlepat wailed a protest, holding on to the bolt. "You bully me because you're the older. It isn't fair."

"It'd look better on me than it would on you. You have fine clothes in plenty because you're the prettiest. And you have a whole counterpane, the newest in the household. I do not. This will do me well. You can go without, for a change."

Marm pushed his way between the two of them. With a reproachful look at each, he unwound the bolt, found the midpoint,
and tore it into two equal pieces. Eying each other like a pair of
angry hens, they accepted their halves from him, and went on peck-
ing through the contents of the sacks. Marm himself nodded pleasantly over a short piece of tweedy brown, and tucked the end into
his tunic belt.

The floor was soon strewn with lengths of cloth, most of them
loud and gaudy to the humans' point of view, but obviously attractive
to their smaller classmates. Laniora was cooing over a length of white-
starred blue. Maura had out the lone bolt of blue denim fabric and
was holding it up against herself, mentally measuring for an outfit. She
skillfully twitched the end out of Catra's hand when she reached for it,
and appeared to be entertaining some pleasant thoughts on decoration. Catra looked up only once to see that it wasn't her sister competing for the piece of cloth, and went back to her own browsing. Holl,
after exchanging unspoken communication with Maura, draped the
blue cloth over his arm and approached Keith with it.

"What'll you trade for this one, eh?" Holl asked, rescuing him
from the Elf Master.

Gratefully, Keith broke eye contact and nervously edged out of
his seat. "Ah, I hadn't thought about it, really. It was supposed to be
a gi—Um," he paused, responding to his friend's obvious prompt
for more diplomacy, and rubbed the corner of the cloth between
thumb and forefinger. "What would you like to trade?"

Maura whispered in Holl's ear, and he nodded, fingering the
fabric speculatively. Keith watched him with respect. He didn't look
too keen or too disinterested: a natural garage-saler. "I'd say it might
be worth a small lantern, or a toy, or a carved wooden box this big."
He sketched a form in the air about six inches wide. "There's more
than a single garment's length here, you see."

"Sounds fair. How about the lantern?" Keith asked quickly. Holl
nodded and rerolled the bolt around its flat cardboard core. Maura
took it and the two men shook hands. Patting Holl's arm for thanks, she
disappeared down the tunnel, waving the bolt happily. Taking their friends'
cue, the others spoke up at once with offers for their prizes.

"Look," Keith said, holding his hands palms out to the others.
"I'm no good at this sort of thing. You take what you want, and we
can figure it out later, okay?"

There was a general chorus of agreement, and the elves simply bundled the bags up and carried them away toward their home. In the echoing passage, Keith could hear the shrill voices of the elven sisters, arguing about *who* would wear *what*. Holl had a satisfied grin on his round face. Keith felt pretty good himself. Everyone seemed happy. This was much more what he had in mind. The other students' ire seemed to have dissolved. They had arisen from their seats to watch the bartering, and now came over to praise Keith for his generosity and thoughtfulness. His idea seemed to have gone over well with them all.

Except the Elf Master. He still stood by Keith's desk, radiating disapproval. Keith tried not to look his way. He felt himself cringing away from the stern little man. The other Little Folk were reappearing out of the tunnel and taking their seats. Keith appeared to have broken the ice, and the students, all of them, were chattering to one another, relaxed, the cultural barriers down at last. Marcy distracted him at that moment by grabbing his face between her hands and kissing him right on the mouth.

"You doll!" she said. "So this is what you were being so mysterious about. I've been wanting to do something like that for months."

"Well, why not do it again?" Keith leered, slipping an arm around her waist. He caught a glimpse of Enoch who had a shocked expression on his face. Keith winked at him over Marcy's shoulder, and was rewarded with a cold stare. Oh, well, the little sourpuss never liked him anyway.

"No, not that," Marcy corrected him, playfully but firmly turning her face aside. "You know what I mean."

"Yup," he acknowledged. But he kept his arm around her, and she didn't protest or move away. This was a reward he hadn't expected for his efforts, and he was enjoying it. There was a thundercloud building up over Carl's head, and Keith enjoyed that, too. He was a hero. In everyone's eyes but Carl's, the Elf Master's, and Enoch's, that is. What was eating them?

"What are you going to do with the jeans fabric?" Teri Knox asked Maura shyly. It was probably the first direct question she'd ever asked one of the others.

Maura seemed just as timid. "I don't really know. I would like to make an outfit like the one in green wool you wear."

"Oh, my pantsuit? Well, I could bring it around, and you can copy the pattern." She eyed Maura, estimating her size. "It's too bad they don't make tailored styles that small."

"That's no matter. I'm good at fittings. I can copy almost anything, but there are no books of patterns in all of Gillington. I'd be most grateful." Maura, just as shy, was warming to Teri's friendliness.

"No problem," Teri said. "I'd be happy to. You'd look really good in a blazer, too. You're built just like a Barbie doll. Did I ever wear this outfit down here? I think you'd like it." The two girls bent over a sheet of paper, and began discussing designs.

"Great fellow, this Keith," Marm said, in an aside to Carl, who was sitting at his desk, staring at nothing. "He's a friend."

"He's a phony," Carl growled.

"Not in my books, laddie," the elf retorted, testily. "In my view he's thoughtful, not like some other people who think only of themselves, and scoring off the other man."

"I don't do anything like that," he snapped.

"And you don't do anything else," Marm flung back.

"You think I'm lying?"

"If you say that about Keith Doyle, you must be."

"Marm, bring your voice down," Holl said, glancing over his shoulder at the Elf Master.

"But, Maven, do you hear this fool? Listen to him," Marm said, indignantly.

The Elf Master sat by himself, watching, saying nothing himself. He appeared to be thinking deeply on some subject, one that disturbed him. Everyone else seemed to be pleasantly chatting. It was the most relaxed class meeting he had ever witnessed, especially one that had started so badly. But it boded to end ill.

Marm's and Carl's argument was getting louder, and some of the others were joining in, mostly on Marm's side.

"You really must be dumb if you believe that." Carl had a finger leveled, and was jabbing out for punctuation. Keith was still talking quietly to Marcy, and seemed unaware that there was a battle going on. "After what I've told you? He's not your friend. He's nobody's friend, except his own."

"And why else would he bring us things?" Marm demanded, ignoring Holl's attempts to bring the argument to a close.

"Yes, vhy?" the Elf Master spoke at last, making himself heard over the din, and addressing Keith directly. "For vhat reason do you bring us gifts?"

"Um," Keith was distracted from his private chat with Marcy, and had to think how best to phrase his answer. "Just because I wanted to. No good reason."

"Eh, I told you," Marm said, triumphantly.

"They're bribes," Carl shouted, pushing his way into the middle of the crowd, and sending a forefinger thudding into the center of Keith's chest. "So when you lose your home you won't blame him. But it'll still be his fault. He's the one behind the movement I told you about. He's trying to get the Administration to tear down the library!"

Keith's mouth dropped open in amazement. So that was what was up. The vindictive creep!

The chatter and noise died away without an echo, and Keith found everyone looking intently at him. "Is that true?" Marcy demanded, a hurt expression in her eyes. "He said that at the beginning of class."

"Well..." Keith began, his voice dwindling to a squeak. "Not exactly. The vote hasn't been taken yet."

"*Is* it true that you've been working toward it?"

"It was," he said, uncomfortably. "I did it to annoy Carl. But that's all over. I looked up some facts on the library building today, and I called the Historical Society. They might be able to declare it a historic landmark. If they do, it can't be torn down."

"And if they cannot so declare it?" the Elf Master inquired frostily.

Eyes on the ground, Keith mumbled, "Then I guess it'll be torn down. But I'm sure I can get them to reverse the vote."

"Meester Doyle," the Master said, very slowly and distinctly. "I think you should leaf now." Keith gathered up his books in silence.

"I'm really sorry," Keith said from the doorway. No one looked up, but Holl gave him a little wave from behind his back. Enoch and Carl had identical grim smiles on their faces. Keith sadly pulled the door closed behind him.

"See," crowed Carl, breaking the silence. "He didn't deny it. For the sole purpose of bugging me, he threat—"

Tears were overflowing Marcy's eyes. "Shut up, Carl."

He whirled on her, angrily. "Hey, he's been a pain in the butt as long as I can…"

"I said, shut up," Marcy blurted, sniffing. "I don't want to hear it. I don't want to hear anything you have to say. Big hero. We're through. You can leave me alone from now on."

"Marcy!" Carl looked astonished, then angry.

"Didna you hear what the lady said?" Enoch hissed, springing up and glaring into Carl's face. "Leave her alone."

"Back off, shorty." Carl snapped. "I'll say whatever I feel like." His face went red and his hands tightened into fists. The slightly built elf stood up to him.

"Did your mother teach you no manners, Carl Mueller?" Enoch sneered.

Holl watched the three of them absently, his fingers playing with his whittling knife. He was bitterly disappointed in Keith, not because he had admitted to backing an issue that would inadvertantly evict them, but because he found Keith's methods shy of sense. If I'd been out to even a score with this big stinking fool, Holl thought, I'd've made it more personal. His clan friends had a lot to think about, by the looks on their faces. Poor Marm, getting straight into the middle. He never had more sense than to start a fight without all the facts in hand.

Keith had a good idea, thinking of having the library declared a historical treasure, though the others didn't give him time to explain how it would work. Holl had read about such things in the library books, and in the periodicals, too. At the very least, it would make for all kinds of delay. His people could find a place, given time. They all liked Keith, but now they were confused.

He knew the older ones believed that the Big Ones were dishonest, two-faced. After all, they had history to back up their opinions. A setback like this one could get them all believing that Keith was one of those, but he himself understood Keith's impulses, and that made all the difference. The younger ones might have his own perspective. He'd have to discuss it with them later.

"Class dismissed," the Elf Master said, at last.

Chapter 14

"But you must understand that it was before he knew about us that he was campaigning for the new library," Holl said, thumping the dinner table with his fist. "He's trying to correct his mistake."

"Rubbish," the clan elder said from the end of the table. "He's got caught, and he's covering his tracks. What does it matter what becomes of us, eh?"

"That's not fair, Curran. He has our interests at heart. If you were to give him any credit at all..."

"I am not inclined to do so." The white-haired elf drew his brows into a single furrowed line.

Keva's hard expression showed him how much support he could expect from his immediate family. "You brought him here. A snake in your own nest!"

"It isn't like that," Holl explained, patiently, trying to deal with their fears. What would they do if they had to leave here? Where would they go? He was born here. He had never lived anywhere else. But it was clear that he had a more objective point of view than the others did. They were all frightened by the idea of moving on. Small wonder: the world had changed a lot in the last forty years. "If you'd read the books yourself, you'd understand. 'Historical landmark' stops action faster than a good strong spell halts a cataract."

"These books contain too many Big ideas. You're starting to think like a Big One." Curran spat on the ground.

"Just exchange of concepts. I know my heritage," Holl corrected her sharply. "I know which is magic and which is science and what is untruth. He is our friend. That is the truth."

"Are you forgetting why we live apart from the Big Ones? It is so we will not be absorbed and destroyed. Look how Keith Doyle made up to seduce us," Keva snapped.

"He's just being friendly," Holl said, shaking his head. "He has no other motives. He is much simpler than that."

"He is intruding himself too far into our lives. That is vhy I sent him away. Perhaps you haf had too much exposure to the Big Ones," the Elf Master's voice came from the next table. "You vill stay away from the class for a time. When you remember who you are and where you came from, then you vill understand why it is not good to absorb too much of their culture. And then you may return."

"Master, that is not just," Holl protested, turning around. Maura sat in her place beside Enoch, her head bowed. Strain creased her forehead. Apparently it was not only Holl's clan that had been discussing the events of the day.

The red haired elf rose to his feet. "I decide whom I vill teach."

Holl pushed himself away from the table, and rose to meet the Master's eyes. "It is too bad you can't decide who will learn," he said, fighting to keep his voice level, "starting with yourself." And he strode away.

When he opened the door of their dorm room, Pat found Keith sitting on his bed with all the lights off. "Now what?" he demanded.

"Did you ever have a case of really classic bad timing?" Keith asked unhappily.

"Yes," Pat answered, turning on the lights. Keith not only sounded miserable, he looked miserable. The black arcs underlining his eyes made him look like a red-haired raccoon. "There was this girl in Kankakee once, well…. And so, I repeat: now what?"

"I've made a big fool of myself," Keith said. He seemed truly worried. "I meant to do something nice for someone, and it backfired."

Pat pulled Keith's chair around and sat down on it. "It happens," he responded sympathetically. "What did you do?"

"Some uh, friends of mine may be getting…evicted. They literally have no money," Keith said, since it was the exact truth. "And I walked into the middle of it today with a bunch of presents for them, and they threw me out."

"So? You hit 'em in a sensitive place. You're a have and they're have-nots. You ought to pay more attention to all that sociological research you're supposed to be doing. It's not your fault."

"But it is! And I've got to fix it somehow." Keith put his head down into his hands.

"No way. You're not responsible for their problems. Injured pride's a tough thing to deal with. You can help, but don't try to do it all for them."

"But they have nowhere to go."

"Bull. Everyone can find someplace to go. And you'll just have to curb your generous streak for now, my boy. If they want something from you, let 'em ask."

"I wish I could win the Lottery. That'd solve the problem. I could buy a place for them to live. Or," Keith caught a glimpse of Pat's face, utterly exasperated, "lend them the money to buy one."

"That won't help," Pat said seriously. "Remember self-respect? It's tied to self-sufficiency. Charity is given by those above to those below. Let 'em be your equals. Give a guy a fish, and he'll eat today…"

"I know…teach him to fish, and he'll eat for the rest of his life. You've got a cliché for every occasion, but this time I think you're right. Unfortunately, I don't know how to do anything I can teach them that'll help. Not in time, anyway."

Pat patted him on the top of the head with a fatherly hand and rose from the chair. "Don't worry about it. Maybe they won't be evicted. That'd be the end of the problem."

Keith mumbled through his hands, "I'm not counting on that."

"What choice have you got?" Pat asked, reasonably, picking up the glass carafe from their Mr. Coffee. "Say, have you had dinner yet?"

"No. Not hungry." His stomach felt wrung out with worry.

There was a tap on the door. "I'll get it," Pat said. Keith heard the door open. "It's for you, Doyle. It's some kid."

He looked up. Holl stood on the threshold, in a coat and knit cap, clutching a bag under one arm. "Hi, there, widdy. I've come for dinner, as you asked," he said, cheerfully.

"Sorry. He's not hungry," Pat told the boy.

"Come on in," Keith said. "Welcome. Am I glad to see you."

"It's a long, cold walk from the bus station," Holl said, with a meaningful sideways glance at Pat.

"Sure is," Keith nodded, catching on. "How was your trip?"

"Okay." Holl pulled off his coat and hat. Keith took them from him and hung them up in the closet. When he turned back, Pat was staring with open interest at the elf's ears. Holl stared back, blue eyes innocent.

"Trekkie," Pat announced.

"Yup," Keith agreed.

"Huh?" Holl asked.

"'Scuse me a minute." Pat walked out of the room brandishing the coffee pot. Holl started to speak, but Keith held up a hand to forestall him until Pat was out of earshot in the washroom across the hall.

"What?" Holl demanded in a hiss.

"Too long to explain now. It's harmless. Look, you're my nephew, okay? And when Pat comes back, just say 'Yeah, I really like Mr. Spock.'"

Pat came back into the dorm room with the sloshing pot of water.

"Yeah, I really like Mr. Spock," Holl said, obediently.

Pat smiled and plugged in the coffee-maker. "Aren't you going to introduce your guest?"

Keith sighed, and waved his hands between the two. "Pat Morgan, my room-mate, meet my nephew."

"Holland Doyle," Holl said, extending a hand.

"A pleasure," Pat said, taking the hand with a courtly salute. They shook.

"Say, let's eat," Keith said. "I just remembered I'm starved."

Holl walked wide-eyed down the buffet line behind Keith and Pat. "Do you eat like this every day?" he asked Keith in a whisper.

"No," Keith muttered back. "Sometimes it's even worse."

Dozens of Big People were filling trays in the serving room, and hundreds more of them were sitting out in the vast dining hall beyond the door. Most of them smiled indulgently at the little blond kid in the cap who was sticking so close to Keith Doyle. Possibly they were remembering their own first visits to a college. The sheer number of human beings was sometimes just plain overwhelming. Certainly the boy seemed impressed.

The abundance of food impressed him, too. Not one, but five main dishes, with several steaming pans of vegetables, and a basket of fresh-smelling rolls. Holl sniffed. Not as good as Keva's bread. But everything else wafted enticing aromas his way. It was hard to choose what to take to eat. At least in the clan kitchen the decision was simple. You ate, or you didn't.

Aware that other diners were waiting patiently behind him, Holl pointed to one of the steaming pans at random. A shining white plate appeared, and a heap of small, golden chunks was shoveled onto it. "Potatoes or fries?" asked the white-uniformed woman behind the counter.

"Fries?" Holl said, uncertainly. A scoop of fries joined the entree.

"Peas and carrots?"

"Yes," Holl said automatically, mesmerized by the deftness of the woman's hands.

"No!" Keith exclaimed, overhearing him and turning around. "No. String beans. You want string beans, right?"

Holl shrugged. "Sure." The hand dropped the scoopful back into the cauldron of green and orange, and dipped the spoon into another filled only with green.

"The peas and carrots are left over from the First World War," Keith said out of the corner of his mouth. "At least the beans are fresh."

"Oh," said Holl.

Somehow the plate passed unspilled over the top of the counter, and Holl went on to secure cartons of milk and a piece of cherry pie in a bowl. Balancing the heavy tray uncertainly, he followed the other two through the dim dining hall to a table near the window, and sat down across from Keith.

"These are good," he said, tasting one of the golden chunks. It was a small piece of chicken, covered in batter and deep-fried.

"What's he got there?" Pat asked, peering over his own plate.

Keith was struggling to cut a tough slice of beef with a dull-looking knife. He glanced over. "Chicken McNuggets. At least those aren't regular army issue." The meat slid, pushing his potatoes off the plate. Pat snickered, picking up a forkful of a thin greyish stew with crisp brown noodles and rice.

Holl filed the name and the expression for future use, and attacked his meal. He had started out using a fork, but careful side glances showed him that all of his fellow diners were eating their chicken and fries with their fingers. Nonchalantly, he followed suit. The food was as greasy as it looked, but it tasted good enough. Keith looked up and gave him a wink.

"What's that there?" he asked, indicating Pat's meal.

"Pork chow mein," Pat said.

"Go on," scoffed Holl. None of the library's cookbooks had an illustration for chow mein that looked like that.

"Honest to God," Keith vowed. "That's what they think it is."

"Want a taste?" Pat offered.

"No, thanks," Holl said. "I know when I'm well off."

"Oh, by the way, the ladies sent to tell you that they all think you're very kind." Holl pushed his empty plate aside and leaned forward on his elbows.

"Ladykiller," Pat leered at Keith, who blushed.

"It's not what you think, Pat," he said, with a long-suffering grimace. "What else did they say?"

"Mostly, it degenerated into an argument about whose point of view served the community best. Naturally, I'm of the opinion that mine does. Most of your younger cousins side with me. It's all the aunts and uncles who disagree. And, as a result, I'm temporarily declassified, myself."

Declas—? Out of class? "That's not fair," Keith protested.

"Not fair, but also not permanent. The same is true for you, if you manage to redeem yourself with them."

"This kid is a genius," Pat declared. "I can hardly understand a thing he says."

"Yeah. He's going to college next year," Keith added.

"This one?"

"Not a chance," Keith said. "He'd meet too many weirdos like you."

"Worse yet," Pat told him, "like you." He put his tray aside and stood up. "Enough of haute cuisine. I've got to get to rehearsal. Don't wait up for me, dear."

"Don't worry, sweetie," Keith said, sourly.

"Live long and prosper, kid," Pat waved.

"The same to you," Holl called back.

"You know," Keith mused, when they were back in Keith's dorm room, "it's kind of ridiculous to call you my nephew, when you're twenty years older than I am."

"Not at all, cousin," Holl corrected him, airily. He snatched off his wool hat and threw it on the bed. With both hands, he rumpled up his blond hair into a comfortable bird's nest. "Much better. In our family, it's nothing unusual for a granddad to have a forty-year-old nephew. Or a two-year-old great-aunt, for that matter. Keva's grandson Tay's in that very position right now, with his aunt Celebes, our baby sister. Who, by the way, is dressed in a natty new gown of red and white, courtesy of you. Many thanks."

"You're welcome, I guess. I didn't think it would cause so much trouble," Keith admitted, remembering the source of his troubles. "All I wanted to do was supply a little raw material where I thought it was needed."

"And it was needed. Don't let the old ones distract you from the truth of that. Tonight there're a lot of blessings being showered on your head. Though the main opinion is that in your case, the heart is greater than the head is."

"I know," Keith groaned. "I'm working on my new strategy to swing the Student Senate's vote the other way again. I hope they'll go for it. Everyone wanted a new Sports Center before Pat, Rick and I started our campaign."

"I surely won't bring *that* news home," the elf said, shaking his head with wry amusement. "If they thought you were a widdy before…"

"But if I *can't* fix it, what will you do?"

"What we can." Holl's shoulders sagged. "We don't know, and that's the truth of it."

"Pat suggested I teach you how to fish," Keith said, staring off into space.

"What do you know about the "Art of Fishing" that Isaak Walton didn't?"

"He doesn't mean real fishing. He meant I should use my considerable skills to teach you how to solve your own problem. But there's nothing I know that you don't know how to do better."

"It's a good idea your roommate had, though. You're both kind for caring," Holl said, kicking his heels against the legs of the desk chair. "Truly, it isn't your problem. It could have happened at any time before this."

"Are you sure you haven't got some pots of gold hidden somewhere?" Keith asked. "It sure would help."

"Of course we do," Holl said, sarcastically. "Which we carried from the old place to this on our backs. Have you ever hefted real gold?"

"No. I wish I could win the lottery or something for you. I'm not rich. Far from it. I'm here on scholarship, myself."

Holl saw that Keith was falling into a depression. "Cheer up, Keith. Here you go, then." He retrieved the bag he had arrived with, and tossed it toward the youth's head. "Your payment."

"My what?" Keith caught it and drew out the contents of the bag. It was a wooden lantern about a handspan high, rectangular in shape, with sharply peaked roof surmounted by a stiff ring, and lattice-carved sides as fine as filigree. Inside was a spiral-carved wooden candle topped by a white cotton wick. The bottom panel was one of Holl's 'cohesiveness spells.' "It's beautiful."

"All my own work," Holl told him proudly.

Keith turned the lantern over and over in his hands, stroking the polished frame. "There's no opening. It's just ornamental, huh?"

"No! What good would it be if it didn't light? I promised you a functional lantern."

"I don't get it. I mean, how would you light it?"

"How do you think?" Holl answered the question seriously. "Blow on the wick."

Obediently, Keith blew. The wick ignited. Astonished, he dropped the lantern. It hit the floor with a THOCK! but the flame didn't go out. "That's incredible," Keith exclaimed. "How does it work?— Magic! Is it magic?" he demanded.

Holl regarded him patiently. "Old skills, like carving," he said, picking the lantern up and holding it out. "It's stronger than it looks. All good hardwoods. Go on, blow it out."

Keith screwed up his face like a little boy with a birthday cake. The flame vanished, and the wick showed white again in its wooden cage. It wasn't even hot. "I don't believe it," he said, cradling the lantern reverently in both hands. "This is mine to keep?"

"Of course. We made a bargain. Value for value received. I'm satisfied. Here, there's more. These are from the feuding sisters." From his coat pockets, Holl produced a pair of wooden spoons, a small painted marionette, and a flat hinged box. "From Marm, who still believes in your innocence," he said, indicating the last. "Good work, but nothing fancy."

"Nothing fancy, he says," Keith echoed, mockingly. "It's professional quality stuff. Even better!"

Holl turned the box so the lock was facing Keith, and took hold of one of his hands. "Put your thumb here, widdy." Puzzled, Keith allowed his thumb to be pressed to the lock plate. "Now it'll only open to your hand. Good for things you want to keep private. You might keep the key to the classroom in here, if you choose."

"A magic lock! I love it. Eat your heart out, CIA."

"Will you stop? A simple charmed lock is nowhere near so important as full-blown magic."

Keith flushed. "Sorry. I'm not used to getting anything that's charmed or magical." He picked up the marionette and admired its glittering glass eyes. "What's this do?" He made it dance a few steps, whistling a few bars from the 'Beautiful Blue Danube'. The joints turned smoothly, and the painted wooden shoes beat a delicate tattoo on his coverlet. But when he let go of the puppet's strings, it did a step of its own before dropping nervelessly to the bed. Its bright stare was reflected in Keith's own astonished eyes. He was speechless.

Holl cocked an eye at it. "You've got a bit of energy of your own," he said enigmatically. "It wouldn't work like that for everybody. Amazing."

"You guys are amazing, not me," Keith exclaimed, poring over his treasures. "I know people who would pay anything for stuff like…. That's it!"

"What's *it*?"

"How you could earn money."

"And why do we need money? We don't live in a cash economy; strictly barter."

"Well, don't you understand? If you made enough toys, like these," he held up the box and the puppet in one hand, "and like *this*," the lantern in the other, "you could sell them and earn enough to buy your own home. Then you wouldn't have to worry about jerks like me trying to tear it down around your ears." Keith blushed, having made mention of those very obvious attributes. Holl didn't notice. He was thinking it over. Keith didn't have to. It was obvious. It was right.

That, of course, was the answer. Marketing was one of his skills. Hadn't he just been demonstrating it to his present disadvantage in Student Senate? Had he not done a thorough selling job on Marcy to get him in to meet the elves in the first place? Was he not, after all, a Business Major? He was.

"Come on, Holl," he said, jumping to his feet and shouldering into his coat.

"Where to?" The elf looked up from his meditation in surprise.

"To redeem myself, and maybe you, too."

Chapter 15

Getting through the concealed door in the side of the library building unobserved was the easy part. The sun had set behind a skyful
of rain clouds, and very few students were out on the common. A
few lonely streetlamps draped their beams on the shiny wet pavement, and the tired brown grass lay flat. Keith and Holl crossed
through the gloomy pools of light and eased in behind the paving
stones as simply as shadows. The hard part was trying to convince
the elders that Keith had rational point of view to which they should
listen. Most of them were for throwing him out on the spot. Holl,
who had had the whole concept explained to him on the way over,
was not entirely convinced himself. He had to concur at least that it
was a darned good idea, and managed to convince the clans to give
Keith a hearing at least.

"But why not sell handcrafts?" Keith insisted to an assembly of
the Little People. "Bored housewives make a bundle on color-by-
number tole paintings at craft fairs. You could clean up on your
creative skill alone."

"Exploitation!" one of the white-haired men shouted.

"Not by me," Keith said, frankly. "I can't tell you how sorry I
am about my mistake. But apologies won't really help you. I know I
blew it, I'll admit, but not because I knew anyone was living here."

Strangely, it was the Elf Master who came to his rescue, speaking up from among his fellows. "Is it any wonder, when we haf
gone to so much trouble to prevent detection?"

Keith was grateful for his teacher's intervention. "Right now
you can't afford to buy a new place if you lose this one. The least
you can do is consider making it easier to find a new home. If you
exploit your own talents, you help yourselves."

"We have no wish to expose ourselves. You have already done
enough to jeopardize us."

Full of excitement, Keith threw his arms out toward the little
man. "But that's where I come in. You won't be exposed. *I'll* find
buyers for you. I'll deliver the merchandise, and I'll handle all the
external negotiations. All you have to do is make things."

"What *things*?"

"These!" Keith seized the handful of wooden toys out of his pocket. There was a general outcry.

"You're ridiculous! Toys!"

"You want to stereotype us to your foolish folktales. Santa's little helpers. Big Ones are all alike!"

"Meester Doyle," came the Elf Master's sadly patient voice, "Meester Doyle, where did you get the impression that we are eager to take up handicrafts as a means of supporting ourselves, however covertly, in your society?"

"Well, I…you know, that's how…In fairy tales, like the elves and the shoemaker, they…." Keith sensed the ridiculousness of his words and broke off, bright red. "I'm sorry. Myths and legends are the only stuff I have to go on in common between your culture and mine. You know, like the story that unicorns are only attracted to virgins."

"And supposing the unicorn hasn't read the story?"

Keith took a deep breath. "I assumed that maybe legends were based on observations that had been distorted over time. I'm sorry. I just wanted to be helpful."

"Don't help. Don't get involved. You haf already done enough. Just go."

"Ye should never ha' come in the first," Curran, Holl's clan leader snapped out, stepping forward. "I was agin it, and still I am."

"Wait," Holl said, holding his hands up for silence. "Curran, there are others with opinions. Can we consider it?"

"Ye're too progressive, lad," the old man growled, shaking his white head doubtfully.

"And what choice have I got?" Holl demanded, addressing not only the old man, but all the elves. "The world's not the same as it was. When was the last time that any of you were ever able to walk about in honest daylight? We younger ones can because we look like Big Ones' children, and we can tell you that this fastness into which we've dug ourselves has become surrounded by *city*." He looked around, searching for understanding in his friends' faces. "Have none of you wondered why scavenging parties take so long to return? The farmland has receded away from our door. The natural ways are drifting out of our reach, and a colder way is taking their place." His voice sank to a choked whisper, but the room was silent, aware, listening. "There's no magic out there now, just machines and money."

A plump, elderly woman spoke up. "Then we've trapped ourselves like coneys. Is no open land left?"

Holl looked at Keith, passing on the question, and the tall student cleared his throat. "Sure, outside of the cities. Ironically, this one just grew up around the University because the Agriculture School is so good. It's big, but there's plenty of farmland and forests beyond it."

"Perhaps we should consider it, then," she suggested. Her daughter, or grand-daughter, a child with flaming red curls, nodded vigorously. The elders wrinkled their foreheads, muttering among themselves. "Look you," she exclaimed, "time was when there was plenty and enough for a'. I do not want to live in a maze we canna find our way out of. If we must *buy* a home on a day soon, we'll have to have the gold in hand before then."

"Um, we don't use gold any more," Keith put in. "Not since the 'twenties. Just dollars."

"How much will we need?" Dever, a younger elf inquired. His black eyes were in marked contrast to his ice-fair hair and beard.

"Depends on the land," Keith said, frankly. "I don't know anything about real estate."

"Ach!" spat Catra. "Don't you read the newspapers, Dever? There are advertisements in, every day."

"I don't read them," Dever admitted, shamefacedly. "I only read the comic strips and the columnists."

The room broke up into a dozen arguments.

"I say, do it!"

"No, it would be selling out."

"We could try..."

"Do you know another way? I don't."

The argument got louder and more forthright, shifting into a language which Keith could not identify. There were German words thrown in here and there, and he was positive he heard some slang, too, but the body of the discussion was nothing he'd ever heard before. There really were three distinct sets of accents in the room, when they spoke English. The old ones sounded Irish, or something like it; the middle-aged ones exclaimed their opinions in middle-European; the young ones in Midwestern American, complete with slang. Right now they all sounded exactly alike.

"I do not trust him," Curran growled, and Keva nodded sourfaced agreement.

"What about those newspaper articles?" one of the others demanded.

"He wrote them," Enoch speculated blackly. "He deserves none of our confidence."

"Not at all," Holl interrupted. "And he offers to help us."

"He offers to make a spectacle out of us!"

"Why not discuss it?" Tay said, dropping back into English and thrusting himself forward into the middle of the group. Keva waved a dismissive hand with a sound like she was spitting and turned away.

"The Maven has been rarely wrong," a burly, dark-haired elf said in English with a thick accent like the Master's, stroking his beard thoughtfully.

"He's becoming too like the Big Ones, Aylmer. Best to stick to what we know, and make our own way," Keva said forcefully. She glared over his head at Keith.

"Yes! Why do we need this Big One?"

"Yes, why?" "Why does he have to come into our lives?" "Ask him!"

Aylmer turned to Keith, and fixed him with a stern brown eye. "And vhat do you get out of all this hard vork for yourzelf?"

"Nothing," said Keith, earnestly but firmly. "You're my friends. I just want to help."

"No," the Master said, chopping a hand downward to forestall debate. "That is more of your charity."

"What charity?" Keith demanded. "Even if it is my scheme, you'd be earning your own way. It will be hard work. Like Holl said, value for value received. Okay—you can give me a commission for being your business manager. Ten per cent is fair. Check it out in the business law texts. That's standard."

"I haf," the Master admitted, showing a small glimmering of humor at last. "The usual percentage is thirty to forty."

The young man turned red again. "Maybe. I'd be happier with ten, myself. You're going to need all you can save to buy land. How about it, then? I'll take care of the shipping and you just fill the orders. What more could you ask? You could have a cottage industry with real cottages!" Keith demanded triumphantly. "That's a degree of reality you rarely find today in business."

"It sounds too easy," Marm complained.

"It vill not be easy," the Elf Master said, consideringly. "But perhaps it should be done." He turned a piercing eye on Holl. "Ve can *learn* at least if it is practical."

Holl bowed acceptance. It would be the closest thing he'd ever get to an apology from the imperious teacher. "Thank you, Master." He turned to Keith. "The floor's yours, widdy. What do you want us to do?"

Scratching his jaw, Keith considered. "The obvious market is gift shops, and things like that. I think we'll need at least a dozen to fifteen things to start off for the buyers to choose from. What else can you make besides these?"

Several of the elves ran for their homes, and came back with armloads of wooden implements. "See this," one said. "That's half worn out," another scoffed. "See this!" Tay and a woman, probably his wife, came back pushing a small wheelbarrow.

Holl sorted them into piles. "Cook's tools," he pointed to one group. "Musical instruments. Toys and puzzles. You'll never figure that one out, Keith Doyle, so you may as well put it down."

Keith set the puzzle box back and helped sort out the most attractive items.

"What about the lanterns?" Marm asked. "They're useful."

"Easy to make, too. It's only a case of strengthening the natural characteristics and uses of the wick," Dever explained. He would have gone on, but Keith shook his head wonderingly.

"I don't understand."

"His brain's got enough to do, moving that big body," Holl said, cynically. "He'd need years of instruction."

Keith held up a regretful hand "I don't know. How will I explain magic lanterns to the shop owners? It might seem perfectly natural to you, but they don't believe in magic."

"That's not a magic lantern," Marm said. He picked up a little box with a round window on one side covered by a thin cloth screen. "This is. Like your televisions. Here, look."

He shoved the screen side at Keith, who peered closely.

"I don't understand," said a finger-sized Keith, looking stupidly at a thumb-sized Dever.

"His brain's got enough to do, moving that big body," an image of Holl repeated.

Keith goggled. "I don't believe it. That's impossible."

"But there's nothing to it," Holl insisted. "It's made with the heartwood of a tree. That part can hold memories forever. Not too lengthy an event, but you can make records over and over until you've got one you want to keep. Keva's got one of Tay taking his first steps."

"Sugar," spat Keva, who was ostentatiously not listening to the progressive Doyle and his cohorts, and hated to be considered sentimental. Tay blushed and stroked his beard. Holl smiled.

"Well, I can't take that," Keith insisted, putting down the magic lantern. "I don't think the Midwest is ready for it."

"Well, then," Holl said. "Will these do?" He pointed out his selections.

"Yeah," Keith said, kneeling before the display appreciatively. "All of it is beautiful. These things'll sell themselves." He considered, fingering the little wooden boxes. "I'll need about three samples of each item, in case I have to give some away. Just let me know when I can come and get them."

He had plenty of volunteers among the younger elves who were ready to show off their skills. Some were openly disappointed that their work hadn't been chosen. "Why not these?" Dever asked, sounding hurt, as he retrieved a hand-sized harp.

"I only need a small representative sample to start," Keith explained soothingly. "I don't want to blow their minds out on my first visit. Plenty of time for expansion later on when we see how big our market is. These are so terrific, my big problem is figuring out where to tell people this merchandise is produced. No one would ever believe I made 'em."

It was a popular answer. They redoubled their offers of help. The middle-aged set joined in less enthusiastically, but they were convinced of Keith's sincerity, and flattered by his admiration of their work. The eldest elves still held themselves apart, refusing to participate.

Curran, the white-haired elder, remained unconvinced, even though most of his clan was involving themselves excitedly with Keith's plan. "But what if the inevitable does not happen, lad?" he rapped Keith smartly on the top of the head with his knuckles to get attention. "What be the point of setting ourselves to earn this money, if we may not need it?" He said 'money' as if it burned his tongue. "The resolution to tear down may be dropped."

"If you *don't* have to move?" Keith rose, frowning thoughtfully. "Well, what if the day comes when you *decide* to move, of your own free will? You could. If it were me, I'd rather have the means available than to have to scratch for them in a hurry. It would keep your options open."

"A valid point," the old man said. "I will gi' conseederation to it. Whether or not we follow your scheme."

"Thank you, sir," said Keith. "Well, I'd better go now. I've still got some studying to do before tomorrow." He gathered up his coat and other possessions. Waving his goodbyes to the others, he disappeared into the dark stairway, his heels pattering happily on the floor. Curran gathered up the other elders with a glance, and they drew together in conference. The argument began again.

"Um, there's just one more thing," Keith said, reappearing around the doorjamb and addressing the Elf Master. "Sir? Can I come back to class?"

"Yes," the Master said rounding austerely on him. "Next week. You are still suspended for causing a disturbance. You must understand that a classroom is no place for theatrics. Others are there to learn."

"Yes, sir!" With a wink to Holl, Keith vanished again.

Chapter 16

Behind the protective bulk of Mary Lou, Keith bent over his plan
of attack for marketing the elves' work. Sociology class went on
without disturbing his calculations. Jewelry boxes. Penny whistles.
Puzzle boxes. Miniature marionettes, fully articulated, using nearly
invisible dowels. Love spoons. Spice bottles with the herb leaf carved
into the side or forming part of the lid. Magic lanterns. He smiled to
himself. Those were undoubtedly his favorites.

Holl assured him that it would be only a few days before his
samples were ready, and he could get going. There was an old sample
case in the business major office, but he had been unable to convince
the secretary to let him borrow it. "I'm still waiting for you to return
my stapler, Keith." Abashed, he retreated, and found an old briefcase for two dollars at the Salvation Army store. With a little waterproof shoe polish and a lot of elbow grease, it cleaned up admira-
bly. No sense in letting anyone see what he was doing until the merchandise was on the shelves. Besides, it looked more professional.

There wasn't time to get official business cards printed up. Keith
had spent some time with the school computer and a graphics program running up a few sheets of personal cards on sixty-pound
bond that had his name, address and "Sales Manager," printed on
them. The day's homework, run off at the same time, was unusually
legible. His teachers were pleased.

The presentations shouldn't be too hard. He'd meant it when he said
the pieces could sell themselves. Wooden things had a sort of charm
completely absent from identical items of plastic. He composed a
separate pitch for each that would dovetail with any other. Good
technique for selling: be friendly, brief, and eloquent. Avoids stage
fright. He rehearsed each speech to himself, muttering them quietly
under his breath. Piece of cake; he should know them all by the end
of class.

There was so much to do that missing a week's worth of Elf
Sociology didn't bother him over much. And he was keeping discreet notes on all the preparations he was making, so when the time
came to get his MBA, he'd have all his marketing research in the bag.

The hardest part of his preparations was finding the single iron the dormitory owned to press out the dark blue suit he now wore.

Marcy found herself glancing over her shoulder at Keith. For someone who had caused as much trouble as he had, he didn't seem too repentant. In fact, he winked at her the one time she managed to catch his eye. She was confused. There was no doubt that he had jeopardized the Little People's safety and privacy, but she didn't agree with Carl that it was malicious mischief that would get the Big students tossed out of the Master's class.

All of the humans felt the same way. There were taut nerves at each class meeting since Keith had been suspended. They were afraid of sharing his punishment, though the Little People, even the Master, didn't show any signs of ire. If anything, they seemed positively enthusiastic about something. Even Teri, whose friendship with little Maura was blooming, had no idea what was up. Lee in particular was nervous. He was in the first semester of his Master's program, and he cursed Keith fluently whenever his name came up, yet he refused to side with Carl. Marcy continued to defend Keith, but she was clearly in the minority.

Most incredibly, Lee reported having seen Keith and one of the Little People in the dormitory cafeteria after the classroom debacle, on obviously friendly terms. He didn't feel happy about it, being deeply superstitious on the subject of the elves, as if mentioning them would make them go away. He'd known them the longest, and he seemed to resent Keith's easy familiarity with them. She had scoffed at Lee then, but with Keith, who could tell? Keith's persistent good humor over the last week made her uneasy; it meant he wasn't taking his expulsion seriously. And why was he talking to himself?

Keith was grinning at her again. She turned her back on him, but she fancied she could still feel his eyes on her.

Dr. Freleng made his way down the aisles, passing out the latest graded papers. She received her B in silence, content to be maintaining a standard with Freleng. He had a reputation for being very tough, and she acknowledged his right to it.

"Mr. Doyle," Freleng was saying, "I am puzzled but most pleased as to your improvement in style and quality of research. Your surprising thoroughness is most gratifying, considering your earlier shoddy efforts. My congratulations."

Keith, surprised out of his reverie, accepted his paper with a tongue-tied mumble of thanks. Marcy peeked back. There was a circled A on the title page. She started to mouth her own compliments to him, but he was already absorbed again in his clutter of papers.

"Congratulations," she said in an offhand voice, as the class broke up.

"Huh? Oh, thanks, Marcy." Keith was obviously off in another world. He was gathering his work together, and Marcy caught glimpses of phrases like, "one of a kind," and "quality, handmade," before they were swept into his bookbag.

"What was your paper on?" she persisted, trying to guess what he was working on.

"Rural farmers," Keith said, faintly. "I got into CompuServe on the library computer, and I collected about fifteen articles. Hashed something together. I guess he liked it."

"He liked it," Marcy assured him. "You weren't really listening today, were you?"

"No," Keith admitted. "I've had a lot on my mind."

"It is like pulling out teeth to get any information from you. Is all that stuff for an Advertising class?" She poked his bookbag.

"Not exactly. I didn't know you were talking to me."

Marcy paused. "I'm not really. I just wanted you to know I'm still mad."

"But I didn't *do* anything," Keith protested. "By the way, can I ask you a favor? Will you give this to the Maven? I'm suspended."

"I know you're suspended," Marcy said with some asperity. "You've got a fat lot of nerve asking me to do anything for you. He probably won't want to talk about you at all. And, besides…"

"Oh, I forgot," Keith smacked himself in the head. "*He's* suspended, too. Please ask Maura if she'll take it to him? I'm beggin' ya. It's important."

Marcy opened and closed her mouth, too overwhelmed by his chutzpah to say no. "How would you know that?" Keith didn't seem to hear her. He dug deep into the bag, and produced an envelope, which he tucked into her hand. "And why are you wearing a suit?"

"Thanks," he said, giving her a quick hug before she could avoid him. "I've got to go. Oh," he said, almost as an afterthought, "I never got to tell you what happened when Holl asked me to dinner, and you made me promise. Would you like to go out tonight, and hear it all?"

"Oh, you!…Why not?" Marcy said, peevishly. "I'm not saying I forgive you yet for misleading me."

"Aagh!" Keith yelped, anguished. "For the last time, I didn't mislead anyone, especially not you. My only crime is one of bad timing. As soon as I became aware I was making trouble, I began to undo it. Ask anyone. Ask Carl. No, don't ask Carl. Ask Rick. Ask Pat."

"Never mind," she sighed. "Pick me up after class."

"To hear is to obey!" Keith shouted over the rush of traffic as he pushed open the door for her and trotted off down the street, kowtowing in the rain. She shook her head and put the envelope in her purse.

As he was finishing the seven salaams one makes upon departing the presence of royalty, Keith bumped into something, or rather, someone. "Oh, sorry," he apologized, turning around to see whom he had inconvenienced. His feet were swept out from under him, and his books went spinning into the water-filled gutters. He hit the wet pavement with a painful splat. Scrambling on his knees to retrieve his possessions, he saw Lee Eisley hurrying away. "Wait," he called out, but Lee paid no attention to him.

"Nobody loves me," he grumbled, fishing his papers out of the water.

Chapter 17

Voordman's Country Crafts & Gifts was at the top of his list of good prospects. It was in the middle of the shopping district in town, good sized, well lit, and it had all sorts of wicker and gingham knickknacks on display. After a few minutes of perusing the contents of the show windows, he pushed in through the glass double doors.

A little bell suspended from an arm jingled furiously, and a dark-haired woman behind the counter raised her head. "Be with you in just one moment," she called, pointing to the telephone against her ear. Keith nodded, running his hand through his rain-drenched hair to make it lie flat, and browsed the aisles until she was through.

"What can I do for you?" she smiled, coming over to him. Then she saw the sample case. The smile dimmed and hardened. "Oh. A salesman. Did you call for an appointment?"

"I did call earlier, Mrs. Voordman," Keith began, placatingly.

"*Ms.*" Her fluffy hair stiffened into black glass filaments. So did her eyes. Keith put on a determined smile. His very first words put him at a disadvantage. She was going to be tough to sell. He wondered what Andrew Carnegie would do in a case like this.

"My apologies," he said, trying to look competent and penitent at the same time. "*Ms.* Voordman. Do you have a moment right now that I can talk to you?" He took a look around. The shop was empty except for the two of them.

The woman noticed his surveying glance and the raised eyebrows that followed it. She was on the defensive, but she could choose only to listen or to tell him to go away. "Very well. Come this way."

Keith stood poised over his sample case, his prepared speeches ready, waiting for the shop-owner to make herself comfortable in the swivel chair behind the desk in her little, cluttered office. He opened his mouth to speak, but Ms. Voordman held up her hand.

"Before you start, I just want you to know that I've seen it all already. There's nothing you can say I haven't heard. This business has no surprises. That's one of the reasons I'm in it. I'm not interested in anything you have, and I'm only giving you this time because I'm not busy. Understand?"

Keith swallowed. She was a tough cookie. "Sure," he said. He reached into the case and drew out the items one by one. "I always say, good product will speak for itself." Beside his own trade goods, he had a few small items the elves assured him they had in plenty. Ms. Voordman leaned forward, and began to handle the individual pieces, eyeing them critically.

"Good workmanship," she said. "Is that adzemark hand-done or artificial?"

"They're made by a sort of commune. No electric tools at all."

"Um-hmmm. The cookie cutters are nice. Unusual shapes and designs. I don't mind telling you I'm tired of the same gingerbread men, angels and Pennsylvania Hex symbols. This one's a little deep. Shortbread mold?" She turned it over in her hands, ran a finger around the chiseled inner rim.

"Um, yes," Keith agreed, hoping it was true. His two great scratch kitchen accomplishments were scrambled eggs and fudge. He was pleasantly surprised to see her gaining more interest the longer she looked, and began to hope for a small order.

"And what's this?" she asked, holding up the lantern. "Wonderful screens. To think something this precise is all handmade."

"It's a sort of toy," Keith explained. "But it makes a good reading lamp, too." He blew on the wick, which ignited. By now, he was almost used to the wonder, but his prospect wasn't. Ms. Voordman's eyes went huge. Her hand fluttered away from the screen, but returned when the part of the frame she was clutching didn't grow warm. "Never needs batteries. Patent pending." He blew it out.

"That is something else. What's it run on?"

"Can't tell you that, but I promise it's harmless. See?" He turned it upside down so she could see the inside of the lid. "No scorch marks. All fireproof."

"I've got to hand it to you," she said, after trying it herself a few times, more relaxed than before. "I've never seen anything like this. Ever. And I've been in this business twenty years. I've got customers who furnish in Early American who'd go for these in droves. They're a little miracle. I want a few myself. They'd make a hell of a party gag."

"Ms. Voordman," said Keith, solemnly. "We're *serious* about our knickknacks."

She threw back her head and laughed. "You've made a sale, mister. What's your name?"

Keith felt his face burning. First law of salesmanship down the drain! "Keith Doyle," he said, extending a hand. "With, um…" He remembered at that moment that they hadn't picked a company name yet. Desperately casting about for inspiration, his eye fell on an eight-inch high painted porcelain statue of an elf peering out of a stump. The ceramic imp's red hair and glasses reminded him of the Elf Master. On the tag was printed the same little face. "Hollow Tree Industries," he finished, mischievously. "Yes, you never would believe where those cookie cutters come from." From his case he took one of his ersatz business cards and the list of prices he and Holl had worked out.

The woman shook his hand and glanced over the price list. "I'll take a half dozen of everything here but the lantern. *That* I want a dozen of."

"Yes, ma'am!" said Keith, seizing his notepad and scribbling.

"And when can I expect delivery?" She was watching him write.

"Uh, we're a small, new firm, just tooling up." Keith chewed on his pencil-end. "I'll turn the tables on you: when would you expect delivery?"

Ms. Voordman moved everything off her desk blotter, and drew an invisible line down the calendar with a cookie cutter. "Four weeks. Absolutely no more than that. I've got to stock the store fully for Christmas by the second week of November."

Keith counted in his head. "Okay. Can I get a deposit? Terms are twenty-five percent down and net 30 days."

"Twenty-five and net 60. I'm a small firm, too." She looked at his card. "There's no telephone number on this."

"Well, we're relocating," he explained, jotting his room phone down for her. "This is my home number."

"Hmm," she said, sympathetically, watching him pack up the sample case. "Moving is a real pain in winter." She wrote out a check for him and they shook hands. "First time salesman?"

"Sort of. Does it show that badly?" Keith asked in dismay and surprise.

"You haven't got enough of the paraphernalia. No order blanks. No receipts. Oh, don't worry about it. You're a refreshing change from the usual polished hustlers. See you in four weeks, Mr. Doyle." She stood up, dismissing him.

He smiled uneasily at her as he slipped on his coat and gathered up his case. On his way out, Keith surreptitiously plucked the tag off of one of the porcelain statues.

By the end of the afternoon, Keith's feet hurt, his back was sore, and his palm had three small blisters starting where the stitching on the sample-case's handle rubbed, but he felt good. Inside the sample-case were three orders with checks from three gift shops, and the business cards from two others who promised to think it over. He was astounded how easy it was to convince the shop owners to buy. On the weekend, he planned to drive to a few nearby towns and pick up a few orders at the gift shops there. In the meantime, he needed to get into dry clothes and find something to eat. He was starved.

Marcy was waiting for him in the lobby of Power Hall. She got to her feet and came over to him as he walked in the door.

"Hi," he greeted her. "Just a minute, let me run this up to my room, and I'll be ready to go."

"No," she said, holding him back with a hand on his arm, "I want to know what's going on. Now."

"What's the matter?" Keith asked, stripping off his wet raincoat.

"Everyone's acting so mysterious. I gave Maura your message. And she gave me one to give you. *Sealed.*" Marcy thrust an envelope at him that was addressed to 'Keith Doyle' in flawless copperplate calligraphy. "I don't like playing carrier pigeon."

"I'm sorry. I didn't expect...I don't want you...Oh, well." He hoisted the case and escorted her to the door that led to the cafeteria, wincing at the tenderness of his palm. "After you."

It was getting late, and the cafeteria was nearly empty. Half of the lights had already been turned out, lending the room a dim, intimate character. Food service employees gathered dirty dishes and banged them into plastic trays that resounded like tom-toms. Keith and Marcy picked out an isolated corner table. He tried to slide in next to her, but she gave him an apologetic look and stayed put in her place on the bench. "I'm sorry, Keith," she told him. "I just don't feel like being touched today."

"No problem," Keith sighed, taking his place across from her. "I hope nothing's wrong."

"N-no," she replied, uncertainly. "At least I don't think so. Now wait a minute. You have some explaining to do. "

"I sure do. Here goes."

Between bites, she chewed over his recounted adventures, and he skimmed Holl's note. It was brief, just to let Keith know that the vote to go along with his plan hadn't succeeded, or even come close. It was a landslide for progress. He could pick up the sales samples later on outside of Gillington. They would be in a plastic sack behind the bushes. Keith felt like a bagman for a numbers runner. He looked up at Marcy. She was still digesting his story. He hadn't told her anything about Ludmilla yet, but he remembered the old woman's words. Why would Marcy need to know about the elves' history? He had no doubt Ludmilla had a reason, but he couldn't guess what it was.

Marcy spoke up at last. "I feel so bad. Why couldn't they be left in peace?"

"At least this way, we have some warning. See, if it wasn't me, it could easily have been a bunch of bureaucrats, and we'd never know about it until it happened. Any time the University wanted to get rid of Gillington, it could. Are you still mad at me?"

"No. I suppose I never was really mad at you. I'm just so frustrated that there's nothing I can do to help."

"That is where the nimble brain of Keith E. Doyle comes into play," he said, and explained his plans for Hollow Tree Industries. After a careful look around to make sure no one was watching them, he opened the case and slid it over to her side. Marcy's face lit up as she poked through the wooden gifts.

"These are adorable," she said. "And you're terrific. Who else would think of something like that?"

"Only another deranged mind," he assured her.

"No," Marcy waved that away. "You're not deranged. A little weird, yes. Can I do anything to help out?"

"Not really," Keith said, considering. "Wait. There is one little thing. You could tell me what's going on in class?"

Marcy giggled. "Fashion is happening in class. The Master is using the phenomenon to demonstrate his favorite principle of cultural adaptation to customs. Today, Maura showed up in a blue denim pantsuit. Catra wore a patterned skirt and a blouse made of old sheet material, and Candlepat had on a sundress and headband straight out of a

Vogue magazine which Teri brought for her." She grinned impishly. "It is sort of startling in star-spangled green, but the line is good, and it is *very* form fitting. The guys really noticed. Quite a contrast, since the rest of us are all in winter clothes. How old is she, anyway? Fifteen?" "She'd be a lot more likely to tell you than me," Keith said. Marcy smiled. "It's been very quiet this week. I think everyone misses you. The Master is being very patient with us. Now that I know we're not going to be tossed out of the class, I can relax, and maybe the others will soon. Though I was stuttering so much today that he stopped me and promised he wouldn't bite me even if my ideas were far-fetched. His kindliness frightens me more than his gruffness does."

"I know what you mean. He's a great teacher. I respect him, but I'm scared of him, too," Keith said, earnestly. "I would never deliberately want to make him mad at me."

That evening, he met his roommate coming toward him in the hall, looking furious. Keith started to dodge past him with a pleasant word, but Pat grabbed his arm, turned him around and marched him back toward their room.

"All right, Doyle," Pat snapped. "This is getting to be a habit."

"What is?" Keith asked, trying to free his arm, but Pat's long fingers had embedded themselves in his biceps.

"The room got trashed again!"

"You're kidding!" Keith pulled free and broke into a run in spite of the weight of the sample case in his hand. He dashed through the door, and a deluge of water splashed down on him from above. The case crashed heavily to the floor. "Wa - wa - water balloon," he gasped.

"That's weird," Pat said, coming in behind him. "I've been through that door already. Twice." He squinted over the bridge of his long nose at the lintel, and at the empty scrap of rubber on their rug. "Why didn't it fall on me? There's no tape or anything on the wall."

"I don't know," Keith said, dabbing at his face with a towel. "Maybe it was balanced funny. Or maybe whoever it was just planted it. Someone from this dorm, like Carl, for instance! What is it with everyone and water today?" He surveyed his half of the room. Once again, there was cola on everything, but this time he saw pieces of a book that had been slashed up and stuffed into the plughole of the sink. It was the *Field Guide to the Little People*. He ripped the soaked coverlet off his bed, and found that it had been short-sheeted. "Thorough job," he commented.

Pat snorted. "Why would you think it was Carl? Plenty of people want to kill you. I want to kill you myself. I was planning to get to sleep early tonight!"

"I'm sorry, Pat," Keith said, but his roommate wasn't listening. "I'll keep it down. This'll probably take me all night." Sighing, he went in search of cleaning supplies.

Two hours later, leaving a snoring Pat behind, he sneaked out of the dorm and crossed the campus to the library building. A security patrol car shone its spotlight on him but drove on, disinterested in a single student.

Keith found the plastic sack without difficulty, and pulled it out of its hiding place, brushing drops of water and wet leaves from its surface. As he was walking back toward Power Hall, a knot of drunken-sounding frat brothers turned the corner and started weaving their way toward him. A group that large, especially in their uninhibited condition, spelled trouble for a lone dormie out by himself. They'd probably stop short of beating him to a pulp, but there were other kinds of trouble they could make for him. He didn't want to have to explain his presence or his burden to the security force.

He froze, looking for a place he could conceal himself and his bag of magical toys. This was a path lined with high, thick thorn-bushes that had once been part of the college's formal gardens. He could force himself between the leaf-bare branches, but he wouldn't be able to pull free again without help.

To his surprise, the frats streamed around him as if they couldn't see him. They passed so close he bet that he could guess the brand of beer they'd been drinking, but not one of them touched him. As soon as they were gone, he unfroze and tore down the path toward Power, refusing to question his good fortune, miracle though it seemed. He found that his pulse was racing.

He sneaked back into his dorm room without turning on the lights. A quick peek inside the bag with his miniature flashlight told him that everything promised was there. The white wicks of the lanterns gleamed faintly from their dark cages. "Ha-*HA*," he cackled under his breath.

"For God's sake," Pat yelped from the other bed. "Go to sleep!"

Chapter 18

The New Accounts officer at the Midwestern Trust Bank explained the whole system again patiently to the eager red-haired teenager. He looked as though he had been explaining the same thing to dim customers for the past sixty years or more. "If you want a business checking account, you have to maintain a balance of a thousand dollars, or there's an eight dollar service fee each month. If you want my advice, young man, just open a personal checking account. The bank doesn't care what name and address you have printed on the checks."

"Fine," Keith said, appearing to understand at last. "That's what I want."

"Good," the man said, passing a hand over what was left of the thin brown hair on his head. His round face folded into the semblance of a Parker House roll as he smiled at Keith. "Now, if you'll just fill out these forms, we'll get you your temporary checks." The man swept Keith's three deposit checks away, and took them over to a teller's window. In a few minutes, he was back with an important-looking slip striped in blue and tan. "Here's your new account number." Keith looked up from it at him.

"Um, I want my nephew to be a co-signer on this account, but he hasn't got a Social Security number yet. He's twelve."

"That's no problem," the banker said. "Only one of you needs to have one. I assume you do. What's the account for, if I may ask? Boy Scouts?"

"Junior Achievment," Keith said.

Three days later, two boxes arrived for Keith from the student Print Shop. Cackling happily over the contents, he hurried down to the elf village, the cardboard boxes cradled in his arms. The stone door opened for him, showing him that some changes had been put into operation since he was there last. He smiled and greeted everyone, but didn't explain his presence until he reached Holl's hut. Holl lived alone at the edge of Curran's clan. Like the other cottages, it was built of odd pieces of wood, but they seemed to be arranged in a handsome and subtle pattern that used both color and texture as motifs; most appropriate for a woodworker and the son of a woodworker. The sloping roof was incised with a pattern of rounded slates. There was no need to keep out weather, so its builders could concentrate on form rather than function. Its door stood open.

The young elf was at home, poring over a thick leather-bound book with print so small that Keith couldn't read any of it from three feet above the pages. A carved shelf was fastened to the wall just underneath the glassless window. It was full of books, all borrowed from the library upstairs. Beyond a partition wall from which a curtain was drawn back lay a simple frame bed spread with a patchwork quilt and pillow, and a chest with the lid thrown open. The windows were hung with curtains in a filmy-thin red and blue weave through which the village's curious lighting shone almost unabated. Holl's woodworking tools were neatly placed on a worktable against the wall between the two rooms. The cottage was a neat little bachelor's apartment.

Holl looked up at the gentle tap on the door, and gestured his friend inside. Keith ducked under the lintel, laid the boxes down on the low table and opened them up.

Behind him, anyone who wasn't busy had followed him from the entrance, and milled around outside the low doorway, speculating on what the daffy Big One was doing now. Even some of the elders, without abandoning their poses of disinterest, found a reason to hang around the neighborhood.

Holl closed his book and pulled the boxes across the table to him. Examining the contents, he paused to peer up at the tall student. "An appropriate conceit, though bold," he said, tapping the letterhead and the line artwork which accompanied it with his fingertips, "but has he seen it yet?"

Keith had no doubt as to which 'he' his friend meant. "No," he admitted guiltily.

Holl rose from the backless wooden bench that served as his desk chair. "Well, we'd better go right away, before someone else tells him."

Desperately, Keith threw up a hand to stall him. "Um, there's no need to do that right now. I've got some other things for you, too." Maybe it wasn't such a good idea to use the face from the tag for the logo. He was embarrassed at his own audacity. But it had been almost like a sign to see it there in Voordman's Gift Shop, the little man in the tree, smiling out at him. Looking so much like the Elf Master...

"Oh, no," said Holl, enjoying Keith's discomfiture a little, but also serious about making his point. He waved the order forms in Keith's face. "Now, you can't use them if he doesn't like them. The cooperation would end before it fairly began. You'd have to have them done over. No sense in prolonging the situation." He grabbed one of Keith's wrists and pulled. The blond elf was amazingly strong. "Oh, and bring the stationery, too."

Keith shifted from foot to foot as the elders passed copies of the order forms around. "It's an insult," Aylmer said, thumping the paper with the back of one hand. "Using a likeness. Has he no respect?"

"It was available as stock art," Keith protested, uncomfortably. "Cheaper than a custom drawing." He towered over them, waving his arms for attention, but they ignored him, as they would ignore a tree swaying overhead. "We're on a pretty tight budget."

"What happened to all his easy promises for our privacy?" Curran asked, acidly.

"Ah, go on," Holl said. "Nobody knows any of our faces."

Most of the younger folk were looking over the elders' shoulders, pointing and laughing. Keith felt like an idiot. His fellow students came in to ask what the joke was, and they, too, had a chuckle over Keith's slyness. The room divided into two parties: the Keithites, and the Anti-Keithites. The groups were similar though not identical to the Progressives and the Conservatives. Holl and all the younger elves who were on his side made up the first group. They thought the idea of using the village schoolmaster as their logo was funny. The Anti-Keithites, the elders and those against the scheme, were all for disemboweling him on the spot. Both parties were loudly vociferous about their opinions, and Keith ceased to try getting anyone's attention. There was no way he could be heard over the din. Suddenly, someone let out a piercing whistle, and the whole room fell silent.

The Elf Master appeared at the mouth of the tunnel. Curran called to him. "The Big One has brought something you must see."

"It's just business stationery, and cards, some with my name on 'em, and some blank so anyone can use 'em. And these are the order blanks. Really nothing to look at. Not important." Keith pulled the boxes away as the Elf Master came over.

"May I see them?" the teacher asked, holding out a hand to Keith. The boy blanched, swallowing hard.

"Oh, you don't need to…," he protested weakly.

The Master deftly slipped the box out of his arms, opened it, and his eyes narrowed. "Hmmm." The Anti-Keithites smiled with vindictive satisfaction. This time the Master wouldn't be so eager to defend the irresponsible, irreverent Big One. Keith shifted his gaze from the stationery to the Master's face and back again. Had he managed to alienate his newfound friends yet again? He wished passionately that he would learn to consider consequences before he acted.

The Elf Master didn't say anything for a long moment, and then croaked out one sentence. "Appropriate for the marketing strategy." Keith almost fainted with relief. The Keithites cheered.

But that was not all the Master's thoughts. "And a fine likeness, as well," he said.

Chapter 19

Lloyd Patterson slammed his gavel on the desktop. "Order! Order, dammit!" The roar of conversation quieted, and Lloyd cleared his throat. "I declare that this meeting of the Inter-Hall Council is in session. Vernita, take the roll."

Keith sat in his place next to Rick, staring at a spot in the middle of his desk. He responded with a half-hearted "here," when Vernita read his name, but was otherwise silent. The room was so full some of the student delegates stood around the walls and against the door for lack of seats. Rick had his feet on the chair of an empty desk, and his expression dared anyone to come and take it away from him. He had no takers. The general consensus among those present who followed college sports was that if Number 41 MacKenzie wanted an extra desk on which to rest his feet, he could have it. The RA observed Keith's unusual depression with concern.

"What's the matter with you?" Rick demanded, scratching at the place where the desk arm cut into his ribs. "This is your show. You should be thrilled."

"Rick, maybe I should have talked to you before...." Keith was interrupted by another bang from the gavel. He twisted in discomfort, only partially attributable to the design of the desk, the same iron maidens in use in the hidden classroom. He wished that he didn't have such a vivid visual reminder before him of the spot he'd put himself in. The freezing countenance of the Elf Master stayed before him as he concentrated on putting his arguments in the right order.

"Quiet! Please!" Lloyd shouted. "The sooner we can have quiet, the sooner we can finish this meeting." Vernita handed him the attendance list and he thanked her formally. She simpered, hair swaying, and sat down. "Before we get on to the reason we're all here, does anyone have any *other* business, old or new?"

There was general pandemonium as the delegates forbore to mention any business, but dragged their seats to the two sides of the room, making it clear that they were interested only in the main event. Lloyd sighed, and banged the desk for order. "Okay, already. I can take a hint."

"Go get 'em, Doyle," Rick whispered. Keith didn't move. Across the room, Carl Mueller had a wide smirk on his face as he got up and walked to the middle of the floor. He looked deeply satisfied for someone who had fewer than a third of the delegates on his side of the room. Rick wondered about his apparent confidence, and stared curiously at Keith, trying to decide if there was a connection.

"Mr. Chairman, I would like to have a vote taken on the proposal whether the Administration should build a new Sports Center or a new library building this year."

"Anyone second?" Lloyd asked, looking around the room for raised hands. "Okay, seconded by Woods of Alvin Hall. The chair opens the floor for debate." There was a roar of voices, all trying to make themselves heard at once. "Order! May I remind you that there is a reason why this vote is being taken in full council? This is the first time the Administration has ever really asked for our input on a project of this size. Three million bucks! This is your big chance to make your mark on the University. Now shut up unless you want to offer arguments for debate." There was some grumbling, but the roar sank into murmurs.

"Go!" Rick urged Keith. Reluctantly, Keith stood up, hand raised for recognition.

"Doyle, Power Hall?" It was a tentative question. Keith could feel Rick's eyes on his back. He felt cowardly for not taking Rick into his confidence before but it was too late. He was about to make a fool of himself by reversing his position without informing anyone in advance.

"Go ahead," said the chair.

"I've been in touch with the National Historical Society in regard to the Gillington Library building. In view of its age and intrinsic historic interest, they are investigating having it declared a historical landmark. If they decide in favor, the building cannot be torn down, even to make way for a newer structure. Therefore," Keith took a very deep breath, felt his ribs vibrating with nervousness, "I must withdraw my previous proposal, and let it be known that I have no objection to asking for support for the construction of a new Sports Center for Midwestern University." He turned away from the raw triumph on Carl's face, and finished his speech staring down at the floor.

For a moment the room was silent, and then everyone started talking at once. Rick was at Keith's side, yelling at him, but Keith wasn't even aware he was there.

Finally, the RA's voice penetrated his misery. "What's the matter with you? You've just handed him the victory, you moron!"

Keith went back to his desk, and sagged into the seat. "I know. But I had to, Rick. That building turns out to be really pretty important. I didn't think so before, but…"

"Terrific. You coulda told me." Rick slammed himself into his seat and kicked his feet up. "I feel like a jerk."

"So do I." Keith buried his head in his hands, and didn't bother to come up for air even during the voting. Even that was not the end of his disgrace. To Keith's dismay, in spite of his self-sacrifice the vote came out overwhelmingly in favor of a new library. Keith had done too good a job of promotion. There were cries of glee when the voting results were announced. He felt like drowning himself.

As the meeting adjourned, Carl came over to him, and spoke to the top of Keith's head. "I really enjoyed that, Doyle, I just wanted you to know. It's too bad you won."

"Lay off, Carl," Rick said in a bored tone, but there was no mistaking the fury blazing behind his eyes. "It doesn't matter. I don't know who put the Historical Society on to Gillington, but I'm sure it wasn't Keith's fault."

Carl puffed up with indignation and pointed at Keith. "What do you mean, who? *He* put them on to it, buddy. You thought it was funny to oppose issues just because I was backing 'em, huh, Doyle?"

"Carl," Keith said, looking up. "Shut up. I still plan to campaign against everything you do for the rest of your life. I blew this one, but it's the only one you'll ever get. I don't like you treating me like a weirdo, and I'm a little tired of you trashing my dorm room, too," Keith added, pugnaciously, rising to his feet. Carl stood a lot taller than he did. He felt like the Chicken-hawk threatening Foghorn Leghorn, but he kept his ground.

"What is going on here?" Rick inquired, uncrossing his running shoes and standing up. "We *won!*"

For once Carl looked honestly surprised. "I didn't touch your room, turkey. I haven't done a thing to you. Yet."

"Not once? Tuesday was the second time." Keith was taken aback. "Then, who?" Rick looked at one, and then the other, and back again.

"I don't know. Now, blow, punk, or I'll do worse than trash your *room*." Carl leaned forward menacingly.

"Well, okay," Keith shouted, making for the door with a fist raised. "You won't have Keith Doyle to push Carl Mueller around any more. At least until next meeting. I'm going to get that vote overturned." He left with Rick following right behind him.

"Did I miss something? At least you could tell me what's going on, Doyle...."

"The next thing I have to do is make sure that the Historical Society doesn't do a basement to attic check. It's pretty hard to hide a whole village. I have to get them to declare monument status for Gillington before the committee reports to the Dean, or I won't be able to stop the planning commission. The good news is that I get back into the Master's class just before it's time to study for the Soc. final. I may even pass, considering how lousy I'm doing on practical social interaction. Marcy?" Keith asked, leaning across her kitchen table and waving a hand in front of her eyes. She was sitting rigid, staring down at a spot. "Hello?"

Marcy blinked. "Sorry."

"Tell old Uncle Keith what's on your mind," he wheedled, patting her hand gently. She endured three pats, then drew away. "I don't like to see my friends miserable. Unless I make them that way myself."

She smiled sadly at that. "No, you didn't do it. The truth is I'm sitting here feeling like a pervert."

Keith did a double take. "Say that again? No, don't. I heard you. Tell me why."

"It started the day you got thrown out of class. Maybe a lot sooner, I don't know. Carl said something insulting to me. I really hate him. He's got such an ego. Enoch jumped on him for it. I think he would've hit him if Carl hadn't backed off. Carl was really surprised. I was, too. He's been...protective of me, lately. Enoch, not Carl." She was having to fight to get the words out. "I...I feel, I don't know..."

"...Like you've got something going for him?" Keith finished, a little light going on in his mind. "That's why you've been sort of backing off on me?"

Marcy nodded, miserably.

"Great!" Keith exclaimed.

"But I feel like I'm cradle-robbing, or something."

Keith's eyes went wide. "What? Is this the author of the Marcy Collier paper on the sociological stresses of racial dwarfism? The person who stood up to Doctor Freleng when he suggested that there wasn't enough statistical evidence to make a sociological premise out of it? You are treating short people like children." He pointed a finger toward her nose. "*You're doing it.* Enoch is *forty-six* years old. He told me so himself! If anything, you're a little young for him. *He's* cradle-robbing."

Marcy's mouth fell open. Her tongue felt dry, and she swallowed. "He is?"

"Scout's honor," Keith held three fingers up. "That's fact. Would you like to have *me* play carrier pigeon for a change and find out how he feels about you? Although I can guess already, from what you just told me."

Marcy flushed at his last words, the red suffusing her fair skin to the hairline. "I'm sorry I said that to you about carrier pigeons."

"I'm sorry I didn't tell you everything at first."

"And I'm sorry, because I think you like me, too."

"I do," said Keith, standing up and taking her hand. This time she didn't pull away. "Enough to want you to be happy. So, are we sorry enough? Shall I go?"

"Yes!" Marcy squeezed his hand, and her eyes were bright.

"Miles Standish to the rescue!" Keith assumed a heroic pose and strode out the door. The hallway rang with his triumph.

"What a weirdo," observed one of Marcy's roommates from the living room.

Chapter 20

Something seemed different about the hidden entrance in the block in the library wall. There seemed to have been some kind of erosion, or a more minor disturbance of surface dirt. "Sandblasting?" Keith asked himself. Apparently, it had caused some internal disturbance as well. The passage wouldn't open up to him. It took some time before someone heard him and let him in. Marm appeared, peering cautiously around outside before he shut the heavy façade.

"There was scratching on the wall last night," Marm told Keith, guiding him by lantern light down the ladder inside. "We listened, but decided it couldn't be you. You'd just come in the other door then. The old ones were pretty worked up."

Keith was disturbed by the news. "You don't think someone else knows you're here?"

The bearded elf spat. "O' course they do. You know, and pretty Marcy knows, and fair Teri knows, and staunch Lee knows. All those do."

"I meant strangers. None of the other students know about this door. Not from me."

Marm looked very worried. "Perhaps from one of us, then. There's been a bit of coming and going of late. More than in past years, I can tell you. Are you going to want the same kind of wood for my boxes, or can I use what I can get?"

"Use whatever you want, Marm," Keith said, absently.

Marm shrugged. "What I want is not what I have. Our supplies are not great. Our stockpiles are gleaned slowly, at night and secretly. You must know that the old ones consider you to be wasting our time and our precious resources."

"I don't think it's a waste."

"Neither do us younger ones," Marm declared. "But we don't speak for the clans."

"Just have to use my salesmanship on them, too," Keith said glumly. "Don't worry. It'll all work out one day." He spotted Holl walking by the hydroponic garden and waved. The stocky blond elf nodded and came over.

"Good day to you, Keith Doyle," Holl said. "You're a bit out of color today. Are you not feeling well?"

Keith found it impossible to meet his friend's eyes, and spoke to his feet. "They took the vote. They're going to tear down this library."

Holl nodded sympathetically. "I know. It's almost an anticlimax after that day in class, isn't it? Very brave of you to come and break the news."

Keith was taken aback. "How did you know? I was coming down here to tell you."

The Maven took a piece of folded newsprint out of a pocket. "We all read newspapers. It was in The Midwesterner. Here, 'Student Makes Plea for Historic Gillington.' We're all most happy about it though it went so against you. You did try. That was enough even for some of the oldsters."

"The vote was pretty lopsided. I felt like an idiot," Keith admitted, and thought for a minute. "For once I did something well. Too well. The truth is that I have no idea now when the axe will fall. The Historical Society may not come through for us in time. I'll understand it if you decide you never want me to come down here again." He grimaced. "I *may* be able to pass the Sociology final on my own."

"No need," Holl said, grinning. "You're still welcome, and in the class as well. For the first time in forty years, they're stirred up. And, for the first time ever, by a Big Person. They've decided to follow your idea to stockpile against the future, since we have no pots of gold. We may not be able to avert disaster so neatly if we haven't our able champion. It's an elegant solution, I must admit, to make us work for our own salvation." Keith kicked the pavement uncomfortably, and Holl chuckled. "There's a second reason as well, and it, too, is your fault. They're beginning to see what they've been missing in new goods. We can earn proper raw materials for daily living, and a few luxuries, too, while we save to buy a home. Lee brings some things in with the supplies. I don't mind at all."

"Seeing as you catalyzed them into it," Keith pointed out.

"I just see a bit further ahead than the others. Never having lived anywhere else, I'm not burdened with memories of the 'good old days.' Though I find it hard to picture my home in another place, I can be...more objective. But to the point," Holl finished, rubbing his palms together, "your two dozen lanterns will be ready in a week or so. I'll let you know. We're wrapping everything in newspaper. The librarians microfilm each edition of the daily press and then discard them. Such a waste. But we could use a bit of string or tape."

"No problem. You guys are doing terrific," said Keith, elated in spite of himself.

"May I return the compliment?" Holl smiled. "I do not judge success by the results, but by the attempt."

"You sound like the Master." Over Holl's shoulder, Keith spotted Enoch between two of the small houses. The black-haired elf was sawing wood, scowling at each cut piece as it fell between the saw-horses. "'Scuse me."

"Hi, there," he said, gently, so as not to startle Enoch into having an accident. "Can I talk to you a minute?"

The black eyes rose and bored into him. "You're talking. Go ahead. I need not listen if I don't want to," Enoch said, curtly, and went back to cutting wood. He had on a carpenter's smock with tools poking out of the many front pockets. There was a heap of small tile-shapes, which Keith recognized as the bases for the elf's own specialty, puzzle boxes. The oddly shaped pieces which made up the rest of the wooden conundrums had been sorted into a neat line of baskets beside the squares. It was a tidy assembly-line.

"Well," Keith sat down on the packed earth floor with his back against one of the houses. A spider meandered down from the eaves on a thread and hovered in front of his face and pondered his capture. He wondered where it would be best to begin his appeal. "It's about Marcy."

Without looking up again, Enoch snapped, "What about her?" In an instant, his face and ears had turned dark red with anger.

"Well, I only really met her a few months ago. I like her a lot. I think she's a great person. She's intelligent, she's pretty, and she's fun to be with. More than a little secretive," Keith smiled, looking around at the village, "but otherwise what else could a guy want?"

"I know all of these things."

"Oh, I know you do. I just wanted to let you know…"

"Aye, you don't have to go on," Enoch said, hostilely. "That it's she and you, and you want me to keep my hands off, isn't that it?"

"No," Keith contradicted him. "You're half right. It's she, but it's not me. It's you. I am here to ask you, as a friend, just how interested you are in her. *I* think you are very interested."

"How would you know?"

"Well, right now, it's written on your forehead in bold-face print. Right under 'Doyle go home,'" Keith quipped wryly. "But mostly, it was your standing up to Carl the day I got thrown out of the Master's class. She noticed it then, too."

"It's none of your business." Enoch gestured sharply at him.

"True," Keith conceded, gritting the words through his front teeth. His back teeth had unaccountably grown together, holding his jaw shut, and he couldn't wrench them apart. He ran his tongue around to determine the cause of the phenomenon. Nothing there. It must be something Enoch was doing to him, but he hadn't sealed Keith's lips, so it wasn't enough to shut him up. "But is it doing either of you any good as just *your* business?"

"Go away!" A slice of wood slipped off the end of the block he was sawing, quickly followed by another, and another. Keith watched in fascination as they clonked to the floor. Each section was dead even. Sweat beaded on Enoch's forehead. He wiped it away with the back of his free hand without ceasing work, and left a sawdusty stripe over one eye.

Keith cleared his throat to project his voice over the saw. "I can't; I'm not through. Would it help if I said Marcy and I just had a talk, and she admitted she doesn't want to go out with me any more because she can't stop thinking of you?" Keith inquired, ramming the sentences out so that Enoch couldn't interrupt him. The color faded from Enoch's face until it was as pale as it had been red. He stared at Keith, who concentrated on looking innocent and helpful.

"Is this true?"

Keith's jaws unlocked suddenly. He worked his mandibular muscles stiffly. It must have been a variation on the cohesiveness spell Holl had once described to him. Whew! he thought, I'd hate to get the little guy *really* mad. "Trust me. I'm a carrier pigeon, to coin a phrase. A go-between. Western Union. Cyrano de Bergerac."

"I've read the book," Enoch said, consideringly. There was the beginnings of hope in his eyes. He picked up another piece of wood, put the saw to it, then carefully set block and saw down on the ground and looked up at Keith. "Why did she not speak to me herself?"

Keith decided not to mention details of his conversation with Marcy. "She's old fashioned," he said instead. "And she's shy. You understand."

"That's uncommonly good of you, if you care for her yourself." Enoch eyed him suspiciously.

"I do. You know. It's because I care that I'm talking to you," Keith said. "I'm happy to be her friend. I've decided that's enough for me. I guess I haven't found Miss Right for Keith Doyle yet. If Marcy isn't the one, why should I ruin it for other people?"

Enoch nodded, squinting thoughtfully at Keith, and then he smiled. The expression changed his whole face from that of a sullen little boy to an open, mature man. It was so startling Keith barely stopped himself from gaping at the transformation. "Ach, aye, well. Maybe it's time I talked to her myself, then."

He stripped off the smock and laid it over the saw horses. With a friendly nod to Keith, he disappeared into his little house, reappeared buttoned up a coat with a cap over his ears, and walked purposefully toward the wall entrance tunnel.

"Wait," Keith said, catching up with him. "It's broad daylight out there. They'll see you."

There was determination in the dark elf's eyes, making him look one last time like the headstrong boy who had sized Keith up that first day in class. "They'll get used to it," Enoch said.

A few days later, Keith reached for the phone without looking up from his 'Sociology for the Masses' textbook. With the receiver between thumb and forefinger, he punched out Marcy's number using his pinky. One of her roommates answered, and over the blare of heavy metal music roaring in the background, deigned to inform Marcy she had a call. She seemed a little amused by something. In a moment Marcy answered, sounding breathless.

"Hello?"

"Hi, it's Keith."

"Oh, hi," she said, more casually. "I was doing laundry."

"I was doing homework. I thought you might like to come over and help?" Keith said hopefully. "The final exam is coming up, and all."

"Oh, I can't. I haven't got anything clean to wear that's dry."

"How about tonight, then?"

There was a pause. "No. I'm going out. With Enoch.... Keith? I'm happy. Really happy."

"I'm happy for ya, dollface." Humphrey Bogart was back. "Don't let him get fresh. But where are you going? You're going to attract a lot of attention."

"Well," Marcy paused, embarrassed. "I thought about that, too; so we're going to the movies."

"What's playing?"

There was a mumble on the other end of the phone, the only words of which Keith could distinguish were 'double feature.' "What was that?" he asked, pressing his ear into the receiver. "I couldn't hear you."

"It's a double feature," Marcy announced, louder than necessary. There was a very long pause. He prompted her to repeat, and then laughed until he was out of breath when she said, almost in an undertone, "'Labyrinth' and 'The Dark Crystal.'"

"That's wonderful!" Keith hooted. "They'll think you're dating the star.... Marcy? Marcy?...Hello?"

Chapter 21

"I feel like I've been brought home to meet the folks," Marcy said, bolt upright in the overstuffed armchair in Ludmilla Hempert's living room, squeezing her hands together uncomfortably. She unclenched them to accept a cup of coffee and a plate of cake.

"I suppose I am considering myself to be family," Ludmilla smiled, serving Keith from her rolling tea tray. Keith took his plate and sank happily into the upholstery of the wide couch. He scooped up a large forkful of cake and disposed of it with a blissful sigh. Ludmilla regarded him indulgently. "Are you comfortable, my dear? A cushion, perhaps?" The old woman swept down on Marcy with a pair of ornate pillows and tucked them in behind her.

"Thank you." Marcy smiled timidly, settling back.

Keith was content to sit and eat cake and watch Ludmilla handle getting Marcy to relax. She was a good hostess, and it wasn't long before the girl was talking more freely, asking and answering questions as if she had known the old woman all her life. Keith already felt that way. He'd dropped by to see Ludmilla a few times since Hollow Tree got rolling.

Marcy obviously felt shy about discussing her new relationship, but Ludmilla drew her out naturally, reassuring her. She had stories to tell about Enoch as a child that made Keith gape in disbelief, comparing them to the taciturn adult he knew now. "He has always been most loyal and loving," Ludmilla insisted. "I am the one he confides in. He comes to visit me frequently. He was so jealous when he saw you two out together. I worried he might do something bad. His feelings were most strong."

"When was that?" Marcy asked.

"He visited me that one rainy day," Ludmilla smiled, "when I had baked for them, and he came to bring my cakes and breads away. He wished to talk to me, the only person he knew apart from his family and people. About you, my dear. We talked so long he went home after dark."

"Yeah," said Keith, nodding. "That boy with the grocery bag a few weeks ago, after *Attack of the Killer Tomatoes*. When he made a face at me yesterday, I remembered where I had seen that expression before."

Marcy smiled shyly. "I recognized him, but I didn't know then why he was so angry. We've talked a lot over the last few days. I love hearing about how he grew up. He learned all sorts of skills—" Marcy took off the necklace she was wearing and showed it to Ludmilla. "See? The end beads stick together without a clasp. I don't know if there's magnets in it, or what?"

"Amazing," Keith said, peering at the string of wooden beads between Ludmilla's hands. He accepted it from her and played with the end beads, putting them together and drawing them apart. "It doesn't have to be magnets. You know what's it made of? Um, professional curiosity," he said apologetically, noticing Marcy's perturbed glare.

"If you must know, it's applewood. He had to take care of his sister Maura when she was little while the village was being built. She and Holl were the first ones born after they got here. The bigger children had to keep the babies quiet until they sealed off that part of the basement."

"This I know," Ludmilla nodded, remembering, with a little smile on her lips.

"Boy, wait 'til I bring that one up to Holl," Keith said, filing it for later teasing. "He thinks *I* make noise."

"And he told me how his father came to be sort of the village headman," Marcy went on, ignoring Keith. "Everyone respects his father. They're all so opinionated, and they still listen to his decisions. Enoch wants to earn that kind of respect for himself."

"Who's his father?" asked Keith, trying to place an older Enoch.

"Didn't you guess, Keith, even after telling me Mrs. Hempert's story? I'm surprised. He's the Master's son."

"It figures," Keith groaned, striking the side of his head as realization dawned. "They've got a lot in common. Especially the temperaments."

"But Enoch admires Keith a lot for being gutsy enough to confront him," Marcy turned to Ludmilla, "and for not letting it get to him when Enoch was rude."

"So," Ludmilla twinkled, "I am sorry you are deprived of a girlfriend, but I am happy."

"I'm happy about it, too." Keith admitted. "Really."

"And I am proud of you, too, Keith," the old woman said, reaching forward to pat him on the arm. "You have done a great thing for my little ones. I am pleased."

Keith beamed. "It's nice to hear you say that. I need a reality check every so often."

"In the light of my reality, you are deserving of appreciation."

"Oh, Keith, you are a doll," Marcy insisted, kissing him.

Keith glowed. "Just don't do that in front of Enoch," he told her. "He said he'd paste me one. He's worse than Carl."

"If you are yet admitting that you are talking to me," Ludmilla told them as she escorted them to the door, "give my old friends my greetings."

"Not yet," Keith told her, bending down to kiss her lightly on the cheek. "But I will."

In the dark of night, Keith pulled his ancient midnight blue Ford Mustang around to the side of Gillington Library, and waited anxiously as the little folk stole in and out of the wall, carrying newspaper-wrapped bundles piled high in their arms. He worried that passersby might hear them, but their footsteps made less noise than the fallen leaves whispering over the ground. A haze of snowflakes speckled the beam from the streetlight. The trunk was nearly filled to capacity when Holl signaled that the last of the cargo was inside, and Keith jumped quickly out and slammed it down. He kept an eye out for patrols. As the last of the elves disappeared back into their home, he flicked on the headlights, and idled quietly forward, his tires crunching gently on the freezing pavement. The security patrol passed by him, shining its searchlamp into his window for the college sticker. Keith let out a long sigh of relief when it drove away from him.

He hurried back to the dormitory lots. The shipments to the local shops he intended to deliver in the morning before classes, and the others that had been promised to out of town shops for tomorrow he would drop off after lunch, before Sociology class in the library basement. Hollow Tree Industries was at last under way.

When Keith's car had gone, a single figure slunk out of the bushes where it had been watching the whole operation, and tried to catch the sliding chunk of facade before it closed all the way. Under its clawing fingers, the masonry ground back into place, leaving no sign it had ever moved. Listening to make sure no one was approaching, the figure threw its shoulder against the block, but it held firm. It tried again. No movement. With a growl, the watcher pulled a pointed chisel out of a pocket, and began to pry at the stone block. The tool's blade hopped out of the long groove and screeched across its stone face. With another glance around, the figure continued to scrape and dig with the chisel, attempting to force open the elves' back door.

In the 'Would You Believe' column in the holiday ad edition of the Midwestern gazette, a little girl was quoted as having seen one of Santa's elves. "He smiled at me," she said. "I been a good girl all year, and Santa knows." The columnist didn't appear to take her too seriously, but Catra did. She knew instantly what the source of the little girl's apparition had been. When she brought it to the attention of the elders, they asked Enoch to be more circumspect on his outings to see Marcy.

"We still don't know where the other articles are coming from," Catra told him, "but this one we do. Stay low!"

Enoch agreed somewhat reluctantly to comply. "Perhaps I should have grown a mustache," he said, ruefully.

Chapter 22

Ms. Voordman recognized Keith right away when he called at her gift shop. "Hello, Hollow Tree," she said, appraising the stacked packages in his arms. Her thin black eyebrows climbed halfway up her forehead. "Right this way. I'll be in the office, Diane," she called. "Watch the door."

"Yes, Ms. Voordman," came a voice from between the shelves near the front of the shop. Keith looked over that way. He couldn't see anybody. Whomever had spoken must be on her knees. Or an elf. He grinned to himself as he followed the shop owner. The porcelain figures smiled blithely at him as he went by.

"Good," Ms. Voordman said, gesturing to him to put down his packages. "Let's see 'em." She began to unwind newspaper and drop it on the floor.

When all of the bundles were unwrapped, she pounced on the lanterns, and held them up one at a time. "These three are mine," she announced, separating her choices from the others. Keith couldn't see that there was much to choose between, but he did notice that wherever a section called for a piece of wood larger than five inches square, two or more smaller bits had been neatly joined together somehow.

All of the items had a semi-parquet appearance. He didn't understand why the elves had made them that way, but the effect was kind of pretty. The ones Ms. Voordman had latched onto were the nicest. "I like the way the filigree pattern works with the various grains in the panel. Real artistry. I'll see that the right people get a look at these, and I'll talk to you about another order when I know how they sell. Ah!" she cried with a pleased expression, snatching up a couple of small items. "My cooky cutters!"

On his way out, Keith heard the bump and scrape of items being set on the metal shelves, and craned his neck around the corner to see who was doing the stocking. A slender girl blinked up at him from her seat on the floor, flipping back fine blond locks of shoulder-length hair. She wouldn't quite have qualified for Aristotle's Ideal of Beauty, but she was beautiful. The bright blue-green eyes and well-molded cheekbones of her triangular face were appealing and attractive. Keith blinked stupidly, trying to find his tongue, and finally stammered out, "Hello."

Her lips curved up at the corners. "Hi." The dustcloth she held in one hand dropped softly to the floor.

"New here?" Keith couldn't believe how much trouble he was having speaking.

"Oh, no," she said. "I've been working here all semester. I think I know you from somewhere."

Keith gave up trying to find his tongue and whipped one of his new business cards from his wallet instead.

"Yes," the girl nodded, reading the card. "Wooden handcrafts. Keith Doyle. Ms. Voordman mentioned you." She smiled at him, handed the card back. She had a delightful smile. He liked the way she said his name. They looked at each other, waiting for the other to break the silence.

"Well," Keith swallowed. "I'll see you." He started for the door.

"My name's Diane," the girl called out. Keith looked back at her, but didn't halt his forward momentum, and he and the door met with a bang. He staggered back, looking surprised. The bell jingled indignantly, and Diane laughed out loud.

"Nice to meet you," Keith said, gathering himself together, and pulled the door open. "Can't think what that door was doing there." Still grinning, Diane waggled her fingers at him and bent her head to her work. He made it out the door this time, feeling a deep exhilaration.

He had a bounce in his step the rest of the day. His awareness that his car was badly in need of a tuneup brought no more than a resigned, "Oh, well." The steadily worsening weather affected him not at all. There was no good reason for his high mood. There had been no declaration of undying love between them, no vows of friendship…not even a promise to have lunch together, and yet he knew that he had just met someone wonderful, and he wanted to see more of her.

In Sociology class, Carl found that he was being entirely isolated. That weirdo Doyle was back, and he was deep in conversation with Holl. The two of them were excitedly pushing pieces of paper back and forth between them. Wasn't one of those the elf gave Doyle a check? Where would he get a *check*? There was something strange going on here, and he couldn't hear well enough to tell what it was.

Goodman and Eisley were into another debate about politics. Teri and those elf girls were giggling about something while waiting for class to start. He noticed that the little ones were starting to dress differently than before. Their new clothes more resembled the kind of thing he was used to seeing outside. More changes had taken place over the last few weeks than in the whole year and a half he had been coming down here. Marcy seemed more odd than ever. She had given up her seat next to him in favor of one beside the black-haired boy. Their heads were close together, and Marcy was gazing at the kid with a sort of hero worship in her eyes. If there were no other explanation for it, he'd say that they were...involved. Child molesting. That was too sick for Carl to contemplate. He turned away from them. But now he was facing Keith again. With a growl, he stared down at his books.

He was frustrated. There wasn't any facet of his life which hadn't been polluted by Keith Doyle. The dorm, Student Senate—even though Doyle had conceded the victory on the library, it still showed Carl that Doyle could ruin anything he wanted to, and there wasn't anything he could do to stop him—and Marcy. He wasn't sure how Doyle was involved in making him lose his girlfriend, but he was positive there was a connection. Pat Morgan felt the nerd was harmless, but Carl could have given him plenty of examples of his potential for destruction.

And now the little people were doing something mysterious, and his rival was a part of it. He had seen them together twice now, late at night. How they could trust him, Carl couldn't understand. He was making money off of them, if that was really a check he had just seen. He almost voiced his question, but the only person in the room not engaged in another conversation was Marm, and he had been ignoring Carl firmly for the last four weeks after their argument. Instead, the bearded elf sat with his nose deep in a textbook, making notes on a scrap of paper. Final exams were only a few weeks away, and the Master liked to keep his class ahead of the University schedule.

Lee Eisley looked around him with suspicion. He watched the little ones hungrily, feeling even more than before that they might vanish before his eyes. When he heard Teri inviting Maura and the others to get together with her outside of class, he started violently. If they left the library, they would disappear, and he would never see them again. He felt almost proprietary toward them, and he resented Keith for his easy familiarity, since it was difficult for Lee to conceive of making them his friends. He still hadn't forgiven Keith for the Student Senate debacle. It was working his way through the back of his mind that he might do something about the worry that Keith caused him.

Holl stopped Keith in the middle of his fourteenth description of Diane, and asked, "What am I supposed to do with all the papers you handed me last night?"

Keith, unaware of the ire simmering about him, snapped out of his reverie and got back to business. "As treasurer of Hollow Tree Industries, you need to fill those out so we can send them in. The IRS requires that we have an Employer I.D. number. And we'll need a resale number, too."

"But these are corporation forms, slow child. I read all those booklets from the Small Business Administration. We decided that it would be a better plan to make you a sole proprietorship, in case you don't remember my mentioning it. We cannot be employees since we do not have social security numbers or verifiable addresses."

"Oh, yeah," Keith said, hitting himself in the side of the head. "I've got things on my mind."

"You've mentioned her."

Keith grinned. "Well, I'll get the right forms. Sorry. Thanks for the check, by the way. It takes a big bite out of the advance money, but I really do need it." Keith patted his breast pocket happily. "Is there anything else you need? All tax deductible as business expenses. More tape? Sharpening stones? Glue?"

"Wood," said Holl promptly. "We need wood."

Chapter 23

Saturday morning, Keith drove his car to the rear of Gillington
Library, reached behind him to undo the lock, and kept lookout
until the rear door opened and slammed shut and the car sagged
slightly on its elderly springs. He had company. "Stay down until I'm
off campus," he commanded.

"Just as you say," came a muffled voice from behind him.

When he was well out of Midwestern's environs, he called,
"Okay." Two faces popped up from under the tarpaulin in his rearview mirror: Holl's and Enoch's.

"Hi, Enoch," Keith said, surprised. "I was only expecting Holl.
To what do I owe the pleasure?"

"He's the hardwoods expert," Holl explained. "So long as we
were shopping, I brought him along. I didn't think you'd mind."

"Not at all," Keith assured him mildly. "Strap in, okay? This
state has a seat belt law."

He drove along the narrow country roads as Holl explained the
object of their quest. "We've used firewood, old furniture the University has discarded, scraps of lumber from the woodshop, but at
last we've run out of stock, and there're orders yet to fulfill. There
isn't time to cure cut wood, though we have some aging. We're
about out of anything larger than sawdust." His voice died away as
his head turned from side to side, catching all he could of the scenery. Keith didn't think he had blinked since they left.

"I noticed," Keith said, remembering the patchwork lanterns.
"Although I wasn't sure you weren't making things that way on purpose. They looked pretty."

"There's far more work in little bits," Enoch said.

"True. Wood's the one thing you can't do without in a woodcraft business," Keith acknowledged.

"Yer a master of the obvious," the blackhaired elf complained.

"Yup. We needed a real source anyway. What we want is a lumberyard that sells cheap, or one who won't mind selling to us wholesale. What kinds of woods are you interested in? Enoch? Hey!" He
shouted to gain the black-haired elf's attention. Enoch was staring out
the window with a look of concentration. "Is something the matter?"

"First time in an automobile," Enoch said, hoarsely, watching the telephone poles flick by with alarming speed. His hand clutched the arm rest tightly.

"Mine, too," put in Holl, though he didn't look nervous, only excited. He watched a field full of seated cows go by, his eyes as round as theirs.

"Does it bother you?" Keith asked, concerned.

The two elves' eyes met. "We don't travel much," Holl told Keith. "In fact, this is my first time outside town."

"Ever?" The blond elf nodded. "Why don't you travel?" Keith asked curiously.

"Well, why should we?" Holl countered. "Everything I love or want is right there in the compound. There's no need for me to stray far beyond it. The school has kindly supplied experimental farm fields from which we can...borrow...without going too far. I can't speak for anyone else, though."

"I don't mind traveling," Enoch mused, looking up at the tracery of tree branches on the overcast sky. "So long as I can go home again afterwards."

"There was another break-in attempt," Holl told Keith. "The stonework is marked where our burglar tried to chisel his way in. The old ones are half panicked."

"I don't blame 'em," Keith said, concerned. "It sounds like someone has seen you guys going in or out. Whoever it is might be watching us. You have to be more security conscious for a while. Especially until the Historical Society comes through."

Enoch forgot his nervousness, and scowled. "I'll come and go as I please."

Instead of looking alarmed, Keith smiled indulgently. He felt like a collegiate Cupid. "How're things going with Marcy?"

"Oh, well, well. We get along just fine." Noticing Keith's wry look, Enoch asked, "Is there anything wrong with that?"

"No, nothing, nothing," said Keith, a grin spreading across his face, as he swung the car around a corner. Wet gravel rattled under the tires. "Just looks to her roommates like she's dating her little brother's best friend."

"Hmm," said Enoch, thoughtfully, studying his reflection in the car window. "Think I should grow a moustache? I've considered it anon."

Keith imagined a big black handlebar moustache on Enoch's face, and sputtered helplessly. He didn't want to hurt the little guy's feelings. Their detente was too recent to stand a fresh breach. But his imagination was too much for him, and he burst out with a hearty laugh. To his surprise and joy, Enoch joined in.

"It is a funny picture," Enoch admitted. "But what do you think?"

"No," Keith decided firmly. "Let 'em talk."

"Aye, I'll do that," Enoch grunted, satisfied.

It took them several tries before they found a lumberyard with wood the elves considered to be suitable which was also willing to sell wholesale to an unestablished and undocumented company. Keith waited only long enough in each one to let the other two browse. If they gave him a signal of approval, he'd approach the owner. Many times, Enoch would give the place one sniff and stalk back outside to the car. Keith had to admit that he couldn't tell what it was the little guy sensed, but they had to work with whatever it was he bought.

They reached Barn Door Lumber when the watery sun was at the top of the winter sky. Enoch and Holl fell to examining this place with alacrity, so Keith sought out the owner, Fred Orr, about a discount. Mr. Orr was a burly man, a couple inches over six feet tall, and almost that much widthwise, with his belly trying to make it six and a half. He much preferred to keep his profits intact. Keith, with a good deal of diplomacy aided by his natural enthusiasm, described the project the wood was needed for, and managed to negotiate a small cut in price. He promised they would present a resale number the next time they stopped in. "We really need the wood right away," he explained, plaintively.

"Well…okay," the owner said. While they were talking, Holl and Enoch, both respectably hatted, wove between skids of boards and panels, picking out the best of the raw materials. The man watched them running their hands over the timber and smelling it closely to determine its age. He rocked back on his heels and gave a thoughtful sniff. "Okay," he said, squinting meditatively at Keith. "You look honest enough. But no credit. Cash now, and you've got a deal."

"Will you take a check?" Keith asked, relieved.

"Uh-huh. If you've got some I.D."

The pleasantly fresh smell of sawn wood made Keith breathe in again deeply. The dust tickled his nose, threatening to make him sneeze.

He followed the proprietor to the rolling metal cart on which the two 'boys' had stacked their choices. The bill was calculated, and Keith wrote out a check, cringing at the amount, which brought the balance for Hollow Tree Industries very close to zero. Holl watched closely, his head at Keith's elbow, doing the mathematics in his head and pointing out where he made mistakes in addition. Mr. Orr grinned at them, and held the door as they carried their purchase outside.

"Couple of smart kids you've got there," he told Keith.

"You bet," Keith said. "Sometimes they act about four times their age." Enoch stepped on his foot passing through to the parking lot. "Ouch!"

With the wood secured under the sheet of oilcloth, Keith felt more relaxed, but hollow inside. A glance at his watch surprised him. It was already after one o'clock. He hadn't eaten in hours. "How about some lunch?" Keith asked the others, now seated next to him, as he started the car. The elves again exchanged glances.

"We didn't bring any with us," Holl said, apologetically.

"No." Keith studied their faces curiously. "I meant we could stop in a restaurant. Personally, I'm starving. Yes?"

"Yes!"

They rolled away from Barn Door Lumber, and started looking out for a good place to eat.

They pulled into the parking lot of Grandma's Kitchen, a franchise family restaurant that Keith favored, about fifteen miles outside of town. It was the perfect place for college students, who tended to use it as a distant rendezvous, or a way station on long trips back and forth to school. It was clean, well lit, kept open 24 hours a day, and was fairly cheap in spite of the high quality of food it served. There were a few snickers from the back seat when he drove in. The place was a study in plastic quaintness. It was built to draw potential diners to it by oozing wholesomeness. In point of fact, it looked silly. The green and yellow building façade, visible from a considerable distance, resembled a bastard cross between a Swiss chalet and a thatched cottage.

There were no other students there from Midwestern that Keith recognized. He wondered what he would have done if Carl or Lee, or any other members of the "I Hate Keith" Society had been eating there that day. Probably spun on his heel and walked out again.

If no one stopped him. He was grateful that he didn't have to find out. The last thing he wanted to do was give the elves their first experience in dining out at a McDonalds.

"Kind of a nice clientele we're building up," Keith said in an undertone, while they were waiting to be seated. "Eleven customers, and six or seven others that are possibles, with five more who said they'd wait and see if we died or not. Not shabby for amateurs, huh?" He felt a small surge of pride as the two elves exchanged approving glances. He unzipped his jacket but kept his hat on, to keep the restaurant staff from particularly noticing that the 'boys' hadn't removed theirs. They fumbled with the wooden buttons on the front of their coats, looking around curiously at their surroundings.

"So, the charm worked," Enoch said to Holl, also keeping his voice low. Holl nodded agreement.

"Charm? What charm?" Keith asked. The elves looked guilty, but finally Enoch spoke up.

"Well…it enhances the attractiveness of things, if you know what I mean."

"Is that why everyone made orders so quickly?" Keith exclaimed, disappointed. "I thought it was because they liked the products."

"Well, I'm sure they did, but we wanted to make certain," Holl said. "We have a strong stake in the success of this venture. Have we done anything wrong?"

"Mmm—" Keith squirmed. "Well…not *really*. But it isn't *completely* ethical. I think."

"According to the marketing studies, most companies use a form of suggested selling for their products," Enoch pointed out. "Doyle Dane Bernbach uses images considered to be unexpec—"

"Shall we stop it?" Holl asked, interrupting his friend. "We meant only to help."

Keith sighed. "How strong is this charm?"

"Not very. By definition, it's a compulsion, though not a strong one. What it does is to persuade one to drop the inhibitions against seeing the true beauty and usefulness of a thing. More of a simplification than anything else."

"Doesn't falsely enhance the item, does it?" Keith asked. "They call that 'fraud,' you know."

"Oh, not at all. An enhancement would make a shortbread mold more profoundly a shortbread mold, but not a more attractive one."

Keith thought about it for a moment. "I guess you can keep doing it. Those things wouldn't be yours if they didn't have a little magic in 'em."

The hostess signaled to them, and showed them to a table by the window. The two elves gazed around them with avid interest, taking in the brightly colored vinyl-upholstered benches in the booths, the glass-roofed salad bar, and the six-foot-high glassed-in carousel of desserts that spun under lights in the center of the restaurant.

"Look at that," Holl nudged his friend. "Vardin would eat himself sick."

"Aye, he would," Enoch said, trying to contain feelings of panic. This place was stuffed full with more Big Ones than he had ever seen together in one place. He stuck close to Keith, whom he trusted, and slid into the deepest part of the semi-circular booth by which the hostess was waiting. She beamed down at him, seeing a shy twelve year old boy. He managed a sickly smile in return, and accepted the tall plastic-coated menu she handed him. It was like a picture book of food. The number of choices was overwhelming.

Holl was already perusing his, appearing to compare the appearance of Grandma's Kitchen's food favorably over that of the Power Hall cafeteria. Keith didn't blame him.

On the way over to their table Keith had observed the size of the portions being served to other customers. They were enormous. He remembered suddenly how little his two guests ate. A little self-consciously, he thought of his favorite meal at Grandma's Kitchen: a broad ring of thick-cut french fries surrounding a hamburger covered in cheese and bacon strips that was almost eight inches across. To him or one of his other friends, that would be a decent snack. To Holl or Enoch, it might be a little daunting. When the waitress came by, a tall woman with bleached hair and a dark vestigial moustache, Keith appealed to her to bring a couple of kiddie menus. "They're growing boys," he said, amiably, "but not that fast." The waitress smiled maternally down at them, and departed.

Enoch let out an opened-mouth squawk, but Holl burst out laughing. Abashed, Keith pointed surreptitiously to the tables around them, and both had to agree he had a point.

"Any of those'd be a week's food in the village," Holl calculated. "We've never had a bought meal before."

"Great," Keith said, passing them the smaller children's menus. "Order whatever you want. Try something new. How about chocolate chip pancakes?" He looked up to find both of them studying him uncomfortably. "What's the matter?"

"We don't know how we'll repay you for all your help," Holl said, seriously. Keith didn't think he meant just the meal.

"Repay me?" he scoffed, deliberately misconstruing Holl's meaning and keeping his tone light. "What's with these 'pay me backs'? I'm not laying anything out but some time. Look," he said, pouncing on an inspiration, "this lunch is a business meeting, so it qualifies as an expense. As such it comes out of the company treasury. And, since you own the company, you're really taking me out. Can the company afford it? Shall I pay *you* back later?" The two elves frowned at one another.

Enoch said gravely, "We would be most honored if you would join us for lunch. Please order anything you want. You may use the big menu. You growing boys need to eat."

"Thank you," Keith smiled with equal gravity. The waitress reappeared as soon as they closed the menus, and took their orders to the kitchen.

"We haven't heard lately about the famous paper you had to write or die, Keith Doyle," Holl chided him. "The one about legendary peoples, specifically ourselves."

"Oh, yeah," Keith laughed, self-consciously, caught off guard. "I guess I haven't thought about it too much lately. It's more fun to rub elbows with the real thing. I may write it one day. Maybe," he said dreamily, "as a series of reminiscences. My memoirs." He snapped out of his daydream when Holl gave him the raspberry.

"You missed a lot in your research," Enoch pointed out. "There're a lot of articles in old magazines. All rubbish, of course, but scholars consider it to be proper research only if it's written."

"Of course," Keith agreed politely. "Just like Dr. Freleng, my other Sociology professor. But I'm too busy to write right now. Business, you know." The waitress arrived and plunked platters of food down before them.

Over their lunch, they chatted about the class and their classmates. Keith listened with interest as the two elves discussed facets of his fellow students that filled him with admiration for their perception. Teri acted shallow, but it was all for show. She actually had a fine brain for spatial mathematics. Barry was afraid of women, probably because of his family life. Lee used the class as a sort of security blanket, and the Little Folk were worried about his dependency, seeing as how he was supposed to graduate in June.

Around a mouthful of hamburger, Keith inquired, "Why isn't the class bigger? I can think of dozens of kids who need tutoring as badly as I do, but there's only the privileged 'we.'"

"Because those of us in it stand a chance of actually learning something from what we're told. Would you assimilate as much if the class was big?" Holl asked.

"Probably not," Keith admitted frankly. "I always go to sleep in lecture halls. I meant, why haven't the *students* brought in more students?"

Enoch scratched the back of his neck uncomfortably, and looked out of the window. Holl studied his sandwich for inspiration. "It's got to do with the same sort of…compulsion that's on the shortbread cutters," he explained. "One comes in, and he asks the next one, and that one invites the one after that."

"Oh," said Keith. "Like a chain letter. You're invited, and you eventually invite one person to join the class, and then *they* ask one person. How do you know who to choose? And how do you keep from asking more than one person?"

"Well, it sort of happens to you," Enoch explained, making sure no one was in earshot. "When the need is greatest, the newest of you gravitates toward the student in need, and then *that one* comes in. Marcy fought asking you, partly because she is…inhibited as she is. One day, you'll find someone who needs us. Whether or not you know they need help.

"The Master accepts only serious students. We have had a bad one or two, but the ones who come to gape never stay long. Their memory fades away, until they don't really believe that they've seen us."

"They might remember a discussion group, but to them, it was taught by a short man with red hair who brought his kids with him to class." Holl indicated Enoch and himself. "Not very interesting."

"Ah," Keith nodded, comprehending some of it. "A geas. This magic stuff is complicated. But interesting. I want to know all about it. Can you grant wishes?"

Enoch sputtered. "Do we look like genii?"

"Nope," said Keith gaily. "Leprechauns."

By the time they left the restaurant the sky had cleared. Keith calculated there would still be two or three hours of sunlight. "If you're not in a hurry to get back, I could just drive you around the countryside for a while. Since this is your first looksee at the world outside Midwestern, that is." He gestured invitingly at the road ahead.

"Yes," said Holl, without hesitation. "Absolutely." Enoch nodded enthusiastic agreement.

At random, they took a road leading west, and turned corners when it pleased them. For the most part, Keith followed his nose, keeping track of the route only enough to be able to find his way back. Some snow had already fallen hereabout, but it remained only in gullies and hillsides sheltered from the sun. In the cold wind, the countryside looked lonely, but there was an occasional house set far back from the road with cheery yellow lights showing through the curtained windows. Cats watched them go by from comfortable seats on top of gateposts and mailboxes, or folded into gaps in the bare, black flowerbeds. Dogs barked at them from fenced yards, and one bold collie, smiling, with his tongue hanging out of his mouth, paced the car along one long slow stretch. On more than a few properties, 'For Sale' signs quivered hopefully in the wind over fields cleared of crops. Barns with the paint peeling off the walls appeared unexpectedly over the rise, and a few cold cows huddled together on the ground in the corner of a fenced meadow.

A few miles after passing through a small town with only two traffic signals and one strip of stores on its main street, they took a sharp right turn onto a half-paved county road that led them up a low hill past leafless trees. Keith spotted a narrow track leading off to the left that wound around, diving into the crease between two high fields where the cornstalks lay in broken rows. They crossed a bridge over a shallow brown river, and watched a tributary flowing diagonally away from them the length of the heavily wooded lot on their right. Lights winked from the windows of the big house, standing on its own hill deep within the boundaries, almost invisible behind the trees. There was a 'For Sale' sign next to the road there, too. Holl, Enoch, and Keith sighed in unison.

"Nice place," Keith decided, pulling over to study it.

"That'd be a perfect place to live," Enoch said longingly.

"It would," Holl agreed. "It has good spirit about it."

"Yeah, but it's probably fifteen hundred dollars an acre, and we don't know how big the parcel is. Land isn't cheap, especially with its own buildings."

They traveled further as the light began to disappear, perusing Keith's Illinois road map with interest by the light of a hastily-twisted wick Enoch made from the rag Keith used to check his oil. Keith watched the process with interest. "It looks so easy," he said wistfully.

"It is easy," Enoch assured him. "A matter of practice, naturally, much like your driving this car."

"Want to swap lessons?" Keith offered hopefully.

"One day, when there is more time," Enoch considered.

"Go on," Holl urged his friend, with a twinkle in his eye. "I'll get you a box to sit on."

They looked at large farms with 'For Sale' signs on them, especially those on lots with heavy forestation. The two elves looked at the farms speculatively. The real estate idea had been firmly planted by Keith, and it was germinating.

When it started to grow dim, the Mustang turned back toward town. "The others might like to have a drive around to look at things," Holl said. Enoch nodded.

"Sure," Keith said, pulling into campus. "Happy to oblige. Doyle Tours, Limited, a division of Hollow Tree Industries. We cater to Legendary Beings."

Chapter 24

When he turned the corner to drop them off at Gillington, he spotted a crowd milling in the common outside the building. "Gack!" Keith exclaimed, and slammed on the brakes. The elves were thrown forward, but Keith was too distracted to apologize. A huge crowd of students and a bunch of police cars, with their blue lights revolving, were clustered around the corner of the building near the elves' back door. Campus security was there, too, keeping the curious onlookers out of the way of the police.

"What is it?" Holl demanded. "What's happening?"

"Did they get in? Is the doorway open?" Enoch barked worriedly.

Keith signaled to them to lie down flat, and got out of the car. He boosted himself up on top of the hood and squinted through the revolving lights at the building. "There're a bunch of people at the wall," he called down to them. "They're looking at the stonework. It looks like it's damaged. But I don't think it's broken through. All surface damage, but it's really extensive." One of the men in gray overalls felt around inside a crater about the size of Keith's head that had been blasted out of the masonry.

"Hey, you!" A security guard in a green uniform came striding over and glared up at Keith. "What are you doing here? There's no parking!"

"I'm, um...." Keith said, glibly, scrambling down.

"What's all this back here?" the security officer snapped out, yanking up the bulky tarpaulin in the back seat of the car. Keith's heart stopped. "*Wood*?"

"I'm taking it to the woodshop, officer," he croaked out. "It's for a project."

The man nodded, waved a dismissive hand at him. "Good. Then take it over there. Move your car out of this vicinity. Say," he said abruptly, with a searching look at Keith and his Mustang, "do you live on campus? I think I've seen that vehicle...."

"Yes, sir," Keith said, immediately, interrupting him. "Thank you, sir. I'm going." He jumped back into the car and backed it away

from the officer, who was still studying him. "Why didn't he see
you?" he asked the back seat in astonishment.

"He wasn't looking for us," Holl explained.

"Magic?"

"Park the car," said Enoch's voice, tiredly. "We'll have to hide."

He followed the two elves across the Student Common to a man-
hole cover well hidden behind a clump of bushes. There was still
enough of a crowd to put Keith in panic. He was afraid that someone would spot them, but the mob's attention was still on the library
wall. Now, men in coveralls were bringing forward a wheelbarrow
containing a bag of cement. It looked like they were going to fix the
break on the spot. A mini-cam crew from the local news station
positioned itself near the damaged wall and began rolling tape. A
commentator placed herself in plain sight, and spoke earnestly into
her microphone. The crowd moved in closer.

It took the combined strength of both elves to pry up the heavy
steel cover. Keith kept a lookout as they slid down into the dark
hole. He let the lid down as gently over his head as he could, and felt
his way down an iron ladder made of staples hammered into the
wall. When he reached the bottom, he discovered that it was not
entirely dark down there. They were in a portion of a steam tunnel.

"The way is blocked," Holl explained, pointing along a spotlit
walkway to the distant end of the tunnel, "but at least we can let
them know that we are all right. I will signal."

"They're sealing that block of wall up there with cement," Keith
told him. "Someone was definitely trying to get in. He did a lot of
damage. You won't be able to use that door."

Holl looked worried. "That means that someone else *was* spying
upon us. There's no mistake now. I thought so. Wait here." He strode
down the hall through the patches of light and darkness, his figure
strobing in and out of existence.

Enoch looked around him with a sort of nostalgia. "This is my
earliest memory of Midwestern University. We found this place. I
stole food from maintenance workers so we could live."

"I know," Keith said, absently, surveying the place curiously.
"Ludmilla told me about it." He realized what he had just said, and
froze. He glanced at Enoch, and the elf had stopped in place, too,
with open shock on his face.

The pose broke, and the brows drew down over Enoch's nose. "You know about her." It was an accusation. Enoch's hands closed into fists, and Keith wondered if he was going to hit him. He considered, uncomfortably, that he probably deserved it. Never could keep a secret from birth, he chided himself. "How did you find her?"

"Lee told me," Keith admitted, meekly. "I needed to know things. I've taken Marcy there, too. Ludmilla asked to see her."

"Ah," Enoch said. He pursed his lips thoughtfully and the fists unballed. "I would suppose it is all right, then."

"She said to say, 'hi,' to her oldest friend."

The elf nodded, friendly again. "I say 'hi' back to her, then."

"Maybe you'd better say it yourself," Keith said, looking around him. "There's no way you can get back into the library through the main door with all this ruckus going on. And it's closed tomorrow, Sunday. This place doesn't look too comfortable. Maybe you should stay with her overnight."

"That is an idea with merit."

"So it is," said Holl, coming back through the lights. "We are accounted for. The elders were worried to death when they heard the scratching on the stone. It must have been a hammer and chisel that did all that damage." He examined his knuckles. "I've never tapped so long a message. My hand is scraped sore."

"We will stay here until it is full dark, and then go. It is a good thing that we had such a good midday meal. We may have a long wait."

"Well, I'd better get out of here. They'll be keeping a close watch on anyone wandering around after dark, and I've got something to hide."

"Leave me the keys to your car, Keith Doyle," Holl said. "We've still got to get the wood. We've a business to run."

As Keith started to shinny up the ladder, Enoch looked up at him. "By the way, Keith Doyle, I'm sorry I made a mess of your dormitory room. You're a good fellow after all."

Keith did a double-take. "It was you?" he demanded, dumbfounded. "Both times?"

"Well, certainly," Enoch said, with asperity. "Perfectly understandable in the circumstances. Don't you agree?"

Holl chuckled. "It's a good thing there's peace between you now."

Two men in green security uniforms stood up as Keith entered the foyer of Power Hall. He recognized the shorter of the two as the guard who stopped him outside Gillington Library. "Keith Doyle?" one of them asked.

"That's me."

The bigger man behaved as if he was uncomfortable. "We're here because we received information...You understand we're not accusing you, but we have to check every lead on something like this."

Keith felt his throat go tight. "On something like what?"

The other guard felt it was time to speak up. "I saw you over by the library. In fact, I've seen you there a lot. You know what was going on there?"

"It looked like someone bashed a hole in the wall."

"Right. Know anything about it?"

"No, sir. I've been out all day."

The big guard jumped on his phrase. "And how did you know it happened today?"

Keith swallowed. "Well, I meet my...girl there. A lot. That's...where we meet."

"Very sweet," the guard said, unsympathetically. He'd broken up a lot of necking couples in his time, and enjoyed it. "Our source said he saw you hiding around there this morning around dawn."

"What? Who?" Keith demanded. "Who was hanging around at dawn? Why?"

"Jogging," the guard said, glaring at Keith. "And we're not identifying him to you at this time. I'm asking you again: what were you doing?"

Keith got away somehow, leaving the guards only marginally convinced of his innocence, and fled to his dorm room. Pat was there, lying on his back reading with the stereo headphones on. Setting the book down on his chest, he looked down his long nose at Keith. "The cops were up here looking for you. Where'd you hide the body? I told 'em I didn't know when you'd be back."

"They were waiting for me in the lobby."

"What have you done? Stolen the kiddies' milk money?"

"Nothing." Keith scowled, shucking off his jacket.

Pat levered himself up onto an elbow. "Doyle, I don't believe you. What is going on? Carl told me about the Senate thing and the Historical Society. What is there about the library and you, anyway?"

"Nothing I can explain right now. I would if I could. I will, as soon as I can."

Pat raised his eyebrows into a thin, dark arch. "Don't do me any favors."

Keith shrugged, flopping into a chair. "I don't know how, but I'm sure that Carl helped set me up for the security guards."

His roommate threw back his head and groaned. "Will you lay off Carl? You must think he's really out to get you. It bugs him. And he's still pissed at you because you accused him of trashing the room."

Keith considered. "Maybe I should apologize to him for that. I found out who did it."

"Oh? Who?"

"A guy who thought I was trying to steal his girlfriend."

"Is this the girl from Sociology class?" Keith nodded. "Does he live on campus?"

Keith shot Pat an enigmatic look. "Yes."

"Well, then you can return the favor some time. I'll help," Pat offered. "Gladly. I think we got ants from the last Coke spill."

"We've come to an arrangement. Besides, I'm not interested in her any more."

"What, after all semester of dreaming and bellyaching?"

"I've found this wonderful girl...."

Pat raised a hand to halt the babble. "Don't tell me. I've got better things to do."

Keith grinned at him, and reached for his homework.

His anxiety over the anonymous informer made him sleep badly. He was sure in the back of his mind that the vandal and the informer were the same person. Security would have noticed if the damage had been done later in the day. Surely it was just one person. Whoever it was serious or desperate enough to draw the attention of the whole world to the elves' retreat. His nervousness was compounded by his concern for Enoch and Holl, but a call from Ludmilla Hempert early the next morning helped to assuage his guilty feelings.

The local newspaper's headline announced "Vandals Deface Historic Gillington." Keith went through the story a dozen times, and walked as near as he dared to the building, itching to get inside. He felt frustrated because the way was blocked, and he knew he was being watched. He was still concerned about the two elves, but it was a needless worry. They knew their way around the campus better than he did, and ought to have no trouble staying out of sight. He could be their biggest hazard.

Chapter 25

It wasn't until Tuesday evening that he managed to get down to the village through the classroom passage. To his relief, Holl and Enoch were both there, no worse for their adventure, and had somehow managed to transport the supply of wood inside without attracting notice. When Keith pressed them for details, Holl would say only, "Old skills," his favorite answer, and Keith's least favorite.

They had discussed all of their sightseeing with the others in their clans, and most of them were keen to take a tour themselves, with Keith's fellow students wanting first go. He promised to figure out some way to do it, as soon as it was safe.

"I don't think it'll be a good idea for a few weeks," he insisted. "There's somebody out there who knows you're here, and just wants to cause trouble."

"No. The sooner the better," Catra insisted. "We can't find a new home by inspiration. We need to see what is available to us."

"I'm concerned about is the break-in. Who was it? Did anybody see him? Whoever it was must have been hammering on that stone for a good long time."

"Of course we heard it," Tay snapped, tugging distractedly at his beard. "Short of going up to ask who it was, there was nothing else to do."

"I think you ought to have an evacuation plan, or something."

"I think," said the Elf Master, coming up to the little group, "that ve can take care of ourselfs, and perhaps you should think about the examination that is about to take place."

With a twinge of guilt, Keith and the others followed the red-haired teacher up the tunnel to the schoolroom.

If the other Big Folk students were surprised to see Keith emerging from the little door behind the elves, they didn't show it. If anything, most of them took it in stride as a natural occurrence, based on what they'd come to know about Keith. Keith exchanged smiles and greetings, and made his way to the desk between Holl's and Enoch's.

In spite of his anxieties about Hollow Tree and the attempted invasion, Keith relaxed when he read the essay questions that the Elf

Master scratched on the upright slate. Though he had been too busy to study over the weekend, he found the answers forming themselves in his mind almost quicker than he could write them down. As his confidence grew, inspiration took over, and he wrote faster. Even with the greater part of his mind involved with the test, he was aware of how the clarity of the teaching affected the amount of information he was able to retain. Holl was right: a smaller class gave the students an advantage in learning.

The Master promised to evaluate their papers right away. Keith felt smug. After this test, Freleng's final would be no big deal.

Thursday afternoon, he sailed blithely past the librarian on duty, carrying a plastic bag which seemed to be very light for its immense size and kept trying to get away from him; and a box which he took great care to keep balanced. The woman waved away his explanations, obviously tired of hearing them, and watched him ring for the elevator.

Keith shifted from foot to foot with excitement. Even if he had blown the test completely, which he doubted, the end of such a stimulating semester was deserving of some kind of celebration. The doors finally opened, and he maneuvered the cake and his bag of helium-filled balloons and party hats inside.

The classroom looked a little bizarre with balloons floating drunkenly all over the ceiling and bumping into each other where they were tethered to the backs of chairs. Keith presented the cake to the Elf Master with a little speech he had prepared ahead of time and thoroughly rehearsed, remembering his usual incoherence.

"I want to express how grateful I am for being allowed to join this class. I think I've learned a lot more about Sociology than I thought I could. Shock does a lot for opening the mind to new experiences." The others snickered, glancing sideways at the Master.

"It has not been one sided," the Master said, "but I am surprised you did not submit to me your thesis on interplanetary relations."

"I thought about it," Keith admitted. "Only I figured that the next time I opened a door in the library, I might find a lot of little green men and bug-eyed monsters."

"I know of none here," the Master assured him, over the class's laughter.

"Well, all I have to say is thank you for drumming the subject into my head…and I'll be happy with any grade I get—so long as it's an A." The rest of the class clapped and cheered. Keith bowed and sat down. The Elf Master got up, shaking his head in mock despair, and handed the papers out to the students one by one.

Beaming at the teacher, Keith took his, and looked it over. "But there's no grade on it," he protested.

"Meester Doyle," the Master sighed, rapping him on the head with the roll of exams. "I do not understand vhy you are trying so hard to impress me. You have demonstrated ample knowledge of your subject. If all you vish is a letter by which you can compare your attainment with that of others, then you have learned little."

Keith turned red. Sometimes the Master reminded him of Professor Kingsfield from the *Paper Chase*. "I'm sorry. Maybe I should have asked what your method of grading was." Carl and the other male students regarded him smugly.

"I vould be happy to explain. I have marked on your test papers where your theory is false, or vhere your argument fails to support your premise."

Abashed, Keith turned his paper over, and went through the pages. "Well, you didn't mark anything on this at all."

"Then you demonstrated no false theories, and defended those you did propose well."

"Oh," Keith said in a very small voice. "I guess I got an A."

The Master sighed, this time in exasperation. "If you must express it in that limited fashion."

"Yahoo!" Keith cheered. The others joined in.

"I vish only that I could be assured you were as delighted vith having accomplished learning as you seem to be vith a mere symbol."

"How about it?" Keith asked Marcy, as the cake went around. "Can you take this one home to your parents?"

"Yes," she said, happily, displaying pages free of marginal comments.

"I meant the test," Keith chided her mischievously, taking a fingerful of icing from her plate of cake. She blushed. It made her look prettier than before.

"Yes, that too." Marcy glanced over at Enoch. The black haired elf smiled back at her.

As the other human students drifted out, Holl beckoned him into the passageway for a private talk.

"There's a problem. I didn't want to bring it up in front of the others. We've the rest of that order to finish before you leave for the winter break, and there just isn't any way it can be done in that little time."

Keith made a wry face. "So how can you speed it up?"

"I don't know. We just cannot make our hands move any faster. I put in an order for power tools, but they ask payment in advance, and we have no reserves in the account. Also all are concerned about losing what money we have made so soon."

"I know where you can get jobs," Keith said, grinning, making points of his own ears with his forefingers, "with Christmas coming so soon. The work's seasonal, but at least it's high visibility, and the pay is good." Holl groaned at him, smacking him on the arm with an open hand.

"Will you stay with the matter at hand and stop recruiting for Santa Claus, you widdy?"

"I am. I'm thinking. Power tools...?" The tall student snapped his fingers suddenly, the sound echoing down the hall. "I know where there are some we can borrow."

"I don't know about this, Keith. The school is fussy about insurance, and things like that."

"Don't worry about it, Mr. Scherer," Keith said, reassuringly. He patted the wood-shop teacher on the back. "We'll give you a 'hold harmless' letter of agreement, if anyone asks. But since it's the end of semester, no one will pay any attention anyway."

Scherer looked around his workshop. He was a middle-sized, middle-aged man with a bald spot beginning in the midst of his black hair, and pretensions toward a pot belly. His usually good-natured face showed an uncharacteristic expression of worry, as he watched a whole bus-load of little kids messing around with his power tools.

It had taken a large dose of the famous Doyle diplomacy to arrange it, but half the habitants of the elf village were occupying the school woodshop. They had acceded grumpily to Keith's insistence that only females and beardless males should go with him, even though

Keith acknowledged that he would be leaving behind some of the top craftsmen. That still left him with fifteen or more workers. With admirable presence of mind, Keith taped a square of paper over the window in the door so that passersby couldn't see in. Mr. Scherer, eager to avoid trouble with the Administration, not only allowed him to block the window, but locked the door for him as well.

"So what's this all for?" the teacher asked curiously, walking among the behatted youngsters. The crease between his brows deepened as he watched his precious table saws run under the leather-gloved hands of a couple of preteenage girls, but a few moments convinced him he had nothing to worry about. He was impressed with their deftness. Keith was right. These kids really knew how to behave around dangerous equipment. And fast! He never saw anyone so quick to learn before. It had only taken one demonstration with the punch press, and the black-haired kid was handling it like he had lessons from nursery school on. Too bad he never got students like this for his classes. He averaged about one accident a week with the usual gang of idiots who took wood shop.

"Junior Achievement," Keith said, gesturing broadly at the roomful of boys and girls. "I got involved last fall."

"Oh, yeah?" Scherer replied. "I used to be the adult advisor for a JA group. Only mine sold toilet roll covers and towel racks and easy stuff like that. So, how much is your stock selling for?"

"Stock?" Keith echoed blankly. "Right, stock."

"Yeah, stock. The way they establish a company."

"Oh, yes, of course, stock. I know that. Well, we haven't printed the certificates yet, because we haven't raised the money for the printer. That's what you're helping us to do right now. We sell these, and we're on our way."

"Awright," the teacher said, approvingly. "And what's this? Ornamental lantern, huh? Nice, simple design: pierced screens, four pillars, peaked roof." Candlepat smiled politely at him as she took the frame out of his hands and put the wooden candle into its socket inside. She gave the teacher a coy wink. "Pretty."

"Uh, they're children's night lights," Keith explained, over the buzz of the table saws. "Their own design."

"Oh," Scherer said, looking admiringly at Candlepat. She raised a hand, delicately flicked her long, golden hair back over her shoulder, and gave him a big, wide-eyed gaze. Catra hissed a warning at her from the next table where she was attaching hinges to boxes. "Yeah, very pretty." The man didn't notice that the other 'children' were moving in more closely around them, prepared to defend the girl with their lives, no matter if it was her own fault. It always was.

Keith, who knew how little they trusted Big People, leaped in to disarm the situation, and did his best to distract the teacher. He waved the others away with a hand behind his back. It occurred to him that they might have knives. He didn't want one of Candlepat's flirtations to turn into disaster.

"Mr. Scherer. *Mr. Scherer*," Keith said, getting the teacher's attention and dragging him away from Candlepat, with whom Keith exchanged black looks. She pouted after her admirer, but went back to work. "Sir, she's twelve years old!" The teacher blanched, realizing how close he might have come to a fatal indiscretion. The administration frowned on statutory deviance. He didn't look at her again. With the threat allayed, the defenders eased back into their places. Keith took a deep breath.

"Stupid!" her sister growled under her breath. Candlepat put her nose in the air and pretended not to hear.

"Didn't mean nothin' by it," Scherer grumbled, hoping Keith wouldn't misjudge him. "Twelve, huh? Regular little siren. Wow! Think what she'll look like when she's eighteen."

"Huh! She'll never see eighteen again," Catra growled into her work.

"You gotta promise to let me know when you're ready to do business, Keith," the teacher urged him as they finished cleaning up and prepared to leave. "I've never seen such good, fast work in my life. It's almost magic."

"Sure is, Mr. Scherer."

"They look like Santa's little helpers in their little caps," the teacher chuckled, heartily, patting one of the blond boys on the head. The kid wielding the broom turned and gave him a dirty look. Scherer shook hands with Keith and smiled at the others as they marched out into the snow. "Merry Christmas, kids. And good luck."

Chapter 26

"He didn't mean any harm by it," Keith said, following the elves back toward the village. The bags of wooden toys and knickknacks were already in the trunk of his car, and he was planning out a route map for the next day in his head. Holl pulled out a glowing blue key to open the side entrance to Gillington. They stayed on the cleared path as far out of the street lights as possible, avoiding the scanty new fall of snow on the grass.

Keith was still a little alarmed at their reaction to the wood shop teacher. It hadn't struck him before, but he'd been underestimating them. Now he saw them as he should have, with a full range of feelings, defenses, worries. And there was nothing wrong with their sense of self-preservation. They might look like kids, but they weren't. Not just cute mini-humans, but adults older than he was, and he of all their acquaintance should have known better. He wanted to kick himself for falling into the trap of anthropomorphic association. Wasn't it just a little while ago he'd called Marcy out for doing the same thing?

"I know," Holl said at last, making a face. "Ach, that man. I hate stereotypes!"

"Just call me Santa," Keith chuckled, feeling relieved. "You weren't really putting a spell on him, were you, siren?"

Candlepat was still offended. "*You'll* never know."

The door closed behind them just before the security patrol passed by on its hourly cruise of the Campus Common area.

"Well," Keith said, a little wistfully, "I guess I won't be seeing you guys again until January. Holl, will you stop by and pick up my mail every day? I am still waiting for our Employer's I.D. number, and things like that. We're not official yet."

"Of course," Holl assured him. "But don't be in such a hurry. We've got a custom of present-giving in this season, too. The most of us feel that we owe you something. Not that a small present would pay you back, but call it on account."

"Thanks," Keith said, flattered, "but you don't owe me any-thing. When I was a little kid, I believed in brownies and gnomes. I never found any, but it was just because I was looking in the wrong places. Now I know: I check the basements of libraries every time. I feel that I owe *you* for my dream becoming real."

Enoch wasn't satisfied. "That's not much of a gift."

"It is to me," Keith said. "I don't know what else I'd want."

"Name it," Holl insisted. "We'd feel better."

"Well," Keith thought for a long moment. "Some of the things which you make have obviously got some sort of magic. Would you do a little magic for me?"

"Little is what it would be," Catra told him. "There's just not enough energy to make a great working last a long time."

"It requires concentration beyond the simple existing life force of the creator," Holl explained, but Keith still looked blank. "Look, it's like this: Sion here could make his ears look rounded, and they would always look so if he wanted them to, without his concentrating, because his mere existing would supply the necessary energy for the spell to continue."

"I wouldn't do it, though," Sion protested, fingering the points of his ears. "It's a matter of pride."

Holl nodded agreement. "Same with us all. Now, if Enoch wanted big fluffy wings…"

"Go on!" Enoch scoffed, putting aside the notion.

"…We'd all have to concentrate, and they wouldn't last too long when we stopped. His own force isn't enough to maintain that kind of circuit. Think of electricity. We're all little batteries. Even you."

"Wow," Keith said. "Can you do something for me that would last?"

"What would you like?"

"Oh, I don't know. Well, my mom always said I was so curious I should have had cat's whiskers."

"Visible or invisible?" asked Dever.

"Invisible, of course," Keith answered flippantly. "I'd never get another date otherwise. But you're not serious."

"Sure, we're serious," Holl said. "You wanted a little magic. Sit down here." The blond elf stood facing Keith, his face eerily half shaded in the light from the streetlamp coming in through the crack between the door and lintel. One eye socket looked empty in the shadow, with a glint of silver deep under his brow. Keith felt a shiver go down his spine as Holl touched forefingers to his cheeks just an inch or so from the nose, and drew invisible lines outward. The fingers touched again, a little higher up and further out, and moved again, out of the line of Keith's peripheral vision. He felt a third touch, below the second set. The others were gathered around, watching with interest, giggling.

"That's it," said Holl, dropping his hands to his side and shaking his wrists to relax them. "You can't see them, but we can, and there they are."

"Come on," said Keith, reaching up to touch his face. "Without any magic words? Nothing happened, right?" He twitched his nose. Something tickled his palm. He tried the other side, and his look of bewilderment made the young ones laugh even more. He felt around the sides of his nose, and discovered two sets of thin, stiff wires, about the same diameter and texture as broom bristles. He bent one upward to get a look at it. There was nothing to be seen, but he felt the pull on the skin near his nose. "There *is* something…" There was an impression in his fingers where the whiskers pressed, but whatever was making it was definitely invisible. He was delighted. "How long will it last?"

"Only until you can convince yourself that they don't," Holl said. "Maybe all your life. It wasn't a difficult request."

Keith wiggled his nose again, laughed with joy. "Well, I couldn't have done it." The headlights passed by again, drawing a long ribbon of light between them through the gap in the doorframe and sweeping it across the floor. Keith looked up, and glanced at his watch. "Uh oh. I'll have to sneak back. Thanks for everything, all of you," he said, his eyes going around to each of the elves.

"Save the soap," Enoch said, brusquely. "We're in your debt."

Keith twitched his whiskers, and with a salute to the elves, slipped out of the door. They were gone into the darkness before the door boomed shut behind him.

The periodical librarian at Gillington had a secret magazine subscription which was charged to the library budget, but never actually appeared in the archives. Since she had total charge of the mail, no one knew about it. So, every week on Wednesday, she would open and carefully abstract her copy of the *National Informer* and secrete her illicit 'research digest' in her locker until she took time off for lunch. After lunch every Wednesday, she would hide the magazine again among her things, and go about her business. Within minutes after it was placed under her coat, it would be removed by careful elfin fingers and carried off to be perused by other eyes.

The librarian was aware that her magazine was being borrowed, but she never dared to say anything. For all she knew, it was Mrs. Hansen herself reading up on what it was inquiring minds wanted to know. Best not to rock the boat and have to pay for her own subscription.

Holl took it out of the locker on his way back from Keith's mailbox in the second week of winter vacation. The collection in the box included a host of get-rich-quick schemes, ads, and three brown legal-sized envelopes with a box number in the corner and 'penalty for improper use, $300' printed on each one. "IRS, eh?" Those would have to be answered, with his new supply of postage stamps and his hasty lessons from Keith on the workings of the U.S. Postal System. He tucked the mail under one arm, and thumbed through the digest on his way back home. There was a funny story on the second page about an actress who believed she was going to have alien twins, and the stacks of Gillington rang with ghostly laughter that sank into the lowest levels and then became silent as Holl passed through the hidden door. The librarian returning from her lunch heard the last echoes, and decided that she would be best employed spending the afternoon sorting the card catalog in the main lobby.

Usually, the village had a good laugh over the illustrated adventures of the spoiled and the gullible, but Orchadia, Enoch's mother, was the first to notice one small article on page five. "Sightings of small alien humanoids rock college town." In spite of the reporter's vague style, there was no mistaking whom he must have meant. "Now they're appearing in a national magazine!" Catra wailed to the Master, showing him the photocopied story, which she kept in her folder with the other clippings.

Holl begged her to be calm. "It's a guess," he assured her. "One of those jokers at the Informer picked up on that little girl's story and improved on it, that's all. Just another literary echo."

"It's that Doyle," the elders agreed, and nothing Holl said could shake their opinion.

"It must be," Curran said. "Who else ha' seen us so close?"

After that, there was a careful perusal of every periodical that came into the library. Anyone leaving the village had to make doubly sure he or she was unobserved. The craftsmen were still working on reopening the back door, so they had to exit by way of the library stacks. It was more difficult during the holiday break with fewer bodies on campus. Any movement was notable. "We have no choice," Curran said at last to his gathered clan. "We canna live on vegetables for three weeks. If the snow comes again, we'd be too easy to track."

"I don't want my children taking the risk of being carried off," Shelogh said, indignantly. Her brown hair had a thread of grey at the temples, but her face, in spite of its set expression, was as smooth as a child's.

Catra sighed at her. "Mother!"

"When he gets back, we can have Keith Doyle look into that story," Holl told them confidently. "I've heard nothing on radio or television. Could be someone caught a glimpse of one of us without the hat on and had a 'hallucination.'"

"No one vould be dot careless," Aylmer insisted.

"I hope not," Candlepat said, alarmed. "When we three visited Teri Knox, we were all most careful. Swore to her companions it was too cold to uncover our heads."

"Were they not suspicious?" Keva asked.

"No," the blond girl giggled. "We're her old summer campers, she tells them. Big Folk don't look for difficult explanations. They're so simple. She dined us on pizza, served from a flat box. It was very tasty, though untidy. May we make pizza some time for supper? The Big Ones would never know it wasn't some of theirs. I can get a box."

"No," said Shelogh firmly.

"What kind of pizza was it?" demanded Dola, Tay's only daughter, and Keva's great-grand-daughter. She was ten, and had a crush on Keith Doyle. Anything the Big Folk did fascinated her.

"*Carryout* pizza."

"Oooh."

"I dinna like having adults masquerading as children," Curran complained. "And as for Keith Doyle, who's to say 'tisn't he spreading the story himself." The old elf snorted. "By purpose or no. He's a fool."

"And all from one unsubstantiated story," Holl sighed. The Anti-Keithites were unappeased. "I wonder if he's the only fool." He put away Keith's letters in a box in his hut.

Chapter 27

"I got your Christmas card," Keith told Marcy.

"I got yours, too," she said. "Did you have a nice holiday?"

"You bet. Everyone was home, so it was a non-stop parade with brass band."

"With your family, I'm not surprised."

"Playing in seven different keys, I'll wager," put in Holl, stepping over to greet them both.

"Hello, Teri Knox," Maura left Holl to touch her friend gently on the sleeve. "It is good to see you."

"Maura! Hi! God, what a wonderful dress!" The blond girl stepped back to admire the little elf as she twirled, billowing out the skirts of a parti-colored dress, white on one side and red with tiny stars on the other. "That's more of Keith's weird Christmas materials, but wow! I love what you did with 'em. I ought to have you make my clothes."

"Hey, Barry!"

"Hey, Carl, how was the vacation?"

"Great. Went cross-country skiing. My mother broke her leg, so we went out for Christmas dinner. My folks gave me a color mini-TV for the dorm."

"*Hand*-sewn?" Teri squealed. "My fingers would fall off!"

"If you please?" the Master said, coming into the room from the tunnel and holding his hands up.

Nobody heard him.

"Mom tried roasting a goose this year. It wasn't done for hours."

"Got a new snowmobile. It does zero to—"

"If you please!" he raised his voice over the din, banging a pointer against the easel chalkboard for emphasis. "The hour is long past vhen ve vere to begin the class."

There was more socializing and good cheer before the Elf Master was able to call the class to order. Nobody mentioned the wall outside which had been damaged and repaired, and Keith didn't want to voice any suspicions in class about the vandal. The spring semester was just beginning at Midwestern, and everyone was fresh and full of new energy from the vacation. Most of the human students were laden down with new books from their other courses. The Master was starting a new course, too.

"The topic is biology," the Master announced. "The science of the life of plants and animals."

Keith was nonplused. As a business major, biology had limited application for him, unless he went into selling medical equipment or something. He had done all right in high school biology, but it hadn't thrilled him much. Still, anything the Elf Master taught was likely to be interesting, whether or not he had any use for it. It was clear that other humans had different feelings about the change in subject. Teri was happy. She had a new Bio textbook already under her desk. Barry looked queasy and ambivalent.

"Do you mean we'll be dissecting things?" Barry asked, raising a hand for attention.

"No. Ve haf not the laboratory facilities for practical study, though microscopes and prepared slides are available to us in the science department. Ve vill be exploring the theory only."

"Oh. Good."

"Um, Master?" Keith raised his hand.

"Ye-es, Mr. Doyle?"

"Will we be examining elf biology, too?"

The teacher looked at him over the top of his gold wire glasses. "In theory only, Mr. Doyle. Haf you any specific questions?"

"Uh, no, sir." Keith subsided. "Just general curiosity." Holl elbowed him in the ribs with a snicker.

"Gut. There is nothing random about the accrual of knowledge. There is always a purpose to vhich research can be put. Curiosity can be a useful tool. If you think of your questions, ask them."

"Keith Doyle!" Holl leaned out the door. Keith turned back. The elf waved a rubber-banded bundle at him. "Your mail, saved faithfully throughout the vacation. There are some letters here that look important."

"Thanks for taking care of it while I was gone," Keith said.

"My pleasure," Holl assured him, letting the door swing closed behind him. As the light vanished, Keith dashed along the aisle toward the elevator. In the darkness ahead, he could hear Barry exclaiming over his good luck. "I'm really weak in science. I'm going to see if I can drop into a basic biology course for the credit." Keith remembered that he was a Liberal Arts major, and had to have one lab science to graduate.

"We'll help you out, too, won't we, Carl?" Teri asked.

"Sure," Carl agreed amiably.

"See if you can get into my class," Teri went on. "I'm registered in BIO 202, Tuesdays and Thursdays at 11 A.M, Dr. Mitchell. He's a doll."

"I think I have that free," Barry said.

"That's what I like about this group," Keith declared, joining them just as the elevator rolled down. "Teamwork."

Teri took him aside on the steps of Gillington as the group dispersed. "I just wanted to tell you how much I appreciate what you're doing, Keith. I saw the wooden stuff in the gift shop in town. I knew it came from...there." She tossed her head meaningfully in the general direction of the stacks.

"You did? How?"

Teri leaned close to him, lifted the wave of hair away from the side of her face. Attached to a scented earlobe by a hinged wooden clasp was a small ring and carved bead of the same shade of wood. "Maura gave me these earrings for Christmas. I love them so much I wear them all the time. The design is of a style that's kind of hard to miss. And if there's one thing I do know, it's style." Keith recognized the twisting ivy pattern Holl favored, and acknowledged that it appeared on a lot of the Hollow Tree merchandise.

"I'd never deny that," Keith said, giving her an appreciative up and down glance. "I didn't think that anyone would really notice things in gift shops."

"Why? Your customers have to come from somewhere," Teri pointed out. "Not everyone goes to Chicago to shop. Can I suggest adding jewelry to your inventory? These are nicer than anything I've ever bought in a store. I was interested, so I did a little detective work." Teri smiled, "I know Diane Londen over at Country Crafts. When I asked her where the great boxes and things came from she described you." Teri paused, her head cocked to one side. "Why don't you ask her out?"

"I don't know." Keith was enchanted, the bundle of mail clutched forgotten under his arm. "What makes you think she'd want to go out with me."

Teri dimpled. "Just call it a little more detective work."

"Hi, Ms. Voordman," Keith sang, in tune with the jingling door bell the next day. He stamped the snow off his shoes with a happy little one-two dance step.

"Oh, Mr. Doyle," the shopowner said, straightening up from a shelf she was arranging. She pushed aside a metal cart with discarded price stickers stuck all over it, and came over to shake hands with him. "I was just thinking about you."

"Keith, please. Only teachers who hate me call me by my last name," Keith assured her with a smile.

"Keith. Do you want to know why I was thinking about you?"

"Yes, ma'am!"

"Come this way." He walked behind the black-haired woman to a small end-cap of shelves. "This. This is where I had the Hollow Tree display all through the Christmas season." It was empty, except for a porcelain statue. Keith grinned at it. It was the elf-in-a-tree that had inspired him to name the company. She waved a hand through the space between the shelves. "I have never seen anything go out the door so fast. It was like magic! The customers loved everything. How quickly can I get another shipment?"

Keith considered. "I'll have to ask my craftspeople, but it shouldn't take too long. I hope."

"And I'm sure you want the balance on my account." Ms. Voordman led him to her office, took out her checkbook and a pen, and wrote the date on a long blue check. "It's been sixty days. I presume that's why you're here." She noticed Keith's attention turned out toward the main room of the shop. "Or is it?"

"Is Diane here today?" he asked, accepting the check with an absent little grin.

Ms. Voordman smiled back at him. "Two birds with one stone, eh? She's doing inventory, but I suppose she can take her break. If she wants to."

"Thanks," said Keith.

"Hi, there," Diane said, coming into the back room. Seeing her boss, she flipped her hair back over her shoulder, looking studiously nonchalant. "Ms. Voordman, may I…?"

"Yes, of course," the shop owner smiled, and turned to Keith. "I would say she wants to."

"I hope orange juice is all right with you," Diane asked, opening the refrigerator behind the shelves in the stock room and drawing out a plastic quart bottle. "I get so sick of sugary stuff I could barf. And the water here is too mineral-heavy to drink." She set the bottle and a couple of styrofoam cups onto a low, battered coffee table and plumped onto an ancient brown satin-upholstered couch. Dust flew up from the cushions and they both coughed. "So, what are you doing selling handcrafts door to door?"

"Helping out some friends. And the commission doesn't hurt," Keith admitted, sitting down next to her on the couch. Dust flew up from the cushions and they both coughed.

"Sorry. This thing smells mouldy, but it was free. We're going to recover it one day," Diane apologized, fluttering an annoyed hand under her nose. "Your merchandise is great. It has class. Believe me, you see the height of tacky come through a gift store. You should have seen what the last salesman wanted to sell Ms. Voordman: ashtrays made of little seashells glued together and shaped like houses. Yuck!"

"My friends couldn't picture their work in the same shop with that sort of thing, but it makes a great contrast, though. So," he asked, toasting her with his cup of juice, "How about…"

"Diane!" Ms. Voordman's voice cut him off. "Customers!"

"Sorry," she said, gulping down her juice and shoving the bottle back into the refrigerator. "I've got to take care of them. Coming, Ms. Voordman!"

"Hey, wait!" Keith pleaded. "Would you like to have dinner with me at Frankie's tonight? I just got my commission check. The sky's the limit. Anything up to three bucks apiece."

"I can't. Busy tonight."

"Tomorrow?"

Diane laughed. "Yes, that's fine. I'd like that. I get off at six every day."

"I'll be here," Keith promised.

"Diane!"

"Aargh!" Diane cried in exasperation. She gave him a friendly smile and ran out to the front of the store. Keith threw her a silent toast with the last of his juice.

Chapter 28

Keith's cheerful mood lasted until he returned to his dorm room, when he discovered that his bed had vanished. In its place lay a ton of announcement flyers circulated by the Power Hall management, telephone books, and a variety of notebooks, plays and drama digests.

"Hey," Keith protested, pointing. It all belonged to Pat, who was piling more possessions on his own bed.

"Sorry," Pat said, dropping the stack of books. "Ungh! Rick came by, said the administration lost all record of our damage deposit, and wants to collect it again."

"What? Why?" Keith joined in and helped him move everything off his desk.

"Your pal, the one who trashed our room twice? He owes us. The rug is ruined under where the Coke dripped off the wall. They want us to pay again to replace it. I'm trying to find the receipt. You know, you're expensive to live with. You could funnel some of your new business profits back to deserving folk like me."

"No way," Keith asserted. "Are they sure the rug's ruined? I know you can get pop stains out of carpeting. My mother does it all the time. Wait a minute, here it is." He brandished a flimsy piece of paper stamped with the University seal.

"Than-kew!" Pat plucked it out of his fingers and stalked out of the room to find Rick.

Keith bent to clear his bed off. Pat hadn't started with his own desk. Under the first layer of papers was the detritus from Keith's. In the midst of a heap of books, he found the bundle of mail Holl had set aside for him. Ignoring the rest of the mess, he slumped down on the floor to go through his mail. The package contained the usual mix of junk mail and advertisements aimed at the college community. "Students—earn up to $6.00 per hour!" "Word processing, $1.00 per page." Holl had been right, though. Keith noticed a few unfamiliar and very official looking envelopes with official looking return addresses in amongst the others. They were addressed to Keith Doyle, D.B.A. Hollow Tree Industries. He tore them open, letting the remainder of his mail drop to the bed. Two of them contained copies of IRS tax forms; one for paying in quarterly income taxes, and one that informed him he had been granted an Employer's I.D. number. Attached to these by a paperclip was a note in Holl's perfect handwriting that the originals had been filled in and sent out.

The third contained a computer-generated form letter, checkmarked in ink on the third possible clause, advising him of penalties he owed for not submitting a quarterly return for the fourth quarter of last year. These penalties were being levied because of an administrative crackdown on small businesses. An immediate reply was requested. A pre-addressed envelope was enclosed for his convenience.

There was a phone number for the local IRS office on the letter. Hurriedly, he grabbed for the phone and dialed it. The IRS wasn't in a hurry to hear from him. He sat through an endless pre-recorded message, before there was a click, and a nasal female voice from very far away said, "Internal Revenue."

With panic rising in his belly, Keith explained that he had received the letter and needed to talk to someone about it. With a "just a moment, sir," the voice clicked off. Keith sat on hold for another eternity half-listening to another pre-recorded message advising him to file his 1040 early while he fought down mental pictures of anonymous men in dark, narrow lapelled suits and sunglasses taking the elves away in handcuffs. Another click came. A dry voice informed him, "This is Mr. Durrow."

Keith swallowed. He hadn't realized before how terrified he was of the IRS. His voice came out in a squeak as he introduced himself. "Mr. Durrow, I got this letter, telling me I'm liable for a tax penalty for not filing a fourth quarter quarterly return. My associate filed that while I was home for spring break. Can't you check to make sure that you have received the form?"

"Who is your 'associate?'" the dry voice wanted to know. "You have filed as a sole proprietorship."

"Just a matter of speaking, uh, sir. It's a sort of wholesale manufacturing operation, and we haven't brought in any profits yet. I take things on consignment. You see, I had to...in the beginning it was necessary to give away a lot of merchandise...you know, woodcrafts...so I'm in the hole. All expenses, but no profit. I live in a college dorm," he explained. "I only just back to school today."

Durrow's tone told him he'd heard those excuses before. "I see, Mr. Doyle. You must understand that we cannot afford to make exemptions. Except the standard one per person, of course." It was a joke, and Durrow let out a little snake's hiss of a laugh at his own wit. "It is admirable that you have started your own company, but you are responsible for your debts as much as for your successes."

"Yes, sir. Just send the forms again," Keith pleaded, "I'll be more careful."

"See that you are. The first quarter estimated tax is due April 15th."

"I know that, sir. I'm doing better," Keith promised him, eager to sound as if he knew what he was doing. "Lately, business has been improving. Black ink is actually appearing on my books."

"Fine," said Durrow, his tone indicating it was nothing of the kind. "We like to see small businesses doing well. You will need to file a 2210 stating you had no income during the last quarter, and make sure you keep up with the tax payments over this fiscal year."

"Yessir, I won't make that mistake again," he vowed. Then Keith hung up the phone and dashed off to find a 2210 before going to Voordman's to pick up Diane for dinner.

"Haven't I seen you before?" Diane asked Keith, putting down her soup spoon and looking at him closely across the restaurant table.

"Sure, yesterday," Keith insisted playfully. "Remember?"

"No, I'm sure..." she studied his face. Keith gazed at her, wiggling his eyebrows. "I know. You rescued my term paper. That day in the street."

Keith's facial contortions stopped as his jaw fell slack. "You're right. The girl in the pink jacket. How could I not remember someone as beautiful as you?"

"You must have had something else on your mind," Diane said gravely. "I could tell by the look on your face. Of course, it could have been pain. Your ears were sort of a dull red."

Keith grinned at the memory: standing outside Marcy's apartment in the wind and the blowing leaves, waiting for her to lead him into the library basement, and finding what he found there...It might have been a million years since he had met the elves, seeing how completely his life had changed. In fact, he had been sitting at this same table in this same restaurant with Marcy.

It felt different with Diane, though. He liked Marcy, but she had never been his girlfriend. She had deliberately avoided having him think of her as one, first because of Carl, and later, Enoch. He was glad she had. The look on Enoch's face when he told him what the score was... *Those two really do belong together.* Now Diane was sitting here, waiting to hear what he was going to say next. She was interested in him. He twitched his invisible whiskers happily.

Diane watched his face with amusement. "Doing a spell?" she inquired, imitating him.

"Nope. Just checking the results." She noticed things easily, Keith observed. *Better be careful not to lead her unintentionally to the elf village*, he thought, *if we're going to spend a lot of time together.* He rather hoped they would. He understood very well how Marcy had felt that evening, trying to decide whether or not to tell him about the class. "What year are you?"

"Freshman," Diane grimaced. "Before you say it, I know. 'There's nothing lower than a freshman.' Except pledges," she finished, with satisfaction.

"Not joining the Greek tradition?" Keith teased.

Diane waved sororities away. "No time," she stated. "I've got to hustle if I want to stay at Midwestern."

"Is that why you're selling handcrafts?"

Diane shrugged. "It's a job. I suppose you're from Illinois?" Keith nodded. "Well, I'm from Michigan. It costs a lot more for me to go here than for you. I have to pay out-of-state tuition. And I really wanted to come here. They have the best Health Sciences school in the country. I'm going to be a dietitian. I'm on a grant from a local merit scholar's association, and the National Merit Scholarship Program, but it is really tough to pull it all together without outside income. Even with it, it's tough. I may have to go home to a Michigan school, where I can afford the tuition, and maybe live at home." She made another face. "But I don't want to. I like it here. It's the first real privacy I've ever had. I have three sisters."

"I have two. I hope your folks have got more than one bathroom," Keith said sympathetically.

"Well, no. We fight about it a lot. I pleaded with my father to build on another one. You know what he said? 'It's too expensive. Next fall you go to college. Why bother?' I really don't want to have to go home."

"I'd hate to see you leave, now that I've found you. Maybe we can get in some of the same courses. What are you taking?"

"Oh, English, European history, biology, Mythology 248—"

"No kidding!" Keith exclaimed. "Me, too."

"Terrific," Diane said eagerly. "Want to study together?"

"You took the words out of my mouth, gorgeous." He regarded Diane with growing affection. The thought of having her vanish next year was too much for him. He put two and two together and came up with an interesting sum. In seconds, his imagination formulated a shiningly brilliant idea to keep her at Midwestern. The obvious solution. "If you're having trouble making it financially, what about other grants?"

"I've tried. There's no such thing as a grant for Nutritional Sciences."

"You're a mythology student." Keith took a deep breath. "Why not apply for the Alfheim scholarship?"

"Alfheim, like the Norse myth?" she asked. "I've never heard of it before."

"No," said Keith, though it had been that which inspired the name. She *was* quick. "Frederick Alfheim is a renowned scholar of mythology. It's a national grant. If you get a recommendation from the Myth professor and apply, you could get it."

"That would be great," Diane said, her blue eyes brimming with hope. "How much do they offer?"

"Oh," said Keith airily, "full tuition. You still have to pay for your books and room and board, but it helps."

"It sure would! Where can I find an application?"

"I'll bring you one when I see you tomorrow."

Diane tilted her head and peered at him through her eyelashes. "Who said we were getting together tomorrow?" she asked, tossing her hair back. The gesture reminded him of Candlepat. He clamped down instantly against any thoughts of the elves as if he believed she was a mindreader.

"I did, just now. Any objections?"

"None at all. Uh-oh," she caught sight of his watch and grabbed his wrist to get a better look. "My God, ten-thirty! I've got to get out of here. I'll turn into a pumpkin if I don't." Noticing the worried look on Keith's face she sputtered, "I'm just kidding!"

"I hope so," Keith said, recovering. "'There are more things on Heaven and Earth than are dreamed of in your philosophy, Horatio.'"

"You're weird, Keith, but I could get to like you." Diane chuckled. She pushed back from the table and let Keith help her on with her coat. Blowing him a kiss, she whisked out into the darkness. He glowed after she left for a long while. Then he started to worry how he would approach the Little Folk about what he had just done.

"This is vun of your more disastrous feats of inspiration, Meester Doyle," the Elf Master said, when Keith went to see him the next day. Holl was already in possession of the whole story, but even he had to admit that Keith's imagination might have taken him too far. "Creating a mock scholarship, tch! The resources of this infant company vill not be able to bear many of your ideas, if they are like this. Have you so easily forgotten your concern over the taxes?"

Keith hastened to explain. "Of course I haven't, but we don't have to give her the money right away. It can wait until the fall when tuition is due. I'll buckle down. I'm sure we can bring in enough extra by then. She's a good student. She deserves a break, and I couldn't think of anything else except inventing a phony scholarship." The Master didn't look convinced of the idea's value. "She works for one of the stores selling our stuff. You wouldn't be wasting money. It'd be just like paying another employee. And," he played a card he hoped would be a trump, "you told me that I could reasonably expect thirty to forty per cent of the profits from Hollow Tree, and I only took ten. Out of state tuition doesn't come anywhere near the other twenty to thirty percent."

"I can add, Meester Doyle."

"He could be right. He is working hard enough, Master," Holl put in. "Widdy, are you sure? Did you have to promise this girl? You've only just met her."

"You haf only just met her?" the Master echoed, aghast.

"No, wait," Keith insisted. "She's special."

"You are infatuated."

"It's not like that. I thought about it. I just, uh, talked before I thought." Keith appealed to the Master, who stonily shook his head.

"I cannot consider it. You must take back your promise."

Keith sighed. "I didn't promise her anything. I just said she could apply to you for a grant. And she really does need the money." The

Elf Master looked him up and down, and Keith fidgeted, ashamed of being so greedy. "I'm sorry. It was an impulse. It was just that I didn't want to lose her after just one semester."

"Your feelings are that strong?" the Master leaned back in his chair to study Keith's face.

"I didn't know, Keith Doyle," Holl added, softening.

Keith waved their sympathy away. "You'll need all the capital you can get to move out of here. Forget it. I know I shouldn't ask."

"Since vhen haf you not asked vhen you vanted something? Very well," the Master waved a hand to forestall interruption. "You haf done a foolish thing, but you mean vell. Certainly if ve can be imposed upon by your generosity, ve need not suffer alone. She may haf her scholarship, if I meet her and I like her."

"You will," Keith promised. "You will."

Chapter 29

Jubilant, Keith set out the next morning with his head full of plans for legitimizing the Alfheim Scholarship. The Elf Master would surely like Diane, and then she wouldn't have to leave the University next year. It was a perfect solution. He whistled a tune to the birds perched in the thornbushes. What a perfect day. If it hadn't been for his problems with the IRS, Carl, and the Historical Society, the world would have seemed perfect to Keith.

He crossed the campus, cutting behind the cafeteria annex of Power Hall, and headed for the entrance. Absently, Keith ducked a fast frisbee game that was going on in the sunshine right under the windows of the Food Service office. His mind was deeply concerned with how to sell enough Hollow Tree merchandise to make up for the hole in the bank account that Diane's tuition would leave. They needed another good idea for new product. Keith knew there was a goodly balance of cash building up, but that a bad month could kill their advantage. Catra still complained that they weren't making money fast enough. For a culture that never used money, they sure took to the concept in a hurry.

"Keith Doyle?" asked a man's voice from behind him. "Keith Doyle of Hollow Tree Industries?"

"Yeah?" Keith answered, turning around.

He caught a brief glimpse of huge meaty arms just before his back was slammed painfully into a shadowed corner of the dorm wall.

Keith looked wildly at the two burly thugs holding him and at the mustachioed man in the neatly tailored spring suit behind them. Standing away at a respectful distance was a middle-aged policeman in uniform. "Who are you? What do you want?" Neither of his guards spoke. The tailored suit gave him a fierce white-toothed smile that made Keith very uneasy.

"I'm Victor Lewandowski. I'm the president of the Local #541. I've seen your goods. Nice stuff. But there's something missing from your stock. No union label."

"Union?" Keith asked. "I don't have to put union labels on merchandise to sell it."

"If it's made in this state it does. This is a closed-shop state. That means your employees have to belong to a union. I want a list of your workers so we can make sure they're getting fair representation."

"No! I mean, I don't have any employees. I make some of it and I sell stuff on consignment for friends." Keith squirmed uncomfortably in the grip of the two men and watched hopefully over their shoulders for anyone he knew. Maybe he could telegraph S.O.S. with his eyebrows or something. The cop, who was standing with his thumbs hooked into his belt, looked sympathetic but stayed neutral.

"I don't believe you. You got stuff in maybe twenty stores. You restock quickly. Nobody's got that many friends." He nodded to his henchmen, who dragged Keith a few inches away from the brickwork then dashed him back against it. Keith wheezed, the air knocked painfully out of him. Lewandowski waved the policeman over, who unbuttoned the upper right hand breast pocket on his uniform shirt and drew from it a paper which he unfolded and handed to Keith.

The man on Keith's left let go of his arm enough for him to bend it toward the policeman and take the paper.

"This is a court notice signed by Judge Arendson, ordering you to release to me a list of the names and addresses of all persons working for you, doing business under the name Hollow Tree Industries," Lewandowski said. "If you refuse you will be considered in contempt of court. You understand?"

Keith nodded weakly.

"Good." The union boss raised an eyebrow and the two men let go of Keith. "I'll expect to hear from you. My people will be keeping an eye on you. Just remember that. You look worried." Lewandowski smiled his shark's grin again. "You shouldn't be. Just cooperate with us, and we'll cooperate with you."

They left him clutching the paper in the shadows.

Keith spent a good part of the day in the college computer center studying the Illinois Business Statutes on unions and coaxing the school's mainframe computer through its graphics program. He wondered if he should tell anyone about the union men. The Little Folk were already worried about the proposed demolition and the mysterious magazine articles being published. The thought of anyone else snooping around would likely be too much for them.

"I've gotta tell Holl anyway," Keith resolved, typing furiously. "And the Master. They'll have some ideas on how to deal with it."

After a few hours work, he was able to produce some realistic looking forms on a laser printer that bore a reasonable resemblance to the handful of scholarship applications he had picked up that morning at the Guidance Center. 'ALFHEIM SCHOLARSHIP,' the letterhead announced proudly. Keith blew the computer a kiss and tucked two copies of each page into his briefcase.

Diane met him that afternoon in a classroom on the 10th level of the library and filled them out. She was excited about meeting the mysterious Mr. Alfheim. "It's such a great scholarship I wonder why I never heard of it before."

"You're not a mythology major," Keith pointed out. While she was writing he read over her shoulder. "Londen, Diane G. What's the G for?"

"Grace," she explained, "and boy, were my parents wrong."

"No," Keith assured her. "They were right. You're beautiful. And graceful."

"But look at me," she said, with a nervous giggle. "I'm so nervous I'm trembling. Look at my hand." She held it up for Keith's inspection.

"You'll be fine," Keith assured her, sidling around the table and sitting down across from her. He kissed the hand, unsuccessfully avoiding the point of her pen. "Mr. Alfheim will like you, I'm positive. You have the recommendation?"

She giggled, and leaned over to wipe his face with a kleenex. "You have a blue spot on your cheek. Yes, I've got it right here. Mr. Frazier didn't know what I was talking about, but he gave it to me. You're sure you have your facts right? Mr. Alfheim is coming here? Today?"

Keith nodded. "Absolutely."

"But *why* is he here? I haven't even applied yet."

"Oh, he's here to interview me," Keith said, watching out the door for the Master. "I'm an applicant too. You'll have to hurry. I don't know when he'll get here."

Diane slapped her pen down. "*You're* applying? Then I won't. I'm sure you need the money as badly as I do."

"*No!*" Keith whirled back to her. "If you don't get it you won't be back next fall. It's okay, I'm really in better shape." For several seconds they just stood there.

Diane blushed and reached out to touch his hand. "I didn't know it meant that much to you."

"Um...I guess it does." He squeezed her fingers and leaned across the table to kiss her. She didn't protest, but she did lean forward, eyes closing, until their lips touched, joined. Keith felt skyrockets going off in his head.

After a little while, Diane giggled. "Your mustache tickles." She opened her eyes, fingers tracing his upper lip. "That's funny. You don't have one. Must have been your hair...."

"Ahem!" said a voice from behind him. Surprised, Keith jumped to his feet. Diane did the same. The Elf Master stood in the doorway, looking as uncomfortable as Keith had ever seen him. The little teacher was wearing a grey pin-striped suit, white shirt, tie, shiny black shoes, and a fedora. His lips were pressed together. Keith stared, his own lips quivering with amusement.

"Mr. Alfheim, I presume?" he said with the utmost control, when he recovered his voice. *If I laugh*, he thought, *he'll kill me.*

"Zo, Mees Londen, tell me about yourself." The Master was making himself comfortable. With his air of confidence, it didn't matter that his feet couldn't quite touch the ground from the seat of the old padded armchair. Diane didn't notice. Her eyes were fixed on his.

"Well, I'm from Michigan. I'm the eldest of four children, all girls. My father works for Ford. I'm majoring in the Health Sciences. I have a GPA of 3.47 on a four point scale." At that point, her confidence broke down, and she appealed to the Master. "I don't know what else you want to know."

"What do you think?"

"Well...I was fascinated by the customs that evolve in primitive cultures which bring out their hopes of life after death, and how little a person changes even though he no longer has a corporeal body."

"Yes, although it is said...." The Master began, but Diane never slowed down enough to let him speak.

"And in the Hawaiian myth of the tree with fragile branches, that only an old spirit can attain the journey's end obviously shows that they didn't believe any death brings wisdom to anyone but those who died of old age."

"I do not believe so. In *The Masks of God* by...."

"Joseph Campbell. Yes, that's where I read it. It's really deep stuff. And I've read Bulfinch, and all the Avenel books, but my...."
It was the little teacher's turn to interrupt.

"How interesting that you have gone into so much depth," he said gently, "but I am asking about you."

Diane seemed flummoxed by his question, and Keith came to the rescue.

"I think, Mr. Alfheim, that she is demonstrating her knowledge of the subject. For the mythology scholarship. Isn't that what you want to hear?" Keith prompted him.

"No." The Elf Master coolly stared Keith down. "I vish to hear about her, personally. Mythology does not change over the centuries. It is only added to and interpreted. Your turn to speak will come next." He turned back to Diane.

"Well, I've filled out the forms. And here's the recommendation from my mythology professor." She handed them over to the Elf Master who gave them a cursory glance, and laid them aside.

"What brings you to Midvestern?" he inquired.

"It is the best school in the country for my major. I love to cook, and I was good in Chemistry. It seemed logical to combine the two in my career."

"Yes, that smacks of logic," the Master nodded, approvingly. "To combine vocation vith avocation. But how do you plan to extend your education through the study of mythology?"

Diane noticed Keith watching her, and was suddenly conscience stricken. "Look, here, Mr. Alfheim, I feel bad. I've been talking about myself, and Keith is really the applicant. I just found out about the scholarship yesterday. It's him you should concentrate on."

"You are qvite right, Mees Londen. But soon. Meester Doyle, von't you excuse us?"

Keith didn't want to go, but the Elf Master peered at him over the rims of his gold glasses, and he remembered that this was supposed to be the first time they had met. Clearing his throat, Keith stood up. "I'll be in the next room if you want me."

Forty-five minutes later, the door opened.

"Meester Doyle, come in here, please?" The Elf Master gestured him in. "No, don't leave, Mees Londen. You may find this interesting and instructive."

"Yes, sir." Obediently, she sat, hands folded nervously before her while the Elf Master enjoyed himself, grilling Keith on his fund of mythical knowledge.

Keith spent the next half-hour having his brain turned inside out on every facet of mythology that he had ever heard of, and a lot that he hadn't. The Elf Master solemnly corrected him on minor points, shook his head sadly at mistakes on major ones, and penciled little notes on the back of Keith's carefully forged forms. Keith was frustrated, because he wanted to be alone with the Elf Master long enough to tell him about the union organizers and ask his advice.

At last, after Keith had reached a state of unbearable discomfort, the impromptu oral exam came to an end.

"I haf heard enough!" the Elf Master announced, folding the papers and putting them in his pocket. "Meester Doyle, it was most enjoyable talking to you. Mees Londen," he stood up and took her hand, "you are a charming young lady. I approve you."

"Does that mean you're giving me the scholarship?" Diane asked, hopefully, standing up to shake hands, and found herself towering substantially above the head of her benefactor. He appeared not to observe the discrepancy in their heights. Keith stood up, too, towering over them both.

"Yes. That is precisely vhat I do mean."

"Oh, thank you....Oh, Keith, I'm so sorry!" Diane rushed over to condole with him, and turned back to the Master to explain. "I mean I'm grateful, but I'm sorry for him, too."

Keith made a show of looking disappointed. "Uh, yeah, that's too bad," as Diane expended sympathy on him, but inwardly he was cheering. The Elf Master hmmmphed to himself as he went out the door. "Caught in your own net," he said over his shoulder to the room at large. Diane threw her arms around Keith and the door closed on them.

Chapter 30

When at last he was able to seek the Master out to ask his advice, the red-haired teacher nodded solemnly at Keith's caution.

"You vere correct not to announce this generally. Very vise. Mit care, it should not become necessary to alarm the others."

"But vhat…I mean what do I do?" Keith pleaded.

"My suggestion is that you obtain legal advice. There is nothing you can do to discourage them by yourself. Call a counselor. Yours is not an isolated case. There must be legal recourse."

The ad in the Yellow Pages pinpointed attorney Clint Orczas as a labor relations specialist. Keith had no trouble getting an appointment to discuss his problem.

"No fee for consultation," Orczas said cheerfully, showing Keith into a handsome walnut paneled room lined with thick books. He had smooth dark hair slicked back over his forehead, and smooth, swarthy skin. "I don't start charging until after we decide if you need me." He gestured to a deep leather chair and sat down at a shiny black onyx-topped desk, tenting his fingers.

"Thanks," Keith said. "Because I don't have a whole lot of money."

Orczas spread his hands. "Who does? Please, tell me your story."

Keith described his encounter with the union organizers and handed him the court order. Orczas examined the signature closely and put the paper down with a sigh.

"That's Arendson, all right. I've seen a lot of these in my day. What they're doing is considered legally questionable, but it takes a long time and a lot of courtroom gymnastics to fight."

"That isn't fair."

"I know," the lawyer said solemnly. "But there's a loophole that keeps allowing such abuses to go on. Ideally, you know, these unions defend the rights of their members."

"Can you help me?" Keith asked.

"Well, probably not. Some of these cases take up to three years to resolve. By then, a lot of the businesses go under. I would have to ask you for a $5,000 retainer just to get going. It could cost as much as ten to twenty thousand dollars more."

Keith blanched. "I can't afford that, not in a million years. So what can I do?"

"Free advice," Orczas said, handing back the court order. "You have two choices: beat 'em or join 'em. I'm sorry."

"It's not my day," Keith complained to Rick as they sat in the first Inter-Hall Council meeting of the new year. "Well, it started out being my day, but it isn't now."

"Probably someone else's day. Try the lost and found," Rick said offhandedly while taking a huge handful of potato chips out of a bag they were sharing. "No, it's Groundhog Day. That's your trouble." He stuffed the chips into his mouth and reached for more.

The Council was engaged in a huge fight over the parking lot distribution. Keith and Rick weren't interested, and were watching the bloodshed with glee. To Keith's relief, Rick had forgiven him for turning his coat at the fall meeting, and now offered to back him up on reversing the vote. "You understand it's because I don't really care, don't you? 'Cause if I cared a damn about the library or the gym, I'd probably have broken your nose for screwing around like that." Keith took a handful of chips and crunched them one by one.

Carl, as usual, was in the thick of the argument. Keith hadn't seen much of him since Marcy had started going out with Enoch, which suited him fine. Nothing new was being proposed during the debate by either side. It seemed to go nowhere. To Keith it confirmed all the worst and most humorous theories about committees. Instead, he sat back in his desk and thought about Diane. He called up before him her face and figure, and the sound of her voice, her laugh as he bashed himself against the door.

"Thank you, delegates," Lloyd Patterson said, finally getting the contenders back to their sides of the room. "We'll take a vote on that. Now, all in favor...?"

More arguing. Keith wondered what he should do about the list the union man wanted. The last thing he wanted was to have attention drawn to the elves in any way. They were paranoid, and with reason. He was very proud of the trust they had in him. He liked them all, even the ones that didn't like him. They had so much character, if that was the word he meant. They seemed more real than the other people with whom he interacted every day. He wished that the first thing he had ever done that they'd heard about wasn't a speech advocating tearing down their house.

"Okay," the chairman said, standing up. "The vote is about evenly split. No clear majority. We'll have to get votes from the members in absentia. You know who they are. Tell 'em to get in touch with me. Any other old business?"

Keith was on his feet, arm in the air. "Doyle, Power Hall."

"Chair recognizes Doyle."

"Regarding the new library project?"

Patterson raised an eyebrow at him. "Something new, I hope, Doyle?"

"I would like to move that the previous ballot be set aside and the vote taken again on the measure."

"On what grounds?"

"Well," Keith urged, as if it was obvious. "In light of the interest shown in Gillington Library by the Historical Society, I think we have to hold off on any action for when they come through. Nobody's interested in preserving the old gym building, so we could approve that one right away."

"I see. Has the Society sent any guarantee of its protected status yet? We don't want the old dud standing in place of progress if there isn't a guarantee that they want to declare it a monument."

"No," Keith admitted. "I've been phoning, but they haven't returned my calls." The last time he had tried, he been handed the runaround by a secretary who tried to convince him the Director was in a meeting, when Keith was sure the guy must only be out to lunch. The delegates weren't impressed. A few of them heckled Keith, calling for him to sit down. He tried again to make them see sense. "Look, wouldn't you feel really stupid if we tore down Gillington just as they declared protected status for it?"

Lloyd asked him in a bored voice, "Do you move for a second vote?"

"Yes."

"Seconded," said Carl Mueller, standing up. Keith was gratified until he saw the look in Carl's eye. The big student wasn't doing it for him. He wondered who Carl was doing it for, and why.

"Fine. Vernita, call the roll."

In a few moments, it was all over, again. The Inter-Hall council, with the exception of Rick, now loudly in favor of the new gym along with Keith, voted precisely the same way it had the last time. Keith felt cast down. Lloyd Patterson acknowledged the count, and ordered it noted for the minutes.

"You might also be interested to know that the other voting bodies in the University are split on the subject," he said. "I'm proud to say that we will cast the tie-breaking vote when our delegation joins the Administrative council this spring. Movement to adjourn?"

Keith left feeling lower than before. He went out the rest of that week to canvass the rest of his customers for February orders and the January receipts. Diane was working, so it seemed the most useful thing he could do with his time.

Among the Little Folk, the real estate frenzy was on. Over the weekend Keith took out three tours of little people, and all of them insisted he pass by the same piece of property he and the other two elves had found: the forested plot with the house on the hill and the stream flowing through. The place just cried out 'privacy,' surrounded as it was by fields with pale blonde rows of winter wheat showing on them and a nature preserve on one side, and the river on another, and more forests and hilly fields all around. There was a tinkling little cascade from the tributary as it fell into the icy waterway, sort of a miniature waterfall, and everyone stopped for a longing stare. Keith had to admit that it would be a perfect place for the elves to live. They never saw anyone in the house or on the road, so no one remarked on Keith's repeated presence.

A few of the older ones, openly enjoying their trip, mellowed by the wintry sunshine, forgave Keith for his recklessness, understanding now that he had been acting from ignorance, and that he was trying to amend his mistake. The collie was back during his third run, panting at them in red-tongued good humor, his breath clouding in the cold air. Keith waved out the window at it, and it barked playfully at him.

Curran, Keva and a few of the others sat huddled in the back seat for the last trip on Sunday. They had issued bitter complaints to Keith about having to hide under the tarpaulin on the trip out of town. Wisely, he put their ire down to nervousness at riding in an automobile and ignored it. Other than gripes, they were stonily silent all the way out to the rural roads, until he began to drive past the farms. Some of the old ones, who remembered having their own animals and fields, chatted among themselves in wistful undertones, too low for Keith to overhear. They never spoke directly to him. At odd moments, he called out a sort of running travelogue, telling his passengers where they were, how many people lived in this or that town, and inquired whether or not anyone needed him to stop. There were no replies to his pleasantries. He felt as though he was talking to himself. He resented that he was no more than a taxi driver until he looked in the rearview mirror at the back seat. All of the oldsters were quiet, and one of the old ladies was weeping into a corner of her apron. Keith was touched and a little embarrassed for his now-evaporated ire. Turning back toward home, he found that he was feeling sorry for the people who had lived for forty years in a concrete cellar.

Holl was waiting just outside the wall when Keith rolled up. The old ones debarked, and Holl rode with Keith to the parking lot. "You look as though some conversation would be welcome," he told Keith.

"Hello!" Keith said, rubbing his ears. "Is that a voice? I just wanted to make sure I wasn't going deaf. I haven't heard so much silent disapproval since I was in fifth grade math class."

With a nod, Holl studied the snow-covered street, pawed the puddled slush with his toe. "Those others can be trying. Come back with me. We'll have a drink. There's something I wish you to see."

"Oh, no," Keith said, remembering the little old lady and her quiet tears. He didn't feel equipped to deal with more emotions. "Thanks anyway."

"I insist," Holl stated. "You need one."

In a short while, they were seated around one of the long tables in the dining chamber with cups of spiced cider. Keith was pleased to accept one that held about eight ounces, and had evidently been made particularly with him in mind, being about half again larger than the one Holl held. He fingered the carving, which showed Holl's favorite ivy pattern.

"It's a gift to you," Holl asserted. "It will wait in a place of honor until each time you come to drink with us. You're popular.

They talk about nothing else than their outings, leaving us younger ones to work on woodcrafts. I thought this last group would be the hardest, but there's those of us who don't want you to go away with a sour taste."

"Not after this stuff." Keith turned the cup around approvingly. "It's very smooth. Not too strong, is it?"

"It's between weak and strong," Holl admitted. "Home pressed. You've been past that place again?" Keith knew which one he meant.

"Three times today."

"We've kept up with the real estate news. The very size of the numbers in each advertisement have us all scared."

"I know." Keith sipped his cider. "Me, too. I haven't got a hope to get a mortgage for you while I'm still in college. I don't know what else to do."

"That's for later. For now, we have an order to make of power tools," Holl said. "How shall we get them?"

"Where are you ordering them from?" Keith asked.

"Martin Tools. The address is Little Falls."

"That's just down the street," Keith told him. "It's a suburb of this town. Why don't I just pick them up?"

"That will do nicely," Holl nodded, refilling their cups. "You are very good to us. The Master has told me about the nosy men from the union. If we can do anything to help you avoid them, let us know."

"I will," Keith said fervently, remembering the rough hands of the president's henchmen.

"I have a theoretical case to put you," Holl continued. "What would you do if you liked something that was plainly out of your financial reach?" Holl peered at him. "Speaking theoretically, that is."

"Oh, I don't know. If it was that far away, I'd kiss it goodbye."

"But if you truly wanted to have it, come what may?" Holl pressed him. "A very attractive purchase, one that many people would want to possess as well. If it meant everything to you."

"I'd see if the owner would take a down payment," Keith said promptly, joining in the spirit of Holl's question, and trying to imagine a *thing* of his dreams, something that would tempt even the thrifty Holl. "before anyone else could sweep it out from under me. I could secure it that way, and then I'd figure out some way to take out a loan. Sell the family jewels. Steal candy from babies."

"Ah." Holl said, meditatively. "The elders think down payments are too modern. In their day, as they are so fond of telling me, you bought only what you could pay for on the spot with cash, truck or hard work."

"Things were cheaper in their day," Keith moaned. "Now trying to pay up all at once takes a miracle."

The phone rang and rang at the Historical Society office. Keith counted sixteen burrs before the secretary picked it up. "Hello, Historical Society."

"Hello? My name's Keith Doyle, and I just want to know...."

"Just a moment please," she said pleasantly, and put her hand over the phone. Her mouth twisted sourly. "Chuck, it's that kid again."

Charles Eddy, director of the Midwestern Illinois Historical Society, barely looked up from the Chicago Tribune crossword puzzle he was doing. "He must think this office is full of self-righteous little old ladies running around inspecting houses. We haven't made the decision yet. I don't know when we're making the inspection on which the decision will be based. Other matters take priority." What Eddy meant was when the inspector came back from vacation, and when the departmental Buick was back from the shop, but the secretary couldn't say that, and she knew it.

"I'm sorry, Mr. Doyle," she told the receiver. "We will most certainly be in touch with you when anything is happening. Yes. Thank you for calling." She put down the receiver. "Whew!"

Eddy smiled, filling CHRONICLE in six down for 'historical account,' "Perhaps we should hire him. I don't have the energy to make that sort of fuss any more."

February and most of March passed by. Keith was busy, sandwiching his schoolwork and the Master's classes with sales sweeps to increase the Hollow Tree customer list. He had the uncomfortable feeling that he was being followed on his rounds, but he said nothing of his suspicions to anyone but Holl and the Elf Master. All the rest of his available time was spent with Diane.

He would have considered the rest of the school year perfect, if it hadn't been for his worries about time running out on the library. The Historical Society, after much pursuit by Keith, had promised to take the matter up no later than early May, and with that Keith had to be content. He knew he was pushing it with them, but profits weren't rolling in as quickly for Hollow Tree as he hoped. The elves who were making the merchandise began to look tired, and Keith avoided asking them to hurry any more.

On the profit side of the ledger, there were more of them making things. After Keith's spate of tour-guiding, a substantial number of the oldsters began to participate. Holl had reported to him that they were still talking as if the Big Person was selling them out, but they were working harder than any youth, and with more experience. In some cases, centuries more, Keith suspected. He was delighted. And the union seemed to have backed off from harassing him.

The semester broke for Easter vacation, and the students vanished from campus like smoke in the wind. In spite of their concern for their home, the elves still insisted on presenting Keith with his commission check before he left for the holiday break. A glance at it assured him that it was enough to pay for next semester's books and fees. "Say, we did really well this month."

"It's not enough," Catra said sadly, looking over Holl's shoulder as he showed Keith the ledger books. "It takes such a long time for the balance to grow."

"Wow! I didn't know we were making so much!" Keith exclaimed with pleasure, whistling at the total.

"You don't know what you're collecting?" Enoch was scornful.

Keith shrugged, stroking his whiskers with a bemused forefinger. "Well, picking up the checks one at a time, I don't really notice. By the way, Teri Knox suggested an idea to me for some new merchandise that would probably just walk out the doors. I wanted to ask what you thought of producing jewelry." He smiled at Enoch, inviting him to speak up. "I've seen the necklace you made Marcy. It's terrific."

"It'd be easy enough to make more," Enoch admitted. "But I'd make none as special. That's for her alone."

"A new idea wouldn't go amiss," Sion agreed. "Something to catch the eye. It is a concern that we do not want to reach market saturation. I was reading in the Journal…"

"As to that," Catra said, turning to Keith, "I want to ask if you'd read…"

"By the way, I might be nosy, but are you ever going to bring Marcy down here to meet the folks?" Keith asked, unaware that he was interrupting.

"Ye're being nosy," Enoch asserted, "but the answer is, not until all you Big Folk have cleared out of campus. And the sooner you go, the sooner that'll be."

"I can take a hint," Keith said cheerily, and strode away.

"Wait up, Keith Doyle," Catra called, but he was already out the classroom door.

The phone rang at the home of Clarence Wilkes. The old man was watching television. He had it up loud because he was getting a little deaf, and if it hadn't been the station break, he would never have heard it ring. He levered himself out of his rocking recliner, as creaky in its joints as he was himself, and answered it. "Hallo-o?"

"Is this 543-2977?"

"Yes. Who's calling, please?" Wilkes asked, trying to place the voice.

"I'm interested in the piece of wooded property you have for sale. I saw your sign out in front. How much are you asking?"

"Wa-al," Clarence calculated. The caller sounded like a city man. He talked clean, no drawl. "Thousand an acre, twenty acres. You interested in buying, mister?" Might as well throw in a little padding for the years he'd spent farming it.

"I might be. Let me see. A thousand dollars an acre, eh?…Um…" the voice became thoughtful. "I'm not that crazy about banks. I do as little with them as I can. How about a contract between just us? I'll pay *you* the interest instead."

This caller was kin to Clarence Wilkes under the skin. Banks had been the source of half his troubles all his adult life, but he learned their lingo down pat. "Me neither," he admitted. "Two thousand down. Two hundred a month with five percent simple interest after that. You can move in after I've seen the down payment, and your check don't bounce. Taxes is your problem."

"I'll be getting back to you, then. I'm interested, but there's people I've got to check with."

"Suit yourself," Wilkes said. "By the way, I'm Clarence Wilkes."

"Pleased to know you," said the voice on the phone. "I'm…Keith Doyle."

Chapter 31

"You're crazy," Diane told him as the Mustang hummed along the country roads. "You can't drive me all the way to Michigan. Drop me at the bus station in Joliet, or something."

"Why should I?" Keith glanced away from the road.

"Don't do that!" Diane pointed back at the steering wheel. "You'll hit something. It's not that I'm ungrateful, but isn't it a silly thing to do? It's six hours out of your way!"

"I'm famous for being silly. How else can I monopolize your company?" he asked, skimming around a file of children on bicycles. "Besides, why go Greyhound? It takes longer than I will, and you can't get all the way home on a bus."

"Oh, all right," Diane grumbled, sitting back in resignation.

"I have a quick detour I want to make. We can catch the highway just north of here."

"You're driving."

Keith steered through the two-signal town and looped around the roads until he was on the wooded stretch near the farm the elves were so crazy about. He liked the place, too. It had a good aura. No…good spirit. Who had told him that? Holl. Holl had said it, that beautiful cold day out looking for wood. His car's springs would never be the same. The second trip to Barn Door Lumber had yielded just as heavy a load. He hoped he wouldn't have to buy new shocks too soon.

He pulled up in front of the farm and took a quick look out the car window. It had been several weeks since he had been here last, and now the leaves were bursting on the trees, almost hiding the house on the hill.

"Nice place," Diane said. "Who lives here?"

"I don't know," Keith told her, "but it's for sale. I like it."

"Me, too." Diane thought about it a moment. "You mean you brought me out here to look at a farm?"

Keith looked a little ashamed of himself. "It's my friend's dream house. I'm just…making sure it's still here."

"It isn't, you know. It's been sold."

"What?" Diane pointed and Keith stared. The "For Sale By Owner" sign had a sticker across it which clearly stated that the property was 'Sold.' "Oh, no." Keith collapsed against the steering wheel. "It can't be sold."

"I thought you said it was just a dream. Keith?" Diane shook him. "What's wrong?"

Keith groaned and threw the car into gear. How can I break it to Holl? his mind cried. "Everything," he sighed.

After a few miles, Keith was resigned to losing the chance at that farm, and cheered up enough to be charming to Diane. She was easy to travel with. She understood that the task of the passenger was to keep the driver from being bored, and told him stories of her life and her sisters and brother, discussed her hopes and plans for the future.

"My dad is really proud of me for winning that scholarship," she said happily. "I called him up right away after we talked to Mr. Alfheim. It takes a lot of pressure off of the family."

"That's great," Keith agreed, pleased as to the success of his subterfuge. Unfortunately, the pressure was off for the elves, too. They didn't have to worry about buying that particular piece of property any more. Well, others would come along, although he was sure they couldn't be as perfect. He hoped that one would before the sheriff showed up with the eviction notice. Shoving the thought forcefully to one side, he thought of a funny story Diane would like and told it to her. Laughter helped to pass the time on the way to Michigan.

"Diane!" Her mother called to her through the kitchen door. Keith's car was just turning out of sight at the end of the street. With a sigh, Diane left the curb where she had been waving good-bye, and went up the stairs into the white frame house. "Telephone, honey." Her mother was waiting with her hand over the receiver. "Keith gone? He's a fine boy. Your father likes him so much. They had such a nice chat last night."

Diane took the instrument with a little nod and smile. "Hello?"

A male voice, Diane couldn't tell how old or young, asked, "May I speak to Keith Doyle?"

"I'm sorry, but he just left for Chicago. He'll be home in about five hours. Is there an emergency?"

The voice sighed. "No. I'll see him when he gets back. Thank you so much."

"You're welcome," Diane acknowledged, puzzled. "Goodbye." The receiver on the other end clicked off.

Chapter 32

The first piece of mail waiting for Keith in his pigeonhole at Power Hall after he returned from spring break was another of the brown envelopes with the warning notice in the corner. Keith shuddered before opening it. All of those envelopes had so far brought him bad news. This one was like its predecessors.

The Internal Revenue Service invited him to call the office to arrange an appointment for an audit of his account. Keith read the letter over and over on the way up to his dorm room, and tore at his hair in dismay.

The letter reminded him that he also had quarterly taxes coming due, and those would have to be paid promptly by the deadline. He made a whirlwind search of his dorm room, desperate to find the new estimated tax forms, but he couldn't remember seeing or receiving them, though the letter made clear mention that they had been sent to him.

Keith sweated over the mathematics, trying to remember exactly how much Hollow Tree had made before the end of the year as he ran downstairs to the dormitory office, hoping to track down the papers.

"Don't know nothin' about it," Anton Jackson said defensively. He was the permanent dorm supervisor of Power and nearby Gibbs Hall, and lived on campus all year round. He aimed a long brown finger at Keith. "This little blond kid picked up your mail every day. He had a letter signed by you. You telling me he was a phony?"

"Oh!" Keith exclaimed, recognizing the description. "Um, no, sorry. He's all right. I forgot all about him. Thanks." Keith shot out into the sunny street.

The sunlight in the elf village matched that upstairs with amazing faith to detail. Keith had to blink, passing through the darkness of the stone stairs and into the clan precinct. He found Holl sitting in the classroom, whittling and distractedly throwing the shavings on the floor. "Hi. I'm back."

"I can see that," Holl said, without glancing up.

"Have you got my mail? I just got another love letter from the IRS. We are in deep trouble. They want to do an audit on us for last year. Did you send in my tax return late or something? That's going to get us nailed, you know."

"No. I sent it in plenty of time." Holl turned toward him, finally letting Keith see his face. He looked worried and unhappy. "Follow me, but wait in the tunnel. Big Folk are not popular today."

All around them, there were signs of activity. Some of the minute elf children were wrapping individual wooden items in newspaper, and carrying them to bigger children, who packed them in boxes or paper bags. The young adults wielded carefully muffled power saws and drills in clouds of sawdust. Others, obviously detailed as caterers, coughed and waved hands before stinging eyes as they brought baskets of food to the workers. The oldsters, eschewing modern equipment, put delicate fragments of wood together with glue. "God, it's Santa's workshop," Keith observed, trying to cheer Holl up. He didn't have the heart to get excited about the missing forms when his friend looked so low. "Where's the reindeer?" he asked under his breath.

"More alien oddities?" Holl sighed. Keith noticed a deep line furrowing between the blond elf's eyebrows.

"What's that mean?"

"Shhh! Here. I've carried a copy with me since it appeared." He handed Keith a sheet on which two slips of newsprint had been reproduced. Keith read them quickly and scoffed.

"The National Informer? Holl, this is a load of crap. Nobody believes them."

"Why then do they have a circulation of over two million? There are the gullible out there."

"Oh, come on," Keith scoffed. "I admit it sounds like a thinly disguised Midwestern, but still!"

"It isn't the only one," Holl corrected him. "There are several others, and have been more since. Catra has them all. Most are revises of this same one, with the words changed around. I keep this one to remind me of the date on which it first appeared. But it's the most recent one," he pointed to the second story on the page, "that worries us the most. It all but identifies Gillington as our base! The others are all but for decamping tonight."

"What do you want me to do?"

Holl considered Keith's offer for a moment. "I thought you could approach the Informer to discover from whom this story comes. They were written by someone who is personally familiar with us."

"I bet it was Lee," Keith said, speculatively. "He's a journalism major, you know."

Holl shook his head. "I doubt that as much as I doubt that it was you who did it, which is what the elders are saying."

"What?"

"They're desperate," Holl offered, turning up his palms in appeal. "They have no other explanation. Will you find out for us, so we can put a stop to it?"

"I'll try," Keith promised, "but first, can we solve *my* little problem? What about the IRS?"

"Your pardon," Holl apologized, embarrassed. "What do you need?"

"Records. Estimated Tax forms," Keith replied. "Can you help me? I've been trying to figure out everything we've done, and I'm confusing myself."

"You're good at that. I'm pleased to see you're not immune to your own skill," Holl said wryly, sounding more like himself. He walked to his hut, emerged with a box of letters, and beckoned Keith back up the tunnel to the classroom. "Come with me, and we'll see what we can see."

The editor to whom Keith spoke at the National Informer was smugly pleased to inform him that they always protected their sources. "The First Amendment, you know," he cackled. "Threats and pleas have no effect on me." He refused to give Keith the name of the anonymous source.

"Well," Keith offered, "what if I said I could get you another article, but I had to make sure I wasn't intruding on your writer's territory? I mean, he might want to send you more, right? But if we're not in the same town, it would be poor journalism to let a corroborating story go…"

"Hmmmmm…" the editor mused. "Mr. Doyle, you're very persuasive, but I still can't give you our source's name. I will tell you he filed the story from Midwestern University."

"Oh," said Keith, not surprised, "that's where I am. I mean, I suppose that you can't give me any other information…?" he inquired hopefully.

"Nope, sorry," he was told. "That will have to do you, son. Can you provide us with corroborating evidence? We pay free-lancers well. Your by-line on a national gazette...." the editor said temptingly.

"Um, no. I, uh, only heard a story from a guy. I'd be a lousy writer. Thanks."

"Okay," the editor said before he hung up. "But if you change your mind, gimme a call."

"Here you are, sir. From November to now," Keith said, spreading his receipts and papers out on a table in the IRS office. He gave one last, longing glance through the storefront-style window at the deep blue spring sky, dotted with fluffy cumulus clouds, before the door of Agent Durrow's cubicle swung shut, cutting off the view. He plumped his briefcase from his lap to the floor, heard the unmuffled *clack* of unwrapped samples banging together. With a quick glance to make sure nothing was broken, he gave all his attention to the IRS agent across the table from him.

When he called to make an appeal for help, it was suggested that he come in to talk to Agent Durrow, who had Keith's file in his possession. That way, it was explained, he wouldn't need to give all the facts of his case all over again. It made him nervous that an IRS agent knew all about him, but he tried to conceal his apprehensions. He turned the slim envelope upside down and shook it to ensure that it was empty. "Like I said, I didn't open until late last year."

"Why didn't you file for a different fiscal year? Say, November to October?" Durrow asked, sifting through the papers. He was a thin-faced, thin-voiced man in a black suit with lapels sharp enough to cut fingers. "You would not have had to send in a 1040 until next year."

"I'm used to filing in a January to December fiscal year, sir. I didn't really think of it as an option."

"Few do," Durrow admitted. "Very well, I will help you with the papers just this once, but I suggest you send for these forms." He opened a drawer in his desk and withdrew a gray pamphlet on which he circled several numbers. "They will assist you in figuring your estimated tax. I regret to say we do not have extra forms here at this time. We are waiting for a shipment. New tax laws. Beyond that, I suggest you find yourself an accountant."

While the agent noted down the figures from Keith's receipts on a legal sheet in his quick, neat hand, he went on with his suggestions. "You should concentrate on keeping track of your expenditures in a ledger…. My, my, isn't that a tidy sum. What did you say are the goods you manufacture?"

"Woodcrafts," Keith said.

"Average price?"

"Oh, five to twenty dollars or so."

Durrow turned a razor-edged glance on him. "How can you have generated so much income by yourself? You are certain you are not using employees to supply your inventory?"

"Why do you ask, sir?" Keith asked.

"Information received," Durrow said austerely. "Well?"

"I make 'em myself, during spring break, Christmas break, you know," Keith said firmly. "Except for things I take on consignment from friends, but they're not working for me. I get ten percent."

"You have income from commissions, then." Durrow jotted that down.

"Yes, sir," Keith said, watching the pencil fly down the page in bewildered concern. "My 1040's there."

"Out of curiosity, I wonder if you know the zoning laws for this town, young man." Durrow acknowledged a shake of Keith's head. "Aha. That school is not zoned for cottage industry. You could be fined for violations if the zoning commission cared to make a fuss."

Keith held out his hands in protest. "Oh, I don't make anything here, sir. I use a…friend's house. And…is there any problem with my finishing things in the school wood shop?"

"No," Durrow allowed, somewhat reluctantly. He looked askance at Keith, having developed skepticism about student businesses in general. "Very well. Based on the income so far this year, you will need to pay in this much per quarter," he jotted down another number, "and if there are increases, you will divide up by the remaining quarters and pay them in that way. Providing there are no irregularities, your account will be entered in our computer files. Your next quarterly payment will be due by the quarter, April 15th."

That gave him a couple of weeks to work it out. Keith agreed, and Durrow went back to the papers. The thin pen scratched out more numbers, adding up the accounts receivable, then the expenses, which he divided into several categories, with remarkable speed. To Keith's eye, it was working out very well. He began to think he might get out of that stifling office and back into the fragrant air, perhaps to take a walk later with Diane; when the approving 'um-hmm's' ceased abruptly. "What's this?" Durrow asked, going through the canceled checks in the latest bank statement, and holding one out to him. "This is a check for $2,000, made out to Cash, and the memo line says only 'down payment.' And another check, 'property tax escrow'?"

Keith goggled at it, forgetting all about the air, the sunshine, or Diane. Two thousand dollars? That was nearly the whole balance! "I don't know."

"It's signed Holland Doyle. Who is Holland Doyle?"

"My nephew, sir." Keith swallowed miserably. "He must have bought something with the company money...a machine, or a car, or something..." He took the check. There were two signatures on the back, and he could read neither of them.

"How old is your nephew?"

"Um...twelve. Almost thirteen."

Durrow's thin eyebrow raised, wrinkling the hairless forehead in precisely two places. "Why do you allow him to sign on *your* checkbook?"

"In case of emergency," Keith said. "He's got more common sense than I have."

"I see." Durrow was amused. A tiny crease appeared at the corner of his mouth. That meant he was smiling. "I strongly suggest that you find out what it was he spent your funds on, so you can submit quarterly taxes. If it is not an appropriate expense, you must pay tax on it as income. That is all for now. You may go. We will be in touch with you."

"Yes, sir." Keith gathered up his papers and fled.

"They must have paid out Diane's scholarship already!" Keith exclaimed out loud, going over the papers again and again on the way back to campus. "Well, I can't ask *her* about it." The fact which worried him most was the huge discrepancy between the tax which was about to fall due, and the size of the remaining balance in the checking account. They weren't even close. The elves certainly wouldn't have any reserves, and his own checking account balance contained only the remains of the commission check he had received before vacation. He thought of calling his father and asking for a loan, but put that aside, recalling a discussion about money his family had had while he was home on break. Any savings in expenditure would be appreciated, Mr. Doyle had said, since Keith's sister Karen would begin college that fall.

"I don't have any choice," he said, resolutely turning the car away from campus. "I've got to save my own skin. The Little Folk are counting on me." It sounded very heroic in his own ears, but he was aware how much of a long shot it would take for him to raise that much money in so little time.

The signs leading up to Matt's Cheese Chalet and Snack Bar mentioned that it sold gifts, so Keith followed an impulse and stopped in. The place, an obvious tourist trap, was made up to look like a Swiss gingerbread building, and screamed 'tacky' at the top of its lungs, but it did indeed sell knicknacks of every description. Keith began to admire the taste and forbearance of shop owners like Ms. Voordman, who showed restraint in her choice of merchandise, if garbage like this was available wholesale. Idiotic little cedar boxes held together by tin hinges and varnish, and stamped with 'Matt's, Illinois,' lay between iron trivets shaped like Pennsylvania Dutch hex symbols and porcelain spoon holders with calico geese painted on the bowls. He sighed, but Matt's was the only new prospect he had been able to turn up all afternoon, and it was already getting close to evening. He had some new ideas, but nothing would bring in cash right now but orders.

"Think of how items like this would jazz up a display," he told Matt, who looked like an ex-truck driver now gone more to fat than muscle, and who liked cheap cigars. Keith smelled the stale smoke in the air when he came in. There was no way he would ever eat a meal in a place like this. He had already lost his enthusiasm for the sale, and was wishing that he hadn't come in. But since he had begun, he might as well finish. "It's for a good cause."

"Nah," Matt said, rubbing his cigar out on the snack counter, narrowly missing one of Maura's precious cooky cutters. Keith cringed, and moved everything subtly away from the restauranteur. "This kinda stuff doesn't *sell*, ya know what I mean? I got troubles with the merchandise I've got, and it's all good stuff. Didja take a look around?"

"Yeah, I did. I don't see how I could compete with what you've got out already." Matt's line featured the very ugliest in junky little gifts. Keith figured he was about a hundred classes above it.

Matt rolled his belly to one side, scratched at his ribs with satisfaction. "Right. So, what's the good cause you were talking about?"

"Oh, nothing," Keith said, preoccupied, starting to put his samples away. There was no hope of a sale here. He had wasted time here, and the IRS was getting impatient. He could feel the hot breath of the auditing computer on his back at this moment. "Junior Achievement."

"Oh, yeah?" Matt stopped scratching. "Where from?"

"Local," Keith said, preparing to trot out his now well-rehearsed tale. "I'm at Midwestern."

Matt's face lost all semblance of joviality. "Really? I think that's interesting. It so happens I have been the local president of the Junior Achievement chapter for the last twelve years, and I know everyone, every single senior advisor, every single kid in the whole organization, and I have never seen you before in my life." He plunged a forefinger against Keith's chest, punctuating every syllable with a stab. "They call that fraud, when some guy tries to make money off the kids. How would you like it if I called the cops, huh?"

"Uh, please don't do that," Keith said, frantically, picturing the officer who had accompanied the union thugs. "Uh, really...my group picked up the skills in a Junior Achievement group in the Chicago area. I buy things from them on consignment. Here," he thrust one of the charmed cookie cutters into the man's hands. "Nice workmanship, isn't it? And if it wasn't for good old J.A., we'd never have gotten anywhere."

Tension eased out from between the man's thick grey brows as the cookie cutter did its magic. Keith breathed again, pulling air into his constricted lungs. "Okay," Matt growled. "But I don't ever want to hear that you're representing yourself as J.A. again, or I'll wanna have a talk with you face to face, get it?" He brandished the cutter in Keith's face.

"Got it," Keith said. Matt slammed the wooden mold down on the counter, heaved himself off the pink plastic stool, and waddled away.

Keith snatched up the cutter and hurried out into the clean spring air. He was happy to have escaped, but he was still without money to pay the quarterly taxes.

Chapter 33

He let himself into the village by way of the class room. The hall-way seemed more remote than usual. It wore an air of forbidding, and Keith felt more than once a compulsion to turn around and leave.

"Security measures," he decided, since there was actually nothing more threatening in the passage. It was protective magic; no, a charm, he corrected himself. He was glad they'd finally taken his advice.

"Hi, Enoch," he said, seeing the black-haired elf reading at a table in the dining hall. "I had a great idea I wanted to talk to everyone about. I figure we can increase our sales, without it costing a penny. All we need to do is get grass-root papers to do writeups on the merchandise. They don't have to focus on the 'factory' at all. They can wrap us by doing the story on the shops we sell to. Ms. Voordman would probably go for it like a shot. Can you tell me where...." His voice faded away as Enoch regarded him in open-mouthed shock.

"Your nerve, Keith Doyle!" Without another word, the elf rose and walked out without letting him finish his question.

"Enoch? Something wrong?"

There certainly must have been. He followed into the sloping passage which led to the clan enclosure. Faces turned toward the entrance when he emerged, to see who was coming down, and turned away again, as if they had all been on one control, as soon as they saw him. He was puzzled and hurt. "Dola? Hey, honey," he began, approaching the child, whom he knew liked him. She was jumping rope and counting out loud near her mother's hut. He bent down to her eye level, his hands on his knees to speak to her. "What's going on down here?" Dola went wide-eyed at his question, pressed her lips together, and kicked him solidly in the shin. While he hopped up and down clutching his bruise, she fled inside, shutting the door on him.

Keith was beginning to get frightened. He hurried over to Curran's clan, and tapped on Holl's door. "Hello? Anyone home?"

"He'll no' be in. Ye may go away now."

Whirling, Keith found himself face to face, or rather, shirt-button to face with Curran himself. The tiny clan chief had never quite gotten over his dislike of the Big Man, and he wore his jaw in a set that would put up with no argument.

"Will he be back soon?" Keith asked, backing away.

"No' soon enow for ye to be waitin' fer him. Go." Keith started to speak, but the elf turned his white-maned head away, refusing to hear Keith's questions.

Keith kept moving, hoping to find Holl or the Elf Master, to ask them what was going on. He needed to find out about the missing two thousand dollars, and fast, but it looked like he wasn't even going to get the time of day. The usually effusive villagers were taciturn and quiet. Conversation stilled as soon as he got near. The only face he saw that didn't blanch on sighting him was Marm's. The bearded elf stood in front of his clan houses, sweeping the pounded walkway with a wisp of straw.

Keith went over to talk to him, willing him to stay where he was until he got to him. "Hi, there."

"Greetings, Keith Doyle," Marm replied, resting his broom on his bent arm. Keith almost fainted with relief to get a friendly response.

"Nice day, isn't it?" he asked. Marm grunted, his usual reply to questions about the weather. Keith pressed on. "You know, I just came down to talk about income taxes, and a great idea I had for publicity, but everyone is acting like I have the plague!"

"What great idea is this one?" Marm asked, friendly as usual, but there was strain in his voice. Whatever was bothering Enoch and Curran seemed to have rubbed off on everyone. Keith swallowed his discomfort.

"Free publicity. What we need are writeups in the local paper," Keith began again with as much enthusiasm in his voice as he could muster, but as he continued, Marm's face turned the color of a boiled beet.

"There you go, and aren't you ashamed of yourself?" Marm demanded, and tossed the broom aside. It clattered on the packed earth floor.

"What?" Keith asked, agog. "Nobody is talking sense today."

"You made the local press. I expect you'll have a hundred copies of your own. Here!" Marm rummaged through one of the huts and emerged with a beechwood stick with a long slit in it, which he thrust into the human's hands.

Keith recognized it as the kind of stick libraries thread through the daily papers, so that no one will steal them and save a quarter. In this case, it had never left the library, so it really hadn't been stolen. "This page, here!" Marm pointed to an article entitled fantastically "Elves Discovered Living In Downstate Illinois!" Keith stared at it, astonishment growing. This one was just like the stories Holl had shown him, but it was in the city newspaper. Alarmed, he began to read.

A source, who asked not to be identified, told the syndicated press that there is proof that a colony of heretofore-believed-mythical creatures is living somewhere in one of the buildings on the Midwestern University campus. And, more damning still was the description of their cottages. There was even an artist's sketch with the article of a small wooden hut, which Keith had to admit did look like one of the clan homes. Marm pointed to a paragraph. "'Witness the wonderful 'nightlights' being sold in the gift-shops. No known science can duplicate such things. Surely they are evidence of magic?' No other has seen our homes. You did it, did you not, you fool? Do you think if they know that they'll be satisfied with toys? No, no, grant me a wish, it'll be! Three wishes! Aren't we under enough pressure already, having to leave our home?"

Keith was dumbfounded. "*I* didn't do this," he protested.

"Then who did? They are saying things here that only you would know. The other stories might have been guesswork, I grant, but you're the one who began to call us elves!"

"I didn't write that article. Look, it mentions the date it was submitted. That was over spring break. I was somewhere between Chicago and Michigan all vacation."

"Ye could have *mailed* it," Marm said darkly. He had never written a letter, and clearly hoped he never would. "I should have believed Carl Mueller the first time when he called you treacherous."

"I swear, this has nothing to do with me!"

"Can ye prove it?" the little man demanded.

"Well, no. Newspapers won't tell who their sources are. You just have to take my word for it. I swear I'd never jeopardize you guys like that. You're my friends."

"So you can't prove it?" Marm picked up his broom. "Well, no one else will talk to you, but I will tell you what they say. They think you are guilty. Until and unless you can prove you are innocent of this mischief, we will fulfill no more orders."

"But wait! You promised," Keith protested. "We have contracts to fulfill. Customers are waiting!" He had visions of Mr. Durrow cranking the wheel on the rack to which a screaming Keith Doyle was tied.

"It is no good," Marm assured him. "You promised, too. You promised us security. Now we will take care of ourselves." The elf went back to sweeping the walk and ignored Keith until he went away.

"Needs work, but it's in pretty good shape," Lee Eisley said, pounding on the walls of the farmhouse. "You're going to have to do something pretty quick about the ceiling in the back, there. There was a lot of leaking."

Holl walked around wonderingly around the place. "Hard to believe it is ours, eh?" he asked softly, more to himself than any of the others. His voice echoed in the empty rooms. Dust mice rolled away from his feet on the polished wood floors. "Ours. Our home."

"How bad is it?" the Elf Master asked, looking over the blueprints.

"Well, If it's drywall, no problem. That's cheap. If it's plaster, that's cheaper, but it takes a lot of patience to get right."

"Ve haf much patience," the Elf Master assured him. "Vhat ve do not haf is much time."

"I've got some tools outside in my station wagon."

"No need," said the Elf Master dryly. "I vill test it for you in a moment."

"Has Ludmilla seen this place yet?" Lee asked. "She'll love it."

"No. No time haf ve had to inform her. You may, if you like." The Elf Master put his nose back into the plans.

"Nine large rooms. One clan will have to share if we are to keep the biggest room as a meeting place," Maura reported, showing them her notes. "The cellar will make a good workshop, since we have no need to place the garden there. Of course, the attic is habitable. The kitchen is of a good size, with a flame stove, but everything is so high."

"Our crafters will take care of that," Holl assured her, taking her hand. "But will they give up each their own roofs after such a long time?"

"Before ve came here, it vas all one roof," the Elf Master assured him. "And in time before that, many roofs. Ve vill adapt. As always ve haf."

Holl peered out the window down the slope of the hill behind the house. Among the weeds were useful herbs and blooming tulips and hyacinths. "There's no reason we can't build if we need more room. I for one would like to see the workshop in the old barn. I don't like sawdust in the bed, nor listening to power tools while I sleep."

"You are correct," the Elf Master nodded, his lips pursed. "It is time ve lived mit confidence, and less like refugees."

"We ought to start moving some of the Folk here right away," Holl suggested. "If we want our own vegetables, we need to plant immediately. And the leak in the roof, and the weak flooring upstairs won't wait long."

"Very vell. I vill ask for volunteers to come out right away to begin vork and set up their homes. If you vill oblige us mit more taxi service, Mr. Eisley?"

"Sure. I'd be happy to. 'Old Farmhouse Becomes Model Craft Community.' It'd make a great magazine story," Lee grinned, looking over the plans and calculating the amount of work the old place would need. "Too bad I can never write it."

Keith slunk out of the library so engrossed in his depression that he walked past without seeing Diane. Clouds were gathering from all corners of the sky, and decided it was going to rain pretty soon. She ran up to kiss him, cheeks flushed red in the brisk spring air. "Hello there, stranger! How about helping me study for Biology? Would you like to have dinner with me tonight, and go on from there? With biology, I mean?" She gave him a slow wink. "Since it's going to be rotten outside."

"Oh, yeah, sure," Keith accepted with a grin. "I think I could eat a horse. At least I think that's what they're serving tonight."

Diane laughed. "You're funny. It's buzzard on Wednesdays."

"You're absolutely right," he said, taking her books and sticking out an elbow for her to grasp.

"I really need help. I think I'm failing the stupid course. Can you believe that? It's no different than high school bio as far as I can tell. What were you doing in the library today?" Diane asked, as they walked toward the dorm.

"Oh, studying," but something in his voice didn't convince her.

"Studying? Studying what?" she asked, sharply.

"Marketing...and a little Sociology," he said sadly. He had a far-away look that puzzled Diane, and she pressed him for more information.

"Keith, I thought we agreed we were always going to be honest with each other." There was a long pause. "Keith?"

"Really, I was just studying," he protested.

"Sure. In the deepest part of the stacks? Come on. You must think I'm really stupid," Diane was annoyed. "*I* know what goes on down there. I was on Level Twelve and I saw you come up the stairs. You never spoke to me, so I followed you out here."

"Diane, I—I wasn't doing anything you would disapprove of, I promise."

"So what were you doing?" she demanded, but before Keith spoke, she held up a hand. "Never mind. I don't want to hear anything you'd say. I'm sure it would all be lies. I thought you really cared for me." She snatched her books out of his hands and stormed away.

"Diane!" he called after her, but she shook her head and kept moving. Keith watched her go with resignation. "I wish a car would hit me right now and end my misery," he said morosely. "There's nothing more that could happen to me."

There was no answer at the office of the Historical Society. Keith spent the evening with his thoughts racing between the quarterly taxes, the mysterious articles, and the elves' unfriendliness. On top of that was Holl's unexplained absence, and his frustration in not being able to explain to Diane what was really going on in the library.

He sighed, gazing out the window from where he lay, watching lighting sear the clouds. Maybe if it rained had enough, he could drown himself without ever getting out of bed.

It was raining the next day, too. Keith dashed between his classes with his head down, as much from unhappiness as the cold wet wind. He spent most of Mythology class watching Diane, who sat four rows ahead of him, with sad, soulful eyes. She noticed his gaze, but turned away with her eyes down. It reminded him of the mass shun in the village, and it depressed him further.

"Keith?" Diane followed him out of the classroom when it was over, and drew him close to the wall. "I just wanted to apologize."

"You don't have to apologize," Keith said, steeling himself to tell her the true story.

"No, I do." She held her hands over his mouth. "I'm sorry. I should believe you. You're a lousy liar. I wouldn't get so upset if…I wasn't so involved. I do trust you. If you say there's nothing to be worried about, I'll believe you." She threw her arms around him and kissed him soundly.

Shedding his gloomy mood all at once, Keith got enthusiastically behind the concept of kissing. "You know," he breathed when they came up for air, "this is the first decent thing that has happened to me all day. Maybe all week."

Diane pouted. "Only decent?"

"Well…" Keith took another sample of longer duration. "A lot more than that." A further kiss assured him it was the best possible anywhere. "Look," he said. "The rain is stopping."

The door at the bottom of the fourteenth level of the stacks creaked open, and Carl hid his key so the distinctive green light wouldn't give him away. He left the classroom door propped open for a quick getaway. It was Wednesday, so there wasn't supposed to be anyone in there. If Doyle or anyone was here, Carl could just say that he forgot something. He was sure that he could get out of any situation.

He felt his way in, hands out for the iron maidens. The room seemed much wider in the dark. Once he touched the wall, he eased first one way, then the other, feeling for the low door. His fingers showed him the lip of the entrance, and he crouched down and walked hunched over along the tunnel's rough cement floor. His soft-soled shoes made a tiny 'tok' sound each time he set down a foot, but he congratulated himself that he wasn't making any noise.

Down at the tunnel's far end, Dola, and Moira and Borget, two of her friends, were playing in the empty dining hall. They had already detected his presence and reported it to the Elf Master down in the village, who was giving a lesson in map reading to a group of volunteers who had offered to be the first to move out to the farmhouse.

"It's not Keith Doyle," Dola said. She still had a minor crush on the tall Big One. She was sorry she was not allowed to talk to him any more, but he hadn't come back since that day she had kicked him.

"Zo?" enquired the Master, setting down his atlas and looking at them over the tops of his glasses. "Go and ask whomever it is vhat he vants." His eyes twinkled. "But quietly. Other people do not vish to be disturbed."

The young ones looked at each other gleefully and dashed back to the passage.

Dola waited by the entrance to the village, concentrating hard on a linen cloth woven by her mother, while the other two silently sneaked up on Carl in the passage. Though she was young, Dola's talent of weaving illusions was one that the elders insisted she begin developing immediately. She was rather proud of it herself, but as yet couldn't design anything in mid air. She still needed a 'canvas' on which to draw her magical pictures in mid air. Dola preferred to create beautiful pictures, but the elders had decreed that for distracting intruders, she had to make an ugly, boring image. As Carl turned the corner and looked the rest of the way down the passage, Dola held up the cloth.

Looking straight at her, all Carl could see was a store-room, dimly lit by bare bulbs hanging on cords. Scattered on the floor were elderly cardboard cartons festooned with cobwebs and dust. Concentrating very hard, Dola made the image of a great, black spider walk across the floor. "Huh?" Carl gasped, then realizing he had spoken, clapped his hand over his mouth, willing the sound to come back. He knew he must have missed the entrance. It was somewhere behind him. He turned and began to feel his way back up the corridor. Moira and Borget were huddled together against the wall behind him, holding hands. As soon as Carl passed them, Moira squeezed Borget's hand.

"Eeeeeeeeeaah!" shrieked Moira at the top of her voice.

"Hmmhmmhmmhmmmmhahahahaha…" laughed Borget, in as sinister a tone as he could manage.

In spite of himself, Carl straightened up to his full height, and bashed his head on the ceiling. There was another burst of ghostly laughter. Clutching his head with one hand, he felt his way out of the tunnel and school room, hotly pursued by his banshees. He screamed curses back at them, but they only laughed. An elvish trick!

"I'll get you, too," he swore, as he ran up the stairs. He wasn't going to get his evidence this way, that was sure. The two young elves laughed and ran back to Dola to share the joke.

The Elf Master was thoughtful as they reported their guest's identity and actions. "This one will bear watching," he said. "A burglar is the only guest who does not knock."

"But what would be here to steal?" Moira asked. "We have no fancy possessions."

The elder elf shrugged. "Our privacy is very valuable," he said, with a sigh.

Chapter 34

Something of great importance was definitely going on in the village, but Keith was being kept in the dark. Worse yet, he hadn't been able to catch Holl outside of class. Every time he tried to strike up a conversation, one of the others would head off the blond elf and lead him away from Keith. The tall student felt it was important that the two of them should talk. Quarterly income taxes would be due soon, and by Keith's calculations, the amount would far exceed the balance presently in the checkbook which Holl held. Though to be fair, Holl had the forms in hand, too, and he had been faithful about sending them in on time. If it got too close to the deadline, Keith would simply swallow his pride and ask the Elf Master for intervention.

Since he was deprived of his friends in the village, he had been spending more time with Diane, but as his anxiety increased, Diane complained that he was becoming distant.

"You've got something on your mind. Is it the craft business?" she demanded as he walked her home from Mythology class one evening. "How's it doing?"

"I'm not too sure." Keith replied, running a mental inventory of his available merchandise and groaning over the total. He wished he could ask someone if everything would be ready when needed. Diane studied him, and he flashed her a quick smile. She shook her head.

"Now I know something is wrong. You used to have every single fact at the tip of your tongue. It's a sign that you're probably doing too much." She leaned down from the steps and kissed him. "If you want to talk, or if there's anything I can do, just let me know."

"Mmm." Keith reached for another kiss. "That helped a lot. Good night."

"Good night. Oh, I just remembered. Ms. Voordman wants you to stop by. She wants to talk to you. Good night again."

Diane disappeared behind the frosted glass of the front door and Keith turned away into the twilight.

The evening was quiet, with the hint of scent in the air that proved Spring had arrived and it meant business. A few late birds chorused with the crickets that lived in the cellars of the ancient brownstones. Keith thought of stopping in to see Ludmilla and telling her his troubles. Her kindness and her warm sympathy were very soothing to miserable souls. She didn't live far from Diane's. He smiled. The two of them would probably get along very well. They were both strong and caring women.

A few early bicyclists whizzed past him along the curb. Keith heard the whirr of spokes and a burst of swearing as one of them accidentally flashed in front of a pedestrian in the crosswalk. He glanced back. There were two men at the intersection about half a block behind him. One of them was still swearing, and his buddy was holding him back from giving chase. It would have been pointless. The bicyclist was probably half a mile away already.

Keith had expected more foot traffic on a nice night in a campus town, but he put it down to the indoctrination of the elves that he walked more than he ever had before he met them. Most of his Big Folk classmates still drove wherever they could. Self-locomotion was only used when nothing else was available. He thought it was weird that these same students would jog or run eight miles every morning before dawn, but they'd rather die than walk to the movies. He turned a corner onto Ludmilla's street.

After a while, he began to have a funny feeling between his shoulder blades. He looked back. The two men were still walking about half a block behind him. They weren't exactly casual strollers. There was purpose in their stride. He thought that he recognized their forms: they looked like the union president's men.

It could have been a coincidence. Keith walked past Ludmilla's brownstone and turned left on the next street, reluctant to lead them to his friend. The men kept pace. He turned another corner, and another, and still his shadows stayed the same distance behind him. The streetlamps sprang alight high over his head. It was growing darker, and Keith found that he was nearly back to the Midwestern campus. The buildings were closer together here. He could hide. Closing the distance between them, the two thugs passed under a light and Keith caught a glimpse of their faces. It was the union men.

Keith panicked and started for the alleyway between the Science Building and the faculty garage. His only thought was to find a security guard, who would drive his pursuers away. There was a cry behind him. He threw a glance over his shoulder. The men had seen him break into a run and sprinted after him.

Keith ran down the ornamental paths on the other side of the Science Building and leaped over a marble bench onto the lawn next to the library, avoiding the thornbushes that flanked it. He could open the stone façade and escape into the elves' village. If he was fast enough. He didn't know how far behind him the men were. Safety was getting closer. He ducked around the side of the thorn hedge, and swung past the sycamore tree by the boulder. There was rustling in the shrubbery to either side of him. To his dismay, the thugs had separated. One was bounding toward him across the grass, and one was heading off his other escape route, past the main entrance to Gillington. He couldn't open the façade now; he'd give the elves' secret away.

Rough hands caught him from behind and held his arms as he turned back into the thornbushes. Keith cried out and kicked, striking his captor in the kneecap. The man swore and kicked back a few times, staggering Keith to his knees with the angry blows to his calves and buttocks.

The other thug moved in slowly, like a boxer under water. He smacked one gigantic fist into the other. It sounded like a pistol shot. Keith winced. "Mr. Lewandowski has been waiting for your list. It is bad business to keep him waiting."

"Sorry," Keith grimaced. "I haven't gotten around to it yet."

"Wrong answer," the man told him, and the giant fist took Keith in the stomach. He folded over, gasping, seeing black stars against the darkness.

One of the ham-hands clutched his hair and his face was dragged up, away from the agony in his midsection. "You get that list, or you're going to have real trouble, you hear me?" Keith nodded weakly. The man let go, and Keith sagged down against the thug behind him. He stared at the ground, trying to get up enough strength to say something, when he noticed that the thornbushes were moving.

For a moment he was so fascinated he forgot about his pain. Thin switches of thorn, with the buds of new leaves gleaming at alternating intervals along their lengths, were weaving out of the hedges, along the ground, and twining themselves up around the legs of the man in front of him. And the man behind as well. The vines pulled taut.

"Didn't you hear me, punk?" The man grabbed Keith's hair again. When his face came up, Keith could see two pairs of bright eyes behind the bushes. Or rather, one pair of eyes, and one pair of spectacles. The Master, and possibly Holl. "We mean business."

"Yeah," Keith grated out, not recognizing his own breathless voice. "I see what you're doing." The spectacles in the shrubbery glinted. Message received. With a heroic effort Keith straightened up. "No sale. Tell him I'm not interested."

"I'm warning you, punk," the man growled. He reached for Keith with both hands.

With a swift jerk, Keith pulled both arms free from the grasp of the gorilla's assistant and jumped to the side. Both men twisted to grab him, and ended up flailing their arms wildly in the air for balance. They fell forward, emitting ululations of pain and obscenities; the dormant thornbushes had nothing on them as yet to conceal or pad the inch-and-a-half-long thorns as sharp as roofing nails that grew between the buds.

Keith was not going to wait around for them to get free. He took to his heels and fled, searching for the security patrol. A mighty wrenching and ripping of cloth, accompanied by much swearing, suggested to him that one of the thugs was abandoning modesty and stripping off his trousers to come after Keith.

While they struggled, he dodged between the hedges and pelted down the ornamental path to the street. To his everlasting gratitude, a patrol car rolled into view as he rounded the corner of the library building. He leaped into the street to flag it down. The car screeched over to the curb. He dashed over to it.

"Help!" Keith yelled in the window at the two security guards, waving back toward the library. "Officer, two flashers out there near the library! Muggers! *Perverts!*" Steadying riot clubs and flashlights on their belts, the uniformed officers followed Keith's energetic pointing, and were just in time to intercept the union men as they appeared around the angle of the building clad in jackets, socks, shoes and undershorts.

Spotlighting their captives with flashlights, the guards shoved the men against the wall of the library and started to frisk them. The senior guard shone his flashlight on the torn backside of one man's peacock blue shorts. "You a streaker, bud? I don't think your butt's so pretty that you ought to show it. I wanna see some I.D. What are you doing on this campus without authorization?" He noticed Keith hanging around behind him, and shone his flashlight into Keith's face. "What's your name, son?"

"Keith Doyle, sir. Power Hall."

"Okay, Doyle. We'll want a statement from you in the morning. In the meantime, get out of here. Thanks for alerting us."

"Sure thing!" Keith waved a jaunty salute, half to the security officers, half to the invisible figures in the bushes. "Thanks again."

"I'm gonna get you, kid!" the muscular thug shouted. "Now it's personal!"

"Up against the wall, you," the guard growled, shoving him back into place.

Chapter 35

"Keith!" Marcy came running up to him as he walked Diane toward the Science Building for her Biology class. "Oh, Keith, I'm so glad to see you!"

"Hi, Marcy," Keith greeted her warmly, and turned to Diane. "Diane Londen, this is Marcy Collier. We're former fellow sufferers in Sociology class last semester. Marcy, Diane."

"Hi," Marcy said, a little offhandedly. It was clear she had something on her mind, but didn't know how to convey it to Keith.

"Pleased to meet you," Diane returned, somewhat suspiciously.

Keith saw the danger signals flaring in Diane's eyes, and hastened to ask Marcy, "So how's Enoch?"

There was nothing false about the glow which lit Marcy's face. "Wonderful. I had the most marvelous time over the break. My mother didn't understand why I didn't come home, but…." She smiled again, and blushed. Beside Keith, Diane relaxed.

"So how's everything else?" Keith asked, meaningfully. "I haven't seen the Folks lately. Most of them aren't speaking to me."

Marcy nodded her comprehension. "Keith, I think Carl is planning to do something horrible. He wrote an article, a lot of unsubstantiated rumors…"

Keith nodded. "I know someone did. They thought it was me." Diane, puzzled, looked from one to the other, but didn't interrupt.

"Well, it was Carl! There are going to be more. Lots more. Says he's got *evidence* to support his case. If it wasn't about *family*, you might almost call it an exposé."

"Oh, no!"

"He's got an investigative reporter coming, Keith. Steven Arnold. You've heard of him?"

"Yes, I have! Have you told the family?"

"You must have some strange family," Diane commented to Marcy. "This Carl your cousin?" They both looked at her. "Sorry. Just an impression."

"I can't. They wouldn't believe me." Marcy sounded desperate.

"Well, don't worry. I'll take care of it. And Carl, too," Keith promised, with a glint in his eye. "I'll upset all of his plans."

"Good evening, Keith Doyle," Holl said quietly from the doorway.

Keith looked up from his books and beckoned the young elf into the room. "Hi! I'm glad to see you. You weren't home last time I dropped in."

"No. We have business to straighten out." His manner was stiff and strained, and Keith felt instantly uncomfortable.

"May I offer you something to drink?" he asked, formally, gesturing Holl to a chair.

"No, thank you," just as formally.

"Holl, you can't honestly believe that I'd do anything...."

The elf held up a hand. "I know what I believe, but I must side with my folk. No other way would I be allowed to come here." He brought out a handful of papers from his jacket pocket. "We have work to do."

Keith struggled to keep his voice level and reasonable. "We have a problem. There are a lot of people we promised merchandise to, they're going to get upset if we don't deliver."

"They are only in contact with you. It doesn't concern us directly. I have brought these papers by to do you a favor, as it's your name on them."

He tried again. "Marcy stopped me today. She told me that Carl was working on exposing the village."

"Do you wish me to carry this tale back, so the pressure will be taken from your back?" Holl asked angrily. "Do you have any proof?"

"There's no pressure on my back," Keith shouted, "except the IRS and a bunch of short-sighted short people!"

"Do you imagine that is funny?" Holl demanded.

"Look, I wanted you to come by today so I could give you the proof."

"If you could do that," Holl said, hope brimming in his eyes. "You'd restore their faith. How?"

"I've got a plan." Keith pricked up his ears. "Carl's going to stop by. We'll let him hang himself. You hide in there." He pointed to his closet.

"Not for you or any other Big—"

"Shh! I hear—"

Holl promptly interrupted him. "I want to hear more—"

"Shh!" He swept Holl up and shoved him into the closet. The next second, as he pushed the double doors shut, there was a rap on the door. Keith swung it open. Carl strode in, suspiciously looking this way and that. Keith wondered if he was looking for contraband legends.

"Yo, Carl," he said, running a hand through his hair and hoping Holl hadn't left any recognizable possessions in the room.

"Hello, Doyle," Carl said, eyeing him with amusement. "You left me a note. You say you've got something for me?"

"Started any good rumors lately?" Keith asked, with his best village idiot expression.

"Nothing I can't handle," Carl replied smugly. "Thanks for bringing out the Hollow Tree stuff, Doyle. The best thing that ever happened to me."

"Like it, huh?"

"Yep. Just the sort of thing successful news articles are made of. Proof."

"So you DID do those articles I read, huh?" Keith asked, his voice full of surprise and admiration.

"Yeah," Carl admitted proudly. "And there'll be more. I called Steve Arnold, the investigative reporter from the paper, to come and interview me on Friday about legends and stuff."

There was a gasp from the closet. Keith's smile widened. There was his proof, right from the horse's mouth.

"I'd sure like to come and hear what you have to say to the guy," Keith gloated, rubbing his hands together. "You were certainly around there a long time."

Carl was clearly preening. "I figure I know enough. I tried to get into the other part of their complex twice without their knowing, once through the classroom and once through the wall but I muffed it." He gave a shamefaced little laugh. "I nearly blew myself up with a couple of M-80's. That wall must be really strong. They have got to have a really powerful mechanism. I bet the construction industry would like to know about it." He eyed Keith. "If you helped me find out, I'll cut you in for ten percent of my profits. I'd get you into the article, too."

"Hey, thanks. I've always wanted to have my name in the papers."

"No problem. It's a piece of cake. Those elves are going to make me a lot of money. And they don't even know it. They're so dumb. Every time they wander around town and someone sees 'em I can sell another story to the papers. No wonder fairies are extinct."

Behind Keith, the doors gave a convulsive shove. Keith threw himself backwards, dislodging Holl who, judging by the sounds, sat down backwards on Keith's boots. There was some muffled swearing, and Holl started pounding on the doors from the inside. "Stop it," he hissed.

Carl blinked at the closet Keith was guarding. "Is someone in there?"

"Yes," said Keith, thinking quickly. "It's my girl, Diane, and um, we were interrupted…So if you wouldn't mind?" He gestured toward the hall. "You know, nice talking to you and all."

Carl smirked. "Try a rubber band on the door knob next time, Keith. This being subtle stuff just gets you in trouble. See you on the front page."

"Whew!" Keith turned the lock, and opened the closet. A furious Holl sprang out into the room and reached for the door.

"We'll get him!" he vowed, starting after Carl. "It was him all the time. I'll take care of him, the traitor! I'll make him stink!"

"No, you won't," Keith cautioned, hauling him back. "That'll blow everything. He wants you to be seen. It'll give credence to his newspaper stories. If that happens, it'll never stop. Help me, and we'll destroy his credibility."

Holl regarded him with shame. "You knew, Keith Doyle. Why didn't I voice my trust in you, as I have before? I knew you were honest. On behalf of myself and my folk, I apologize."

"Save it," Keith said flippantly. "I might need a real apology some day."

There was a cautious tap at the door. "Come in," Keith called out without thinking. Pat pushed in.

"Yo. Oh, hi, kid. I met Carl in the hallway. He said he was just by here. Where's the girl?"

"Um, she went home," Keith babbled out.

"Oh. Minute-man, huh? You know, Carl is starting to sound just like you," Pat told him, putting his books on the floor and stretching out full length on the bed. "Legends and fairy tales. Too bad he doesn't like you. You could babble at each other, and leave me in peace. Giving me all this razzmatazz about legendary elves. In fact, he claims the campus is crawling with the little suckers."

"Do tell," Holl inquired blandly.

There was something about the way the boy spoke that made Pat really look at him. Something was different about him than the last time the dark-haired student had seen him. New haircut? No. He wasn't wearing a hat now, so you could see his ears. Boy, what big ears the kid had...! "Those ears!" Pat gasped, sitting up. "Doyle, what on earth? I've been thinking all this time that your nephew here..."

"Holl," said Holl.

"...Yeah, *Holl*, is just a kid with a Trek complex, but you're one of 'em, aren't you?" he asked, taking in Holl's appearance carefully for the first time. "Carl's right. You're not a kid at all." Pat got up and looked closely at the side of Holl's head, tugging on the point of one ear.

"Ouch," Holl said distinctly. "They're attached, you know."

"They're real," Pat breathed. "God damn."

"Yup," Keith told him. "Holl's one of the 'legendary elves' Carl was writing about. At least I call 'em elves," he finished, doubtfully. "Can't seem to get any confirmation from them on a scientific classification."

"It's all empirical anyhow," Holl said casually.

"Wow," sighed Pat, sitting down on the coffee table. "I suppose he isn't really your nephew after all."

"Nope," Keith said, regretfully.

"Fear not. We're most likely distant kin," Holl assured him. "Ten thousand research books can't be all wrong."

"Hey, great," Keith crowed, diving for pen and notepad. "Can I quote you on that?"

"How's it feel?" Pat wanted to know.

"Never a problem to me," said Holl. "I was born normal, same as you. Oh, no," he held up his hands, palms out, seeing that Pat was misinterpreting his words. "Not an oversized babe like yourself. A normal, healthy squaller that drinks milk and pulls hair."

"Keith," Pat said faintly, "I take back almost everything I ever said about you."

"Carl is causing Holl and his family a lot of trouble."

"Who's his family?" Pat looked at him in amazement. "You mean the stuff with the investigative reporter? And the Inter-Hall Council?"

"They live in the basement of the library. For more than forty years now," Keith added. "Their village chief is the reason I passed Sociology last semester."

"Jeezus!"

Holl nodded. "It's not easy finding housing for eighty. We must be able to escape notice."

Pat eyed Keith. "So what's your role in all this?"

"I went into business to raise money so they could buy a place to live."

"You're the ones he was going to teach to fish."

Holl bowed to Pat. "I understand we owe the suggestion to you. It's a good one, and perhaps Keith Doyle would never have come to it himself."

"Much obliged. You know," Pat said thoughtfully, "if Carl had told you what was going on in the beginning, you would never have come out in favor of tearing the library down."

"That's just one score of many we need to settle with him," Holl said seriously. "You see how *you* react to encountering me, and Keith trusts you. I've no wish to be the object of gapers."

Pat was still overwhelmed. "After living with Keith for two years, I should be better prepared to deal with you guys. Although this is the first time he's actually brought home a research project. What can I do to help?"

"We're planning," Keith said. "But now that I think of it, you could help out if you want to. I'm happy that I can ask you openly. Meantime, there's a few more people we ought to get involved with this. What we need to do is to call a council of war." They sat down to conspire.

"Why'd we have to meet down here?" Teri said, hugging herself and looking around nervously at the steam tunnel. "Brr! I got dirt on my new toreador pants coming down that ladder. I bet it's all grease. I'll *never* get it out."

"Shh!" Barry hissed. "These tunnels echo. We had beer parties down here my freshman year."

"Mine, too," Pat said. He was still watching Holl and the other Little Folk with open fascination. "That was normal. *This* is freaky."

The elves stood away from the humans in a knot under the light of a hanging bulb. Maura, Holl and Keith conversed quietly with the other students near the entrance. Marcy and Enoch stayed together off on the side between the two groups.

"May ve know vhy ve are assembled in this place?" the Elf Master requested in a quiet voice.

"Just a moment," Keith said. "Are we all here?"

"Two more coming," Lee's voice said from above them. They all looked up, expecting to see the big student backing down the ladder, but to everyone's surprise, including Keith's, a small elderly lady descended first.

"Mrs. Hempert!" Keith exclaimed, his sibilants echoing in the lonely hall. Lee came down next, grinning.

"She didn't want to be left out."

"But naturally," Ludmilla said, smiling at Keith. She walked over to Marcy, kissed her on the cheek, and gathered her protectively under her arm. "Hello, my dear."

Keith gestured to them all, gathering them closer. "Here's the problem," he said. "The elf village is about to have its cover blown," he had to hold his hands up to silence comment. "But not by me, or anything I'm doing. You'll notice that Carl isn't here. He's the one causing all the trouble. Just recently, he published a few articles," Keith nodded to Catra, who held up a folder of news clippings from her archives.

"I heard him confess it," Holl called out.

The murmuring grew louder. Keith raised his voice just a little to be heard over it. "And on Friday, he's going to talk to a reporter whose job is to ferret out facts and make a big deal about them. They call him an exposé writer."

There was a lot of muttering as the two groups, still separate, mulled over the information. Keith waited a moment for them to digest it, and then went on. "Now, there's been a lot of hard feelings lately, with everybody suspecting everybody else. The only way that we can fix that is with cooperation. In fact, that just happens to be the only way we can get Carl to back off."

"What can we do?" Teri asked, concern in her eyes.

"I thought, between the bunch of us, we could come up with a creative way to queer it with this reporter. It's important to me to make it go wrong for him."

"I intend to help," Ludmilla said immediately. "I *know* it is important. You haf but to ask me."

"Me, too," Lee told him, and turned to the others, unconsciously echoing Holl. "I apologize for Carl on behalf of my species."

From the isolated group of elves, the Master stood forth. "It is our species, too," he said. He took Ludmilla's hand and bowed over it. "Danke shoen, mine old friend."

She put her other hand on top of his. "It is gut to see you again."

"They talk alike," Teri said, amused.

"I think we should all have a chance to help," Barry said, making the accord unanimous. The elves drew closer, mixing again with their friends. The girls hugged Teri and Marcy, and the men all shook hands.

"There is a time limit, you realize," Holl said. "We don't have as much time as we'd hoped, and we can't move while there is a watch out for us."

"Move?" "Where?" Everyone asked at once.

"To a place. Keith knows."

Keith realized he did. "You bought the farmstead! I was really worried when I saw the 'Sold' sign. So that's where that money went."

The elves were visibly ashamed. "Of all folk, it is you we should have trusted," Candlepat put an appealing hand on his arm. He smiled down at her.

"You would have found out sooner or later," Holl put in apologetically. "I tried to call you after the sale was agreed, but you were in transit. After that, I was prevented from meeting with you."

"I took 'em there the other day," Lee grunted approvingly. "Nice choice. Needs work, though. I'm going to help out, too. If you don't mind, that is. It's all 'Keith Doyle this', and 'Keith Doyle that' to them." He made a face, drawing his voice up into a falsetto.

"I'm sorry for the things I thought about you, Keith Doyle," Marm said, slapping him on the back, reaching high enough to hit between Keith's shoulderblades. "I'll pass it to the others to begin production once again. We have commitments to meet." There was a wholehearted murmur of agreement.

"Good," Keith said. "Now, here's what I have in mind. A few little surprises, that's all."

On the way back to campus, Holl looked up the street, and blanched. "Uh-oh." He stuck his hand into Keith's.

Keith looked down in surprise. "What's this?" he asked playfully. "I thought you had a thing for Maura."

"There's a security officer down there, you had-a-thing," Holl growled out of the side of his mouth. "At least in this twilight he can't see me clearly. Now escort me safely across the street, Uncle Keith."

"Naturally, Holl, my dear boy," Keith said indulgently. "Look both ways."

"We do," Holl muttered in an undertone. "I look uncomfortable, and you look like a fool. As usual."

Chapter 36

As promised, the elves had geared up to full production again, and reported to Keith through Marcy that they would have all orders filled within the week. Keith was pleased, because was able to reply to a mayday call from Ms. Voordman, pleading for her shipment. "It's gift season, Keith. If I wait too long I'll miss the window."

"I'll get it to you today, Ms. Voordman," Keith vowed, smiling at Diane who disappeared into the back room to put away her purse. Ms. Voordman was his best customer, and he felt bad about letting her down.

"And by the way, Keith, there was a man in here last week looking at your merchandise. I would call him a snappy dresser. He made a fuss about union labels." Ms. Voordman's eyes grew cold, and Keith swallowed, suspecting that Lewandowski hadn't forgotten about him. "He didn't say anything openly, or I would have gotten a restraining order, but he suggested if I kept buying non-union goods I might have a fire."

"What?" Keith squawked.

"Oh, I've heard it before, but this is the first time at Country Crafts. He particularly wanted me to pass it on to you."

Keith nodded, his mouth in a grim set. "Don't you worry, Ms. Voordman. I'll do something about it." He turned and strode purposefully toward the door.

"My shipment!" she called out to him.

"Oh, yeah!" Keith swung around and kept moving toward the street. "This afternoon, Ms. Voordman. I promise!"

Holl's estimate on completion of the orders was right on the money. Just after Mythology class on Wednesday, Keith picked up a colossal bag of newspaper-wrapped bundles from the elves' newly opened back door and started for his car.

Suddenly, he spotted a broad figure in a black suit. He turned around on his heel and pushed himself and his bag back through the doors of the building.

"Hey!" Diane squawked, all but knocked off her feet. "You sure know how to impress a girl."

Keith dropped the bag and helped steady her. "I'm sorry. I owe a guy some money, and I'm trying to avoid him."

"A lot of money? I could lend you some."

"No, thanks," Keith assured her. "I don't think you'd have enough." He peered out the window, but the man in the black suit turned out to be a Jesuit theology teacher walking to class. He panted a sigh of relief.

"It's because of me, isn't it," Diane asked woefully. "I've impoverished you forever by taking that scholarship away from you."

"It's okay, really," he assured her. "An investment of mine will pay off in a few days. I just have to wait for it, and everything will be okay. I just want to avoid some people 'til then."

"Are they looking for you? Do you need to hide out?" she asked, anxiously, fearing for his safety. She moved protectively closer to him.

"No," Keith said, appreciatively, slipping an arm around her waist. "I can handle it. But there is something you can do for me."

"Anything."

Keith shifted the bag into her arms. "Keep your boss from wringing my neck."

"Why not? Count on me," Diane said, moving out the door Keith opened for her. "Don't let 'em get you."

Leaning around the bag, he kissed her on the cheek, and started out the door behind her. Suddenly, he spotted another burly figure on the common, coming toward the classroom building. The union man whom he'd gotten arrested for indecent exposure. It was clear the thug had seen him, too, for he had quickened his pace. He was back here to make it 'personal.'

Keith could hear the man's promise of revenge ringing in his ears as he fled back into the building and began to look for some place to hide. There was nothing on this floor but classrooms and storage rooms. Behind him, the man opened the door and stepped in, stopping at the top of the hall to let his eyes adjust to the dimness. Keith picked a door at random and pulled the door open.

A class was in session. "Yes, young man?" a thin, elderly professor asked him. "Can I help you?"

"Sorry," Keith said. "I guess not."

The union man walked swiftly up the hall toward him, an expression on his face which Keith equated with murder, but his pace was even, as if he belonged here.

Keith swallowed. He had to find a place to hide. He thought hopefully of finding a security officer, but they rarely patrolled the classroom buildings.

Glancing frequently over his shoulder, he walked rapidly away from the union man, trying to seem nonchalant. He ducked among a crowd of students who emerged suddenly from a study room, and started running down the hall.

His pursuer dropped pretense and ran after him, roughly shoving the other students out of his way. Books flew out of arms, and the girls shrilled protests.

Keith flew down the corridor. There was one solid wood door near the end of the hall that he believed led to a storeroom in which he could hide. Reaching it only a few feet in front of his assailant, he flung open the door and shot inside, slamming it closed behind him.

It was filled with filing cabinets and boxes. There didn't appear to be anywhere he could stay out of sight that he would fit, as thin as he was. He heard footsteps in the hall, and willed himself to come up with an idea fast. There was a lot of dust in here, and his eyes watered. He knew just a moment too late that he was going to sneeze.

"Aa-choo!" His whiskers twitched, tickling his ears.

The footsteps outside stopped, and the door creaked open. "All right, Doyle. I saw you come in here. Come out and I'll make it quick."

Keith plunged between a pair of filing cabinets. His whiskers extended the width of the space, dusting long lines in the grime on either side. It had looked like he wouldn't fit, but it was just wide enough for Keith, who was of no great bulk, to move through. He reached the back, and poked his nose into first one and then another possible hiding places, measuring them with the whiskers, which were exactly as wide as his narrowest dimension. He flattened himself in the niche made by one of the files and an upended metal-topped desk into which his whiskers fit snugly, if not comfortably.

Malcolm was used to clients being reluctant to cooperate with Mr. Lewandowski, but never had a reluctant client managed to get Malcolm and his partner thrown in jail for the night, either. Mr. Lewandowski had been justly pissed off to hear that the two of them had gone down for a simple scare visit and ended up bare-assed before the night magistrate. Malcolm's pride was bruised. That kid had to pay.

He'd had no trouble finding where Keith was going, either, thanks to a large young man with a brown crewcut in Power Hall who was happy to give him Keith's schedule. Sure enough, he'd spotted the red-haired kid leaving the big building. Too bad the kid had seen him so soon.

With a quick look out to make sure there were no nosy security guards walking around, Malcolm slowly pulled open the door to the storeroom and put an eye against the edge. The room was dim and full of tall, blocky shadows surrounded by darker striped plat-forms. Creepy. A glance to the left showed him the light switch, and Malcolm reached in to flip it upward. In the light the tall figures became stacks of desks and tables ringed with filing cabinets. To Malcolm's eye, there wasn't room to fit a playing card between 'em, let alone a teenager.

He heard the rasp of a shoe on the floor somewhere in the back of the room behind a row of folding chairs. With a malicious smile, he flexed his shoulders and moved in on the chairs, picking them up by the dozen and depositing them behind him, like John Henry forc-ing his way through the mountain. If the way out was blocked, Doyle would have to come past him to escape.

"I'm gonna get you, kid," Malcolm whispered. The hiss of soles brushed the floor again. Must be the kid shaking in his shoes. "I'm gonna tear you apart."

At the back of the row was a dead end. Filing cabinets had been laid in a column all the way to the ceiling on every side. Malcolm looked around, wiping his dusty nose on the back of an arm. No Doyle. There wasn't room to hide a rat among the heaps of furni-ture. Angrily, he flung the chairs back to fill in the gap. The ringing of metal on metal echoed deafeningly in the room, and Malcolm re-membered too late he shouldn't attract any more attention. He didn't want the security force to find him before he taught that Doyle some manners. Leaving the remaining chairs in a heap, he slunk through the door and out of the building as casually as he could.

Keith heard the door slam behind him, and let go the breath he was holding. When the thug had started to push between the rows of chairs, he had passed right by Keith. Only the most incredible kind of luck kept him from looking to the right, straight into Keith's cramped niche. There would have been no escape, and that man would have torn him into little pieces. He vowed to do something about the union men, just as soon as he could get back to his dorm in one piece.

He counted up to a hundred before squeezing out between the cabinets, just in case the union man came back. Cautiously, slowly, he eased out of his hiding place with the ease, if not the grace of a cat. "Thanks, guys," he said fervently, fingering his invisible whiskers and sending the elves grateful thoughts. "They worked!"

"So, kid? You called me yesterday for a meeting. You wanted to meet in a neutral location. So here we are. What do you want?"

Sherman Park was virtually deserted during business hours on a Thursday. And yet, Keith figured, if Lewandowski's two hoods started to beat him up, the chances were better that someone would come to his rescue here than in some secluded alleyway.

"I asked you to meet me because I want you to leave my friends alone," Keith said furiously, standing before the union boss, his arms crossed firmly over his chest.

Lewandowski ate some peanuts out of a cellophane bag and threw a few to the squirrels who surrounded the park bench under the brilliant green of the maple trees. He seemed unimpressed with Keith's bluster. After all, the skinny kid wasn't likely to try to pick him up and deck him with the two union enforcers standing so close. If he could pick him up at all, which Lewandowski doubted. "Where's my list?"

"You threatened one of my customers with a fire if she continued to carry my goods. And one of your goons there," he pointed to Malcolm, who still wore the scabs from the thorns in the hedge, "chased me around the campus in his underwear. Why should I cooperate? I thought you were going to do this legally."

"Chased you around the campus—? Wait a minute," the union president held up a hand, glaring at his employee. "Is he wired? Did anybody search him? He could be recording this."

"No, sir," said Malcolm, avoiding Lewandowski's eyes. Nodding to his fellow, they went over Keith, patting down the windbreaker and jeans.

"I got something," the other thug said, unzipping Keith's jacket and stiff-arming the student in the face when he tried to get his property back. "A camera." He pulled the woven strap from around Keith's neck and dangled the object before Lewandowski.

"It's not real. It's a toy," the union president complained, poking at the small wooden carving with the circular cloth window where the lens should be. "You think you're funny or something?"

"That's one of my samples," Keith said. "I call it a magic lantern. Can I have it back?"

Lewandowski sighed and nodded to his man. Keith looped the strap around his neck and sat down next to the union president.

"So, where's my list?"

"I don't have one," Keith said. "I don't have any employees."

"Oh, yeah? Where do you get your merchandise, then?"

"They're made by elves," Keith stated. "Look, Mr. Lewandowski, I don't like the way you do things. I can't afford to fight you in court. I'm too small for you to bother with. Why don't you just leave me alone?"

"It's in the interests of the members of the union. They've got families to feed. Scabs like you take sales away from them. That's what we protect them from. Listen, kid," the union boss got suddenly bored with the smart-assed college student defying him. "You had just better play along with me. I've got police and judges and elected officials on my payroll who could see to it that you won't get a job in this state for the rest of your life, let alone a lousy diploma. Judge Arendson gets plenty from me every month to sign court orders, and well, he sees the court cases go my way. I got insurance adjusters who never settle arson claims for the insured, not if they cross me, so warn your lady friend. Even a stooge in the police office, so it won't do you no good to call them."

"I'm impressed," Keith said.

"You ought to be. If I don't get that list from you pretty soon, you'd better never get a traffic ticket in this city, or my man on the force will write up every ordinance they can find on that blue eggbeater you call a car. You may as well let yourself get organized. Save yourself a lot of trouble."

"Well...I didn't know what I was dealing with before," the boy admitted. "I'm awfully busy right now. Let me have a couple of days to decide. Okay?"

Lewandowski crumpled up the cellophane and tossed it aside. "Sure. I can wait that long. I'll be waiting to hear from you."

Chapter 37

The next day, Friday afternoon, Keith tripped into Carl's room, ignoring the death-dealing looks with which the other student burned him. Pat had given him the tipoff that Steven Arnold had already arrived, and gone back to the dorm room to help with his part of the 'surprises'. There was a man sitting on the edge of Carl's desk, jotting things down in on a legal pad whom Keith guessed must be Arnold. He was about thirty, with dishwater brown hair beginning to creep backwards from his forehead, and wore a skeptical expression that went well with his slightly slanted eyebrows.

"Hi, Carl," Keith said cheerfully. "Heard you had company." Keith carried a glass flask, containing a potently stinking liquid (Holl's inspiration) with a long piece of white cotton twine coiled up in the bottom, which he waved at the reporter in greeting. Some of the liquid sloshed up, creating a miniature miasma. He coughed. "Hi. Keith Doyle. Fellow student of Carl's."

"Steven Arnold. Nice to meet you." The reporter gagged and pointed to the flask. "What's that?"

"Oh, lantern wicks." He cocked an eye at Carl to see if the big athlete caught the hint. The fish went right for the bait; not even a fight. Carl caught him by the upper arm and dragged him over.

"Doyle here knows the little folk. Tell Mr. Arnold about the elves. We're both in the class taught by one."

"Well," Keith said brightly, "Mrs. Depuis is really short, but you couldn't call her an elf." He wrinkled his nose. "Maybe a dwarf."

"No," Carl urged. "The group in the library."

"Well, yeah, we were in a group for a while. But it was a sort of encounter group," Keith told the reporter. "The stuff we talked about is private. I mean, what did *you* dream about when you were thirteen?"

"No, it wasn't," stormed Carl, finally deducing that Keith was making fun of him. That was the end of any ten percent of merchandising profits for Keith. "It was the little folk. Look!" He reached in a drawer and produced one of the Hollow Tree lanterns. He blew on the wick and it lit. Another puff and the flame went out.

"Lemme see that," the reporter said, fascinated.

"Do you like that?" Keith asked, full of pride. "I make 'em."

"You what?" Carl interrupted him incredulously.

"Yeah. I sell them to the gift shops around town. The string is treated with a chemical. Look, I was just whipping up some more. Got the raw materials for the wicks right here in this bottle." With a long pair of tweezers, he fished an end of the cord out of the liquid. Exposed to air, the chemical compound was horribly pungent. Both Carl and the reporter choked and backed away. Keith, even though he was prepared for it, felt a little faint. One of Teri's little concoctions. All he knew about it was that it contained nail polish remover and vinegar. What else, he had no idea. For all he knew, she'd cornered a skunk and persuaded it to contribute to the cause.

"Sorry," he said. "Brings tears to your eyes, doesn't it? It doesn't stink when it's dry. Here. I'll show you." He picked up Carl's blow dryer and turned it on the cord full blast. Hot, the smell was close to unbearable. Over the roar of the motor, he told the reporter, "It's 99% cotton and one percent I can't tell you, because that's what makes the magic work, so to speak. It's nitrogen/carbon-dioxide sensitive, but perfectly safe."

"Doyle!" shouted Carl. "Get out of here!"

"Wait a minute, Mr. Mueller," said the reporter, pointing his pen at Carl. "I'd like to see what he's got there."

Keith beamed at him. When it was dry, he picked up the tweezers and held the long piece of twine out to Carl. "Blow on it," he suggested to the reporter. Doubtfully, the reporter obliged. He puffed at it. The whole length caught fire. With a curse, Carl jerked his hand back, dropping it, and stamped on it to put the fire out. "Don't do that," Keith admonished him. He knelt and blew on it. The rug was unscorched where the burning cord had fallen. Carl studied his unburned hand and regarded Keith with enmity.

"That's wonderful," gasped the reporter, both eyebrows reaching for the ceiling. "Can I have a piece of that?"

"Sure," said Keith magnanimously, cutting off a few inches of the cord with a pocket knife. "But please don't try to duplicate it. My patent is pending. They last for a decent while before the chemical is all used up."

"Thanks. I might like to order some of your merchandise," the reporter said, carefully putting the string away in an envelope. "I've heard of you, now that I think of it. My editor will love this. You could get a science award for that fluid."

"Nope. I'm in it for the money. My card," Keith flourished it, with a dramatic expression. "Hollow Tree Industries. Woodcrafts and wonders."

"Nice name," the reporter said. "How'd you like to talk to me a little later? It'd be some free publicity for you."

"Sure." Keith beamed. "Always happy to meet a member of the legitimate press." Arnold beamed back.

"Damn you to hell," Carl snarled, hating Keith for wasting his time. "Well, come on, Mr. Arnold. I'll show you where the Little Folk meet for those classes."

"What sort of classes?" the reporter wanted to know.

"Biology, Philosophy, uh...Sociology."

"Interesting curriculum," Arnold said. "Who teaches this class?"

"One of the older ones. He's called the Master."

The reporter scribbled that down on his pad. "Uh-huh. Humans and, uh, elves both in the class?"

Carl scowled, suspecting he was not being taken seriously. "Yes."

Keith was delighted: the reporter was a skeptic. He made Keith's job a thousand times easier. With an air of ennui, Keith announced that he wanted to come along for the ride. "I have to see this," he insisted, a mischievous grin on his face. "Never heard of elves associating with college students."

Carl was about to retort, but he noticed the questioning expression in the reporter's eye. His credibility was already on the line. Doyle he could take care of later.

"Uncle Keith?" Holl tapped on the door, right on cue.

"Oh, wait," says Keith. "I'm babysitting for my nephew. He's a Trekkie. You don't mind if he comes, too, do you?"

"No, not at all," the reporter assured him.

Holl came in, hatless, casually dressed in a new pair of jeans made by Maura and a windbreaker borrowed from Keith's younger brother. He could easily have been a member of the Doyle clan. There was theatrical latex smeared all over his ears, courtesy of Pat, which made them look larger than usual. Holl scratched fitfully at the rubber goo, which was dried to a matte finish. "Uncle Keith, can I have a can of pop?"

Carl jumped to his feet and pointed. "That's one of them. That's not a kid. He's an elf."

"He's a Trekkie," Keith explained. He gestured at Carl, then made a spinning motion at his temple with a finger.

"Oh, I see," the reporter nodded.

"Fascinating," Holl intoned.

"For God's sake, his ears! Look at his ears!" Carl dragged Holl over to the reluctant reporter, and turned the elf's face sideways. Holl put on a convincing demonstration as the uncooperative adolescent. "Lemme go!" He struggled and kicked at Carl until Keith interceded.

"Look, you'll pull them off. Watch it," Keith said, moving Holl away. "They're expensive."

"I shall have to stun you," Holl threatened in what was obviously an excited child's attempt at a Vulcan monotone, pulling a toy phaser from the pocket of his borrowed windbreaker. Keith pushed the barrel of the toy gun toward the floor.

"Never point guns at anyone, Holl," he admonished his 'nephew' solemnly. "Not even toys."

"They're latex and rubber," the reporter said to Carl coldly, after examining the plastic coating with Holl's grudging cooperation. "You'll have to do better than that to convince me you've got something, Mr. Mueller. Two articles in the National Informer do not constitute proof to me. The library, I think you said?"

"After you," Keith said, courteously bowing Arnold and Carl out before him. He hung back until he was sure they were well on their way down the hall. With a maniacal chuckle, he tilted the flask at eye level, and very carefully poured about an ounce of skunk cocktail into each of Carl's track shoes. Holl gave him a wink as they pulled the door closed.

A guest pass was secured for Arnold in the office of the library. The plump administrative assistant on duty recognized the name when she stamped the card with the date and hour. "Steven Arnold?" she asked almost flirtatiously, smoothing her flowered print dress. "I've read everything you've published. You have a fine mind."

"Thank you, ma'am," Arnold said politely. "Takes one to know one."

She blushed and giggled, for a moment looking far younger than her fifty or so years. "Are you going to write a piece about our library, young man?"

"I sincerely hope so," Arnold said. "I've been promised a special exclusive." He gave Carl a this-had-better-be-worth-it look.

"Come on," Carl said, impatient with protocol and all librarians. "This way."

"Just a moment," the librarian on duty stopped them as they reached the checkpoint for the stacks.

"They're with me," Arnold said, flashing his pass and a big smile. The librarian perused them indifferently and let them by. Holl lifted an eyebrow at her as he passed.

"Fascinating." Holl was really catching on to the Trek jargon, Keith thought approvingly.

"My nephew," Keith said, as he went in behind Holl.

They took the elevator to the twelfth level, and walked down the stairs from there. There was no screech or struggle as they entered Level Fourteen. Carl had obviously set it up beforehand; the security door had been left propped open and the hinges oiled. The lights were on, but the place still had an air of eeriness.

Arnold scribbled on his legal pad, having no need of illumination to write, a talent forged over long years of experience. He looked around at the tall shelves of books looming over him forbiddingly like giant librarians. After a moment, he wrote the image down in his notes. It would make good copy for the sensationalist editor to whom his work was frequently assigned.

The corners of the chamber were dark in spite of the fluorescent lighting, which was inadequate for the expanse it had to cover. Arnold had to admit that willing suspension of disbelief would be easy to accomplish in such a spooky location, but he was still waiting to be shown.

Carl marched his little train proudly down the aisle to the wall that separated the classroom from the rest of the library. It was his moment, and he was going to enjoy it. Doyle and the elf kid with the stupid glue on his ears were in the back watching him, looking like they might laugh. Doyle was a jerk to miss out on bringing the Little Folk to the attention of the world. Now it was Carl Mueller who would get all the kudos. And all the rewards.

"Now, watch." The reporter leaned in as Carl gestured them closer. The burly student took out his green glowing key, and felt the invisible door in the wall for the smooth metal scratchplate. It was still too dark in this corner to see what he was doing, but never mind. He'd been doing it without light for years. With a deep breath, he put the key to the keyhole.

There was a blinding green flash, and the green light around the key went out like a birthday candle. Keith, the reporter, and Carl all rocked backward as they were momentarily dazzled into shocked blindness. They scrubbed at their eyes, seeing red flashes that faded slowly back to normal vision. Holl, who knew what to expect, merely looked Vulcan and imperturbable. He had had his eyes closed.

When Carl could see again, he looked for the keyhole. He scrabbled at the wall. The doorplate had vanished completely. "What happened? Where did it go?" He looked down at his key. It was cold and dead again, just a piece of metal with nothing special about it but the shape.

"Where did what go, Mr. Mueller?" Arnold asked, watching the big student's antics with an air of displeasure.

"Phasers on stun," intoned Holl, from behind Keith. He resheathed his toy gun, which he had drawn when they boldly went where no man had gone before. "Request permission to beam up."

"Sorry," said Keith plaintively. "I shouldn't buy him toys his mother hates. She always gets even with me. I've got him for a whole week."

"What the hell happened?" demanded the reporter. "Is this some kind of elaborate college prank? My editor is going to be furious. You promised him an exclusive on alien beings living on this college campus. I don't waste my time on student rookery. If you got me down here on a false pretense, I'm going to report it to your dean. I don't work for the National Informer, you know!"

"Where's the door?" Carl felt the wall wildly, sounding desperate. He was nearly sobbing with frustration. "You did this, Doyle. Somehow I know you did." His voice reverberated hollowly in the concrete room, but the echoes sounded like the voices of children laughing.

"There's no door here. This is the oldest part of the stacks," Keith explained, patiently. "The walls are solid." He knocked on one, and it gave out with a flat THONK. "Everybody is always blaming me for things I haven't done." He turned back to the reporter, who was putting his pencil away in his breast pocket. "Did you know that the Historical Society has declared Gillington a historical monument? I have been in touch with them over the past months, and they have finally reached their decision. We're looking forward to the restoration committee's recommendations."

"I'd heard," Arnold said, taking the pencil out again. "Well, since I won't be getting the story that I came out for, I might as well hear about your library."

"Well, we're proud of it. Built in 1863 during the Civil War...." With an arm around the reporter's shoulders, Keith led him and Holl back up the stairs to the ground floor. Carl didn't follow immediately. There was a wild yell and a thud as the burly student hit the dusty floor face first. From somewhere behind the American History section, Enoch had thrown a minor cohesiveness whammy, and stuck Carl's shoes to the floor.

On the way out of the stacks, Keith gave Steve Arnold a quick rundown on the history of the library. They parted with a friendly handshake before the disapproving eyes of the stack librarian. "I think you can count on seeing this Gillington article some time next week, Keith. And I'll be sending you an order for Hollow Tree pretty soon. Sure you can't spare free samples for the press?" Arnold asked persuasively, putting his notebook away.

Behind them, the elevator door opened. Carl emerged, red-faced and fuming, and stalked across the floor to just behind where the three others stood. He had to walk with some care because he was shod only in sweat socks, but they helped him to move with greater stealth. His shoes still lay stuck to the floor on Fourteen as though by industrial-strength Crazy Glue. He didn't know how he was going to blame Doyle for that, but it had to be his fault, just like the way Doyle made a fool of him in front of Steven Arnold.

"I would if I could, but I have a really high overhead and a loan to pay back," Keith said, regretfully. He liked Steven Arnold. "The best I can do is a discount."

Arnold shrugged. "It was worth a try. No hard feelings. Goodbye, kid," the reporter waved to Doyle's nephew.

Holl raised his hand in the Vulcan salute, in which he had been carefully schooled by Keith. "Live long and prosper."

Arnold left the library with Keith waving him a friendly farewell from the entryway to the stacks. Carl waited until Arnold was out of sight, then he sprang out and grabbed Keith by the front of his shirt.

He had recovered from the shock he'd received downstairs, and now he was going to get even with the person responsible for ruining his plans. The satisfied look fled from the red-haired youth's face as his air was cut off.

"Ulp!" Keith protested, trying to free his collar. He glanced over at the fire door.

Carl followed his gaze, then glared back at Keith. "You've got a heck of a lot of nerve," Carl said, shaking him roughly. "It took me forever to set up that interview. I'm going to beat the funny stuff out of you. Yeah. Come on." He dragged Keith back into the stairwell and let the door whine closed. Carl pushed him to the wall. "It's just you and me."

"Wrong," said Lee, stepping out of the corner and dragging Carl away from Keith with ease of a man used to flipping around fifty-pound sacks of flour. "It's you and all of us. We've been waiting for you."

Carl stared at him in disbelief. "Where...?"

"I'm disappointed in you," Teri said, appearing from behind him and shaking her head. "I'm the one who brought you in. I'm so ashamed. I thought he'd ruin it because he's such a nut," she pointed at Keith. "But *you* tried to do it. You know what this means to the rest of us. How could you?"

Carl goggled like a fish. A sentence forced its way out. "I didn't think anyone would care. It was my chance..."

"You're crazy," a voice grunted from the other side. Barry stood there in the shadows with an arm around Marcy, holding her, keeping her from springing out at Carl. She looked ready to explode, and Barry seemed dubious about his ability to keep her where she was much longer. "Mister Hotstuff," Barry spat. "As if you don't owe them, the same as the rest of us."

"We do care," Teri tossed her head. "In fact, we care more than we really knew. When it looked like we might lose our friends and teachers, it tore us to pieces. We blamed the wrong man because you *accused* him. And we believed you! You won't ever be able to betray the Little Folk again, because you won't know where they are."

"No one will believe you when you talk about 'em. And none of us will back you up." Lee punctuated his statement with another push.

"From now on, the Little Folk will just be a legend as far as you're concerned," Marcy said, throwing off Barry's arm, her eyes glowing fire and stepping right up to Carl. She drew back her hand and slapped him ringingly across the face. He was so surprised he backed up a pace. "*That's* for that day in class. Maybe you'd better study up on it, big man. Come on, Keith."

Rubbing his shoulder, Keith turned out the door, side by side with Marcy. As one, the students walked out behind them, leaving Carl stunned on the landing, rubbing his cheek. "Hey!" he called.

The hinges squeaked faintly as the door sagged shut behind the other students, drawing the attention of Mrs. Hansen, who was discussing changes of assignment with the librarian on duty at the front of the stacks. "Oh, no," she said, catching a glimpse of the fire door swinging closed. "Not again." She shot through the chamber, pulled the door open, seized Carl by the shoulder and marched him out into the lobby. "If I have told you students once, I have told you a thousand times. That stairwell is OFF LIMITS! Come with me. I want to talk to your student advisor!"

Surreptitiously, Keith examined his own key. It was still glowing.

"Don't worry," Holl said, peeling off at his latex disguise. "Yours will still work, always. We'll just be opening a new door. Here," he handed him the phaser. "I do not need this any more."

Keith twitched his invisible whiskers in satisfaction. "By the way, I have a present for you," he told Holl. Digging into a pocket, he came up with a small piece of beige paper. "It took a little conniving, but I pointed out you have got a bank account and a job, however nepotistic." It was a Social Security Card made out to Holland Doyle.

"Thanks, Uncle Keith," Holl said, reverently handling the card as if it was printed on crystal.

"Don't mention it, nephew," Keith replied, knowing that the breach between them was completely healed now.

Chapter 38

Five after three. The union president waited in the middle of the Sears television department for Keith to appear. It wouldn't have been such a bad wait if there was any place to sit and watch the thirty or forty sets on display. Besides, with ten of 'em tuned to each of the four local stations, the place sounded like a zoo anyway. The manager had recognized him and was getting nervous. Sears employees were represented by a different union, but you never knew: they might be thinking of a change of organization. The wait didn't bother him, because he knew he was going to win. Hollow Tree would join the happy membership roll of Lewandowski's union.

Ten after. His bodyguards were watching two different soap operas on the most expensive receivers in the place. Lewandowski casually leaned against a big cabinet set as Keith came running up to him.

"Sorry I'm late. I couldn't find a place to park."

"No problem, kid. Well, what can I do for you. We're private." No one could hear a thing over the racket.

"Well, I just wanted you to know that there's no hard feelings," Keith began, removing the toy camera from around his neck, "but I'm not going to join your union."

Lewandowski's blood pressure went up twenty points. "Are you nuts? Didn't I tell you what I can do to you?"

"Sure you did," Keith agreed. He set the toy down on top of the nearest console television. Suddenly, all forty sets showed the same scene. It was a man on a park bench under a maple tree with pigeons and squirrels all around him. Lewandowski glanced down curiously. The man on TV was himself. And he was talking, on every set in the store.

"...I've got police and judges and elected officials on my payroll who could see to it that you won't get a job in this state for the rest of your life, let alone a lousy diploma. Judge Arendson gets plenty from me every month to sign court orders, and he sees the court cases go my way. I got insurance adjusters who never settle arson claims for the insured, not if they cross me..."

Lewandowski's bodyguards looked up with shock as their programs were interrupted by their boss's confession. They noticed Keith and started toward him.

The manager of the television section was beginning to get interested in the sudden change of programming on his sets, and was coming over to ask Mr. Lewandowski what was going on. The union boss grabbed Keith's arm.

"Stop it! Shut it off!"

"Sure, Mr. Lewandowski." The kid moved the camera away, and the taped confession was immediately replaced again by the soap operas. "See? I remember *everything* you said."

Lewandowski narrowed his eyes at Keith, who still looked innocent and stupid to him. He waved away the bodyguards, who were within inches of grabbing the college student. "All right. You win. You're not worth it. I'm a businessman, too. I know when I've lost. Gimme that tape."

"I can't," Keith said firmly. "I think I'll always keep it to remind me of you. But you'll never hear from it again if you leave my customers alone." The union man nodded reluctantly and Keith smiled. "Just one more thing," he pointed out. "Please keep your gorillas off campus. We have an ordinance against wild animals in the streets, leash laws, you know."

Keith watched the thugs' faces turn red.

"Nice doing business with you," he said cheerfully. "Excuse me. I've got another appointment I've got to keep." The union boss was still staring at the bank of television sets as Doyle went out the door.

"You wanted to know where I was studying down in the library." Keith said, guiding Diane down the stairs to Level Fourteen on that Tuesday afternoon. "So, I'm showing you."

"What's this got to do with my failing Biology?" Diane wanted to know. She looked around anxiously for any library personnel. They could get in trouble for being down here. The level was restricted, but Keith seemed to be pretty well at home.

"Well," Keith began, "that just happens to be what I'm studying this term. The very thing."

"Uh, Keith," Diane babbled uncomfortably, clutching his arm as they crossed the dark floor. "I don't think that, um, *practical* instruction in biology is what I need."

"Don't worry," Keith said. "It's not what you think. Trust me. Please." He walked her through the stacks and took out the glowing key. Diane stared at it disbelievingly. Keith put the key in the lock and turned it.

"What IS this? This is just to scare me, right? It's a makeout corner," she determined pugnaciously.

"Nope," Keith said, pausing. "I want to present you to the greatest teacher in the world on ANY subject, *including* biology."

"You mean you?" Diane asked, with mock skepticism, turning into the bright room. "Hi, there, Mr. Alfheim," she called. "How nice to see you. What are you doing down here?" Then her eye took in the unique characteristics of the room's inhabitants. Her jaw trembled and fell open. "Oh, my," Diane said. Keith gently propelled her inside and closed the door.

"Good afternoon, Mees Londen. Von't you sit down?" the Elf Master suggested, pointing to an empty desk next to Marcy. It was Carl's.

"If it's all the same to you, Master, I can move," Enoch volunteered, lifting his books and leaving the desk next to Keith's vacant. Keith winked at him. Enoch smiled as he settled down between Marcy and Lee.

Diane's eyes followed the child-sized figures with wondering fascination. "I don't believe it."

"You'd better," Keith informed her. "These are my best friends."

"I know what she's thinking," Marm complained. "'Those ears.'"

"They all do that," Holl chuckled as the Master rapped on his easel for order.

To Keith's delight, Diane fitted in with the current class as if she had always been there. Teri gave him a silent thumbs-up behind her back, and he grinned. When the session broke up for the day, Holl suggested that she would be welcome to help box and wrap orders, since extra hands would be useful. Keith was delighted. Holl always voiced the others' opinions, and their opinion seemed to be that they were happy to have Diane with them.

Keith was pleased to have gotten his secret off his chest to Diane, but he was equally pleased as to how well she was handling getting to know everyone. She had an easy facility for making friends, and it didn't take long before she stopped noticing the differences between the Big Folk and the Little. Within an hour, she was chatting as freely as she would anywhere else. Maura and Candlepat liked her immediately, and involved her in a passionate talk about fashion that made Keith want to flee the room. The look on Holl's face told him probably he'd have company.

Diane instantly agreed to help pack up Hollow Tree's merchandise, "to make things move more quickly," she said. "Ms. Voordman'll have a fit if the Hollow Tree shelf drops empty again." She went through the new items with careful, awed hands. "Ms. Voordman's going to love this jewelry," she said, holding a necklace of tubular beads up to her throat, and then reading the tag. "She won't be able to keep it in stock." She paused and stared. "Diane Teri Designs? What's this?"

"Well," Keith admitted sheepishly. "Teri gave me the idea, but they thought they should put your name on them, because you're my lady. In the end we compromised."

"Take it," Maura said, thrusting the necklace on her. "We'd be pleased if you accepted it as a gift."

"Oh, I can't," Diane protested, admiring the tiny lady timidly, almost afraid that by looking at her she might break her. "What about you? You'd look beautiful in something like this. You should have it instead."

"My man is the one who makes them," Maura said, proudly glancing at Holl. "I can get others."

"So," Diane asked Holl over a packing crate full of bundles, "why do they call you the Maven?"

The next morning, Wednesday the 15th, Keith and Diane cut all their classes, and spent the day taking the parcels around to his many clients. They waited impatiently at each stop for the owners to write out checks. "I don't know why you're in such a hurry," one shopkeeper admonished him, looking up at the two nervous faces across her counter. "I always pay within thirty days."

"Taxes, Mrs. Geer," Keith answered pathetically. "They'll skin me and hang me out to dry if I don't get in a quarterly payment."

"Of course. I understand perfectly." She bent her head over the checkbook and plucked the pink slip away from its perforations. "Many happy returns of the season."

It took them hours to get around to all of Keith's scattered customers. Most of them were as understanding as Mrs. Geer had been, but others had passed over tart remarks about economy along with their checks. Only a few were unsympathetic enough to insist on the standard 30 days, but in the end, there was enough in their hands to make the payment. At five minutes to five, Keith roared up to the front door of the Midwestern Trust Bank, and leaped out. "Sit in the driver's seat, will you?" he shouted to Diane as he ran inside, not waiting to see her if she moved.

There was a long line for the tellers' windows, and Keith nearly died of impatience before a teller beckoned him over. He drummed on the counter while the girl counted the checks and then added up the total on her machine, until she stopped and looked annoyed at him. He flashed her a toothy smile, and put his hands behind his back. She went back to her addition.

At last, all the paperwork was finished. Keith stopped at one of the convenience tables and wrote out his checks to the IRS and the Illinois Department of Revenue and sealed them with the appropriate forms into stamped envelopes. He saluted the guard who opened the door to let him out into the street, and heard the click of the deadbolt lock behind him. Throwing an OK sign to Diane, he trotted over to the mailbox, yanked down the handle and threw the envelopes inside.

"Good evening, Mr. Doyle," a thin voice said from practically next to him.

"Yaah!" Keith jumped in surprise. Mr. Durrow stood there, his lips pursed in a tiny smile. This was the sort of effect IRS agents lived for. He was pleased.

"I just mailed the check, honest to God," Keith wailed in protest.

"I know," Durrow said, austerely. "Your next payment is due June 15th." And he walked away without changing expression.

The Historical Society met with the press on campus. Director Charles Eddy was pleased to announce to the newspaper-reading and television-watching public that "Gillington Library has attained monument status, and it will be cared for in perpetuity. It is my honor to have discovered this worthy structure in our midst and brought it to the attention of those who care about the history of America."

There was some scattered applause. Eddy smiled fatuously, posing with a broad gesture to the high doorway. Several cameras flashed in his face. "We are proud to have such a fine example of Civil War era architecture in our own little town, and we want to make sure it will be available for our children to appreciate." There was much cheering and confetti-throwing as Eddy presented a small plaque to Mrs. Hansen, and they shook hands for the cameras. Eddy was pleased to note that he would have his picture in several papers by morning.

Brushing confetti out of his hair, Keith went to announce the good news to the little folk.

"That's a blessing," Holl told him. "Now there is no need to hurry up to get to the farm. It will take quite a lot of work before it is habitable to our standards."

It hadn't struck Keith until that moment that his friends would be moving just that much further out of reach. His heart sunk in his chest. "How much time before you go?" he asked with a long face.

Holl chucked him on the shoulder. "Cheer up, widdy. The Master won't leave the students while the course is in session. Perhaps we'll go in the summer. We'll be staying a good while yet."

"Just as well," Diane put in, coming over to them with a handful of flowers from the village garden and a paper-covered bundle, "since I need to finish the Biology course. Don't abandon me now, just when I think I could pass!"

The Master regarded her. "Ve keep our responsibilities in mind, Mees Londen."

"We can't do without you in any case, Keith Doyle," Holl continued. "We'll need help getting there and moving all our things, and finding sources for wood and plaster and the like."

"You bet." Keith got a dreamy look on his face and studied the glowing ceiling. "I've been formulating a plan to help with that. I have these friends..."

"My dad drives a big van," Diane interrupted eagerly. "I'm sure he'd lend it to me if I tell him I'm helping some friends move house."

"Uh-huh, and I think I can get a deal on bulk plas—"

Holl searched the heavens in exasperation. "We didn't know when we were well off. Now we have *two* like Keith Doyle."

"Now how bad could that be?" Marm inquired, frowning at his neighbor. He flipped a hand out and enumerated the blessings of Keith Doyle on his fingers. "Look at all the good he's done us. Found us a new home and the means to acquire it. Been a good friend."

"I agree," the Elf Master added. "I do like him, but I must admit he drives me mad."

"Me, too, but I like him anyway," Diane said, agreeably. The Elf Master didn't seem to intimidate her. "I have a present for you, Keith. From Ms. Voordman and me." She handed him the bundle, and he stripped the paper off of it. "This is thanks for everything, including the scholarship. Even though I know now it was phony." She looked at the others regretfully.

"You may still haf it at least for this year," the Master stated graciously, sketching a little bow to her. "I haf not changed my opinion of you, though I know not how finances will fall out in the years to come."

"Thank you," Diane said gratefully, turning to him. "I didn't know how I was going to break it to my father." Behind them, Keith let out an exclamation.

Underneath the wrappings was the original ceramic elf-in-a-tree from the Country Craft shop. "Now that I've seen the original, I know where he got the logo for your company. It wasn't just a fantastic myth." Diane grinned, winking at the Elf Master. He gave her a stern look, which made her smile more.

Keith hugged her. "Thanks, Diane. Listen, I have to tell you. Wait 'til you hear about my project for next year," Keith said enthusiastically, holding the figurine carefully. "I'm going to be taking archaeology, you know. There are still reported sightings of the fair folk that no one's ever been able to disprove. Maybe I can find historic traces. *You* know—and, Holl, you haven't heard this one yet. I figure, if I can get up high enough in a hot air balloon—an airplane is too noisy, you'd scare 'em off—I can find out if there are really air sprites up in the clouds. There's much more atmosphere than there is surface on this planet, and I'm sure Nature never wasted it. But if I don't find anything *there*.... Wait, Master! Where are you going?" The Elf Master turned and walked away, shaking his head as if it hurt.

"Progressive," Aylmer stated, teeth clenched around the stem of his pipe. "You are too progressive."

"Perhaps we should make statues of you, Keith Doyle," Holl said wryly, "as a fantastic myth."

"Yeah," Diane agreed. "But it shouldn't be an elf for you, Mr. Keith Doyle. I looked it up. It ought to be a gremlin. I found it when I was researching my Mythology paper. There you were, right in the dictionary. 'Gremlin: Mythical creature. Meddling spirit.'"

With a mischievous grin on his face, Keith bowed to them. "That's me," he said.

Mythology Abroad

Chapter One

"Now, now, my wee darlings, get along. This isn't for you, as well you know." Mrs. Mackenzie gently shooed her yowling cats out of her path as she pushed open the kitchen door. Sniffing the sweet, heady scent of milk in the bowl she held, the four Siamese cats followed her out into the garden, their erect tails hopeful. "Enough of your din. You'll have your tea in a moment, my lovelies," Mrs. Mackenzie chided them, laughing. "This is for those who haven't got a mum to give them meals and treats." With her free arm, she held back a low branch of a stunted apple tree and scooted by between the tree and the garden wall. The blossoms had just begun withering away, and tiny green knobs swelled behind them. Mrs. Mackenzie started to count them, and smiled. Even in the wild Atlantic winds that crossed over and over the Isle of Lewis, her garden prospered well enough, as did their small hayfield, fenced in to guard it from the sheep. For this she gave thanks in her church on Sundays, but since she had lived here all her life, she knew better than to ignore the other powers of the land, and offered them thanks as well.

At the end of the garden path sat a square stone with a bowl-like depression in the top. The stone had sat there for heaven knew how many centuries and generations. Its rough, yellowed sides were covered with moss, and its corners had been shaved round by the wind. It was thought to be cut from the same stone which formed the forest of man-made monoliths on the hilltop above their farm, but was probably far older. She stopped in front of it and waited until the liquid in her bowl had stilled. The cats rubbed against her ankles and set up a fresh wail. Paying them no attention, Mrs. Mackenzie poured the bowl of milk into the hollow. "There. The first milk of the first milking from our Flora."

The moment she touched the stone, the cats lost all interest in her or the milk, and wandered back up the path. The chief cat and only female started a game of Tag with the youngest male, and the other two joined in, racing up and down between the plantings of young carrots and strawberries. Mrs. Mackenzie followed them toward the house, calling at them impatiently to go inside for their tea.

Chapter Two

"Do you want to sit by the window or on the aisle?" Keith Doyle
asked Holl as they struggled toward their row on the 747 aircraft.
The flight attendants smiled at the thin, redheaded youth and the
blond, apple-cheeked child in the baseball cap who followed him,
and directed them across the body of the big jet and down another
aisle. Keith ducked around a well-dressed man who was removing
his coat in the Business section. "At least they said the flight isn't too
full. We should get the middle seat of our row, too. Then we can
stretch out. Can you believe how small these things are? How do tall
people sit in them?" Another smiling attendant bowed them past
her into the Economy section and pointed further down the body
of the plane.

A wide-eyed Holl stared distrustfully at the paneled plastic walls
as he trod, zombie-like, behind Keith. All around him, Big Folk,
strangers, stowed their possessions in high-set boxes and sat down
with expressions of expectation in endless rows of identically colored chairs with metal armrests. The chairs creaked as the big people
sat in them. Holl shuddered. Though the other passengers ignored
him now, eight hours of boredom might draw their attention to the
sole representative of the Little Folk on the plane, and he'd be trapped.
Keith called his people elves, which just went to prove how little
even the Big Ones who understood them best knew them. He felt
immediately claustrophobic. Statistics he had researched over the
last few weeks on accidents involving commercial jet aircraft flashed
alarming red numbers inside his head. The two hours they had had
in the terminal before the flight's scheduled departure was too much
time for him to sit and consider the dangers of the trip. Perhaps
sometimes it was not a good idea to have been raised in a library. He
had access to too many alarming facts. "Keith Doyle, I no longer
think this is a good idea. Can I go back?"

Keith looked back at the mob of passengers following them
along the narrow passage from the jetway, and sighed. "I think it's
too late. We've gone through passport control and x-ray. You'll just
have to hang on the best you can, and keep your mind occupied. Try
and sleep, or something."

"This feeble little box will carry us safely four thousand miles?" Under the brim of the Cubs cap he wore to disguise his tall, pointed ears, the young elf's eyes were big and round with fear.

"The aisle," Keith decided firmly. "Wait for me to get in. Here we are." Their row number appeared on an overhead bin to Keith's left, and he shot his suitcase into the compartment. He took Holl's small bag and tossed it up next to his, then squeezed into the window seat. "Hey, we're not over the wing. Great! We'll be able to see everything!"

"Don't ask me to look," Holl said, settling down into the aisle seat. It squeaked alarmingly, and the smooth armrests were cold. "Sticks and stones, these chairs are uncomfortable!"

"There are pillows up there," Keith offered, then he caught Holl's outraged expression. He measured the distance with his eye, and pulled himself to a standing position. "Never mind. I'll get them."

"Talk about your artificial environments," Holl said disgustedly. "Did you take a look in their lavatories?"

Keith was relieved that his friend had recovered enough to complain. The takeoff had been a trauma he didn't expect. Keith himself enjoyed the pressure when the jet was racing down the runway, building momentum, and the breathless feeling of weightlessness he got just as it left the ground. It was fun, the way that the drop-off over the crest of a rollercoaster track was fun. He'd forgotten just for that second that Holl had never been on a plane before, let alone a rollercoaster. He was as innocent of modern transportation as the ten- or twelve-year-old Big Person he seemed to be. No one from Holl's village ever traveled anywhere except on their feet. In a brief glance toward the seat on his left, Keith saw Holl's face go chalky white, eyes squeezed shut, and he was gripping the armrests with his fists.

"Hey, it's over," Keith nudged him gently. "We're airborne."

"My stomach's still down there somewhere," Holl replied apologetically, opening his eyes. "And you talk about my people's magic. This thing oughtn't to be able to fly!"

"Well, we're defying gravity at about 500 miles per hour, and we're heading for the clouds. Wait, don't look. I'll keep the window shut. Do you want to get up and look around?"

"Need I?" Holl asked, nervously.

"No, but others are getting out of their seats and stretching. Why don't you take a quick look around? We've got lots of time before we get to Scotland. Hours, in fact." Keith grinned. "You ought to see what you're traveling in. Consider it research. You can tell the others all about it."

Holl considered. It was true that few of his folk would ever have the opportunity to do what he was doing: flying in an aircraft across the Atlantic Ocean. His friends and family would demand detail of his adventure, and if he didn't have it, they would be disappointed. Watching other passengers negotiate the aisles without care, Holl flicked open the catch on his safety belt, defying his own fear. "All right. I will, then."

As Keith kept a surreptitious eye on him, the young elf paced out the length of the aisle and doubled back through the back galley to the other aisle. He had a look into the cockpit, where the pilot and crew smiled at him, seeing only another youngster curious about the workings of the jet. Holl even took a peek into the upper level of the aircraft, into the First Class lounge, before the steward on duty up there chased him down again.

"No one else seems worried," Holl reported, returning to his seat just as a flight attendant rolled a beverage cart into their aisle.

"They're not. They do this all the time. It's almost safer than walking," Keith promised him, and looked up at the attendant's prompt. "What'll you have? Everything's free but the liquor, and I can't give you that anyhow. You're underage, my dear nephew."

The attendant helped them to plastic cups of soda and two impermeable packets of sugared peanuts. Keith turned the knob in front of him to let the table down for his drink. Holl was pleased by the design of the fold-down tables, and examined the suspension mechanism closely.

"First flight?" the stewardess asked Keith, glancing at Holl.

"Yes, ma'am. He's twelve." They exchanged smiles. "Hey, Holl, your drink."

The elf received his refreshments and put them on his tray table. After a few attempts to tear open the plastic package of peanuts, he reached surreptitiously for his whittling knife and poked a hole in the celluloid. He caught Keith gawking at him.

"How did you get that through the security check?" Keith demanded, staring at the long, gleaming blade as his friend tucked it away in its sheath. "The buzzers should have gone crazy with a long hunk of steel like that passing through them."

"They just didn't notice, that's all," Holl replied, offhandedly. "And it isn't made of steel. You know what too much steel does to us. It's titanium. I made it from scrap lifted from the Science Labs, and difficult it was to do, I will tell you. I wasn't leaving home without it. You never know what you'll need. Money can't buy it all."

"I don't know," Keith said dubiously. "I still think it would set off the metal detectors. You must have done something magic to them." He waited for Holl to clarify, but the Little Person wasn't talking. Another thought struck Keith. "Speaking of not being able to buy it all, how'd you get the money to come with me?"

Holl made an offhand gesture. "From sweepstakes and the like. At first, we had to figure out which ones actually had drawings after the entries were sent in instead of choosing them in advance."

Keith sputtered. "You can't use magic to win contests! That's cheating!"

Holl was nonplused. "We didn't use magic to win. You should see the things professional contesters do to their envelopes to get them chosen. Ours were innocent by comparison. We just wanted to ensure that our envelopes made it to the final draw. We had every chance to lose after that point, one among thousands in a turning drum. But when we had enough money, we stopped. Lee Eisley said the barn roof needs repair, and we can't make tar paper for ourselves. We won a good bit, but only out of need."

"In my name, I suppose." Holl nodded. Keith groaned. "Pray the accounting companies never check the system for magical intervention. I hope you have enough left over for me to pay the income tax on the winnings."

"The Master says so." The village headman, who also taught one of Midwestern University's more interesting and exclusive study groups, was known only by his title. Keith respected the Master's encyclopedic knowledge, but was just a little put off by his formidable personality. He nodded.

"If the Master says it's okay, I guess it is, the way you guys research things. I oughta let you just take over my life. You make more money in my name than I do. But where did you get a passport?" Keith continued in a low voice, glancing over his shoulder between the seats to make sure no one was listening. "Without a birth certificate, without any identification?"

"Don't ask how and I'll tell you no lies," was all Holl would say. Keith shrugged and sipped his drink. He watched the sky through the window next to the seat in front of him. Through breaks in the clouds, he could see the green checkerboard pattern of farms and roads. Holl quaffed soda and ate the peanuts methodically, one at a time, staring straight forward at the bulkhead.

"Okay, I've waited to ask," Keith said at last, "but I guess you're not going to tell me. Why are you coming with me?"

Holl raised his hands, palms up. "You're a trend-setter again, Keith Doyle. When they heard that you were making your way to Scotland and Ireland, there was much discussion."

"I'm going on an educational tour. Archaeology. For credit. I don't see what use that would be to you."

"But afterwards? When you visit Ireland to look for your distant relatives? The old ones have decided that it's important we make contact with the ones that were left behind—if there are any still alive, and where we left them. We're tired of being isolated. If there are Folk left to find, in this day of easy global communication, there's no need for them to remain isolated any longer."

"Yeah, I've heard this thesis somewhere before," Keith said drily. "I think it was mine. But Holl, you were born at Midwestern University. You're what, forty-one? Your folks left home lots longer ago than that. You don't know where to go to find them, do you?"

"I can find them," Holl stated, "with your help."

"Bring 'Em Back Alive Doyle, that's me. But wouldn't it have been easier to send one of the old folks back to look? There must be plenty of them who remember how to get there. What about the Master? Why you?"

"I volunteered to go," Holl said firmly, as if that should settle the matter.

"Uh-huh." Keith could tell Holl was hedging by the way his invisible whiskers twitched, and searched his friend's face for clues. The very idea of hunting for more Little People in the wilds of Ireland intrigued him, but there had to be more to it than that. "Okay...but your Irish relatives have never seen you before. They may not trust a strange face, even if you have the pointy ears to prove kinship. Why not someone who remembers them? Anyone still alive from when your people left home? People who know the homestead on sight? Can you help me find it?"

"Well, I might." But Holl sounded unsure.

Keith picked up on his tone immediately. "Okay, if you're as lost as I am, there must be another reason." Holl started to speak several times, but stopped short before uttering a word. Keith waited.

"My reasons are my own," the elf said, and fell obstinately silent.

"C'mon, Holl. I'm your friend," Keith wheedled. "You're not like me. You don't blunder in and get lucky. You plan. There's got to be a better reason than 'it's important.'"

The buzz of the steward's cart grumbled toward them, breaking the concentrated mood. The attendant leaned over to collect their cups. Holl instantly stuck the earpieces of his headphones into the entertainment system and stared straight ahead, ignoring Keith. Keith sighed and settled back into his seat with a book. Presently, meal service passed through the cabin and dropped trays in front of them.

"You'll like the food." After taking a bite of the entree, Holl pulled the earpiece away from his head and nudged Keith. "It tastes exactly the same as what you eat at school."

While they ate, Keith talked. He could see that his friend was still anxious, but he was negotiating the jet's aisles without lurching, and he handled the air turbulence over Nova Scotia without comment or color changes. So what was bugging him? He looked haggard, more tired than he had ever seen him. Something wrong in the village? Or something more personal? "I'm really looking forward to exploring Scotland, aren't you?" Keith babbled. "I can't rent a car 'til I'm 25, so that's out, but there are buses, and we can get bicycles. Can you ride a bike? I'm especially anxious to see the standing stones at Callanish. It's supposed to be Scotland's answer to Stonehenge— you know, really magical."

No response. "The Hebrides are so far distant from everything, that they haven't been spoiled by development yet. The syllabus said there are five dig sites currently under investigation, though we won't know which one we work on until we get there. I've got lots of books with me about the area, and the local legends. Of course, all of them are about half read. But I expect to have them all finished by the time I go home. We travel to the islands by ferry boat, you know, same as when we leave for Ireland. No more flying."

Holl, made more comfortable by food, and the fact that night had fallen, obscuring the view from 37,000 feet up over open water, shook his head wryly. If he couldn't trust Keith Doyle, whom could he trust? Besides, he needed the boy's help. "You've worn me out, widdy. I'll confess. I've been through a trauma the likes of which I never want to repeat in my lifetime. It's well that you've provided an opportunity for me to remove myself from the situation for a while. I just asked the Master for permission to marry his daughter, and you can imagine what that was like."

"Holy cow!" exclaimed Keith, sympathetically regarding Holl. "You've still got all your hide, though. I take it he said yes? Congratulations! When's the wedding?"

"*Maura* still has yet to be asked, foolish one. But that's not all we discussed, hence my departure with you to discover our original home." Holl sighed. More and more in the recent past, he and the Master had butted heads over issues, and Holl had come in second each time. Experience and logic won over youthful energy and good intentions over and over again. "There's the welfare of the other Folk to be considered. Did you know there hasn't been a wedding since we came to Midwestern, more than four decades gone?"

"Really? Wow! So you'll be the first. Great. When are you going to ask her? Can I come to the wedding?"

"*If.* If I can. There's something I need to find before I do."

"In Ireland? What? The Ring of Kerry? A four-leaf clover?" Keith laughed.

Holl glowered. "Your interminable questions, Keith Doyle! I almost wish I'd not told you. We've always had the custom that a wedding couple wear white bellflowers. No one has married since we came to Midwestern. We'll be the first in a string of decades. It sounds squashy and sentimental when I think about it, but there you are. But no white bellflowers survive among our plants. My mother's sister was in charge of propagating of all the seeds our folk would need, but that one slipped by, whether dying off infertile or simply being left behind in the old place, she can't say, it's been that long. Many of the kernels and seeds she's preserved have never been grown, since the bottom of the library building is no fit place for them. And there's been no need for the flower in all this time, so it wasn't missed."

"That vital to the process, eh?" Keith asked.

"We've never done without it. They're imbued with a charm of joining, among a host of other useful natural properties, good for healing wounds or curing the tongue-tied."

"Yes," Keith nodded solemnly. "I can see where you'd want to be holding one of those before you propose."

Holl ignored the jibe. "Of course, this is all before my time. I've not witnessed a wedding myself. But I have a feeling that many of my generation have only been waiting to pick white bellflowers to ask their loved ones to marry."

"And the Master made it one of the conditions of his approval, didn't he?" Keith asked shrewdly, and was rewarded by an expression of summing respect on his companion's face. "Well, you did say it was for the welfare of everyone else, too. What do they look like? There's a lot of different kinds of bell-shaped flowers in the world. Lily-of-the-valley, bluebells, foxglove, you name it."

"I'll know them when I see them," Holl said, uneasily. "They probably are similar to any of the other *campanulaceae.*"

"So where do you find them?"

"I don't know, exactly, but the Master felt I should look in the old places from where our folk come. They might be in fairy rings, well-guarded earth mounds in hidden places, and the like."

"I suppose you know it's illegal to carry plants back into the U.S. without a license?" Keith asked. Holl nodded. "Well, I don't know that magic flowers count. Now that we've cleared that out of the way, let's open the atlas and find our most likely prospects."

Holl and Keith discussed the subject well into the night, until the in-flight movie was announced. At the stewardess's request, the lights were shut off and the window shades pulled down. The movie played on an easel-sized screen at the front of the section. Through his rented headphones, Holl listened to the tinny soundtrack, and relaxed back into his nest of pillows. It wasn't half bad, really, watching a film this way. There were no extraneous noises to distract one from the program, barring the constant atonal whistle from the air system. He glanced over to ask Keith Doyle a question, and saw that the boy had fallen asleep, head back and jaw open, in his corner of the row. Holl grinned at him paternally. The lad had been so intent on making sure he, Holl, was comfortable that he wore himself out. Gently, Holl eased the headset off Keith's ears and hooked it on the cloth pocket of the seat in front of him.

The Big Folk took their technology so much for granted, they didn't realize how much of a miracle it would seem to someone else, Holl thought. If it wasn't magic to fly through the thin, high air, in relative comfort with hot food and entertainment, then it was a near cousin, and it took not a whit of energy out of one's own aura to be a part of these marvels. Holl could feel the threatening presence of too much metal under and around him, though it was unlikely to break through the protective cloth and plastic coats in which the Big Folk clad it to attack him.

It did indeed make him nervous to be surrounded by so many strange Big Folk. He realized how sheltered he had been all his life, coming into contact only with the few who could be trusted. He had to keep reminding himself that no one knew him, and that none would observe that for which they weren't looking. Trying to put that thought from him, he reminded himself he was on a mission of great importance. Strange as it may sound, he couldn't be in better hands than those of Keith Doyle. If something came too close to him, Keith would draw away attention and make a joke out of it. There was surprising safety in humor. Holl took off the baseball cap and ruffled his hair with his fingers with a sigh of relief. No need to put it back on until the lights came up again. Now was his chance to do something about the uncomfortable seat. He unbuckled his belt and scooted forward off the pad. A searching tendril of knowledge he put into the cushions suggested that there was just enough fiber to be comfortable, but it had been flattened down by who knew how many bottoms before his. He forced them to repel from one another, springing out against their covering, puffing the cushions up from within. The charge abated swiftly, for the fibers were poor conductors, and Holl was able to settle back in the seat without feeling the bars and rods poking at him any more.

The film's plot was predictable, one of the nine plots repeated over and over throughout five thousand years of literature and ninety of filmmaking, so Holl's attention wandered. Looking around at his fellow passengers to ensure he was disturbing no one, he reached across Keith, slid up the shade and looked out of the window at the night.

He had heard of all sorts of terrible accidents in planes, owing to bad maintenance or fatigued metal. Holl preferred to live long enough to see the far lands on the other side of the ocean, and return home again. There was so much that was precious to him, only the thought that he would return allowed him to wrench himself away. Feeling outward gently with a cohesion spell, he touched the braces and bulkheads of the giant airliner, seeking weak spots and untightened bolts. The jet's complexity of construction amazed him. Not surprisingly, the massed metal repelled his touch, but reassuringly sent back impressions that it was solid and whole, needing none of his magic to finish its journey in safety. Holl relaxed, satisfied. This jet was well built and correctly maintained. As a craftsman, he approved such work.

The stars were remarkably clear up here. The disturbing sight of the far-distant surface was covered by a soft carpet of white clouds, ghostly fleece under the moon. Holl spotted constellations and counted stars until he fell asleep with his face toward the moon.

Chapter Three

"Good morning!" The sheer power of the loudspeaker over their heads belied the flight attendant's friendly greeting. "We will be landing in just about an hour, so we'll be serving breakfast and distributing landing cards now. Please have them with you when you pass through Customs."

Holl woke up like a shot at the first blast of sound. "They dole out sleep in grudging amounts, don't they?" he asked grumpily, planting his cap on top of his disordered hair. Keith had been curled up like a grasshopper with his thin knees against his chest until the flight attendant's voice shocked him awake. Both legs shot out and banged into the seat in front of him, earning a sleepy grunt from its occupant. "Sorry," Keith murmured. He focused his reddened eyes on his friend and ran his hands through tousled hair.

"Good morning," Holl said politely.

"I guess they don't want us to get too comfortable." Keith noticed the glare of the sun coming over his shoulder. "Sounds like we crashed straight into tomorrow. Oops, I must have nudged the shade open while I was asleep. Sorry." He glanced down at the shimmering gray sea far below them, visible through thinning white clouds.

"Don't bother," Holl said, catching his hand. "I don't mind any more. It doesn't look real up this high. There, I see coastline, clear as I can see you. Which is it? Can we open up your maps?"

Breakfast was a basket containing a cold, sweet pastry, fruit cocktail, and a sealed cup of orange juice, and accompanied by a white document identified by the flight attendant as a landing card, which all non-United Kingdom residents needed to fill out. Holl tasted a single bite of the pastry and rejected it, as he read the card.

"Newsprint mixed with sugar, and topped with more," he complained. The fruit was pronounced edible, but the orange juice proved to be as difficult to open as the peanuts. "They must have an endless supply of that plastic."

"Don't worry," said Keith. "I have emergency rations in my bag. Cookies, candy bars, and sandwiches. Do you want peanut butter and jelly, or ham, tomato, and mustard?"

"I apologize, Keith Doyle, for all the bleating," Holl admitted, shamefacedly accepting a sandwich. "Grousing about such trifles as food, when I've just flown three thousand miles and more. A wonder, and I'm not even properly grateful. Your pardon."

"I promise, I would never have assumed you were scared out of your skull," Keith replied, very solemnly, but his eyes twinkled. "If I didn't know better, I would have put it down to that."

Holl laughed. "That's the truth of it. I don't react well in crisis, do I?"

"Lack of experience. You're much better on your home ground," Keith reasoned. "Why not let yourself go, and take the adventure as it comes? The food wasn't poisoned or anything, just not that good. I prefer home cooking myself." Keith, who prided himself that he could eat anything, had finished both their pastries and a sandwich, and was rolling down the wrapper on a candy bar. "It's a whole new experience for me, too, traveling to another country. At least this one speaks the same language I do."

A flight attendant appeared beside them to take away their trays. "Well, how are we this morning?" she asked, brightly. Her swept-back brown hair looked freshly coifed, and her makeup had been newly applied.

"Better," Keith smiled up at her, wondering how she looked so good when he felt so lousy. Maybe their seats were more comfortable.

"Good! The captain would like your little brother to have his wings, for completing his first flight across the Atlantic." The woman handed Holl a small card to which was pinned a pot-metal representation of pilot's insignia. "Thank you for flying with us, young man. We hope you've enjoyed yourself." Holl stared at the card and then up at the woman with disbelief in his eyes.

"Say thank you," Keith urged him, with an elbow in the ribs.

"Thank you," Holl gritted out. "I suppose I deserve a medal for living through this," he said under his breath as the flight attendant walked away.

"Don't hate it too much," Keith cautioned him. "We have to do it all over again on the way home."

Within the hour, the plane touched down, and the passengers debarked into Glasgow Airport. In the midst of the milling crowd, Keith and Holl followed the signs for Customs. The longest line in the Customs hall proved to be that for U.S. and Canadian citizens.

"It's tourist season," Keith reasoned, glancing covertly at the loud, obscene, or torn tee-shirts in which his countrymen were clad. He winced, and then wondered if he would be considered overdressed in his short-sleeved button-down shirt. It was close in the hall. The heat was not as much a problem as the humidity, which made breathing a task in the stagnant air, especially for travelers short of sleep. They shuffled back and forth in the serpentine queue, which was bounded by colored ropes and bronze posts. "I feel like I'm on Mulholland Drive in the middle of an L.A. summer."

"No air conditioning," Holl observed. "When it's there, you complain of it. When you don't have it, you miss it."

"Passports?" said the man behind the narrow desk, with little to no inflection in his voice. Obediently, Keith and Holl handed over their dark blue booklets and white landing cards. "Business or playsure?" The final 'r' rolled off his tongue in a rumbling burr.

His was the first real Scottish accent they had heard, and Keith's ears perked up. "Uh, we're here to join a university class," he explained, hoping the man would say something else.

The deeply etched mouth lifted slightly in one corner, and the dark eyes twinkled. Keith saw that they were actually dark blue. "Taychnically, that'd be playsure, do you no' agree; still it might be a bit o' a job?" Keith absorbed the tones with avidity, and nodded. The man stamped their passports with a square and a line of print and waved them on to the baggage hall.

"Whew! Did you hear him? Great!"

"Fascinating," Holl agreed. "He sounds like and not like Curran, the chief of my clan. Are we that close to Ireland?"

"We're separated from it only by a narrow sea and a sense of direction. Remember King James the Sixth and all. Hey, come on. Our bags won't be on the baggage carousel yet. I want to call home."

There was a money-exchange inside the baggage hall which took Keith's traveler's checks and provided him with a receipt and a handful of very colorful paper money and coins of several sizes and shapes.

"Uh-oh. I hope the phone doesn't just take…what is this?—" he wondered, examining a small silver coin with seven sides, "— twenty pences."

Holl looked through the collection of cash with fascination. "They're all different, and graduated in size by value, I see. Would you mind lending me a bit of that for the duration of the journey, Keith Doyle?"

"Sure—Whoa! Didn't you bring any money with you?" Keith asked, aghast. He experienced a moment of panic, calculating his meager supply of liquid cash, and dividing by two. It wasn't a comforting total. "Who the heck travels without spending money?"

"And how should I know, when I've never been ten miles from my home in my life?" Holl defended himself, and produced his wallet, which he thrust at Keith. "You should have warned me, Keith Doyle. All I've got with me is this."

Keith counted the money in the leather folder and sighed with relief. "Holl, they'll take hundred-dollar bills, I promise."

"I don't need the blue money?" Holl asked meekly.

"Nope. Those are traveler's checks, which I bought at home for green money. The exchange rate's a little lower for cash. I might even ask you for a loan later on. I don't have anywhere near seven hundred bucks on me."

Returning from the exchange desk with a fascinating handful of British money, Holl found Keith reading the instructions on long cards surrounding the pay telephone.

"Piece of cake," the young man called, as the elf caught his eye. "It takes all the coins." Keith fed in the change, punched in the International Access Code, 1, then his home phone number. "It's ringing...Hi, Dad. Yeah, we're here. The flight was fine. I'm on a pay phone, and it's ticking off the money pretty fast. I'll call again in two days. Give my love to Mom. Sure I'll send postcards! 'Bye!" He punched a square blue button under the hook marked 'Follow On Call,' and dialed again. "Whew! The sign says that's what you're supposed to do to keep from losing your change. Dad says hi, and hopes you're okay. Diane? Good morning!"

"Keith?" Diane muttered sleepily into the receiver. "Hi. I'm not up yet. Can you call later?"

"Whaddaya mean you're not out of bed yet?" the cheerful voice demanded. "It must be four in the morning!"

Her eyes flew open. "Are you guys okay? How's Scotland?" Diane asked anxiously. Unable to restrain a yawn, she covered the receiver with the other hand, and gaped at the clock. She peered out of her apartment window at a gray false-dawn, and groaned.

"Haven't seen it yet. We're still waiting for our suitcases. Say, can you let them know on the farm that Holl is okay?"

Diane clicked her tongue in exasperation. "Don't you have their phone number? Call them yourself. They'd be thrilled to hear from you. Can I go back to sleep now?"

"Be my guest," Keith said magnanimously. "Call you again later in the week?"

"Later in the week *and* the day. Bring me a souvenir. A pot of gold would be nice. Love you."

"Yeah, love you, too," Keith echoed, fondly. He winked at Holl and pushed the blue button again and dialed another number. He waited for it to begin clicking through to the American exchange, then handed the surprised elf the receiver. "Here. Phone home."

"They thought it was a young miracle, hearing my voice travel four thousand miles," Holl told him, impressed by the feat. "They're all well, though Dola has the sore throat again."

"Probably still. You've only been gone a couple of days," Keith chided him lightly. "Not much usually happens in that short a time. Sorry I ran out of coins, there."

Holl waved a dismissive hand. "Ah, they'll never know the difference. Having never received a call of this distance, I don't think they know how one should end."

"Did you talk to everyone?" Keith grinned, picturing a crowd of fascinated elves around the phone.

"Nearly," Holl returned the impish smile. "Those I missed this time will demand their turn when I call again."

They followed the crowd past the baggage carousels to the two wide doorways marked Red Channel and Green Channel. As they had nothing to declare, Keith and Holl obediently joined the queue going through Green. At that time, it wasn't moving at all. They stood yawning behind a family wheeling a huge number of bags, and waited for the way to clear.

"They must have just returned from going around the world," Keith muttered behind his hand to Holl. He shifted his weight from one foot to the other.

Holl was becoming impatient. "Wait a moment." He left his bag beside Keith and ran forward to the edge of the Green Channel. Surrounded by Customs men opening a host of matching luggage, a woman in a fur coat was gesticulating with an official in shirtsleeves. Her face was bright red. One by one, the Customs men set bottles of liquor on the metal tables. There seemed to be dozens in each bag.

He marched back to Keith, and explained what he had seen. "The whole channel is constricted by Customs Agents helping to move her bags aside. Come with me."

Seizing Keith's arm, he marched them around the queue and into the Red Channel.

"What are you doing?" Keith demanded in an undertone. "We can't go that way. They'll search us."

"They won't even look at us," Holl promised. "I'm putting an aversion between us and them."

It was true. The agents in the Red Channel seemed to look everywhere but at the two youths walking between them. They passed unnoticed by everyone, and abruptly found themselves amidst a huge, busy crowd in the waiting room of the airport. Everyone else seemed to know where they were going. A number of the people waiting for passengers had small white signs of cardboard in their hands. Keith peered at them all as he went by, looking for the Educatours representative.

"Now, where to?" Holl asked, feeling lost and helpless among all those Big Folk.

"I don't know," Keith answered, casting around.

A tall, thin, elderly lady with silver hair tied back in a knot scurried up to them. In one hand she held a clipboard; in the other, a cardboard sign which read "Educatours." She peered at Keith through thick, round glasses which magnified eyes of flower blue. "Doyle? Are you Keith Doyle?"

"Yes, ma'am," he answered politely, hoisting the strap off his shoulder and setting his bag down on his foot.

She thrust the sign among the papers on the clipboard, took Keith's right hand and pumped it enthusiastically. "I'm Miss Anderson. How do you do. And is this Holland?"

"Holl," the elf said, extending his hand to her. She gripped it, and Holl winced in astonishment.

"How do you do, Holl. I'm the Educatours director for this tour. Nice to have you with us. The weather's not as fine as we could have hoped, but it may improve as the day progresses. I often find that it's foul before noon, and fair afterwards." Keith was fascinated by the perfection of her diction.

"Perhaps it has the same trouble I do with getting out of bed in the morning," Keith joked.

The blue eyes gleamed behind the glass circles. "Hm! It wouldn't surprise me at all. If you tend to be a slugabed, you'll have to scotch your tendencies over the next six weeks. We get an early start every day. This way. Our motor coach is waiting in front of the terminal building. You look tired. Let me take that. I must meet one more flight, and then we may leave for Glasgow proper." She hoisted Keith's large bag over one shoulder without the least suggestion of effort and strode ahead. The electronic-eye doors parted before her.

"Boy, if that's an example of the old ladies of Scotland, I don't want to get in any fights with the wee lads," Keith muttered under his breath to Holl as they scurried behind with their carryons.

"She's likely an example of why they're so polite," Holl suggested. "All bones and wires. She must have ten times their energy."

"Michaels here, sir. We caught sight of him on his way through Immigration: Danny O'Day." The mustachioed man in the nondescript tweed suit spoke into a telephone at the front of the airport. He sent a suspicious glance around, watching out for illicit listeners, but no one seemed interested in a middle aged man who looked like a retired mathematics professor lately returned from a fishing holiday. "Aye, it had to be him. Face like the very map of Ireland, and a midget with him pretending to be a kid, on a plane from the States. Oh, yes, big bill-cap and all. Cool as you please. They came through the Red Channel, if you like. Yes, incredible. No, no one on the floor saw them. I got word from the operator minding the security cameras. The bloke got all excited when he watched those two trot unmolested through the channel, and made me a phone call. Left here with a tour group led by an old bag. Wondering what he's smuggling in this time. Whatever it is would have to be light. They have no sizable luggage. The airline said there's nothing in 'em but clothes and books. A lot of books."

"No idea, Michaels," said the Chief of Operations. "Might be disks or microfilms of classified information hidden away, like the last time, but it's just as likely to be diamonds. We're fortunate you spotted him. The gen was that he'd be entering from the U.S. either here or Manchester."

"Shall I have him stopped?"

There was a pause on the other end of the telephone line. Michaels eyed a woman who was waiting impatiently for him to finish, and then turned his back on her. "No," the Chief answered, reluctantly. "They'll laugh themselves sick at Scotland Yard at our expense if we stop him, and he's here empty to make a pickup instead of a delivery. Keep an eye on him, will you? Report anything he does that looks suspicious."

"I will, sir." Michaels pushed the Follow-On Call button, and punched 100, requesting Directory Inquiries to tell him what it could about a company called Educatours.

Miss Anderson shepherded them into the waiting motor coach, painted a natty silver and blue with "Educatour" blazoned in white across the sides and front of the vehicle. "Keith Doyle and Holl Doyle," she said formally, indicating the other passengers with a sweep of her hand, "meet your classmates for the next six weeks."

The group assembled on the coach was a mixed one. A cluster of college-age male students huddled together at the back of the bus. They stared blankly through a haze of acrid cigarette smoke at Keith when he was introduced to them. Max, Martin, Charles, Edwin, Matthew, and Tom came from the same college at Edinburgh University. Alistair was one of Miss Anderson's own pupils at Glasgow University. In spite of their casual insouciance, they were dressed in button-down shirts with identical ties. Keith was glad he hadn't given in to the temptation of comfort and worn a tee shirt. Two middle-aged women, Mrs. Green and Mrs. Turner, whom Keith guessed to be teachers, sat together in the second seat behind and to the left of the driver. They gave him polite, shy smiles, but positively beamed at Holl. Miss Anderson dashed off and returned with a petite Indian girl dressed in a sari.

"There. With Narit's arrival, we have our full complement." Miss Anderson plumped herself into the seat in front of the pair of teachers. "Open the windows, extinguish cigarettes, thank *you*! It's too nice a day not to take the air."

Keith and Holl took a seat on the left side halfway back, between the Scottish students and the English teachers. Even though he had seen the driver seated on the right when he got on, Keith still did a double take when the bus pulled out to the right, with apparently no one driving it. They left the one-way system in front of the airport, and pulled onto the motorway.

"Now, now!" Miss Anderson clapped her hands at Keith. He had just settled back with his head on his rolled-up jacket. "No naps yet. We've too much to do!"

"I can hardly stay awake," Keith pleaded.

"Nonsense!" cried Miss Anderson. "Today is your first day of class!" There was a chorus of groans from the back of the coach. "Now, pay attention, and I will begin. The area of the island of Great Britain known as the Highlands had a surprisingly rich Neolithic culture, which was during the period between 4400 and 2400 B.C. In the ensuing millennia, the population in many of these centers has declined. As a result, a number of the Stone Age and following Bronze Age sites have remained relatively undisturbed, because until air transport and surveillance became a reality, they were unknown. That feature which our ancestors have left for us in the greatest abundance is the tomb. It was the custom for most of these ancient peoples to bury substantial goods with the dead, and from these goods, we are able to deduce as much about the way they lived as we can from the remains of the people themselves.

"The first site we will explore is just southwest of here in the portion of the county of Strathclyde which was known as Renfrewshire, in which Bronze Age settlements were common. Alas, this area has been heavily settled through the ages since the beginning, so we are hard pressed to discover undisturbed sites near here. In this case, we're immediately in front of the bulldozers. There will be construction on the site in ten months time unless something of significant cultural or historical importance is unearthed, so time is precious. The team do not expect such a find, so they are working quickly to document the site while they still can."

"Do they hope that they'll find something that will save the site?" Keith sat up, remembering Gillington Library on the Midwestern campus and how he had worked to prevent its demolition.

Miss Anderson shook her head. "Indeed, no, not really. In this case, we're merely record takers, making notes of what was where, and when, for future historians. We can't hope to preserve all the sites where our ancestors lived—we'd soon run out of places to live! Most of what we find will be reburied *in situ*. The second and third digs, both in the ancient province of Alban, now known as Inverness-shire and the Islands, are much better. Neither is immediately subject to development."

She went on with her lecture. Keith strained to comprehend and remember what she was saying, but realized, hopelessly, that the words were bouncing off his jet-lagged ears. Holl had dozed off miles back. Maybe one of his fellow classmates could help fill him in later.

The coach turned in off the main street and passed by an arched stone gate. Keith glimpsed relief carvings on the archway and a square surrounding a grass sward, banked by solid walls of buildings inside of the same soot-darkened stone as the arch. He was awed by the antiquity of the University buildings, compared with those of Midwestern University. What they offered here was Education, with a capital E, tried but untroubled by the passing ages. He was enormously impressed, and couldn't wait to explore.

"That is the MacLeod Building," Miss Anderson pointed out. "We'll have seminars in the Small Lecture Room once a week, where those of you taking this tour for credit will present weekly essays, which I'll explain later. The University is not in session during the summer, so we've got the place pretty much to ourselves. You'll all be staying in rooms in the Western Residence Hall just along this road for the next two weeks. Meals are in the refectory. Your names are on the doors of your dormitories."

The party clambered out of the coach before a gray granite building with no windows on the ground floor. Checking Miss Anderson's chart, Keith and Holl found they were sharing a suite with Martin and Matthew on the second floor, which, translated for them, meant that they had to climb two flights of stairs to get there. "We're on the ground floor, now," the teacher explained, as they pulled into the car park next to the gray stone building. "First is just above us."

"Miss Anderson," Keith began apologetically. "Can I get a review sheet or something of the lecture you gave on the bus? I don't think I absorbed very much of it."

"Never mind, lad," the teacher smiled brightly. "I was talking simply to keep you awake on the coach, though it won't hurt if you retained some of it. We'll be reviewing the same information tomorrow morning before we go out. Wear old clothes; we'll be getting a bit mucky."

Keith enkindled instant admiration for the wiry instructor. "Yes, ma'am!" He pulled a smart salute. Holl groaned.

With a smile, she shooed them away. "Get on with you before your room-mates scoff the best beds!"

Chapter Four

The accommodations were comfortable enough. Holl and Keith shared a tiny bedroom that bore a striking resemblance to Keith's dormitory room at Midwestern. "Even the dressers are in the same place," Keith pointed out with amusement. "I bet they stamp them out of a mold in Hong Kong."

"Keith Doyle," Holl spoke up suddenly from behind him. "I've been meaning to ask—those rows upon rows of houses in Illinois and those we saw on the way from Glasgow Airport? Are there really molds large enough to make houses?"

Keith, turning around to face Holl, tried to stifle a grin, but was unable to do anything about the twinkle in his eye. "They don't stock much in the way of architecture texts in Gillington Library, do they?"

"No...." Holl admitted, thoughtfully, turning red. "They've a subscription to Architecture Quarterly, but that deals mostly with unique structures. Not the mass-produced ones we saw."

"It's just an expression," Keith assured him, going back to unpacking his suitcase, "although they sometimes make them out of prefabricated sections. It would save a lot of time if they could cast a whole block's worth of houses at once."

Holl's jaw dropped. "Do you mean those identical, cheap-looking boxes are constructed one by one? On purpose? There are frauds passing themselves off as craftsmen, then."

A rap sounded at the door, cutting off further exclamations of outrage. Holl sat down on the bed with his cap pulled down over his forehead, and yanked a half-whittled stick and his knife out of his jacket pocket.

"It's open," Keith called over his shoulder.

Matthew and Martin leaned in. "Are you settled now?" Matthew asked. He was about Keith's height and build, but his face was sharper in outline. His hair was black and smooth, but his pale skin seemed curiously thin, showing pink through it over the cheekbones.

"Just about," Keith said, shutting a drawer full of t-shirts.

"If you do' mind it, we can show you about the town. Maybe nip into the pub for a quick one. It's well on into lunchtime, though they'll serve meals until two," Martin grinned, exposing crooked,

white teeth. His hair was taffy-colored, similar to Holl's, cut short in
the back, but long enough in front to droop over his eyes. "We
know where to find the best cider in Glasgow."

"Cider? Sounds good. I'm thirsty," Keith said.

"It gets dry on those jets," Holl added, sliding the cap's bill further back on his head with the point of his knife.

"Um, he's your nephew?" Matthew asked the American youth,
aiming a shoulder at Holl. The lilting cadence made it a question,
though he had none of the broad accents of the Customs officer
or his roommate. "We've got legal age limits in the pub. How old
is he?"

"Twelve," said Keith.

"Fourteen," said Holl at the same time. With a long-suffering
look at Keith, he handed over his passport. The date of birth bore
him out. Keith looked at it curiously, but said nothing.

"You certain he's a relative?" Martin joked.

"Well, I suppose he could have aged while I wasn't looking,"
Keith defended himself lamely. "It seems such a long time since he
was born."

"Small for your age, my lad. Still, that's old enough to get in,
though not to drink cider," Matthew affirmed cheerfully. "There's
squashes and other things for you. Come on, then."

"What made you come to Glasgow for the summer?" Matthew
asked, when they plumped into a booth in the Black Bull pub in
Byres Road, just outside the grounds of the university. Glasgow was
a city of four-hundred year old golden sandstone and gray granite
buildings standing alongside new glass and chromium-tube construc-
tions. The whole seemed to fit together fairly well. The walking tour
had taken them over an hour. They had been on and off the cylindrical orange trains of the Underground transportation system three
or four times at different points around the city. Keith was ready for
a snack and a drink.

"Curiosity, I guess," he admitted. "My best excuse is that I get
college credit for this tour, while getting to know another country."

"The same for me," Holl put in. "I've never been away from
home before."

"Well, we don't have the endless money you Americans do, so
we have to get our education at home," Martin said darkly. "No
jollicking off for us."

"Hey, I work for my tuition," Keith retorted. "My family isn't rich. You've been watching too much American television."

"What's your job?" Matthew asked, hurrying to make peace and defuse the argument.

Keith, always eager to talk about the success of Hollow Tree Industries, began to explain. "I sell handmade woodcrafts to gift shops, made by some friends of mine. Holl, here…" his voice dropped when he realized what he might have been about to say. "Holl here has seen some of the items. Shortbread molds, toys, boxes, jewelry like necklaces, and so on. They're pretty nice. Very good workmanship. I get a commission on the sales so my crafts-men don't have to go out and find buyers themselves." Holl nodded approval, and Keith beamed.

"That can't be easy," Matthew acknowledged. "I work in a bak-ery near my home half days, starting early in the morning. I'm on holiday for the next month. Two weeks pay I'm losing at the end of this course, but like you, it's credit toward graduation."

"You get four weeks vacation a year?" Keith gawked. "Wow. We only get two weeks."

"Have you ever had cider?" Martin inquired, getting up to put in their order at the bar. Hanging signs under the inverted bottles be-hind the counter advertised Tennant's Ale and Strongbow.

"Oh, sure. There's lots of orchards near where I live," Keith said. "You can get fresh cider every fall." The two Scots exchanged glances, and Martin chuckled.

"I'll get the first round. We can order from the bar menu for lunch while we drink it."

"This is a St. Clements for you, lad," Martin said, returning with a small round tray full of glasses. "Fizzy lemonade and orange, nothing toxic."

Holl took the light orange drink, and sipped cautiously. He nod-ded happily and ran his tongue across his lips to catch the thin foam. "That's refreshing. Thank you."

"I got you a mild cider, Doyle," Martin continued, innocently passing him a large glass of a cloudy, burnt gold fluid.

Grinning at Holl's watchful gaze, Keith drank. The other boys sat back nonchalantly, only their eyes alert and mischievous, waiting. "That's good!"

Martin did a double-take. "You knew it was alcoholic, did you?"

"I do live near orchards, I told you." Keith lifted the glass happily, and studied the color against the light. "This is the smoothest applejack I've ever tasted."

"Well, watch it," Matthew warned him mildly, holding no grudge for being cheated of his fun. "You may think you know your capacity, but don't trust cider. It sneaks up on you. You get apple-juice palsy well before you know you've had a drop too much."

"No problem," Keith assured him. "Next round's on me."

Holl took an interested sniff of the cider. Pity about the drinking laws, but he didn't want to cause a fuss and draw attention to himself. Still, he felt the need for a calming drink after the trauma of plane travel. When the second round of St. Clement's came to the table, he concentrated quietly on his glass, *enhancing* the sugars until they fermented into alcohol. He took an investigative sip. Not as good as one of Marm's brews, but passable. The others, deep in their conversations, took no notice of him.

They talked about their homes, comparing the differences between their early lives, and exclaiming over the many similarities. Keith found his two room-mates to be outgoing and curious, and thankfully, less reticent than he'd been warned. He didn't press them for details, and found that once the boys relaxed, they told him all about themselves without urging.

"You're not like we thought Americans would be," Matthew admitted, candidly. "I was sure you'd be posing us for pictures in front of every stone building and bobby. You know." He pantomimed frantic snapping with an invisible camera.

"I probably would have, but I haven't got any film left," Keith confessed, putting on an abashed expression, and the others laughed.

"You're a friendly lot, you Yanks," Martin said. "If you'd been English, we'd probably not have talked to you."

"Too shirty and superior," agreed Matthew, hoisting his nose in the air with a forefinger.

"With a name like Doyle, there's not much chance of that, is there? I don't want to be offensive, but you sound almost English to me," Keith continued, apologetically. "You don't have a burr in your voice. You talk like the BBC announcers. Cultured."

"We've gone to English day schools and colleges," Martin explained. "I come from a wee place near Edinburgh." He pronounced it 'edin-burra,' and Keith marked it for future use. "My dad's in finance, and if I want to follow him, I can't keep my old regional, even if I wanted to."

"Speak for yerself," Matthew said, dropping into a thick burr. "Hey, Keith, hae you ey'r heard o' Billy Connolly?"

They chose their meals from a long list of entrees, each of which came with chips—French fried potatoes—and peas. Keith looked down the menu for fish and chips, but to his surprise, it wasn't listed. "Have plaice, if you want good fish," Matthew said, answering his tentative question. "It'll be fresh, at least. Fresher than the cod."

"Why does everything come with peas?" Keith asked. "Was there a bumper crop this year?"

The other two laughed uproariously. Baskets of greasy chicken and chips and peas, fish and chips and peas, and, to Keith's amusement, lasagna with chips and peas, were set down before them. They washed down their lunch with more cider. The other youths seemed in no hurry to leave, and the bartender ignored them as long as they were relatively quiet.

"Everyone comes into the pub. If you don't know anybody in a town, you can wander into a pub for society. There's not much else for young people without a lot of money to do in Glasgow, unless you want to skate at St. Enoch's Center," Martin explained.

Holl chuckled, sharing the joke with Keith in an undertone. "I'll certainly pull his leg hard when we get home. Saint Enoch."

"Though they're all not as friendly in the wee places," Matthew corrected his friend. "We're in the local pub at home almost every evening. You'd like it, if you care for old places. The building is a restored inn, over 350 years old. You ought to come home with us some time at the week end for a visit."

"You bet! Thanks," Keith exclaimed.

"But leave your camera at home," Martin warned. "It's not Trafalgar Square. Start making a place a tourist attraction, and the locals stay away. It defeats the whole point of a pub."

The Black Bull was a companionable place. Keith felt very much at home, surrounded by dark brown wooden paneling and beveled mirrors. No yuppie plants in the windows; this place was functional, not just for show. The only thing he couldn't identify were designs cut out of circles of brass that hung on leather strips over the stone fireplace and from the ceiling beams. The colorful machines in the corner with whirling wheels and strips of lights that read "10p" had to be the local equivalent of arcade games. Matthew and Martin began to discuss Rugby football, which sounded more brutal even than American football. They explained the British game to Keith, who listened closely, and offered comparisons.

"What's this apple juice palsy like?" Keith put in, setting down an empty pint glass. He was starting to feel a little light headed, but put it down to jet lag. According to his watch, it was just after noon at home, but it felt as though he'd been awake for days. Holl reclined limply under his cap in the corner of the booth, offering a word or two when one of the others spoke directly to him.

"Ach, you know," Martin gestured, trying to conjure an image out of the air with his hands. "You go weak at the knees, and you see things like little pink lizards."

"Lizards?" Keith exclaimed, squinting impishly at the table. "Pink ones?"

"Aye." The boys' cultured voices were sliding into homier dialects as their blood-alcohol ratio went down. "Snakes and bugs, too. And then you feel like your head wants to come off."

As Holl watched in horror, a finger-long pink lizard rose out of one of the spilled puddles of cider on the table and scooted toward Martin. It made a run of about a foot before it reached a dry place on the table and popped. Martin jumped, and Keith grinned.

"Did you see that, Matt?" the youth demanded, clutching his friend's arm and pointing. "Lizards!"

"Nae. Just a bit of reflection from the street," the other reassured him, distinctly. "Maybe from a lorry. I saw a little flash of pink in the slop. This table wants wiping. What a clumsy lot we are." He rose unsteadily and went to the bar to borrow a towel.

"You're probably hallucinating," Keith added. "This cider is insidious stuff, isn't it?"

Holl wasn't fooled by Keith's innocent expression. and eyed him as the other lad blotted up the spills. Enoch, the Master's son, had been trading driving lessons in Keith's car for magic instruction over the last few months. Evidently, the Big Person was getting good at simple tricks like cohesiveness and shaping. Holl was surprised and dismayed by his proficiency. Maybe there was something after all in the boy's insistence that he was related to the Little Folk. But the red-haired student was losing all his inhibitions as he got more drunk. In a moment, he'd do something stupid, and expose them. Holl had no wish to wind up a museum exhibit in a foreign country thousands of miles from home, doing charms and tricks for a lot of scientists. The "extraterrestrial" movie Keith had brought once for the Folk to see had opened their eyes amazingly. Holl had had nightmares for weeks.

"I've got to get some sleep, or I'll be sick," he spoke up suddenly, as the others were discussing another round of drinks. "My head's pounding, and *I* haven't had any cider."

"He can't be sick here. You'd better take him back to the Hall," Matthew told Keith, worriedly.

The American youth looked at Holl almost as if he'd never seen him before and shook his head to clear it. "Right. C'mon, Holl. I wouldn't mind an hour's nap either." He slid out from behind the table and attempted to stand. His knees buckled, and Holl sprang to catch him as he clawed at the dark wooden walls of the booth for support.

"There go your knees," Martin crowed. "Apple juice palsy it is."

"Up you go, Uncle," Holl gritted, supporting Keith's weight on his shoulder. "You've had too much for one day."

"How do you feel?" Matthew asked Keith the next morning on the way down to the refectory for breakfast.

"I'll never do that again," Keith vowed. His face was pasty, with green showing just below the skin. "What a hangover. I think I was sick on the way back, but I don't remember. My knees didn't follow me back to the dorm until about 3 A.M. I saw the sun rise then. It was blinding."

"You might have a little less until you get used to it," Matthew suggested kindly, without a suggestion of "I told you so".

"Maybe. Maybe I'll just go teetotal for a while," Keith said, meekly. Holl had lectured him fiercely on the walk back to the dormitory on the responsible use of talent, and he felt contrite for his indiscretion. Secretly, he was pleased to have created such a realistic illusion, but after last night, he vowed to practice only in private. He felt thoroughly ashamed. After all, he had spent nearly a year making certain that no one would discover the Little Folks' home and helping them move to a new place on Hollow Tree Farm, isolated from Big Folk. He had nearly blown it all in one night.

"If you can't hold your liquor better than that," the elf had hissed at him, "then I'll have to put a block on you so you can't use charms at all. I don't want to have strangers look too closely at me when queer things happen."

Keith could only agree. He carried his plate to the table and sat down gingerly next to Holl. His head hurt when he moved too quickly, and the sound of forks ringing against plates reverberated between his ears like the clapper in a bell. Holl didn't say a word to him when he sat down. Keith poured himself a cup of dark brown liquid from the metal pot on the table and let the steam bathe his face, relaxing a knot or two behind his forehead. He shot a glance to his left, but Holl, focused on his breakfast, paid no attention to him.

"Try the tea. It's strong, but it's pretty good," he said to Holl. No answer.

"Are you still mad?" he asked quietly, as he sawed a piece of bacon with his knife. It was louder to him than a hacksaw going though wood and he winced. The taste was like boiled and salted leather, but he felt he deserved no better. A glossy fried egg shone up at him like a plastic display dummy. He shuddered at it, and reached for a piece of toast from an upright rack on the table. It was cold. He scraped butter on it to the tune of Brazil nuts cracking in his ears.

Holl sighed and set down his fork. "No. Do you feel as poorly as you look?"

Keith grimaced. "Worse, I think. They were absolutely right. It feels like your head will come off. There's got to be more than apples in that stuff. This never happened at home."

His friend clucked his tongue and shook his head. "Here, then." Holl spread his fingers and planted his hand against Keith's cranium. "Breathe in and out, and forget about me."

Keith closed his eyes gratefully. Instantly, the agony began to slip away from the inside of his head, like wax melting out of an inverted glass. In a few moments, he drew a deep breath. "Oh, that's great," he crooned, rocking his head from side to side and enjoying the sensation. "That's terrific. My headache's completely gone. I wish you could market that. You'd make a mint."

Holl watched him with a wry smile curling up one side of his mouth. "I can't market it. But I'll give your headache back in full force if you do such a silly thing ever again."

"I promise," Keith said fervently.

As she had assured Keith, Miss Anderson repeated her lecture of the day before, and dismissed the class before noon. "We'll be taking the coach out to the dig site later, to meet the team of archaeologists, and begin work. You may not understand what you're doing unless you've read the text, but please remember to follow their every instruction. We are there to make an accurate record of the past, and any errors, any deviation from the correct steps, could have long-range ramifications. Go have lunch, and meet me in the quad at half past one."

Like all the rest of the smaller information gathering branches, the Secret Intelligence Service was second or third priority in getting their questions answered or their projects funded. A lot more attention was paid to the electronic wizards and their toys, but where would they be without the hard work and footslogging of the SIS, Michaels wanted to know. With difficulty, he had managed to get assignment of a small car and set out along the M8 in pursuit of the Educatours vehicle. In the most ordinary way possible, the coach had deposited its passengers, O'Day and his accomplice among them, in the heart of Glasgow. With the way the old buildings echoed, it was no problem to hear everything that went on in them. Michaels learned that the 'boy' was carrying a formidable knife concealed in a pants pocket. O'Day was not notably a violent man. Perhaps his small associate was the one he ought to watch in a close up fight. Personnel checks on the others in the tour would have to be made a priority. Unlikely as it seemed, one of them could be O'Day's contact

Chapter Five

The coach transported them along the M8 motorway leading to the southwest. Except for Keith and Holl, who were wearing jeans, the boys were dressed in corduroy or twill. To the surprise of the others, Narit had appeared wearing jeans, too, and her long hair was braided into a tail that hung down her back.

"Where's the sari?" Keith had asked. "We half expected you to be formal."

Narit had laughed prettily, a quiet, tinkly sound. "I wear the traditional dress only to please my grandmother, when I visit her. I much prefer English fashions. They don't get caught in doors."

The seating in the coach had worked out much the same way it had the day before. Keith, armed with his camera and a new roll of film, had a seat to himself, and took pictures of the landscape through the thick plexiglas plate windows.

"Look, there's nothing special out there. Just houses," Matthew, behind him, pointed out.

"They're different from American houses," Keith said happily. "The slope of the roof is a lot sharper. And you don't see that many stone buildings around us. Nearly everything is frame and brick. And the color of the grass is different here." He glanced upward. "So is the sky, though it's hard to tell through the safety glass. Look! A milestone!" Keith crouched over his viewfinder, fumbling with the focusing ring on the lens.

"Please yourself," Matthew grumbled, sinking back into his seat. "It's your film you're wasting. *Milestones*."

Holl sat on the opposite side of the coach from Keith, also watching the scenery. They had quickly passed out of the city limits and into reassuringly rural countryside. None of the land lay in the ironing-board flat plains of the American midwest, so it was unfamiliar and interesting to the eye. When he had excitedly named the characteristics of the hills and valleys they were passing to Keith Doyle, that one had teased him, accusing him of learning them out of a book. It was a fact. He had. So far in his short life, the geographic features he was seeing had been flat pictures to him. He was storing up all his impressions of the wide world, to bring back to the other Folk. So far, this part was big and wild and empty. Keith was correct about the houses, too. They had an air that held them apart from American construction, what little he'd seen of it. But they were hauntingly similar, in a generations-removed way, to the houses of the under-library village in which his Folk had lived. He wondered if Keith had seen the likeness. What connection was there between his folk and the people who lived here? What would his clan say about the resemblance? The younger ones would likely speculate, while the old ones, who might actually know, would very probably say nothing at all. It was frustrating how they kept the younger generations in the dark. But with evidence, he could start a controversy that might bring out useful revelations.

"Say, Keith Doyle," Holl called across the aisle. "There's an interesting house coming up here on the side of the road. Take its portrait, will you?"

The hot summer sunshine slanted down across Keith's shoulders and burned the tips of his ears while he worked on his patch of earth. The grass on the broad hilltop had been cleared in a section about twenty feet long by six feet wide. The exposed area was divided into sections three by three feet, by pegs to which string had been tied. When the group arrived, each student or worker was issued a pan, a loosely woven sieve, a trowel, and a pair of brushes. Under the supervision of Dr. Crutchley, the Professor of Ancient Studies from London University, they were expected to scrutinize the earth for artifacts, brushing away particles of earth from the marked patch to uncover each layer. The brushings were to be dropped into the sieve and broken up gently to see if there was anything hidden in them. If an artifact appeared, the site was measured and a note was made of where it lay. At least, that was what Keith understood them to want. He had been working for hours on his section, and had found nothing worth measuring or noting. He carefully brushed away the surface of the dirt with the larger, stiff brush, and scooped it into his pan, sifting through it for particles of metal or pottery. At times he would see a spot of another color and work feverishly to uncover it, but it would never turn out to be more than a pebble.

"Not even a toenail clipping," Keith grumbled to Matthew, whose pitch was across from his. "I never realized that scientists came up with their impressions of our ancestors based on such thin evidence. It's like finding photographs, when you were expecting a movie. There's so much in those exhibits in museums I supposed there would be more to see in a site. I think this part must have been the garden. Are they sure this was part of the site? The building boundaries are way over there." He gestured with his trowel toward the tables where Crutchley's assistants were sorting potsherds and animal bones. Behind them, inside a square pavilion tent, more of the professor's team, nearly invisible in the shadows, moved back and forth with flat trays, filled with the results of other days' successful searching.

"Don't give up," Matthew said, absently. "They wouldn't still be here if they thought the site was milked dry."

"Well, this is where Professor Keith Doyle says that they didn't have either the cooking or sleeping quarters," he said emphatically, gesturing at his patch with the trowel. "Or anything else of importance, except maybe a footprint from the family pet dinosaur."

Matthew grinned without looking up at him, but then his expression changed. He began brushing furiously with the stiff brush at a spot in the earth before him, his cheeks pink. "Hoy, help a body here, eh?"

"Do you have something?"

"Here I thought it was one of the ever-present pebbles, but this one's not shifting," Matthew explained, his voice increasingly more excited. "It's red-brown in color. Do you see it?"

Keith dived over to help. "Yeah. Brush away from it. Clear the earth level. Hey, it's round."

"What's there?" Holl asked, from partway up the row of workspaces.

"Don't know yet, but it looks like Matt struck gold," Keith said, his eyes shining. What disappointment he had been harboring evaporated in the excitement of an actual find. No matter that it was in someone else's section, it was an archeological artifact, and he was watching it—no, helping it—be uncovered. He grinned widely as the edges began to emerge. "It's a covered pot of some kind. And it's intact."

The dig staff saw the crowd gathering at the end of the site and hurried over to see what was going on. Miss Sanders, Professor Crutchley's assistant, a middle-aged woman with light ruddy-brown hair, leaned over Keith's shoulder to watch as the pot emerged.

"Carefully now. It could be very fragile. Stop using the brushes now, and use your fingers instead. Clear away the earth from its sides with your fingers. There might be small handles, and you could break them."

"Yes, ma'am," both youths breathed, working more slowly.

"Stop, Keith Doyle," Holl's voice came softly in Keith's left ear. "I can feel cracks in the fabric. It's only hardened clay. Stop now and move outward. You'll have to pick it up from below."

Keith glanced up at Holl, and pulled away from the edges of the brown jar's rim. "Matt, let's move out and break up the dirt. It might widen out further down. We don't want it to smash just as we're getting something at last." He dragged his fingertips along the ground until the pressure of Holl's hand on his shoulder told him to stop. Matthew, shooting him a curious glance, followed suit, and started breaking up the soil.

"Good, good," the assistant encouraged them. "Now, *lift*...."

A collective sigh of joy gusted from the crowd. Between their fingertips, Matthew and Keith held a glazed clay jar with a small round lid crusted in place by more dirt. Its shape was slightly reminiscent of an amphora, except that the foot was flat, and instead of the earlike handles, it had only pinched-looking tabs under the curled rim. At Miss Sanders' instruction, they set it down in an empty pan on someone's outspread handkerchief. The assistant dropped to her knees beside Keith and whisked at the jar with a soft brush until the lid came free and rattled in place.

"Well done, you!" Miss Sanders exclaimed. "Someone get the camera."

Another assistant hurried up. The jar was photographed in the pan. A ruler was laid and chalk powder dribbled around the location in which it was found, and the assistant took another exposure. Dr. Crutchley beamed down on his workers as proudly as if he'd thrown the pot himself. He was a man in his late fifties, with perfect wings of white in his dark brown hair. Between those dramatic temples, wiry eyebrows stood out, just barely not touching above a beaklike nose.

"A perfect example of corded ware, Miss Sanders. I never did expect this site to be another Jorvik, but it is encouraging to find fine specimens of this nature. Very gratifying. It's an Irish style vessel, isn't it, except that there are well preserved traces of paste ornamentation, and the firing is much finer than you would expect. And a lid...not a seal or a stopper. Most unusual."

"There's something broken off inside," Keith said. "I felt it sloshing around when we picked it up."

The professor gently lifted the lid, and set it down on the cloth. With two fingers, he extracted from the jar a long string of globular, translucent golden beads. "Amber! An amber trading string." The aged, blackened cord began to deteriorate as he lifted it, and he scooped his other hand underneath to catch the beads before they fell. "A small fortune in tally beads. Well, a good omen as a first find, I'd say."

"Someone's cache, sir?" Miss Sanders inquired, picking up the pan containing the jar and lid.

"Impossible to say until we've examined the entire site. "It might have been interred with a shallow burial, not uncommon for wealth as grave goods..." The two scientists drifted away to the table, offering speculations to one another, and exclaiming over the artifacts. The second assistant followed respectfully with the camera. Matthew and Keith watched them go with open mouths.

"They've forgotten all about us," Matthew said, a little indignantly. "We passed a miracle, and they've forgotten we exist!"

"Oh, carry on, you lot!" Miss Sanders called over her shoulder.

"There," Keith grinned at him. "That's better."

Enthusiasm rekindled, Keith doubled his efforts at searching, breaking up even the tiniest pieces of earth in his sieve and shaking them through. Miss Sanders had hinted of a shallow burial. There might be a skeleton here some place. Most likely, it would be cremated fragments in a funerary urn, which was relatively small and easy to overlook if you weren't digging smack over it. The others were coming up with small artifacts, or fragments of larger items. With respectful hands, Holl was turning over a green, flaking piece of metal that could have been a bronze axehead. The two ladies and Edwin were standing back so the assistant could sprinkle chalk along the outline of a long bundle that lay exposed across their three sections. Keith's patch still showed no signs of yielding up anything interesting.

He went on digging, undaunted by failure. Since his patch was adjacent to Matthew's, it was possible that there was something hidden there, another clue to the solution of the puzzle of the Bronze

Age settlement that had once been there. With a mighty heave, Keith tossed the earth from his sorting pan over his shoulder and bent down, trowel in hand, to start over filling it up.

"What are you doing, lad?" a voice roared from behind him. "More care! more care!" Arrested, Keith tilted his head back until he was looking straight up into the face of Dr. Crutchley, face red above the collar of his white short-sleeved shirt over which he was wearing a sleeveless knitted waistcoat. Over which someone had inconsiderately sprinkled a truckload of dirt. Keith swallowed guiltily.

He sprang to his feet and began to brush off the protesting professor. "Uh-oh. I'm so sorry, sir. I wasn't watching where that was going."

"Take it more slowly in future," Dr. Crutchley ordered, batting irritatedly at the front of his waistcoat, which sent clouds of gray dust floating into the air. "I came over to compliment you lads on the skill you showed at bringing out that pottery piece, but it may have been a fluke! You could be missing something working at a pace like that, or worse yet, destroying it in your haste. More care is needed. Or perhaps it would be better if you stopped what you were doing and helped to catalog our finds instead?" He pointed the stem of his pipe toward the table. Keith followed his thrust and shook his head vigorously.

"Oh, no. I'd rather help out finding things, sir. Normally I'm good at digging things up."

Crutchley flicked particles of dust off one arm with a decisive finger. "Yes, though more like a surgeon exposing tissues, boy, and less like a dog burying a bone."

"Yes, sir. Sorry, sir."

"I admire your initiative, but keep the energy for endurance, not speed. Carry on." The professor walked away, reaching into his back pocket for a tobacco pouch and plunging the bowl of his pipe into it.

"Ooh, that was a rough ticking off," Edwin said under his breath.

"Hah," said Keith, going back to digging, but much more slowly. His face was invisible to the others, but his ears were red. "That was nothing. I've been chewed out by experts."

As the sun began to throw longer shadows over the dig, the team called a halt to the work. Some contrast was useful, as it threw the edges of hidden objects into relief, but if the angle was too great, pebbles began to look like potsherds. Gratefully, Keith and the others creaked to their feet and exercised stiff legs and backs. Miss Sanders and the male assistant made tea inside the square tent, and distributed it to the workers in stained, chunky pottery mugs.

"From the look of these," Mrs. Green quipped, "ceramics skills haven't changed much in forty centuries."

"Man hasn't changed significantly over the ages," Dr. Crutchley replied, settling down in a canvas director's chair with a sigh. "In my opinion, only his tools have advanced in sophistication. Well, that was a good day's work. I thank you all, especially our newcomers. Now we like to sit down and have a chat over what we've done today. What you Americans would call the 'recap.'" Keith grinned at Holl, and the others chuckled.

"Before you came," Miss Sanders began, "my lot were turning over the rubbish tip. Once we had an idea of the perimeter of the settlement, we started nosing about downwind. There it was, just about twenty paces behind one of the structures. Fairly extensive."

"You can't still smell any of it, can you?" Mrs. Turner asked in alarm, wrinkling her nose.

"Not at all," the archaeologist answered, impishly. "Kitchen refuse becomes quite sanitized after four thousand years. We've come up with the bones of many herd animals, and an enormous quantity of remains of fish and shellfish. We take that to mean that the settlement was prosperous, since they weren't dependent upon a strict diet of fish. Herd animals would be more rare in a poor environment."

"Doesn't the amber necklace prove that they were wealthy?" Matthew asked. He took a proprietary pride in his find, and no one seemed to object.

"Amber," Dr. Crutchley began, in a lecturing air, "was both an irreducible tally and in itself valuable. Our ancestors weren't utter barbarians. They were attracted by the beauty of the substance. Now, without any other evidence to support it, what do you think the pot was doing out there at the bottom of the settlement?"

Encouraged by the professor, the students offered their own conclusions. The professional archaeologists took their theories seriously, discussing the pros and cons of each suggestion. Keith found the give and take stimulating, and volunteered his own theory.

"Maybe that amber string was somebody's ace in the hole. You know, cookie jar money; and he wanted to keep his advantage hidden."

The others laughed. Dr. Crutchley let the corners of his mouth curl up. "Very interesting, Keith," he said. He seemed to harbor no ill will for Keith having showered him with dirt, and even confessed that not only had it happened to him before, but he'd done it to others himself.

"Am I right?" asked Keith, eagerly.

"Probably not, son," said the archaeologist, grinding ash out of the pipe bowl and tamping fresh tobacco into it with his thumb. Keith's face fell. Dr. Crutchley went on. "But you make me think that you're heading in the right direction. I am reminded of a book in my library—I must send for it from London—that mentions a similar artifact. You may not have the right answers, but you function nicely as a catalyst for others by making them think. Do remember, there's no theory so silly that it hasn't been proposed in quite serious scientific papers by my learned colleagues." He lit the pipe and drew on it, watching the others humorously through the thicket of his eyebrows. "We are coming to the conclusion that this was a trading village. By its placement, and by the types of artifacts we are finding here, our theory continues to be borne out. What I would like to find, though it is nearly impossible with the dearth of evidence, was what early man thought about." He looked around at his circle of listeners. "What inspired him? What brought him here? Whom or what did he blame when it rained? Luckily, the Celts and Saxons were inclined to tell stories to us, their extreme descendants, through the decoration and ornamentation of household goods, what they ate, what things they held dear and," with a wave toward Keith, "what they kept hidden. Yes, I will have to send for that book."

"I've made a note of it, Professor," Miss Sanders said, flourishing her pen.

From the crest of the hill where they sat, the students could see the shining ribbon of the river leading down to the sea. The hills around them were similar to that one: scattered scrub along the sides and clearings of wind-brushed grass atop the flat bluffs. Most of the land was marked off as restricted sites, cordoned off at road level by twisted wire fences and red printed signs warning away trespassers. Theirs was the only one of the peaks which was unmarked and unfenced.

"This is not a terribly important site, but it is a nice one," Crutchley continued. "Good, defensible location, but still reachable. As the population grew upriver, the shipping trade routes dealt with cities so much further inland. Wool and iron rejuvenated this area in the Middle Ages, so this site became obsolete. Lucky for us, since we can now investigate a stopped moment in time."

The tea cups were gathered up and washed in a tub behind the tent. Keith and the others picked their way down the hillside to wait for the Educatours coach. Everyone else was chattering excitedly about the day's work. He sat next to Holl in the tall grass, playing with a straw between his fingers, gazing at nothing, and thinking about Dr. Crutchley's lecture. To understand a site, you had to make up a story using what was there, artifacts, layout, weather patterns; and hope that nothing you excavated later made the story invalid. The work was backbreaking, but it was fun. He was fond of making up theories. If he was a better catalyst than a scientist, then he'd better come up with some good suggestions. To stimulate the others' minds, of course.

"Doesn't really tell you who they belong to, does it?" Keith asked. Holl followed his eyes, and read the Restricted signs swinging on the barbed wire across the road.

"Perhaps the owners want privacy," Holl reasoned, peering up between the thick bushes and waist-high grass on one obscured hillside. "What could they possibly be building out here among all these private sites?"

"What?" Keith asked, not really paying attention. "Who?"

"Don't you remember the reason they're hurrying with this excavation? 'Right in front of the bulldozer' was the way Miss Anderson put it. Someone's building something among all these unfriendly neighbors."

Keith walked backward and squinted under the flat of his hand toward the crest of the hill across the road. "I don't know. No buildings. Not even a tent. No one *lives* there, anyway. Maybe it's a nature preserve of some kind. There's a path leading up the hill. I'm going to have a look." He started for the fence.

"A preserve, preserved one hill at a time? What has that to do with bulldozers? In any case, you shouldn't touch, Keith Doyle," Holl warned him. "I don't know what they'll do to you if you're caught meddling over here. Think of me stranded here by myself in a strange place before you decide to get yourself tossed in jail."

Keith grinned. "I guess you're right. Hello, Mom?" he pantomimed a telephone receiver, "can you send me five hundred pounds bail?"

"You'll have to bail out later. Get up. The coach is coming."

Chapter Six

The dig was the exclusive topic of conversation in the coach all the way back to Glasgow. Miss Anderson circulated up and down the aisle among the tour group, chatting and asking questions. She gave Matthew hearty congratulations on his find, and discussed funerary customs with him. After a hasty dinner which no one really tasted, Keith and Holl joined the other young men for a celebratory pub crawl around Glasgow. Miss Anderson, the two schoolteachers and Narit stayed behind to talk quietly among themselves.

"And I vote for a good pudding, too," Alistair suggested, as they emerged on the street.

"Huh? Oh, not custard: dessert," Keith translated. "Sounds great to me. How about the rest of you?"

There was a chorus of approval, and Alistair nodded decisively.

"I know a place nearby with fine sweets and a cellar second to none." He steered them out of the university complex and around the corner into an alley. An unobtrusive doorway let into a quiet but crowded establishment, with the risible name of the Ubiquitous Chip. The host looked them over cautiously, judging them to be sober enough not to make trouble, and escorted them to a long table.

The restaurant, uncomfortably like an American fern bar in decor, proved to have a genius making desserts in the kitchen. Keith licked his spoon thoughtfully and wondered if he should order a second selection. He decided against it, and amused himself throwing leftover crumbs to the enormous goldfish in the fountain that ran along one side of the main room.

On top of homemade ice cream, mousses, and tortes, the others poured down wine and liqueurs, and discussed with great interest the events of the day. Matthew was acclaimed a hero for his great find, and decided on his own reasons for the interment of the covered jar. He was in a mood to take no prisoners, which the others took as a personal challenge.

"Well, what do you know about it anyway?" Martin asked, challengingly. "All you've ever dug up before is your Mum's tulip bulbs."

Keith and Holl plowed straight into the thick of a loud and passionate argument about whether or not the professor was right in his theories. The languid, sullen pose assumed by most of the boys turned out to be nothing more than a pose. Something important had actually happened, progress had been made, and they were a part of it. Their daily lives must have fallen into one unmarked by change or excitement. They were bored, and pretended they didn't care. Hard work did bring out the best in some people. Keith grinned to himself. No one who felt like taking it easy would have joined a tour like this to begin with.

As the wait staff began to clear the surrounding tables, Edwin rose to his feet. "Let's go. We can talk in the pubs until closing time."

"Where should we go?" Matthew asked. The others started to argue for their favorites.

"How about the King's Head?" Martin suggested.

"Why not the Black Bull. It's only across the road."

"What about the Curlers?"

Keith snickered at the names. "What's that, a combination pub and hairdresser's?"

Charles pushed him toward the door. He was a big youth with heroic looks: a sharply planed jaw, curly brown hair, and mild blue eyes which wore a glint of amusement. "No, you silly git, curling is a sport. You take a big round flat stone, and hoik it up and slide it across a frozen lake, sweeping the ice as you go..."

"No, they've only got Tennant's lager," Max said, interrupting them. "Come on, I'll choose the first one. We'll go down to City Centre and stop in at the Skye Boatman, and make the rounds from there." On a chorus of approval, the party turned toward the stop for the Strathclyde Underground.

"Nine for the orange caterpillars," Edwin shouted, letting his voice echo in the brick-walled station. They trotted down the stairs toward the trains. A man in a rumpled suit detached himself from a group at the ticket machines and followed them unobtrusively into the bowels of the station.

The Skye Boatman was crowded and jolly, mashing its patrons into two small, smoky L-shaped rooms which surrounded the bar. The party had to shout at one another just to be heard over the clamor of the fruit machines and the canned music. Though it was early in the week, the pub was full of men and women laughing over glasses of cider or a brown-red brew which the other students told Keith was bitter ale. Keith tasted a mouthful and ordered some for himself. He was much more cautious this time with his liquor. Where the others finished one pint and ordered another, he nursed a single pint of bitter throughout the evening, and then switched to a St. Clement's with Holl when they moved on to the next pub.

"That's no way to drink," Alistair chided him, when he ordered his fifth orange-and-lemonade. "One minchy pint, and you're calling a halt? Ooh, you Americans are made of weak fabric."

"I'm working up my tolerance a little at a time," Keith replied, good-naturedly, refusing to be drawn into a contest. For all the kidding they gave him, Matthew had confided that they did drink a lot every night. This evening was by way of being a celebration. A good thing, too. The dark ale was rich and heavy, not bitter at all, but Keith could tell by the light feeling in the top of his head that the alcohol content was a lot higher than beer back home. "There is no way I'm going to relive this morning's headache. That was one hell of a hangover." And a close shave with disaster, he reflected, catching Holl's eye. The young elf seemed relieved by Keith's prudence, and was considerably more relaxed, even among the ever changing mob of strange Big Folk. The others had long ago forgotten his ostensible youth, and had accepted him along with Keith as one of them.

At eleven o'clock, the publican of the Black Bull rang a bell and called, "Time, gentlemen, time. Your wives are waiting for ye!"

Seeing that no one was taking the initiative, Keith got to his feet. "Come on, guys. Someone is going to have to direct me back to the Underground station."

"I can feel me right leg, but I think me left one's gone to sleep," Edwin said, looking surprised as he tried to lever himself out of the booth.

"Don't you hate when that happens?" Keith asked, helping him up. "That means it's going to be awake all night."

With Holl's aid, Keith managed to steer the others back to the train and home to Hillhead Station. There were few passengers on the late train. Only one man rode all the way to their stop with them, and trudged up the stairs in their wake. The light drizzle that met them as they emerged from the station was bracing, and woke everyone up enough to stagger the rest of the way to the residence hall.

"Whew!" Keith blew a lock of hair out of his eyes with an upward gust as he sagged onto his bed. "And I thought American college students were party animals. Matthew said they do that almost every night!"

"You'd hardly connect the serious archaeologists of the afternoon with the drunken louts we just put to bed," Holl agreed. He yawned. "It's late, and we've had an eventful day. I could sleep for weeks."

"Could still be some of the jet lag, too," Keith reasoned, pulling off his sneakers. "Look at that. My feet are swollen. By the end of this trip, I'm going to be wearing clown shoes."

"And I'm going to be wearing your discards." Holl rubbed his own toes. "Blisters. This is my first pair of hard-soled shoes, and it may well be my last if they don't soften soon. I may survive well enough, as we're doing all our work from our knees."

"Are you enjoying yourself?" Keith asked, anxiously. "I know this kind of trip wasn't exactly your choice, since you signed on at the last minute to go with me."

Holl waved an impatient hand. "I am interested. Realize how little practical experience any of us young ones have with the outside world. I'm as keen as your fellow tourists to see what else we can find up there. It's nice to know that there's a past that stretches back beyond the date of my birth, one for which there's tangible, if unreadable proof."

"Hmph. Won't the old folks tell you what life was like before you came to Midwestern?"

"Not much. You can tell it isn't something they want to talk about. And the younger ones just tell of extended travel and wandering. They're home and secure and happy now, so the past doesn't exist. That's shortsighted, in my opinion." Disgusted, Holl dropped his shoes on the floor, and lay down, hands behind his head. "I find it frustrating, as do the rest of us born at Midwestern. Don't you find it an interesting place we're digging up? You can see why the settlers chose to live there. They get the full sun every day, but they're not exposed to the high winds. Small game would be plentiful, as would be fish. The fields are sunny. The place is defensible, but not unreachable."

"Do you suppose that they had any dealings with your ancestors?" Keith asked hopefully. "I mean, I noticed that you could tell that the pot we were uncovering was cracked, without touching it. Did you see something? Was it made by one of your Folk?"

Holl chuckled. "Ah, no. It was just a craftsman's instincts. I could feel the weakness in the material. It was nearly crying out its infirmity. It had no essence of magic or charm to it. But it was well made, and all of four thousand years old. I admire that."

"Is there anything in the site which has got the essence of magic?" Keith pressed. "I mean, what do you think? Would these people have had any contact with yours?"

"I don't know," Holl mused. "The site is not inimical to it. And there's almost no iron among the remains, and it's ages too early for steel. All their metals are bronze or softer, which you might have noticed doesn't hurt me. That would make it more comfortable for contact...but this is all speculation, Keith Doyle."

"That's what I'm best at, speculation and guesses. Besides, the professionals are guessing too; that's what Dr. Crutchley said. The more evidence we get, the more accurate the picture they can put together."

"Well, I don't know what to look for. I've barely seen the habitations occupied by Big Folk *this* century, let alone one forty times as old." The Little One sighed. "There's no sign of anything belonging to my people. In a way, it makes me feel lost and alone. It's true that we tend not to leave many marks of our passing, just out of self protection, but I wish that they would have. That site is dry and cold and empty, so far as I can tell. You're the expert bogey hunter; what do you think?"

"Well..." Keith mused. "You know, the Little People are hardly likely to have set up shop right next to the Big Folk's town. You, I mean, *they* would be unnatural creatures." A sly smile. "They didn't have the benefit of a library full of...texts, like we do. If they had, they would have been blamed for all disasters, whether or not they were responsible. You guys would be easy scapegoats, if for no better reason than size. You know, they might have lived further inland, in the woods, or in one of those little valleys we passed surrounded by scrub...?"

"Dells," Holl supplied.

"Right. You can hardly see a hundred yards in any direction. The locals wouldn't bother to punch through that, not with meadows and bluffs already cleared for them by nature."

Holl cheered up. "It doesn't mean they mightn't have been nearby. We can have a look, if there's time."

"Yeah!" the red-haired youth agreed. "According to my legend books, this is the kind of place where wood elves and certain kinds of brownies can be found. They seemed to live just about forever, getting older and more crotchety, or wiser, take your pick. If there's anyone still here, we can ask them about what life was like 4,000 years back, and give Dr. Crutchley something he can use to spike his competition."

"If they don't give us the spike first. I have a feeling that after four thousand years, they won't likely be too talkative."

The rest of the week went on like the beginning of the first day. To Keith's relief and joy, he was moved off his patch to a new one at Matthew's left, clearing the grass downslope from the site of the lidded pot's discovery and beginning an excavation there. "We must find that urn, intact, if possible," Dr. Crutchley pleaded. "If the small jar was undamaged, the chances are good that other artifacts nearby will be in a similarly well preserved condition. I am sure this was a burial, not a cache, and this grass appears to be undisturbed. My textbooks suggest that these amber beads were not personal ornamentation, but the bookkeeping strings of a wealthy trader. I believe some similar pieces are on display in the British Museum."

The group was impressed. Closer personalization of the people they were investigating evoked a deeper involvement on the part of the team. Keith vowed to find the trader's burial site, or die trying.

On Wednesday, Miss Anderson made an announcement on the way to the dig. "Anyone who is taking this tour for credit should be prepared to give me his or her weekly essay on Friday. Verbal is acceptable, though handwritten or typed would be welcome. There are typewriters we may use in the Archaeology Department office. I'll schedule individual appointments this evening." She smiled around at them, her eyes twinkling behind her thick glasses. "That will give you a day to decide whether or not you wish to go to the extra trouble."

"Why not?" Keith said. "It's one fewer course in basketweaving I've got to take to finish off my college credits."

"Well, Keith, come in," Miss Anderson invited him. The Archaeology office, set in a row of terraced buildings to one side of the common square, was a couple of cramped rooms filled with books. The teacher had cleared a place at one of the battered desks for her records and the small pile of essays. Keith sat down in a time-worn swivel-back chair beside her. "I have read your paper with interest. I find that your writing style is clear, which is gratifying, but your thesis leaves more to be desired."

"I researched my facts from the books in the library," Keith pointed out, a little disappointed. "I do a lot of research at home."

"Yes, I see that. It isn't the research which I find faulty. It's your conclusions. You're jumping to them." She turned over the top page and pointed to a paragraph alongside which she had drawn a red line. "You don't have any basis for making the conclusions that you do about the size of the settlement or its relative prosperity."

"A lot of the books I checked suggested that some of the things we found were unlikely to turn up in poorer places, like all the jewelry. Sure, they could have been the craftsmen who made them, but if they needed money, they would have sold the goods, instead of keeping them. The village must have been large, because of the number of bones in the garbage dump. I pieced things together from a lot of sources, not to mention the things that Dr. Crutchley has been telling us. I think there's a similarity between the way we work at home on research papers and the way the archaeological team does here."

"Keith," Miss Anderson said firmly, "This course is intended to teach you to respect facts, not hare off after assumptions. For example, the size of the rubbish tip may have been the product of years rather than population. You are on a strict fact-finding expedition. Theories are for those in full possession of those facts."

"Dr. Crutchley is making speculations," Keith offered in his own defense.

The teacher sighed, as if she had made this point many times before. "Yes, but he labels them as speculations. He does not *know* anything for which he hasn't got proof. If you find a jar in an ancient village site, you may assume that one of the ancient folk had *a jar*. You don't state baldly that they kept stoats in it, unless you have pictorial proof, such as art or hieroglyphs, or actually find a mummified stoat inside one. Dr. Crutchley can make educated guesses based on experience and research. This could be a good learning experience for you. It wouldn't hurt your everyday life to learn the difference between blind belief and supported theories for which evidence exists."

"Like whether or not there are really leprechauns and things like that, you mean?" Keith asked innocently, accepting his paper back from the teacher.

Miss Anderson nodded, her eyes twinkling. "Yes, I suppose that would be a good example. Evidence separates fantasy from fact."

"Okay, I get it." Keith smiled sweetly, feeling as if he had made a point, even if the teacher didn't know it. "Do you want me to rewrite the paper?"

"No, that won't be necessary." Miss Anderson stated. "You do understand the principles of the expedition, and your guesses are fairly intelligent, though I want you to understand that it is far too early to make such firm assumptions. It smacks of scientific irresponsibility."

"It won't happen again. I'll be as cautious as if I was walking on dinosaur eggs," Keith promised. "Um, Miss Anderson, how do you handle the grades? I'm carrying a pretty good average at Midwestern, and I'd like to maintain it."

Her blue eyes twinkled up through the thick glasses, reminding Keith irresistibly of the Elf Master. "The first essay carries far less weight than the following five. It gives us a chance to know one another. Or, you can elect to have the grade recorded as Pass/Fail, if you like. If you're the sort prone to ulcers over marks, we can make a gentleman's agreement that you will pass so long as you do any work at all and take part in the discussions."

"I'm not that bad," Keith said. "I'll take my chances."

"Good for you," Miss Anderson replied, cheerily. "I thought you had the stuff of fighters in you."

Keith rose, and rolled up his paper. "I'm really enjoying this tour, Miss Anderson. Even the dirt feels more historical than the kind I usually get under my fingernails."

The teacher laughed. "I'll look forward to what you have to tell me next week, when your muscles are really sore. Just send Alistair in on your way out, won't you?" She swiveled her chair to face the pile of papers, and Keith slipped through the door.

Chapter Seven

Keith bought a handful of postcards and wrote enthusiastic messages to his friends and family as the coach carried them toward the dig early on the second Monday. One for his roommate, Patrick Morgan, one for his parents, one for his resident advisor, Rick, and one for Diane, over which he lingered lovingly, crowding all the detail he could in the small message square. He had saved a special card for Ludmilla Hempert, the old woman with whom he shared the Little Folks' secret. It was a hot, sunny morning, with just a striping of clouds arching overhead. Slung across his back was a straw coolie hat he had found in one of the souvenir shops the week before and had worn every day since burning his ears and neck. The others laughed at him for worrying about a little sun, and turned down his offer of hats for each of them. None of them wore hats, sunscreen, or even sunglasses.

"No sense worrying about what doesn't stay long, or hadn't you noticed?" Edwin asked, deprecatingly. "This isn't the tropics, laddie."

"Americans worry too much about natural things," Charles added.

"Skin cancer is natural?" Keith asked pointedly.

"Oh, come off it. In this soft light? You must be made of wax," Edwin laughed.

"Look at Miss Anderson," Keith defended himself. "She's got a hat on."

"I rarely stay through the afternoon," the teacher said, mildly, adjusting the confection of straw and flowers on her head, "but I concur with Keith. I feel that hot heads make for hasty judgment. But don't take me as an example. I'm prone to sun-stroke."

The coach turned off the road and pulled up behind a queue of unfamiliar cars parked at the foot of the hill along the narrow lane. The driver looked quizzically over his shoulder at Miss Anderson. "No place to pull up," he announced.

Miss Anderson studied the line of cars and bobbed her pointed chin vigorously several times. "They must have the press or guests here today," she said. "Reverse out, and take the small road to the left. You can let us off there. I saw another path on the leeward side of the bluff."

"Yes, ma'am," the driver said, nudging up the side of his cap with a forefinger as a sort of salute.

Her students groaned audibly as they saw the path Miss Anderson meant them to climb. It was a muddy, slick trench, almost perpendicular to the road.

"Now, now, you're all younger than I am. You've got the energy to make it up there. Go on, and I'll be up after you in a wee while," the teacher urged them cheerfully.

"Holy Mother, we'll need a ladder," Matthew complained, standing and gazing upward. Narit, who never complained, pushed past him and started to climb the hill, clutching the long grass as handholds. The boys looked at one another, half amused, half outraged, watching her long plait of hair swaying above them.

"I'm not going to let a mere girl clinch the title," Martin said, starting after her. "Hoy, it's not so bad. Come on, lads!"

"The sheep can get up there, and they weigh more than you," Edwin called.

"Smarter, too," Max chimed in, and glanced at the others. "Well, what about you slackers?"

"Yar boo sucks," Matthew answered, good-naturedly. "Coming, Keith?"

"Right behind you," the American said. "Hey, Holl, do you want to go up ahead of me? That way I can catch you if you slip."

The elf snorted. "More likely it will be so you don't fall on me from above with your big clumsy body. I'll be fine. After you," he gestured toward the slope, with a slight bow. Keith saluted wryly and jumped for the first foothold, grabbing sheaves of grass with both hands. Holl followed him, less energetically.

"Hey, this is a view we haven't had before," Keith said, stopping on a relatively level part and looking around. The others had disappeared over the crest of the bluff, and their voices faded into distant echoes like the cries of gulls. "More fences. I swear that this is the only piece of ground for ten miles that isn't roped off." Holl, toiling up behind him, grunted his acknowledgment, but didn't look up. Out of the corner of his eye, Keith caught sight of a depression in the grass on the hillside across the road, which had been invisible from the road behind stands of underbrush. He squinted under his hand at it. It was the shadow thrown by a small hillock. The inverted bowl-shaped mound was almost perfectly

round, and it was surrounded by woodland plants that didn't encroach on the smooth grass thereupon. Something in his memory
went *ting!* "Hey, look over there, Holl. It's a fairy ring."

"What?" Holl struggled up to stand next to Keith. "Go on with
you."

"Well, it's got all the right characteristics. It's a low, rounded grassy
mound, surrounded by little purple flowers and mushrooms." He
wrinkled his nose, wishing he could see more detail under the shadows of the low trees on the other side. "And I think there's something
on the top. Some kind of flower with bell-shaped cups on tall stalks."

"What? What color are they?" Holl demanded, brimming with
hope. Could the object of his quest be so close? Right under his
nose?

"I'm not sure. But I've got to have a look." Keith skipped down
the track, past an inquisitive sheep or two, and ducked under the wire
fence on the other side. His long legs took the slope in easy strides.

"Wait for me!" Holl half-slid, half-ran after him.

As soon as he crossed the road, he felt a wave of malignity
smack into him, as if he had hit a wall. Ignoring it, he pulled up the
loose wire strand and hurried to catch up with Keith. There was
something about the hill he didn't like, something sinister. It was
the same sort of suffocating wash he had experienced on the jet.
Perhaps Keith's fairy ring had its own defenses, a guardian of some
kind.

"It's pink!" Keith's voice came from above. "Does pink count,
or do your flowers have to be white?"

"White's all I know of," Holl called up to him. "Wait, and I'll
come up and see." He reached out to grab a handhold among the
plants, and came away with a handful of tiny, red, stinging blisters.
"Ow!" A fierce guardian, if these inimical plants were anything to
judge by. Hoping he could keep his balance, he wormed his way
through the undergrowth.

Keith circled around the low mound, his invisible whiskers erect
with excitement. He knew that most things ancient humankind thought
of as fairy rings were actually the outward growth from successive
generations of some kinds of plants, like mushrooms, but this
couldn't be in that category. The hillock was too perfect to be completely natural. Six inches above the ground, there was a barrier encircling it, consisting of a single wire attached at intervals to small

wooden posts, and smaller signs that read "Restricted." The flowers in the dead center of the mound stood defiant amidst the low grass. That grass was strange in itself; the natural growth on the rest of the hillside would be almost knee high except that it lay flat on the ground. Holl appeared through the underbrush.

"Here, look!" Keith called. "Come on over and tell me what you think!"

Holding his stung hand gingerly, Holl came over and peered at the tall flower stalks. As he approached the mound, the feeling of ill-will was stronger, almost overwhelming. His face fell as he got his first good look at Keith's quarry. "It's pink foxglove," he said. "I've seen it before. It wouldn't be of any use at all. That is to say, it has some medicinal uses, but it isn't magical."

"Are you sure?" Keith asked, disappointed. "Well, I'm not going to write the whole experience off as a waste. I've never seen a fairy mound before. How about a closer look?"

"No, thank you!" Holl said, warily. "Keith Doyle, there's something about this hillside, something I feel is wrong here."

"You're just nervous," Keith chided him. He peered up at the inviting green grass, hoped that there weren't dire consequences for intruding. With a quick apology to whatever powers had designed it, he stepped gingerly over the perimeter and up onto the green.

Holl's mouth formed an O of horror. "What are you doing, you silly fellow?"

"It's okay!" Keith assured him. "Nothing's happened to me yet. Hey, the hill feels strange under my feet." He stamped on it, felt the reverberations through his feet. "Almost hollow, like a drum. Come on in, the magic's fine!"

"Out, you widdy! The place is surrounded by "Restricted" notices. Someone doesn't want you tramping around on it."

Struck by a curious thought, Keith looked up. "Yeah! Do you suppose that means the British government believes in magic? Why else would they rope off a hill? What do they know that they're not telling?"

"Perhaps the grass you're stamping out of existence is an endangered plant," Holl pointed out acidly. "Come down from there." The effort of shouting made him feel faint, and he sat down in the long straw. He felt cold chills, though the sun was shining directly down on them.

"Holl, what's the matter?" Keith asked, leaping down from the mound. The little man didn't answer. His chin sagged onto his chest, and he shuddered. "Holl?"

"There's something powerful in there," Holl whispered, trying to project his voice. A buzzing started in his ears, and grew louder and louder until he could hear nothing else. He knew Keith was shouting at him, but he saw only the young man's mouth move. He couldn't understand the words at all.

Keith reached Holl just as the other started to slump over onto the grass. His skin was red and hot, as if he had been sunburned, but they had hardly been out under the sky long enough to get warm. Keith felt for a heartbeat, and found it: rapid, shallow, and unsteady. What kind of attack was this? Had something evil under the hill reached out at the more sensitive one of the two when Keith broached its barriers? "Holl, can you hear me?" The elf made a sort of choking noise, and Keith pried the jaw open with a thumb, and looked down the throat. His breathing didn't appear to be blocked by anything physical. "I have got to get you to a doctor. Oh, my God, where am I going to find a doctor out here?" He settled Holl gently into the long grass with the coolie hat over his face to keep the sun off. "You wait here. I promise I'll be right back."

He ran down the hill and around the bend, looking for the tour bus. It was long gone from its temporary parking place. Desperation dragged him scrambling up the hill to the dig site. He stumbled over his feet at the top of the rise, and practically fell over the project coordinator's table, which lay at the end of the site. "Ah, there you are, Keith," Dr. Crutchley said cheerfully, from the edge of the cut turf where the boys were digging. He waved to the young man to join him. "I wondered what had become of my most energetic worker."

"When do Miss Anderson and the tour bus come back?" Keith asked breathlessly. The rest of the team stared at him.

"Why, not for several hours, at least, son. Haven't you just arrived? We have a lot of work to do."

"Holl, my nephew, he just passed out. I have to get him to a doctor!"

"What's wrong?" Miss Sanders rose from the table, and laid a concerned hand on Keith's arm.

Keith started, wild-eyed. "He's got a fever, he's gasping, and his skin is all red. I don't know if he had some kind of attack, or what." He willed himself to calm down. The others hurried over to him. "Did he swallow something? Is his throat obstructed? Time is crucial if someone is choking!"

"He just said he felt funny, and passed out," Keith explained, helplessly, surrounded by the crowd. He felt he had to move, to do something quickly, or burst. He was responsible for Holl. Holl trusted him.

Matthew came up, offering Keith a small cell telephone, and yanked up the antenna wire. "Here, use my portable. Dial 999 for the rescue squad. They'll send someone."

Miss Sanders waved the phone away. "It would take too long for them to find us. I have a car. We'll take him to the National Health Service clinic. It isn't too far. I'll drive you. You bring him to the side of the road, and I'll pick you up."

"Thanks, Miss Sanders, I appreciate it," Keith wheezed, and dashed back to where he had left Holl lying. The others dropped their pans and followed him.

Keith hurried up to Holl. There was no change. Holl was still in a near-somnolent state, responding only with fluttering eyelids to Keith's voice. The American stuffed the fallen baseball cap in his pocket and picked the young elf up. To his surprise, his friend was very light. "Well, I guess personality doesn't weigh anything," he joked out loud, but his insides were twisting in panic. There seemed to be nothing he could do for Holl. What would he say to the Elf Master, to Maura, if something happened to Holl while in his care? Then reality intruded. The others were right behind him. There was no way for him to hide Holl's most characteristic features. He dropped to his knees, and turned his back on the advancing crowd, laying the elf on the grass, and raising his head gently. "Holl, can you hear me?" he pleaded in a rushed undertone. "I'm going to ask you for the biggest favor ever. I promise, I'd never ask this if it wasn't vital. I mean, a matter of life and death. Please, make your ears look round." Holl didn't respond. "Darn it, do it!" Keith insisted. "You've got to hide those points. Otherwise they'll know what you are and we'll never get out of here. You don't want that to happen. If you won't do it for me, think of Maura."

The Little Folk's breath caught once, and Keith held his breath. Before his eyes, the ears changed, shortening, shrinking, the tips receding into the pinnae as if they were withering. Keith touched one, curiously. It felt exactly as it looked. Keith felt a little bit of a shock go through him. That was all it took to remove the Little Folks' specialness. Without the ears, Holl was a kid. A short, blond-haired kid. Mentally, Keith kicked himself, having fallen into that trap once before, with embarrassing results, and had promised it wouldn't happen again. It hadn't, but boy, how deceiving looks could be! Keith hoisted the disguised Holl off the grass and bundled him into the back of Miss Sanders's small Fiat Uno as the others crowded around him, clucking their concern.

The doctors at the National Health clinic were firm and kind. "An attack of some kind? Does he have any allergies?" a white-coated man asked, writing down facts on a history sheet. Holl's discarded cap and Keith's coolie hat lay on a table behind them.

"I don't know," Keith answered, helplessly.

"Fourteen. Hm, small for his age, isn't he? Looks about the same age as my nephew, eleven or twelve." The doctor took Holl's chin in his hand and moved it from side to side.

"Well, it's not really unusual," Keith said, hurriedly, wondering if Holl had a weird blood type or some other indicator showing that he wasn't exactly human. "Not in his family. I mean, his side of the family. My sister's in-laws. They tend to be short. What's all that swelling, doctor?" He pointed to the reddening on Holl's cheek.

"That looks rather nasty, but it's only nettle rash. As for the burning, I'll want to keep him here for observation. A few days. We'll admit him immediately." The doctor clucked. "Look, you're all over nettles yourself, lad. Your skin must be burning you. You're brave to ignore your own hurts to look after the boy. Sit down, and let the nurse put a deadening cream on it."

Obediently, Keith sat down, and let them fuss over him. He was too bound up in guilt to notice any stinging. He was desperately worried about his friend. He had never known one of the Little Folk to be ill before. He felt guilty for not having gotten off the mound when Holl told him to. Holl was probably right, that whatever possessed that mound got upset about trespassers. He might have been responsible for the attack Holl had suffered. But how could he tell the doctor about a speculation like that?

Keith felt as if he had betrayed a trust, and it was tearing up his insides. He sat and stared at Holl, head lolling to one side on the examining table, and willed him with all his heart to get well. He knew Holl had never wanted to leave Hollow Tree Farm. Traveling shook him. He even disliked car trips. He was an old homebody, but he had volunteered to make the trip, insisted on it, because he trusted Keith to look after him. It was like the blind leading the blind, really, because neither of them was too worldly. Always said he had no wish to go away. Enoch was the one who was interested in going out and seeing the world. Keith kept wondering what had hit them on the hillside. Could it be a spell that someone put on the hill before, as Puck of Pook's Hill said, all of the *sidhe* left England? Or was it something more mundane and sinister?

"You can go now, Mr. Doyle. You can visit your nephew later, when we've had a chance to observe him. We have the telephone number, and we will call you when we know anything." The nurse escorted him firmly to the door and into the reception room. Keith tried vainly to keep Holl in sight until she closed the examining room door on him.

Chapter Eight

"O'Day was spotted cavorting on top of the buried dome of the satellite tracking system, just like he knew it was there. The hidden cameras are on totally silent swivels. They snapped his photo, and the johnnies in security were on to us in a flash. They've got copies of all our advisories. And then the kid had some kind of attack. Instead of intercepting them, I followed them to the Health Service. I've been keeping a close lookout ever since, in case he tried anything suspicious. He might be here to bribe one of our men to look the other way when a Russian satellite is launched." Michaels squirmed uncomfortably in the office chair. The seats in the Chief's office were not meant to encourage long stays. The room was nondescript and cluttered, but probably chocked to the rafters with listening and recording equipment behind the walls. "He seems so normal, sir, and genuinely concerned about the kid."

"Even spies have relatives, Michaels," the Chief reminded him. "That's how the Rooskies keep their operatives' loyalty. Have you any hard information on them?"

"Aye, sir. He's traveling on an American passport under the name of Keith Doyle," Michaels reported. "I've got the numbers out of the medical history the clinic took. It's a clean one, fairly new, with a few trips on it, legitimate, to Canada. The 'boy' is going as a Doyle, too. By the report from the medico, the lad was genuinely ill. Except for some nettle rash on his hand and face, he can't figure out quite what was wrong with him. Is there a loose nuclear source at that site, chief? He had what looked to me like mild radiation sickness: red, burned skin and fever, lightheadedness."

"Can't be too careful," the Chief agreed. "I'll have it checked out. The boffins up there have probably built up so much of an immunity they don't notice what would be a dangerous dose for normal people. I think perhaps our smugglers might be doing us a service after all, pointing that out for us."

"They do seem like a pair of personable chaps."

"So were Mungojerrie and Rumpelteazer," his supervisor pointed out, sternly. "A couple of charming thieves. Well, now we've got them on a genuine charge of criminal trespass, if we need to swear out a warrant for a quick pickup. Stay close and keep an eye on them. They've obviously been in no hurry up 'til now. They may be preparing to make their move. And when they do…"

Michaels rose, decisively. It was more comfortable to stand. "I'll lower the net on them smartly, sir. Count on it."

Holl, languishing in a bed in the corner of a hospital ward, stared at the white walls and the blank, curtained windows. He had never felt so lonely in his life. There were others in the beds around the room of the ward, Big children, all his own size or larger, but clearly younger than he and frightened, and none of them with a thought for anyone else. He had to admit that he was frightened, too. He couldn't recall clearly what had happened to bring him here. He had already examined his ear-tips, and discovered that they were round, instead of pointed normally. At first he thought it was Keith Doyle's doing, but a hazy memory reminded him he had done it himself at the Big One's urging.

His skin under the white cotton robe was tender. His arms were slightly puffy, as they had been once when he had gotten sun poisoning. That was before Catra, the archivist, had issued an advisory about sunscreens and vitamin B5. Then he remembered the burning and choking feeling he had suffered on the hillside. The absence of pain was a chilling void.

"Good morning, Holl," caroled a woman in a stiff-starched white dress. "Have a good sleep?" Her warm voice had a burr in it, which was the friendliest thing he had found in this strange place so far.

"Yes, ma'am," he said, looking up at her. "How long have I been here?"

She took his wrist in a businesslike grip and consulted the watch on her other arm. "You were admitted in the afternoon the day before yesterday. You've slept the clock 'round, and half again. I'm surprised the usual tumultuous clamour of this ward didn't rouse you at dawn. Pulse normal, but you've still got a nasty burn. You'll be staying with us at least one more day, for observation."

"Two days? Does K…does my uncle know I'm here?" Holl asked, pushing himself upright. The nurse took the pillows from behind him, plumped and replaced them, settling him back against the head of the bed.

"Good Lord, yes. He's probably out in the corridor now. We've had to chase him out at the end of visiting hours already. I'll send him in just as soon as you have had breakfast."

As soon as the cart containing the dirty trays was wheeled through the swinging doors, Keith slipped into the ward. He had an armful of books, which he shifted to one elbow to wave. "Hi! How are you feeling?" he asked in a low voice, as he sat down on a chair beside the hospital bed. He settled his burden on the floor underneath his seat.

"Fine, I think. Well enough, though I can't remember anything that happened after I climbed up the hill. Must I stay here?" he asked plaintively.

"You're still pretty red. Do you know what happened to you?" Keith asked, studying his face closely.

"No."

"Then I think you ought to stay, just in case." Keith explained the events of Holl's collapse, and ended by saying, "I would rather you were where they can treat a convulsion instead of worrying if you're going to have an attack in the middle of nowhere. When they say you're all right, then you can get out of here. It shouldn't be more than another day."

"I don't like the hospitality of strangers," Holl said darkly. "Most especially strange Big Folk."

Keith sighed. "I know, but they're professional medical specialists. I'm just your ordinary cub scout who had CPR training once in swim class. Come on, humor me. How would I explain to the Master if I came back with you on a stretcher? He'd probably make me sit in a corner and write five page essays on health care for the rest of my life."

Holl threw up his hands. "Very well, I submit. I'll stay until they release me. But with a protest."

"Fine. They have vaccines for that sort of thing. I brought you a few things to make your incarceration more interesting." From under his chair, Keith retrieved a small hardcover book, which he gave to Holl. "This book will eventually be a Doyle family heirloom. My cousin gave it to me when I was six and home with chicken pox. My mother put it in my suitcase at the last minute as a sort of traveling talisman. I think you should keep it with you while you're here."

"'How to Go About Laying An Egg'?" There was a cartoon drawing of a white chicken on the paper dust jacket.

"Full of good advice," Keith insisted, airily. "Very Zen."

Holl looked from it into Keith's twinkling eyes and fell back on his pillows laughing. "I like your family, Keith Doyle. They all seem to be a little mad, but in a good way."

Next, Keith handed him a yellow paper envelope. "Here. More surprises. I brought you the pictures I took at the farm, during the going-away party your folk gave me. I mean, us. Look, here's Maura. And there's the Master in the corner with his wife."

"See him glare," Holl noted with amusement. "He didn't care for that."

"Told me to go away and play," Keith averred with satisfaction. "Well, he wouldn't pose, so how else was I going to get a picture? There's Enoch and Marcy, and here's Dola, pretending to be a movie star. She's going to be a knockout when she grows up. What is she, ten?"

"Just about," Holl said, taking the photograph from Keith and adding it to the stack.

"Here's your baby sister. The next picture was nothing but a big blob because she put her hand in the lens. Almost gave me a black eye."

Holl laughed, but then the laughter constricted into gasping breaths. Keith, still seeming jolly on the outside to hide the worry on the inside, sprang up to press the bell for the nurse. Holl forestalled him with a wave.

"No, leave her be. I'll be all right. I'm just out of energy. So strange. There was some truly malign force on that hillside, but whether it was natural or not I can't tell." He sat upright again, and with Keith's assistance replaced the pillows propping him up. "Do you know, I haven't been this ill since I was a tot. That was in the days when the steam tunnels were still exposed near our home. We had to be so quiet all of the time. My mother sat by me, soothing and silencing." He gave Keith a wordless look full of woe.

Keith smiled sympathetically, and moved from the chair to the edge of the narrow bed. "You want your Mom. I know how you feel."

Shamefaced, Holl nodded. "I guess I'm hearkening back to my childhood. I've only just realized that I can't sense any of my Folk this far away. I *know* they're there, so I understand the link's still good, but I can't differentiate between them, if you see what I mean. There's a tiny dot on the horizon, and I know it's them. I didn't mind it while I was well, but being feverish leaves me gloomy and sorry for my-self."

Grinning, Keith passed his hands in the air a few times like a conjuror and produced a small, narrow, black box from his jacket pocket. "The pictures and books weren't all I brought. Would it help if you could talk to them?"

Holl eyed it warily. "What's that?"

"Matthew's portable phone. He said you could keep it here until you're sprung. I think you was framed," Keith went on, in his bargain basement imitation of Humphrey Bogart. "But we'll have you outa here and playing the violin again in no time. International Access Code, then 1, then your area code and number." He handed the small phone to Holl. Holl dialed.

There was an audible click from the receiver, and the distant sound of ringing, and then a another click. A shrill voice, audible even to Keith, demanded "What is it?"

"Keva," Holl explained, his hand over the mouthpiece. "She's never learned just to say 'hello,' as the etiquette manual suggests." Keith grinned. Keva was a law unto herself regarding manners, or anything else. Holl uncovered the receiver. "Keva, this is Holl speaking. Can you ask our mother if she'll come to the phone?"

There was a long wait, and then Keith could hear the overtones of a more gentle voice. Holl's mother Calla was a tiny woman, small even for the Little Folk, with a very young face under a wave of soft, silver hair. Keith guessed that she was a bare eighteen or twenty years older than her outspoken daughter. That was unusual enough. Normally, the Folk only thought of getting married in their fifties and sixties. Babies came much later on. At forty-one, even Holl was pushing it a little to be thinking of engagement.

"Mother? Yes. I know, I'm far away, and the link is weak. You sound as clear if you're standing here. A miracle, these small machines." Holl dropped from English into the Little Folk language, a tongue Keith was becoming used to hearing, though he couldn't understand it.

It was boring to listen to a conversation in a foreign language. Keith tried to make sense out of the tone, instead. At first, Holl seemed to be merely exchanging news with his mother. After a while, though, the subject changed, and Holl's voice became angry, then thick. Something his mother was telling him bothered him very much, nearly choking him. Keith felt he was intruding on something private, and got up to leave, but Holl waved him to stay. After a while, the conversation must have turned to more cheerful topics, which he was willing to share with Keith.

Holl translated a phrase from time to time, moving the receiver aside. "The she-cat has had kittens, Mother says. There are six of them. The well has been cleared out at last, and is flowing so generously it threatens to burst the old pipes. Deliveries are keeping apace of orders, and Ms. Voordman has sent word through Diane that if you are really in Scotland, you must send her a postcard."

"That sounds like an order," Keith joked, snapping off a salute.

More words were exchanged in the Little Folks' language. "Dola wouldn't look askance at a small present, but is too well brought up to ask," Holl told him, with a wry grin.

"Now, that's a hint," Keith acknowledged, "but it carries the same weight as an order."

"I'll tell her. And many photographs of the strange places we visit would be welcome." More talk. Holl's voice fell to soft, nearly inaudible tones. Keith felt uncomfortable, but didn't leave because Holl wanted him to stay.

To break the tension, Keith opened a book of his own, *Popular Tales of the West Highlands*, and read for a while, trying to block out the conversation. He became engrossed in J.F. Campbell's description of the *bodach* of Jura and other tales of magic. Those sounded friendly. He wished he could find one of those to interview. Interesting also how the stories coincided so neatly with other books he had read.

Thoughtfully, Holl took the phone away from his ear and pushed the Off button. Keith closed his book on one finger. Holl looked depressed, but he mustered a grateful smile.

"Thank you," he said. "That helped. There's...a lot going on at home. Express my gratitude to Matthew, and let me know what it costs for the call."

Keith quickly judged that Holl didn't want to talk about his call until he had had time to digest it, and cast about swiftly for another topic of conversation. "So, when you get out of here, should we go and find whatever it was I offended and apologize to them?"

"I wouldn't if I were you," Holl warned him, momentarily distracted by Keith's endless interest in his hobby, though his eyes kept their troubled look. "Most of the hidden ones want to stay hidden, without your great feet tramping all over their privacy."

"Well, we were always brought up to think that Americans abroad should act as good will ambassadors wherever they went. Don't you want to be the ambassador for your people wherever you go?"

"No," Holl answered, keeping the banter going, but without much spirit. "Especially not in your company; they'd probably declare eternal war on my folk once they'd met you."

Keith waved away the suggestion that his presence could cause an inter-species feud. "They'd get used to me. I've never asked, you know, but do *you* believe in sprites and fairies and things like that, Holl? I mean, what I'm looking for could be fantasy to your folk, as much as it is to mine."

"I don't know. I've never made a study of it. But I'm here. And since the legend writers group my Folk in with them, I suppose there might be others out there. You're counting on it, aren't you?"

Keith considered the question. "I'm looking for whatever is out there, but naturally, I'd prefer them to be my kind of Little People, who consort with dragons and do magic." He pointed out a passage on one of the pages. "This J.F. Campbell compares legends of the Fair Folk with actual people he met in Lapland. The way he describes them, they could walk under his outstretched arm with their tall hats on without bending over, but never touch him." Keith measured his friend with an eye. "Just about the right size. Do you think you're descended from Laplanders, Holl?"

Holl snorted. "I don't know where my people are from, if not from the old place we're trying to find. So far as I know they've always been there. All my father would say was that it was terrible when they left it, without much helpful detail. We didn't spring out of the ground, so I expect we came from somewhere. You'll need to ask one of the old ones. Why?"

There was a long pause. Keith's eyes twinkled. "I read this feature article about a man in Lapland who everybody thinks is Santa Claus," he offered, impishly. He grinned at the expression on Holl's face, who realized he'd been led into a trap. "Even the adults who meet him think so."

"Aargh! Be off with you before I have a relapse!" Holl seized his pillow and yanked it over his face. Keith shut his book, and stood up to go.

"Oh, by the way," he said casually, "I found the body. It was in a funeral urn, about five feet down the pike from where Matthew dug up the lidded pot. He's dead all right. It was moider. No doubt about it. Moider. Case closed, shweetheart." Running his finger along the brim of an imaginary fedora, Keith winked at Holl and swaggered out the swinging door.

Holl pushed the pillow back into place behind his head, and settled back with a sigh. "Thank you, Keith Doyle," he said softly. "You're a host and a cure in yourself. I have a lot to think about now."

The guard at the quadrangle gate had become used to seeing Michaels walking in and out of the University grounds. Perhaps the guard thought the old boy in the tweed suit was a visiting doctor. The way the National Health chopped and changed, he could have brought in a host of agents and never been questioned.

Surveillance on the portable phone link the blond lad had been using revealed one interesting fact: the boy's first language was not English. The lingo boffins hadn't pinned down the root language yet, but it sounded halfway between Icelandic and Balkan. Were other powers involved in O'Day's latest pickup? Michaels hoped the answers lay in Inverness, the tour's next stop.

Chapter Nine

"This is a great place," Keith exclaimed, all but hanging out the coach window to get a good look at Inverness. Where Glasgow was gray granite and yellow sandstone, Inverness was red sandstone and black iron. He snapped pictures with the lens focus set on infinity so he wouldn't have to keep changing it and risk losing his subjects. It wasn't a perfect system, but it worked most of the time. He had taken three whole rolls of new scenery in the last two hours alone. "That's weird. This castle looks almost brand new. It's almost exactly the same color as cream-of-tomato soup."

"I'm sure that's precisely how they put it in the travel brochures," Martin quipped sarcastically, from two seats behind Keith. "'Our national treasures and how they compare with canned goods.'"

Inverness was hilly, set along the deeply cut bed of the river. With passersby wearing shirtsleeves and light dresses, it was hard to believe that the city lay 200 miles further north even than Glasgow. The hot summer weather was a surprise to the Americans, but it was more of one to the English school teachers, who exclaimed over it with pleasure.

The storefronts were trim and clean, and painted hoardings disguised construction sites. Flowerpots made a colorful contrast to the wrought iron lightpoles from which they depended. From pegs in the walls around some of the shops, lengths of tweed and woven shawls flapped gently in the breeze like plaid pennants. Above the buildings in every direction, distant mountains, the snow topping their peaks a shock in July, arched broad green backs to the sun and clear blue sky.

Holl leaned against the window across the aisle, and soaked up the new sights. He was feeling much better, and after a few days of forced inactivity, was ready to do some exploring. The others had been solicitous of him, cheering him up with stories of the dig. Matthew especially had been kind. He waved away the idea that Holl should pay him back for the telephone call home. "It was necessary medicine," he assured Holl, "and we'd never stint you that."

The camaraderie of the little group, the unquestioning acceptance of Big Folk toward complete strangers touched Holl. Beside his own village, the Big students in the Master's course at

Midwestern had been his only real outside contact. The ancient Conservative faction within the village held that the seeming friendliness of Big Folk was a sham. He was pleased to be bringing back to them proof that that was not so.

What did not delight him was the memory of the mysterious attack he had suffered on the hillside. If this was what happened to trespassers on charmed soil, he planned to keep Keith off any fairy mounds in the future. Thank heavens that nothing like this existed in Illinois. On the other hand, at home he would have had the experience of one of the old ones to hand, and there probably would never have been such a trap sprung from which he would need rescuing.

Though he was at pains to conceal it from Keith, he was troubled, and had been ever since he had called home. There was gossip going around the farm about Maura and Gerol, another male a few years older than Holl. They were spending a lot of time together, and the attraction seemed to be both obvious and mutual. She hadn't said anything to Calla to the effect that her 'understanding' with Holl was off, but that was the way many of their clan read it. Holl was very hurt. He had taken on this quest so he would have the right to ask her to marry when he returned, following all the traditional forms. Apparently, she had taken his departure as a rejection. The impulse returned again and again that he should go home immediately, abandon the search for the white bellflowers. But did he give up his quest, thereby abrogating his right to be headman of the village one day? That was never an ambition he had intended for himself. It was merely what others had always expected of him. They were counting on him. If he went home now, there would be others who would lack the bellflowers for their weddings, and he felt somewhat guilty about that, but he didn't want to be outmatched by a rival when he couldn't be there to defend his suit. The Conservatives would attack him as a culture-killing Progressive, sucking up to Big ways, but he wondered if he cared about that if he lost Maura. Still, the Elf Master had made it a condition of his proposal to find the flowers before he could marry Maura. Holl wished he had taken her aside and told her his intentions before he had left, but that wasn't the way the Little Folk did things. Until her parents said he had their permission, he had to hold his tongue.

There wasn't so much bad about the Big Folks' life. Would he wed instead after their fashion, making up their own ceremonies when it suited them, and when convention couldn't apply? They seemed to get along fine. And yet, had Maura rejected the old ways? Was she choosing her own mate over her long-time suitor in defiance of tradition? He wished he could talk to Keith about his worries, but he wanted to think it through further first. It was important not to let the situation at home drag down his spirits.

"We are now passing over the River Ness," Miss Anderson put in. The sunshine was brilliantly reflected off the flowing water. Small, black-headed gulls swooped around the coach as it drove over an iron bridge.

"Have they ever decided what it is that so many people report seeing in the Loch?" Holl inquired, and wondered why everyone else laughed.

"Do you mean Nessie?" Miss Anderson asked brightly. "No, there are ten times as many theories as there are reported sightings. You'll have a chance to look for yourselves. You're on your own for today, ladies and gentlemen. Dr. Stroud would prefer that we start with him Tuesday. He wants only his team on site this afternoon. I believe they are at a delicate stage of the proceedings. I am sure you wouldn't want to interfere."

There was a chorus of amiable protest. "We're more like day trippers to the profs," Edwin said, speaking for them all. "If they're doing something serious, we won't get in the way."

"Somewhat inelegantly put," Mrs. Green added, smiling over her shoulder at the tall young man, "but essentially what I would have said."

"Those of you taking this for credit are not excused from your essays, though," the tour director warned. "But allow me to suggest a topic you might explore. Picture yourself as far forward in the future as we are now to our Bronze age subjects. What would you be likely to find left of Inverness in the 60th century?

"I think you will find Inverness worth your exploration. I have a schedule of day tours available, if anyone would care to inspect it, and there are more to be had from the Tourist Information Centre. We'll be staying in a guest house this time, instead of a residence hall. Evening meals will be provided for you as well as breakfast. If you want to make your own arrangements for supper, please let the owner know early in the day."

The weather was fine and warm, with a hot sun persuading the tourists to leave their coats behind in the guest house, and a breeze promising that the heat wouldn't be too oppressive. Keith found a reasonably respectable tee-shirt to wear among his belongings, and joined his friends on their way out for a look around.

From their lodgings to the city center it was downhill, via a long flight of narrow stone steps and a broader, sharply turning staircase. From the head of the twisting steps, they found they were on a level with the red stone castle, which gave them a good view to the east. Most of the section of Inverness in which they were staying appeared to be laid out along a similar plan to provide access to the higher neighborhoods. Down on the long High Street, Keith would catch sight of endless stairs reaching up and back into the shadows between buildings.

As in Glasgow, the traffic was fast, with taxis taking death-dealing turns around corners under the noses of wary pedestrians. Except for the perils of traffic, Inverness was easy to get around in. Keith found it cheerful and clean. The group stopped for lunch in a small family style restaurant by the side of the River Ness, just out of the shadow of the main bridge spanning it. The Hearty Trencherman boasted a sign showing a plump, happy diner beaming over a huge plate and brandishing a knife and fork.

Matthew made a face at the sign. "Ooh, I hate campy adverts."

"I'd call it the Trench, for short," Martin suggested, as they pushed inside. "Look at the high banks of the river, surrounding us. We're in the bottom of a pit."

"Well, if you look at it that way, anything good you get here'll be a nice surprise," Keith reasoned. He sat down and accepted a menu from the female server standing beside their table. "Hi, beautiful. What's good here, besides the service?"

The waitress tossed a light-brown ponytail and dimpled prettily. "Nearly anything," she said. "The salmon's off, but all the rest is ready."

Keith waggled his eyebrows at her outrageously, collecting a blush. "So'm I."

"Keith Doyle!" Holl exclaimed, shocked. "What would Diane say?"

"Diane?" Keith, surprised, turned innocent hazel eyes on him. "What's this got to do with her? We're just having a conversation. It doesn't mean anything." He promptly went back to flirting, and Holl turned a hot red in embarrassment. The waitress seemed to take the whole business in stride, all the time noting down orders and dispensing drinks.

The menu was predictable, including the ubiquitous "and peas," but the food was well-prepared. The young men leaned back from their empty plates with satisfaction, waiting for the bill.

Keith peered out of the plate glass window at the river. "This would be a good place to watch the sun set."

"Aye," said Matthew. "This is just into Midsummer, and we're far enough north that the sun nearly never sets. We'll go and have a sit down in the nearest local, and when the publican cries closing time at eleven, we'll know it's sunset."

The others agreed that it was a good plan. They paid the bill and walked out into the sunlight. At the first sign of a likely pub, most of the young men turned in. "Aren't you coming in with us?" Max asked Keith, holding open the door.

"Nope," Keith replied, grinning. "We're going to take a tour down to the Loch and look for the monster."

"Oh. Happy fishing," Edwin said sarcastically.

"See you later," Keith promised. "I'll look for you guys here around sunset."

Directed by Miss Anderson to look for the signs with the small script "i," Keith located the Tourist Information Centre on a street perpendicular to the main thoroughfare not far from the Trench. The TICs provided numerous services for travelers, including directions, event schedules, lodging arrangements, maps, and an assembly point for tours.

"The next one sets out in twenty minutes," the woman in the glass-fronted booth told Keith. "You can pay for your tickets now or on the coach."

With time to kill, Keith studied the wall map of the city, while Holl perused displays of handcrafted knickknacks for sale in the front of the Centre. Keith compared the scale from the city to Loch Ness, the long, narrow stretch of water angling southwest from the river which bisected Inverness. It was a curious shape, long and narrow like a spear.

"Keith Doyle?" Holl's voice interrupted his reverie. "Can you come here for a minute?"

Holl gestured him quietly to a small display case which contained ceramic pieces. Behind a tiny card which said "Nessie" were ranged a half dozen separate pieces: a head, four semicircular loops with ridges over the back, and a tiny squib of a pointed tail, which made it appear as if the monster was swimming with half its length submerged in the table. "Is that what it looks like?"

"That's what most of the people who have seen her say," Keith said. "They don't have any concrete proof, of course. Some of the pictures they've got suggest that descendants of plesiosaurs are living in the Loch." Holl's eyes went wide. "The legends also say she might be a selkie, which is a sort of magical seagoing horse. Does that look like a horse to you?"

"Don't you go talking down aur Nessie," the clerk chided them playfully from the other side of the shop. "We're fond of her in these parts."

Keith clapped his spread fingertips to his chest. "Me? I believe in her," he assured the clerk, earnestly. "I know of stranger things in real life. But it's not like she's ever appeared on the evening news."

"There are those who believe and those who doubt," the clerk said offhandedly. "But you'll prove it to yourself at the Official Loch Ness Monster Exhibition. Queue up for the coach just outside the door."

The Official Monster Exhibition was in Drumnadrochit, several miles southwest of Inverness. The guide doing the presentation offered them walls filled with blurred photographs and written eyewitness accounts as proof of the monster's existence. The multimedia program was more interesting, and dropped delicious hints that investigating scientists were on the edge of making an announcement as to Nessie's species and location. They showed the audience films taken by spotters, who had accidentally caught sight of the mysterious denizen of the Loch. After glancing at the displays, which held far less scientific theory than they had hoped, Keith and Holl made their way through the turnstile to the book and gift shop.

"Now here's something that looks like home," Holl said, spreading his arms out to the walls of books.

"Are you going to have trouble living on the farm, since it's exposed and all?" Keith asked. "I mean after living underground in a library, anything is going to feel less solid."

"No, but the walls are awfully bare without books. We're budgeting to start our own collection of books. The Conservatives insist that we get a good grounding of textbooks, to keep up our education. The Progressives want literature, with an emphasis on science fiction. It's still in negotiation."

Outside the Exhibition hall was a pond, in which a twenty-foot concrete dinosaur model was posed swimming. "It's a plesiosaur, all right," Holl agreed. "But is that really what's in the Loch?"

"No one really knows," Keith said, thoughtfully. "But I might come back some day and try to find out."

The tour's next stop was the ruin of Urquhart Castle, a fabulous ruin on the west side of the Loch. Keith slapped a new roll of film into his camera, and crawled all over the stones taking pictures. Holl followed him more sedately, stopping to inspect the layout and read the small signs describing what used to lie in each part of the castle.

"Keith, let me take one picture of you," Holl suggested, when Keith stopped to reload. "That way, you'll have at least one piece of proof you were here along with your camera, instead of it having a nice vacation on its own."

"Great idea," Keith said. "Let's go back up the road so you can get most of the castle into the frame with me." Together, they trotted over the rise and up toward the road.

They gazed appreciatively around them at the scenery outside of the castle grounds. In the thick grass on the roadside, small blossoms of pink and yellow grew abundantly. Urquhart Castle was downhill from the road, so they had to walk some distance from the grounds to where they could see it again.

"I have to have you take a picture so it looks like I'm holding the castle on the palm of my hand, or my father'll be disappointed," Keith explained. "It's an old family tradition."

"Ah," Holl acknowledged, amused. "How about seeming to pick it up between your thumb and forefinger? It's already a ruin. You can do it no more damage."

"Ha, ha," Keith said. He posed, and Holl snapped the picture.

"How are you feeling now? It's only been about three days since you got out of bed again. I haven't given up on trying to find your flowers for you," Keith said, solicitously.

"I'm well enough," Holl replied. "I'd prefer that you didn't go charging up fairy mounds and the like again."

"Well, if I see one, I'll go up it myself, with you out at a safe distance," Keith insisted, "in case there's something mean that just doesn't like other magical folk. I guess I'm immune to whatever hit you in the first site, so you point, and I'll fetch. Okay?"

"Okay. So where's your monster?" Holl asked, teasingly, gesturing with a sweep of his arm. "Now that we have seen the amazingly over-painted model, we know what to look for."

"I've got the bait right here," Keith said, pulling half of a cheese sandwich out of his pocket and unwrapping it. "Just you wait. Here, Nessie, Nessie, Nessie," he called, hurling a corner of it out over the loch. A seagull came out of midair and snagged the scrap of food. "Whoops. Took my bait. I'll have to try again."

Holl grinned sheepishly. "Oh, you can't be serious, Keith Doyle."

"Never more than half," Keith assured him, unquenchably, breaking off a piece of the sandwich and giving it to Holl. "But wouldn't they be amazed if it worked?"

"You'll never die of hypertension, that's certain," Holl said. "Your frivolity is quite an act. You give an amazing imitation of grasshopper, Keith Doyle, but I have always suspected you of being mostly ant."

They threw crumbs into the loch for a while, in no hurry to go back to the castle and rejoin the tour.

"I wish I could drive a car over here," Keith said wistfully, watching the spare traffic race past the lay-by in which they were standing. "If we're going to have a lot of time to kill, I want to get out and see some more of the countryside. It's beautiful here."

"It is," Holl agreed, taking a deep breath of the fragrant air. "I wish I could show some of the others more of the world. They wouldn't be so fearful of going out into it once in a while."

Keith made a noise that sounded sympathetic and derisive at the same time. "It could be 99 percent wonderful, and they'd hate it because of one percent of things that would be off kilter."

"You've shown more than one percent of going wrong, and they still accept you," Holl pointed out.

"By the way, I hope you notice I've been good, not trying out you-know-what in front of other people," Keith said defensively.

"And for which I'm grateful. Such behavior deserves reward, is that your thought?" Holl asked shrewdly. "Never mind. It's all right with me. Since Enoch isn't here to continue your education, I'll give you the next lesson. I've wanted a quiet moment to listen for home. You may as well learn something about that."

"What do you mean?" Keith asked eagerly, sitting down on a low boulder at the edge of the road and pulling his knees up. He glanced around. Behind him, it was almost a sheer drop to the Loch. He scooted forward, keeping as much of the rock between him and the precipice as he could. Holl sat on a rock next to him.

"Concentrate and sit quietly, and think in the direction that the Folk are," Holl instructed him, closing his own eyes. "Send your knowledge toward them. See them."

"With your third eye?" Keith inquired, screwing his eyes shut.

"No, you innocent," Holl said, rapping him on the head with his knuckles. "With your heart. Think of the ones dearest to you to make the best link."

"Well, you're my best friend and the one I know best. Hmm. I don't think I can use the Master as a focus. I think he'd disapprove."

"I'm sure you're right," Holl agreed. "How about Maura? You know her well."

Keith thought for a second, looking uneasy. He cracked one eye and peered at his friend. "Maybe not. I wouldn't be able to concentrate on her with you here."

"Eh?"

"Well, it's like horning in on your date," he explained lamely. "I may flirt, but I don't poach."

Holl snorted. "You're amazing, Keith Doyle. I wish everyone had your scruples. How about Dola? She's fond of you."

"Okay. I'll give it a try." Keith concentrated, letting his body relax. He knew that thousands of miles to the southwest, sort of along the axis of the Great Glen, across the ocean in America, lay the village. He thought for a moment that he could see an infinitesimal golden spark on the horizon that felt right, in the correct direction. "I think I've got—what did you call it, a link? But there's something like radio interference in the way. I'm not sensing anybody particular. Of course, I haven't got tons of magical energy to use."

"All you need is practice, widdy, not tons." Holl closed his eyes again and let his muscles go slack. After a few minutes, he sighed. "You're right," he said, disappointed. "We're so far away I can't touch them properly. There's too much of the world between us. Something's in the way."

"Ireland," said Keith wisely. "Ireland's that way, too." They sat for a moment, quietly concentrating. Holl's forehead was drawn down and troubled.

After a long silence, Keith spoke up. "That sounded significant, the part about scruples," he put in gently. "That reminded me: when you were talking to your mother, you sounded angry. I didn't know what was up."

Holl clicked his tongue. "It was rude of us to speak in a different tongue in front of you."

"Oh, don't worry about that. I felt like a jerk eavesdropping on you anyway. Something I can help with?" When Holl hesitated, he insisted. "Go on, you can confide in me. All discussions become privileged information here at Uncle Keith's Lonelyhearts Club, Fish Market and Filling Station." He presented earnest hazel eyes for Holl's inspection.

Holl turned his head away, and looked out over the loch. "Keith Doyle, do you feel right, going out drinking every night with the others?"

"Well, when in Rome, do as the Romans do. You notice I'm not trying to match them drink for drink, after all. It's the way they socialize over here. The pub really is a great invention. I wonder why nobody has ever tried to import them to the U.S." Keith made a mental note to find out more about pubs.

"What about flirting with the waitresses?" Holl pressed.

"Oh, ho, is that's what's bothering you?" Keith demanded. "It's nothing serious. If it bothered her, I wouldn't do it, but I'm just being friendly. Why?"

"She might have an intended of her own," Holl said significantly.

"If she didn't want me to joke around with her, I assume she'd tell me to flake off," Keith said, confidently. "Just because I'm a customer doesn't give me any special rights to move in on her."

"Oh. So you'd expect her to send you on your way, if she had someone of her own."

"Usually." Keith threw another crumb into the loch and waited. Holl was silent for a while, then sighed.

"It would seem that I have a rival," Holl said at last. "No sooner did I leave the farm than the village is full of talk about Maura spending all her time walking or sitting with Gerol. You know him?"

Keith pictured a strongly built, broad-shouldered elf with a moustache and a sweep of black hair across his forehead who specialized in heavy construction. "Yeah. Nice guy. Reminds me of Ernest Hemingway without the alcohol problem. He's Bracey's brother, isn't he?"

"That's right. I thought he was a friend of ours, but now, what can I think? What can I think of Maura? We had an understanding, or so I believed."

"Have you talked to Maura?" Keith pressed.

"No. It isn't something which I can talk about on the telephone, only face to face. I'm not even supposed to bring up the subject of marriage without the Master's approval. I should go home. Shouldn't I?" Holl looked up helplessly into Keith's face.

"I can't make that decision for you," Keith said, sympathetically but firmly. "I'm on your side, you know. If you want to go home, I'll even drive you to the airport, but you have got to be the one to tell me what you want to do." There was a long pause. "Well?"

"Well," Holl stared mournfully at the waters of the Loch. "I'll stay for now," he said, unsure of his own resolve. "But why isn't she sending him on his way?" Holl burst out.

"Maybe she's lonely," Keith said. "Did you take her aside and tell her why you were going away?"

"No. If I failed, I didn't want too many hopes raised and dashed."

"Did you ask her not to date anyone while you were gone?"

"No. I would never have thought I had to," Holl said, sadly. "It's been an understanding between us, all our lives."

"In my vast and far-reaching experience," Keith said in a ponderous voice that made Holl smile even in his misery, "assumption is the mother of all disappointments. I've heard it phrased differently, but that one'll do for now." That made Holl look even more depressed. "Look, if you've had an understanding all these years, why should she throw it over now? You love her, right?"

"Right," Holl said.

"She loves you, right?"

"Well, I've always thought so."

"*Right?*"

"Right," Holl acknowledged, listlessly.

"So what's the problem? You can't do anything from here. Except trust her."

"I'll stay," Holl said, more certainly.

"Good," Keith cheered. He heard voices, and leaned over the edge of the bank. A couple of men were sitting on the footpath below them, fishing in the loch. Their creels sat beside them, as did a nearly empty bottle of Scotch and a couple of lunchboxes.

"Hey, Holl, how'd you like to help me with magic practice?" Holl looked out across the vast expanse of water, and returned a questioning gaze to Keith. "What, a finding? A calling?"

"Nope," Keith replied, with glee. He parted the tall grass with a quiet hand, and showed Holl the two men quietly fishing. "A forming. On the surface of the water. I don't have enough *oomph* to do it myself."

"It wouldn't last long," Holl warned, skeptically, but his own eyes were twinkling. He was getting caught up in the idea in spite of himself. "It's flowing fairly fast."

"That's okay," Keith assured him. "It doesn't have to last."

"You're a bad influence, my boy."

"Aw, let down your hair a little," Keith returned, innocently. "You're just doing your part for Scottish tourism."

"Ah, there's no harm in it, I suppose." Holl thrust his arm forward. "Lay your arm next to mine, and lend me your strength. Concentrate. There, that's the way. You're not half bad at it, for a beginner." With his other hand outstretched toward the water, Holl drew on the air a half loop, a whole loop, and another, and another, and finished off with a sharp little gesture like an apostrophe.

"Beautiful," said Keith, admiringly, staring at the loch below "I want to be just like you when I grow up."

"You're never going to grow up, Keith Doyle," Holl retorted, but he chuckled, too. "It is good, isn't it?"

"Look!" cried a voice below them, highly excited. "There's *Nessie!*"

Michaels reported to his chief over the telephone that afternoon from Drumnadrochit. "I can't help it if you don't believe me, sir. You'll be seeing the report on the evening news. I wasn't the only one who spotted her. That's right, Nessie. I was observing O'Day and his accomplice. There it was, large as life on the waters of the loch, and neither of them were paying the least attention to it. Very strange, sir. What's that?" Michaels sighed. "Aye, sir. I assure you, I saw it, as plain as I can see…well, this telephone here. What was it? It was a sea serpent, or as close as makes no difference to me. There has to be a logical explanation for it. But it's curious, sir. I can't understand why they weren't excited by it. It's as if they never saw it. They're up to something, sir, and it must be something *big*."

Chapter Ten

Tuesday morning dawned with further instructions from Dr. Stroud not to come to the dig site. So did Wednesday. At the end of the week, the group was allowed to attend for a couple of days. They assembled for the coach to pick them up, radiating excitement and relief.

The settlement under investigation lay to the southeast of Inverness, near where the late-Neolithic Clava burial cairns had been discovered long ago. "It's bound to be fruitful," Miss Anderson advised them. In terms of distance, the location wasn't far from the city, but it was slow going on the roads, which swooped unexpectedly into ravines, and took hairpin turns which the bus could barely negotiate. Amid broken slabs of rock, deep streams of brown water flowed noisily beside to the narrow roadway. It looked pretty, but provided no maneuvering room for the ungainly vehicle. There was only inches of clearance for the coach's tires.

"One slip, and we're fishbait," Keith stated, peering out the window. He was acting as lookout. A low swinging gate appeared ahead across the road. "Your turn, Max."

Low gates like that were common in the area, dividing property in the rural area to allow sheep grazing on both sides of the road. Max swung himself out of the coach, and ran down to open the gate. The coach eased through it. Max relocked the fence, and dashed ahead to climb back on. "That's the last one! Here we are at last," said Miss Anderson, sitting up poker straight to see better. The coach ambled into a pleasant valley with a gentle, almost imperceptible rise toward the distant hills. The group's anticipation was almost palpable as the coach rolled to a gentle stop at the roadside behind a line of automobiles parked on the verge. They piled happily out of the coach. Charles and Edwin both ran to open the field gate for the party.

The sound, or lack of it, nearly stopped them altogether in surprise as they approached the work area. Compared with Dr. Crutchley's small band, the large team working here was a mob, but a quiet one. Thirty or forty men and boys were scattered in the fenced field, working absorbed on their tasks, hardly speaking to one another. Some were in shirtsleeves, but most were bare-chested and pink to the waist with exertion. Only low conversation blended with the sounds of excavation and the clink of stones hitting sorting pans.

"Welcome," a man called, coming up to greet them. He was in his early thirties, of a bull-chested build and fair coloring. Keith had seen a hundred just like him in Inverness. He shook hands with everyone in the party. "I'm Thomas Belgrave, the professor's assistant. I'm happy to see you. Let me give you a quick tour around before we begin. We've had some good fortune here, and we're rather proud of it." He led the way to a pavilion tent.

Matthew's eyes gleamed hungrily as the group was given a tour of the team's gleanings thus far. Among its findings were sealed jars which once contained grain. One of the lids had been replaced with clear plastic film so that the contents could be seen without exposing the team to bacteria or other organic parasites that might be living in the rotted remains of cereal.

"There was a helicopter reconnaissance of the site before we ever put shovel to turf. The village millstone was practically the first thing we tripped over," the assistant confided. "From the air, one could see a dimple in the earth over its resting place. It had come to rest on something soft, like chaff or straw, which deteriorated over time. We more or less expected the typical village outline, animal bones, broken crockery, but never this much, abandoned *in situ*. No one had any idea that such an extensive remnant of this settlement still existed near here. The jars must have been abandoned when the settlement burned. They were in a pit inside the largest hut. We still haven't guessed why the people didn't return for their possessions after the fire went out." He pointed out scorchmarks on the stones and clay items, and brought them to where vestiges of the original circular hut walls remained, standing in narrow knee-deep trenches cut around them in the earth by the archaeological team. The assistant lifted the sheet of plastic covering one as a medical examiner might pull back the sheet on a dead body.

"Dr. Stroud suspects that it was a new colonization, hardly settled yet, as there are none of the characteristic stone buildings of the age, not even a barrier wall. The ditch and bank were only partly formed. Thus vulnerable, they were victims of an enemy attack." The man paused, and grinned long-sufferingly. "As always, he wants more data."

"How sad that it was all destroyed," said Mrs. Green, squatting on her heels to peer down at the walls. The group tried to picture the village as it might have been, wooden walls thatched with brush.

Household items had been found in plenty, and lay on a table in the pavilion, tagged and numbered. There were also a number of what the guide described as children's toys, though to the newcomers, they looked no more than broken bits of junk. A few pieces of jewelry and other small items had been unearthed practically as good as new. The Educatours students were impressed. It was indeed a rich find, and the assistant displayed an excusable degree of smugness.

"What a lot of flint you have here," Miss Anderson said, turning over a stone hand axe. "Wouldn't its presence suggest to you a late Neolithic settlement rather than early Bronze Age?" she asked. "Surely this is part of the Inner Moray Firth culture."

For answer, the young man shrugged his shoulders significantly and jerked his head over toward the team leader.

"You might argue also that the presence of vaissils for storing wheat would make place this in the latter grouping," Belgrave said, apologetically, his diction occasionally falling into broad Highland Scots. "He says it's airly to tell yet." The teacher raised her eyebrows, but said nothing.

Most of the group were given the task of sieving pans of earth already removed by Dr. Stroud's regular team. Huge amounts of it lay in heaps beside each of the excavations, since the floor of the settlement was a few feet under the modern surface. Four of the others, Keith among them, were assigned to help clear the earth inside the boundaries of one of the large huts using brush and trowel. Carefully, they set their new tools down on the grassy edge outside, and stepped down into the knee-high pit. The assistant admonished them not to bump the trenches guarding the exposed walls, and to call for help immediately if they uncovered anything. It got to be monotonous, since Edwin was nearly on top of an 'axe factory store,' a collection of knapped stone and flint, that lay almost waist deep within the earth along one wall, and kept revealing the edges of new pieces. In time, the assistant assigned to the group grew used to them, and was able to keep from hovering while they worked.

Dr. Stroud never spoke directly to any of the tour group. He made side comments to his associates in their presence that he didn't care if they overheard, about moneyed dilettantes wasting everyone's time. He was especially upset that Holl, a child, should have been foisted off on him. The group worked hard, but it never seemed to dent the contempt he showed for them. Matthew and Keith, who were serious about learning more, felt personally affronted by the professor's attitude, though they managed to hold their tongues.

Max was finding it difficult to move the full pan of scraped earth without losing his trowel or brush. Without a third hand to steady his burden, he had to move the heavy pan very slowly to the edge of his patch and over the stub of wall. The brush squirted suddenly out of the crook of his thumb and shot into the grass. Max flailed for it, and accidentally let go of the pan. It slipped awkwardly to the ground, spilling soil everywhere, most of it right back into his patch. He looked up to see the professor glaring down upon him.

"Inexperienced muggins," he sneered to one of his team that happened to be passing by. The assistant looked startled, and Stroud cocked his head toward Max. "Bloody paying guests." Max reddened. Leaving his tools propped against the pan of spilled dirt, he picked himself up and sauntered to the roped-off area at the edge of the dig site which served as No-Man's-Land for the smokers in the group. Very deliberately, he shook a filterless cigarette from a pack in his shirt pocket and lit up. He didn't return to the hut for the rest of the day.

The atmosphere on the coach was far different than it had been in the morning. Several of the boys were ready for an argument, and everyone was out of temper. By then Max had run out of cigarettes, and was rebuffed in his efforts to borrow one from his friends. The refusals made him cross all over again. Blank faced, Narit kept her eyes on her lap all the way back to the guest house. Keith had noticed that there were no women on the site except for the three from the tour group. He guessed that the professor had made some disparaging comment in Narit's hearing that hurt her feelings, and felt sorry for her. Stroud probably didn't like women. Mrs. Green and Mrs. Turner also seemed unusually quiet. Miss Anderson said nothing, but watched them and waited for reactions.

"He's a bully and a louse," Keith said, at last, breaking the silence. "The only reason we're taking his crap is because we thought we could learn something from him. Also, he probably thinks its a crime we see what he does for a living as fun. It's only another week, and then we never have to see him again. I'm not going to let him drive me away."

"Bloody cereal isn't all that's rotten there," Matthew grumbled, but he concurred with Keith.

Grudgingly, everyone agreed to try and hold their tempers, and peace was maintained over the weekend. Keith and the others saw more of Inverness, but spent most of their free time in the pubs carefully not talking about archaeology.

The next weekday, the coach came off the main road into the lane nearest the site and rolled to a stop. Before any of the tour could alight, Dr. Stroud detached himself from his team and strode through the gate toward the coach, waving his arms and shouting.

Miss Anderson swung out of the door and went to meet him. They had an argument in pantomime, since the thick window glass of the coach prevented anyone inside from hearing what the two were saying. Pink cheeked, the teacher returned to the coach and gave instructions to the driver in a low voice. Her lips pressed together, Miss Anderson sat down.

"I'm sorry," she said, tightly. "I have tried, but he pointed out that our contract cannot guarantee us access to the sites. He feels that the presence of non-professionals could jeopardize the safety of artifacts, or accidentally muddle clues. I'm sorry."

"Well, what's wrong with the silly bugger?" Matthew shouted. "Don't these old codgers talk wi' one another? We did a sterling job in Glasgow."

"Aye, we did. Did we make a single mistake on Thursday or Friday?" Edwin growled. "We did not."

"Perhaps one of us did," Mrs. Green suggested mildly, glancing sympathetically at Narit.

"No!" "It's not us, it's him!" Unable to contain their frustration any longer, the others started a shouting match among themselves. There was a consensus that they couldn't blame Miss Anderson or the tour company for their exclusion, but that she ought to be able to do something.

"I think Stroud's a snob and an ass," Martin stated, folding his arms. "I'm not sure I'd go back even if he let us."

Miss Anderson let them shout themselves out, and resumed in a quieter voice. "I remember a group I was leading to South Cadbury where we were similarly driven off. The team leader feared that the 'crazed Arthurians' among us would inadvertently destroy precious and delicate artifacts. In the end, of course, there was little to see but the placement of the walls, buildings and wells. We were fobbed off elsewhere.

"I'm sorry to say that it's a game of chance. Educatours gives an honorarium to the archaeological teams for letting us visit and participate, but it isn't much. In some cases, not enough to stir any consciences when we're denied what was agreed to under contract. Sometimes they give it back if they change their minds."

"Has Dr. Stroud given the money back?" Matthew asked, narrowing one eye. "You deserve a refund from him."

"We'll most likely get it all back in the end," Miss Anderson said, deprecatingly. "I believe that Dr. Stroud has a powerful corporate sponsor, so he doesn't need our few pence."

"Oh, I see," Max said acidly. "Well, why doesn't he just label every fossil with his little corporate logo. That's what I want to ask. That way we'll know what we're dealing with."

"The company has started to negotiate a refund, but that's nothing for you to fret about. But hold on," she requested, extending her hands to them. "I promise that the Isle of Lewis will be nothing like this. In the meantime, Educatours has considered this eventuality, and is putting the coach at your disposal for local touring. Tomorrow," she said, looking around at them brightly, "we'll have a day out at the Official Loch Ness Monster Exhibition and Urquhart Castle. I'm sure you'll enjoy that."

Keith and Holl looked at each other, and exchanged resigned grins.

Chapter Eleven

"Another bloody boring day in Inverness," Charles grunted, throwing himself into a booth in the local pub they frequented a few days later. "I'm ready to go home. If I have to sit for one more day on the steps of Inverness Castle until the sun goes down, I'll just jump off the bank into the river. At least that'll give me a different view."

The weather had continued to be bright and warm, which only exacerbated the boys' annoyance that they couldn't be out at the dig site.

"If it had been gloomy, we'd have a reason to stay off. But you know if he said to come it'd rain every day," Martin pointed out.

"Unless you fish or play golf, there's not much to do, once you've hit all the tourist traps," Keith said gloomily. He propped his chin up on his hands and glanced at Holl. That afternoon, they had been out as far as they could range on rented bicycles, looking for Holl's bellflowers. He was frustrated, hot, and his legs ached. He hated to guess how Holl felt. The spirit of tolerance among the tour group was fast dissipating. It was a good thing that week was coming to an end.

"I knew I could find you here," said a low-pitched female voice. They looked up to see Narit standing beside their booth. "May I join you?"

"Of course," Matthew said, standing up to let her slide in along the bench.

"We thought you liked to spend the evenings with the other ladies," Alistair added, abashed.

She tossed her head, and her long pigtail whiplashed. "It is all right when we are busy," Narit answered, patiently, "but when there is nothing to do all they talk about is ailments and grandchildren. I have neither. I don't care to stay in and watch the *East Enders* so I came looking for you. Do you mind?"

"Far from it," said Keith, gallantly. "We thought you wanted to stay in and talk girl talk."

"Sometimes. I wish there were more girls my age on this tour, because then I would have somewhere I belonged when this happens."

"I know what you mean," Holl put in. Their search for the object of Holl's quest had been fruitless so far. Keith had pushed himself extra miles if they even spotted a glimpse of white in the undergrowth at the side of the road and pedaled back to report, saving Holl the effort. He was grateful, but it would take more than gratitude to solve the knotty problem he was wrestling with. The internal argument still roiled within him. He knew that if he found the white flowers tomorrow, he'd be on the jet home to Maura that afternoon, Ireland or no Ireland.

He had also been unable to make contact with his folk except by use of the telephone. It wasn't easy to conceal from Keith how unhappy it made him being isolated from his family and friends, but it wasn't fair to worry him with a new concern. "You *didn't* do anything wrong at the dig, did you?"

"No!" Narit protested. "I sorted the small pieces exactly the way his assistant told me to, and I entered the notations very neatly, precisely as they were written on the sheets. When I looked up, he was there, glaring at me. I had no idea what he thinks."

"No one's blaming you," Keith said soothingly. "I think he hates women. We've all come to the conclusion that Stroud's an a—uh, idiot."

"Aye." There was a chorus of agreement. Max grinned at Keith. He knew that the American had substituted a last minute euphemism out of consideration for Narit. Holl watched the glance, and added his own smile. These young people had formed a common front against an enemy, and were supporting one another. He enjoyed socializing like this. It was so easy for Big Folk to get to know strangers, to make friends with them. Some of their ways were worth exporting to the Little Folk. If he made headman one day, he'd incorporate some of their notions into daily life—slowly, of course. But that also meant completing his quest. He didn't know what to do.

"You've not been at the Bored Meetings these last couple of afternoons," Charles accused Keith. "We were counting on a full membership on the castle steps."

"Oh, well," Keith said. "Holl and I have been out having a look around. The Highlands have a lot of mystical associations, and I'm interested in that sort of thing. You might call me a…research mythologist."

"Come again?"

"I track down the source of legends. I'm really interested in how those old stories got started. I mean besides Nessie," he said, forestalling Charles from making the obvious association. "There's thousands of fascinating tales in your history. This place is great for legends."

"What, like Robin Hood, or King Arthur?" Alistair asked.

"No, more like magical things," Keith corrected him, warming to his favorite topic. "Dragons, elves, unicorns, banshees, you know. There's legends about things of magic in every early culture. You wonder where they all came from."

"I don't," Martin protested.

"So you go about like Sir Arthur Conan Doyle, eh? Looking for fairies and so on?" Matthew asked, an eyebrow arched cynically skyward.

"Only partly. He believed in those things with all his heart. I do, but I've got to convince my head, too."

"Ah," Martin nodded sagely. He and Martin exchange winks. "Well then. We might have something to show you later, eh?"

"Do you believe in the unseen, Keith?" Narit asked in her soft, lilting voice. She seldom spoke up in the group, so Keith turned his whole attention to her. "My family believe in karma. I practice with the Tarot cards, myself. I find they have great meaning for me. The symbols here are not familiar in my people's history, but they have their equivalents. May I read the cards for you?" She reached for her handbag. From it she drew a silk-wrapped bundle as long as her hand and half as wide.

"Well, uh, why not?" Keith accepted, a little unsurely. "Thanks. I'd really appreciate it. How do you do it?"

"I shuffle the cards," she began, taking the silk off and smoothing the edge of the deck with her fingers. The backs were a plain bi-colored design, but the faces were exotic and colorful. Keith peeked at them as Narit shuffled. She separated the cards into two piles and sifted them together again and again with skillful motions. "Cut."

Keith gathered a third of the deck between thumb and forefinger and handed it to her. Narit took the remainder and placed it on top of the smaller section. "The last card of the section you chose is your significator, the card which represents you in this reading." She pulled the card from the bottom of the combined deck. It showed a young man with a hobo's bundle over one shoulder and a dog romping behind him up a craggy path. "The Fool."

The others laughed. "Good choice, Keith," Charles crowed.

"He represents potential, substance rather than form." She dealt the cards into a cross and to its right an extra column of four starting at the bottom up. "That's interesting. You have several of the Major Arcana in your reading. This means that much of your situation is not of your own devising, that you're being led by circumstances rather than creating them. Is that right?"

"I don't know. What circumstances?"

"Well, since you didn't ask a specific question, it usually means your life's path. Many things which you think you encounter by chance are karmically arranged. But that is not necessarily a bad thing. It means there is much power in your life. It is far from ordinary."

Keith glanced surreptitiously at Holl, whose eyebrows were in his hairline. The others hooted. "I guess. What does the rest mean?"

Delicately, she turned over the cards one at a time. "Here in your potential future is the Star. Whether that means help will come to you, or that you will provide help for others is yet open to question. Ah!" Narit's voice took on a note of concern as she flipped the card at the right arm of the cross. It showed a crowned turret being struck by lightning. Keith's eyebrows lifted. "The Tower. There will be the abrupt end of a path, and a new beginning. It can mean death, but you needn't take it as that. Your final outcome is the Three of Cups, which shows fulfillment and celebration, so it is doubtful the Tower predicts a death in this case."

"Well, what does Death mean?" Keith asked, poking a finger at another card, which depicted a cloaked skeleton wielding a sickle, the second card from the bottom of the column of four.

"Change," Narit said promptly. "Many times for the good. Death is not a threat if you consider the pitfalls of everlasting life."

"I'd want to live forever," Charles put in. "Who wouldn't?"

"Only if you could get replacement parts," Keith replied, mildly, enumerating them. "Teeth, hair, eyes, knees...."

"D'you really believe in this stuff?" Martin exploded scornfully, amused by the serious acceptance Keith offered Narit.

"Karma works in your life whether you believe in it or not," Narit said coolly. "Do you want to know your own future?"

"Not me!"

"I would," Holl piped up.

"Think of a question, if you have one." Narit gathered the cards as she had before, and shuffled them deftly. Holl reached out to pick up half of the deck, and found his fingers only wanted a small fraction. There was something to these cards. They weren't charmed themselves, but felt rather more like a conduit of power. He leaned forward curiously.

"The Hermit. You seek, as Diogenes did," Narit said, her voice seeming to Holl to come from far away. "He is alone in all ways, in his mind, his heart. This is a very old card for a child."

Holl ignored the inference. "What do the others mean?"

Narit turned them all face up before speaking again. She pointed to a card with the face of a jolly, fat man among some cups. "Your finish is the Nine of Cups. It is also known as the wish card. You will have all that you require at the end. But there are many obstacles through which you must pass before getting your wish. It is by no means certain. The cards do not guarantee what you see. They are merely guidelines. You have several rod cards in this reading, trials of the spirit, and you are crossed by the Chariot, which is a balancing influence and an outside force that you might see at first as a barrier, someone or something which has mastery over you. But you will be aided in the end by the Star. Help from a friend."

Overwhelmed, Holl could say little more than "Thank you." He retired back in his corner with his St. Clement's to think.

"That sounded a lot of mumbo jumbo," Matthew said, but his face was uncertain. Narit glanced at him reprovingly, and mixed the cards once more.

"Go ahead, cut," she ordered. "I think I can do one more tonight."

Tentatively, Matthew reached out to the long deck, picked up half and set it firmly on the table next to the other half. Narit picked up both halves, and began to deal them. "You are the Page of Swords. In the past you have been the Knight of Pentacles, interested in the material world and somewhat advanced there, but here at present, you're the Hermit, looking for something else," Narit said, pointing at one card after another. "Crossing you is the King of Pentacles."

"What's that mean?" Matthew asked, interested in spite of himself.

"A master of Earth, a teacher, a father, a man of authority with regard to the physical world, also the material or financial.

Ah, here, where you appear once again, is the Knight of Swords. The seeker of Air."

"Oh, that's the truth," Martin said cynically. "Hot air, it is, too." Matthew's elbow took him in the midriff. "Oof!"

"Air is intellectual attainment," Narit continued, as if Martin hadn't spoken. She had a quiet authority when she handled the cards, and the boys were impressed. "Here is Death, who may be changing your life. If you win through your struggles," the forefinger picked out a sword card and a pentacle card showing a man hugging sacks of gold, "you will come to the Four of Rods, which is contentment. Rods deal with the attainments of the spirit." She met his eyes and studied him closely. "You have decisions to make soon."

Matthew glanced at her with new respect. "Thank you," he said sincerely as she bent her head to gather up the cards. He fell silent, and studied the far wall. In a moment, he realized the others were staring at him.

He drained his glass, noisily. "I'll get the next round, shall I?" he asked the table. "Narit, what'll you have?"

"Well, that's it. I'm clappit out," Charles said, at about ten o'clock. He felt around in his pocket for money and came up with only twelve pence. "Until I find the till machine, that's it for me."

"I'm skint, too," Martin said. Hopefully, they both turned to Keith.

"Hey, don't look at me," that youth said, flinging up his hands. "I'm broke for tonight, too."

"Ach, you rich Americans," Edwin said scornfully, looking up from the glass of beer he was nursing. It was down to an inch or so of dark amber fluid. "You know you're rolling in it. You could cough up a little for one more pint."

"Look, this rich American had to buy a plane ticket here," Keith protested. "You guys only had to buy three pound train tickets from Edinburgh."

Matthew cocked his head wryly. "Not even that. Martin's father motored us down here."

"See?" Keith said, defensively. "Look, I'm sorry, but what money I've got has got to last me another three weeks. I haven't even bought my girlfriend a present yet. Not that I have any idea what she'd like. She's hard to buy for. But she'll kill me if I come home empty-handed."

"Yer a stingy old goldpockets," Edwin slurred, leaning toward Keith threateningly.

"It takes one to know one," Keith shot back, angling toward the other. "Isn't it supposed to be Scotsmen who can squeeze a penny until it screams?"

"You—you *capitalist,*" Edwin spat, raising his fist. Keith braced himself.

"Hey!" Shocked, Alistair rose and put an arm between them. "None of this, now. Sit down. Perhaps we've all had a drop too much."

Keith felt a tug on his sleeve. "Keith Doyle," Holl whispered. "To quote your Robin Williams, doesn't the name General Custer mean anything to you?"

The red-haired youth was overwhelmed by a wave of shame. "I'm drunk. No doubt about it. I'm only this tactless when I'm blasted." He put out a hand to Edwin. "I'm sorry, Ed. See, Narit was right. I am the Fool. That was a stupid remark, considering I'm surrounded by thousands of people who would be totally right to mash my head through the pavement for spouting stupid stereotypes. I am a dunce. But honest, I've really got to stretch my budget."

Edwin buried his head in his hands. "I'm plain mortified with myself." He reached up tentatively to Keith. "Truce."

"Nope," Keith insisted, collecting a round of astonished gazes. "Peace." He took Edwin's hand and they shook. The others pounded the two of them on the backs.

"And to celebrate," Holl spoke up over the hubbub, "I'll stand you all to black coffee. Then a good, brisk walk back to the guest house will clear everyone's head."

"Oh, but we've got something to show Keith, first," Matthew said, eagerly pulling the American down the street. Holl trailed behind, puzzled.

"Yeah. Since you're a specialist, you might be interested in this," Martin added. "Come on."

"Not me," said Edwin. "I'm for bed. My head's about to explode."

"We've got to walk Narit back. It's about dark," Alistair explained.

"Suit yourself," Matthew called, guiding Keith around a corner.

Keith tried to free his arm from the other's tight grasp. "Hey, guys, where are we going?" They crossed the main bridge over the Ness and hurried down the street on the west side.

"We saw the very thing you're interested in," Martin assured him, after a few blocks. "Right in there." He stopped out of the street light in front of a gate. The sign beside it said "Bught Park."

When they departed the pub in such a hurry, none of them noticed the shadow which followed them to the bridge and over it to the Ness Road. Michaels hunched his shoulders into his light coat and tried to look as if he was minding his own business without losing sight of the three young men and the boy nearly half a block ahead of him. The Educatours people had been happy to give him the itinerary for their Scotland summer expedition. A pity no one had kept him apprised of the fact the man in charge of the Inverness dig was an obstructive bastard. Michaels had put miles on the Bureau car he'd borrowed morning after unconscionably early morning, until he realized that O'Day and the others weren't going out there at all.

The directional microphone he had clipped inside his coat wasn't powerful enough to pick up what the boys were saying, only that they were talking. He'd have to be closer than sixty feet to get clear transmission. It was almost the oldest equipment of its kind available. The local office refused to devote much of its stretched resources to the pursuit of an international smuggler who might or might not be making a pickup in their demesne. Even a boom mike was out of the question for him. Privately, he cursed the field operatives of the American service, who got all the powerful miniaturized toys they wanted, in tie clips and eyeglass frames, with recorders or transmitters in, just for the asking.

He wormed his way into the park as the young men settled themselves into concealment about twenty yards from the park gate. There was nothing he could do to hear better. Was the pickup tonight? He'd have to search the young bloke's room later, after he'd gone to sleep. Michaels fervently hoped O'Day had had enough to drink to gag him soundly. Sleeping gas was another thing the James Bonds of the American service could get, practically delivered by the pint bottle on their doorsteps every morning like milk. If he bagged O'Day, they'd allot a good deal more money to the department, and about time, too. Uncomfortably, he eased himself behind a clump of bushes and aimed his microphone.

Later, he would tell the Chief that this stakeout had all been a great waste of time. "There was no acceptance or delivery, sir," Michaels assured him, wearily. "They might have been setting something up, but it sounded like code to me. Nothing I've ever heard before. I couldn't get much of it on that bloody Stone Age mike, but they all seemed to understand one another. It was a great big joke between them. We still don't know what the hell's up."

"Did you see that?" Matthew hissed into Keith's ear, pulling his arm and pointing down the field toward a clump of tall flowers and a pond which reflected the city lights in its depths.

"See what?" Keith demanded, trying to follow Matthew's gaze in the dark. He parted the bushes, spitting out leaves and twigs that brushed his face. His invisible whiskers didn't protect him from the waving shrubbery.

"There goes another one!" Martin poked him in the side. "And another. Oh, you'd better look quicker than that!"

"Wait," Matthew said, his voice dropping to a conspiratorial whisper. "Now wait for it, here comes one. Yes! Look there, Keith!"

"Where?" Keith wailed, desperately. "What? What are we looking for?"

Matthew stopped and gawked at Keith. He rolled to one side to regard him with mock amazement. "Do you mean to tell me quite seriously and with no deception whatever," his voice started to crack as a broad grin forced its way past his teeth and plastered itself across his face, "that a great big investigator like you has never heard about there being fairies at the bottom of the garden?" He collapsed to the ground, giggling. Martin threw himself onto the ground and howled hysterically, flapping limply at Matthew's legs with one hand.

"Ha, ha," Keith retorted sarcastically, glowing beet red in the dark. He glared at Holl, who was doubled up, too. "And what are *you* laughing at?"

The little man wiped his eyes on the back of his hand and swallowed his hilarity enough to speak. "You have to admit, Keith Doyle, you left yourself open to it. Conan Doyle couldn't have made his own trap and fallen into it any neater than you did yourself. Led straight up the garden path by the hand, in fact, just like he was in the great fairy hoax."

Caught off guard, Keith rubbed his lip, beginning to get the joke. He grinned and threw up his arms. "All right! All right, I've been had. Royally. What can I say? I guess it just goes with the name."

Chapter Twelve

Miss Anderson's word was good: Educatours kept them occupied. She guided the tour group out on short trips throughout the Inverness region every day until Sunday morning, when the coach was loaded for its final destination, on the Isle of Lewis, northwest of the coast of Scotland.

If the Scottish landscape had been dramatic before, it had become breathtaking. North of Inverness, the land rolled away from the road in curving valleys and fields, and changed gradually to sweeping glens and expanses of forest cradled between mountain ridges shaded in distant blue, dark green and gold. The road followed river valleys cut deep into the heart of the land, or broad and shining like strips of silver painted on the green earth. Few habitations lay beyond Garve, thirty miles northwest of Inverness, but the highlands were far from lonesome. Instead, they radiated an ancient, eternal patience that was soothing and awesome.

"'My heart's in the Highlands, my heart is not here,'" murmured Holl, gazing wonderingly out of the coach window and drinking in the feeling that beauty was a palpable thing. "'My heart's in the highlands, a-chasing the deer.'"

"Isn't that William Saroyan?" Keith asked, squinting through his viewfinder at a photogenic ridge.

Holl's mood was broken, and he felt suddenly as if he had lost something precious. "My Heart's in the Highlands is by Robert Burns," he said, long-sufferingly. "Don't you read any poetry that's not on the syllabus, you cultural infant?"

"That's what we keep a Maven like you around for," Keith pointed out unquenchably, ratcheting the film noisily forward in his camera. "Isn't it great up here? I love it. I could stay up here forever just staring at the scenery. The mountains and clouds are sort of *unreal*, like someone's paintings. Look, stuffed animals."

To the right of the road, a herd was grazing calmly. Except for pairs of wickedly pointed long horns bobbing close to the ground, the broad, short animals were undifferentiated mounds of ochre hair. One lifted up its nose at the passing coach and revealed huge, mild brown eyes under the yellow thatch.

"They're cows!"

"Highland cattle," Miss Anderson corrected Keith.

"I thought they might be woolly mammoths without trunks. I should yell 'moo' out the window at them," Keith pondered, playfully. "My dad always does. They're cute, but I bet they could stomp their weight in cattle rustlers."

"You're perfectly safe if you come upon a herd," Miss Anderson said, conversationally, beaming at them one by one. "The bull is peaceful except when one of his cows is threatened. If you come upon a bull alone, keep moving."

"Move?" asked Martin, astonished. "I'd fly! How long until we get to the ferry port, Miss Anderson?"

"Another hour or so to Ullapool," the teacher replied, checking her wristwatch. "Should we have a song to pass the time? Who would like to start?"

"How about the intrepid fairy hunter here?" Martin asked, mischievously, glancing sideways at Keith. The American student turned red, remembering the garden episode. Once his hobby had been revealed, they seemed to recall and repeat every detail of the things he'd said offhandedly throughout the trip. He wished the novelty would wear off already. The ladies and the coach driver had already heard the story and dismissed it, but the boys continued to remind Keith mercilessly whenever it occurred to them. "Bring-'em-back-alive Frank Puck here must know something."

"Such a hobby for a grown man," Matthew appealed to Holl. "Have you ever heard such foolishness?"

"No," he replied, calmly. "And the widdy's always going on about it. It's an obsession with him."

Keith turned to Holl, an acid retort half formed on his tongue. Then with a shock, he noticed that Holl's cap was off, and the short blond hair was neatly brushed. The elf's ears were still rounded like a human's. In fact, the more that he thought about it, he realized they had been ever since Holl got out of the hospital. What was going on with him? He couldn't draw attention to the aberration now. He would have to wait and tackle Holl privately. "Okay," he said, weakly, feeling betrayed, "I can take a joke. Um, does anyone know "Take Me Out to the Ball Game?""

The ferry was scheduled to depart at 5:00 A.M. The group spent the night at a small hotel in the port of Ullapool. In the morning half-light, under a homogenous sky of light gray stratus clouds, they sat aboard the coach, waiting their turn on the pier to drive into the hold of the ferry. The ship bobbed gently at the pier's end, a massive inverted wedge of black and white.

Once on board, the passengers left their vehicles and ascended to the upper decks for the 3-1/2 hour passage. Shivering with fatigue from their short night and early rising, Keith and the others scrambled down from the coach in the narrow space left between two small cars and a dust-covered minivan on which someone had scrawled with a fingertip "Also available in *clean*." Following a herd of silent fellow passengers, the group found a small lounge at the rear of the ship's restaurant, and settled down on the leather-covered couches with hot drinks to try and wake up. Other passengers slipped through the glass-walled lounge and into the cafeteria beyond it like bats: silent, avoiding their chairs and the laden tables with weary expertise.

"The Outer Hebrides have yielded up the oldest samples of rock in the British Isles. Some of them have been dated at 2,800 million years," Miss Anderson stated, as the ferry's engines thrummed to life beneath them, awaiting departure time.

"Or two point eight billion years in American," Keith calculated, yawning, and wrapped his hands around his cup of tea. A British billion was one million million. "That's only two hundred million years or so younger than some of the upthrust they've found in the Rocky Mountains. Old."

"Not as old as I feel," Matthew said, peering into the depths of his coffee as if he expected the steam rising from it to revive him. The two English ladies sat nearby, huddled over folded arms and blinking owlishly at the others. "You remember the chap we unearthed on top of the hill in Renfrewshire?" he asked Keith, who nodded. "My grandson."

The others chuckled. A huge grinding noise interrupted them, and the ferry lurched suddenly to the right. The land visible out of the broad windows lining the lounge began to move, and the noise moderated to a hum. They were under way.

Tired though they were, the group was already in better spirits than they had been in Inverness. Keith taught them and the rest of the passengers in the lounge how to play Buzz-Fizz. "It's a counting game. Buzz is five, and seven is fizz. You keep going until you make a mistake, and the next person takes over where you left off. Don't forget about multiples. I'll start. One, two, three, four, buzz, six, fizz, eight, nine, buzz-buzz, eleven, twelve, thirteen, fizz-fizz, fifteen..."

"You mean buzz-buzz-buzz," Edwin triumphantly corrected him. Keith grinned sheepishly and made an over-to-you gesture in the large youth's direction. Edwin started, counting carefully with his eyes on the ceiling, a broad smile on his lips as he tried to remember what was a multiple of what. When he got tangled up amidst the z's, Max took a turn. They played until no one could shout out the right buzzes and fizzes for a high number over the laughter from the rest of the crowd.

"Thank you, dear," Mrs. Green complimented Keith, as he brought her a fresh pot of tea when the game broke up. "You're good at traveling with a group,"

"I'm one of five kids. My father taught us these games as a matter of self defense on long trips. Otherwise, we would've driven him crazy asking 'are we there yet?'"

"My two sons liked to ask us that," Mrs. Green acknowledged with the corners of her mouth turned up. "Somehow we managed to stave off the question until we actually were *there*. And Holl is your elder sister's son?"

Keith gulped, trying to remember what he'd told whom. Mrs. Green was stirring sugar into her cup, head bent over her task. She didn't seem to notice any hesitation. "Right. You can see the family resemblance."

"Yes, I can. It's very strong, especially in the jaw and ears. Your foreheads and noses are very different, though."

"That's heredity, I guess," Keith said, lightly, wondering what the older woman would say if he speculated on how far back in history the resemblance would have to reach. He stood up. "Excuse me, please. Hey, Holl, let's go up on deck and watch the scenery."

"A fine idea." The Little One extracted himself from a group having a discussion around one of the small cocktail tables. He gathered up a sketch he had been making, and followed Keith. "I'll be happy to get out of this big metal room. How do you stand it?"

They made their way up the stairs, and together forced open a door on the uppermost deck of the ferry. The wind was still whistling up a gale, but the dull, leaden grey of the sky was brightening steadily as they sailed westward. Keith could feel his invisible whiskers whipping sharply against his cheeks. He concentrated on making them lie flat, and then gave up. The coast of Scotland had dwindled to a dark, irregular line nestled on the horizon far to the east, indistinguishable from the dark sea and the waves of clouds overhead.

"Look how murky the water is," Holl shouted, pointing over the rail. "It must be icy cold."

"Well, I wouldn't want to get out and swim," Keith admitted. He decided to bite the bullet, and find out the answer to the ear question as long as they were alone. "Hey, Holl…" he began, but cut off his sentence as a gaggle of tourists came out of the stairwell and passed within earshot. The elf looked at him questioningly, but he waved a dismissive hand. "Never mind. I'll remember later what I wanted to say."

Holl nodded. "There's nothing in sight to the west. The Isle of Lewis must be more than seventeen miles away. That's the distance you are able to see at sea level before the curvature of the Earth drops the edge out of eyeshot. I've never been anywhere I could test the hypothesis."

"Are you doing okay?" Keith asked, with sudden solicitousness, remembering how little traveling Holl had actually done. "I mean, I know you've never been on a boat before, and lots of people do get seasick."

"I thank you for your concern, but I don't feel a thing out of the ordinary," Holl replied, leaning comfortably on the rail and squinting at the horizon. So long as he kept his jacket sleeves between his arms and the metal, he was all right. "I'm having a very good time, as well. From what the old ones told me, I thought sailing would be terrifying. I don't find it so. It's no worse than riding in a car on bumpy roads."

"Smoother," Keith said, after a moment. "I've got to get new shocks." He thrust a hand out across the sea, and waved a finger. "Hey, look at that."

At the edge of the expanse of smooth, silver ripples lay a low mound, growing gradually larger. "Land ho!"

"Seventeen miles, and a small bit more, of course, allowing for the extra elevation of the ship," Holl said, satisfied. "My ears are freezing in this wind."

"Mine, too," Keith agreed, wondering if that was an opening for a discussion. No, the elf's face showed only curiosity and excitement as he stared out over the water at the island. Keith shrugged, and folded his elbows on the rail to watch Lewis growing nearer. He yawned. "I wonder if anyone there besides us is awake at this hour."

Michaels sat at the rear of the lounge with his coat buttoned up to the chin and watched the two smugglers go above deck. O'Day must suspect that he was under surveillance. Why else would he go to the far end of nowhere with the tour group? Unless the Isle of Lewis was *it*, the pickup site where his contact was waiting. It seemed like a mucking great lot of trouble to waste four weeks—four weeks!—hoiking about Scotland to establish his bona fides as a tourist. The research boys suggested that there was a major scientific discovery for sale. If he kept his eyes open, he should be able to bag O'Day just as the information changed hands.

After Glasgow and Inverness, Stornoway was a small town. Before Keith and the others on the coach had had more than a quick glance at the city, they were out of it, and following a narrow road into the countryside. A thin curtain of trees parted suddenly, revealing a rough, torn landscape. Outside of the capital city and the tree farms, the Isle of Lewis seemed to be little more than rock and peat with grass and heather growing on it. At first glance, it looked almost like a war zone. The shelves of banded metamorphic rock which made up the island were highly friable, and left fantastic splinters piercing through the undergrowth and tumbling down the slopes. Miss Anderson described the mineral development to her open-mouthed group as Lewisian gneiss, unique to this part of the world. Rocks turned up all over the dark-hued ground as if careless giants, rummaging through geologic drawers, found what they wanted at the bottom and then departed without cleaning up after themselves.

Thousands of sheep, some sheared and recognizable, and the unsheared looking like shaggy hassocks with tiny pipestem legs sticking out from underneath, grazed calmly on the backs of the hills. Half grown lambs galloped crazily up and down, venturing out from the ewes long enough to get a look at the world, and hurrying back every time something surprised them. Their placid elders cropped the greenery or stared off into the distance with nobly thoughtful expressions.

Rounded valleys between the hills were filled partway with water, as if the island was porous to the sea. Every so often, the coach would pass a small farmhouse or newsagent shop, but between them was the endless sea of peat under an almost peat-colored sky.

"My God," said Matthew, despairingly, looking out the window at the scenery. "It's a desert island. I haven't seen a single pub for the last twenty miles!"

Keith shrugged. "It's just like middle Illinois in winter," he said. "A thousand miles of open, uninterrupted countryside. No pubs. You'd just pick up a sixpack if there's no place to go."

"There, I knew the colonies were backward," Matthew crowed. "Bottled beer! But what do they do for fun here?"

"We'll be in Stornoway for supper every night," Miss Anderson pointed out imperturbably. "There are plenty of public houses and shops there. We're here to learn, not carouse."

"I'd rather carouse," Martin muttered defiantly under his breath. "Have you ever seen such desolation?"

The wild ruggedness of the island did take some getting used to. After driving through Illinois wheat fields, Keith was accustomed to long stretches of nothingness, but the dramatically sharp rise and fall of the dark land was new to him. As they drove west, the wind whipped up more fiercely, soughing among the fences and shrubs, and causing the hanging fleece on the sheeps' backs to sway like wash on a line.

"This is Callanish," Miss Anderson announced, as the coach suddenly came upon a double row of small houses and farms. "To save a long, long drive every morning from Stornoway, everyone has been assigned to bed-and-breakfast establishments right here." The coach slowed down sharply as they rounded a high curve. Suddenly, on their left was a low building with a peaked roof, looking as if it had weathered millennia. Ahead of them was a tiger-trap of pointed, weather-worn monoliths.

"And there," Miss Anderson continued, pointing unnecessarily, "are the standing stones. The arms of the cross point toward the compass directions, though all but one of them are out of true. In the center of the inner ring is a round chambered tomb. The monument dates to approximately 2000 B.C."

As they drew closer, the undifferentiated cluster spread into two thin arms of stones. Another double axis of tall stones pointed from the curve in the road toward a hill topped with more blocks. Several stones were missing from the pattern, but the effect was still impressive. Keith snapped away happily at the monument with his camera.

Two at a time, the group was dropped at the doors of farm houses that boasted small 'B&B' signs in their front windows or nailed to the fences facing the road. For their housing among the spare population on the island, Keith and Holl were instructed to get out at the door of a small, trim house with a large, hedged garden that looked down over the western sea. Miss Anderson pushed between them, and knocked briskly on the door.

A slender, black-haired woman answered. "Mrs. Mackenzie," Miss Anderson said. "These are your two young guests, Keith and Holl Doyle. When you've settled, meet us at the tea shop at the top of the hill," the teacher instructed them.

"Yes, Miss Anderson," they said in unison. She smiled. The boys watched her climb back aboard the bus, and shouldered their bags.

"Ah, come in, come in," Mrs. Mackenzie urged, shooing them like chickens. "Close the door. The wind is strong today. There's a fierce cold bite to it."

"Yeah," Keith said, pushing the door to with some effort. "And I thought this was July."

"Well, come in and warm up," Mrs. Mackenzie invited them. "Do you want some tea?"

"Uh, no, thanks," Keith smiled, feeling his cheeks thawing already, once they were out of the wind. "This is a nice place."

"Thank you. We like it here," the slim woman said, ushering them through a doorway. "Make yourselves at home."

An electric fire was glowing in the hearth of her sitting room. As they entered, four plump, tan cushions on the very edge of the woven oval hearth rug moved, arose into tall, smooth silhouettes, shoulderless like wine bottles and crowned with triangular sable ears.

"Hi, kitties," Keith said, dropping to his knees beside them. The Siamese cats regarded him with cool, summing, blue eyes. All of them blinked once. "They're beautiful." He reached out to stroke one on the end, and the cat in the middle of the rug emitted an inviting, throaty groan.

"You may as well fuss Her Majesty first," Mrs. Mackenzie warned him, indulgently. "She's in charge here."

"Sure," Keith said, scratching the cat behind her ears. She was slightly smaller than the other three, and her mask and paws were darker. Keith moved a finger around to scratch under the angle of the cat's jaw. She purred, lowering her head to give his hand a wet, fishy-smelling kiss with her upper lip.

Holl approached the cats more cautiously. "They're like Lladro statues," he said, touching one with gingerly care. It leaned into his hand and slitted its eyes. Encouraged, he rubbed his knuckle softly around the pointed cup of its ear. His caress was answered by a huge rumble, surprising in such a slim beast. "Friendly."

"Aye, well, he knows what you are," the landlady said. "So do I."

Aghast, Holl stopped playing with the cat and looked up at her. "He does?" The cat bumped impatiently at his hand, demanding more petting.

"Aye," Mrs. Mackenzie repeated, with satisfaction. "You're cat people. They always know. Cats are wise. Will you come this way now, and we'll see you settled?"

While Holl mentally counted his pulse and commanded it to slow down again, Keith grinned and picked up all their bags. Their hostess led them into a long hallway and pushed open the levered handle on one of the doors.

The room had been decorated in yellow and white, with sheer drapes over a wide window which faced the sea. The beds were deep twins covered with thick yellow and white flowered quilts. "This will be your room. Lav's up the way. Breakfast is served between 7:30 and 9:00 in the morning. Will that suit you?"

"Sure," said Keith, exchanging approving glances with Holl. They dropped their bags in the corner, and took turns in the bathroom washing off the grime of travel. Then, gathering their strength, they pushed out once more into the frigid wind.

At the top of the hill, Michaels waited in his rented car. At last, his two quarries emerged from the farm house at the bottom of the hill and started toward him. His thermos of coffee was chilling down quickly in the unseasonable cold. He wished he could go into the Tea Shop, only a few feet from the car, to warm up, but there was a fifty-fifty chance that his subjects were going in there, too. It wouldn't do to get close enough for them to identify him later.

Chapter Thirteen

If anything, the wind had become worse while they were inside the house. There was no movement amidst the clouds to tell from which direction the wind was coming, or any glimpse of the blue sky they had seen on the sail toward the island. They hiked up the hill against a downward gale.

"There's ice in this wind, Keith Doyle," Holl gritted, pulling his collar up around his face to just under his eyes. "The tide must be turning, or it would be blowing inland, following us."

"I feel like Nanook of the North—no, I wish I *was* Nanook," Keith grumbled pulling the hem of his light jacket as close to his thin frame as he could to keep out the gusts. "*He* had a warm fur coat."

The low, dark silhouette of the Tea Shop was in plain sight on the right side of the road they were climbing. Keith focused on its curious peaked roof like a rock formation to mark the end of a long hike. About twenty feet further up the steep path, the road leveled out somewhat, and Keith stood erect for the first time.

Before him, the stones of Callanish marched across the fenced-in field of grass. He was so fascinated by the formation that for a few moments, he forgot how cold he was. There was a clear and deliberate purpose in the way the stones had been laid out. He was curious who was so important in the ancient days that they buried him in the round cairn Keith knew to be in the middle of all that stone. It had to be the product of maybe thousands of hours of work, and hundreds of workers' sweat. There was a feeling of power in the air, perhaps emanating from the stones themselves. Maybe the deceased was the priest of whatever this temple signified, or the chieftain responsible for its construction. Well, it wasn't the Great Pyramid, but Keith was impressed. The Egyptians didn't have to deal with ice storms in July when they built the Valley of Kings.

A few figures in colorful clothing were wandering among the dentine monoliths, stopping to touch the stones as they passed. Another small knot of people were sitting in a circle on the grass between the stones, talking earnestly, ignoring the wind blowing around them. Keith shivered, and wondered how they managed that. He had only been out a few minutes, but his ears and nose were already whipped into red icicles.

Huddled along the side of the Tea Shop was a cluster of grimy tents. More men and women, wearing odd combinations of garments, such as long skirts and surplus army jackets with shawls flung over, or loose cotton trousers with leather coats and wool hats, sat or lay full length near a fire set on stones in the midst of the grassy common. They glanced up disinterestedly at Keith and Holl as they passed.

The door was on the far side of the croft. Keith and Holl fled another gust of cold wind and all but tumbled inside through the narrow doorway.

The room within was low and modestly lit, but it seemed bright after the lowering sky outside. The thick walls held enough heat to thaw their faces and hands almost immediately. Keith let the surroundings register to his returning senses. On the left, the long chamber was lined with tables and benches of golden wood. His friends were seated at one of these, cradling tea cups between their hands. They waved to Keith and Holl to join them. Immediately before them was a glass-topped counter, over which a girl was squinting at them.

"Close the door, then," she ordered. She had dark hair and lashes, sharply contrasting with her pale skin, and eyes which tilted up slightly at the corners.

"Is it usually like this in summer?" Keith asked over his shoulder, as he pushed the door shut.

"Sometimes," she admitted.

Keith rubbed his cheeks and felt his nose. It was still there, though numb. "Wow, what's it like in winter?"

"More of the same, but livelier," the girl said, smiling. Keith glanced to the right, and discovered that the rest of the Tea Shop was a small dry goods and souvenir store. A tall shelf unit filled with bolts of fabric stood next to the door, and beyond that was a rack of sweaters and coats.

"Coats! Great. Maybe I'd better buy a warm jacket," he said, impulsively. "That is, if you're sure it won't get nice tomorrow."

"It might, and it might not. I can't promise."

"Hmm, I thought so." Keith grinned. "Well, I'll never make it home alive in this thing. How about you, Holl?"

But the young elf was already inspecting the rack of garments with interest. Keith shot a smile to the girl, and started pushing the hangers along one at a time. All the coats and jackets were made of the same kind of woven fabric. It felt coarse and smooth at the same time under his hand. A label fluttered from the neck of one hanger. Keith straightened it out to read it. "Harris Tweed," it said.

The fabrics were surprisingly complex. The rough wool, which looked solid-colored from a distance, had dozens of colors blended into each piece. In a fabric which seemed made up only of shades of red, tiny hints of gold and blue like hidden jewels winked out at him between single black threads, invisible unless he stared at it closely. One bolt rolled up on the rack near the door had as part of its pattern vertical stripes of grey which were made up of twisted fibers of pink, black, and green.

There was a little pamphlet about the history of Harris tweed on the wall. He read it, and then picked up a few of the coats to try on for size. Holl was silent in fascination, letting out only an admiring hiss as he browsed. "The coats are made by hand by a few local people," the girl's voice came from behind them. "The weavers are all locals, too."

"You mean there are people weaving this stuff at home?" Keith asked, surprised, turning to face the young lady.

"Um-hm, and selling it, too. Stop anywhere you see a sign that says 'Harris tweed'. The genuine fabrics are stamped with the orb-and-cross Association insignia by an inspector. But I'll warn you," she shook a finger in Keith's face, "you'd better like what you buy, because it will wear forever."

"Wow." Discarding garments of red and black, or peat brown, Keith chose a jacket of a blue and green tweed that sparkled with red, black, and gold, and paid the young woman over the counter. "I feel warmer already," he assured her.

"Hey, Doyle, come on!" Charles called. "You're the last ones."

"Thanks again," Keith said, and headed toward his friends.

"I'll bring you some tea," the young woman told him.

"What's that for?" Edwin asked, as Keith sat down with his new purchase across his lap.

"Staving off death by hypothermia."

"What for? It'll be nice again in a few days, and you'll have spent all your beer money."

"I'm not betting my chances of getting pneumonia against two weeks of drinking. I only brought a windbreaker with me." There was a gasp of laughter, and Miss Anderson corrected him, without a hair out of place.

"I think we call the same thing a windcheater, Keith. Your term has an indelicate meaning over here." Her voice was stern, but her eyes twinkled. Keith tilted his head apologetically.

"I'm going to write a book comparing the logic of British slang with American," he insisted, with a sheepish grin. "We're only pushing the wind aside. You're cheating it. Hey, Holl, come and sit down! You can shop later."

Reluctantly, Holl pulled himself away from the shelves of tweed fabric. "They'd love that at home," he told Keith, meaningfully. "Especially if it lasts forever."

Keith waved a generous hand. "Bring some back. Bring lots. We're going to have plenty of time to look around at the other weavers' shops over the next two weeks. I'm going to wear this one on the dig. The lady said that it's windproof."

"You're going to look a prize Charley in a tweed jacket and a coolie hat," Martin assured Keith.

"Yeah, but at least I'll be unique. You're going to look like everyone else on this island," Keith jeered playfully.

Over tea and cake, Miss Anderson outlined their activities for the next two weeks. "The team works down in the valley, but none of us will be going down there today. They left word with the tea shop's proprietress for me." Over the groans of the group, Miss Anderson raised her voice and coaxed them back into silence. "Now, now, I promise this won't be like Inverness. You'll like Professor Parker. He's a friendly man."

The boys remained unconvinced. Matthew and Martin exchanged sour glances and ate cake with grim ferocity. Keith thought of Dr. Stroud and wondered how he would tolerate two more weeks of unappreciated slavery.

The door opened to admit a small, roundfaced man with a scarf holding his tweed hat onto his head. "Miss Anderson," he crowed from the threshold, unwinding the lengths of wool with his large hands. "Penelope Anderson! How lovely to see you. You look most attractive in blue, did I ever tell you?"

Clearly pleased, Miss Anderson's face compressed into a warm smile. "Professor Parker. Now here's a nice surprise. This is your new workforce." She fluttered a delicate hand toward the group, who stopped what they were doing and sat up at attention.

The man's long face glowed with good humor, and he came toward them with his arms outstretched. "I apologize for being late. I rather underestimated the time it would take to drive here in the rain. I am so pleased to see all of you, you have no idea." He descended the two steps down into the croft, and the level of his eyes fell nearly below that of the party seated at the table. Keith realized with amazement that Professor Parker was a dwarf. He looked at Holl, who was staring wide-eyed. "It's a completely ordinary variation in the gene pool," Keith hissed. "Don't stare."

Holl forced himself to blink and look away. "My apologies on a breach of good manners," he muttered. "For a minute there, I thought it was one of my folk."

"No kidding," Keith said. "It was like seeing the Master come into the room, wasn't it?"

"He's even smaller than we are," Holl replied, astonished, as the man approached them. Keith poked an elbow into his friend's ribs. "Shh. Later. He's talking."

The professor clambered up and settled himself on the bench beside Miss Anderson, and addressed the group very seriously. "You must understand how important we feel this site is."

"Here it comes," said Matthew audibly. He was unimpressed by the archaeologist's appearance, and was obviously wondering when Parker would lower the boom on them. Any good-natured trust he had had at the beginning of the tour had been evaporated by Dr. Stroud. It wasn't fair to Parker, but Keith couldn't really blame Matthew.

Parker enveloped all of them in his wideflung arms. "We're counting on you to give us your best. I always feel that some of the greatest enthusiasts join these Educatours outings. You're all welcome. I hope we can get to know one another better."

That was so far from what Matthew expected the professor to say that he gaped openly at Parker. Miss Anderson looked pointedly at Matthew. She put a forefinger under her chin and pushed her own jaw upward. Matthew understood the pantomime and closed his mouth. "I did promise a different experience from the one in Inverness," the teacher said.

"Hurray," cheered Edwin. Max twisted his lips into a satisfied grin and leaned back, arms folded behind his head, against the wall of the croft.

"Would there be some cake left for me, I hope?" Parker asked, as the dark-haired girl appeared to clear away the plates. She smiled down at him and nodded toward the covered plates near the till. "Thank you," he said, as a dish and cup were swiftly placed before him. "As the area is somewhat isolated, we have arranged with the kind and indispensable ladies of the tea shop to provide lunch for my team every day." Parker aimed the point of his fork toward them. "Of course, now that includes all of you. As the weather is so inclement, the rest of my people are spending today in Stornoway. The site is down at the bottom of the hill, across the road, and there's no protection from the wind. You'll have noticed that there are almost no trees on the Isle of Lewis, no windbreaks. It isn't sensible to allow the wind to damage the very pieces we're trying to unearth whole, is it? The others are doing a little shopping. You'll meet them tomorrow. Allow me to describe just what it is we're doing here."

With the help of a small chart he unfolded from his coat pocket, Professor Parker outlined the project, and detailed how much had already been done. With jabs of his fork, he indicated what he hoped to have accomplished every few days. "But you have to understand that the peat makes it very hard work. Between the time the Leodhas Cairns were built and the present day, the Isle of Lewis has undergone several climactic and topographical changes. There was thick forest here, once, and when that died, the heather began to cover everything. I'm counting on all of you to have patience. You've had a month's experience already at hard labor, so you know what is needed here." The others chuckled. They had already forgotten the professor's stature, and were genuinely listening to what he had to say.

Holl watched him closely. This Big Person's size made Holl feel a sudden kinship for him. He felt guiltily that he shouldn't be permitting such a superficial similarity to make a difference, but it did. He smiled whenever Parker met his eyes, which the professor did frequently with all the members of the group, drawing them in and making them feel accepted.

This one's a born leader, Holl thought. I wonder if I will make the same good showing when my turn comes to lead.

The next morning when they came out of the Mackenzie house, the sun was already high in a bright blue sky.

Keith stretched, and listened to the vertebrae in his back click into place. "I'm stiff. The cats got into the room last night and sat on me in a different place every time I turned over."

Holl grunted, stumping down the hill beside him. "You're a magnet for lower life forms, Keith Doyle. They feel a kinship with you."

"Ha, ha," Keith said, refusing to acknowledge a putdown. It was a bright morning, and there were songbirds trilling in the distance. It was unbelievably pastoral. He felt relaxed and energetic at the same time. He couldn't wait to get down to the site and start work.

The day was not as warm as one in Inverness, but it felt springlike. The sun was trying to burn its way through the thick layer of cumulus clouds that interrupted its beams from time to time, but it was there. Everything looked and felt so sharp it crackled. At the bottom of the hill, the sea had been hewn out of silver-grey flint, and polished into waves. The noise of waves crashing seemed detached from it. In the field next door, the sheep sang them a morning chorus in baritone and alto voices, drowning out the birds.

"Morning, ladies," Keith called, feeling expansive after a big hot breakfast. "These are all shorn," he observed to Holl.

"You were wearing their winter coats on your back yesterday," Holl pointed out. "I'm sure they're relieved now, but they'd have been glad of it a day ago."

"I know, can you believe the change?" Keith said, looking around him at the hills, and taking in the beauty of the land. He stretched out his arms and felt the heat of the sun through his thin sleeves. "Yesterday it was next door to a blizzard, and today it's summer again. I thought only the Midwest did this much of a quick change act. Of course, Lewis might have been at it longer. This place feels *old*."

"Aye, it does," Holl acknowledged, concentrating. "Old bones, and little to keep the skin from sloughing away in the wind."

"I feel that there's something deeper to this place than it looks. Don't you feel it? Maybe there's magic here," Keith suggested hopefully.

Holl shook his head. "I don't sense much of it, myself."

"Well, what about that circle of stones up there? We walked through it yesterday. That's supposed to be a temple or something."

"As nice an office building as I've ever been in," Holl said flatly, ignoring the bait Keith had laid before him. "But I do like this island. It isn't a bad place at all."

"Nope. I like it, too. All browns, greens, and dark blues. It's kind of a macho landscape," Keith added, trying to sum up the sensation. "It's beautiful without being full of little roses and daisies. You know, I think we're going to have to forget about your bellflowers for the time being. There's hardly anything growing around here except for heather and yellow gorse."

"I know it," Holl said mournfully. His hair fluttered in the wind, and he pushed it out of his eyes with an impatient hand. Keith noticed that the ears were still in their Big Person form. He decided to brave the question.

He cleared his throat, and tried to sound casual. "Say, Holl, why haven't you changed your ears back?"

The elf started, and then shrugged, his shoulders sagging low. "Oh, I intended to. As soon as I got out of the hospital, I was going to change them back. Our ears are badges of pride to us, as you know. I realized that you had urged me to alter them to save my life, but I'd sooner evade detection by wit."

"Yeah, but you were in no condition to use wit. It was the best thing I could think of with you lying there unconscious. So why are they still round? Going native?" Keith asked, forcing his voice to be light.

Holl was silent for a long time. The words stung him, because that's just what Curran and the other Conservatives would say to him back home. "Well, it's easier this way to get along," Holl said uneasily, but he was as little satisfied with the answer as Keith.

"You're getting along fine. The other guys like you just as you are."

"They don't know what I am. They accept me well enough," Holl acknowledged, grudgingly, "so long as they think I'm one of them, and a child at that. Only now, I can take off my hat in company. Imagine what they would say if I went bareheaded among them in my normal state."

"I can't imagine you doing that," Keith said, truthfully. "But the guys are used to your hat, too."

"It's artificial in this culture. It was easier in downstate Illinois, where many men wear their caps in diners and stores. Here, I stand out too much. It's considered an affectation for my head to remain covered all the time."

Oh," said Keith, sadly. "Well, *I* like you the way you were, bull-headed tradition and all. I admired the way you survive by sneaking around but never pretending to be different. I'm sorry you've lost pride in yourself, denying your elfhood."

"Elfhood! Your terms, Keith Doyle...Well, I haven't!" Holl protested hotly, kicking stones down the hill. "It's just...easier to be this way."

"Forever?" Holl gave him a sad look which made him wish he had kept his mouth shut. The mixture of unhappy emotions that had surfaced in Holl's face for that brief moment surprised him. Keith would have offered an apology, but they had nearly reached the site, and other people were now within earshot. There was nothing Keith could do to take back his words. The discussion was over.

Chapter Fourteen

"Good morning," Dr. Parker hailed them. "I cannot get used to having the sun up so early. How strange to have it light nearly the clock round! It makes me feel as if I should be up and doing at what usually proves to be an ungodly hour. As you can see, we're a small group, so we greet your arrival with pleasure, as we will miss you when your time is up. By then, we're expecting a group of students from the University of Wales, but that's let's see, nearly three weeks away. Ah, but let me introduce you to your coworkers. Mind the gate there. The latch sticks."

A waist high wooden fence of pickets and wire had been driven into the tall grass, encircling the site and dipping down the shallow slope to where the land fell off abruptly into the sea. The half-revealed mound they were investigating, which seemed set in a depression lower than the surrounding terrain, lay nearly on the shore of a small inlet west of the standing stones, which were visible above them on the high hilltop. Parker hurried forward to open the gate, nearly disappearing behind it, and admitted Keith and Holl with a wave. By its pale, unweathered color, Keith judged that the fence was recent.

"Why is this here?" Keith said. "The area seems pretty deserted to me."

"Oh, I don't mind the curious onlooker," Parker said, expansively, latching the gate behind them, "so long as it's human. I don't want to have to pay the local sheepherders for the loss of a nosy ewe. The sheep are everywhere on this island, if you hadn't noticed. You're the last two to arrive, I think." Parker screwed up his long face and did a mental count. "Yes. Please, come with me.

"Not much of the Neolithic culture remains on view here, except for cairns and round chambered tombs, which is what we have on this site. The Leodhas Cairns have had rather an interesting history. They were built long before the peat covered Lewis, and were shown on topographical maps to be no more than irregularities in the gneiss. Can you imagine? They were already two thousand years old when the Romans came to this island." Keith and Holl waited while Parker clambered over a low projection under the grass. Keith started almost guiltily when he realized that he had just stepped over the same ridge without conscious effort. He and Holl slowed their pace until the small professor caught up. Parker didn't seem to notice any hesitation on their part or expect any special consideration, and continued his chat.

"You'll have noticed on the way here from town how very much construction is going on here on the Isle, haven't you?" He met their eyes again, in his friendly way, and waited for nods. "Ah. Well, demolition here above the western shores of Loch Roag caused subsidence in the neighboring fields. The sea was much lower when all these monuments were built. Air pockets and water pockets have been waiting for just such a momentous disturbance, and some of them burst. The outlines of long-buried stone structures were exposed in the peat, like a furniture in an empty house under bedsheets."

Keith could easily see what Parker was talking about. The other two low mounds lay revealed some yards away from the one which the party was excavating. He had seen similar lumps of peat and grass in a dozen places between Stornoway and Callanish, and wondered just what it was that told the scientists they were different from all the other lumps. The marks of tearing and wrenching were just a little newer than most of the features of the Lewisian landscape.

"There's bound to be some damage to the structures underneath, since what these poor old fellows have just experienced is tantamount to an earthquake. That's one of the things we need to determine. We hope it won't be much. It'll be some years before we've uncovered all the secrets of this place, but it's rather exciting to be the first to open the box, if you see what I mean," Parker continued, engagingly. "Now, some underground caverns may have collapsed. The sea has been nibbling away at Lewis for ages, drowning farmland, and possibly other burial sites. Those small islands you see out there were once simply high ground. Hence our haste to uncover the secrets of the past in the low places. We don't want it to disappear before we've had a good look, eh? Nor you to disappear into the bowels of the earth. I caution you to pick your way warily, because we don't know if there is further instability under the site itself. There's strange stories told of the Western Islands, and of the Long Island in particular."

Keith felt his whiskers twitch in anticipation. He wondered if Dr. Parker knew any of those stories, and if he would tell them.

The group was divided among the professor's regular assistants. "Can any of you type?" Parker asked, hopefully. Of the ones who raised their hands, Holl and Mrs. Turner were chosen, and paired off with a blond-maned young man. Their job was to organize the data and transfer measurements and notations from penciled notes into a personal computer right there on the site. Keith was relieved. He didn't feel he could work the whole day with Holl, unless they could talk without fear of being overheard. He wanted to settle their argument and undo the tension. There was more going on with his friend than mere unwanted cosmetic alteration. He was moody, and he seemed to walk around in a daze half the time. Still, that wouldn't have to be resolved immediately. Work would keep them both busy, and maybe Holl would have a chance to cool off. Keith knew that he wasn't to blame for his friend's mood, that the ear thing was just the tip, so to speak, of Holl's troubles. Holl was just going to have to call long distance and see what was really happening on the farm. Maybe one of the others, Marm or Tay, perhaps, would give him a true report.

Keith found that he and Narit were assigned to work with Dr. Stafford. This man, Dr. Parker's second in command, was a giant, with rough blond hair and beard, and a deeply tanned, lined face, giving him the aspect of a lion walking upright. He had returned only a few weeks ago from an archaeological exploration in Africa. While they worked, The Lion described in a booming voice the investigations in which he had participated near a site known as Great Zimbabwe. "I'd have been there longer, but the governments down there tend to limit the amount of time that foreign scientists can stay each year. It means you've got to pass the baton on someone who joins you partway into the dig, like in a relay race, to look for things you were still seeking when your time ran out. No continuity. Still, I don't see that there isn't some sense in that. No one can become proprietary about a site, and science doesn't have to come to a stop because the one man who knew it all dies." Keith glanced occasionally over his shoulder at Matthew, who was listening to Stafford with a sort of hero worship written indelibly all over him like tattoos, while hoisting buckets of the heavy peat out of the pit.

Dr. Stafford treated them all with a dry, humorous affection that Keith found appealing. He could see that the big professor's calm, matter-of-fact manner soothed Narit so that her hands stopped darting tentatively, and became deft and sure as she picked stones and shards out of the nearly rock-hard peat. The Neolithic era was positively new minting as far as Stafford's usual specialty went, but he had come to the Hebrides to assist Dr. Parker, who had been his tutor thirty years ago. Now he was a tenured professor in the department which Parker chaired. Stafford clucked over Parker protectively when the small professor was trying to do too much. It had been some months since they had seen each other, and they were catching up on past times. "And he hasn't changed his ways at all. He's still not taking care of himself," The Lion complained in his booming voice.

Keith liked Stafford instantly, and he started watching Parker, too, turning the director away from treading on loose rocks that would plummet him into the depths of a pit. Parker tended to work like a kitten, expending all his energies in great bursts of activity, and then sitting down exhausted. The man was so involved in what he was doing that he came across as absentminded. It was mere appearance, though. Anyone who moved a stone or a shard of pottery or a bone without marking the site found Parker at his or her shoulder, fitting the piece back into the enveloping peat, signaling for the measuring rods and camera.

Parker had evidently attracted young scientists who were of a similarly intense but easygoing nature. The Educatours group found they were working very hard, but their questions were never treated as stupid or a waste of time by the team. The core group was small, a fact which worried Parker, when he reflected openly how little time he had to examine this site.

As Keith worked on the open mound, and saw the outlines of the tombs begin to emerge more clearly in his eyes, he sympathized with Parker's longing to stay. Keith himself probably wouldn't be satisfied until he had explored all three structures. The wind played gently with them that day, sending tentative breezes among them instead of the forceful gales. As the sun rose higher, it got warmer, burning off the morning mist. The birds' morning song changed to conversational trill, and the sheep, sounding strangely distant, could be heard adding their music to the chorus.

"If there's any luck, we'll find an intact version of the chambered tomb which is up there," Parker told them, pointing up at the standing stones. "I'd give my eyeteeth for a few unspoiled artifacts as well. Peat is anaerobic, and does kindly by organic compounds, but with the sea so close, I've no idea what will be left."

Under the noon sun, the colors in the landscape were even more pronounced, greens and yellows drenched with light. When he paused for breath, Keith started picking out the colors that echoed the ones that he had seen woven into his tweed jacket, in the things that he could see growing on the land.

"Are the dyes made from these things, like the peat for brown, and the heather for purple and green?" he asked the tea shop ladies at lunch. "I couldn't help but notice that what's out there ends up in there." He pointed to the shelves.

"You'd better ask the weavers that question," the dark-haired girl said, serving him a sandwich and a bowl of soup. "I know only that they design their own patterns, and mix the colors to suit themselves. You might ask old Mrs. MacLeod about it. I'm sure I don't know."

Holl paid little attention to the discussions going on behind his back. Ignoring his lunch, he fingered the lengths of cloth on the shelf again and again, trying to make up his mind what might best serve the needs of those in the village. "You've got to like something which is virtually indestructible, sews well, is remarkably warm, and has a natural waterproofing from the lanolin," he had explained to Keith over and over again in the B&B. "You don't see sheep with such a long wool staple in the Midwest as you do here. We're not yet self-sufficient enough to be making our own cloth, but it would still take years to achieve a quality like this."

Now Holl was using his interest as an excuse not to sit down and eat with Keith. "You've got tons of money with you," Keith pointed out, patiently, coming up and leaning over his friend's shoulder. "Why don't you just make up your mind and bring a lot of cloth back for your folk? They sell it by the yard here, and it isn't that expensive for the value."

"It's remarkable stuff," Holl said, almost to himself. He had fallen in love with the multicolored fabrics. He was inspecting each bolt, and making sketches of the various weaves with color notations.

"He's right," Keith commented to the Tea Shop's ladies. "This stuff is so good it's a wonder why you have any left on the shelf at all"

The young woman made a friendly grimace. "Ah, well, if we had more customers like you, we might sell out more frequently. But I think that *those* people scare away the tourists." Keith didn't need to ask who *those* people were. The unkempt band hanging around the tents behind the shop had put some of their group, Mrs. Green and Mrs. Turner particularly, on edge, though they never actually accosted any of the party. The ladies would only approach the croft with escorts. Keith had seen worse, but he didn't say so. The girl seemed genuinely distressed.

"Who are they?" Keith asked.

"Traveling folk, mostly. Gypsy folk, harmless. But they're a damned nuisance, and we wish they'd pull up their tents and move on."

"What are they waiting for?"

"They're Worshipers of the Old Way. They've been here for the solstice, since the Wiltshire England police have blocked them out of Stonehenge for their destructive habits, and now they say they are waiting for the full moon. Their dirt and disrespectful attitudes chase away the shyer customers." The girl sighed. "Oh, some of them are probably genuine worshipers, but there's bad apples in every barrel. Look out for them."

"We will." Keith paid for their meals. He picked up Holl's sandwich and wrapped it in a paper napkin. On the way out of the building, he plumped the small package into Holl's hands. "Eat. You need strength to worry."

The elf regarded him with cynical amusement.

"Point taken, Keith Doyle."

Investigations on the others in the Educatours party came through from the Home Office, and were posted to Michaels on the island. Michaels perused them impatiently. None of the students or the adults had a criminal record, or in fact any notations of subversive behavior at all. None of them were likely to be his contact. They all seemed to be 'above suspicion.' O'Day had chosen his camouflage well.

There was another element present, one which Michaels suspected might prove to be the mysterious contact. The dirty lot of traveling folk who were camped out behind the Tea Shop were a possibility. But if he had been chasing Danny O'Day for a month for a mere shipment of drugs or stolen jewelry, the chief would go spare. No, Michaels's intuition told him there was more to O'Day's visit than ready valuables easily disposed of for cash.

The week began auspiciously, but the weather was not always as clement in the following days. Usually it was calmer in the mornings, though the moist dew clung to everything, making the peat cold and slippery. During the afternoons that were too windy or rainy for work, the boys spent the better part of the day sheltering in the Tea Shop before the coach took them to Stornoway for the evenings. There, they discussed the dig, with the same gusto that they had evinced in Glasgow. Miss Anderson was pleased to see that their good spirits had had a resurgence. Matthew and the others still complained being in the Western Islands was like exile, but it was good-natured griping. It wasn't really as if they had been entirely deprived of beer for a fortnight, what with all the pubs in Stornoway. They were vitally interested in what was going on at the site.

Professor Parker was almost apologetic that almost no perishable grave goods were turning up. He had been hoping for some examples of craftworks to augment the funerary materials that were contained in the cairns. What they were finding was mostly fossilized bone and pottery. Keith knew that Matthew was disappointed. He had hoped to recreate his Glasgow experience, unearthing a successful find. Matthew was working hard to find something the professor would be pleased with.

"You have a true talent for this job," Holl told the young man, sincerely.

"Yeah, you sure do," Keith chorused.

Matthew's oddly thin skin blushed scarlet. "I'm enjoying it," he confessed.

Martin elbowed him. "Pretty soon the hols will be over, though, mate."

Matthew nodded sadly. "I know it. I thought six weeks would be a long time, but it's not."

The Tea Shop served only tea and soft drinks, and it became crowded several times a day by the many coach tours that visited Callanish, so the group hung about there only when there was nowhere else to go. On the proprietress' part, the students were allowed to stay there only because they were well groomed and clean, a contrast to the unwanted guests behind the shop, but it was made clear to them that they, too, remained under protest. Keith and the others tried not to wear out their welcome, but they could tell that the ladies would prefer it if the whole lot of them would clear off at once.

Holl's gloom had worn off by the end of the first day. In an effort to keep his friend from falling back into a gray mood, Keith asked Miss Anderson about setting up a tour of Lewis and Harris, the southern half of the Long Island, one that would include a lot of wool shops, but the teacher reluctantly had to refuse.

"The coach's brakes aren't in the best condition right now. We're doing pretty well in making it safely between Callanish and Stornoway every day—well, wait until you see the roads in the interior of the island before you protest that we could do it. They are steep and very narrow. I wouldn't advise trying an extended trip until the vehicle is fixed. The driver is awaiting a part to be sent to a garage here. Perhaps later, near the end of the tour."

"I tried," Keith reported back to Holl. "We'll have to wait for a while."

"Ah, well," the Little One said, resignedly. "Still, I appreciate you trying to cheer me up. It means a lot."

The U.S. Passport office, in a pointed example of hands-across-the-water, had come through with the files which Michaels had requested. The chief's secretary read the details to Michaels over the phone. The agent stood in the only public telephone in the village. It was a new telephone and worked a treat, but the booth was unaccountably open to the elements six inches from the ground, like a lady holding her skirts up off the floor. It gave the wind a perfect chance to freeze his ankles while holding him virtually immobile.

"The passport issued to Keith E. Doyle is fairly recent, issued only weeks before he arrived in Britain." The chief's secretary read the information from the sheet over the phone to Michaels.

Michaels huffed into his moustache. The pay telephone from which he had placed his call was situated halfway between the Mackenzie farm and the dig site. From it, he could keep a reasonably constant eye on his quarries. "He mustn't have made up his mind on a pseudonym until the last minute."

"The one for Holland Doyle, aged 14…"

"Ha ha. If he's fourteen, I'm Winnie the Pooh."

"Yes, sir," the secretary continued. "…was issued even more recently, only a day or two before departure from the U.S."

"It seems there is a real Keith Doyle. We haven't been able to locate him, though. He's got two addresses, one in the north of the state of Illinois, and one in midstate. The FBI is sending an investigator to look into it."

"Could it be a full-fledged plot, I mean the family's name is Irish, after all," Michaels pointed out significantly.

"We hope it's not that, sir."

"Aye, I hope not, too. Probably we'll find the boy is dossed down with a bird somewhere in between one place and the other."

"In the meantime, we want you to keep a close eye on those two."

"Well, I wish they'd go ahead and make a move. I haven't seen a trace of any stranger yet who might be O'Day's contact. The weather's a great bloody mess, and there's hardly a pub in the place. Praise God the coach takes them off to the town every night, where there's a little civilization. Regular old package tour, this is becoming. I feel like a gypsy."

"The chief asks that you keep him posted, sir."

"Thanks, love. I've already asked the local constabulary to lend me a hand if I have to lay gloves on our boys. More tomorrow."

Chapter Fifteen

"There'll be a full moon tonight," Keith said, early one morning when they were dressing for breakfast. He reached over the edge of the bed for his old pair of socks to toss them into his suitcase. They weren't there. "Holl, did you pick up my socks?"

"I'd sooner handle nuclear waste, and well you know it," Holl said, indignantly. "You must have stowed them somewhere yourself."

Keith glanced under the bed, and then sifted through one side of his duffle for a clean pair. "Oh, well, I must have put them away last night without thinking. I'm about due to hit the laundromat again, unless Mrs. Mackenzie will let us use her washing machine. I was really beat yesterday. Dr. Parker is working us like robots, but you know, I'm enjoying myself, and learning a lot on top of everything. I'm going to have muscles in my brain as well as on my arms when I go home."

"At least that'll give your skull some makeweight," Holl said, tartly, but his heart wasn't in the banter. While working on transferring Parker's minutiae, he'd had plenty of time to think about his troubles. Holl had no idea whether his life as he left it would be ruined when he got home. Nothing could be done while he was here but worry, so worry he did. Whether he completed either half of his quest now was immaterial to him. He had considered over and over again phoning Maura at the farm as Keith Doyle suggested, and demanding to know what was going on. But if there was nothing to know, no truth to what his mother had said, then it would be a slap in the face of distrust to Maura, and shame to him. In the meantime, he had plenty of occupation for his hands.

"You know, I think this is probably what they mean by the midsummer full moon, Holl," Keith offered again, fastening his shoes.

"Midsummer Eve is the summer solstice, the 21st of June. Any buffoon knows that."

"No, but look: summer is June, July and August, right?" Keith argued. "This is July, so it's the middle of summer. That makes tonight midsummer. Right?"

"As a syllogismist you're correct, but custom has dictated otherwise for centuries."

Keith made a face at him. "Yeah, I know, but it sounds like a good excuse. I want to go up to the stones under the full moon. If any of the faerie folk visit that circle, this would be the time of the month when they'd do it. You could come with me…" Keith hinted temptingly.

"Hmph! Well, give my regards to Oberon and Titania if you see them. I'm going to stay and get a quiet night's sleep without you thrashing in the next bed."

At midnight, armed with a camera full of very fast film and a notepad with pencil, Keith made his way out of the B&B. The moon was a burning silver disk high in the twilit sky. It threw a sharp shadow behind every stone and pebble on the road, and made the shallow potholes appear bottomless pits. Keith trudged up the hill to the circle of standing stones, listening to his feet crunch on the pebbled road. It was very quiet, and only a soft breeze ruffled his hair. The sensation of still, sleeping power came to him again. He imagined it surrounding and lifting him up, until he could dive into the milky heart of the moon. He glanced back over his shoulder toward the dig site. It was dark, with the sea tossing up occasional white glints in the distance. Every light in the village was out. Though he could see every house and barn, there was no illumination in any of them, except for one white dot, like an eye, at the bottom of Mrs. Mackenzie's garden. Keith blinked at it. It was probably a birdbath, or something else which was reflective.

As he came over the breast of the hill, he saw the Callanish stones gleaming like candle flames under the moon, reflecting its silver light. It was hard to believe how few the stones actually were. In the sharp black and white it looked like there were thousands. Keith saw a sudden movement under the tallest monolith, heard a snatch of vocal tone like a shout and then a rhythmic booming. He pricked up his ears. Suddenly, white figures burst from the center circle and melted into the darkness between the other stones. Keith ran the rest of the distance to get a better look. Could this be the fay, rising from the center of the hill to its peak to dance in the ancient temple?

Then one of them tripped on a rock, and hopped around, uttering a curse. Keith blinked and shook his head. It was only the hippies who had been living in the parking lot for the last month. This was their long awaited full moon ceremony. They ran forward again, raising their arms and touching hands at the height. Their voices carried to him. They were chanting and dancing in a circle around the tallest stone. Once again Keith wondered at their ability to ignore the temperature. They were all stark naked.

Their ceremony appeared to be breaking up. Keith was relieved, since he had felt like an intruder watching. The sensation of mystic power hadn't passed yet. He waited until they were all back by their campsite before he crossed the gate and entered the monument at the south end.

He followed the broken avenue slowly, and stopped at the edge of the circle. With a mental apology to anything he might be disrupting, and a quiet prayer that it wouldn't be something as cranky as that fairy mound in Glasgow, he stepped forward.

Keith wandered around the circle, listening and waiting, the camera hanging by its strap from his shoulder. The sound of the sea and the low chatter of the worshipers reached him as a soft undercurrent to the silence. He waited at each compass point by the inner perimeter of the circle, looking around for any clue that there might be something else here, something he hadn't seen or sensed yet. The west was barren. So was the north. He was doing a full rotation on his heels at the east, when a tall, dark figure, the moon behind it casting a ghostly outline, rose before him from the cairn. Keith gulped, and fumbled one handed for his camera. The other hand was steadying him on the monolith behind him. Abruptly, the figure stretched out a hand and spoke, but not in staves of poetry or syllables of the wild magic.

"'Ere, gi'es a hand, mate. I fell on my ruddy bum in here. Wot time is it?" So he wasn't faced with a prince of the underworld, or one of the returning dead. This was only a human being like himself, one of the hippies. Disappointed but vastly relieved, Keith waited for the hammering of his heart to stop.

He extended a hand, and helped the man out. One warm hand clasped his fingers, and the other grasped his wrist. Unlike his fellows, this traveler was clad in the usual daily mix of odd garments.

"Just after midnight," Keith said, squinting at his watch, as his new acquaintance beat the dust out of his clothes.

"Yank, are you? Hoy, I got an uncle in America." The lanky man caressed his temples with both hands. "Christ, I've been passed out for hours. Me head feels like it's been detonated. Where'd everyone go?"

Unwilling to trust his voice to perform without a squeak, Keith pointed toward the campsite, where the others, once again robed, were sitting around the fire. Now that their devotions were ended, they were breaking out cans of beer, and having one heck of a party.

"Ta," said the tall man, and stalked expertly between the stones to rejoin his friends. "Y'can come sit with us if you want. Plenty for everyone."

"No, thanks," Keith said, shaking his head. "I'm driving." The man lifted his hands palm up, and clapped Keith on the shoulder as he went by.

Dejected, the American left the circle and walked back to the B&B. Holl was right. There was nothing there. He let himself into the room and walked on tiptoe, trying to be quiet.

"Well, was there a dancing circle of magic elves under the moonlight?" a wry voice asked out of the darkness.

Keith felt for his bed and sat down on it. It gave under him with a wheeze and a thump. "I guess Shakespeare was wrong." Moodily, he pulled off his shoes and pushed them to one side with his foot. One by one, his socks went off in opposite directions.

"Did you see any fairies?"

"Nope. Just hippies."

"Hm. Not the same thing at all. Perhaps you should come next year in June, when it genuinely is midsummer," Holl suggested in a gentle tone. "The Fair Folk likely have rules, too."

Keith shrugged, disappointed. "I didn't feel a trace of anything out of the ordinary up there, not in the circle. But I can't believe that there's nothing here to find, I mean not just on Midsummer Eve. It's such an amazing structure. This place feels so old, and magical, that I expect something. If it's here, though, I'll find it," he finished, with determination.

"I count on you for that," Holl said drowsily, and turned over to go back to sleep. "Good night, now."

The next morning, Keith arose feeling a little sleepy, and wondered if even the hippies had been a product of the moonlight and his own imagination. Yawning, he glanced at his watch, and blanched. "Hey, Holl, it's late! Breakfast is almost over."

"Eh?" The elf blinked at him, and sat up.

"Quarter to nine!" Keith seized his shaving kit and hurried out to the bathroom. When he returned, he started throwing on his clothes distractedly while Holl went out to take his turn under the shower. He came back, well-scrubbed, and feeling much more alert. The red-haired student was on his knees casting around under the bed.

"Have you seen my shoes?" Keith asked.

"I did. They're just outside the door, where you left them." Holl started dressing, much more calmly than his roommate.

Keith looked puzzled. "I didn't put them outside. I remember sitting on the bed to take them off. I think." He tilted his head, trying to bring back the events of the last evening. "Oh, well." He opened the door and dragged his shoes back into the room, and sat down on the bed to put them on.

"Holl," he said suddenly, in a strangled voice. "Now I'm sure that something is happening. Look!" He held up one of the shoes.

"It's clean. What about it?"

"No, but look. The heels are whole. And my socks are gone again. Boy, after the letdown I got up in the stone circle, it's hard to believe. I wonder if there isn't some kind of Wee Folk right here, who does little jobs around the house."

"Oh, come now!" Holl scoffed.

"They might take the socks as a fee," Keith continued thoughtfully, as if Holl hadn't spoken. "I didn't leave any money in the shoes. I mean, I didn't know that anyone would come by to fix them, so they took whatever else was around. They're nice socks, one hundred percent wool."

"Nonsense. What a lot of silly legends you do attribute to folk like mine," Holl said, exasperated. "Making supernatural fixit men out of us. Shoemakers and housecleaners!"

"Okay," Keith demanded, rounding on him, "if the old story isn't true, how did you people get a reputation for fixing shoes and so on? You're master craftsmen, you might have wanted to do favors for some Big Folk, who, it turned out, knew a writer."

Holl was adamant. "Nothing to do with us. We're natural creatures. We've always kept to ourselves, live and let live."

Keith shook the shoe at him. "Well, what about this? You saw what they looked like yesterday. They were about to fall apart. Now the heels have grown back. Where there's smoke, there's fire," he reasoned.

"Yes, and where there are balloons, there's hot air," Holl retorted.

"Well, do you have any idea what to look for, to tell if there are other Little Folk in this place?"

"No, I have not. You're the one with all the experience with looking for bogeys. I've lived in one place all my life, and you've been everywhere else I've visited so far, and that's not much."

"Maybe Mrs. Mackenzie knows about her little helper. I'm going to ask her."

"She'll think you're as mad as I do."

Keith grinned. "You know, that's exactly what everyone used to say, and somehow I connected up with you guys, so I'm just going to keep on asking."

He put the question delicately to their hostess, expecting her to be disconcerted by the concept of magical folk, but instead, Keith was the one surprised. As soon as she ascertained what her American guest was asking, Mrs. Mackenzie burst into merry laughter. "Have I got a *what* roaming around my house? *I* polished your shoes, lad. They were in foul state after your night on the stanes, when you came in so late. My poor clean floor! I'd also bought a repair kit for my boy's boot heels, and there was enough left to patch yours. They were all to pieces, I saw. So, you were looking for the whippitie-stourie, were you?"

Keith seized his manual of Scots dialect from his back pocket and started to thumb through it. "A 'house brownie'? Um, I suppose something like that."

Mrs. Mackenzie kept on laughing, wiping tears from the corners of her eyes, until Keith had turned as red as his hair. "Nowt of it, lad. Look here." She led them through the dining room to the kitchen. Keith and Holl followed the sound of her chortling down the hall.

"I didna ken this oun, so I guessit t'be yours. It's too late to rescue."

From her nest next to the stove, the slim female Siamese blinked adoring blue eyes up at Keith. Under her sable paws, she held her prey, one of Keith's gray wool socks. Delicately, the cat dipped her head, and dragged a few fibers out of the sock, swallowed them, and did it again, like a child playing 'he loves me, he loves me not.'

"She's eating my sock," Keith said incredulously.

"Ach, she does that," complained the landlady. "Loves wool, she does. There's nothing we can do about it. It's scold her and scold her all the time, and nowt comes of it. It's a wonder she doesn't chase down the sheep for their fleece. She must have slippit in when I fetched out your boots. I'll clear out a drawer for you to keep them safe from now on."

Holl started laughing. Keith was outraged at the destruction of his clothes, but disappointed that there was no more to the mystery than a shoe-shining landlady and a sock-eating cat. "There you go, Keith Doyle. One more legend of the Fair Folk relegated to children's tales."

"Ah," Mrs. Mackenzie nodded. "If you wanted the true Fair Folk, you ought to look for them under the moonlight when the milk runs. That's what my gran used to tell me. Now, come and have breakfast. All this wild jumping at conclusions has no doubt left you ravening."

Chastened, Keith went back into the dining room, and took his place at the table. A homely clatter erupted from the kitchen. Soon, heralded by the appearance of the female cat, who was still holding part of Keith's sock in her mouth, Mrs. Mackenzie emerged with a tray. Keith matched stares with the cat, who took her prey out into the hall.

"There, that ought to fill you," the woman said, maternally, setting a full plate before him and ruffling his hair.

Keith took some toast out of the toast rack before it could cool, and buttered it. "Thanks. By the way, what's the holed stone out beyond the garden? There's traces of white in the bowl. I saw it sort of reflected in the moonlight from above on the way back from the circle, and I went down to look at it…. Um, did I say something wrong?"

Mrs. Mackenzie had started like a rabbit. Before she answered, she looked right, left, and over her shoulder as if someone might be listening to her right there in her dining room. "It's old," she said at last. "Ancient as time. My gran, who owned this farm, had the custom passed to her by her gran, and so to me, to pour the first milking there every full moon. I've done it for years."

"For prosperity, and so on?" Keith asked, surprisingly calm. She nodded. "To propitiate the *bodach*? And the cream of the well, too?"

"The what?" Holl asked, skeptically, looking from one to the other.

"Water drawn from a well on the first night of the new moon," Keith explained.

"That's right." Mrs. Mackenzie was embarrassed. "It's my ain silly superstitions, but I'm amazed that anyone understands how it is."

Keith put on his most persuasive and trustworthy face. "Come on, Mrs. Mackenzie. Tell me the rest. I study this kind of thing. I'm interested in it. I read a lot about legends and things. I promise we won't laugh. We take it very seriously."

She seemed a bit shamefaced, twisting a fold of her tweed skirt between her fingers, and wouldn't meet the boys' eyes. "Seems silly to tell you all," the landlady continued, "but I haven't stopped doing it for fear there's aught to it. It's there for the wee ones, to keep off the dark and help the farm along." Keith glanced triumphantly at Holl, who rolled his eyes impatiently at him. "They don't do jobs, but they do look after us. I put the milk by, and it's all gone in the morning. It might be cats, but I've never dared to stay and look."

"Does it have to be you who leaves the milk?" Keith asked.

"I don't ken it matters, so long as it's left," she replied, surprised. Keith pressed his advantage.

"It's the full of the moon tonight. Can I do it tonight? Please?"

Holl rose out of his seat and shook a finger in the young man's face. "Oh, no, Keith Doyle," he cautioned. "Don't you dare. Remember what the Master said. No meddling."

"It might be nothing at all, just some neighbor's cat, like Mrs. Mackenzie says," Keith informed him. "All I want to do is see what's out there, talk to whatever it is, and maybe take a few pictures."

"I wouldna mind," Mrs. Mackenzie added. "The creepity feelings of that stane make me nervous. If he's a mind to try, I've no objections."

"There, you see?" Keith finished, triumphantly. "And she thinks I'm brave."

Exasperated, Holl threw up his hands. "I'm against it, and so would any other creature of sense. My family tells stories of this kind of spirit to scare the children, not to encourage them to waylay it. You don't know if it's hornets or kittens making the buzzing, but you want to stick your hand into the nest. Please yourself."

"From ghosties and ghoulies and long leggity beasties/ And things that go bump in the night, Good Lord deliver us," Keith declaimed in a spooky voice. Mrs. Mackenzie nervously gathered up the tray and went back into the kitchen.

Holl pursed his lips. "You're mocking me. If you want to take your own silly risks, go ahead."

"How bad could it be? It might be nothing. I've followed up dead end leads before. This is probably just one more." Keith quoted the research books he had been reading. "Remember the *bodach* of Jura. They're good guys. The little wise men of the oak trees, and so on. You'd want to meet someone like that, wouldn't you? This guy might be nothing more than a house brownie, like Mrs. Mackenzie says. Look, if I leave out their fee without trying to do them a kindness, I might be able to talk with them and get a few pictures without 'laying' it."

"Chasing it away," Holl translated. "But this isn't Jura. The *bodach* of this land might be quite a bit different than the ones there. And Mrs. Mackenzie won't be pleased if you scare off her household protector."

"Well, she doesn't actually know if he does anything for them now, or if there's anyone who comes for the milk. This way, I'll settle the matter quietly for the lady, and prove its existence for her, and for you, too."

Chapter Sixteen

That night, as soon as the moon appeared, Keith promptly took himself outside, and made himself a comfortable nest in the grass next to the weathered stone at the end of the garden path. Mrs. Mackenzie came out with a bowl of milk balanced carefully on her hands. The cats followed her hopefully, but veered away as soon as she stopped next to the stone.

"It's from the first milking, that I'll guarantee," Mrs. Mackenzie said, looking a little nervous. "Everything should be proper."

"Thanks," Keith replied, blithely, pouring the milk into the depression on top of the stone and handing the bowl back to her. "It'll be all right. There's nothing to worry about. I've brought something extra, in case your visitor's upset that someone's here waiting for it." He produced a bottle of whiskey, propped it on top of the stone. His camera was loaded and waiting. There were new batteries in both the flash unit and the electric torch on his knee.

Mrs. Mackenzie was hesitant. "I'll leave ye to't, then, shall I?"

"Yup," Keith said happily. He felt confident. This was much better than the night before—his intuition told him so. "I'll be in later. Thanks again."

The landlady retreated along the path, followed by the cats. Keith was alone. It was only about eight o'clock. He figured he would have a long wait until the *bodach* thought everyone was in bed and came to claim its tribute. Keith had looked up the illustration of 'whippitie-stourie' in one of his guides. It showed a small figure with a slim torso and tiny, long fingers. He was certain he could handle something like that. After discovering a whole village full of Little Folk who were a lot bigger than that, a brownie should be an ordinary night's work. On the other hand, there *was* something supernatural about shivering in high July in the Northern Hemisphere in a tweed jacket and a woolly hat as if it was December, Keith thought, as he hunkered down between two apple trees to wait.

"Sir, I think we've got something here," Michaels whispered excitedly into the pay telephone at the bottom of the hill. "I've been watching O'Day closely, and there's no doubt about it, he's up to something. He's been acting pretty strangely all day, hieing about with his camera. Can you get me clearance on whether there's a secure installation hereabout he might be preparing to photograph?"

On the other end of the line, the chief became very agitated. "I'll inquire of the Home Office in Edinburgh. Where's O'Day now?"

"I think he's waiting for a contact, sir. There's a bottle of whiskey on the stone he's sitting beside, and he looks settled in for a long night."

"Aha! This is probably the contact," the chief said. "Well done, Michaels. Take him. As soon as possible before our security is breached. Move in. You have our full support. If nothing comes of it, we can say he was detained to help us with our enquiries."

"Yes, sir." Michaels hung up, and moved purposefully to his observation spot. At last, there was going to be an end to his vigil.

Holl, denouncing Keith's antics as a waste of time, declined to wait outside with him. Instead, he had gone into the sitting room and opened one of Keith's storybooks to pass the time. Two of the Siamese cats sat down on his legs, holding them in place with slim, dark paws and narrow chins. In a short time, Mrs. Mackenzie had appeared with a tea tray, laden with steaming pots, cups, and a plate of small cakes.

"I always have a wee bite when I'm up late. I don't think I could sleep! Whew! It's like the best ghost stories, isn't it, with him sitten out for the spirit's rising? You don't feel as your cousin does, then?" she asked, offering him tea. "You don't think there's a Presence out there?"

"No, I don't," Holl said firmly, stirring his cup with a minute spoon. "It's a lot of nonsense. He's going to spend a long cold night. But at least you'll both be satisfied at the end of it."

"Aye," the landlady said. "Well, I don't believe it, but he does shape a convincing line of talk. I'm quite enjoying it." They sipped tea for a while in silence. Holl read his book, and Mrs. Mackenzie stared calmly at the electric fire. At last, she gathered up the tea things and rose.

"Any road, I'm going to me bed. I have early mornings."

"Good night," Holl said, and looked after her thoughtfully when the door closed. He folded the book over on his thumb.

So Keith Doyle looked as silly to his own kind as he did to Holl's, playing about with stones and such. Why was Keith so willing to take foolish chances? Did he feel he had nothing to lose? Or did he consider himself so lucky that there was nothing he couldn't do?

That was one of the differences between them. Well, it made one think. Keith Doyle seemed to see small adventures like this as part of his life, not an unwelcome intrusion or an overwhelming spectre. If nothing happened, he didn't even feel he had wasted his time on the caper. "You can't learn from your mistakes if you never make any," he was fond of saying.

Holl felt that the parts of his own life were much too precious to risk. This trip was the largest departure from his normal routine that he had ever made—that he had ever thought of making—and look what it did to the rest of his comfortable existence.

Sticks and stones, I'm starting to think like Bilbo Baggins, Holl chided himself. Adventures which made one late for dinner! How hidebound I am, really. He decided all at once that it was silly to let Keith take such risks by himself. There was something about that garden place by the stone he disliked. He finally admitted to himself that he hadn't wanted to wait with his friend because it made him uncomfortable. And if it did, might there not be something to his feeling? Shaking off the cats, he went to wash his hands.

In the bathroom, he confronted his own reflection in the mirror. It angered him to see the simple, soft, rounded eartips pushing through his hair, where tall, elegant, sharply pointed ears ought to be.

"What an idiot I've been, hiding behind the semblance of one of the Big Folk. Enough of this masquerading!" Holl spat. "I'll be myself, with all the silly things I do, and whether or not they're right, I'll stand by my decisions." With an effort of will, he concentrated his energies on his ears. Like corn growing in time action photography, the simple round buds opened, and sprouted into tall, backswept points. Holl smiled at his reflection. "Better." He couldn't wait to tell Keith about his decision.

"If there's nothing to it, at least I'll keep him company. There'll be one supernatural being in the garden this way, at least in the eyes of Keith Doyle." And if it really was dangerous…. He hurried out to join his friend. There was a lot to talk about. They had the whole night through to debate.

Comfortable with his new resolve, he let himself out the kitchen door to the garden.

The moon was full above him, giving the garden a diffuse glow. The path split just outside of the door, and took right angles around the rectangular lawn, past dark flower beds full of nodding bushes of blossom translucent in the moonlight. From the far edge, it continued in a single line between a line of slim apple trees with hard half-grown fruits clinging to the boughs. At the end of the path, Holl could see the white-washed stone, and a dark form next to it with a gleaming red crown. As he walked toward it, the figure became animated, raising thin limbs to its head. There was a brilliant flash of hot white light and a second in quick succession. Then the shouting started. It wasn't Keith's voice doing the yelling.

His blood drained suddenly into his feet, making him feel faint. There was someone out there. He ran the final distance to the stone. Keith had stood up and was grappling with a figure slightly smaller than he. Holl dashed through the apple trees, beating the branches out of his way with an impatient arm. By the time he reached the stone, both figures were gone, and the garden was silent. Holl hadn't seen them go. He crossed the last few feet to the stone. The whiskey bottle was smashed on the paving stones, and the camera lay in the grass beside it.

"Keith! Keith Doyle!" Holl cried, casting around desperately. No answer. He had been taken away. But where? Oh, why, why was it that that foolish boy always had to suffer to prove his principles?

"Lad, lad, what is it?" Mrs. Mackenzie called, emerging from between the trees. She was in a long cotton nightdress, and was hastily wrapping an overcoat about herself. "Why are you shouting? Where's your cousin, hey?"

Holl turned wild eyes on her. "He's gone! I think he's been carried off!"

"What?" Mrs. Mackenzie looked at him curiously, scrutinizing the side of his head. His hair was well back from his ears, which were anything but hidden in the bright moonlight. Holl hastily blurred her vision, and guided her gaze to focus upon his eyes. She blinked, not sure she had seen anything out of the ordinary, and continued speaking normally, having hardly missed a beat. "Taken by the Wee Ones? Oh, no, lad. Look here." She led him to the edge of the garden. "See how the ground drops away right there? He tumbled down the hill, I'm certain. Ye can't see the bottom from where we're standing, what with the gorse being that thick. He'll be back up after he's gathered his wits." She pulled a protesting Holl away from the edge. "There's no sense you falling down after him. The ground is unchancy where they've been digging it up. You can lose a leg in the peat. Wait for him. See, there's his torch, here next to the stane. He's no light to lead him upward. Wait a while, eh? If he's not back until morning then my husband'll help ye. Come on back inside. I'll give you a coop o' hot milk. That'll settle ye to sleep."

Numb with shock, Holl followed her to the house. His brain raced as he sat in the kitchen while the kindly woman bustled around him. Where could Keith be? Did he just fall down the hill? Surely he would have answered if he was able, if he hadn't been knocked unconscious. The strong sensation of power he had noticed by the stone during the day was amplified now.

"Now you drink that, and off ye go to bed. Your cousin will be in soon." She left him alone, and padded away down the corridor. Obediently, Holl drank the milk, which relaxed his tightly wound insides, and listened closely. The woman had shut her door and was already lying down in bed. In a moment, all was silent except for the gentle breathing of the others in the house.

"Oh, I've missed my ears," Holl said, clapping his hands over them. "Imagine having to live with the sorry level of hearing the Big Folk have." Feeling somewhat restored, Holl slipped toward the door, and eased it open. He heard an inquiring sound near his knees. It was the female cat.

"Now don't you hinder me, miss," Holl commanded her. "You're part of the reason he's in trouble." The cat sat down on her haunches with an 'I don't know *what* you're talking about' expression, and began to wash her breast fur with nodding licks. Holl closed the door behind him and hurried down across the grass to the holed stone.

He couldn't shout for Keith Doyle again, not unless he wanted to raise the household. He and Keith hadn't yet met Mr. Mackenzie, but they had seen him once or twice from the back as he left the house early in the morning. He had an uncompromising way of walking. Holl got the impression that Mrs. Mackenzie's husband didn't approve of her telling silly folk tales to strangers.

More than anything else, Holl didn't want to be hindered in his search. If Keith had been swept away by a *thing*, Holl needed to be able to deal with it and not have to worry about Big Folk bystanders wandering into the line of fire. He unsheathed his whittling knife, and started poking around. Between the knife and his own abilities, he should be well able to take care of himself.

He had better night vision than the average among his Folk, and there was a full moon overhead, with only wisps of clouds across it. The sun was out of sight now, but the sky still wore a dawn-colored cloak that made it nearly as light as it had been at eight P.M. They were far enough north that there was no true night during the summer months. He tried *listening* for Keith, but he realized that he was too shaken to sense properly, so he would have to seek him in the mind-blind, Big Folk way. Still, Holl had his hunter's training and all the book learning available to him from the stacks of Gillington Library.

The site of Keith's disappearance had little to tell him. The white-washed stone bowl was dry. Somehow, the *bodach* had taken the traditional offering without actually touching the stone. The whiskey bottle lay smashed into glistening fragments on the pavement nearby. Holl hadn't noticed it before, but there was no smell of spilled liquor. The bottle, like the bowl, was dry. The tax seal on the neck hadn't been broken, but there wasn't a drop of liquor left on the grass or the ground. The *bodach* had taken Keith Doyle's gift, and Keith Doyle as well.

The ground had sealed up seamlessly above them, if this was where the two had vanished. This place had nothing more to tell him. Perhaps he could try Mrs. Mackenzie's suggestion, and examine the scree outside of the garden. He hoped that Keith might be there, nursing a sore leg or arm, but in his heart, Holl doubted it. He smelled magic. Not the simple tricks and bending of rules that his Big friend called magic. This was the real thing: the raw, wild power.

"Keith Doyle, you were right," Holl said out loud, "and I'm sorry you're not here for me to tell you so." He clutched Keith's camera at his side. Whatever was on the film would tell him a lot about what he was dealing with. Holl slipped out of the garden and went to have a look.

Michaels emerged from the bushes, and surveyed the ground next to the stone. That was a pretty trick. Must have been something to do with the light. One minute O'Day and his contact were on the top of the hill in plain sight. A bright flash, and suddenly they were nowhere to be seen. Good optics, and good timing with it. He hadn't had even so much as a glance at the face of the contact. The chief wouldn't be pleased about that. The office still had no clue as to whom O'Day's client was. Michaels had missed his brief chance to make an identification.

"Hey, presto, and they're gone." O'Day and his contact had eluded him, their minder, and gone off somewhere to have their private chat. Obviously, they hadn't let the boy in on the secret of the vanishing act, from what Michaels could see of the lad running to and fro on the hilltop. He seemed genuinely worried. Well, better to have one than neither. He would get what he could out of the boy. Certainly neither of them could have seen Michaels. The agent prided himself that he had been completely discreet in tailing them, even down to watching them at their third, interminable archaeological dig. Here was a perfect opportunity to approach the young one and take him into custody. No fuss, no fight. He could get the older one when he turned up again.

Chapter Seventeen

Holl left the farm by the road and trotted downhill until he found a break in the fence that would let him in under the bottom of the garden. Stones and chunks of peat lay tumbled in a heap against a sheer face at the top of the field. Evidently, one of the hidden air bubbles in the uneven gneiss had given way in the same explosion that had exposed the Leodhas Cairns. It had crumbled away the edge of the bluff on which Mrs. Mackenzie's garden rested, leaving a dangerous patch that could cause any unwary walker to tumble over. Easy to see why she thought Keith had simply fallen.

No footsteps, no signs were here at all to suggest that anyone had been here in the past week, let alone the last hour, but that also could be a trick of camouflage played by the *bodach*. Holl started poking through the tumbled rocks, hoping to find the way into the earth. The shifting mass was too heavy for him to deal with on his own. He didn't feel any natural openings in the stone wall behind it.

He stood up, unsatisfied. For all appearances, the *bodach* must have opened up the ground and gone straight through it with Keith Doyle in tow. That smacked of true experience, familiarity with the terrain, and great power. Holl's heart sank. He didn't have enough of what Keith called 'oomph' to open the way for himself, even if he knew where to start. Once he had rested and calmed down, he *might* be able to trace where Keith had gone by listening for him, and try to figure out what to do from there. Holl felt very small and alone. The situation was too much for him to handle by himself; that he knew.

Resigned, he left the field and made his way down to the telephone booth at the bottom of the hill. He would have to call home. It griped at his very sense of independence, but there he was. There was no good reason to put off the inevitable, humbling as it would be. He had plenty of change in his pocket. He calculated it was no more than mid-evening at home. He didn't want to alarm the other Folk unduly, even if it was an emergency. The only person who could be hurt by a delay was Keith Doyle. It wouldn't serve the Big Person at all for Holl to be proud and stiffnecked. He owed Keith that, at least.

His heart was beating like a bronze gong in his chest as he dialed the international number, and waited for the distant phone to ring. It didn't bode well for his hope of future responsibilities to have to cry for help, but he knew he was too much a stranger in the outside world.

One of the children answered the ringing. Holl cleared his throat. "Good evening, Borget. It's Holl." He spoke in the Folks' own language, in case there was anyone near to overhear him. "It is late; shouldn't you be asleep?...Ah, how is Keith Doyle?" Holl grimaced, and quickly devised a phrase that wasn't a falsehood. The Folk never lied to children. It was counterproductive to their development. "Well, he is much as you would expect he is." *In trouble, as usual,* he thought. "Can you fetch the Master and tell him that I would like to speak with him? Thank you."

The Master came on the line, and Holl explained the situation to him, keeping his voice under tight control. "I've done all that I can, except continue to search and hope I am lucky," he concluded. "I could go on until I stick my foot in it, but if the *bodach* takes me, too, then there's two of us lost, instead of just one, and no one will be left to look. I'm unequal to the problem, which is well out of my ken. I would welcome any help or suggestions you can offer."

There was a long silence on the other end of the line. Holl shifted uneasily, waiting.

When at last he answered, the Master sounded curiously distant. "I vill see to it that help vill reach you within a day."

Holl felt a wash of relief. "Thank you, Master."

He hung up, buoyed up by lighter spirits than he'd felt in hours. Who would come? Probably Aylmer, or Dennet, Holl's own father, two who were good at hunting and tracking. Possibly Enoch, the Master's own son, who had been giving Keith lessons, and with whom the Big Person might have a traceable bond. In the meanwhile, Holl had best keep trying to pick up a trail. There was no sympathy to be had for one of the Folk who met a situation without having all the facts at hand. He decided to go back and examine the fallen rock again.

In thirty paces, it hit him again that he had abrogated his responsibility for finishing his task on his own. Someone older and wiser was coming to take over. He felt suddenly that he had failed in his mission by calling for help, showing that he was really in tow to his

Big Person protector, and not out on his own. He kicked a stone, which skipped noisily over the road and into the nettles at the side. Well, he couldn't just abandon Keith Doyle, no matter whether his pride was whole or in tatters.

A few minutes more careful examination of the field convinced Holl that there was nothing more to be learned from the scree or the garden. The *bodach* had hidden his path well. The whole hill was imbued and riddled with old magic, the product of thousands of years. Holl needed to catch the precise end of the latest thread to have it lead him back to Keith Doyle. That would take time. He stood up, wiping his hands forlornly on his trouser legs and directing a sensing around for clues. He wondered where to start, for there was a lot of geography to cover. "Thank heavens you didn't vanish in Asia, Keith Doyle. I'm fortunate this is only an island."

"Hallo?" A man's head appeared through the break in the hedge. "Lost something, my lad?" The man stepped over the fallen bracken and approached him. He was a kindly-faced, middle-aged, middle sized Big Person with a droopy moustache and spectacles. He was wearing a rumpled tweed suit and carrying a walking stick.

"My cousin, sir," Holl answered. He combed his hair down with his fingers and concentrated on keeping the man from looking at his ears.

"What, down here?" The man surveyed the scene with an eye of concern, and poked at the tumble of rocks with his stick.

"I don't know!" Holl lost control of his voice, and the reply sounded like a wail.

"Now, now," the man said soothingly, hooking the cane over his wrist and patting Holl on the back. "None of that. We'll soon turn him up. You come with me, and we'll find him. What's your cousin's name?"

"Keith Doyle. He's an American." Meekly, Holl accompanied the man down the edge of the field. Big People certainly could be kind. It was very fortunate that this man had turned up when he had. There was sure to be a procedure for finding missing persons, though he didn't know how much good it would do if the person had been kidnapped by a mythical being.

Together, they searched the farm and the area around it, calling in low voices for Keith. It turned out that the landscape lent itself amazingly well to concealing things. There were places among the boulders and shallow ravines where an entire house could be hidden, invisible from all eyes except for those of birds. It promised to be a long job on foot.

Michaels was still convinced that O'Day must have disappeared to make a rendezvous with a contact, but the boy was genuinely upset by his companion's disappearance. It began to occur to him that perhaps O'Day had been abducted by someone who didn't bid high enough for his services. On the other hand, it might be that the meeting with the mysterious contact was still going on. That wasn't uncommon in these illicit matters. Where there was little trust, negotiations could take hours, or more. Michaels himself had sat surveillance on days-long 'stake-outs,' as the Americans liked to call them. Or perhaps he had just gotten lost. This island had fewer signs and directions than any place he'd ever been, and that included London. Michaels could understand his being lost.

Delicate questioning of his young associate revealed that the boy didn't seem to know that he'd been under scrutiny. In fact, he seemed grateful for Michaels' assistance in helping him to look for O'Day. He was refreshingly naive. It was almost as if he didn't realize that there was any reason to hide their presence in the island. Michaels was struck by a horrific thought: could O'Day have brought this innocent with him, and not revealed the mission to him? The boy would be in genuine danger, with a prison sentence at one end, or death at the other, never knowing he was a target. That was monstrous! Indecent! He wanted to find O'Day now to give him a piece of his mind.

Together, Michaels and the boy explored the fields nearby. They scrambled over huge hillocks of peat, calling Keith's name among herds of huge, somnolent sheep. Holl skidded to a halt and clung to a wet clump of heather when a voice that sounded like Keith's answered their call.

"Do you hear that? I think that's him!"

"Yes, I do. Which way is he?"

The cry came again, sounding more distressed. Holl clambered almost on all fours over the next rise, and dropped flat on his belly. On the other side, there was a pit six or eight foot deep. In the bottom stood a half-grown lamb. As Holl appeared, the lamb started calling again, in a consonantless cry that sounded just like the one they had been following. "Eeeehhhhhhhh-hhhhh!"

The ewe was on the lip of the pit, peering through the heather fronds at her offspring, wondering how he got down there.

"That's...my cousin, without a doubt," Holl said disappointed, slumping partway down into a sitting position. "The lost lamb." He slid down the slope, and dropped cautiously into the pit. With a heave, he boosted the young sheep out. Both it and its mother ran away while Michaels gave Holl a hand up. "But no Keith, anywhere around here."

"You'd very likely need a helicopter to survey the place properly," the man said resignedly. "If you broke a leg, no one might find you for weeks."

Holl thought about spending weeks searching the island, and his heart sank.

"By now, he'd have wandered farther afield," Michaels speculated. "We can describe a greater radius tomorrow. I'll lay on a car. You'd best get some rest now, lad." There was no fear that he'd run away overnight, the agent told himself, or wonder where Michaels had come from. The boy's concern was genuine.

Holl was too exhausted by the end of the day to do more than thank his newfound friend and stagger back into the Mackenzie home. Disorientingly, the light was no different than it had been early that morning when he had begun his search. He had the hopeless feeling that no time had passed at all, and that all his efforts were in vain.

Mrs. Mackenzie caught up with him as he was making his way back to his room. She was taken aback by his ragged and dirty appearance, but more concerned by the worried look on his face that made him look many times his years.

"Lad, where have you been? Your Miss Anderson's been here seeking after ye. Where's your cousin Keith?"

"I'm not sure," Holl croaked. His voice was worn out from calling Keith's name. "I hope he's all right."

The landlady looked him up and down with a calculating eye. "Ah, he's just gotten himself lost. Possibly a thump on the heid, and he's mooching about. You've had nothing to eat all day, I'll gi'e odds. Hmm?" Holl nodded. Suddenly he was hungry. The delicious aroma of the family dinner was still in the air. "Well, there's a bacon sandwich or so that needs a home. I'll bring you a plate in the sitting room, with some tea. Go and sit down, and warm yourself."

"Mrs. Mackenzie, would you have another sleeping room?" Holl asked, hopefully, trying to hold himself upright though exhaustion was tugging at his muscles. "I think there's going to be another one of us here by tomorrow."

"Of course I do," the woman asserted heartily. "And happy to have him. Now, you go and sit down, and eat, and then you sleep a good sleep. You must think of nowt more to worry you. All will be well in the morning."

"That's what I'm hoping," Holl said, wearily.

Michaels picked up Holl the next morning in a small car requisitioned from the local authorities. There was only time for a quick circuit of the area before the boy directed Michaels to drive to the Stornoway airport.

"Some of our relatives have heard that Keith has gone missing. They're concerned. I think one of our cousins is coming to see if he can help," the youth explained enigmatically.

Michaels shrugged. It was a transparent story. Without a doubt, this was the original contact coming to verify O'Day's disappearance for himself before the youth would be let off the hook. Best to stay on guard, or he'd likely be missing this lad, too. At the youth's request, Michaels stopped at a chemist's to let him drop off a roll of film. It was Keith's, the boy explained. Michaels began to think that the next time that film manufacturer declared a stock dividend, they could attribute it solely to Danny O'Day.

The airport was small, and not set up for international travel, so Michaels was stunned when the passenger turned out to be two, not one, and both had foreign accents. The caper had begun to take on more and more of an international flavor.

"Holl!" a girl cried. She was a pretty thing, slim and fairly tall, with blue-green eyes and long blond hair unimproved by nature, so far as Michaels could tell, and quite young. She and the boy met halfway in a warm embrace that all but swept the lad off his feet. An American. "Oh, Holl, what happened to Keith?"

"Wait until I tell you. So they've sent you?" Holl asked, eagerly, inadvertently ignoring his escort, who stayed close by, listening.

"Not exactly sent," the girl said, glancing sideways at Michaels. "I came along with him." She gestured by tilting her head at the gate door through which a short man was entering.

The second passenger had red hair and a silky red beard. Michaels was taken aback by the cool, summing glance that the small man gave him through a pair of gold-rimmed spectacles. Those cold blue eyes had considerable intelligence and determination behind them. This must be the spymaster.

"Diane, this is my friend," Holl said, fluttering a hand toward Michaels, and then realized he didn't know the man's name.

"Michaels," the agent supplied, extending a hand to the man and girl in turn. "How do you do?"

"Well, this is my...uncle Friedrich," Diane said. There was something about this man she didn't like, even if Holl did seem to trust him. "My name's Diane Londen. I'm, I'm Holl's sister."

"A pleasure, Miss Londen. I'm no more than a Good Samaritan, encountered upon the road. I'm helping the lad here to find his cousin." Michaels realized that he really towered over the red-haired man. He started to say something, but Diane interrupted him, and dragged him to one side.

"He's very sensitive about his height, you know. Please don't mention it."

"I wouldn't think of it," Michaels promised her. "Is he, er, Keith's father? I couldn't help but notice the, er, similarity of coloring."

Diane raised her eyebrows at him curiously, but smiled winningly. "No, he's our uncle. Cousin Keith takes after his mother. She's *really* tall." Diane sketched a ridiculous distance above the ground with one hand.

"Friedrich Alfheim. How do you do?" the small man demanded in a Teutonic accent, shaking Michaels's hand.

"Alfheim?" Michaels asked, appealing to Diane. "I thought you said he was a Doyle, too?"

"He writes books, you know," Diane whispered, thinking fast. "It's his pen name. Shh. We don't want his fans to know he's here."

"How did you come so soon?" Holl demanded, taking Diane's bag. Michaels relieved the older man of his suitcase, and led the way out to the car park.

"We came standby," Diane explained. "We just caught the jet; they held it for us while we ran for the gate. It didn't make us very popular, but we made it. If your call had been ten minutes later, we would have missed it completely. As it is, we've been on four planes in the last twenty-four hours, and I'm pooped. What exactly happened to Keith?"

"I'm not sure." Reluctant to mention anything to do with magic in front of a stranger, Holl gave them a bowdlerized version of Keith's disappearance. "There's been a lot of earthmoving in the area, and Keith might have fallen into a pit where there was a lot of subsidence. As we discovered in our searches yesterday, there are thousands of places where things may be concealed. This island is made up of geological odds and ends, with a high water table, where the peat has it stored up like sponge."

Once again, Michaels was impressed by the midget playing the part of Holland Doyle, and wondered if he had been wrong thinking that he was a kid. He sounded too intelligent to be a youngster, but you never know with young ones these days. He was concerned— what could have happened to Danny O'Day? Left the boy here to hold the bag while he headed for greener pastures? But this older one, now he was something to watch. A formidable old bastard. He reminded Michaels of his fifth form master.

Chapter Eighteen

"Of a' the scunnersome, junting fuils to interrupt a ca'm evening with a nasty licht like tha'," the mocking voice, as brown black as mascara, echoed in Keith's head, as the skinny figure wrestled with him. "A curse on ye, then. A curse!" It was amazingly strong, and hard to get a grip on. His hands always seemed to miss the hold he aimed for.

Keith had already dropped the camera somewhere in the grass. A tiny, unoccupied part of his mind hoped it was all right. The rest of him was involved actively in wishing he could get away from this angry thing, but it was a lot stronger than he was.

Both of them had been surprised when the mysterious figure popped right out of the ground next to the stone and reached for the milk. Keith was amazed that anyone had really come for the offering, but the *bodach*, if that's what it was, appeared completely thunderstruck that anything should be there waiting for him.

Keith had unwound like a spring, bounding astonished to his feet. He realized he should have been expecting an entrance like that. You could hardly expect a mystical household guardian to use a gate. The reality stunned him. By comparison, discovering the Little Folk in the bottom of Gillington Library was ordinary. *They* used doors. The Little Folk were a heck of a lot more friendly to strangers than this creature was. It sure didn't look like the illustration in his guide book. There was nothing benign or playful about this creature. He wondered what they would call it. The being's coloration seemed to blend with the landscape, so Keith couldn't get a very clear idea of what it actually looked like. It didn't resemble the picture in the book, or the old man that some of the fairy tales referred to. It was creepy looking, and wasn't at all pleased to see him. Their eyes met in the shadowy light, the stranger's round and dark, with hidden lights like obsidian. Before it could move again, possibly disappearing through the ground again, Keith had raised his waiting camera, and snapped its picture. The figure was flooded with the hot, white light. It threw up a limb, a skinny arm, in front of its eyes, and then lunged for Keith, shouting. Keith tried to hold the being off at arm's length, but it let him have it with all four limbs, kicking and scratching with long nails like talons. He pushed it away, but it sprang back to him like a yo-yo. They grappled all around the end of the garden, and then something hit Keith solidly on the side of the head.

He cried out. The landscape around him, the house, the garden, the sea and the stone, faded away into darkness. As he felt himself losing consciousness, the angry voice muttered in his ears. "No speech ye shall have ever in your life of three of the pleasures: women, wine, nor gold. I curse yer tongue as so ye've cursed my een!" The voice grew into a wail, and died away.

When he came to, Keith was lying on his side in a shallow puddle of water. His head felt like he'd spent the night drinking rotgut, or maybe cider, but he couldn't remember a day in the last month when he'd had more than a beer, two at the most. He pried his eyes open. That was no help. It was just as dark outside as it was under his eyelids. The summer sun hadn't left any part of Scotland in absolute darkness for the last month. So where was he? Or was he blind? He held up a hand in front of his nose. Nothing. Not even a shadow. Groaning, he started to sit up.

Suddenly, his invisible whiskers broadcast an alert to his brain: Don't move any further to the right! Keith raised a tentative hand toward his right shoulder. A quarter inch beyond it was a rough stone wall, damp and slimy. Ech. Keith's fingers recoiled. So he was inside something, he thought. *Well, that's progress. Nothing's wrong with my eyes. Where is this place? And what?*

Using hands and whiskers, he explored his new environment. The invisible wiry hairs spread forward as well as to the side, kept him from smashing his nose into the stone walls. It was a tiny chamber, roughly round like a flattened sphere, almost four feet high, and about five feet in diameter, too small for him either to stand up or lie down in any comfort. The slimy stuff smelled fresh and green, like moss, so he stopped flinching from its touch. Two feet up in the middle of one side was an irregular hole as wide as his shoulders and approximately the shape of an inverted triangle. Apart from several smaller holes on the opposite side of the floor, it was the only thing which suggested an exit from the bubble of rock. He was alone, but that, he reflected, depended on whom you're alone from. Holl was nowhere nearby, which was bad, but then neither was the *bodach*, which was good.

"Oh, well, I had no idea the little guy would get so mad. I must be right under the hill," he reasoned, turning his head upward to gaze blindly into the darkness. He wondered how long he had been down there. A good deep yawn summoned up no sensation of fatigue, suggesting that he had slept at least a few hours. It was probably near dawn outside. He felt for his watch. It was gone. For a wild moment, he considered pounding on the ceiling of his chamber and shouting for help. "Nope, I'm probably halfway to Australia. No one would hear a thing. I've got to get out of here on my own."

It was cool in the chamber, but not too oppressively so. Keith had read somewhere that the constant temperature underground was 57° Fahrenheit. The scientists who had discovered that never accounted for the subjective reaction to damp, which made it feel more chilly. Keith was glad of his tweed jacket and woolly hat, but suspected that those garments were going to make it difficult for him to wriggle through the passageway. If only he knew how far the passage extended, or what it looked like. It could be a long narrow tube, or it might drop off suddenly if this was a small bubble on the side of a larger cavern. He wished he hadn't dropped the electric torch. It would be so comforting right now to see.

What he needed was some alternate form of illumination. He wondered if Enoch's lessons in magic extended to providing light in slimy, moss-covered underground caverns. Keith stuck his head through the opening, and felt a tiny breeze of cool air. There was no source of light anywhere nearby, but he wasn't imagining it: the air was moving. He raised two fingers to feel its strength and source of direction. "Great!" he said out loud. "This opens out into the upper air someplace. I'll just follow it. Ow!"

Keith pulled his head back, clutching his jaw. It felt like something had just socked him on both sides of his face. One of his teeth had just suffered a stabbing pain in the cold air. It hurt abominably. He probed it with his tongue. The top surface of the tooth felt rough, and his tongue dipped into a depression that hadn't been there earlier. "I think my filling fell out when I hit my head," Keith moaned. "Great. Here I am being Darby O'Gill, or maybe Rip Van Winkle in the depths of the Scottish mountains, and I've got dental problems." On further investigation, he discovered that every one of his silver fillings were gone. They couldn't all have fallen out. There had to be another reason, maybe a magical one.

Keith grimaced. The *bodach*, teaching him another lesson. That was probably where his watch had gone, too. Well, fixing his mouth would have to wait until he got the mouth, and the rest of his body, out of this cavern and back in civilization.

"No offense!" he said hopefully to the air, wondering if the *bodach* was listening. "Sorry I spooked you! I was just being curious." No answer. He sighed. It was probably long gone, sulking in a hole somewhere. He wished Holl or Enoch was with him. He thought of Diane, too, and wondered if he'd ever see her again. Well, there was no use being morbid. Either he would get himself out of here, or he wouldn't. It wasn't hopeless, he told his twisting stomach. He had a lot of resources he hadn't even used yet. So with that firm resolution, why did he feel like he wanted to cry? Light, that's what he needed. It would lift his mood if he could see.

To make light, he needed something that had natural tendencies toward giving off light. Crystals of some kinds did, when you crushed them. Unfortunately, if the rock around him was of the same type as the stuff on the surface, and he had no reason to believe it wasn't, the matrix was too flimsy to have very productive crystals, and he had nothing with which he could crush it. It ought to be granite or quartz, not shale. So what else was there with him?

He shifted to get out of the puddle, which was getting deeper— probably because he was sitting on one of its drainage holes—and moved closer to one of the moss-covered walls. There was a soft gurgle as the water ran out. Keith sat idly playing with the clumps of moss. Didn't decaying vegetation have light-emitting qualities? Unless this chamber flooded completely at times, washing away all the dead stuff, there should be plenty here to make a light.

Nervously, he stroked a bit of moss and thought about how to construct the magical process around it. This was the first time he had tried to do anything serious without supervision. On the outer surface, the moss was like damp fur, but it got more fibrous inside where it hung on to the rock face. Keith tried to think of the dead fibers as bulb filaments. Reaching down deep inside himself, he worked at *knowing* that it was right for moss to glow in the dark, that it did it all the time, and shaped his energies to fit that thought.

He opened his eyes. It was still dark. He sank back, feeling defeated. Doing magic took a lot out of him. Well, there was no point in waiting for the cross-town bus. He'd have to make his way out in the dark. Keith started to feel his way toward the opening, and then realized that he could just see it, as a blacker darkness at the other side of the bubble. There was the faintest, spooky glimmer everywhere in the chamber, just on the edge of vision, like fluorescent lines in a haunted house. It wasn't a dramatic difference, but it was good enough. He had light! Now, to get out of here.

Once he could distinguish the shape of the triangular passage, it occurred to him how uncomfortable it would be to crawl through. He'd have to keep one knee on each of the sloping faces, and hope he didn't get stuck anywhere. His own weight would press him into the trench like peanut butter in a celery stalk. It was a wonder to him how the *bodach* had gotten him in there. Never mind; he was leaving.

An absurd litany sang itself in his head, "You'd better go before you go." Feeling a little foolish, he relieved himself over one of the drainage holes. The simple, natural action took part of the urgency off his need to get moving, and gave him one fewer concern to think about.

"Okay, here goes." Expelling a deep breath, Keith crawled into the passage and, with an effort of will, dragged the spell in after him. The faint glow touched the walls of the narrow tunnel wherever there was moss. It extended the full length of his body behind, but only a couple of feet in front of him. He convinced the glow to move further forward, illumining more of the passage ahead. His legs and back could take care of themselves. There was so little room he could hardly turn his head to look back over his shoulder.

He found as he went along that he could see better as he became accustomed to the fairy light of the moss. The light didn't extend far enough to give him much view ahead, so Keith let his whiskers guide him through the zig-zagging tube. His hands and knees shifted and slipped on the slick stone. Several times his supports shot out from under him, dropping him painfully onto his stomach in the narrow crevice between the rocks. Below him in the angle of the slabs, a trickle of water flowed back toward the way he had come. "At least I can tell I'm going uphill," he reasoned.

Sometimes the tunnel was so tight that his nose was only an inch from the streaks of mosslight. The layers of rock were neither smooth nor evenly laid. The upthrust which had exposed this interstice through which he was crawling had also splintered pieces which shifted suddenly under his hands. More than once, Keith had to catch himself to keep from sliding back toward the round chamber. He edged forward, concentrating on keeping the fairy light in sight. Suddenly, he found a place where the glow was interrupted, and resumed a few feet further along the tunnel.

He lowered himself and crept up to the dark spot on his belly, and peered over the edge. Perhaps it was just a dip in the path, and he could drop into it on his feet, and hoist himself up on the other side. There was no light beneath him. He felt the stone with his fingers, and discovered that the slab he was on ended. His fingers walked downward until his whole arm was extended into the abyss. Nothing at all lay within reach. He called down into it, but no echo came back. With his thumb, he loosened a pebble and dropped it into the gap. A long, long interval went by before he heard the faint *plop* as it struck, but it was so far away he couldn't tell if it had hit water or more stone. That was *deep*. He squinted up at the mosslight on the other side of the gap. It would take almost a running start to get over it, and he was already traveling uphill. Once committed to crossing, he would be unable to pull himself back again.

Keith rose to his knees. He was thankful that he couldn't see the sheer drop into the pit. It would only frighten him to know that what he was about to do was impossible. He pushed back half a pace, and then with all his strength, flung himself across.

He landed on the other side, and hastily scrabbled up onto the new slab, bracing his knees against the side to keep from falling backwards. His legs slipped partway into the gap, and he flailed his arms for anything to grab onto.

A long splinter of stone protruding from the right side of the tunnel met his grasp. He battened onto it like a sea urchin clinging for dear life to its ship. Just as he slipped past his waist into the pit, he got his arms around the stone, and hauled himself upward. The stone wrenched partway out of its socket, but by then Keith was sitting on the far side of the gap.

He sat on the edge of the pit panting. His heart was beating so loudly it was pounding in his ears. He had to go on.

Crawling over one of the gigantic splinters, he found that the passage had leveled out. The stream issued from beneath a new slab in a different direction, which had only a handspan's clearance. He could no longer follow the flow of the water.

"Last oasis for twenty miles," he told himself. This junction was the largest opening in which he had been, with just enough room to stretch. He wiggled his shoulders, feeling the cramp relax slightly. Twisting and maneuvering in the narrow tunnel with difficulty, he reversed his position so his head was hanging over the edge of the slab just above the source of the stream. With a cupped hand, he scooped up water. It was cold, and except for being mineral heavy, tasted pure. It was probably rainwater, precipitating down through the porous construction of the rock.

He became conscious of a panting, gasping noise echoing around him, and felt hot sweat break out on his forehead in fear. Was there something following him? Was the *bodach* there right behind him. Keith felt a wash of terror break over him. He held his breath to listen, and the sound ceased. Keith expelled air in a gasp that turned into relieved, nearly hysterical laughter, and heard the gasping start again. "It's me."

It was his own breathing, magnified by the enveloping walls. The *bodach* was certainly seeing to it that he was sufficiently punished for disturbing it. He had nearly scared himself to death.

At the top of the next slab, he came to a dead end. Keith was forced to snake his way downhill slightly and to the right, where he had seen the blackness of a new passageway. His sodden jacket caught on a projection. Keith stopped to pull it loose. It didn't want to come. He yanked. The fabric came free suddenly, sending him sliding quickly down the tube on the mass of wet wool as if he had been greased.

"Help!"

Keith tried to stop his fall by sticking out his hands and feet into the tunnel's narrow sides, but that only got them bruised. At last, with an effort, he rose to his knees, bracing his back against the top of the sloping tunnel. He knelt there panting for a moment, before cautiously beginning the climb back to his turnoff. He was getting tired, and, he hated to admit, hungry. He had been too excited to eat much dinner. How long ago was that? A few hours or a few days?

The passage to the right led him to a perfectly level T-junction. Keith waited for a moment, feeling for the air currents before he decided which way to go. The only clue he had for leaving this labyrinth was the wind from the outside world. He put his chin down on his folded arms to rest.

It was only the faintest hint, but the breeze felt stronger against his left cheek and whiskers than his right. In a moment, Keith picked himself up and rubbed his palms together. They were raw and hurt, and he knew that if he could see them, they'd be red. He thought about taking his socks off his feet and putting them on his hands.

"So long as I'm walking on them, that is. I'm not up to crawling like this any more," Keith admitted to himself. "It's just not a habit that stays with you." He decided against it only because he needed the sensitivity of his fingers to help guide him through this labyrinth. Somehow, he'd make it up to his shredded palms later.

There seemed to be more moss wedged into the crevices of the stones. Some of it dangled in his way like ghostly spider webs. The glow had increased to where Keith could distinguish the outline of his own hands and arms. Realizing that he couldn't go on indefinitely without food, he decided to try and alter the spell. If the spelled light could follow him so easily, maybe a ring of the glow could go up toward the sunshine outside, and come back toward him, over and over again, like a neon sign arrow in reverse. He could follow that out. Of course, there were dangers in an idea like that, if the end of the line terminated in a hole too small for him to crawl through, or over a sheer cliff face. Or maybe he was so far underground it would take forever for the light to get back to him. But if the idea worked, Keith felt it was worth the risk. He concentrated, and the glow diminished around him to total darkness.

He waited. Nothing happened for a long time, and Keith felt his hopeful mood start to ebb. "I didn't know when I was well off," he groaned, and started to reverse the spell.

A tiny light appeared just out of the edge of vision, and crept toward him. It was no more than a bit of spidery tracing on the floor, but Keith stared at it with growing joy. "It worked!" he crowed. He crawled energetically along it, as it faded out beneath his hands.

Periodically, his neon sign would disappear completely. Keith took these opportunities to stop and rest until the sun-line renewed itself again. He was making progress steadily upward. Without a regular source of light, he had to rely more heavily than before on his whiskers. He blessed Holl for giving them to him as last year's Christmas gift. At the time, they had been a kind of running family joke. Now, they were saving him.

"I wish Holl was here. No, that's rotten. I wish I was with Holl. He's probably drinking tea and playing with Mrs. Mackenzie's cats." The discomfort in his hands and knees was increasing, but he ignored it. He had to.

As Keith had feared, the next turnoff ended in a T-junction at a solid stone wall with a hand-sized hole in it. The light, instead of following either of the available paths, came through the wall. In dismay, Keith slapped at the rock. His palm stung, and he winced.

"Now what? Hey, spell, this doesn't help!"

The mosslight continued to glow dispassionately through the hole in the wall. Apparently, this was all the aid his spell could muster. Keith put his eye to the opening and squinted through.

There seemed to be a passageway on the other side, because the light followed the thickness of the wall and then dropped off. He could see a thinner line reappear at some distance away, but that was all. Flipping a mental coin, he chose to turn right. The fine yellow glow died away again as he crept away from the T-junction, leaving him in the dark.

This path turned unexpectedly again and again, growing smaller all the while. Keith had to pay close attention to his whiskers to avoid bashing his head on the irregular ceiling. The tunnel had narrowed to barely a foot in diameter. In the end, he was reduced to creeping forward on his belly like a snake. He had to crawl with one arm extended forward to keep from getting his shoulders wedged.

"I feel like I'm being swallowed by the mountain," he thought. He put his head down and scrabbled his way out of the tight spot. Without the light breeze playing constantly on his face, he knew he would go out of his mind with fear. He had to keep from thinking about the tons of rock, poised above him only by a fluke of nature. If they did any more blasting nearby, the strata could come down on him and squash him flat, and no one would ever know.

The passage led him steadily around in a loop that went in the general direction of his mosslight. Any minute, he expected to see the burning yellow-white line. That hope was almost all that kept him pushing forward through the stone tube.

Keith crept over a slight bump in the passage floor, and down again. As soon as his hands touched down, he realized he had found the stream once more. There was two inches of water pooling in the worn floor of the tunnel, only this time, it was flowing in the direction he was going. Miserably, he plowed through it, feeling the water soak in through his clothes to his chafed and chilled skin.

He came to a Y-shaped intersection. The left-hand side of the Y leveled off, and its ceiling rose to nearly three feet in height. Keith measured it with a tentative hand following the wall in the darkness. It was a much more inviting tunnel than the right turning. Keith blinked. There was a tiny spark of light down toward the left. That was the way back to his mosslight! Happily, he rose to his hands and knees, and crawled as fast as he could toward the light.

The golden glow grew much faster than he thought it would. I must be a lot closer to the way out, Keith thought, cheerfully. Hot bath and food soon! He was able to urge greater efforts from his hands and knees by promising them that their ordeal would be over very shortly. Head bent to take the strain off his back, Keith made his way along the tunnel. Strangely, the air was heavy and damp here, instead of fresh, as it had been all along the way the mosslight took before.

A sudden roar shook the passage under Keith's knees, like the sound of thunder. His eyes flew up in horror. There was a golden glow only a few feet before him, but it wasn't his little line of spelled moss. It was two points of light like eyes, and the rest of the fearsome face was coalescing around them as he watched. There was a brief suggestion of fangs, then horns, then a loose and stringy mane. He had blundered into something's lair. What was it? The creature roared again, right in his face.

Keith let out a yell and turned almost double on himself to get away from the wide open maw. He backpedaled in the tunnel, flipped over like a cat in a box, and fled back up the passage. The apparition pursued him, its roar causing the whole mountain to vibrate. Pebbles worked loose from the ceiling and fell on him as he scrabbled toward the lower tunnel.

Maybe it's too big to follow me, he prayed. He couldn't make any speed in the low tunnel, not on his elbows and toes, not in the water. All too soon, his whiskers signaled that there was an obstruction in his way. He ducked, and squirmed into the low passage, huddling his body into the smallest knot he could.

The bellowing face was almost on top of him now, bearing down on him like an approaching express train. Keith had nowhere to retreat. The yellow fangs clashed against one another like a boar's tusks, and the hot strings of the mane whipped like summer lightning in the utter blackness of the tunnel, leaving burning afterimages. Terrified, Keith threw his arms over his head and waited for the inevitable. He was going to die.

In his ears, the roaring grew and grew, buffeting his ears with sound. Keith imagined the fangs lowering toward his back. His skin tautened, waiting for the first points to tear through the cloth, and then his flesh.

Nothing touched him. His whiskers didn't so much as twitch. The beast's noise died away suddenly, leaving silence in its wake. Keith looked up. The beast was nowhere in sight. It had vanished.

If something that big was heading straight at him, and it didn't pass him, and it didn't have room to turn around, A) it must have been an illusion, or B) it went right into one of the stone sides of the tunnel without using a door. Keith was pulling for option A with all his might. In any case, he recognized it as a warning. He'd have to follow the right fork, water, low ceiling and all. The next time, those fangs probably wouldn't be illusionary.

He wondered briefly if other magical things affected each other. Could passing through another magic field possibly have taken off the spell that the *bodach* laid on him? It was worth an experiment. He felt in his mouth for his fillings. Nothing. His teeth were still hollow and aching in the cold. He tried bucking the terms of the curse. "Say, mister, can you give me change for a d—, d—, doh—." He attempted heroically to force the word 'dollar' out of his mouth, and his teeth still ached horribly whenever the cold air hit the open cavities. "No way," he said unhappily. "I need expert help."

The right passage bore a striking resemblance to household plumbing. Keith found himself snaking through smoother tunnels than before, though they were low and narrow. His jacket and trousers were no longer catching on the stone.

Something clicked as he put his hand down on it in the water. It felt like a flat stick. It was too knobbly to ease his way over, so he elected to push it along in front of him in the extended hand. As he crept downhill, the flow of the water started to become stronger. Little trickles joined the main tunnel from small cataracts that rained down on Keith as he passed. Now there was a genuine stream gurgling around him.

Keith's whiskers broadcast an emergency message as soon as his hands touched a ring of rock ahead of him. This was going to be a really tight fit. Gently, Keith eased forward, trying to ignore the water building up behind him. First one shoulder passed through, then the other. He pushed all the air out of his ribcage, and got his chest through next. Everything was going fine until he tried to get his hips into the hole, and remembered too late about his Pocket Scots Dictionary. It stuck up like a deadbolt in his rear jeans pocket, holding him pinned head down under the lip of the rock. Keith's heart started pounding. He bit his tongue. His legs were now awash in stream water. He kicked.

Bracing his elbows on the other side of the ring, Keith took a deep breath and shoved *down*. There was a rip as his jeans pocket tore loose. He was free! With nothing left to hold him in place, Keith tumbled over the lip of the rock and down, followed by a cataract of water.

He landed with a splash in a fast-flowing pond several feet deep, which swirled him around and then dragged him into a broader stream leading further into the bowels of the mountain. Keith banged into rocks and projections sticking out into the water. Gasping, he fought to stay at the surface, but not too high, fearing there might be a low ceiling above him.

His mind started composing epitaphs for an empty tomb in his family cemetery back in Illinois: "Keith Doyle, Died Aged 20. He Rediscovered the Little Folk." "Keith Doyle, Died Aged 20. He Duked it out with a Bogey and Lost." "Keith Doyle, Died Aged 20, Drowned...."

Boy, am I morbid, he thought. At that moment, the stream turned, and deposited him, along with a lot of other debris, in a small hollow. Gratefully, he crawled onto the small bank and held tightly to an outcropping of coarse rock as a shower of small pebbles cascaded down on him from higher up. Every square inch of his body felt as if it had been bruised. I wonder if I should be talking about muchnesses or something, like Alice in Wonderland down the rabbit hole. He coughed up stream water and gasped, tossing his wet hair out of his eyes.

He remembered the voice of the *bodach* as it threw the curse on him, which would prevent him from talking about liquor, money, or women ever again. *I can live with it*, Keith vowed. All he could think of were longing visions of food, warmth, and not being wet any more. *Maybe Holl can find a way to take the curse off before I have to deal with it in public.*

He realized that he could think about the future again. Though he was still lost, he was safe for the moment. Even exhausted, that thought gave him some hope. So long as the *bodach* didn't pop out of nowhere again and put him back in the round cave.

Chapter Nineteen

"Now, vhere exactly did you lose him?" the Master asked, pausing at the gate to the Mackenzie garden.

"This way," Holl said, leading the others down to the holed stone. Though he still resented giving up authority, he had to admire how quickly the Master could sum up the facts of a situation. It was possible for him to walk in cold and instantly take over in a crisis. Holl was still a schoolboy in comparison. The Master studied the holed stone with interest, but then focused on the whiskey bottle, as Holl had done, as a clue to the way the *bodach* worked. He stood rubbing a fragment of glass between his fingers, thinking.

Holl could sense the directions his thoughts took. He had some finding process he wanted to try, and he didn't want the strange but helpful Mr. Michaels to watch him. That meant Holl had to remove the stranger. Fine and good. With two parties searching, the chances of finding Keith Doyle were raised significantly. He cleared his throat and spoke up. "We'll continue looking in Mr. Michaels' car. It was his suggestion the other day that Keith may have become lost and strayed further. I'll let Mrs. Mackenzie know you're here."

"Gut," the Master said, seeming to come back from very far away. "You go that vay, and ve vill start to familiarize ourselves vith this area. Ve can meet later and share our impressions." He pottered around the garden, and looked over the edge of the field.

"Dismissed, are we?" the Big Person asked, feeling left a little behind by the conversation. "Come on, then. I've got a topo map of this part of the island." He led the way back toward the house. He wasn't sure what the other two actually had to do with his case, but so long as he could keep his quarry under his eye, he was happy.

Diane stood under the apple trees, swaying slightly with fatigue. She had had little sleep in the last twenty four hours, but she was too worried to go lie down and let the Little Folk alone. The Master noticed as she tried to stifle a yawn, and smiled.

"Mees Londen, I vould be grateful for your assistance, but it is not necessary." As Diane tried to protest, he interrupted her. "I know vhat promises the others extracted from you to look after my vell-being, but I assure you, I vill be fine."

Diane forced her brain to clear, shoving down the sleep toxins like coffee under a plunger. "No, I can't do that. A promise is a promise. Your son Enoch would slice me into little bits and build lanterns out of me if I didn't make sure you were all right. I don't know why they asked, because you'll probably end up looking after me. Besides, I have *got* to know what's happened to Keith. Is he alive?" she asked plaintively.

"Yes, I belief he is, but he is a long vay from here. Let us go into the house and find our starting point."

When he felt like making the effort, the small teacher could be charming. In Diane's opinion, the Master positively buttered up Mrs. Mackenzie while she was showing them the house in general and their rooms in specific.

"Qvite a lofely place," the Master insisted. "A hafen uf calm and beauty against the backdrop uf the vild sea outside."

"I wasna expecting two, since the lad only asked for one extra room," the landlady said, much flattered by the little man with the thick German accent. "It's good fortune I've just seen off one of my other guests. Pity about the young man, is it not? The local constable is having a wee look around for him. He's likely gathering his wits. So easy to take a wrong turning when you don't know the way. The road dips away when you're no more than a few paces doun it."

"Funny he couldn't see those creepy stones on the top of the hill," Diane mused.

"Ah, weel, they're not visible from every side," Mrs. Mackenzie explained.

"Thank you," the Master said. "Ve vill endeafor not to be in your vay."

The landlady left them alone in the room shared by Keith and Holl. It was an airy, pleasant chamber, the twin beds covered by yellow and white. With the small suitcases zipped closed, it looked as if both occupants had just stepped out for a moment. Diane flopped woefully on one of the beds and folded her arms.

"Now what do we do?"

The Master, who was rooting through Keith's belongings, didn't answer her. At last he rose, brandishing a gray wool sock. "This vill do."

"What for?" Diane asked, casting a skeptical eye on his discovery. Above the ankle, the sock featured a grimy brown ring that matched the dark soil outside.

"It is for the finding," the Master explained, beckoning to her to follow him out the door.

In the garden, he brushed away the broken glass from the place in the grass nearest the low stone plinth. While Diane watched curiously, the Master knelt and placed the sock on the grass, and held his hands over it, as if he were warming them.

She stared at the sock when he moved his hands away. It looked no different than it had before. In a moment, it began to twitch. Diane checked for a breeze, but the air was fairly still. In any case, it couldn't have made the sock do what it did next.

As if had been pulled by a magnet, the sock started to slide along the ground, very slowly and jerkily at first, and then with increasing speed.

"Ah, I vas not expecting such a strong response," the Master said, rising swiftly to his feet and trotting after the sock. "This is fery gut. Keep an eye on it." It disappeared around the corner of the garden and under the bushes toward the road. They ran after it.

"I've heard of laundry walking by itself, but this is the first time I've ever seen it," Diane admitted.

The Master, who was rather fond of Diane but did not show emotions easily, grunted a bit at her witticism. The matter was too serious to admit humor. The grey sock, moving as fast as a snake, had gained the road, and was already yards ahead of them when they emerged from the garden. Diane, with her longer legs, paced the sock as it took a sharp right at the bottom of the road and slid across to the left side.

"Where's it going?" she shouted back to the Master, who was huffing to catch up. The wind, now coming in off the sea, whisked away his words. "What?"

"Follow it!" the Master called. "Don't lose it! It is taking us to Meester Doyle!"

Holl felt in much better spirits this morning. Perhaps it was just the arrival of the Master which gave him confidence, but he had an indefinable feeling that Keith Doyle was alive, well, and not too far away. Mr. Michaels had driven him inland several miles, and they had explored the narrow tracks which led off the main road. Keith was nowhere in sight, and no one they met had seen anyone answering to his description. Michaels seemed concerned for him.

Holl, preoccupied with organizing his thoughts, put off his attempts at cheerful conversation.

Instinctively, Holl knew that they were going the wrong way. As soon as they had circled back through Garynahine and were once again approaching Callanish from the south, the fragmented senses he had thought too scrambled to do him any good suddenly pulled together. They were now going the right way. He could almost imagine he heard the American student's mind somewhere ahead.

"I think we'll find him in this direction," Holl suggested.

"How the blazes do you know that?" Michaels demanded, slewing his gaze left at the vivid young face next to him.

"Only a feeling," Holl answered absently. He could sense the Master's strong personality nearby. It was on a vector to intersect with the way they were driving. Fairly soon, he and Michaels would pass by him. 'Triangulation' was what they called this process, and it seemed to be working. "I think he's near the sea. I think he'd head for the water."

They drove back into Callanish by the lower road, which took them past the public telephone booth, and the intersection that led to the farm. Before too long, he noticed a fall of blond hair deep in the field to the left.

"Stop! That's Diane," Holl said. Michaels pulled to the side of the road, and the Little Person jumped out. Once he stood up, he could see the Master. They were climbing over a hillock of peat. Another moment and they would have been out of sight on the other side. He pushed through the wires of the fence and ran to them.

"What news?" Holl shouted.

They looked up at the sound of his voice. Michaels had parked the car, and was climbing over the fence to join them. Quickly, Diane picked up the topographical map she was carrying, and pretended to sight down it over the edge of the sharp fall of the land to her right.

"Keith Doyle is here," the Master announced.

Holl leaned under the lip of rock and shouted into the dark tunnel entrance he found there. "Keith Doyle! This way. Come out, Keith Doyle."

Keith clambered up further into the fall of pebbles, and drew his legs out of the stream's flow. With blind hands, he patted the mossy wall over his head, seeking an escape from the underground river bed. He knelt suddenly in a trickle of water traveling across his shelf.

There had to be a way back to the source, perhaps big enough for him to fit through. Hopefully, he followed the flow upstream. About five feet from where he had washed up was a large opening. The sides were rough, but it was more than adequate in size. He leaned through it, prepared to crawl onward.

"Yahoo!" He let out a shout of delight, which echoed in the cavern. On the other side of the opening he could see the golden lines of mosslight, banking the narrow cataract of water. The magic was gleaming more brightly than ever. He was never more glad to see anything in his life. It seemed the stream had not dragged him out of his way. He had probably been paralleling the airway all along.

Hands and knees straddling the cataract, he scurried along the floor of the cavern. Every muscle protested.

"Boy, after this, a marathon actually standing up would be a piece of cake!"

The passage twisted and wound upward in a more sinuous, smoother fashion and at a more gentle angle than had any of the tunnels he had been in yet. Keith had a hopeful suspicion, but was trying to keep from believing in it, in case it was another disappointment. In a few more turns, there was a glimmer of light ahead of him, not the gold of mosslight, but the genuine white glow of sunlight. Excitement spurred him the rest of the way. His hands and knees slipped painfully into the stream bed once and again, but he splashed his way out and kept going.

What if the bright light was a decoy, he thought suddenly, stopping in midcrawl. What if the bodach had decided to keep him running around in circles for the rest of his life, which wouldn't be long, stuck underground as he was. Confused and exhausted, he collapsed down full length on the wet stone.

Holl's voice intruded itself into his consciousness, almost like a sound heard in a dream. "Come out, Keith Doyle." It had to be an illusion, but he was willing to grasp at straws. With one more effort, he pushed himself forward.

He emerged into the brilliant day. The moss under his hands changed suddenly to cress and then to warm grass. The sky seemed blinding white at first, but resolved through a squint into blue. Keith drew a huge breath. He was out! Grateful and exhausted, he threw his hands out in front of him and flopped onto the grass. The wind sang Hallelujahs in his ears. In a moment he would get up, he promised himself.

Something smooth under his hand moved. He thought it was a stone, but stones usually didn't move by themselves. Nervously, he raised his head to look. In front of him was a shoe. A woman's casual shoe. There was a woman's leg in it, and another one with a matching foot and leg beside it. He raised his head further. At the top of a much foreshortened body surrounded by a corona of tossing white light was a face that he knew. It was Diane. There were tears in her eyes as she stooped down to him.

Surprised, he stuttered out a greeting. "H-hi, there." His voice sounded rusty in his own ears.

"Hello, sailor," she returned, relieved to find him safe, but quick enough to throw him a line. "Buy a girl a drink?"

Snappy retorts having to do with money, women, and liquor swirled through his mind, but because of the creature's mocking curse, none of them would go anywhere near his mouth. In the effort to say something, ANYTHING, in reply, Keith passed out.

Michaels joined the others in jubilation as they gathered up their lost lad, patting him on the cheeks to bring him back to consciousness. The young man's clothes were torn and wet, and the red waves of his hair lay plastered to his head. There were streaks of moss on his clothes and skin, but he was alive. Michaels found he was a relieved as the rest to find that Danny O'Day was all right. The youth had been abducted, all right, by one of his scummy compatriots, and then pushed out into one of these littoral caves. Can't trust 'em even when you have to work with 'em, he thought. Good thing they'd been there waiting when the youth crawled out of his hidey hole. Sun blinded as he was, he'd have fallen smack over the precipice only a few feet beyond the cavern mouth.

"Meester Doyle," Mr. Alfheim said patiently, as they raised the youth to his feet, "I see I find you as I have always found you, prostrate and half in, half out of trouble."

Michaels chuckled. "Come on," he said. "It's only a few hundred yards back to your B&B. I'll give you a lift."

The young man seemed astonished. "D'you mean after all that I'm *walking distance* from the garden?" he croaked.

As he helped hand the young man into the car, Michaels gave him a quick pat down. Nothing on him. In fact, his clothes had been half torn off him, leaving no way to tell if there had been a drop or not. There was no money on the lad, not a coin—literally empty handed except for a broken stick. Time to report back to the chief.

So long as O'Day had been recovered alive, he had to remove himself and go back to observation. His well-being was no longer Michaels' concern. He'd already jeopardized his cover enough.

In a daze, Keith, kept upright by Diane on one side and Holl on the other, wiped his shoes carefully on the mat.

"They're just about hopeless," Diane said, looking at the worn shoes. The toes were nearly worn away, and something had ripped off the metal buckles. She squeezed Keith's arm. His hands were still half-balled up, probably a muscular spasm of some kind, and he was clutching a piece of old stick. She was trying not to cry at the pitiful picture he made. "So are your clothes. You look half dead."

"I feel great," Keith insisted, smiling brilliantly at her. He made his way unsteadily into the house.

"Is that you, Keith dear?" Mrs. Mackenzie called from the sitting room.

Keith cleared his throat with difficulty. He remembered he hadn't had anything to drink in hours. "Yes, ma'am."

The door to the front room swung open. Instead of the patient face of Mrs. Mackenzie, Keith was confronted with the furious countenance of Miss Anderson. Professor Parker appeared under her arm, and studied Keith with sympathetic eyes. Keith goggled at them.

"Where have you been?" the teacher demanded. "I have had the Educatours main office calling every few hours wondering if you have been found! When you hadn't reported to the site for two days or been seen by any of the others, I came here. Mrs. Mackenzie told me that young Holl had been beside himself because you took it into your head to go wandering in the moonlight two days ago. Your irresponsibility has caused a great deal of inconvenience and worry for a lot of people. I've been concerned for you, too, but the contract you signed specified that you would behave with care because Educatours is responsible for your welfare while you are part of one of our groups!"

Keith tried to explain where he had been, with an occasional astounded glance back at the Elf Master, who was standing in the doorway, out of the line of fire. He still couldn't believe the little teacher was there with him. Miss Anderson let him get out half a sentence, and then started her lecture off anew. Educatours couldn't be responsible for such inconsideration. If he had been seriously hurt or killed, the company was liable for damages to Keith's family.

He waited for her to run down, and tried to apologize when she paused for breath. "I got lost, Miss Anderson. I'm sorry. I don't know this area at all." He started to put down the bit of old stick in his hand. Holl reached out to take it from him, but Professor Parker beat him to it with a swift grab that surprised both of them.

"Miss Anderson!" the archaeologist yelped. "Look here!" With careful fingers, he brushed away the traces of mud caking the flat stick. A pattern of lines began to emerge. "Forgive me making a mess of your rug, Mrs. Mackenzie," Parker said, without looking up. "What a wonder! It's a comb! Horn, with sawn bone teeth inset. Dear, dear, dear, look at it! This is a very important find. It's contemporary to the Cairns, I'm certain of it, and in such fine shape. Yes, look at those markings. How fortunate it isn't broken."

Miss Anderson stopped her tirade, and looked down curiously at the object the professor was holding. "Keith, where did you find this?"

"In a…a streambed," Keith said carefully, not wanting to explain how his adventure actually began. "I guess I forgot I was holding it."

"He found the underground tunnel system on the shores west of here," Holl explained, pointing out the location on his map for the two Big People. "He must have become turned around down there after he found it."

"That was very dangerous," Miss Anderson said sternly. She had been somewhat appeased by the find of the comb, but was still concerned for her company. "Even if you are an expert spelunker you could have died down there."

"I was fine, until one of the tunnels flooded behind me," Keith said truthfully, hoping he appeared to be more of a hero than he looked. His stained and torn clothes looked even more pitiful in daylight than he had feared. His jaw was aching in the cool air, and his eyes were going nuts trying to keep out the blinding light of midday.

"Off you go to bed, then," Miss Anderson ordered. "I will tell everyone that you are back. Everyone has missed you greatly. I hope we can expect you back on the site in a day or so? Going into caverns without a helmet, hmp!"

She exited magnificently. Parker followed her out, chuckling and cooing over the comb, now cradled protectively in a handkerchief.

Stripping off his sodden, torn clothes, Keith staggered through a hot shower and collapsed into his bed. The softness of the mattress and pillow came up to meet his shoulders and head. He scrunched his fingers into the clean sheets, and grinned with pure pleasure.

"No moss," he said happily.

Holl sat on the edge of the other bed and watched his Big friend's face. "Mrs. Mackenzie has bought the story that you went treasure hunting for the dig and lost yourself, my lad, and she's making you tea and a hot meal. Now, what really happened to you?"

With the help of a pad of paper and pencil, and a lot of humorous sallies at his expense from Holl, Keith managed to explain his problems while avoiding any references to the three conditions of the curse. He discovered he couldn't actually mention the curse either, but Holl guessed the problem from context.

"You've come to no real harm," Holl announced at last, very amused. "What a thing for a lad like you to be unable to speak of three of the pleasures in life. But a typical Gaelic curse. Those...*bodach* have a sense of humor."

"I don't think that could have been a *bodach*. They're supposed to be beneficent, and this one sure wasn't," Keith said emphatically. "Ooch." He clutched his jaw.

"'*Bodach*' means not only 'old man,' but 'spectre or bugbear,' if you'd read up on the Gaelic, Keith Doyle. In any case, it was something that you Big Folk can't classify with ease. And why do you expect beneficence, surprising a millennia-old hermit entity with a flash camera in the middle of the night?" Holl was enormously relieved, but not above taking a little of his anxiety out on Keith to teach him a lesson. "He's probably never been so taken aback in his long life. By the way, you owe me a few pounds sterling, too. Your pictures came out. I've got them right here." He showed the two frames to the red-haired youth, whose eyes widened with excitement. They showed Keith's quarry turned captor, standing up from a crouch, and then coming toward the camera with its skinny arms outstretched. Both were perfectly in focus. Keith was jubilant.

"Thanks, Holl! Those pictures are worth a mi—a mi—," Keith stammered. The word 'million' was stuck in the top of his mouth like peanut butter, and his tongue couldn't dislodge it.

Holl grinned. "Yer welcome, widdy." He got up to go.

"And Holl? It's nice to see you back in one piece again." Keith tugged the lobe of his own ear significantly, and smiled. Holl returned his smile, and closed the door behind him.

Chapter Twenty

Diane and the Master looked up as Holl joined them in the sitting room. The fire was turned on, warming the room pleasantly. Holl spread out his chilled hands before its glow. Two of the cats got up to salute the knees of his trousers with their cheeks.

"He's tucked in and resting," Holl announced. "He won't need anything but a quick trip to the dentist. All his fillings are gone, but there's nothing wrong with him that a meal and a sleep can't fix." He explained the details of the *bodach*'s curse.

"So," said the Master. "Ve must now study how best to dispose of the curse. I observe that it comprises the classic forms of three prohibitions…"

"Wait!" Diane interrupted him, outraged. "How can you sit and analyze it so coldly when it's Keith's welfare we're talking about?"

The Master eyed her over the tops of his spectacles. "Analysis vill help us to determine the structure, and perhaps suggest the means of ridding him of it. It appears to be no more than a geas, a prohibitive statement, vhich exacts a penalty for violations. In any case, this vun is not harmful. Fery Gilbertian, this *bodach*. The punishment seems to haf done no more than fit the crime."

"Thank God," Diane sighed, and then sat up straight. "Say, Holl, I never thought of him until now; where's your friend Mr. Michaels? He didn't come in with us."

Holl looked surprised. "You're right!" He ran to the window, and glanced up and down the road for the car. "He just went off. I never had a chance to give him my thanks for his help."

"Where did he come from?" Diane pressed. Holl frowned thoughtfully at her.

"I…I don't know. He came up to help me when I needed transportation. I never questioned where he came from. Should I have?"

"No, he seems to have been a nice man," Diane said, hoping she wouldn't have to eat her words later. "He seemed to know a lot about looking for missing persons." It all seemed a little too convenient. Diane couldn't get over wondering how Michaels had known what Keith looked like, without ever having met him. Was Keith in some kind of trouble? She wondered if Michaels wasn't some sort of official, but she kept her misgivings from the Little Folk.

Holl turned to the Master, who was sitting complacently on Mrs. Mackenzie's couch, drinking tea. "I'd like to thank you for coming to help me, sir," he said politely.

Without a word, Diane got up from her armchair and went to the window to look out. With her back to them, she could pretend she wasn't listening. Holl was grateful for her discretion. It wasn't pleasant to be called on the carpet, and to suffer before witnesses only made the ordeal worse.

"You do understand that the process vith vhich I located Meester Doyle vas vun you yourself know?" the Master asked.

Holl studied a spot on the wall. "Yes. But I wasn't sure I had enough energy or experience to overcome the local interference."

"Are you certain that your concerns were not simply the product of letting your emotions run avay vith you? You spent two days running around physically, not to achieve the purpose vhich took, by my estimate, under two hours when properly performed."

That stung. "No. I've thought about that. In time, I might have realized the truth of that, but by then Keith Doyle might have fallen over a cliff." Holl tried to keep his voice from sounding defensive, but the matter did disturb him. He had foolishly run his feet off searching, when all one had to do was employ the Law of Contagion, and call like to like. He deserved to look a fool by comparison with his teacher. "It seems also that Keith Doyle did his own spell, to make light. He would probably have come out by himself in time, under his own power."

The Master stared at him with half-lidded eyes. "It vould be the mark of an immature ego to try and achief the impossible all alone," he said calmly, "instead of svallowing vun's pride and admitting the situvation is too much for vun. I consider that you haf used good judgment in calling for aid."

"Thank you, sir," Holl said, gratified. He had thought he was behaving like a helpless babe, but he was being praised for it! The situation put him one more down to the Master, which galled him, but he was so grateful to have Keith Doyle back again in one piece that he didn't care. "Would you like to see the photographs Keith Doyle took?" He displayed the small envelope he had picked up from the developer.

"No. It is his honor, as he took the risks to obtain them. I vill vait until he may offer," the Master stated, and poured more tea.

Parry and riposte, Holl thought. Bested again. He studied his feet, feeling ten years old all over again.

"But thank you," the Master said, his blue eyes glinting through his gold-rimmed spectacles.

Diane escaped from the sitting room, and went in to see Keith. She couldn't pretend to be invisible any longer, and she wanted to make certain for herself that Keith was all right.

"Do you want visitors?" she asked, leaning halfway into the room.

"This feels like deja vu," Keith said. "I was just visiting Holl in the hospital about two weeks ago."

"It was longer ago than that," Diane corrected him. "You probably don't realize how long you've been away."

"I've missed you," Keith said, looking up at her fondly. "How are you doing?"

Diane leaned over to give him a kiss. "There. Better. Other than suffering from oxygen deprivation and partial deafness from the flight, not to mention worrying half to death about you all the way here, I'm fine."

Keith gave an apologetic and sympathetic grimace. "Well, time is having fun when you're flying," he quipped. "What's it like traveling with the Master?"

"Not bad. You know he's never been on a plane in his life, but he was so cool about the whole thing, you'd think he does it twice a day. Everybody in the village volunteered to come when they found out you were in trouble, but he said he would be the one to go. We had lots of time to talk, just sitting there," Diane explained. "I like him. You know, he seems to think Holl has done something really great."

"What, by attempting to find the old folks? He hasn't found them yet. Unless you count my *bodach*," Keith shuddered.

"Nope, I mean by making the *attempt*."

"Whether or not he succeeds?"

"I think so," Diane answered, thoughtfully. "You know how they feel about going anywhere out of sight of the house, let alone halfway around the world. And then there's the small matter of his having saved you."

Keith looked amused. "That's the way it's been reported, huh?"

"That's the way it IS," Diane snapped back, impatiently.

He smiled ruefully. "I know. I can take the lumps, if it'll help him look like a hero."

Diane relented. "Whether Holl will feel the same way, I don't know."

"I doubt it myself." Keith told her what Holl had heard from the village going on between Maura and Gerol. "He doesn't talk about it, but it's been on his mind a lot. He went away to sort of achieve the adulthood quest, and someone steals his girl behind his back."

Diane whistled through her teeth. "That's something Holl is going to have to work out for himself. I think the Master feels sorry for him, but he's not going to lift a finger to help him with his own daughter."

Keith sat up to protest. "That's not fair!—Now, wait, that's probably the best thing. There I go, being knee-jerk protective again, and Holl's twice my age. He's a lot more sensible than I am."

"Practically everybody is. What was it like, being underground?" Diane asked curiously.

He shivered, remembering the lion-headed apparition that charged him, the crowding of the damp stone walls, and the tunnel full of water where he tore his trousers. "Wet. Cramped. If Mrs. Mackenzie had been leaving a dry towel outside along with the bowl of milk every month, he'd be so grateful she'd probably be raising tropical fruit in her garden right now."

"Holl's got your pictures. I want to see your bogey man when you're out of bed," Diane said.

"Sure. Now, how did you get here? I mean, where..." The prohibition on talking about money hit him and turned the rest of his question into numb-tongued gibberish. Diane listened carefully for a moment, trying not to giggle, then held up a hand to stop him.

"I'm being mean. Holl told us what happened to you—all of it. Never mind, I get what you're asking," she assured him. "I think you paid for it. The Master said something about winning a lottery?"

On top of the contests they had entered in his name to send Holl with him? The IRS was going to love that. Keith groaned and threw an arm over his eyes. Idly, Diane turned over the sorry heap of clothes that Keith had been wearing in the underground tunnels. "All this stuff needs to be washed yesterday." She picked up Keith's wool jacket, which though filthy, was virtually unscathed by its ordeal. "Look at this. Is it made of iron or something? Your jeans are ruined, and this just needs cleaning. Are you really doing magic? Holl said you did a kind of spell, or something. I want to hear all about that. Is this part of it?"

"Oh!" Keith remembered. "It's not magic, it's Harris tweed. You know, local handcrafts. Did you get any of my postcards?"

"Yes, I did. So this is Harris tweed," Diane said, interested. She examined the jacket speculatively, humming as she turned it over in her hands.

"Do you want this one?" Keith asked generously. "You can have it if you want. I was going to buy some fabric for your gift, maybe enough for a skirt?"

She nodded approval absently, holding the garment before her in the mirror, though careful not to let the muddy cloth touch her blouse. "I might borrow this once in a while. You were going to choose my gift?" Keith nodded earnestly. "You chose that jacket yourself, huh? No help from Holl?" Diane demanded.

"Yup."

"Okay, I guess you have good taste. You can come with me and pay for my choice."

"Fine," Keith said. The curse limited him considerably in his responses. He hoped he didn't sound too abrupt. Besides, his teeth hurt when he tried to talk.

"So what's my limit?" Diane asked, careful not to mention money.

"The sky," Keith gestured gallantly. "Anything for my rescuer."

Diane shook a finger in his face and dropped the coat on the chair. "That's Holl, and don't you forget it."

"I'm not. I never will," Keith assured her seriously. "But right now, there's nothing he needs that I can give him."

"I'm going to go and see if someone can get you to the dentist." Diane said, briskly gathering up the pile of clothes and rolling it together. "And then I am going to take a nap. I don't think I've slept in two days now. And it's all your fault." Keith lowered his eyes meekly and tried to look abashed.

"Well, now, laddie," Mrs. Mackenzie said as she bustled into the room with a steaming tray. "Did you see your little man, then, out in the garden? After all this, I'd near forgotten why you were out there."

"Um, not exactly," Keith stammered. Diane grinned over the landlady's shoulder as she settled the tray over Keith's knees.

"Ah, well, it was a braw try of yours. You've had an adventure, from all accounts. Have a sup of this, and then a long sleep. The best medicine in the world for wear and tear."

"I'd better go," Diane said. "Remember, except for now, I'm not letting you out of my sight for a minute. You can't be trusted out by yourself. I mean it."

"Hey," Keith whispered as she started to slip out of the door. Diane looked back at him. He smiled up into her eyes. "Welcome to Scotland."

Lacking other transportation, Keith had to wait until the evening coach trip into Stornoway to see the emergency dentist. His friends clustered around him, demanding to hear his adventures in full before they would let him go up to the small medical office.

"You won't believe a word of it," Keith warned them. "I mean, it's full of mystical things and fairy folk. You know, what you've been razzing me about for three weeks!"

"Oh, get away," Max said, disbelievingly.

"We've been working our fingers off shifting peat, and you've had a soft adventure," Martin chided him. "You must be chuffed, finding a rare artifact like that comb. The Professor was all over the place about it. Locating that must have been exciting."

"Well..."

"Pay the bard, pay the bard," Edwin shushed them all. "We'll wait until you've seen the dentist. We'll buy the drinks, and you can tell us all about it, eh?"

"That sounds fair," Keith acknowledged, happy to have some windfalls descend from his mishap. The fewer times he had to mention money, the less of a fool he would look in the pub.

"I'd like to hear all about it myself," said Holl, teasingly joining the clamor for Keith's story. "Make it a good one, Uncle Keith. Full of ghosties and ghoulies...."

"Later, later," Keith promised.

Miss Anderson said nothing to him, but she was no longer looking as stormy as she had. Keith took that as a good sign. The Master had decided to stay behind in Callanish and get some sleep. The redhaired teacher hadn't confronted him yet. Keith had some time to compose an apology and a speech of thanks before actually having to face the formidable Master. He was glad he only had to deal with Miss Anderson that night.

Mr. McGill, the emergency dentist, was amused by Keith's predicament. In a soft Scottish burr, he told his assistant to mix up a large quantity of amalgam. "Yer fillings seem to hae evaporated. There's not a sign that they were dug out, and the traces of tooth sealant are still there. What have ye been doing to your teeth?"

Keith rearranged the suction hose in the corner of his mouth. "Would you believe the fairies took them?"

The dentist laughed. When the assistant returned with a small white bowl, he cleaned and refilled all of the rough holes, and smoothed them with a scraping tool. "There's been no decay since they've gone; you're lucky. I'm using porcelain amalgam here, to match with your enamel. No more temptation there for the selkies, eh, son?"

"I hope not," Keith agreed, giving him one of his best village idiot smiles, and unhooking the paper bib from around his neck. He tried his bite, grinding his molars together. It seemed to fit okay.

"Give it an hour before you eat or drink," Mr. McGill said. "And don't annoy the Little Folk any mair, eh?" The dentist laughed until he closed the door of the office behind Keith. Still chuckling, he stripped off his thin rubber gloves and went into his private office.

Michaels stood up from the chair in which he'd been waiting. "What do you make of it?"

The dentist was distrustful of the man in the tweed suit, even though he'd seen the important-looking identification card in his pocket, and knew he was bound by the law to help him. "I've never seen such a case in all my life. There was no digging, and not a fragment of metal left clinging to the enamel. It was as if they had never been put in."

"Curious," Michaels mused aloud.

McGill spoke up indignantly. "I demand to know if there's a new secret weapon that caused the boy's fillings to vanish like that. I don't approve of nee-uclear teechnology."

"That'd be classified information, Mr. McGill," Michaels said, patiently, his voice devoid of inflection. He had a lot to report back to the chief.

"Oh, aye, so you'd say, until we're all dead in our beds," the dentist raged. "Then what do you do? You blame the Americans or the French, don't you? Good day to you, Mr. Michaels." He stood by the door until the agent took his leave.

"It might be a taunt to us, Chief," the agent said quietly into the telephone. "They might know we're shadowing him. He didn't have a thing on him except a ratty old comb. His pockets were stripped, his clothing was tattered. No microfilms, no packages."

"Sounds like he double crossed by his contact. Say he made a pickup of a formula, but there's no proof. There can be no arrests without proof."

"Unless you'd call this process for dissolving metal and leaving tissue intact behind it proof, sir," the agent reasoned.

"That would be handy. Defense would love us for it, wouldn't they. Upstairs doesn't want this lad getting away, Michaels."

"If proof is there to find, sir, I'll find it."

The tour bus took only a small party around the island for what Keith dubbed the Tweed Tour that Saturday. The other young men, though relieved to see Keith back and in one piece, would not be persuaded to join a sightseeing and shopping tour under any circumstances. As one, they elected to stay in town for the day. They teased Keith mercilessly over having a girlfriend who was so devoted that she would fly halfway around the world to see to his welfare.

"Throwing money around again," Edwin chided him, but the teasing was affectionate now, "and all for your sake. As if you were worth more than ten pence. You didn't tell us she was such a knock-out."

"There's some secrets I can keep," Keith returned, waggling his eyebrows. "I didn't want to make you poor dopes jealous."

Mrs. Green expressed herself interested in joining the bus tour to look at scenery, but not at dry goods. She was coming along for the ride. Mrs. Turner, by contrast, was a keen craftmaker, and was eager to see what the locals had to offer. Narit and Diane had hit it off right away, and settled down in the back of the bus to talk.

Keith loaded up his pocket with three new rolls of film, and took over the seat behind Holl and the Elf Master, camera at the ready.

Though the day was fine, the sea wind made it 'windcheater' weather again. Keith had on his old jacket with a sweater tucked underneath, leaving the new one behind at the laundry with his other sodden clothing.

The range of geography throughout just the few miles of land comprising the Isles amazed the tourists. Only a short distance from the rocky hills lay long valleys of marsh grasses and wildflowers, a temperate environment attached at odd angles to the tundra-like terrain of the peat bog.

"This is nothing at all like the land we've been seeing," said Mrs. Green enthusiastically. She and Keith stopped to take photographs as they rolled along the narrow roads. "How lovely it all is."

"That bird you hear is a shore lark," Miss Anderson said, looking pleased, when they stopped to listen in the middle of a huge, flat plain completely full of tiny daisies. "They are extremely rare. Look, there he goes! The little brown bird. See him!"

"That's one for my bird book," Mrs. Green said, breathlessly. "A shore lark!"

"Too quick for my camera," Keith announced regretfully. "But I did see him, anyway."

Further south, quiet sandy streams flowed down the hills and spread out across astonishingly white sand beaches. The brilliant aquamarines and blues of the water made the inlets look like they belonged in the tropics, instead of less than a thousand miles from the Arctic Circle.

"We ought to go for a paddle," Mrs. Green suggested. "That water looks marvelously refreshing."

"I don't know whether I'd advise that," Miss Anderson clucked. "The water might be bone-numbingly cold."

"The climate here is moderated by the current of the Gulf Stream," the Elf Master intoned austerely. "It is far varmer here than in the similar latitude on the vestern side of the Atlahntic. Certainly vhere it is so shallow vill be varmed by the sun as vell."

Keith snickered at the preponderance of 'v's' in the Elf Master's little speech. Miss Anderson stopped and looked at the small, redhaired man, the surprised expression on her face revealing that she knew the Master was absolutely right. "Well, that's true. If any of you would like to try, we can wait here."

"No, thank you," Mrs. Green bubbled, snapping a picture of the sea. "It was only an impulse. But it does look so nice."

Chapter Twenty One

The first hand-painted sign advertising Harris tweed appeared on their left. At the top of the long unpaved drive was an ordinary house, but next to it was a smaller building with the door open, and colorful swags of cloth hanging in the window. Everyone, including Mrs. Green, came in to see what the first weaver's shop was like. Thereafter, the Englishwoman stayed outside to take photographs and chat with the coach driver.

In most of them, the displays were like that in the Tea Shop. In only a few was the weaver actually at work. Most seemed to have their looms in a different building than they kept the goods for sale. Shelves and tables were set up to show off the cloth to its best advantage. Some of the weavers had ready made garments for sale, and a few offered colorful sweaters knit out of the same wool.

Holl and Diane were the keenest customers at the various stops. Holl's fascination with crafts intrigued Diane, and she watched as he made endless sketches of looms and spinning wheels. Together, they examined the various weaves made on the complicated mechanisms. They watched for the signs that directed them to the next weaver's place. The coach driver, amused, stopped looking out, and let his self-appointed navigators direct him.

Narit admired the colors, but said the wool was too scratchy for her. "It's warm. My skin gets hot with it just resting on my hand." Narit shivered in horror. "I would hate to feel that next to my skin."

"Lining, dear, that's the secret," one of the weavers told her patiently, patting her arm. "Lining and a wee bit of interfacing."

Diane hadn't yet made her choice, so Keith followed meekly along in her wake as she plowed through the shops. There was only the faintest idea in her mind of what she wanted to have made of the cloth, so she kept changing her mind as she looked. One fabric would make a beautiful coat, another was perfect for suitings, and still others suggested skirts and waistcoats, blazers, and heavy man-like trousers. She was looking after Holl, too, who seemed tentative and indecisive, unable to make a definite choice.

"This color would be nice on Maura," Holl said, shyly, "but I have no idea if I should bring it home or not." He blushed, and looked helplessly at Keith.

"Oh, buy it," Diane urged him. "*I'll* take it later if you don't have any use for it. It would look so good on her with that gorgeous auburn hair," she added soothingly, "but don't keep beating yourself up. You'll kick yourself later if you miss out getting something here that you want later. How often are you coming all the way to Scotland?"

"I bow to your judgment," Holl said, happy to have the decision made for him.

Leaving Holl on his own, Diane walked away to have the weaver cut off skirt lengths of cloth as gifts to her sisters and mother. In a very short time, she nudged Keith. Holl had started showing some initiative, and even seemed to be having a good time. He was actually making a purchase. Keith squeezed Diane's hand for joy, and leaned over to give her a kiss.

Once they were back on the coach, Holl approached the Master with a paper-wrapped package on his outstretched hands. "This is for Orchadia," he said.

The Master tilted his head curiously, his spectacles glinting, but put out his hands for the parcel. "Thank you, on behalf of my vife," he accepted, with a ceremonious nod. "I shall not mention this to my daughter."

"Don't," said Holl, evenly. "I hadn't so much as considered the possibility that you would." The truth of that showed in his face, and the Master was inwardly pleased. "I don't want it to affect Maura's judgment. But the Illinois winters are cold. I believe that Orchadia will find this a useful gift."

The Master peeked under an edge of the paper at the folded cloth. It was a good choice, both in color and weight. He nodded again at Holl. "So she vould. My thanks. But let me gif this back to you, so you may present it yourself. She vould be pleased to know this thoughtfulness came directly from you."

With no one supervising the driver, he found the next sign on his own. The bus took a turn onto a narrow, unevenly paved piece of road, which dipped up and down toward a sunlit sound. On either side of the tarmacadam were pools of standing water of peat brown, with the dark blue sky reflected in them. When the little drama in the middle seats came to an end, his passengers were once again watching the view, but he was already slowing down for the stop.

The coach pulled up a steep graveled drive, and rumbled to a halt in front of a cluster of older wooden buildings. The weaver, a tall man with grizzled salt-and-pepper hair, came out to meet them, and showed them into his workshop.

The building was an old barn that had had a concrete floor poured in. It was kept spotlessly clean, except for hanks and shreds and bales of wool stored anywhere there was space to rest them. In the center of a wall was a huge mechanical loom, set so that the light from the window poured over the weaver's shoulder. He had been working when they arrived, and the roll of red, blue, and dark green cloth gathering on a spool underneath the loom was already a handspan thick.

"Hands back," the weaver commanded, taking his seat. He started the loom. Six shuttles, set around on a wheel like rows of corn on a cob, flew crashing back and forth in turn.

They watched the weaver work, asking a question now and again, with their eyes fixed on his hands and the web of cloth growing between them. By this time, Holl was sketching out the structure of the loom, and making small observations about technique. The village would have its own weaving equipment by winter, or he'd know why not. The Master caught his eye and raised one carrot-red brow with an approving nod.

"Do you dye all the wool yourself?" Narit asked, keeping a wary distance from the clashing machine.

The man paused and the din died away. "Ah, no, that's all doon on the mainland now."

"Europe?" Keith asked, puzzled.

"Scotland," the man replied curtly, as if that should have been obvious to anyone but an idiot. Keith shrugged, with an apologetic grin. "The fleeces here are sheared off the sheep's back and takkin' awa'. We see them next in clean hanks of color."

"Doesn't anyone do it the old way anymore, making the dyes themselves?" Keith asked, disappointed. He had been picturing huge bubbling cauldrons of thick, brightly hued glop.

"Aye," the weaver said, offhandedly. "That's Annie MacLeod you want. She's kept all the old ways gaeng. Boils her own dyes from natural plants, and so on the like."

"Mrs. MacLeod. That's who the ladies in the shop said to look for," Keith affirmed to Holl.

"Good," Holl said. "I want to get all the information I can to bring home."

"You pay her a visit," the weaver encouraged them, dictating directions to Holl. "But dinna believe oot she tells ye, especially nor when she says she's seventy nine. She's been sayin' that for ten years and maur." Since he never cracked a smile, Keith couldn't tell if the weaver was kidding them. They thanked him for the tour, and left. He grunted a farewell without looking up. Behind them, the hammering noise of the loom began again.

At his most persuasive, Keith convinced the weary coach driver to take the next precarious turnoff to one final destination before going on to town and his tea. Diane hadn't made her choice yet, and Holl was still keen on fact gathering. The others, too, were tired. Only Mrs. Green accompanied the four travelers off the coach into the low black house.

Keith could feel something different about Mrs. MacLeod's place the moment he set foot inside. There was a sensation just hanging in the air he couldn't identify, one that made his whiskers twitch. He could see that Holl felt it, too, by the catch in the young elf's step as he crossed the threshold. Nothing ever fazed the Master, at least not openly, but the teacher approached the small woman seated behind the great wooden loom with open respect. They made a strangely mismatched couple, but Keith sensed between them an inexplicable kinship. Their eyes were the same penetrating blue, but he felt the similarity went deeper than that. Physically, they couldn't have been more unlike. The Master was small, potbellied, upright, while the woman behind the loom had been tall, but had allowed the years to bend her spine at the shoulders. Her hands were huge and strong; its fingerpads were flattened into broad, spatulate disks.

Around the walls of the croft room hung floating hanks of unspun wool, dyed in dozens of colors: browns, reds, greens, golds, and one mass of electric blue, which Keith suspected wasn't entirely made of natural dyes, but had to admit he liked. Rolled bolts of fabric were stacked neatly on deep, low shelves built against the walls. The frame of the loom came within inches of the high, beamed ceiling.

This machine was simpler than the others they had seen. It appeared to be made almost entirely of wood, something Keith could see interested Holl closely. The blond elf had flipped over to a new page in his notebook, and was drawing with concentrated speed. Keith took a quick picture of the loom for his own records.

"This loom is more than a hundred years old," Mrs. MacLeod said, without preamble. Her voice was very clear and low. "My father built it. Over years, the worn bits and pieces have been replaced. It works in this way." The old woman reached up to a group of cords hanging over her head, and pulled one after another in a pattern her hands knew so well she didn't have to watch them. The loom responded, shooting the polished shuttles back and forth across the web.

"That's marvelous," exclaimed Mrs. Green. "Did you make all this cloth yourself?"

"Ach, of course," Mrs. MacLeod smiled, her eyes crinkling. "When I'm going well, I can make two pieces a week."

"That doesn't sound like a lot," Keith frowned, looking at the piles of fabric. "It must take you ages to make this much cloth."

"A piece is seventy to eighty yards, lad," the weaver said, eyeing him humorously.

Keith's eyes went wide. "Oh. Wow. Excuse me and my big mouth."

"Do you blend all of your yarn yourself?" Mrs. Green asked, sorting busily through the selection. The old woman nodded. "Wonderful! You hae a lovely sense of color, Mrs. MacLeod. How much do you charge per yard?" The Englishwoman turned over one bolt after another, holding a fold of cloth up to the light to see it better. Diane joined her, exclaiming over the variety of weaves and hues. Holl chimed in, asking about recipes for natural dyes. Keith decided not to enter the fray. At a safe distance, he took a picture of the ladies, and then turned to photograph the rest of the inside of the croft. To his surprise, when he stopped to take a picture of the loom from a different angle, he noticed that the weaver was no longer in her place behind it. The old woman had instead appeared at his elbow. He raised the lens to snap off a closeup of her, but something in her expression stopped him. Keith waited while she studied his face.

"Ye've been fairy-nagged, lad," she said suddenly.

Keith's jaw fell open. "How did you know?"

"I see the marks on you. Weavers are some of the makers on Earth. We see the strands which go into the life around us. Yours have been tangled a bit."

"Like elf-knots?" Keith wanted to know.

"Aye. That's one of the ways. Been poking yer lang neb in where it oughtn't to go?"

"I suppose so," Keith admitted, humbly. The memory of the bogey's voice rang in his ears, and he shivered.

"What did it do to ye? Never mind," the woman forestalled his attempt to explain with a toss of her head. "I suppose ye canna say."

Keith sighed, relieved, saved from trying to figure out how he could explain the thing's curse without stuttering like a jackhammer. The old woman gave him a searching look and wrapped one broad hand in the fabric of his jacket. She pulled him over to her work-table, and, one handed, rummaged through the scattered bits of fleece and spun yarn, talking all the while.

"Well, it might wear off in time. You ought to walk a straight path until then. But if you're fixed on doing things like twisting the tiger's tail, you need a bit more protection than you have in yerself. I'm likely locking the barn door after the horse is gone, but you never know. I see you have an aptness for wandering into such places."

She released him and selected three colors of unspun wool. Holding the ends together between her ring fingers, she braided and twisted the mass into a nearly solid knot of complicated design, and tied it off. "I'll gi' ye a wee bit of yarn to wear it about your neck, but ye should find a sma' poke of yer ain to keep it in."

"Will any kind of little bag do?" Keith asked, clutching the little mass of wool in his fist.

"Aye. Any will do. One more thing," the woman said, sounding a little hurt as he started to turn away. He faced her again, puzzled. "Dinna you not want to take my picture?"

Keith brightened immediately, and cranked the film forward in his camera. "You bet I do. I wasn't sure if you'd let me. Say cheese!"

"Wensleydale," the old woman said dourly, but her eyes twinkled in their network of lines. "You're like a monkey. I've seen plenty like you in my seventy-nine years. Go with good luck." She shook hands with him. Her broad, strong fingers closed on Keith's like a bear trap, and he concentrated on not wincing. "Dinna disturb the fair ones' nests again," she warned him in a low voice, pitching it so that Mrs. Green, only feet away, couldn't hear her. "That'll save ye only from glamours, not foolishness."

Keith fingered the wool charm, now safely tucked in his pocket. "I promise."

"That's good enough," said Mrs. MacLeod. "Now, ladies, what have ye found?"

"Keith," Diane bubbled, grabbing his arm with excitement, and pushing a mass of bittersweet, oatmeal, and blue tweed under his nose. "This is it. This is perfect. I mean, picture a suit made of this stuff. My sisters will just die of jealousy!"

Keith snickered, taking out his wallet. "So long as they don't kill me, too."

As soon as the purchases were counted, and the yardage cut and folded, Mrs. MacLeod sat down again behind her loom and reached for the cords above her head. The shuttles began their rhythmic pattern once again. Keith tried to form some suitable words of thanks, but Diane grabbed his arm and yanked him out of the croft.

Chapter Twenty Two

On the last night of the tour, Educatours liked to host a special dinner as a farewell party for each group. The coach delivered the tourists, Professor Parker's team, and Diane and the Master, dressed in their finest, to a hotel in Stornoway they hadn't passed by or seen before. Holl and the Master were suitably hatted for the trip into town. Keith recognized the fedora the redhaired teacher sported as one he had once worn back home.

They were directed to a long table along one side of the elegant, high-ceilinged restaurant. Candles burned in crystal chimneys in the center of the table, their light glinting off silver and crystal. Keith seated Diane courteously, and settled down in the chair next to hers. The menus were passed among them, and everyone fell silent, contemplating their choices. The lights were turned fashionably low, making it a little difficult to read. "What's good, Miss Anderson?"

"Everything is good," the tall woman said. "This hotel has a superb reputation. I have had it highly recommended by several people."

The food was excellent, and there was a small room in the center of the dining room which was used as a self-serve dessert bar. There was a good deal of toasting one another over the meal.

"I have got to ask something," Diane said tentatively. "I know I'm new around here, but does everything come with peas?"

Everyone laughed. At last, the group moved somewhat unsteadily to the lounge bar to finish off the evening in greater comfort. The party commandeered several tables, and pulled all the chairs around them.

"So what are your plans from here?" Matthew asked Keith, across the table, where he was sitting between the Master and Diane.

"We're going on to Ireland for a week," Keith explained, "but as soon as I get home, I'm going to write a book that will be a revolutionary best seller over here, a high-moraled self help tome."

"Oh, what is it about?" Charles asked innocently.

"Cooking Without Peas," Keith announced, describing the sales banner with a highflung hand. "I'll sell a million of 'em."

The others laughed. Keith exchanged addresses with everyone, writing them in a brand new book purchased especially for the occasion. Because of the *bodach's* curse, he was forced to stick closely to mineral water and a half-soda, half-orange juice combination the bartender recommended. Holl, who had long been relegated to non-alcoholic beverages he altered himself, met Keith's eye with a sympathetic and humorous expression.

"And what are your orders, gentlemen?" the waiter asked, leaning over them with a pad.

"S—s—cider." Keith found to his pleasure and amazement that he could still ask for the hard drink, by concentrating on the nonalcoholic variety. The word had actually emerged with relative coherence. Take that, *bodach*, he thought.

"I'm sorry, sir. We haven't got any," the waiter apologized.

Keith's face fell. He thought longingly of bitter ale, which he could see on tap behind the bar. It was meaty and rich and almost like a food, and he could just about taste it. "How about a b—, bi—, birale, no, I mean a btitaler, um—" He turned red, seeing everyone staring at him. He must have sounded as if he was having a seizure.

The waiter glanced at him sadly. "Ye've had too many, laddie. How about a nice coop o' coffee?'

"Um," said Keith decisively, peering into the wooden shelves beneath the hanging decanters. "Is there another Orange 50 back there? Make it a double."

"Cooming right oop," said the barman, relieved.

"What's the matter," Edwin asked. "Taken the pledge?"

"I can't keep up with you guys," Keith answered evasively. "I've given up trying."

"Keith," Miss Anderson began. "Normally I wouldn't think of passing anyone who missed as much class time as you had, but under the circumstances, if you would care to sit an oral examination—and pass it—I think I can guarantee you a suitably acceptable grade. In light of your accident, I am willing to take your past performance and your remarkable find into consideration." As Keith tried to protest his gratitude, she held up a hand to stop him. "No, don't thank me. I promise you the test will be a difficult one. Come and see me tomorrow morning."

"My father is going to be very displeased with me," Matthew announced, suddenly. "I'm not going into finance after him. I've been in touch with Dr. Crutchley on the phone, and he's agreed to take me on as a pupil if I transfer down to London University. I'll be going out with his team when he's on a dig."

"Most commendable, young man," Dr. Parker said. "You're a hard worker. I'm sure you're bound for great things. I wish I had a dozen like you myself. If you choose not to work with Dr. Crutchley, I'd be happy if you would join our little band. I'll give you a written recommendation, and look forward to seeing you at our meetings and conventions in the future. "

"Your health," Martin said, raising his glass to his friend. Matthew made a half bow.

"Hear, hear," called Miss Anderson, applauding him.

Martin grinned, before touching his glass to his lips. "And believe me, you'll need it when your dad finds out you've chucked it all for some dry bones and old pots."

Everyone laughed, but they raised their glasses to Matthew.

"Dr. Alfheim," Parker began, turning to the Master, "I am curious to have your impression of the find made by young Mr. Doyle. Perhaps I swept it away too quickly the other day, but I am really so delighted that such a piece has come to light. You'll have to forgive an enthusiast."

"I qvite understand," the Master agreed. "I vould appreciate a chance to examine the artifact. Such jewels look like vorthless discards to the untrained eye. I am not surprised you recognized its quality."

"My dear sir, how kind." Parker was warming up to his favorite topic. Keith had noticed when they were loading on the coach to come to the restaurant that the Master was a couple of inches taller than Parker. They still looked like different species to Keith's educated eye, but Parker helped hide the reality that the Master was much smaller than a normal man. The other lads didn't seem to have looked twice at him.

"What's he do for a living?" Alistair asked, nudging Keith and gesturing subtly at the Master.

"He's a teacher," Keith said, trying to decide which of the many subjects he'd studied in the underground classroom to mention, and decided to let the statement stand as it was.

Alistair eyed the small red-haired figure. Keith caught a glint of blue behind the Master's gold-rimmed glasses as he looked their way. The little teacher had a clairaudient's knack for knowing when he was being discussed. "Looks a tough old bird, too."

"The toughest. But you really learn from him. He's the best."

"That's the important thing," Alistair acknowledged. "Miss Anderson's like that during Term time. I'd rather have one I curse every day of term than one I curse later on for not drumming the facts into my head."

Keith winced at the word 'curse,' but he nodded. "I couldn't agree with you more."

At the other end of the table, Matthew turned his glass in his hands, pensively watching the liquid slosh in the bottom. "You don't think I'm wasting my time, do you, lad, budging into archaeology instead of banking?"

Holl looked up, and realized Matthew was talking to him. He was puzzled why Matthew addressed him so seriously, when he was supposed to be only a half-grown Big One, but he remembered he had been one of the ones to praise Matthew for his hard work on the site. He stopped to consider the question. "If you find merit in that course, pursue it. I think my own father would be proud that I was finding my own way in the world instead of following him blindly into a path on which I'd be unhappy."

"Very profound, small boy," Matthew said, blinking reddened eyes at him. "I raise your hat to you."

Before Holl could grab his hand, Matthew lifted the Cubs hat off his head. The points of his ears promptly poked through the waves of damp blond hair. Holl said nothing, but he could feel his cheeks burning. Fortunately, it was fairly dark in the lounge, and no one else was paying attention. Matthew stared, and looked him carefully up and down.

"Well, wrap me in brown paper and ship me by Datapost," he murmured, impressed into a hushed whisper. "My, what big ears you have, grandma."

Worried inside whether Matthew was drunk enough to make an outburst, Holl smiled sweetly at him, and spoke in a quiet voice. "There are fairies at the bottom of the garden."

"I never saw them, myself," Matthew said, eyes misted with drink. "No wonder Doyle is so keen. Where'd he find you, then? Under a toadstool?"

Holl groaned. I will not leave a string of Patrick Morgans behind me! he thought in exasperation. Keith's college roommate had discovered what he was, too, but he was unlikely to talk. *I can't let it become a precedent, leaving people behind who have seen me and have a fair idea what it is they're looking at.* "Under a building, if you want to know the truth. I live in the sub-basement of his school library." Surreptitiously, he inched a hand forward and wrapped it around Matthew's pint glass. "Keith Doyle's been helping us keep our noses hidden. It's not so easy to get along with all you Big Folk chopping and changing everything." He let a 'forget' seep into the amber liquid in the glass, hoping that it wasn't so strong it made the youth mislay his name, but not so weak he'd remember boys with pointed ears.

"Here, drink up, my friend," he suggested. "The waters of Lethe are good for you. The next round will be on me." Digging into his pocket for a few pounds, he signaled to the bartender. "A St. Clement's here, and another pint of whatever it is he's drinking."

The man looked from Matthew to Holl to the money in Holl's hand. "I shouldn't do it," he warned them. "I could lose my licensing privileges for selling to a minor."

"Go on, he's older than he looks, he's a short eighteen," Matthew said, playfully, winking. He held up the half empty glass, toasting the bartender and Holl. "Your very good health." He drank the whole thing in a few well practiced gulps and puts down the empty glass. With a resigned air, the bartender took it and Holl's money, leaving them with the fresh drinks. Holl held his breath as Matthew studied his ears closely and handed him back his cap. He snapped his fingers. "I have it. Star-Trekker, right?"

"Right you are," Holl agreed, with a gusty sigh. "Pity there aren't many Vulcans in the new television series."

"Aye?" Matthew inquired, taking the fresh pint of ale and sipping through the foam. "I haven't seen it yet, myself."

"Forgive me," Dr. Parker stopped himself in midstream and studied his new guest. "I've been er, hogging the floor, as they say. Please, Dr., er, Alfheim, tell me, where do you come from? You seem to be well up on the latest finds and techniques. I don't remember hearing of you or meeting you at any of our conclaves. I, er, would remember anyone who comes close to meeting me at my level, if you will excuse the pun."

"I am at an American University, Midvestern," the Master said with perfect honesty. "Allow me, though, to gif you my home address. I should be fery interested in continuing our confersation by mail, if you would like."

Parker's long face shone. "So should I. My, my, I am sure we've been boring our companions, talking shop at table." Stafford and the others nearby shook their heads. "You are too kind. This object most likely came from a similar burial to the one we are excavating. I wish we had time for you to see our work."

The Master seemed full of regret, too, handling the comb with careful fingers. "I am so sorry, since ve must leaf early tomorrow, vith the others."

"I wonder if there were more of these here once, before the waters rose," Parker said, getting a dreamy look on his face. "Combs were rare, and considered to be valuable. They were made heirlooms among our Neolithic ancestors. Probably the last owner was not the original maker. He may have been given it or traded for it. Did you know, some were considered to have magical qualities."

"Yes, so I understand," said the Master. Keith looked up at the teacher's tone.

"Oh, really?" Holl said curiously, and reached out. "May I see it?" He had a close look at the comb and nodded significantly at the redhaired student.

Keith nearly went wild waiting while Holl passed nondescript conversation with Parker, and handed back the comb. He tried to catch Holl's eye, but the Little Person ignored him. Distractedly, Keith answered a question from Alastair, and got drawn into a conversation to which he gave only half of his attention.

"What's going on?" he demanded in a whisper of Holl when the party broke up for the evening.

"Congratulations, you widdy," Holl said, calmly. "You've hit the jackpot. That comb does have a charmed aura about it. That's why it's still intact after so long."

"One of the Little Folk made it?"

Overhearing them, the Master came up. "I vould estimate that that is correct."

Keith was shocked for a moment, wondering if he'd been talking too loudly. "Boy, I forgot how far away you people can hear. Was that made by some of *your* folk in particular?"

The Master was noncommittal. "It is possible. The carvings are not unfamiliar."

"But he's going to put it in a museum," Keith yelped, and clapped his hand over his mouth. He looked around to see hastily if anyone had heard him that time. No one was paying much attention to the antics of the odd Keith Doyle. "A magic comb, right out there in front of everyone."

"Who vill know?" the Master asked mildly, turning up his hands.

"Well, *I* will," said Keith, concerned.

"And who vould you tell?"

"No one, I guess," Keith said, after a moment's thought. He grinned impishly. "Well, they say three can keep a secret...if two of them are Little Folk."

"And I would like to thank all you ladies for producing my coat, which kept me warm through the middle of summer. I know my friends feel the same as I do, but are too shy to present their thanks in person. Ladies, I salute you."

Keith's audience set up stentorian bleating of what he hoped was appreciation. He bowed to the field of sheep, and prepared to declaim further, when he was interrupted by a shrill whistle.

"That's enough, you widdy!" Holl called from the window of the coach. "Come on, we're all waiting for you."

"That is all," Keith said to the sheep. "Carry on. I know you'll make me proud."

Chapter Twenty Three

"Sir, I'm speaking to you from Northern Ireland," Michaels said, and then held the receiver away from his ear, wincing. "No sir. I didn't have a chance to call before. They just vanished from Stornoway, and I had to check every passenger list leaving the islands before I found them. They knew where they were going, I assume. This blighter is bouncing from place to place like a bloody Phileas Fogg. No, he left the bloody comb in the hands of the archaeologist. It's a real item, a coup for the old man. You'll be seeing writeups on it in the journals.

"Once I got here, it wasn't hard to track them. O'Day isn't going to a lot of trouble to be inconspicuous. No, sir. I've got a positive identification on his passport photo. Apparently, he bent down and kissed the ground upon arrival." Michaels chuckled, echoing his employer's amusement. "Yes, sir. There were several witnesses."

Michaels looked up at the Departures board on the Terminal wall. "Oh, chief, must run now. The train for the south is about to pull out. It looks like he must have achieved his purpose in Scotland, doesn't it? We thought it was a drop at first, but I'm assuming a pickup, or else why is he going into the Republic? For payment? Aye, I'll look for the best opportunity, and apprehend him and the other three. There'll probably be a scuff-up about extradition, but what's new about that? Report back soon. Bye."

"People do look a little different here than they do at home," Diane said, surreptitiously people-watching from behind her magazine on the train. "Only, they look a lot like each other, too."

"I noticed that," Keith agreed, looking away from the window. He had been studying scenery, admiring the Irish countryside. He was out of film, and felt disappointed at missing photographing the first sunrise he'd seen in a month—not that he hadn't been up early every day. They had bundled aboard the train from the ferry at about six o'clock. It was not quite seven. Most of their fellow passengers were lounging listlessly in their seats. "I guess your basic gene pool is limited to whatever conquerors zoomed through here over the centuries."

"Yes, but you fit right in. I could lose you on a crowded street corner."

"Many have tried, my sweet," said Keith blithely, "but I've always found my way home again. Um," he said, seeing the worried look resurface on Diane's face. "I didn't mean to bring that up." He truly hadn't intended to refer to his misadventure. He was still having nightmares about being blind in a knee-high tunnel with hideous laughter echoing around him.

"See how you like being walked on a leash after this," Diane shot back, her eyes suddenly filling with tears. "Darn you, being lost and almost *killed* didn't even dent your sense of humor."

"Best armor plating in the world," Keith quipped. He poked around in his jacket pocket and came up with a handkerchief, which he offered to her. She shook her head.

"I'm okay. Come on," Diane said, suddenly, blinking her eyes fast. "Let's see some of this magic you're supposed to be able to do."

"Well, if you want," Keith said. He looked around. "Ah." There was a trash container behind their seat. From the top, he fished out a beer can and shook it. "Still a few drops left. Good."

He spilled the beer on the table in front of them. "Hey!" Diane protested. "Yuck!"

"No, really, this is how it works," Keith said. "You have to have something to work from. I do best with liquids so far."

"Well, all right." Diane was dubious. Keith winked at her, and then put his cupped hands over the small puddle of beer. With his eyes closed, he concentrated on the principles Enoch had taught him.

"Okay," he said, dropping his hands back into his lap. There, on the table, in the place where the golden beer had been, was a coiled bracelet. It was made from a rich, deep gold, and it sparkled with rubies and emeralds. The clasp was only partially hooked.

"Ooh," Diane breathed, reaching for it to try it on. As soon as her fingers touched the chain, the whole thing popped, and dissolved again into featureless beer. "Very funny!" She shook her dripping fingers.

"It's only an illusion," Keith said, apologetically. "That's all I know how to do so far."

"But that's wonderful." Diane gestured at the pooling liquid, now starting to run toward the edge of the table. Keith fished out his handkerchief and mopped it up. "The clasp was a nice touch. I couldn't resist it."

"Thank you, my dear," Keith replied, wiggling his eyebrows lasciviously. "We aim to be irresistible. Wait until I start working with solids."

"I know where you're going on this trip," Diane murmured softly. "But where are *they* going?" She tilted her head toward Holl and the Elf Master, who were sitting in the seat across from theirs. The two Little Folk were looking out of opposite windows, not talking, and appearing not to be aware that Keith and Diane were discussing them.

"I'm not sure," Keith replied. "Come on, let's get some sandwiches or something. Everyone else is going by with bacon and eggs, and I'm getting ravenous." They rose to their feet in the swaying aisle. Holl looked up at the movement. "I'm getting food. Want some?"

Listlessly, Holl lifted his shoulders and let them drop. "If you please."

"Okay," Keith said, cheerfully. "Breakfast for everyone."

On the way toward the buffet car, he explained what he knew of Holl's quest to Diane. "Do you know exactly what's going on here?"

"Not so's you'd notice," Diane said, pushing through the sliding doors between the cars. "Something to do with Maura, I thought."

"Sort of." Keith explained what Holl was looking for, and why. "He's been hounded to prove himself worthy of being the next headman, the village leader, not that the Master looks like he's stepping down any time soon. It's been like a charm said over his cradle, that it would be lucky to have him as leader because he was the first one born in the new place."

"Well, that's not a bad destiny," Diane replied. "All things considered."

"If it wasn't enough on top of all that, he's got to have one great deed under his belt to claim the leadership. Talk about performance pressure."

"How did the Master claim it, then?" she asked.

"I suppose because he brought the Little Folk to Midwestern, where they had a safe place to live. He's never said how or why, but I can guess that that was his big accomplishment."

"Isn't that enough?"

"It would be, in my book," Keith said, arriving at the end of a long queue of people waiting their turns at the buffet counter. "Here we are. A full breakfast for me, please?" He passed Diane his wallet, and gave her a beseeching look.

"All right. I'll take care of the money," Diane said, grinning wickedly, taking bills out of the leather fold and handing it back to Keith. "Do you think you should ask Holl to make part of his quest getting you back to normal?"

"I don't know," Keith said. "I think he might find it an advantage to have me permanently silent on at least three topics."

"I've always wanted to go to Ireland," Diane said, sighing happily as the train passed over a river. She put down her tea cup and pushed the empty tray to one side of the table. The sun was higher, and there were more signs of life in the countryside surrounding the tracks. "I hate clichés, but I can see why they call it the Emerald Isle."

After the remoteness of the Hebrides, Ireland was almost unbearably noisy and crowded. Backed by the smooth hills, which were clad in a brighter green than those of Scotland, children, clad in school uniforms, raced their bicycles alongside the train, shouting happily to each other. Dogs, running through yards facing the railway cut, barked as they rumbled past. Dozens of slender-hocked horses, nearly absent in northwest Scotland, grazed calmly in their paddocks. Men in flat woven caps chatted on the street corners, and women in skirts and knitted sweaters went about their business among the shops or hung up washing on the lines in their gardens.

"Sort of the national uniform," Keith observed. "But it's nice and homey."

Just outside of Dublin, Diane poked his arm and cried, "Look!"

High on the side of the railway cut was a billboard. In bright letters two feet high it advertised the Doyle Hotels. Within a hundred yards, they could see signs on shopfronts for Doyle's Estate Agency, The Doyle Bookstore, and Doyle's Grocery.

"Enterprising family I've got," Keith said proudly. "Wouldn't you say we're in the right place?"

In Dublin's Connolly Station, they left the train, and checked their bags in Left Luggage. Keith had unearthed from his suitcase the pages of notes on his family tree, and was eager to get started on his research. "I'm going down to the Genealogical Office. I've got all the facts my grandparents could remember from their parents, and some other stuff that's been handed down. Would anyone like to come with me?" he asked the others.

"Not a chance!" Diane said. "I didn't expect to be coming over, but as long as I'm here, I'm going to go do tourist things for a while. There might be a tour leaving from one of the hotels."

Keith looked hopefully at the other two.

"Not I, Keith Doyle," Holl said. "I want to walk in the sunshine. I'm not taking a Roman holiday with dusty books and tomes. I live in a library."

"He puts it vell," agreed the Elf Master, amused.

"Whatever," Keith said, somewhat crestfallen because no one wanted to join him. "Look, we'll meet for lunch at noon." They agreed on a meeting point, and Keith mounted the steps into the building.

The Genealogical Office offered help to people looking for their family lines on a per hour basis with one of their researchers. Keith was assigned to a slender, fair haired man named Mr. Dukes, who looked at Keith's records, and made some notes on a yellow pad.

"You've got more than some and less than others," Dukes said. "Pity you couldn't have thought of bringing the family Bible."

"My dad has it," Keith admitted, "but he didn't want me to take it with me. If anything happened to it, he'd be furious. I wrote out everything it said, though, all the births, deaths, and marriages."

"Good, good," said Dukes. "Let's see, now."

"The father of my ancestor who came to America was a land-owner. We have a couple of his letters," Keith said, showing the fragile slips of paper to Mr. Dukes, "and it sounds like he never got over being upset that his eldest son left the country, not keeping his skills as a doctor where his own people could benefit from them."

"Well, let's see what can be done with what is here." Dukes twisted his chair to face a computer terminal, and glancing at Keith's notes and sometimes to his own, brought up reference numbers, which he jotted down. "Some of this you'll have to look up at the Archives, but I think we may have a lot of what you need right here."

Typing expertly on the keyboard, Dukes requested cross-references to the data Keith had provided. He turned back to chat with Keith while the computer was digesting the information.

"So, are you enjoying Ireland?" he asked.

"For the few hours we've been here, yeah," Keith said, cheerfully. "It's beautiful. We took the train down from Larne."

"Well, that's only the north you've seen," Mr. Dukes chided him, deprecatingly. "Wait, here we are." The printer next to the workstation began to clatter, and ejected several sheets of paper. Mr. Dukes tore them off and separated them. He ran down the data with a pencil. "Good, this is what you'll want. We've got a match on several of your entries. Don't go away. I'll be right back with you. There's coffee over the way." The researcher left through a door at the other end of the room.

Keith waited at the desk, idly pushing his notes around, and reading the other papers upside down that lay on Mr. Dukes's desk. Soon, the researcher returned, pushing a library cart on which were stacked gigantic leatherbound books.

"The parish records for those entries we have," Dukes explained. "All the births, baptisms, deaths, and marriages recorded there, up to the present records, which are still in the parishes. We get them when they're through."

"How old are these?" Keith asked, touching one of the big books reverently.

Mr. Dukes turned to a page, and passed his finger down it carefully. "Some of these go back to 1800. These are the original documents, you understand. I can't let you take them out of the building, but I will give you copies of the entries, or you may write them down." He stopped at one line. "These are all in Latin, but this is the marriage record of a Fionn O'Doyle who married a woman named Emer O'Murphy on the fourteenth of June, 1818."

Several pages further on, he came across a baptism record for her firstborn, a boy named Emerson, born in 1820. Keith scribbled down the dates and names.

"Gee, that's creative," he observed. "Emer, Emerson. Wait! Aha, it's a family name. And I thought it was all rock and roll. I saw it in the family Bible, and it never dawned on me."

"A good match?"

"One I didn't expect," Keith said, pointing. "That's my middle name. This has to be the right family."

Mr. Dukes marked it with a tacky-backed tab for copying. "There's no death registered with that same name, so it looks like Emerson O'Doyle was the one who left."

"That's right. Grandpa said that he was a doctor," Keith added, referring to his notes.

"Possibly, but the birth register won't say so," the man said impishly, "and it's all we have to go on."

"You mean they didn't know at birth?" Keith innocently carried on the joke. "I thought second sight was run of the mill here."

The man ran through the file once more. "It seems he married a Miss Butler. Yes, this entry does note him as a Dr. O'Doyle. Well done. Now we can trace back through to see the rest of your lines. The Butlers and the O'Doyles are both from just north of Arklow near the coast, but more O'Doyles and the O'Murphys come from the north end of County Wexford above Gorey."

Keith soon had a pile of photocopies with a list of addresses of the parish churches. Mr. Dukes directed him to a nearby Ordnance Survey bookstore for maps of the area south of Dublin. "I hope you find what you're looking for. The best of luck to you," said Dukes, shaking his hand. "If you've any questions, come back again."

"Top of the morning to you," Keith said cheerfully, gathering his papers under one arm. "And thanks a lot."

Keith emerged from the Genealogical Office and found his way to the rendezvous point where the others were waiting. Diane steered them to a place that was serving lunch. As soon as they had given their orders to the waiter, Diane pointed at the pile of photocopies under Keith's elbow.

"Is all that from the Genealogy Office?" Diane asked.

"Yup. I have a few starting places," Keith said, patting the sheaf of paper. "I've got a list of parish churches and an abbey which might have records of my ancestors that can fill in holes in the stuff we've already found. The rest of this is copies of the birth and death registers for a lot of my multiple-great-grandparents and their children. If we take the train south from here to Bray or Arklow, we can start out looking around there locally."

"It's still the season for wildflowers," Holl said meaningfully. "If there's no trouble involved, I'd like to keep a close watch out for the bellflowers. It is the reason I came here, after all."

"Of course," Keith assured him. "I think it'll have to be on bicycles, though, and that will take a lot of time, not to mention muscle power. I'm too young to rent a car over here. They want you to be twenty-five."

"Ah," said the Master. "I can solf that problem."

"You'll really be the first couple married in Illinois?" Diane asked Holl, sentimentally.

"Yes, indeed, as well as the first ones to be born there. Because we're beginning a new page in our history, it's important to us to have a touch of the old ways about it. Maura and I have had a bond between us all our lives, and I want it to be a permanent one. I love her," he ended fiercely, looking off out of the restaurant window. No interloper will have her, he promised himself. I will win her back.

The Elf Master took off his spectacles and polished them with a pocket handkerchief. For the first time Keith had ever seen him so, the Master looked distressed.

"What's the matter, sir?" he asked.

"Ach, nothing. Both of my children are thinking of marriage. They grow so qvickly. I hardly think ve haf had enough time to enjoy them."

"Enoch is talking about getting married, too?" Keith asked, astonished. "Is he still dating Marcy?" Marcy Collier was a Big Person. She had been the object of Keith's affections for most of a school year. He had stopped chasing her when she had revealed a preference for one of the Little Folk. Keith knew about her and Enoch, and applauded it, but the idea of matrimony between them amazed him somewhat.

"Yes, he is," the Master confirmed.

"You're just going through empty-nest syndrome," Keith said, thinking out loud. "Maybe you should have some more kids."

The Master glanced at him, looking for evidence of flippancy, and found none.

"You're younger than Holl's folks, and they have a three-year-old," Keith pressed.

The Master shrugged. "Perhaps ve vill consider it. But I do not think that is the answer, vith so much vork left to be done on our new home."

Keith thought then that it would be politic to change the subject. Holl was still staring off into space. He tried to catch the Little Person's eye, and decided to let him come back to Earth at his own pace. "So, what did you see in Dublin?"

"Trinity College is walking distance from here. I had a look around. That's where they keep the Book of Kells. It's kind of a pity," Diane complained. "The books is shut up in a glass case in a fairly dark library. You only get to see whatever page the curator decided to show off on a day. I mean, I didn't expect to get to handle it, but it would have been nice if they had someone up there who could answer questions. I think he was having his tea."

"It is a mastervork," the Elf Master put in. "This vas a splendid opportunity for me. There were other illuminated manuscripts on display, vhich I examined closely. I haf purchased a complete reproduction of the Book of Kells itself for class study on medieval art."

"I thought you might say that," Holl groaned. "So that is what made you put in an Interlibrary Loan request for works by the Master of Sarum."

"That is true," the Master said complacently. "I alvays seek new subjects to explore. Research is the backbone of knowledge."

Leaving the restaurant, the Master took the lead. He guided them along the street, into the next block, and over the threshold of a glass-fronted showroom on the corner. The sign over their heads read Ath Cliatha Auto Rentals. Keith caught his arm.

"Where are you going?" he yelped. "The train station is the other way."

"Solfing the problem of transportation. You can drive vun of these autos?" the Master asked calmly.

"I think so," Keith said, involuntarily glancing at the traffic. "It's on the wrong side of the road, but it looks pretty straightforward."

"Gut. Then come vith me and choose. I am certainly old enough to sign the contract."

Thunderstruck, Keith followed the small teacher into the agency. Holl and Diane tagged along behind. A slim woman with dark brown hair and dusty green eyes stood up as they entered.

"Back again, Professor?" the woman greeted him cheerfully, putting out a hand for his. The Master clasped it. "We have two four-passenger vehicles on the lot now." She named two manufacturers. The Master looked back at Keith.

"Uh, either one, I guess," he said, and then watched as the young woman filled out the contract.

"May I have your driving license, please?" she asked the Master. Without murmur or hesitation, he duly produced a small card with a photograph in one corner. She turned to Keith. "If you're driving as well, I'll need to take your details, too." Keith handed his wallet card to her, and waited while she copied down his name and address.

He said nothing until the woman went for the keys to the car, and then leaned over the Master's head. "I'm going to tell the Department of Transportation on you."

The Master glanced up at him with a conspiratorial wink. Keith was delighted.

"Here you are," the young woman said, leading them outside to a small blue two door compact. She put the keys in Keith's hand and opened the door for him. Keith slipped into the driver's seat and looked for the rearview mirror. It was on the wrong side. So was the leftview mirror. It was on the right. Panicking, he looked up at the young woman for help. She smiled, crinkled lines gathering at the corners of her eyes.

"Let me go over the controls with you. There's a full tank of petrol. The rest is fairly easy to understand…"

Chapter Twenty Four

Keith's first few miles driving the car were as tentative as the first flight of any baby bird from a nest which was surrounded by asphalt and wild birds zooming by at top speed within inches of his wings. He made his way cautiously into the lane of traffic to the tune of racing engines and screeching brakes. The Dublin drivers didn't give an inch among themselves, and the roads seemed unaccountably narrow from his point of view on the wrong side of the car. Diane, navigating in the front passenger seat, was huddled as close to the center of the vehicle as she could be without obstructing the rear view mirror. Shortly, as Keith began to relax his driving improved, but his passengers took some time to lose the white around their eyes.

"Who says the Irish don't believe in magic?" Keith demanded, once they were out of the city and onto the smaller southbound roads. "Look at that. This road is almost as narrow as my bed. They paint a yellow stripe down the middle, and presto! Two lanes."

He glanced in the rear view mirror. His back seat passengers were not impressed by his levity. His jaw set, Holl was clutching the rubber loop hanging from the ceiling, and the Master simply sat looking pale. "Do you want me to stop and pick up some four leaf clovers?"

"No," the Master said. "Drive more slowly."

"Okay," said Keith imperturbably, without turning his head. "So where do we go?"

Diane handed the map into the back seat, and the Master opened it up. "I do not know," he admitted, after examining it closely. "It has been a long time, and the names have changed somewhat. Mere lines on paper mean nothing to me. I think I may haf to see landmarks to be certain."

"You didn't see anything familiar on the train ride south into Dublin, did you?"

"Of that I am certain, no. I do remember Dublin, and it vas most definitely to the north of vhere ve lived."

"That's okay," Keith assured him, following a fork in the road to the left. "I'll just head toward where I'm going, and if you have a place you want to stop on the way, then tell me, and we'll check it out."

With Diane directing him from the map, Keith drove through County Wicklow. The land changed gradually as they left Dublin. On the west side of the road, low mountains began to appear over the tops of the trees. They were not the dramatic black and gold peaks of Scotland. Instead, they were more gently rounded, with bright green grass and darker green trees covering their expanse. A high, nearly conical mountain passed by to their right, casting a long shadow across the road. At times they emerged into flattened valleys where the road was edged with trees, or wound along through small villages with signs written half in English and half in Gaelic. The iron mailboxes, which in Scotland had been red, were painted bright green.

"This is where you leave the Arklow road," Diane said, reading from the map, as they came to a sharp intersection to the right. Cutting across the right lane swiftly while there was no traffic, Keith turned inland, and started looking for the way to the first parish church on his list.

The road narrowed immediately to an unstriped lane between high hedges. Cautiously, Keith hugged the shrubbery on the left side. Though the road was frighteningly straitened, there always seemed to be enough room for two vehicles to pass one another. After one panicked moment when he had to dive into a blackberry thicket to avoid a farm vehicle and an old woman on a bicycle, their progress was much more calm.

"Hey, I'm getting the hang of this," he said happily, and then glanced at his passengers, who were hanging on in silence. "Hey, don't you all applaud at once."

Through the brush bounding the road, they could see farm houses and manor houses, and well trimmed fields with sheep or cows placidly grazing. A cluster of small cottages emerged among a stand of trees. "Look, Holl, it's your house," Keith said, cocking his head toward the roadside. A tiny white cottage with a high peaked roof of red slates lay nestled amid a wreath of rosebushes. Ivy climbed one wall and twined around the base of the chimney. A sheepdog lying in the middle of the drive regarded them with professional disinterest.

"It's amazingly similar," Holl said, staring as they passed the cottage.

"But old," Diane commented. "Really old."

"Vhere function does not change significantly, form rarely alters," the Master said, enigmatically.

"We're getting close to your village, aren't we?" Keith asked, excitedly.

"I am not certain," the Master said, without inflection. "I have seen nothing yet which awakens memory in me."

At last, a churchyard appeared on their right. The church, a fairly small building made of time-darkened stone, raised a square tower surmounted with a cross over the peak of the roof. The headstones, tilted this way and that in the tall grass around the building, were mostly flat and white, with sharp edges that made them look as if they had been cut out of a cake of wax. Beyond it was a residence, much newer than the church, but with the air of age. "This is it," Diane announced. "St. Michael's of the Downs."

"This is where I make sure that the Butler who I think married the grandfather who came to America actually left the area," Keith said, trying to avoid mentioning his female ancestor, but still get his meaning across. This curse was getting to be a pain.

"If I may understand your circumlocutions," Holl said, "you wish to find that the great-grandmother was not buried here, so that you have a match against the name of the one who left for America."

"Right," Keith said, relieved that someone understood his problem. "If the parish clerk is in, he or she might be able to give me some help finding the name."

"I'll help you," Diane said.

"I'm staying here," Holl declared. "I don't feel much like being exorcised today."

"Oh," said Keith, curiously. "Well, okay. I'll leave the key in the ignition in case you want to listen to the radio." He and Diane disappeared through the creaking wrought iron gate.

As soon as they were out of sight, Holl threw an aversion around the body of the car to drive off the gazes of idle passersby.

"To vhat purpose do you do this?" the Master asked curiously, observing Holl's handiwork. "You know ve haf nothing to fear from their priests."

"I know," Holl said, and steeled himself. "But I wanted a chance to speak with you privately. It is important that we come to an understanding. I have thought long and deeply on the subject, and I am determined to follow the old ways—where they are good ones.

Though I don't see why a bunch of simple flowers should be enough to prevent marriage among our people, I will follow the tradition set down. I am grateful that you came to help me when Keith Doyle was lost, but I feel that you have taken over the entire direction of this journey. All the decisions that have been made since you arrived have been yours. What about my task? How can I complete it if you take control?"

"I?" the Master asked, looking puzzled. "I shall do nothing to abrogate your task from you. Vunce ve are in the correct location, I intend that you shall complete your task on your own. My only concern is similar to that of Meester Doyle's. I vish to find our old home, and ensure that our folk still live. Vhether or not you haf a use for the flowers yourself vhen you return home, you have undertaken a responsibility on behalf of the others. I expect you to fulfill it."

Holl was mollified, but only just. He nodded.

"After all, unless you finish vhat you set out to do, you cannot reap the rewards of that action," the Master continued. "And it has alvays been my intention that you should do so."

Holl tried to find something to say in reply, but he found himself gaping at his teacher. So the Master was in favor of his match after all. He quickly turned away and went back to looking out of the window. Behind him, the Master chuckled softly.

A loud creak of protest from the churchyard gate heralded the return of the two Big Folk.

"Whew!" Keith said, swinging into the driver's seat, after he had unlocked the passenger door for Diane. "There was no one in the church, so we had to go over the tombstones one by one by ourselves. That was like taking attendance in a study hall. I counted a hundred and fifty seven names."

"Were any of them the one you were seeking?" Holl asked.

"Nope," Keith replied, happily. "In this case, no news is good news."

"Well, it's getting pretty late. We'd better find a place to stay for the night," Keith said. "I have a booklet of B&Bs and guest houses from the Ordinance Survey office. We'll see if any of the ones near by have room."

They pulled over beside the nearest green and yellow telephone box, and Keith started phoning down the list in the book. The first two had no room, and the third didn't answer. Keith grimaced apologetically to his passengers while waiting for the fourth to answer. There was a click, and a voice.

"Hello, Mrs. Keane? My name is Keith Doyle. I got your name from a tourist booklet. Do you have room for four people for about five nights? A twin room and two singles or a triple and a single is what we need. You can? That's terrific!" He scrawled down directions on the back of the book. "Right, see you soon." Keith returned to the car. "Voila. It's not far away, either. We're staying right in the middle of the clan area."

Under Diane's direction, Keith descended from the mountain valley and into the plain looking up into the heart of the range between the foothills. They followed the roads into a small town and out again, looking for the unmarked turnoff. Once they found it, they drove for a mile alongside a stretch of croplands interrupted only by telephone poles and odd lines of trees. They came to a gravel drive between white-painted gateposts, and drove through.

The house in the center of the grounds was a large manor in the Georgian style, with pillars around the entrance way. Keith parked next to a few other cars and stood up to stretch his legs.

"This is the place," he announced.

"Yes," said the Elf Master, getting out of the car and looking around him with evident satisfaction. "This *is* the place."

Keith eyed him. "Is there any more significance to that phrase than simply 'we are here'?"

The Master gestured with his chin toward the horizon. "Those mountains are to the north of us, are they not?"

Keith glanced to his left and then back at the Master. "Unless the sun has started setting somewhere else, yes."

"Then this is the correct area. The village lies to the south of the mountains you see before you, and not far away. The angle is correct."

"Yahoo!" Keith said, eagerly. "Are you sure? Right here in the middle of Doyle country? Terrific! We'll get an early start tomorrow, and find your old home. I knew it, we're neighbors." Holl groaned.

Together, they climbed the broad stairs between the pillars and into the front hall. "Hello?" Keith called softly, hearing his voice echo in the high, ornate ceilings above.

Suddenly, there was the sound of activity deep inside the house. One of the heavy wooden doors burst open, and a woman bore down on them, beaming. She was a handsome woman in her middle forties, roughly cylindrical in shape, with dark hair piled high on her head and milk white skin. The woman glanced at Holl and Diane, stared curiously at the Master for a short moment, and then her dark blue eyes fixed on Keith. She shook hands with him.

"Mr. Doyle, is it? How do you do. I'm Amanda Keane. Let me show you to your rooms."

The family occupied only the ground floor of the grand house, leaving the upper floors available for numerous guests. Keith and the others had a small wing almost to themselves. Diane was installed in a corner room at one end of a corridor. Keith and Holl were to share a twin room a couple of doors down, next to the bathroom. The Master was given the other corner room. Each was furnished with antiques and handmade rugs. Diane was breathless with admiration.

"There's tea-making facilities in each room," Mrs. Keane explained. "The bath is here. You should have it to yourselves, at least for tonight." She held out the keys to Keith.

"They're terrific, Mrs. Keane," Keith began, reaching for them, "but I guess I forgot to ask how muh—, how muh—"

Holl swiftly stepped in to rescue him. "He was asking what the tariff is? We forgot to inquire."

"So that's what the young lad here was asking," Mrs. Keane laughed, patting him on the back. Keith shot a pleading look at Holl, who opened the tourist booklet and showed a page to the guest house owner.

"By the way, I notice that here in the book you have a weekly rate, which is less than we would pay for five nights' stay. May we pay that instead?"

"Done and done," Mrs. Keane agreed, shaking his hand solemnly, and putting the keys into his hand. "Breakfast at eight, if you please."

"Thank you," Holl said. "And now, can you tell us a good place near by where we can get a meal?"

"Well, you might try the White Wolf. Their food is good, and it's only just up the road," Mrs. Keane instructed him, watching as he wrote down the directions. "But there's no sign on the road, and it doesn't say White Wolf. It says "Gibson's," and only on the glass. You have to watch for it."

Holl thanked her and accepted the keys. She bid them good night and went down the stairs. He watched her go. How good it was to be treated as an adult again! Perhaps Keith Doyle was correct, and the people around here did know the look of his folk. Then he heard her voice say to someone below stairs in a highly amused voice, "Such a *serious* child, you can't think!" He smiled to himself. And then again, perhaps not.

"Well, that's all too complicated for me," Diane yawned. "I still have jet lag. I'm going to bed."

The others went off in high energy to find the White Wolf and discuss their search for the village. Diane took the opportunity when the house was quiet to have a long, hot bath and wash her hair. While she was toweling her hair dry, there was a tap at one of the doors down the hall.

"Mr. Doyle?" Mrs. Keane's voice asked.

Diane opened the door and leaned out. "They've gone to dinner, Mrs. Keane."

"Ah, well, there's a man on the telephone for him," the landlady said.

Diane shook her head. "It's got to be a mistake. No one knows we're staying here yet. I haven't even called my folks."

"It's likely a wrong number, then," Mrs. Keane said, reasonably. "Certainly our telephone system is none of the best, but I am sure he asked for a Mr. Doyle."

"Well, it's not like it's an uncommon name around here," Diane smiled. She closed the door and went back to drying her hair.

Michaels had got no joy from Genealogy Office. It seemed that O'Day had embarked on what would be a legitimate ancestor search. He must be planning to keep the Keith Doyle persona for a long time. Michaels was reassured then that O'Day and the others were unaware that they were being followed, or he would have discarded the pretended identity like a used tissue.

The Ordinance Survey Bookshop in Dublin had been much more forthcoming. The clerk remembered the red-haired American. O'Day had purchased a list of guest houses in the area south of Dublin, and if he was staying with his assumed identity, would be putting up in one of them. All Michaels had had to do was call down the list of numbers until he found them.

Chapter Twenty Five

The four travelers spent the next few days searching the countryside for anything which sounded a chord in the Master's memory. Keith worked out a system of triangulation by which they circled an area, covering all the small roads within it, and were able to reduce the area of search considerably. Still, the process was slow.

The weather contrived to cause the search to be more slow still. It was nice the day after they arrived, but thereafter, a low front moved in over Ireland, dousing them in rain every day and raising the ambient humidity considerably. Keith kept the defogger running constantly to keep the windows clear, so the passengers had to shout over the noise of the fan. He knew the Master was looking for particular landmarks, some of them small. One for which he kept his eyes peeled was a rockfall. There were plenty in this part of the country, and the Master looked at them all, rejecting one after another.

"It could be ground up into pebbles by now," Keith said. "It might not be here any more."

"They von't haf moved it," the Master assured him. "But I am not sure I remember vhy."

Diane checked off another small section as they turned off one of the narrow roads marked on the map, and noticed an interesting entry. "Well, that's that for this part. Say, did you know that those mountains out there are supposed to contain gold mines?"

"Yes, of course," the Master replied absently. "It vas a valuable resource to us. Though the mines were not safe after a time, and they began to yield less. They kept out the Big Folk, but of course ve did not ask their permission."

"Uh huh," Keith said. "And that's where you got your pots of gold, eh?"

"Keith Doyle!" Holl exclaimed, outraged, quickly deducing where that line of logic was leading. "In your own research, leprechauns are reputed to be hand high."

"Depends on how high you hold your hand," Keith replied, blithely.

"Stop the car," the Master ordered suddenly. Keith coasted to a halt, and the Master got out. Among a crowd of smaller trees down the slope from the roadside, two huge oak trees stood, seemingly sprouted from the same root. Keith followed him partway, to make sure nothing happened to him. Ignoring the rain, he watched the Master hurry toward them, almost sliding down the hillside, which was ankle-deep in last year's leaves. The teacher examined the trees, walking around them, and reaching as high into the fork as he could. Then the little man's shoulders slumped, all the starch gone out of them. He turned back and walked back, not looking up at the car. By the time he ascended the slope, Keith was sitting behind the wheel, waiting politely.

"Shall we go on? I think you wanted us to try this way next."

From then on, Keith kept an eye out for twinned oak trees. As they drove higher, trees became fewer. He took the next road which sloped downward. Ahead of him, he could see the brilliant green of leaves once more. The road twisted and rose higher, but this hill was copiously forested and blocked them from seeing more than fifty yards ahead. Keith felt hope stir when he saw the Master's face out of the corner of his eye. The little teacher wanted to smile, but he didn't dare. Keith felt his heart start beating faster. This time, it was the real thing. They must be close.

They passed several huge trees to which had been tied red and yellow signs. Keith couldn't read them through the rain, but they appeared to be protesting something to do with the Council.

"Take the next turning toward the hilltop," the Master ordered. "Tvin oak trees. Ah! Those are the vuns. They vere smaller vhen I vas last here." Holl gazed at the trees, as if being remembered by the Master somehow ennobled them above all other oaks.

Keith pointed. "Is that your rockfall?" he asked. Across the valley to their left, half a hillside had collapsed, leaving a heap of gigantic boulders. A rare angle of perspective through the rain and the clear air made the monument seem to be much smaller, and immediately beside them. "So that's why you were so sure no one would move it, over the years. It's a mountain! Here we are!"

Keith steered the car into a small turning, slick with mud, and stopped.

"Vhat's this?" the Master demanded. Before them was no village of cottages, but a small street of newly built houses, surrounded by churned-up earth.

"This is the hilltop," Keith said, looking around him in confusion.

"This vas not here before. Vhat is it?" the Master asked in an agitated voice.

"It's a housing project," Keith replied, reading a yellow sign tied to a tree at the entrance to the site. "Really recent. There's still mud all over the streets, and no grass yet. And I guess it's not a very popular project. Look at that."

Holl read the notice. "It asks the local folk to rally against the council and the developers. They wish others to boycott the project, and not buy the houses or prevent others from taking residence, 'because only Peeping Toms would live here.'" Several other signs had been tied up all over the street. They were visible on the young trees planted in front of every house, and tied to almost every doorknob.

Behind them, an engine raced, and a voice shouted at them through the rain. Keith glanced into the mirror, and hastily moved the car aside. A lorry thundered past them into the development, carrying a gang of skinny trees.

"Where are your folk?" Keith asked the Master.

"Gone." The Master climbed out of the car and walked blindly along the muddy street. Keith and the others followed him. The new houses watched them with blank glass eyes like rows of mannequins.

"Gone," the Master said forlornly. "All has been destroyed. Are they all dead?"

"It was a nice place," Keith offered, following the little teacher and trying to be soothing. "There's a great view."

The Master stopped and looked away, reminiscently. "And the river vas only a hundred paces away. The vells vere sweet. The air is as I remember it. There is as yet only the faintest stink of cifilization here."

"It looks like this place isn't happy," Keith said, wondering what made him think that.

The Master turned a penetrating gaze on him. "It is not. You can sense it. Imagine vhat anger *we* can sense. The Big Folk down there think that it is bad because these new buildings overlook them. That is incorrect. It is because a magical place that has been here from the beginning has been uprooted. They shall have no joy of it. But it is too late." He raised his hands helplessly to encompass the muddy streets. "Too late. It is ruined. They do not know what they haf done, but the earth vill tell them."

Keith remembered being swallowed up by the earth on the hill-top in Callanish, and stopped the small teacher with a hand on his arm. "Is there, um, something sentient underneath there? Like a monster?"

The Master smiled sadly. "Ah, no, merely the Earth. Only Nature. But ve treated it vith respect, and they have not. Vill not," he added.

"Should we warn them?" Keith asked, with concern.

"Vhat good vould it do? Can you warn the developers in your own country that what they are disturbing is vengeful?"

"No," Keith admitted, honestly. "But what about the tenants? It's not their fault they're going to be living over a magic volcano."

"They'd call you a nut if you told them that," Diane said firmly. "Nobody is moving in here against their will. They'd think you owned one of the houses down there." She pointed to the offended neighborhood.

Together, they walked the perimeter of the entire housing estate, looking for anything which had been left undisturbed. The area around the streets had been piled high with the earth excavated from the building sites. Mature trees had been pushed down and left in scattered heaps like jackstraws.

"They must haf left directions to where they had gone," the leader said sadly, "if there vere any who could leaf them. But it is all destroyed, beyond where they beliefed it might be, by the bigfooted fools. Are ve the only vuns left?"

"Maybe they're still close by," Keith suggested, hopefully, unwilling to declare the Master's folk dead. He threshed his way out into the nearest large field and called out a halloo with his hands cupped around his mouth. "Yo! Little People!"

"Oh, stop that," Diane said impatiently, running out after him and bringing him back. "This field is full of nettles. Let's get out of here. You're soaked, and so am I. So are they." She nodded back at the Master, who was standing in the growing downpour looking lost. "This place is too creepy to stay in."

There was silence in the little car for a long while. Keith turned the heater on full blast to try and dry them, but succeeded only in making them feel sticky and uncomfortable. He rolled down the window a crack, and let the coolness of tiny drops of rain come in.

"Do you think they stayed close by?" Keith asked the Master, who was sitting deep in thought, stroking his beard. "I mean, you guys are not too big on travel."

"I haf no idea. There is no vay to tell vhen the village vas abandoned." The Master stared sadly into space.

The rain began to break up. Brave spears of sunlight poked between the clouds and lit up that much of a hill or this much of a valley, striking up the golds and greens in the landscape, and dropping curious shadows down the valleys. The photographer in Keith refused to be contained any longer.

He pulled the car over near a likely field, where the hedge was low, and climbed up. Beneath him lay a broad and handsome valley like a sampler, dotted with sheep or stitched with growing crops. Clusters of woods lay at the right intersection of the perfectly straight lines of trees and brush which separated fields.

"Yoo-hoo! Little Folk!" he called down, waving his arms. "Hey, Holl, how do you say "where are you" in your language."

"I don't," the Little Person shot back. "Don't waste your time. Take your picture and come down."

"All right, spoilsport," Keith said. "I'm only trying to help."

Michaels huddled over the wheel of his car and wished again for the omnidirectional microphones of the American secret service. O'Day was signaling to someone, with an air of expectancy. He feared that it was quite likely to be the connection that would make this entire investigation worthwhile, and his elderly listening mechanism couldn't pick up a sound. The small blue car rolled again, and Michaels followed, careful to keep his distance. An unexpected turn could throw him into line-of-sight, or lose O'Day in the distance. Something was sure to happen imminently.

At any likely point when he wanted to take a picture, Keith repeated his antics on the hedge, and called out to any of the Little Folk who might be listening. Holl had given up trying to stop him, and sat in the car patiently with Diane, waiting for Keith to run out of film.

They stopped on a ridge of land that overlooked two points in the great valley, both satisfyingly picturesque. Happily, Keith got out, and leaned over the gorse-covered wall on one side to take an exposure. The hedge on the other side was too high and too flimsy to climb. Eyeing the nettles and gorse cautiously, Keith walked back to the car. Bracing one foot on the car bumper and the other among the heather, he hoisted himself up far enough to see over the wall.

Below was a broad sward of green populated by a herd of cows, who stood or lay on the flattened, wet grass, ignoring the waving and shouting of a figure like a demented scarecrow.

"Hello there," a voice called from behind him. Keith twisted his spine around and glanced back. There was a tan car parked about fifty feet behind him. A man had climbed out of it, and was walking toward them. He was of middle height, and had wavy red hair.

Keith jumped down with his hands on the car roof for balance. "Hi!" he called back. "What can I do for you?"

"Nothing for me," the man said, cheerfully, coming up close to him. "Having a bit of car trouble? I saw you waving. I thought you might be signaling for help."

Keith laughed. "Oh, no. Everything's fine. We're just taking pictures. Beautiful day for it."

The man looked up and down at his sodden clothes, and grinned at him. His eyes were hazel-green. "It is now. Goodbye, then."

"Thanks anyway," Keith called. The man threw him a salute and drove off.

"Didn't he look like the map of Ireland?" Keith commented. "As my grandmother would say."

"I would say he looked just like you, plus ten years or so," Holl called through the window in amusement.

"I noticed," Keith said, winding the film forward in his camera. "My uncle Rob and he could almost be twins."

"But what I found more interesting is that the sticker on the back window of his car said 'Doyle's Garage,'" Holl pointed out. "He did offer to help you fix your car. I wonder if he owns the place, or merely rents from them."

"What?" Keith leaped into the driver's seat. "Why didn't you say something?"

"I thought you could read that for yourself," Holl protested.

The others braced themselves as the little blue car leaped forward. It raced down the road in pursuit of the sedan. Keith thought he saw the tan car ahead of him.

"We'll catch him at the next turning," he said.

The next intersection was a blind angle to a crossroads. Each of the other three branches was empty. "We lost him," Keith said sadly.

"Never mind," Diane said. "If you had any doubts before if we were in the right place, you better have lost them now."

"Oh, well," Keith said, pulling over to the side of the road. It was narrow, so the left wheels were wedged up among the nettles and gorse. A quick glance in the mirror showed the Master's crest-fallen face. He was still hurting after finding the old homestead abandoned. Keith needed a distraction, any distraction. He looked up at the wayposts at the crossroads. "Look, that way is Killargreany. Isn't the next place on my list there?"

Diane found the sheet of paper in the map compartment and read it. "That's right. Boy, that must have been right up the road from your family. Married, born, married, died, born, born, born, married, born...." she ticked off the highlighted entries in the sheaf of parish records. Keith took off the parking gear and headed toward Killargreany.

The Killargreany church was larger and more elaborately decorated than the small parish church of St. Michael's had been. Set in a valley embraced on two sides by the glowing golden-green mountains, it had a serene solidity that made the travelers stop simply to look at it. The stone walls had long ago gone green with lichen. The shrubbery around the churchyard side had been allowed to grow wild, but it had done so artistically. Birds sang from the great yew trees clustered within the low stone walls.

Numberless generations of local men and women had attended this church and had been buried here with its rites. Large tombs, some new, some old, and some decrepit, jostled elbows with every description of memorial stone, some of which stood at drunken angles in the ground. Keith took one look at the extensive churchyard, and made straight for the church door. "I've got to have expert help on this one. I wonder if anyone's here."

The huge wooden door opened quietly on its hinges. Inside, the church was cool and dim. Diane shivered once, violently, and felt all right after that. They stood for a moment to allow their eyes to become accustomed to the light.

Above them, the high, vaulted ceiling began to emerge from the gloom. It was held up by heavy beams of blackened wood. The door through which they had entered was at the rear of the right side of the building. At the front of the church, to their right, a window of jewel-colored stained glass glowed with warm blues and reds.

"How beautiful," Diane breathed. "This place is old."

At its foot, there was an altar, covered with an embroidered cloth and bedizened with colored dashes and dots from the window above. In the middle of the tabletop stood a gold cross with a circle set at the juncture of the crosspiece and upright.

Rows of carved wooden pews marched back toward them along the aisle. Keith stepped forward to caress the smooth polish with the palm of his hand and wondered what Holl would think of them, and why he wouldn't enter churches. That was something which would warrant investigation when he had the time to think about it.

A table stood at their side of the church, behind the last row of pews. On it were arranged stacks of small pamphlets. One showed a line drawing of the church, and said in two languages "The History of Our Church". There was a box with a slot in the top nearby, which read "Pay Here Please" in black letters.

"Honor system," Keith noted, digging in his pocket for change.

The large coins falling into the box sounded like chains clanking, echoing in the quiet building. Keith was reading one of the flyers by the light from the door when he heard bustling near the altar place. A door opened, and a elderly priest in long black vestments emerged, straightening his glasses on his nose.

"Visitors, by the look of you?" the old man said, a question and a statement in one phrase. "Welcome. Ah, it's getting late, and I'm behind in my duties. It's no excuse, but it's a sleepy summer day. The lights should be on by now. I'm Father Griffith." He smiled at their surprise. "One Welsh ancestor, and it's followed me for eight generations."

Keith introduced himself and Diane, and explained his reason for visiting. "I'm hunting down my family line. I think that this is the area where my folks came from. The Genealogy Office told me this would be the first place I should look, and then branch out into the smaller parishes around here."

The priest shook their hands. "I'm pleased to meet you both. Do you know, we get many visitors over the year, most of them from America. And where is it you might be coming from?"

"I live outside Chicago. Diane is from Michigan."

The priest nodded expansively. "Ah, Chicago. A great place. I've never been there myself, you understand, but so I've been told, and the films that are made there! Shocking, some of it."

"They're all true," Diane said, impishly.

"Doyle, Doyle," Griffith mused, studying Keith's face. "There's enough of those, to be sure. What's the names you're looking for, then?" He took Keith's hand drawn family tree and began to peruse it, steadying his thin rimmed glasses with one hand. "Ah, well, you'll not find this one here," he pointed, and then read the small penciled notation underneath. "I see you know that already. Good. I'm a great historian, if I am going to have to say it for myself. I'm always browsing among the stones out there, getting to know my parishioners, even the ones who are not precisely with us any more, if you understand me."

"It looks like my three-times-great grandfather, Emerson O'Doyle, was the one who moved away from here. He was born in this parish, and married here, too, I think. It looks like he went to open a practice in Arklow, and left from there to go to America," Keith explained, pointing out the names in the family tree.

"You don't know why they left, then?" Griffith asked, looking at him over the tops of his glasses.

"No," Keith said. "We've only got a few letters and things that were saved. None of them say why."

"You can make up great stories and all, but it's usually a fundamental thing which drives a family to leave the land of their birth. I think I know the reason for this one. The name stuck in my mind, which is why I remember it. It's this way." Griffith beckoned them around to the aisle and along the wall. He stopped before a white, engraved stone only a few inches square.

"Pray for the soul of Padraig Thomas O'Doyle, Died April 5, 1855, aged sixty-three days," Keith read. "Beloved son of Emerson and h…" His voice stopped on the reference to the dead child's mother.

Diane finished for him. "…His wife Grainhe Butler O'Doyle."

"How sad, to have survived the Famine, and lose his first little son like that," Father Griffith said, sympathetically. He nodded when Keith held up his camera, giving silent permission to take a picture of the cenotaph. "If it's a happier note you'd be wanting, I can show you where his uncle is buried: Eamon. He lived to be seventy-eight."

In spite of himself, Keith laughed. "I'd be happier if you could tell me where to find the living half of the family, Eamon's children—or great-great grandchildren now. My folks would like to get to know them. Do you know many Doyles?"

"Ah, yes, I know everyone. In a small place like this, we all know the ins and outs of each other's business. I've got to look up me records. It occurs to me that I might know someone who's come down from the family of Eamon O'Doyle, second son of Fionn," Griffith recalled suddenly, one finger in the air to mark a mental place. "And you might think of putting up a notice on the board with your name and address. That may stir memories I lack."

He guided Keith back to the pamphlet table, and gave him a sheet of paper, and then disappeared into the rear of the church. While Keith was printing his message, the priest arrived with an armload of big, leather-bound books. "These are the current birth and baptismal records, along with the marriage and death registers for this parish. The old ones go to the Central Archives when they're written to the last page. My clerk will as likely have my ears for pulling them out of her office, but as you've come all this way I'm not wanting to stand on ceremony."

"Thank you, Father!" Keith began to thumb through the pages. Here and there he spotted the name Doyle. Furiously, he jotted down names and dates and the names of babies' parents. "I should have given myself a lot more than one week for this job."

"Well, you'll be wanting to come back, then," the priest said hospitably, and dropped a fingertip on Keith's notice. "Just scratch down there the place you're staying while you're in Ireland. You'll excuse me now, as it's nearly time for evening prayers. You might think of staying yourself, if you have the time. And good afternoon, Mrs. Murphy. How are you this fine day? Not a drop of rain or a wisp of cloud." The priest moved away to place a hand on the arm of a very old woman walking slowly into the aisle of the church. Squinting through filmy blue eyes, she smiled up at the black-coated clergyman, who helped her to a pew. After he tacked up his notice, Keith waved a silent farewell to the priest. Father Griffith nodded companionably to him, never breaking off his conversation with the old woman.

"That's a great piece of luck," Diane said, as they wandered around the churchyard. "There were their names, right there, together, even carved in stone. Hmm!" She stretched out her arms in the sunshine and turned up her face to be warmed. "What a nice place to be buried, if you have to be dead. It's really lovely here."

Chapter Twenty Six

They walked back to the car. Keith was jubilantly buoyant with the success of his visit. Holl listened to the narrative intently.

"So what will you do with the birth records you copied down?"

"Mr. Dukes suggested that I look in the phone books, and send letters explaining what I'm doing. A lot of the people might consider a phone call to be intruding, so I should just approach them politely from a distance."

"That sounds sensible," Holl agreed.

The Master, now seated in his old place in the back seat, said nothing. He seemed to have retreated inside himself to think. As they headed back to the Keane home, Keith tried several times to start cheerful conversations. After the Master ignored his questions and remarks, he decided wisely to leave the leader alone with his thoughts.

"I'm still soggy," Keith said. "We're not far away from the guest house, but why don't we stop and have a drink or something, and warm up? Then we can go back and change for dinner." On the backdrop of the still-gray sky, Keith had noticed a glow of white light over the treetops which might mean a pub or a farmhouse in the distance. He was hoping for a pub.

Following the glow, Keith wound upward through the two-lane roads, and arrived in front of a white-walled building that announced itself proudly as The Skylark, which was The Highest Pub in Ireland.

Keith coaxed the reluctant Master into the pub's lounge.

"There are many of your folk in this place," the Master said. "Are you not concerned that they vill see us?"

The American peered around the corner. "It's pretty dark in there. Look, there's a fireplace with no other lights around it. We'll go and dry out a little, and then if you think it's safe, we can have a drink. If not, we'll just go before there's any trouble."

"That sounds prudent," Holl said. He pushed the door open and stood by as the others passed inside.

"Ach," said the Master. "You are behaving like vun of the Big Folk. Too bold!"

Rather than being oppressed by the dimness of its lights, the Skylark was made cozy and inviting. A coal and peat fire glowed red in the ornamental iron firebox and touched lights in the complicated patters of the enameled tiles with which the hearth and wall were lined. Overstuffed chairs and sofas sat under the curtained windows, which were shut tight against the cool evening wind. There were knickknacks on the walls, some of them unidentifiable even in full light. With Keith between them and the customers at the rectangular bar, the Little Folk made their way toward the old fashioned settees near the fireplace.

"Oh, that's better," Diane said, shaking out the legs of her jeans. "I wish I could wring out my shoes. They'll squish for a week."

Keith watched the bartender inside the bar moving back and forth between customers in the light of the single orange lamp behind the bottles. He was a burly young man with curly, dark hair and a beak of a nose between straight, dark brows. He set down glasses, and exchanged quiet jokes as he cleared away empties. Conversations between the locals, though animated, were in low tones.

"How about it?" Keith suggested.

He walked over and casually took a seat at the darkest corner of the bar, far removed from the next customer. Diane sat down next to him, and gave him a conspiratorial wink. In a moment, Holl joined them, sitting on Keith's other side. He was followed by a reluctant Elf Master, who wedged himself between a post and the wall.

"You are unreasonably bold," he told Holl sternly.

"They think I'm a child, Master," Holl replied reasonably. "They'll give me a fruit soda."

"Welcome," the server said, coming over and giving the bar in front of them a wipe with his towel.

"Hi," Keith said. "It's a wet night."

"Oh, I don't mind," the man said. Keith could see that he was quite young, not too far from his own age. "I was planning to swim home tonight. I brought me water wings." Diane laughed, and the young man smiled at her. "Americans, are you?"

"That's right."

"Over here for the holidays?"

"Sort of," Keith said, wondering where to begin. "Well, I'm researching my family tree. I was here for a combination tour and college course for credit. We both go to Midwestern University in Illinois."

"Do you?" the young man said, pausing in his polishing. "I'm at Trinity College in Dublin. I'm happy to meet fellow students."

"We were there," Diane said. "I went to look at the Book of Kells."

"What are you studying?" Keith asked him.

"I'm reading history," the young man said, with a wide grin on his face, "but I'm learning Mandarin Chinese on the side."

"Go on," Diane said, sensing a joke, "drop the other shoe. Why?"

"Well, me mam's expecting her fourth, you see," he told them seriously, "and they say that one out of every four babies born in the world is Chinese. I want to be able to understand him when he starts to talk."

"So why don't you move next door to a Chinese family?" Keith asked, joining in the game. "That way, if they get one of the other three, you can just swap babies with them."

"That's a grand idea," agreed the young man, just keeping a straight face while the others laughed. "The truth is that I'm learning Chinese to be a translator. It'd be a grand job. I have three other languages as well."

"That's great," Keith said. "I know a little Spanish, but that's all."

"And what's her name?" the lad asked with a wink, and presented Diane with a guileless mien. "Just in fun, miss."

Diane gave him her best image of outrage, and then cracked up helplessly into laughter at the youth's wide-eyed innocence. "I know."

"What may I bring you?"

"Two pints," Diane ordered for herself and Keith. "Is it still called a pint here?"

"More than ever," the young man said. "You ought to have a Guinness. It's good for you."

"Sure," Diane said, looking at Keith for his approval. He nodded, eyes shining. "Hmm. Must be good stuff."

"Oh, it is, it is, miss," the bartender assured her. He reached for two pint mugs and set them under the pumps.

Diane gestured toward the two Little Folk. The young man glanced at them and back at her. "And I think they'll have..."

The bartender stopped her short, and turned to Holl and the Master. "I beg your pardon, miss," he said deferentially. "Gentlemen, what is your pleasure?"

The two Little Folk looked at each other. Some thought seemed to pass between them, and the Master nodded. As one, they removed their hats and set them on the bar. "A Guinness," Holl said, tousling his hair furiously with both hands and fluffing it out. "Thank the powers, maybe now it'll dry."

"The same, please," the Master said, watching the young man curiously. The bartender gave them a wink and stepped over to the pumps. Carefully, he drew half a glass of Guinness into each pint mug and put them on the back of the bar to settle. The mocha froth slowly began to separate into chocolate beer below and cream foam above. The Master nodded approvingly.

"It takes time to pour one properly," said the young man. "But it's worth it for the taste." Holl pushed a few pound notes across to him, but he pushed it back, with a shake of his head. "Oh, no, it'd be unlucky to take your money from you. My compliments to you, sir. It's on the house."

"Thank you kindly," Holl said, in surprise.

Keith watched this performance with a kind of outraged concern. He looked hastily around the bar to see if anyone had observed them. It was impossible now to disguise the fact that two of the customers in the Skylark had ears almost five inches long that ended in points on the top. Strangely, the Little Folk didn't seem to be worried. Keith wished that he could feel the same way. He was so used to protecting his small friends and drawing the attention of others away from them, to keep them from being carried off to be used for strange experiments or museum exhibits. He had no idea that it might be all right to expose the truth in some places, but apparently, they did. No one at all had turned their way. Maybe it was more of the aversion spell that Holl had used in the airport, and, now that Keith looked back, in the town around Midwestern University. Their own sort of protective coloration, he acknowledged.

The Guinness was topped off, and in a few minutes, set before them. Keith picked his up and offered a silent toast to his friends. He tasted it, and let out a sigh of satisfaction. It was rich and tasty, with a sort of astringency that in a poorer drink would be bitterness. Diane handed the young man a banknote, and picked up her mug.

"This is better than we got in Scotland," Keith said, sipping carefully through the foam. Diane tasted hers, with an expression of pleased concentration on her face. She nodded.

"Ah, it doesn't travel well," the server said. "You have to come to Ireland to have real Guinness. The brewery is not far from here, just down the road a bit. They say that it's the best when you can see the smoke from the chimneys from where you're drinking it."

"Can you see it from here?" Keith asked. The young man nodded, his eyes twinkling. "Have one yourself."

"Not at present, but my thanks to you," the server said, taking the banknote and turning to the cash drawer. "I have to give it all my attention when I drink—in appreciation, you understand—and that's bad for business."

Keith was relieved to be just sitting still for a moment, and not staring at anything through fog. With one hand on the handle of his glass, he watched the goings-on in the pub. A giggling couple came in at the door and made for the fireplace. The girl unwound a scarf from her hair while the man came up to the rail to order from the bartender. He returned to her, sipping the top off an overfull glass, and disappeared into the red-tinged shadows next to the hearth. Other customers looked at their watches, and flicked money onto the bar top, calling farewells. The server picked up the change and bade them return soon.

A bandylegged figure in a leather coat and woolly scarf emerged from a darkened corner on the other side of the lounge and waddled silently toward the door. Lit only by the fireplace and the orange lamp, the bearded face under the flat cap bore a slight resemblence to the Elf Master. Of course, half the men over forty in this part of the world did. That didn't make him any different from most of the other gaffers in the bar. What made Keith take notice was when the bearded man opened the door to leave. He seemed to be no more than eyelevel to the doorknob. Keith blinked. It was probably a trick of the light. Keith caught a glimpse of bright blue eyes glancing his way, lit by the swinging lanterns outside. He turned back to the bar, shaking his head.

"I think we just saw one of your relatives," he said in a voice pitched only for Holl and the Master to hear.

"This is no time for one of your jokes, Keith Doyle," Holl said in a frosty voice.

"I mean it," Keith persisted. "I'm not betting my Uncle Arthur's hotel towel collection on it, but I really think so."

Holl lowered his glass, with eyes narrowed. "I thought you said your family broke no laws."

Keith assumed an expression of wounded innocence. "I did. He's in the textile business. He gets one of each as samples."

Holl looked over his shoulder. "Then where is the man you saw?"

"He's gone now," Keith said, glancing back, too. The outer door had swung shut. "Really, he could have been your cousin."

The Master said nothing, and drank his Guinness gloomily. Frivolous references to his loss thickened the shell around the small leader. He ignored Keith and Holl stolidly.

"We ought to think about finding a place where we might be able to have dinner," Diane said, and did a double take. "God, I'm starting to talk like the locals, with the eightfold sentences. I'm getting hungry."

"Me, too," Keith said, referring to his watch. "It's just about the time they start serving. We're dry now. I think I could face the car seats again. Come on." Diane smiled at the bartender, and the four of them stood up.

Amid merry calls of farewell, Keith assured the publican they would stop by again soon. "We'll get back here at least once before we go home," he promised. The door swung shut behind them. The moon overhead was not far from full, and Keith felt alive and full of good spirits, both figurative and literal.

He jingled his car keys, and started across the car park to the blue compact, followed by Diane and the two Little Folk. It was full dark, and the sky overhead was clear and spangled with stars. As they passed under the shadow of the brick arch, a voice issued from the darkness, smooth and warm like melted caramel. It asked a question in an unintelligible lingo. The Master's head went up. He stopped, and replied tentatively in the same language. A small figure darted from behind the wall and waylaid the Master, pulling him to one side. Keith jumped forward to defend his teacher, but the Master held up a hand.

It was the small man in the cap. He slapped out a barrage of words, his nose within inches of the Master's, who replied to him slowly in the same tongue, without a trace of the Deutsch accent with which he spoke English. Keith hovered nearby, getting more and more excited.

"Listen!" he hissed to Diane. "Listen!"

"I think they know each other," she murmured. "Is that your little man?"

"Yup."

The small man turned his head to glance at the Master's companions. The two Big Folk he dismissed immediately, and ignored thereafter, but Holl he studied. He asked another question, a short one, and Holl, clearly fascinated, approached more closely to answer. The stranger clasped his forearm and drew him forward, looking him carefully up and down. Keith was burning with curiosity.

The stranger made a final exclamation, and guided the two Little Folk under the archway toward the road. Keith, with Diane holding on to his arm, started to follow them. Holl heard the crunch of gravel behind him and looked over his shoulder.

"Go home," he ordered. "Don't follow us."

"But, Holl, I want to know who he is, and where...."

"Go home, Keith Doyle," Holl repeated, seriously. "This is not Gillington Library. You might wind up with your teeth pulled, not only your fillings. We will be safe, and we'll find our own way back."

Keith's hand flew protectively over his mouth. Diane tugged him back into the car park.

"Come on," she said. "He's right. Let's go have dinner." Keith stayed next to the car until the three small figures disappeared into the darkness. Glumly, he unlocked the door and climbed in.

After changing out of their sodden jeans and running shoes at the guest house, Diane asked the proprietress for recommendations of good places to eat. Mrs. Keane had flyers from a number of restaurants, but she pointed out two as being the best of the lot. They chose the one that was the easiest to find, a small restaurant named The Abbot's Table a few miles to the north.

The daily specials and their prices were chalked on a black slate over the hearth in the small dining room. The candlelit tables, about twelve in number, were crowded fairly close together, but there was still some elbow room left over. They slid into their seats, and read the menus in silence. Diane ordered their meals for them, and chatted for a few minutes with the waitress. Keith sat looking glumly out of the window at the darkness, wondering what Holl and the Master were doing. Who was the little man? A relative or a friend? Did he know they were going to be in that pub that day, or was it chance?

"Come on," Diane said, breaking into his thoughts. "You're obsessed. Let's just have a nice time, and you can interrogate Holl tomorrow morning. Let's talk about something else other than them."

"Sorry," Keith said, apologetically. "I'm only half human, you know. The rest is pure curiosity. I won't be rotten company any more, I promise." Keith roused himself, determined to be entertaining. Over the excellent dinner, they talked about the countryside they'd seen, and travel in general. He was fine so long as he avoided any of the *bodach*'s prohibited subjects.

"My dad always wanted to come here to Ireland. I think with all the stuff I've found for him, he'll be even more rarin' to come over and pick up where I left off," Keith said. "There's a list of Doyles in the phone book a mile long. Dad will be thrilled. I found two Eamon Doyles. You know, given names sometimes run in cycles, skipping generations, so one of these guys might be a direct descendant of my multi-great-granduncle."

"It's fun to watch you working on your family tree," Diane confessed, after they had ordered dessert. "I don't have the energy, or maybe not the interest, to do my own. Part of the problem is that I don't speak Swedish or Danish, or any of the other parts of my family's background. I could do the maternal line, I suppose. Some of my mother's family is English."

"Shh!" Keith silenced her playfully, looking suspiciously around the restaurant in case they were overheard. "Don't talk about that here!"

"Oh, knock it off," she retorted, shaking her head at him affectionately.

"Excuse me," said the older woman seated at the table next to them.

"See," Keith told Diane. "Now you've done it."

"Oh, shut up. Yes, ma'am?"

"You're Americans, aren't you?" They nodded. "I thought so," she said to her husband. "How are you enjoying Ireland?"

"Oh, tremendously," Diane enthused. "It's gorgeous."

"I just had to ask, watching the two of you. You're so happy together. Are you on your honeymoon?"

"Um, no," Keith said, hurriedly, shocked all the way down to his new shoes. "I mean, no. We're here for research, and some sightseeing. We're not married."

"Well, then, you could hardly choose so lovely a young lady as this one when you come to be settling down, now could you?" the old man said, nodding charmingly to Diane. "So, when are you going to declare yourself?"

Keith looked helplessly at Diane, but she gave him an expectant blank stare. On that particular subject, she wasn't giving him any assistance. Anything he wanted to say about that was going to have to come out of his own mouth, however garbled. Mustering his words carefully, Keith tried to make some nondescript compliments to Diane without falling headlong over his own tongue. The *bodach*'s curse seemed to see them coming, and stuck out a foot. What Keith sputtered out sounded like gibberish.

The old man and his wife exchanged knowing glances. This young man's tongue-tiedness must mean that he had honorable intentions sometime in the future. He was certainly in love.

"Your very good health, young man, young lady," they said, toasting them with glasses of wine.

"Um, the same to you," Keith said, raising his own glass. He looked back at Diane, who was still watching him. He did a little pantomime, spreading out helpless palms toward the older couple, and pointing at his mouth. She shut her eyes and shook her head, long-sufferingly.

The waitress returned with their desserts and refilled their glasses, rescuing Keith from his efforts to explain himself. He let out a relieved sigh. Diane relented, and gave him a warm smile.

"That's all right. It would be nice to know where I stand. But I'll wait until you can tell me what you're thinking yourself," she said.

"Thanks," Keith offered humbly. He wished he could tell her how lovely she looked in the candlelight, or how much he cared for her, but he knew none of those phrases would ever make it out of his mouth alive. "To you," he said at last, raising the full glass to his lady. There was no stammer or stumble over the two simple words. Ha, ha, bogey, he thought. I'm showing *you*.

Chapter Twenty Seven

"A pity you had to struggle to find us," said their new companion, whose name was Fergus. "We'd never have left our home, as well you know, only the honest country folk were moving out, and the fast-moving ones coming in their places. It was only a matter of time before they'd want to intrude upon us, so we made tracks first."

Fergus led the two Little Folk down the road and through a break in the hedge. There was a small pathway that led downward.

"Watch your footing, if you please. It slips a bit."

The moon disappeared as they passed under a canopy of boughs. Fergus went first, indicating that the other two should stay as far to the left of the pathway as they could.

"It's a wee bit wet," he explained, enigmatically.

It was wet where they walked, too. The water in the sopping grass soaked through Holl's sneakers. He wished he had Wellington boots, like their guide's. They had covered nearly half a mile when Holl felt some sort of compulsion to turn back which grew stronger as he struggled forward, and then suddenly, he pierced through a nearly tangible, fearsome curtain of sensation, emerging into clear air once more. Panting, he looked around to find that he was at the top of a street overlooking a country village. It was like the Big Folks' ones they had been passing through for days, but scaled down to size, his size. The humped shapes of ordinary farm animals, pigs and sheep and geese that rested in paddocks and folds between and behind the houses, were almost comically huge in comparison. Holl could hear ponies snorting in the darkness beyond. Torches and lanterns burned at the doors of most of the cottages. Along the lane which ran between them, lanterns on standards lit the way for pedestrians. Cats slunk across the path on business of their own. There were no dogs that Holl could hear. Nothing in this place made a noise that could be heard at a distance to attract attention, but still, the village was of a fairly good size. In fact, it was a lot like the one in which he grew up, but there were differences.

"Aren't you afraid the Big Folks will find you here?" Holl asked.

"Oh, sometimes they can see the vale from the road, but you can't get to it on foot, there's nowhere to land by hellycopter, and somehow you and your poor little computer forget all about the coordinates when you want to find it later."

"It vorked for years on the hilltop in this vay," the Master put in.

"I'll take you to see the Niall, then," Fergus told them.

"The Niall?" asked Holl.

"Aye. We like to think of him as the last King in Ireland, but his title is merely the Chief of Chiefs, which he considers is quite important enough. But you should know all that, laddie."

Holl shook his head. Fergus shot a puzzled look at the Master, but dropped the topic.

"He'll be curious to see *you*, and how you grew up! Eh, you were such a wild one. But I'm glad to see you back and all, and so will he be."

"A wild one?" Holl whispered to the Master, whose face had twisted into an expression of disapproval. He waved Holl away.

"How many live here?" Holl asked, looking around in awe, trying to count the houses as they walked among them. No one was outside in the lane, but in the windows he could see shadows of figures thrown up on the curtains by firelight within.

"As many as there are," Fergus answered vaguely. "Eh, you're only a child, to ask so many questions. Have a look about, if you please, but it'd be better in daylight. Why not wait until then?"

"I haf not been here either," the Master reminded Fergus.

"Ah, that's right, then. You went off long before we moved here." Fergus moved ahead of them, chuckling.

"Vhen vas that?"

"Oh, a wee while ago," Fergus replied.

The path continued on down a gentle slope. They came to a fork, where Fergus turned right and continued on past more of the little cottages to a grander, more elaborate residence on the edge of the settlement, two storeys in height. Lanterns burned at the corners of the house, and inside behind the window curtains.

"Well, himself is at home, for a wonder," Fergus said. "Come along inside."

Inside the house, a woman sat spinning at a treadle-driven wheel next to a carved and ornamented fireplace in a large, airy room. Her knee-length dress was of a supple, woven material that flowed around her like water, rippling when she moved her foot. The movement echoed the sway of her long hair, bound back in a ribbon to keep it out of the wheel's spokes. The interior walls of the house were plain except where flowering vines grew and entwined, making a handsome living mural. The woman glanced up when the three of them entered, and her eyes rounded with surprise. The thread between her hands, which had been smooth and thin, suddenly knotted, but she ignored it. She rose from her seat in a single graceful movement and flew to embrace the Master.

"I don't believe it!" she exclaimed, standing back to gaze at him at arm's length. "Niall! Niall!"

"Women are like birds," said a musical voice from the next room. "They're beautiful, ornamental, and they should be kept in yards or cages, so they should. For what are you screaming, my love?" The speaker entered. He was Holl's height, but thinner. His fair hair was of a lint white, something like Holl's grand-nephew Tay's. Holl tried to gauge how old he was, but the face with its sharp nose and chin and equally sharp eyes had only enough skin stretched across it to cover the fine bones. His eyes crossed their faces impassively, until they came to the Master. In a moment, the Niall had recognized him, and his jaw dropped.

Holl saw that the Master had braced himself for a cold reception. When the Niall advanced on him and wrung his hand, the Master relaxed, and returned the following embrace heartily.

"I never thought on this side of life that I would ever see you again!" the Niall exclaimed, thumping him soundly on the back.

"Nor I you," said the Master. He extended a hand toward Holl. "I present to you this young man, whose name is Holland."

"Holl," Holl corrected.

The deepset, dark blue eyes turned to study Holl. "He's not yours, to be sure. This'll be one of Curran's get, will it not?"

"That's right," Holl said. "My parents are Dennet and Calla."

"Ah, of course. And he can speak for himself. I remember your sister, and a sharp tongued young wench she was. Very good! So, my dears, sit down." Niall gestured them toward the cluster of low, wooden-backed chairs at the side of the fireplace across from the spinning wheel. Fergus, forgotten on the threshold, cleared his throat significantly. "Sit down, Fergus, do. You're welcome, as always. Ah, here are the others. I thought word might spread like a grassfire. Come in, friends." Five or six other men and women had come in from the outside, and greeted the Master warmly. Holl was introduced in a flurry of kisses, pats of the back, and handshakes to the other Clan Chiefs. "Ketlin, will you kindly get us something to drink?"

"Certainly I will. And you hold the talk until I'm back, hear me?" Ketlin insisted.

"Ah, women." Niall saw to it that everyone was made comfortable. "Now, then, the question that's knocking at every lip begging to get out is *why*? Why have you come back to us? Do you need sanctuary? Are you the only ones left alive, then?" the Chief asked, anxiously.

"Not at all," said the Master. "The village is thriving. We haf doubled our numbers. There are many children, and all are healthy."

There were quiet exclamations of "Ah!" around the circle, and a spate of whispering.

One of the women spoke up. "We hoped for word or glance of you, but you went straight out of our ken. Who dreamed you could go so far away that no one could touch you? You were all given up for dead. Many's the curse called down on your head for leading away some of our children and loved ones to die."

"None died in the traveling," the Master promised solemnly. "'Ve lived in many places before arriving in the one we now occupy, but that vill be a home and a haven now forever. The land is good. Ve haf plenty of food, and there is wood for building. Only one house stands on the property at this time, but it is a Big Folk house, vith plenty of room. Others are planned."

"Ah, I feel the truth of your words," the Chief of Chiefs said, with one hand on his heart. "But I'd be content if I could look into the faces of our lost ones."

"In a way, you can," Holl spoke up. The old ones had been ignoring him, treating him as a nestling barely out of the egg, and he found it annoying. He wanted to defend the Master, who was so obviously on trial before them. "Keith Doyle has several rolls of photographs of our folk, taken at the Going Away party."

Memory dawned on the Master's face. "That is true. I had forgotten his posing and prancing. Ve haf the faces preserved. All of them, or I do not know Keith Doyle."

"May we see these preserved pictures?" the Chief asked.

"With Keith's photographs comes Keith," Holl warned the Master.

"That is true," the Master acknowledged. "His curiosity must be past the bursting point already. May he come?" he asked the Niall.

"Big Folk among us in our fastness? Never! We'll have no peace from them thereafter." There was protest among the elders. Holl waited them out. Their curiosity was aroused. They would eventually capitulate.

The fire was replenished many times during the course of the night. None of the chiefs seemed to become bored with having the Master repeat the details of his journey to America. Clan by clan, he ticked off the children that had been born, who their parents were, and what capabilities the children seemed to be showing as they grew up.

"And who has married whom?" asked Aine, another of the female chiefs.

"None in my lifetime," Holl said.

"None yet in the new place," the Master replied.

"None yet?" Aine echoed, disbelievingly. "In all that time? Heavens above, why not?"

Holl thought it would be appropriate to bring up the point of his quest. "By our custom, or so I've been taught," he began, with a seated bow toward the Master, "none of us can marry unless there are white bellflowers to hand to bless the union. We have none."

"The last seeds appear to haf been lost in one of the transits to our present home," the Master affirmed.

"Ah, well, it's impossible then, isn't it?" the Niall said, nodding.

Holl noted the serious expressions on the faces of those seated around him. He had been inclined to dismiss the flowers as a fillip; a gesture, no more; but clearly they were not.

"I know of none at present," the Chief continued. "Fiona, have you seen any weddingbells in the fields?"

"There have been no weddings or engagements planned for the year, so none sought them," one of the female chiefs answered. "It's nearly the end of the season. It may be past their time. I'll have the children go out and seek them in the morning."

Holl felt panic rising in his belly. What if there were none?

"There'll have to be the gathering ceremony," one of the very old chieftains said. The Master turned to him with an expression of annoyance barely concealed. The old man missed none of it. "Ah, don't look at me that way. You've forgotten, have ye? It's been a long time since you married my daughter. Hah! Do you not know about the weddingbells? To take them off the sacred places requires respect to be shown. Never do we hasten the blooming of the bells, never! Three blessings those flowers give. Are you willing to show the proper respect, young one, to receive the benefits?"

"Yes," Holl replied, returning to the present and wondering exactly what was going on between the Master and this man. It must be an old feud. So this was Orchadia's father. Enoch resembled him somewhat. Grandfather and grandson seemed to have identical tempers, at any rate.

"Perhaps if you wait a wee while we can put you on the way to finding some weddingbells," Fiona said, interceding, and turned the conversation to other matters.

Holl understood that there was no point in trying to hurry them. If none were found before the date he was expecting to leave, he would change his plane ticket to a later date. It was that simple. There must be some way to break the news to Keith Doyle.

"I'd be remiss if I didn't ask again on behalf of my Big friend if he may visit your home. He can be well behaved, and it would be a joy to him if he could meet you."

"Certainly not," the old man stated firmly.

Most of the chiefs still protested against it, but one or two held their tongues. They were becoming interested.

"I too must speak on Keith Doyle's behalf," the Master said, unexpectedly. "He is, if not the author, then the director of our present prosperity. Ve owe him much."

"And at present, he's got a tongue-tying curse on him," Holl reminded the Master, who nodded.

"Laid by one of the two of you?" Fiona asked, humorously.

"No, by a being of the earth in the Scottish Islands. He has a photograph."

"Ah, well, we can't touch that, but the weddingbells could take care of it," she insisted. "They cure many ills, you may know."

"Tell us about the haven," one of the other clan chiefs demanded, interrupting them. A rooster, immediately underneath the window, interjected at that moment to announce dawn. Holl looked up. Orange and pink streaks were reaching up from the east to color the sky. They had stayed up all night talking, and at this rate, would be here all day.

The Master gave them every detail that concerned Hollow Tree Farm: how many acres it comprised, how many of each kind of tree, what condition of farmland and how many lengths. They pressed him to know how the Folk lived on the farm, and what that life was like.

"Ve are not yet self sufficient. There's more to be made, and time needed in vhich to make it. Ve could not do all ve vanted in the Big Folks' building, but now ve haf land of our own."

"I would like to introduce weaving and spinning to the farm," Holl put in. "We have never had textile capability of our own, and now that we have room to graze them, we should have sheep. I observed the weaving in the Scottish Islands. There's nothing they do that we can't. In fact, quite a lot of the wool fabric here looks a lot like the cloth that the Hebrideans make."

"We use an old style loom, with several shuttles," Ketlin said. She brought Holl back to examine the one in her workroom, behind the Niall's study. "It's old, but it does its work well."

"It's just like Mrs. MacLeod's." Holl showed off the sketch he made of the Big Person's loom. His notebook, which had been in his back pocket all day and all night, was creased, and some of the drawings were smudged, but that one had been spared.

"So it is," Ketlin said, studying the sketch. "You've got a skilled hand, lad."

"I'm planning to have the others help me to make some of these looms so we can make our own wool cloth, and some finer ones for cotton percale and so on. The United States is great for growing fiber plants."

"You should talk to Tiron," the Niall said when they returned to the front room. "And now it seems we should think of having breakfast. Go back, all of you, and tell your folk we have a couple of honored guests this day. We can breakfast together on the common. I think it will be fair this morning."

"Meet Tiron, who is the child of Ardigh and Gerome," the Niall said, introducing them formally over breakfast. "Holl, son of Dennet and Calla. Holl is interested in the making of looms, my lad."

"Ah, good!" Tiron said. He had brilliant green eyes, and a cap of curling dark hair under a peaked cap with a buckled band around the crown. He wore a short, sleeveless coat over a long-sleeved shirt, unlike many of his seniors, who wore coats and woolly vests, like the Big Folk in the nearby towns. "And I'm pleased to meet you. Well, there's nothing I can't tell you. I made all the looms in this village. My design is better than the one they were using while I was growing up. It took a little persuasion to force out the bad ways," Tiron wiggled a hand sideways to show the direction his machinations took, "but it's been worth it, they say. A wee bit of tinkering was all a loom needed to run more smoothly, with less chance of the web wrinkling or the thread snapping. What's more, I know all there is to know in caring for them. Nearly all the clothing you see here is from cloth woven on one of my looms," Tiron bragged. "I can make one in a fortnight, by myself."

Holl looked around at the others for someone to give Tiron's statement the lie, but no one did. They were all nodding at the young craftsman. "All of it! I am impressed," Holl acceded. "It must be sound work indeed."

"So they tell me. You're from America, are you?" Tiron went on, with interest. "I've wanted to go there all my life. You ought to take me back with you."

"I don't know how that would be possible," Holl said, cautiously. He was by no means eager to take this cocky fellow back to the farm with him, even if he could figure out how.

"If you did, Holl vould haf to fall back on leadership," the Master said teasingly. "He is our finest woodworker and ornamenter." Holl displayed the small box he had been working on in idle moments.

"He *is?*" said Tiron, affecting surprise. "Let's see what you've got there." He twitched Holl's work out of his hands and inspected it closely. The featureless stick Holl had begun with in Inverness had become a cylindrical box three inches high covered solidly with his favorite ivy pattern. He watched Tiron examine it with a gimlet eye. "Well, now what a pretty pattern," the other said, somewhat patronizingly, "but you've forgotten to give the poor little leaves any backbones. Here, now."

He whipped out his own knife, a tool with a simple bronze blade. Holl eyed it. Any fool could make a bronze knife. The titanium blade in his pocket took a considerable amount of work and skill to create. The important thing was what he could do with it. With the knife held an inch from the point with his fingers, Tiron bent over the box. "There," he said after a moment. "If you'd take the trouble to look at that, I'd be most pleased."

Holl accepted the box back. Tiron had carved minute spines and veins on the ivy in the pattern in the lid, swiftly and without error. The leaves suddenly looked real, a monochrome illumination for a calligraphed manuscript, and made the rest of the little carving look clumsy. Holl turned red.

"There's still a few things for you to learn, my boy," Tiron winked at him in a friendly manner. "No hard feelings, I hope."

"None," said Holl, humbly, inspecting the work more closely once the fierce blush of embarrassment had subsided. "It's so easy to enlarge upon the detail, now I've seen what you do, and I never thought of it, never felt to add it."

"You have the look of someone who's done it by rote, from a design or drawing, not the real thing," Tiron said summing him up with a critical but not unfriendly eye. "You've all the ways and skills to be good. Come and see real ivy." He clapped a hand on Holl's back and led him toward a low stone wall that ran around the rear of one row of the small cottages. "Ah, pity. I could teach you so much, but we have so little time. Come and talk!"

The Master and the Chief of Chiefs looked after them. "You've chosen well, if that's your choice," the Niall said. "You don't mind that he isn't your own son?"

"My son is not interested in leadership. He is a fine craftsman," the Master said proudly.

"In Holl I'd say our continued future is well assured."

"Ve knew it almost from his birth," the Master said, with equal satisfaction.

"And so we knew with you, my boy. And so we knew. But we expected you to stay *here* and lead."

The Master clicked his tongue. "There could not be two of us, could there? You had the same promise. Vhy should you not be permitted to use your talents? And I could not stay. I did not vant to stay. There vere too many of us, and not enough room. The rules vere not stringent, they were silly. I could not lead, vith the old men crying for dusty precedent in efery unimportant case."

"You were right to go," the Chief said at last. "When the Hunger came, careful as we'd been to bank our harvests, so many died. If you and the others had stayed, we'd have had too many more mouths to feed. I think some would have followed your trail then if they could have. And I promise you," Niall said slyly, "I've had my own confrontations with those dusty old ones. You might be pleased at some of the progress I've made. Come back again soon—today—and bring along your tame Big Folk. We'll give them greeting."

Chapter Twenty Eight

Keith and Diane waited anxiously for the Master and Holl at the guest house until almost noon. At that time Mrs. Keane had made it clear that she wanted the rooms vacated so she could clean them. She began to vacuum the hall outside Diane's room aggressively about eleven thirty. Keith was so keyed up he leaped in the air when the vacuum started.

"My nerves are shot, too, waiting around. Why don't we go back to the Skylark?" Diane suggested. "They're just as likely to turn up there as here. We can have lunch while we wait. The sign said they have seafood. I wouldn't mind some of that."

"That's a good idea," Keith agreed. He shouldered his camera bag.

"And what's that for?" Diane asked, raising her eyebrows.

"Well…just in case," Keith said. "I'm the eternal optimist."

"I know," Diane said, looking heavenward for patience. "I know. Come on."

The young bartender greeted them as they came into the Skylark and sat down at the bar. "Back again, so soon? You're very welcome. What may I bring you? Lunch? We've a prawn salad on special today."

Diane pulled over the cardboard lunch menu, and ordered for the two of them. "And Guinness. Only make mine half the size of the one I had last night."

The bartender put in the lunch order and came over to talk to them while he pulled the beer. As it was still early, there were only a few people in the pub. "Since we're going to be friends, my name is Peter," the young man said. "Pleased to know you."

Diane and Keith introduced themselves. "There's something I've been meaning to ask," Keith said. "It hit me after we left last night. You didn't seem too surprised when my two friends came in the other day." He sketched a tall ear on the side of his head with a finger.

Peter looked over his shoulder, then shook his head. "Ah, no, they're in here all the time. You learn not to talk about it. It doesn't do to offend the Fair Folk, as my granda always said. They'll wish you bad luck. Did you say now that those two came in with you?"

"Yeah. They're good friends of ours. They live near our University."

Peter was astonished. "In America? Well, fancy that. I thought the only ones in the wide world were here."

"Well, a whole lot of them moved to America. How long have these, er, Fair Folk been coming in here? I mean, into the Skylark."

"Oh, years now," Peter said, trying to count backward. "My da talked about them when I was just a wee one, and my granda before him. It wasn't until I was almost grown that I knew my da wasn't just telling stories."

"How many of them are there?" Keith asked curiously.

"I've only seen a handful, myself. That's enough for me. Some say they're a bad omen, coming in here, though truth to tell, not many notice them."

"I think you should take it as a good omen. My bunch make their own beer. If they like yours enough to come out for it, you should feel complimented."

"That's good to know," Peter said, smiling. "I'll tell my da." He fetched their drinks, and left them alone on their side of the bar.

"Where *are* they?" Keith said to Diane, looking at his watch. "They've been gone all night."

"They're all right," Diane assured him. "They're adults, remember? Older than you?"

"Yeah, I know. I wonder if the others will let me visit them. I'd hate to have come all this way, and never see where they live."

"Trust Holl. If anyone can get you an invitation, he can." Diane patted his hand. "You are not to sit there feeling sorry for yourself. Do something. Call Doyles from the phone book."

"Nope, I've got a better idea. Hey, Peter?" The young bartender came over to them, hands busy with a glass and a towel. "You know a bunch of languages. Do you speak Gaelic?"

"Of course I do. It's me mother tongue," Peter said in an exaggerated brogue.

"Can you teach me how to say something? To greet someone important?"

"Ah," said Peter knowingly. "In case you meet the king of the fairies, is that it? I'd be glad to." He thought for a moment. "It's 'Dia dhuit.' Can you say that?'

"No," said Keith, trying to separate Peter's phrases into manageable syllables. "Say it again, slower."

Patiently, Peter helped Keith rehearse the greeting over and over again. He wrote it out on a paper napkin in Gaelic with the translation in English below, and left him alone to try it out for himself.

"This doesn't look like what I'm saying," Keith said to Diane. "There's way too many letters." Keith tried to pronounce the sentence.

"That sounded more like it. Try again."

"I thought we'd find you here," Holl said, interrupting the language lesson. He slapped Keith soundly on the back.

"Where've you been?" Keith demanded, rounding on him. "Are you all right? Who was that other one? Can I go and see the new village?"

"The answers are, we've been visiting relatives," Holl said, "as well you know. We are fine, though I've not slept all night; his name is Fergus; and yes."

"Yee-hah!" Keith cheered, throwing his napkin in the air.

"That is, they're willing to trust you with their secret, if you can behave yourself," Holl said sternly.

"Oh, I will. I promise." Keith retrieved the little piece of paper. "Let's go!" He caught Peter's eye and showed him he was leaving money on the bar. Peter nodded, and waved farewell.

Fergus and the Master were waiting behind the pub on the side opposite the car park. Fergus shook hands solemnly with Diane and Keith. "He says you're friendly and worthy of trust," the Little Person said, dubiously. "I suppose I must believe him. A Doyle, are you? There are many of that name who live near here."

"I know," said Keith. "I'm descended from some of them."

"Are you now?" Fergus snapped his fingers. "I thought your face looked familiar. The man I knew must have been one of your grandfathers. Ah, but that was a wee while ago."

"It sure was," Keith exclaimed. "At least a hundred and forty years! You sure don't look it."

"Thank you for the kind words," Fergus grimaced, though he was clearly pleased. "A fine man. You're shorter though. That's what threw me off. Come along, then."

The Little Folk turned off the road and down into the little path broken through the growth at the side, and paused to let the Big Folk catch up. Fergus traced its outline with his hands. "The Big Ones think badgers made this, and sheep use it, so we let them think so."

"It's so close to the pub. I'd never dreamed that you'd live so near to hum—I mean, Big Folk habitation."

"Our neighbors don't bother us," Fergus assured him. "We have privacy in plenty."

They made their way down the path until it was interrupted by a tiny stream with a concrete block over it. The block had a semicircular hole in the lower half to let the stream through. Keith helped Diane over it, and then climbed through himself.

The bushes were lower beyond the barrier than they had been on the sheep track. "I can't stand up in here," Keith complained.

"Aye, well, if we knew you were coming to visit us," Fergus said, looking up at him regretfully, "but there! This is our way backwards and forwards, always."

"Not alvays," the Master said, dreamily.

"Well, now it is. The farmers leave the trees and bushes over the rivers to themselves, so as not to run their machinery straight into the water. We like that quite well, for they've left us a covered pathway. We don't have to skulk," Fergus explained, "for no one comes this way but us and a few other natural creatures. There's passages like this all over Ireland. Some join with the Big People's paths, like the *Slí' Cualann Nua*. But mostly they're alone."

"Great!" Keith said, ducking to miss a raspberry cane. He walked half stooped over, watching the three Little Folk make steady progress along the stream path ahead of him. Inwardly, he was thrilled. To think that he was going to visit the Elf Master's old home, and meet the rest of the clans! "That was lucky, finding a river close to where you wanted to set up a home."

"Luck? What luck? We needed water, so by water we must be."

They walked past a low thicket, whose floor was carpeted by wildflowers, most of them white. Keith recognized lily-of-the-valley and a few other summer flowers, but the tall stalky flowers caught his attention next. He recognized the shape in an instant.

"Holl, look!" Keith exclaimed. "White bellflowers! Just like the pink ones in Scotland."

"Ah, no," Fergus corrected him. "That's just white foxglove. It's one of the fairy flowers, but nothing as fine as the bellflowers."

"There are fairies around here, too?" Keith asked, eagerly.

"At the bottom of every garden," the elf assured him solemnly. "But to be serious, you might see a dancing light on the fields of an evening."

"I thought those were fireflies." Keith struggled to understand.

"Ah, well, sometimes they are."

Holl turned to watch as first Diane and then Keith passed through the protective spell surrounding the village environs. Diane was terrified, and started to retreat back into Keith's arms. Holl and the Master hastened back to take her hands and lead her through it. In a moment, she was all right. Keith eyed her, and then took a deep breath. He plunged into the thickest part of the spell, and burst through it, letting his breath out on the other side. He stood with his hands braced on his knees, supporting his back, shaking his head as if to clear it.

"Are you all right?" Holl asked.

"If that's what I have to do to boldly go where no Big Folk has gone before, I can take it," Keith said, stolidly, making a face. "It felt like I rammed my head into a stone wall. I think I broke something. What *was* that?"

"A charm of great strength," Fergus said. "If someone should make his way this far seeking us, we need it to be strong enough to erode even that determination."

"It didn't feel solid to me," Diane said. "It felt like getting smothered in a quilt. Horrible!"

"At the risk of getting my knuckles rapped," Keith asked, "are we there yet?"

"We're there," Fergus said.

Most of the village was waiting for them on the other side of the trees. Murmuring broke out when the two Big Folk appeared. Keith surveyed the faces of the crowd of Little Folk staring up at him. He had a definite feeling of *déjà vu*, experiencing all over again the delight and wonder he felt at discovering the Midwestern village of the Little Folk. He walked among them, feeling as if he must be dreaming, but it was a dream in infinite detail. This hamlet had more of an established air about it than the Gillington Library village did, and the roofs, which were recreated in loving detail in the basement of the library, existed for real here, and kept off real rain and wind.

"Holl, we are definitely not in Kansas any more."

"Illinois," Holl corrected him, with a puzzled glance.

"Whatever."

Keith gazed, taking in all that he could with a feeling that he had never been so happy. There were flower gardens here, something that looked odd next to the houses he had never seen anywhere but on a plain dirt and concrete floor. There were animals, too: sheared sheep grazing quietly in a field at the end of the lane, ponies snorting quietly over their food, and geese and chickens wandering everywhere as if they owned the place. It was more alive than the Gillington complex, and a lot more noisy. There were children laughing out loud, and the sounds of music playing. He realized now that the hidden village was a copy done from memory of this place. He became vaguely aware that Holl was pulling him down the lane by one arm.

"This is the Chief of Chiefs," Holl said, presenting him to the Niall, who was seated on a chair under an oak tree in the middle of the village green. "Keith Doyle."

"*Dia dhuit*," said Keith, bowing low from the waist.

The Chief looked surprised, but he replied in the same way. "*Dia dhuit*, Keith Doyle."

"Sorry, that's all I know," Keith said, with a sheepish grin. "I'm going to have to go on in English."

"But that's grand," the Niall told him, his eyes dancing. "We expected it." He rose before Diane and took her hand in both of his, and said something to her with a very formal bow. She looked embarrassed and glanced at Keith for help.

"This is the Chief of Chiefs," Keith said to her.

"Pleased to meet you," Diane told Niall, unable to think of anything better.

"The pleasure is mine." The Chief effected introductions all around. First, he brought forward the clan chiefs, including one sour-faced squirt who shot a surly look at the Master. Keith found he couldn't keep up with the torrent of names, but he smiled and shook hands with everyone.

"This is Tiron," Holl said, introducing him to one young fellow with a wispy little beard on his chin.

"How do?" Keith asked.

"As well as I can," Tiron replied. Tiron reminded Keith of a young Hollywood actor from the Golden Age, maybe one of the Dead End kids who had worked hard all his life from age ten, and was self-possessed and tough. Not that he looked much older than ten. Like all of the Little Folk, he had the face of a child.

"So we hear you had a bit of a malediction read over you," the Niall said. "We'll see if we can't do something to help you. In the meanwhile, my people would like to get to know you."

"I'd like to get to know them," Keith said eagerly. "Can I take pictures?"

Niall waved a hand grandly. Without waiting to ask twice, Keith started making the rounds of the village, with a whole herd of children in attendance, spouting questions. They wanted to know everything about him, and about where he lived and what he did. As an American, he was a genuine curiosity. He learned that he was the first contact many of them had had with the Big People. "So I'm the good will ambassador after all, huh?"

"More than that," Holl informed him. "You're the representative of your entire race. Keep that in mind."

In the context of the Irish relations, as Keith called them to himself, Holl seemed more than ever to be really an adult. And the Master, the immutable Elf Master, bane of his classroom existence? He seemed younger, and a bit embarrassed. "I vas qvite a child vhen I departed. I think my folk here see me the same vay still. Some treat me as vun. They vanted to meet you, because of the great task I undertook in my youth, to lead my people avay and find them prosperity elsevhere. It vas not actually completed until you provided assistance, Meester Doyle. And for that, I thank you."

"Really?" Keith said, very flattered. "What did the other folk say when you told them you were leaving, all those years ago?"

"They vere shocked because I vas taking away half the population vith me. It vas a hard decision, but to survive we needed to divide. I am pleased to say that it vorked. The anger they felt is gone now. This is the first time that they knew that we survived, and they are glad."

"Wow. How *did* you get to America?" Keith asked.

"On a ship with sails," the Master explained.

"When was that?" Keith asked, but the Master ignored the question. Keith felt frustrated. He was getting to know more about his mysterious friends than ever before, but he realized that there were some things that he wouldn't find out. Their explanations tended to be a little bare of detail.

"How old were you when you led your half of the Folk away from here?" Keith asked him impulsively, trying another tack.

"I vas very young; only a boy. Perhaps twenty, twenty two."

"Mmm." Keith knew that the Master was at least twenty five years older than his son Enoch, who was born in America. Enoch was forty seven. That made the Master seventy at a minimum. But then, they came to the U.S. in a sailing ship. There were no sailing ships crossing the Atlantic during the twentieth century. Unless they built their own? No, that was unlikely. There were hardly any trees to speak of in the countryside. A whole boat's worth would be missed. "So you're about seventy-two, sir?" Keith asked hopefully, hoping the teacher would fill in a number. The Master smiled slightly, ignoring the pry. Holl nudged Keith with an elbow and steered him in another direction.

"Well, how can I learn if I don't ask questions?" Keith said innocently.

"You wouldn't just happen to have your pictures with you?" Holl asked. "The Niall would like to see the rolls of the folk at Hollow Tree Farm."

Keith smiled brilliantly. "I had a hunch I'd need the whole kit," he said cheerfully, swinging the camera bag around. "Here." He dug out the envelopes and handed them to Holl. Immediately, a crowd gathered around to look at the photographs. Holl looked helplessly at the Niall, who waved a resigned hand.

"I can wait. Bring them along to my home when you can wrench them away, and your tall friend, too."

Chapter Twenty Nine

Keith and Diane dined with their new friends, who guided them out of the vale and back to their car by moonlight. There had been dancing and games on the green until it was too dark to see. They were both quite exhausted by the party.

"I think I danced with everyone in town," Diane said, limping up the bank. "But it was fun!"

"The Niall's compliments," Fergus said as he bade them goodbye at the head of the path, "and he'd be pleased if you'd all come back along in the morning."

"You bet," Keith said, enthusiastically. "I'll be there with bells on."

"Eh, there's no need," Fergus said deprecatingly. "They make too much noise. Come as you are."

Holl started laughing. "They'll need a lexicon to understand you, Keith Doyle."

The next morning was overcast and showed threatening signs of rain. With Peter's permission, Keith left his car in the lane behind the pub. He stood in the stone courtyard and looked out over the fields below. There was the village, nestled among trees like an egg in the nest. A few rooftops were actually just visible from there, which made Keith fear for its vulnerability. Holl assured him that no one could reach it.

The only place where the two Big Folk could fit comfortably out of the weather was sitting on the floor in the Chief's front room, so that was where they spent the morning. The furniture looked comfortable, but it was too small for them to sit in. The Niall's wife, Ketlin, piled wool rugs and sheepskins for them to recline upon. What Keith took at first to be bouquets of purple and blue flowers with attendant greens turned out to be living blossoms growing right there inside the house. So was the vine design on the walls and ceiling. A bee actually flew out of one of the trumpet flowers as they watched.

The Niall and his wife had as many questions for them as the children had the day before. Other Little Folk wandered in and out of the great house at will to pass a few moments with their odd guests. Keith discussed the problem of visibility with the Niall.

"It's been no worry so far," the Chief told Keith. "Yet there will come a day when long-held belief will no longer stay the curious, or strangers will stumble on our secret and reveal it to the world of Big Folk. Then we may have to move on."

Keith, keenly aware that he was one of those stumbling Big Folk, assured the Chief that he'd keep their secret. "I mean, except for my father, I don't know who I'd tell, but Dad understands. He knows Holl."

"That's good. We need friends. There was a time when the Big Folk and the Little had a war to divide up all the land in the world. The Big had many more people, and took the best, leaving us what little they did not care to own. In the ripeness of time, and with good health and many children, we came to be at elbow's point," the Niall said.

"The hilltop. We were there," Keith said. "And that was when the Master left."

"Aye, that's a fair summation."

"You know, I don't see a lot of difference between the way you folk live here and they way they do at home, barring differences of surrounding culture, to quote my unlamented Sociology professor. Um, how long ago was that they left?"

"Oh, a wee while ago," the Niall said, disinterestedly. Keith was disappointed again. The way people talked around here, that could have been a year or an eon. Tiron poked his head in.

"Good morning to you all, though I'm disinclined to believe the good. Will it rain or not?" the green-eyed lad asked. "Holl, come and see. I've made you a set of plans for the loom."

Holl rose from the chair next to the fireplace. "With your permission, Niall?"

The leader waved a hand blithely. "Be free as you will."

"Ah, a chair left for me next the fire," said Fiona, arriving as Holl and Tiron departed. "There's kindness itself." She seated herself and spread her skirts around her.

"Fiona is the one of us who seems best to understand the language of plants," Niall explained. "You see a bit of her handwork on the walls here."

"They're wonderful. Um, has Holl mentioned what he's here looking for?" Keith asked diplomatically.

"The weddingbells?" Fiona asked. "Oh, yes. We're trying to find some for him, to be sure. Though we only use them when we find them, I can see that tradition will have to change when you have to come four thousand miles to look for clumps."

"I saw white foxglove on the way here, but they said that those aren't the ones, is that right?"

"Here, now," the herbwoman said, showing him one of the living nosegays. Keith was amused to find clover of the ordinary three-leafed variety growing there. It ought to have been four-leafed. "This is the bellflower wearing its everyday clothes." Fiona bent a stem toward him. Keith saw a cluster of purple-blue flowers. "It's just an ordinary blossom which closely resembles the weddingbells. They call it 'cuckoo's shoe' here," she said with a goatish grin, "but some know it as 'thimble of the goblin.'"

"Appropriate, I guess," Keith chuckled. "You know, I saw some of this in Scotland, just before Holl got sick. We overlooked it for the foxglove. It was on the plain below the fairy mound. I was expecting something a lot more—you know, large or impressive. It looks so tiny and insignificant."

"But it is, except as one of Nature's works. Sometimes the smallest or most unimportant seeming things have the most virtue to them," the Niall said. "We let the Big Folk know the white foxglove is a fairy flower, so they'll let our other resources be. This one has no magic. Only the white variety does."

"How do you know?" Diane asked.

"By the feel," Niall said simply.

"Well, what does magic feel like?" Keith asked.

"Hold up your hands, palms in front of you." Keith raised them obediently. "If you don't look straight at them, you can hardly see a sort of field around them like a glowing glove, can't you?"

Taking 'hardly' to mean 'barely', Keith looked off into the distance, but glanced at his hands in his peripheral vision.

Diane tried it. "I don't see a thing." She dropped her hands in her lap in disappointment.

"There is sort of a glow there. I think," Keith said slowly, seeing a faint halo surrounding his hand. "It could be an illusion, or just my eyesight."

"It's not an illusion. It's part of your body, though you can't see it, feel it, or cut it off," Niall explained. "Now, it's in this glove that lie the senses for feeling magic, and doing some types. Good magic feels good to you, like velvet or joy. Evil magic has a nasty prickle, like nettles."

"I've heard that some people do black magic on purpose," Keith said.

The Niall clicked his tongue. "I can't imagine why, for all of me. There's a lot of power in black magic, and nothing with the senses to feel it will blunder into its sway, so you have less to expend doing it. The workings of all are very subtle, and it changes the character of the worker over time to something twisted and warped."

Keith gulped. "Can you do it by accident?"

"No. There must always be intent expressed when fashioning a spell. There are some charms worked in which the hand of the body never touches the physical form of the subject. The work is all done in the aura, which affects the subject's reality."

"Oh." Keith was beginning to go crosseyed trying not to look directly at his hand but to keep his aura in view.

"Though you can set up a good-intentioned repulsion spell that keeps things out without being evil," Fiona said. "It's a born necessity around the lettuce patch, we've so many rabbits."

"But strong magic," Niall continued, smiling at the clan chief, "that feels powerful, like a white hot fire or a wall or a terrible fall, whether it was designed by good or evil intentions or by nature. It can do as much harm as boon if a charm is too strong."

"So there's everyday magic, like magic lanterns," Keith said, thinking of the Hollow Tree crafts. "And then there's the serious stuff."

"Well put," Niall laughed. "If you're willing, we'll teach you to feel it first with strongly imbued articles, working downward in concentration as you become accustomed to it, to the most subtle, featherlight touch."

"The exact opposite of Szechuan food, huh?" Keith reasoned, giving up the struggle to watch the aura, and rubbed his eyes. "There you start with mild, and end up flat on your back."

They practiced for a while, letting Keith try out his newly trained sensitivity on a variety of objects. The other Little Folk seemed to be impressed that the Niall was taking so much interest in a Big Person, but Keith was so interested and so respectful that they soon got over their resentment. In time, the whole room was coaching him, calling out suggestions as he tried his new skill with varying results. Diane sat back and watched, interested, but not interested enough to try for herself.

"How about this," Ketlin said, holding up a lantern by the ring.

"We have those at home," Keith said. He took it and looked at it, trying to see an aura. "On a scale of one to ten, I'd say this was a two. I can feel it, too."

"Good!" she said. "And this?"

Keith stared at the carved needle case she laid in his palm. "Barely a tickle. Right?"

"Right. Good lad!"

"How about this?" the sour-faced elder said, passing him a bronze key.

Keith felt it and looked at it. Nothing. By the expression on the old man's face, he was expecting something. Keith felt sweat starting on his forehead, and they were all looking at him. "Not a thing," he admitted at last.

"Well, you're honest, at any rate," the old man said, grudgingly. "It's only an ordinary key."

"Not too bad for the first day's attempt," Niall said, praising Keith. "You've a bit of aptitude. If I had twenty years of the teaching of you, you'd be one of us in no time."

A youth running up the path to the house skittered to a halt in the doorway. "Fiona, Niall," he panted, "we've found a wee spot where the flowers are growing."

The Chief of Chiefs led a grand procession through the stream path, up over the road, and down into the next meadow. Everyone wanted to be present when Holl plucked the weddingbells. On either side at eye level, the fields were full of crops. Because of the leafy outcroppings overhead, they couldn't see more until they clambered up out of the trench beyond the next crosspoint.

This little piece of land had been left to grow wild by the Big Folk owner. It was too steep to make good farmland. Bushes and wildflowers sprang through the sparse, knee high grass over most of the rocky ground, but on the far side, under a lush carpet of green, there was the unmistakable shape of a fairy mound. Faint lights floated in the air around the hillock like fireflies, though it was just barely evening.

"There's a lot of flowers growing there," Keith said, squinting across the field, "but nothing special."

The Niall clapped him on the back. "With your new eyes, see!" Obediently, Keith concentrated. It was hard to let his eyes go unfocused and still look at an object eighty feet away. Suddenly, there was a white glimmer, like a candle flame, in the midst of the flowers covering the hillock.

"Hey!" Keith exclaimed.

"Ah, you see it now, do you. And there they are. Not easy to locate, are they?"

"You remember what to do," Fiona instructed Holl seriously. She handed him a small sickle with a crescent-shaped blade. "Concentrate on your purpose. You cannot take them if you are married or promised already. The flowers will stand no nonsense."

Repeating to himself the strictures, Holl walked across the open land. He stopped at the perimeter of the fairy mound, and spoke quietly. "I am Holl. I mean no harm. I crave permission to walk upon this hill. I want to gather these flowers."

A tiny voice like the jangling of silver bells answered him, not in his ears, but in his mind. "Walk and be welcome."

Holl stepped onto the smooth grass. The tiny clump of bellflowers beckoned him. The clustered blossoms were white and shining and more alive than anything he had ever seen in his life. They positively radiated power. Holl understood why no one picked these without a good purpose. He knelt beside them, and glanced up at the waiting crowd one more time. Across the field, Keith Doyle threw him a thumbs-up. He smiled, and grasped the stems with one hand.

Hot power coursed into him like an electric shock and threw him backward across the mound and halfway down the other side. Holl struggled to his hands and knees, and sat up again. Dumbfounded, he stared at the flowers, and down at his hand, which was red and felt burned. Why did they do that? Were they refusing to be harvested? Had he come all this way to fail at the last minute? He moved toward them again, but the flowers emitted an angry noise, like static, as soon as he placed his hand near them. He drew away.

"What's the matter?" Keith called.

"I don't know!" Holl shouted back.

"Tch, tch," Fiona said. "You've gone and promised yourself to your lass before this, lad. It'll never work."

"Do you mean I can't do it myself?" Holl asked, panic-stricken. "After all this, I can't finish my own task?" He looked helplessly at his own hands.

"Holl! A good leader knows when to delegate responsibility," Keith called out suddenly. "Order someone else to do it!"

Light dawned on the young elf's face as Keith's meaning sank in. "Ah. Keith Doyle, if you're willing, would you undertake this task for me, under my direction?"

"I could do it," Keith agreed. "I'm not promised yet. I mean, with the you-know, I can't even say anything."

There was a momentary discussion among the elders. "All right," Fiona said at last. "But be careful. You must wear no silver nor gold, nor carry any iron."

Keith laughed shortly. "The *bodach* took care of my fillings. I can empty my pockets." He handed his camera to Diane, and put all his change and the car keys into her purse.

"I think the lacings in your shoes are steel," Diane said, pointing at his sneakers. He doffed them, too.

In his stocking feet, Keith strode out into the field to where Holl was nursing his palm. "Once again you write yourself into our history, Keith Doyle. But thank you."

"What do I do first?" Keith asked.

"Ask permission to climb the hill."

Keith repeated the phrases Holl had had to learn. "Holl, did something just say to you 'walk and be welcome'?"

Holl raised an eyebrow. "You heard it, then. Go ahead."

The youth stepped up onto the grassy side of the hillock, and started to bring the other foot up behind him. He found himself tumbling backward in a somersault across the field. "Stone wall," he said, shaking his head and feeling his nose to make certain it was still straight. Holl watched him with bewilderment. "I'll try again."

He threw himself against the invisible barricade. Again and again, it repelled him, rebounding him backward like a springboard. He was bouncing off of the fairy defenses like a cartoon character. "Hey, I thought you said I could walk here," he complained to the invisible silver voices. His bones felt as though they had been jarred askew.

"What could you possibly hold that would keep you from entering?" Holl asked.

"I don't know," Keith said. "Pants zipper? I think it's brass." He patted himself down from shoulders to socks. "Wait!" He fished under his shirt and came up with a small bag on a cord. "Mrs. MacLeod gave me this to protect me."

"Well, it is. It's protecting you from picking flowers," Holl said wryly. With a grin, Keith pulled the cord up over his head and dropped the charm on the grass. Now there was no barrier to climbing the fairy mound. He stepped up and joined Holl. The grass felt pleasant and springy under his stockinged feet.

"Hey, Diane, can you take some pictures?" Keith called out. "This could be interesting!"

"You're out of film," Diane shouted back, after checking the indicator on the back of the camera. "I'll go and get some out of the car. Wait a minute."

Michaels had managed to get a positive identification from the bartender in the Skylark. O'Day had picked his place well. No one who hadn't business in the immediate area would ever find this godforsaken hole in the wall. O'Day and the boy were not here, and hadn't been in to the pub that day. The landlady hadn't seen them either. They must be out waiting for the contact to arrive.

Suddenly, the blonde girl appeared out of a break in the hedge across the road from the pub. If she was here, O'Day couldn't be far away. Here was an opportunity to divide the party and conquer.

Diane walked toward the car park, jingling the keys in her hand. She was paying no attention to him. He walked up and quietly put his hand through her arm and leaned against her side.

"What?" she demanded, in surprise, and tried to pull away. She recognized him in a second. "You!" She raised her other hand with nails bared to tear out his eyes. Michaels grabbed her hand and pinned it.

"Please, miss, don't try to attack me. The martial arts I'm trained aren't the slap-the-mat-and-get-up kind. I'm sorry, but that's the way it is."

"You've been following us!" Diane realized. "Why? Hey, I knew there was something fishy about you, Mr. Good Samaritan. Let me go!"

"I thought I must have made some slip up," Michaels affirmed. He palmed his ID out of his pocket and showed it to her.

"British Intelligence. Your boyfriend down there is a smuggler. Tell me, what's he here to get?"

"Keith?" Diane asked, astonished. "Not a chance. He's too honest to cheat on his income tax. You must be mistaken."

"Acting on information received, miss. How long have you known him?"

"About a year, as if it's any of your business." The girl was impressed by the identification card, and very frightened.

Michaels counted back in his mind. The last big delivery carried off by O'Day was about fifteen months back. It had been nothing but small stuff since then. "I think It's quite possible you don't know about it. But I can't risk having you tip him off. This way, please." Diane started to fight free of him. He twisted her arm behind her, and frog's-marched her to his car, parked on the side of the road. "I'm sorry, but I can't allow you to interfere and tip him off. I've got my job to do."

"Let me go!" she screamed. "I'm an American citizen!"

Out of his overcoat pocket, he pulled a pair of handcuffs. He locked one loop around Diane's wrist, and held onto the chain while he opened the left rear door of the sedan. When Diane protested and dug in her heels, he put one hand firmly on the top of her head and pushed down, propelling her into the car. Swiftly, he passed the loose end of the handcuffs over the rubber handle over the car window, and locked up her other wrist.

Outraged, Diane started yelling for help and banging on the door with her elbows. He shut the door on her, and locked it. Her hands were too high up even to roll down a window. Down the road a short distance, he couldn't hear her at all. O'Day wouldn't even know where she had gone. I'll nab the others when they come out.

Chapter Thirty

Keith watched the river path for Diane, and was disappointed at how long it was taking her to get back. Holl jogged his elbow impatiently.

"We can wait no longer. Please," he urged.

Keith sighed. "Okay, but we're missing a great photo opportunity." He accepted the small golden sickle and hunkered down next to the flowers. "These are really pretty. Hi, guys. Look at me, I'm a druid!" He brandished the curved blade.

"More respect, Keith Doyle," Holl chided him.

"Okay," Keith said. "Ready."

"Concentrate on the purpose for which you are taking the flowers," Holl said, staying at arm's distance but watching anxiously.

Keith squeezed his eyes shut and mentally told the flowers that they were being picked to help Holl win his ladylove, and to make him a great leader. He opened his eyes again, and took hold of the stalks, bundling them tightly together in his fist. They didn't kick him backward. He took a breath. "Here goes."

The golden sickle cut through the flower stems as effortlessly and frictionlessly as if it had passed through air. Keith, expecting some kind of resistance, found himself sitting back on his rump, holding the bunch aloft. He started to say "A piece of cake," to Holl, but something exploded suddenly in the middle of his body, and he lost all sensation in a brilliant, white light. The hot light raced through him, reached his extremities and shot off into every direction like a laser hitting a broken mirror.

He could hear Holl shouting at him. "Concentrate! Take control!"

With all the willpower he had, Keith pulled in his thoughts and focused only on Holl and Maura as he had last seen them. While Keith waited in his car for Holl, they had kissed goodbye at the door of the farmhouse. That was a beautiful thing, an event that should last forever. It was meant to be.

In a moment, the fire in his body died away, so suddenly that he shivered. The hot white light concentrated once again in the shining blossoms in his hand. Keith waved them at the others, who swarmed across the field toward the mound. They gathered around him to cheer him and Holl. Keith stood up, and with a flourish, presented the bouquet to his friend. Holl took them gingerly, treating the blossoms with the greatest respect.

"I'm embarrassed to say I thought these were only a gesture," Holl said. "How wrong I was."

"Merely a gesture," Keith squawked. "They're magic flowers! Boy, are they magic." He shook his hand up and down. "I don't think I'll ever be the same."

"Normal for us," Holl said. "But these are of a caliber that even I handle with respect."

"You don't know eferything yet," the Master reminded him, but there was no reproof in his voice.

"I know that well enough," Holl said humbly. "This trip has shown me enough to prove it if I did not."

"The first blessing is yours, then," the sour-faced elder told Keith. "Don't waste it."

"What's he talking about?" Keith asked Holl.

"I don't know, but I am certain you'll find out."

From his vantage point on the road above, Michaels spotted the two Doyles sitting on the grass through his field glasses. He saw a glint of yellow metal pass between them. Michaels smiled to himself. "Being paid in solid gold, eh?" This was the payoff. Good, that's easy to find with a metal detector. "Once we have all four in custody, I'll have no trouble in taking them in."

A crowd, hidden before behind the high hedging, rushed forward. These must be O'Day's local contacts, and they seemed awfully cheery about something. He ought to get some pictures. O'Day was a hero, and here were his employers.

Suddenly, the redhaired man stood up. He was head, shoulders, and chest above the crowd. Michaels reminded himself that the young man had been sitting on a hill. But then O'Day started to walk with them toward the river path, and the bunch of flowers in his hand were glowing. He looked more closely at the crowd through his glasses. Children? More midgets? There was something unusual about their profiles. They looked like ordinary people—except for the big pointy ears.

Flowers that glow? Little people with sharp pointed ears? That was impossible. It must be a trick of the twilight. Michaels lowered the glasses in disbelief. It's the perspective, he told himself. No, it wasn't. Everything looked exactly the same with the naked eye. He peered through the binoculars and had a good stare. *"Up the airy mountain, down the rushy glen. We daren't go a-hunting for fear of little men,"* he recited to himself. "I don't bloody believe it. I wish I had never been assigned to this case."

A thumping sound on glass reminded him that he had a prisoner to release. He walked back to his car. Diane had worked one shoe off her foot, and had her leg hooked over the front seat, reaching for the horn with her toes. Her determination and resourcefulness were to be admired. She'd probably make a fine agent. He opened the front door, grabbed her foot, and tossed her leg back over. While she sputtered and swore at him, he leaned in and unlocked the gyves.

"You can go now, miss," Michaels said, handing her the discarded shoe.

"Why?" she demanded, tauntingly. "What made you change your mind? I thought you were going to arrest the big smugglers."

Michaels started to tell her what he had seen, and then decided not to say it out loud. If I'm mad, I'm mad, he said to himself. No need for two of us to know it. "Go on, miss. It's a mistake. On behalf of the British government, I tender you my sincerest apologies, and I request that you do not take any action against me."

"Oh, I get it," Diane said, fuming, putting her shoe back on. Hanging up in the metal bracelets had hurt her wrists, but anger and the pain kept her from feeling scared. "The secretary will disavow any knowledge of your actions."

"That's about the size of it, miss."

"I suppose you helped rescue Keith in Scotland just so you could keep an eye on him."

The agent regarded her mournfully. "You won't believe me, but I was helping the little lad. He was worried sick, and I hated to see that." Michaels made an impatient gesture. "Look, miss, I can take you in, if you like, and you can spend a lot of time assisting me with my inquiries, which is a code term for wasting a lot of time, when we both know there's nothing to find. Wouldn't you rather spend it shopping in Dublin instead of in a nasty room with a draught?"

Sullenly, Diane said, "I suppose so."

"Good. Then if I hear nothing more from you, then you'll hear nothing more from me."

"Promise?" Diane sneered.

"Yes, miss, I promise you," Michaels sighed. "You won't believe me, but I do mean what I say."

As soon as Michaels unlocked the handcuffs, he stood away, his hands held out from his sides to show he wasn't holding a weapon. With her eyes on him Diane backed off until she was far enough away she was certain he couldn't reach her if he jumped. Then she ran down the road and into the stream path, crying out to the others.

"What's the matter?" Keith said, gathering her into his arms. "Did something happen to you? To the car?" Diane kept shaking her head.

"It was that man," she told them, her words coming out in a rush. "Holl's friend—he followed us from Scotland. He thinks Keith is a smuggler. He's an agent of some kind. I knew there was something weird about him. How he knew what you looked like when he had never met you."

"Ah," Holl said, light dawning. "I remember him saying something about Keith's red hair. I was too worried even to think about what that might mean. You were right not to trust him."

"He's up there," Diane pointed toward the road.

"Well, I want to find out why he's here," Keith said. "What can he do, shoot me?"

"You'll probably want this, Keith Doyle." One of the others handed Keith the discarded wool bag containing Mrs. MacLeod's charm. Another one held up his sneakers.

The Little Folk mustered protectively around Diane as they followed Keith along the path. When they emerged onto the roadway, Michaels' car was gone. Diane looked around vainly for it. "He's gone. He saw all of you through binoculars. I watched him."

"Oh, don't worry about him," the Niall said. "If he goes for a drink anywhere hereabout, we'll drop a forget in his beer. That's a good idea of yours," he said, ruffling Holl's hair. "We'll recall that when strangers see us in the pub or down in town. If I know my Big Folk, he'll probably want a cool sip to clear his throat soon."

"Likely to be the Skylark," Fergus suggested.

"There's a telephone in the Skylark," Keith pointed out. "If you want to keep in touch with us, I'm sure that Peter and his father will make sure you can have some privacy. You can bless their beer or something in return." He jotted down the dialing code for the United States, his telephone number, the number at the farm, and at Diane's request, the one for her apartment. "There. Now you can call any of us, or write to us, too. I've added all the addresses. Um, international calling's kind of expensive. Do you need me to leave you some money?" he asked delicately.

"Ach, money, we've got a muckle of that," the elders said.

"And isn't there a gold mine close by here which we can walk in and out of?" said the Chief of Chiefs. "Do you need some? We have plenty to give."

"It's occupation we lack," Tiron added. "And curiosity, forbye, to see the rest of the world, and to come back again. But it's these passport things and the like preventing us."

"Well, once you're in the States, no one ever asks you for identification," Keith explained. "Unless you try to pay for something by check."

The Little Folk looked at each other, then back at Keith. "Tell us more," they said.

"Now, I'll only remove this curse," the Niall said sternly, "if you give me your word to employ a wee bit of good sense in future when making your inquiries. We're all the better that you decided to take a hand in our welfare, but not all would feel the same to have their privacy invaded. If your *bodach* was something bigger and nastier, it might have eaten you alive for punishment, and then where would you be?"

Keith tried to follow his chain of thought to its logical conclusion. "I don't know. Or I don't want to. I promise. I already promised Mrs. MacLeod."

"Good enough." The Niall signaled for Holl to come and stand by him. "The natural magic can often blunt the wild magic. Now, silence for the ensorcelment." He touched the glowing blossoms of the weddingbells with one hand, and put his other forefinger to the middle of Keith's forehead. Keith closed his eyes.

With a wink to Holl and Diane, the Niall tapped Keith smartly on the head, mouth, and throat in succession, and made a wrenching gesture before Keith's Adam's apple with his fist. "That'll do it. Let that be a lesson to you, my Big friend."

Keith worked his jaw and rubbed his neck with one hand.

"How do you feel?" Diane asked.

"You're beautiful," Keith said, and his eyes lit up as he realized his voice wasn't going to betray him. "By the way, to answer a question you asked me a while back, I'd buy you a drink any time."

"Congratulations," Diane said. "I'll take you up on that."

"I regret that you are leaving us tomorrow," the Niall said sadly. "If you will come back to us in the morning, we have some gifts of friendship we wish to give you."

"I've got something for you, now," Keith said, taking an envelope out of his pocket and presenting it to the Niall. "I've got the negatives, so you can keep the pictures I took of Holl's people. I promise to send you copies of the ones of you in care of the Skylark, as soon as I get home. You can work out the details with Peter."

"May I keep them?" Fiona asked, glancing avidly over the Chief's shoulder. "I've a handsome book they can go into, that I use for pressing flowers. They'll smell sweetly."

"I think not," Fergus said with some asperity. "I brought the Big Folk in, so I will keep them. I'm an old friend of his grandfather." He pointed at Keith. Others spoke up to protest and stake their claims.

"None of you will," the Niall said, raising his voice over all. "The photographic pictures will stay in my house, and any who wish to come and see them may do so at any time. That is enough bickering between you. I have spoken."

"I am ready to go home," the Master said. "This is precisely vhy I left in the first place."

Michaels sat mournfully at the bar in the Skylark, nursing a pint. He was tired of getting the mickey teased out of him by his co-workers for following will-o-the-wisps and Loch Ness Monsters. If he told a soul what he had just seen take place, with fairies and leprechauns, he'd never hear the end of it. They might even send him for psychiatric counseling. He'd be genuinely glad to see the back of his quarries, whatever the chief might say.

He rang through to his office on the pay telephone in the rear of the pub and asked for his superior. "Chief, you know the old story of the lad on the bicycle, who the customs and excise men would stop peddling furiously south over the border, with a heavy bag on the back? Always full of peat. No one could figure out why he was always smuggling peat. It's worthless. There's plenty of peat in the south, there for the taking."

"So?" the chief asked, impatiently. "What has this to do with your investigation? Have you apprehended them? Was there a pickup?"

"Turned out that he was smuggling bicycles, chief," Michaels went on doggedly. "Remember?"

"What's your point?" the voice in his ear roared.

Holl and the others came into the pub at that moment, and the four sat down at the bar. Michaels eyed Holl suspiciously. The blond boy still wore his Cubs hat. Michaels had rather liked the lad, but now he was convinced there was something strange about Holl he didn't want to know. Better to write the whole thing off as a bad dream and take his lumps in the office. "Well, we've been looking at the peat instead of the bicycles, sir. It's got all the form we were looking for, but none of the reality. This one's not our man. He's not a smuggler at all. I'm convinced that our pigeon's name here really is Keith Doyle. Trust me on this one."

"What about his kissing the ground and all that rot?" the chief growled.

"The silly things he does are just because he's a Yank, sir," Michaels said, with conviction. "Danny O'Day is still back in the states, if I don't miss my guess. He must be hanging back waiting for something else. If I were you I'd step up the alert in the airports again. Can I come back home now, sir?"

Keith opened the door of the Keane house with a flourish, and gestured the others through before him. Mrs. Keane looked up in surprise, and her brows wrinkled apologetically. "Mr. Doyle, there's been a telephone call for you. I'm so sorry. He just rang off. I don't know where my mind has been these last few days. He called on the Wednesday, and yesterday, too, though he didn't give me the number."

"Who's that, Mrs. Keane?"

"Well, his name is Doyle, too, fancy that. It must have been he who called the first night, too. Here you are." The landlady rummaged through the papers on her telephone table and came up with a slip which she handed to Keith. "Do go right ahead and call, if you please."

Curiously, Keith dialed the number on the slip. The phone on the other end rang twice, and then there was a click. A plummy voice said, "Hello?"

"Hi, there. My name is Keith Doyle. Someone called and left your number here. I'm returning the call," Keith said, uncertainly.

"Ah, well!" the voice said, pleased. "Greetings, then, cousin. I'm Patrick Doyle. The family dropped the O' about the same time your great-great grandfather left for America. I've been trying to get through to you for a few days now."

"What? Oh, no."

"Yes, indeed. I got word from my sister-in-law's family that there was a notice up in the old church, looking for details of us. So you've come all the way from America to look for us, have you?"

Keith became animated, and began pacing up and down in the hallway, twisting the phone cord nervously between his fingertips. He'd been so involved with the Little Folk, he'd forgotten entirely about hunting down his own family tree. It sounded like a root had sprung right underneath his feet, and he had nearly missed it. "That's right. You're Eamon O'Doyle's great-grandson, or great-great?"

"I am that. Great-great, if you will call it that."

"Can we meet?" Keith asked. "I've got to go home tomorrow morning, but I've got a car. I can drive anywhere."

Patrick Doyle was full of regret. "Ah, well, I'm just out of the door for France this very minute. I do a job in public relations, and I was hoping you'd have called me back sooner than this, but no harm done."

"I guess not," Keith replied, dejectedly.

"You'll only just have to come back again, and meet your cousins then."

The idea immediately perked Keith up. "Yeah! I've just about promised to come back anyway."

"Good on ya. Let's keep in touch, now, shall we? Here's my address."

Seizing a pencil, Keith scrawled down the information. "That's great. My father will be thrilled."

"Must go now. It takes a long hour and some to get to the airport. It's good that you called. I'm pleased to have been hearing from you, Keith. Give my best to your folks, and come again soon!" Patrick rang off.

Keith set down the receiver and looked at the others, who had been watching him curiously. "Well, how do you like that?" He waved the paper at them. "Said he's tried to call a few times, but we were always out."

Holl bowed his head, abashed. "My apologies, Keith Doyle. You've missed your own opportunities by assisting us, once again."

"Oh, it's all right," Keith said, dismissively. "I couldn't have concentrated on what he was saying anyway, not with all the things going on with you and your kin. I'll meet him eventually. It's not like he was going to disappear into the mists," he said playfully. "He's only going to France."

Chapter Thirty One

Holl hummed happily to himself as they rode the shuttle bus to the Dublin airport. He had a packet of white bellflower seeds in his pocket, a gift from Fiona, who had worked hard and at some little risk to cull them overnight. That and the bunch of cut flowers tucked into the hastily sewn inside pocket of his jacket gave him a contented feeling of accomplishment. Diane was twirling a featherlight woolen shawl, woven by Ketlin's own hands, and talking of accessories. Keith was more thoughtful. The Niall had taken him aside and presented him with a pair of golden rings. "You'll know when best to make use of these," the Chief had said, "if you'll allow an old man like me to meddle in your private life."

"Why not?" Keith agreed, lightly. "I meddle in everybody else's."

The Niall smiled. "I agree it's a little soon yet, but one day it won't be."

Keith had accepted them with thanks, and put them away carefully in an inside pocket. He hadn't mentioned the rings to the others. Niall had also presented him with a flat woolen cap like most of the elders wore. He showed that instead.

No one knew what the Master had been given. He had hardly spoken a word since breakfast.

Diane folded her shawl away at last. "Well, now we know where they come from," she told Keith glancing backward significantly toward the direction of the vale. "And the mystery is solved."

"Maybe for you," Keith said, "but for me it's deeper now than it was before."

"What? Why?"

"Well, I learned the Gaelic greeting from Peter, right?"

"Right. You said it perfectly. And Niall repeated it back to you, or something a lot like it."

"But it's not the same thing he said to you when *you* arrived. It's not Irish they're speaking. It sounds like it, with the lilt and all, but it isn't. Probably some Irish words have drifted into it over the years, like 'newspaper' has into our Little Folks' dialect. But they don't belong there."

"You mean it isn't their native land?" Diane asked, puzzled.

"Probably not the same way it is for the Irish. This means their culture comes from some place else, and they've managed to keep it up, inviolate, over the years they've been there."

"So where DO they come from?"

"I don't know, but I'm going to find out."

"I don't doubt that for a minute," Diane said definitely.

"Unless," Keith offered, after a considering pause, "they've been there lots *longer* than the Big Folk. That would make sense. Wow. What a concept. I wonder if the Celtic people mentioned the presence of Little Folk before they settled in Ireland—or if they found them when they got there—or if maybe they moved in at the same time." He made a note on the back of his ticket envelope. "Maybe I should start learning Lapp after all."

"Now I'm really confused," Diane complained.

"So am I," said Keith, thoughtfully chewing on his pen. "I didn't ask nearly enough questions. I'll probably have to go back."

"I'll come with you," said Diane.

"So what do you think of your relatives, after all this time," Keith asked, while they were waiting their turn in line to pass through Airport Security. The Master grunted.

Holl replied instead. "Oh, I like them. They're not much different than the folks at home, only I think the Conservatives more greatly outnumber the Progressives here. Thank goodness the Niall is a strong man."

"I suppose it's easier for the Conservatives, when they've held the home ground so much longer. What about that Tiron? Nice guy. You and he looked like you were getting to be as thick as thieves."

"We became friends," Holl said, shortly. "He knows a great deal about woodworking that I never dreamed of."

"Sure seemed to know it all," Keith asserted. "He'd be a great asset to Hollow Tree Industries. So, did you promise to keep in touch and everything?"

"Oh, yes," Holl said. "We'll be very close in the future."

"It seems like everyone's aspirations came true on this trip," Keith said happily. "But I've got to tell you, I'm going to be glad to get home."

"Put your bags on the belt," the Customs Agent instructed them. Keith hoisted his bag up and put it on the conveyor, and stepped toward the magnetic arch.

"Wait, Keith Doyle, your camera," Holl cried. He took it from Keith and handed it to the x-ray technician seated behind the luggage machine. "Please don't put this through. It has film in it."

The technician looked away from his screen and turned to one of the other guards, who put the camera carefully on a small plastic tray and carried it to the other side.

Keith retrieved his suitcase and demonstrated to the security guards how his camera worked. When they were satisfied that it contained only film, they waved the party away and directed them toward the departure gate.

"Anyone for the Duty Free Shop?" Keith asked.

"Anything to declare?" the U.S. Customs agent asked Keith, when he presented his passport at the glass-sided booth.

"Yep," Keith announced. His nerves were a little strung out. He had spent the whole flight anticipating this moment, knowing that Holl was carrying a packet of highly questionable flower seeds in his pocket. If they were searched, the Little Folk were through. He knew he was babbling, but he couldn't help it.

Holl, waiting behind the red line five feet behind him, was thrown into a panic. He wasn't sure whether to grab Keith's suitcase and bolt, or just brazen it out. Then Keith grinned foolishly at the agent. "I want to declare that it's terrific to be home."

"Geddada here." The agent had heard this type of declaration before. He stamped Keith's passport for the Green Channel and shooed him away, shaking his head sadly. "Next!"

"How was the trip?" Keith's father asked, peering in the rear view mirror. Holl sat in the front seat between Mr. Doyle and Diane.

"Great," Keith said, enthusiastically. "The tour of Scotland was terrific. I shot about twenty rolls of film. I've got tons of information from the Irish Genealogy Office, and from the priest of the parish where our folks were born, Father Griffith. And I talked to one of our cousins. His name's Patrick Doyle."

"That's wonderful," Mr. Doyle said, cheerfully. "One of Emerson's descendants?"

"No, one of Eamon's, his brother, so he's a cousin something removed. You'll have to see the family tree now. We missed each other a few times, but I've got his address and phone number. We met a lot of other terrific people, too."

"It was full of surprises," agreed Holl, glancing sideways at the suitcase. He watched out of the sideview mirror as the Doyle car turned onto the tollway and pulled into traffic. "We're well away from the airport now," he said loudly.

"Thank the powers," said a muffled voice from inside Keith's suitcase. "Now let me out of here. My spine's at a permanent angle."

Keith stared openmouthed at the suitcase at his feet, and fumbled with the locks. The top burst open, and Tiron sprang out of it, clutching his back with both hands. "Ooh, I don't think I could have waited another tick. Well, what are you staring at?" he demanded of the gawking Keith. "Have you never seen an economy class passenger before, then?"

"What am I running here, an underground railroad?" Keith asked, in mock outrage.

"More on the order of an underground airline," Holl offered, innocently. "Though that is physically impossible, it's the best description."

"You said I'd be an asset to your business. Well, here I am." Tiron stretched up his arms to Keith and the Master. "Help me up. I don't think I'll ever sit straight again, so I won't."

"What happened to my blue jeans?" Keith asked, surveying the ruin of his suitcase.

"Ach, with my folk. They'll keep them safe for you," Tiron assured him.

"Oh, thanks. How do I explain my mother I left my other pants with the leprechauns?"

"And all your books," Tiron added.

"My books!" Keith protested. "Hey! I wasn't finished reading them!"

"You've already promised to go back, to meet your cousin at least," Holl said reasonably, "so they're not really lost."

"I don't see any difference," Keith grumbled.

"Well, you're a hero in my eyes," Tiron assured him, "giving up your luggage space just for me. I've wanted to visit this continent all my life. So, how far is it to the haven from here?"

"Haven?" Mr. Doyle asked, speaking up for the first time, peering back at his new passenger in the rearview mirror.

"Hollow Tree Farm, Dad," Keith explained, and did a double take toward the front seat. He had completely forgotten that it was his father driving the car. "Um, Dad, you don't have any, well, negative feelings about Tiron appearing like this. I mean, I carried him home in my suitcase. He's sort of an...illegal alien."

"So far as I know, son," the senior Doyle said mildly, "the U.S. government doesn't believe that he exists, so what negative feelings could possibly affect me? I've accepted the reality of your other friends without losing my marbles. In fact, I wish I'd been the one who discovered them. I grew up on The Lord of the Rings. Personally speaking, I'm delighted he's here. Tiron, eh? Pleased to meet you."

"And I to make your acquaintance, sir," Tiron replied, settling into the car seat.

"I want to hear more about your vacation. When you come back from the farm, that is," Mr. Doyle finished, politely. "I think these gentlemen want to get home as soon as possible. You all look beat."

"That is true," the Master affirmed, nodding to Mr. Doyle. "Ve should be very grateful for all speed. My thanks."

"Definitely the block you were chipped from," Diane crowed gleefully to Keith.

"But, Keith?" his father put in.

"Yes, Dad?"

"Please don't bring home any dragons."

"No, sir."

Keith turned his blue Mustang into the gravel drive under the trees. It was very late, but lights still burned in the windows. The headlamps dipped down into the slope of the drive and up again, illuminating the side of the old white farmhouse. "Wake up, everyone! We're here!"

A head peered around the curtains inside the house, and a cluster of laughing children poured out of the door to greet them.

Holl looked up at the old farmhouse with a feeling of completeness. He had traveled far, and was in possession of the object of his quest, but oh! it was good to be home. With the trees in full leaf, the outside world was hidden from view. He had had enough of it for the time being. Only a little of the sky showed overhead. He couldn't help but feel trepidatious about seeing Maura again. He had played scenarios all the way across the Atlantic of her refusing his formal proposal, of meeting her and hearing her say that she had already chosen a new lifemate or worse—accusing him of abandoning her deliberately to break it off.

"So this is it," Tiron said, taking it all in. "A lovely place. Quiet, though. Are there any pubs nearabouts?"

Aylmer, a stocky, dark-haired elf, and his quiet wife Rose came out of the house to shake hands with the Master and Holl, followed by a handful of children. "We've missed you," Rose said, sincerely. "But who is this?"

"This is Tiron," Holl announced, presenting him. "He is without a doubt the finest woodworker in the world." The Master looked approvingly at Holl's statement, and nodded.

"Thank you for your compliments," Tiron said flippantly, sketching a bow. "I assure you they're no more than true."

"All has gone vell," Aylmer assured the Master. "It is in your hands vunce more."

"Thank you for taking charge in my absence. But all is vell now. I haf messages from the old ones, and many gifts."

"I've got lots of pictures," Keith said, patting his camera bag.

"Come in, come in," Rose urged them, slipping her hand around Diane's arm as far up as she could reach. "Marcy is here. There is coffee, there is cider, and fresh milk, too."

"Cider!" Keith exclaimed. "It's been weeks since I had some of that."

"We want to hear all about the old place," demanded Borget, a boy of seven years, tugging on Holl's sleeve.

"All these stories vill be told in the fullness of time," the Master assured him.

"Hi!" Another Big Person, a girl with black hair curling around her shoulders, walked into the room wiping paste off her hands. "Welcome back!"

"Well, if it isn't Snow White and the Eighty-Seven Dwarves," Keith said, mischievously, as the girl's cheeks reddened prettily. "Hi, yourself, Marcy."

"How was your trip?"

"Great! Have I got stories to tell you!"

"Wait for the others before you start telling them," Marcy pleaded. "Enoch is in the attic fixing the chimney. Some of the bricks fell down inside the fireplace."

"I'm not in a hurry, believe me. Where's Dola?" Keith asked, looking around the faces of his friends. "I brought her a tam o'shanter doll. That is, if it's still in my suitcase."

"Aye, that's there," Tiron assured him.

"She's coming," said Catra, the village Archivist. "I called the others down from the sleeping rooms."

"I have gifts to present, too," Holl remembered, following the others into the common room. While his friends watched curiously, he unpacked his case. There were sighs and exclamations as each item appeared.

"Well, you might have brought some of this lovely cloth for all," Catra's sister, Candlepat sniffed, upon learning all the pieces were spoken for. She fingered one hopefully until Holl picked it up again.

"I've brought something better," Holl stated. "We'll have lengths of our own making in a few weeks' time, with Tiron's help."

"That's right, fair colleen," Tiron said, looking at Candlepat with interest. "Though you must understand it will take time and skill to make any which will properly adorn your beauty." She preened herself and looked coyly at him under her long blonde lashes. Catra sighed heavily. Tiron made her a gallant bow, too, and she smiled at him.

"Excuse me," Holl said, not wanting to be in the middle of another battle between the rival sisters. Tiron could no doubt take care of himself. "I must find Orchadia."

He encountered the Master's wife as she was coming out of the kitchen, with her daughter behind her. He was so taken by surprise to see Maura, he all but shoved Orchadia into the sitting room and closed the door. Maura looked at him with hurt shock on her face, and he was sorry.

"I wanted to give you this," Holl said, handing her the tissue wrapped bundle of cloth, "before I spoke to Maura—in case she isn't speaking to me, that is."

"Haven't you gone to her yet to find out?" Orchadia asked, taking the bundle and giving it only the most cursory glance. For a moment, the snapping eyes were like those of her son Enoch, or her imperious father. "Do you mean you shut the door in her face that abruptly? For shame! You're getting to have too many of the Big People's ways. Now it's all hurry up and wait, and tomfoolery. Get along with you!"

Maura must have run away as soon as the door closed. Holl ran through the house to find her. When he discovered her, she was standing by the window in one of the upstairs sleeping chambers, very still. As soon as he could see her, Holl knew she was on the edge of weeping, curtaining her face with her long red-brown hair. "So you come to speak to me last, do you?" Maura asked, standing with her hands folded at her waist.

"I have thought about you a lot while I was gone," Holl said, at last. "And all that when I went away so that when I came back we could be together for all time. I was distressed to hear that you were spending a lot of private time with Gerol."

Maura's green eyes caught fire. "Oh, you heard that? Oh, Holl, what sense have you? Sometimes you're as silly as Keith Doyle. You went off, for all everyone knew for ever. You might not know since I didn't complain openly about it, but Ronard made a certain set at me as soon as you left. And Catra is not speaking to me because Ronard was courting her until you went away. Gerol stepped in to help me keep him off. I thought about you, dreamed about you, and who could I talk to about you? Candlepat? Certainly not. She's interested in you herself, as she is in all males. She'd cut me out without a thought. My mother? She's got no patience with mooncalfing. Marm? I know he's your good friend, but all he'd do is agree with me and say 'Yah.'" Maura made a face. "Gerol's a good friend. He listened to me."

Holl dropped his gaze to the ground at her feet, his face red as a rose. "I'm sorry for doubting. But I was so far away, I couldn't hear any of you. I didn't know what you were thinking."

Maura's face softened, and she touched his cheek with tender fingers. "The same thing I've thought all of our lives. We were worried about you, too, off in the great distance. It was only the sound of your voice over the telephone which reassured us."

The flowers were none the worse for their long travel in the inside pocket of his coat. Holl drew out the bouquet, as amazed as before by the purity of the power radiating from the tiny white bells. Even though they had been cut days earlier, and had been without water, the blooms were still fresh, clad in their astonishing glow.

"How lovely," Maura sighed. Holl took one of her hands, and proffered the flowers to the free hand. When she reached for them, it was as if an electrical circuit had been completed. The elders had been right. When the match was true, the flowers sealed the bond. This was the second blessing. The third would come when the flowers produced seeds, continuing the circle of life.

"Will you be mine, then?" Holl asked, tenderly.

"Of course," Maura said, teasingly, her cheeks a becoming pink. "I was never anything else." She turned up her face to kiss him.

Holl pulled her out into the main room, where everyone was exclaiming over Keith's rolls of snapshots.

"Now, wait," Keith insisted. "I got double prints of everything. Let me separate them, and you can have the second set. They'll be yours to keep. Don't mix them up. There's about twenty rolls. Hey, watch the fingerprints, Borget."

Borget's mother pulled his hands away and washed them with a surreptitious cloth. Everyone looked up from the colored squares as Holl held up his free hand for attention.

"May I have the pleasure of announcing that Maura has just consented to be my lifemate."

"As long as life lasts," Maura affirmed, her eyes shining when she looked at Holl. Everyone clustered around them to give their congratulations. With eyes shining, Orchadia kissed her daughter. "Bless you, my loves. May you be happy."

Keith shook Holl's hand over the heads of most of the villagers and then stepped back out of the way to let the others close in.

"I love true romances," Diane said happily, watching the others embracing Holl and Maura and offering good wishes. She clutched Keith's arm. He reached up to twine his hand with hers and squeezed her fingers. "Doesn't that give you some idea of your own?"

Keith pointed to his throat and mimed laryngitis. He produced a thin, squeaky voice. "Sorry," he croaked. "It's the curse. I can't talk about wine, women, or money."

"Oh, you!" Diane exclaimed. "One day…!"

Marcy sighed sentimentally. "I'm so happy for them. I wonder if this might get Enoch thinking along the same lines, eventually. It'll probably take a few years, but if it's right, I'll wait."

Keith was surprised to learn that she was seriously considering settling down permanently with the Little Folk. But why not? She had known them longer than he had. And he knew something that she didn't: that Enoch had already broached the subject with his father. She'd probably be thrilled. There might be another declared romance right here and now. He opened his mouth to speak.

The Master caught his eye and stared him down sternly. Keith closed his mouth again without having made a sound. He understood that perhaps that was another secret he'd better keep.

"Remember the *bodach*," the Master said, warningly. "Vhat he did, I can do, too."

"Curses," Keith said ruefully. "Foiled again."

Higher Mythology

Chapter One

"I always cry at weddings," Diane Londen said, snuffling noisily into her handkerchief. "Oh, God, I only brought one hanky! I'll be a mess by the time the bride comes out."

Without looking up from his viewfinder, Keith Doyle reached into his pocket and passed over to her his own square of cotton. "Here. I can always grab a napkin off the table if I need one."

"Don't you dare!" Diane admonished him, refraining from shoving his shoulder only because it might knock over the video camera he was adjusting. His face was invisible, leaving only a thatch of wavy red hair showing over the body of the camera. She directed her remarks to that. "It looks too nice to disturb."

Freeing his eye from the rubber focusing ring, Keith glanced over at the huge buffet table laden with a feast of good-looking dishes that lined one entire length of the Little Folks' great room. Well, the concept of huge was relative. The tabletop hit him just above knee high, as he had found out to his agony when he had arrived and tripped over it, and the bowls and platters were small compared to what graced the Doyle family table on major holidays, but the feast itself, for pure variety and quantity, was nothing less than spectacular.

The Hollow Tree farmhouse had been transformed fantastically in a matter of only a few weeks after he and Holl had returned from their transatlantic trip, almost more than it had since the Little Folk had moved in at the beginning of the summer. With a special impetus urging them on, the Folk had worked wonders. In one month flat, the house had gone from being a pretty ordinary building where people lived and worked and repaired the neglect of decades, to a fanciful bower, complete with braided arches of vine and flowers over every door, three-dee sculpture pictures in wood, glittering stone, and colorful woven tapestry on nearly every wall, waiting for Titania and Oberon to make their big entrance, stage left.

All the Little Folk were already in the big room. It just about held the eighty-some of them, with a little space left over for the handful of Big Folk visiting for the wedding. Midriff high to a medium-sized human adult, the Little Folk resembled the Big Ones in nearly every way. They were proportioned just like humans, with the notable exception of tall, elegantly pointed ears where their big cousins had to be contented with small, rounded scrolls of flesh, and their faces looked young, almost childlike, even those Little Folk with beards or gray hair. And they could do magic. They assured Keith time and again there was nothing about the wonders they worked that he couldn't do himself with practice and patience, but he still held them in awe.

Not enough awe to quench his delight that his best friend, Holl, was marrying his ladylove Maura, and that he, Keith, was here to witness the event, not to mention recording it for posterity. It gave him a rare chance to see his mysterious friends at their best. Keith knew that this was to be the first wedding among the Folk in over forty years, certainly the first since they had come to the midwestern United States, and the first real celebration of any kind in who knew how long.

Out of pure excitement, not to mention a little pride, everyone had gone all out to deck the house in beauty. Flowers festooned every vertical surface, leaving one to perch well forward on the chair seats lest a casual lean backward crush a careful arrangement and dust the unwary sitter with pollen and petals. The blossoms' scent filled the air. Living vines entwined with streamers across the ceiling and doorways. Each one of the Folk, large and small, had on new clothes, specially made for the occasion. Keith surveyed the range of costumes that embraced styles from a nod to ancient Greece to a whimsical interpretation of modern metalhead.

And there was the feast to come. Among the Little Folk there were some notable cooks. From Keith's point of view, after years of school food, any meal actually prepared for less than a hundred tasted pretty good. Add skill and time to improvise and season, and the results were ambrosial. Keith's belly rumbled in anticipation. On the table, cold plates of meats, cheese and fruit were arranged around big empty spaces awaiting the arrival of the hot dishes, which Keith could smell cooking just beyond the doorway. Big bowls, carved beautifully in some of the elves' favorite designs, ivy and honeysuckle, held their quivering cargo of creamy yellow or ruby red ever so slightly out of reach of the flies that circled hopefully overhead. No pest alighted on the food or dishes. There was a distance beneath which the insects couldn't go, though they kept on noisily trying. Keith sensed a benevolent buffer layer of magic that protected the picnic from the ants. He wondered if it would keep out the questing fingers of a hungry college student hoping to extract an olive from the crudités tray.

To Keith's delight, in the center of the table was a broad, flattened bowl filled with unsliced loaves of fresh bread. He didn't need to see the look of pride on the face of Holl's sister Keva when she caught him eyeing it hungrily. Little old Keva made the best bread in the world. Keith had eaten enough of it to give it his wholehearted approval. To make his joy complete, he spotted butter and fruit preserves in wooden dishes nearby.

Though pastries and other goodies abounded, there was no wedding cake as Big Folk were accustomed to seeing, so he suspected the ornately-fashioned braided bread at the nearest edge of the table served much the same purpose. The wooden-staved keg at the other end, seeming a little self-conscious under its crown of vine-leaves and larkspur, had to be full of home-made brew. Elven hooch sneaked up on you, Keith recalled. It had to be magic, because although it packed a good kick, it didn't leave behind hangovers as a lasting memento. The wallop happened all at once, and got the punishment over with.

Holl and Maura had kindly waited for the fall class session at Midwestern University to begin before celebrating their nuptials so their classmates could join them. That consideration told the Big friends that they were valued as much by the bride and groom as the folk of their own size. Keith thought this was a terrific way to begin his junior year.

A peep through his viewfinder framed some of the Big guests arriving. Keith waved over the camera's top at Teri Knox, a pretty girl who'd been in the secret classes taught by the Elf Master. She was graduating this summer. Her honey-blond hair was almost hidden by a wreath of silk flowers, a medieval accompaniment to her modern sleeveless, soft jersey dress. Teri spotted him and waved, making a deliberate face for the camera. Barry Goodman, next in at the door, echoed the expression. Teri caught Lee Eisley's sleeve and pointed toward Keith. Lee shook his head with a pained, pitying look on his dark bronze face. Keith grinned. This was going to be a great tape.

Lee was the first Big pupil the Elf Master had ever taught. He'd been out of college for over a year now. Though he was a quiet man, Lee's high GPA in journalism had helped him to get a foot in the door at the Indianapolis daily paper. Hard work and talent got him the occasional feature article, each of which Catra, the archivist, had carefully preserved in a scrapbook. The Elf Master was proud of his oldest pupil and was glad that the young man made time to keep in touch. Contrariwise, Keith knew Lee would rather lose his byline and five or six teeth than miss an event like this. All of them had reason to be grateful to the Little Folk for helping them to master difficult academic subjects, but before Keith came along, had never had much social interaction with their small benefactors.

Dunn Jackson was the newest keeper of the secret. He was Diane's addition to the class, as Diane had been Keith's. The three of them shared an Introduction to Philosophy course that threatened to swamp them all in a wave of gibberish. If the Master hadn't begun a parallel tutorial in the basics of philosophical thought, Keith could have kissed goodbye his consistent B average. Dunn's cheeks were flushed red under his light coffee-complected skin. He was excited to be here, too. His eyes were wide, moving here and there, trying to take everything in at once. Keith liked him. Dunn had an enquiring mind that ran along some of Keith's favorite channels. He and Keith had gotten together over speculations that if Little Folk of the Caucasian persuasion existed, there might be some of his own color out there somewhere. It was a concept worth exploring one day.

The other newcomer was an elf from the Old Country. In Keith's opinion, Tiron felt at a disadvantage being thrust into a new country among seven dozen new Folk, and it came across as an attitude problem. One facet of his real personality was as clear as the blue sky: Tiron was a womanizer. Without having to ask for details, Keith could tell Tiron had set the sisters Catra and Candlepat against one another—not too difficult a thing to do—as rivals for the prize of his affections. His direct challenge of Holl's position as an acknowledged leader was going nowhere; Holl was too popular. Pity would have been out of place for the newcomer, though. Tiron wasn't suffering for lack of attention. The older Folk sought him out as a tie to the old country, and the younger ones as a curiosity, someone their own size with whom they hadn't grown up. His skill in woodworking was also a great addition to Hollow Tree Industries, putting him immediately into the first rank of craftsmen and craftswomen. Keith was sure in time Tiron would relax. If he didn't, some of the fathers of daughters would take turns decking him.

Things were so different now that the Folk had a place of their own. The first change Keith noticed was sound. When they were living beneath the Midwestern University library, everyone had been quiet, listening all the time for footsteps, fearful that they would be discovered by the terrible Big Ones. They were liberated now. The twenty acres of thickets and meadows around the house contained the more normal hubbub of eighty or ninety beings, plus farm animals, plus pets. Out in the small Near Meadow just beyond the kitchen door were a handful of sheep and a dog barking at them. And there was music. Tuning up in a corner was a small band consisting of a harp, two wooden flutes, an ancient fiddle, a guitar, and a gadget which looked like a combination of the last two. The guitar player, Marcy Collier, was a Big Person, a friend and former object of Keith's unrequited affection. She smiled at him shyly and bent her head to tune a string. Her thick, black hair was crowned with ivy and roses, like those of the Little People around her. Unlike most Big Folk, Marcy belonged here, on Hollow Tree Farm. She and Enoch, the Elf Master's son, were an 'item.' Marcy took a lot of good-natured razzing on the topic from her friends, but she was learning to defend herself and her choices. In Keith's opinion, the Constitutionally-guaranteed pursuit of happiness included dating someone half one's height. He applauded anything that made Marcy happy. With love and support, she was blossoming into a capable, confident woman.

The music and the noise in the room died away suddenly as Curran, Holl's clan chief, appeared at the door. For once, the sour old elf had a smile on his face. By contrast, Holl, behind him, looked solemn and nervous. His usually pink cheeks were pale. He was dressed in new clothes of russet and dark green that were cut to unfamiliar but ancient-seeming pattern, making him look as if he had stepped out of a long gone time. His dark blond hair was slightly damp and curled up at the ends, as if it had been wet-combed just moments ago. On his head he wore a woven circlet of white bellflowers. The magic blossoms gave off a white light visible to those who could see that kind of thing, gathering strength from and giving strength to Holl. Keith regretted that the video camera didn't have second sight to catch the almost perceptible pulsations of mystic energy. Beside him, Diane sighed. In the corner, the harp player began a soft, winding melody like the memory of a forgotten dream.

There was a whisper of sound from the opposite side of the room. Into the doorway leading from the kitchen the Elf Master stepped, his head held high and proud. Maura was on his arm. Her rich hair, a deep auburn almost the color of carnelian that contrasted not unfavorably with her father's carrot-colored thatch, was braided into complicated patterns and crowned with bellflowers, the blossoms nodding with every step she took. Embroidery ran down the bodice and around the long sleeves blending the green and gray ivy pattern favored by Holl's clan with the green and yellow honeysuckle motif of her own. In her hand she clutched a bunch of the white flowers, their energy gleaming and spilling over her fingers like water. Maura's lips were trembling, caught between a smile and tears. She stepped toward Holl with a look of love and anticipation burning in her deep green eyes that made Keith catch his breath. The Little Folk were so childlike in appearance that sometimes he forgot that they were mature adults, far older and wiser than he. That brief flash reminded him. Holl came forward to meet her, his right hand outstretched.

Candlepat broke through the ring of witnesses and hurried to Holl, clutched his arm, turned him away from his bride. Keith was shocked. The blond elf, a pixie carved by Playboy, had lost her usual self-assurance, and was pathetic, even woeful.

"Holl, don't go to her. I care for you, too. What about me?" she begged, her eyes gleaming with tears.

Keith was horrified. Blindly, he felt his way around the camera and edged forward. Candlepat was such an all-round flirt, even vamping him sometimes, he'd never suspected she had an honest attachment to Holl. This was no time for her to bring it up. He couldn't let her interrupt the ceremony. She probably needed a good heart-to-heart talk with someone. If he got her outside, the wedding could proceed uninterrupted.

Steel-strong fingers gripped his forearm and dragged him back. Keith glanced down. Maura's black-haired brother was holding onto him with all the natural strength of a full-time carpenter. Did he want his sister's wedding disturbed? What was going on here?

"It's part of the custom," Enoch growled under his breath. "Explanations later."

Arrested, Keith nodded, his eyes fixed on the figures in the center of the room. "All right," he whispered. Carefully, he edged back to his post, hoping he hadn't gotten in the way of the lens.

Holl put the girl gently aside, with a tender touch on the cheek. "I want only Maura," Holl answered her softly. His hand came away wet with her tears. "You'll find someone, lass. But not me." Candlepat withdrew to the edge of the ring, her straight back proud as her sister enfolded her in a comforting arm. Keith couldn't see her face, but she was too proud to show disappointment in her posture. He wondered how much of her performance had been sincere.

The couple made a few more steps toward one another, and Enoch shoved forward, moving between his sister and Holl.

"Think, sister," he said, almost hoarsely. "You're too young to make a life's commitment."

Smiling, Maura touched his hand with her fingertips, found and clasped her brother's palm. "Thank you, but I made my choice long ago." She leaned to kiss him.

Enoch nodded, and eyes down, moved out of the way. As he returned to his place, Keith could see him smile. The two pairs met in the center of the circle and the clan leaders put the marrying couple's hands together. Curran and the Master shook hands – the white head and the red nodding politely to one another – and stepped away, leaving Maura and Holl together, joined.

Holl smiled at Maura. "Before our friends, I swear that I will be a good husband to you, support you, and provide for you. Not only a lover I'd be, but a friend and partner in all things. No other will ever supplant you in my heart. I promise to treat your dreams as dearly as my own, to enjoy and suffer life alongside you all the days of our lives."

"Since we were children, I knew we were meant to be together," Maura replied. Her voice trembled as if she might burst into tears. "I've never wanted another for my lifemate, and I come to you with joy."

The audience sighed with pleasure as Holl bent his head and kissed Maura gently. Keith waited, but the embrace deepened, went on and on.

The Elf Master cleared his throat. After a long moment, the couple broke their kiss and came up for air. Maura's cheeks were rose-pink.

"As you haf claimed one another, none of us shall stand between you or compel you apart. I offer my congratulations and good wishes."

Beaming, Holl and Maura moved to embrace him, then turned to enfold Curran. There was a general cheer, as the crowd converged on the couple, shouting well wishes. No longer constrained to silence, Diane honked loudly into Keith's handkerchief.

"You'd think I'd learn to buy waterproof mascara," she said, smiling. Her eyes were rimmed with soggy black. She dabbed it away. "Oh, I'm so happy."

"Me, too," said Keith.

He couldn't stop grinning. Happiness seemed to be contagious, because the foolishly indulgent smile he wore was on every set of lips in the room.

"And now the feast begins," curly-haired Rose called out cheerfully. Like a flock of pigeons abandoning one old lady's crumbs for another, the crowd reversed and made toward the feast table. Keith managed to barge through the throng to Holl and Maura. He knelt to kiss the bride on the cheek and gave Holl a strong embrace and a hearty slap on the back.

He tried to find something deep and profound to say, but all that came out was, "Congratulations and good luck."

Maura squeezed his hand. "It could not have happened without you," she said.

"It was nothing, Maura. I'm a sucker for a happy ending," Keith said, feeling his cheeks burn. "Hey, what was all that about a challenge tradition? For a moment there I thought the whole thing would stop."

"It is one of our oldest traditions, ye ignorant infant," a gruff voice said from behind him. Enoch stepped over Keith's ankle to get to his sister. He embraced her and his new brother-in-law. "I'd never have kept Maura from claiming this grinning oaf if she truly wanted him," he aimed a warning scowl toward Holl, "nor would I let him take a step nearer her if she looked at all unhappy about it." The rough edge in his voice was undoubtedly connected to the bright gleam in his eyes. Keith's mouth was open as he considered the delightful revelation: Enoch was sentimental. When the black-haired elf turned back to him with a suspicious glare, Keith's mouth snapped shut like a trap. "I'll explain it all to you in words of one syllable. Come with me, and listen."

While they stood in line for the buffet, Enoch explained the custom of the challenge. "It's to ensure that each of the pair loves the other without doubt. In the face of the challenge, either is entitled to turn away if they feel they're being coerced into the match or making a hasty decision. We like to take our time to decide things, as well you know. There might be hurt feelings this way, but no lifelong mistakes are likely to be made, and we live long lives."

"I like that a lot," Keith said, nodding approval. "To win your ladylove, you have to be proof against temptations or threats."

"So pretty a custom," said a voice at Keith's elbow, making him start. The elderly woman beside him twinkled at him with mild blue eyes. Ludmilla Hempert must have been standing beside him the whole time, listening to Enoch talk. She patted Keith on the arm with a somewhat large and surprisingly strong hand. "I surprised you? I have been resting in one of these so fine rooms. Ah, my little ones! A feeble, old lady like me, and they must have me by them when they bless the young."

Ludmilla was a retired cleaning woman who had been working for the University at the time the Little Folk had taken refuge there. She was the first benevolent Big Person the Little Folk had ever encountered, and they treated her like a guardian angel. As for her protests as to being a feeble, old lady, Keith wouldn't have bet against her bench-pressing her weight in grandchildren.

"It wouldn't have been the same without you. Can I make you a copy of the videotape?" Keith asked, politely.

Ludmilla beamed. "Oh, yes, I would enjoy it. But how would I explain to my family when they visit?" she asked, with a sly quirk of her mouth.

Keith grinned back. "I'll put opening credits on it. You can tell them it's a Hollywood short subject called 'A Mid-Autumn's Afternoon Dream.'"

Beer would make him too drowsy to enjoy the dancing. He wandered into the kitchen to find a glass of water instead. There were clean cups on the table, but when he reached for the tap, Shelogh called out to him.

"The purified water's in the jug. Have all you want of that. We've a cisternful down below. Don't bother with the tap. The water stinks."

"What's wrong with it?" Keith asked.

"Oh, nicht much," Shelogh said, mixing midwestern English with the Germanic accent the middle-aged Folk had picked up from Ludmilla Hempert. "Just some nasties, smells like it seeped out of a barn instead of from between limestone sheets."

"Bizarre," Keith said, pouring out water from the jug and tasting it: pure, clear, invigorating as wine. "Should I start looking for a water-purifier for you?"

"Oh, no," she cried, "when we can do it ourselves? Ach, Keith Doyle. We haf energy to spare now that it's our own home. Have you not noticed?"

"Oh, yes," Keith said, with a grin. "I have. It's terrific."

Holl came through with a stack of dirty plates and put them up on the drainboard.

"Hey, it's a rotten thing to mention on your wedding day, but what's wrong with the water supply? It smells like runoff from a feedlot, but there's no feedlot within miles. One cow and seven sheep couldn't do that much damage, not to the underground water table."

"Oh, that," Holl said. "Olanda has listened to the water's heart. She said it isn't natural. Someone is pouring an evil smelling mess into it somewhere between the source and our cistern."

Keith's brows drew down over his thin nose. "That sounds like deliberate contamination of the groundwater. That shouldn't be going on down here. You ought to try to arouse some local action to look into it. You should write letters to the editor, or something. "

"Of that wee paper that comes out once a week?" Holl asked, astonished.

"Come on, Holl, you live in a small community yourself. Everyone reads The Central Illinois Farmer because it's more personalized to them than, say, the Chicago Tribune or the New York Times. You could write really stirring letters if you put your mind to it. You're the most environmentally aware people I know. You can *hear* streams and trees complain. You waste nothing. I know your homes in the library were built with scrap, and you use everything to death."

Holl stroked his chin. "Then the ones to blame might be more apt to pay attention to a well-written plaint, eh?"

"Right," Keith said.

"Would they listen to the cries of a mythical person, then?" Holl spluttered.

"No one who can mail a letter is mythical. If it goes that far, I'll come down here when they check out the groundwater on the farm," Keith said. "But hey! I didn't mean to get you off on a tangent. This is your wedding day. Have a blast!" The band in the corner began to play. "Dance with your wife," Keith finished, with a grin.

"Just the thing I was about to suggest to him," Maura said, coming up to claim her bridegroom. She tucked her hand into his arm and drew him out onto the floor. Keith watched them swirl away to the merry beat of the dance band. With all their friends and relatives clapping the beat, the bride and groom circled the room. The music had as much magic in it as the crowns of flowers they wore. Keith found himself tapping his toes with the rhythm, and longing to get out and do the modified polka which was his standard for weddings and other festive occasions.

Pat Morgan, Keith's former dorm-mate with whom he was currently sharing a cheap student apartment just off the Midwestern campus, came over to poke him in the ribs with the handle of his dessert fork. "Look at this," Pat said, gesturing around him with a sweep of his arm. "It's like a Shakespearean pageant, with all the elements of traditional drama—love, suspense, happy ending." He sighed. "It would never make it in the theater today." Pat had a melancholy bent that went with his Ricardian looks.

Breathless, the bridal couple broke apart though the music was still playing. Each ran to the sidelines and joined hands with the parent-in-law of the opposite sex. Then those couples parted to bring others onto the floor one by one. Maura's tiny hands seized Keith's, and pulled him out to dance. His partner looked like the bride on the top of a traditional wedding cake, and was almost small enough to fit. He felt like an uncle escorting a five-year-old niece.

"You look beautiful. Could you possibly be that happy?" he asked, feeling indulgent.

"More so, Keith Doyle," Maura said, her skin fresh and pink, her eyes firelit emeralds. "I feel I owe you much."

"Holl did it," Keith said, hastily, turning away in embarrassment but making it look as if he was making sure they weren't going to bash into the next set of dancers. "Holl did it all. He saved my neck, too, you know."

"He learns quickly, but he had a good example set him," Maura said, not letting him off the hook. "Well, when will we see you as happy as we are? When will you ask the pretty Diane to wed with you?"

"Uh, not yet," Keith said, feeling his cheeks flush. "At least let me get out of school first and find a decent job! Love in a student-grade apartment isn't all that romantic."

"When you're in love, any bower is a palace," the elf-lass reminded him. She fixed him with a searching gaze. "You didn't gainsay me. So you'd actually do it, would you? She's the one of your heart?"

"Uh," Keith said, feeling the floor drop out from under him. He looked around wildly, wondering if anyone was in a position to overhear them. Thankfully, the music was pretty loud. "Come on, Maura, have mercy! I want to do things in the right time. Don't tell her."

"I don't have to," the girl said, coyly. With a gay smile, she spun away from him and chose another partner. Inspired by Maura's last teasing words, Keith turned to find Diane and draw her into the dance, but to his amazement, the Elf Master had already asked her.

"Claim-jumper," Keith muttered. He bowed to Ludmilla Hempert and assisted her gallantly to the floor.

In the second set, he managed to secure a dance with Diane. She was breathless and flushed.

"Isn't this wonderful?" she asked. "I'm so happy for them, Keith."

"Keith Doyle!" Dennet, Holl's father, waved to them from the side of the room. "There's been a package for you, by the bye. Did Rose give it to you?"

"Uh, no," Keith said, puzzled.

"Oh, I'll find it. There's been enough of a stir these last days, so there has." He bustled away and returned with a flat box covered with brown paper and tied with waxed string. "From Ireland, it is. Have you friends called Skylark, then?"

"Mailed from a pub of that name," Keith said, unwrapping the brown paper. He grinned, and showed the contents to Diane and Dennett. The flabby rectangle wrapped up in fine embroidered cloth had a fancy lettered card tucked under the ribbon. "It's not for me. It's for Holl. A wedding present. From the Niall."

Dennett's eyes twinkled. He looked like a teenager letting them in on a prank, in spite of his white hair. It was disconcerting, considering how old Keith suspected him to be. "There's the name of a man whose face I've not seen these, oh, well, how long has it been? Your photographs were like a work of wonder, lad. I thought never to see those likenesses again in life. What's in the package, then? Ah, gifting time won't be far off. I'll have to hold my curiosity 'til then."

"How long *has* it been?" Keith asked, pointedly. He had never managed to learn how long ago the Little Folk had made their way to the New World, nor how old they grew to be. Curiosity made his invisible whiskers twitch.

"Oh, a long time," Dennett said. He smiled conspiratorially at Keith. Maybe he thinks I already know, Keith thought, dismayed. "Gifting time's coming soon, after Holl and Maura have broken their fast together as husband and wife. My son's eaten nary a thing all day, though he's been up since sunrise, he's that nervous."

"I can't blame him," Keith said, and recoiled as Diane socked him on the arm. "Ouch!"

"Well, go and enjoy the feast," Dennet said hospitably. He turned to follow his own advice.

Keith went back to his camera and filmed some of the guests eating, then turned his lens and hastily focused on a full plate moving toward him.

"There," Diane said, putting her hand over the lens. He lowered the camera and she handed him the plate. "Stay out of trouble."

Keith dug in. His anticipation was exceeded by the reality. The food was terrific. Meat dishes were few, leaving a more significant presence by savories that got their proteins from nuts and beans. The vegetables were as ornate as the room's decor: carrots were cut into corkscrews, celery shredded into small replicas of wheatsheafs, relishes and salads appeared as colorful as mosaics and stained glass windows—and everything was delicious.

"Did you see the dessert?" Diane asked, pointing to the edge of his plate with her fork.

Two half-blown rosebuds lay together near the salad. They were nearly perfect, except for the fact that they were larger and transparent. "Those are amazing. What are they made of?" Keith asked.

"Jell-O," Diane said, with an impish grin. She ticked the plate rim with her fingernail, and the gelatin rosebuds quivered. "When I asked how they did that, Calla said, 'Enhancing, lass, enhancing!'" Diane mocked the Little Folk's tone.

"That's all the answer you'll ever get out of them," Keith said, with a grin.

After much of the feast was eaten, the newlyweds were enthroned on the finest of the flower-strewn chairs. At their feet the children placed the colorfully-wrapped packages entrusted to them by the adults. The presents from other Little Folk were few. The Big Folk proffered their large, and in Keith's case, heavy, boxes with a trifle of embarrassment.

"Oh, don't concern yourself," Holl assured them. "It's most generous of you to include us in your custom. Heart's generosity is always welcome. In our ways, which are a bit rusty, as you might guess from forty years' disuse, presents given to the newlywed couple are mostly personal in nature, since everything else is shared for the good of all. But Maura and I are grateful for whatever inspiration you've been visited by. Be sure none are unwelcome. We'll open yours first, after a presentation of my own."

He turned to Maura and lightly held out his hand for hers. When she extended her palm, an inquiring expression on her face, he placed in it a tiny, carved wooden box.

"We work mostly in wood, but I wanted something a little thinner and stronger," Holl said. Maura pressed the miniature button and lifted the box's lid. Inside was a ring made of braided silver and gold. In its center, glowing with the blue of a cloudless sky, was an oval sapphire. Keith and the others let out an appreciative gasp as Maura showed it around.

"But where did you find the stone?" she asked.

Tiron cleared his throat. "A heart's gift from me, cousin," Tiron said hoarsely. "I swear by the trees and the earth that there are no love spells on it to make you turn to me, nor any other influence that would lessen your joy." Surprised, Maura smiled warmly at him.

The sentimental, generous gesture showed a side of Tiron that surprised Keith. The strange elf seemed at times to be the greatest of egotists. He blushed when Maura rose from her throne to kiss him heartily on the cheek.

"We welcome you among us," Maura said, squeezing his hand. "I can't thank you enough."

"Well, it's nothing," Tiron said, blushing.

"But you're trying to denigrate the gift," Holl protested. "He told me that the stone came from the hand of a king in days long gone. This king, a visitor from over the water, gave it to our people in Ireland and promised to keep faith with them, but he was killed soon after by traitors."

"Which king?" Keith asked eagerly. "How far over the water? England? Scotland? Denmark?"

Tiron shrugged. "I'm sure I didn't listen to the old stories," he said. "You can write to the Niall, for all the useless rambling you'll get out of him."

"Well, it's a mighty gift," Maura said. "Thank you. And thank you for the crafting of it into such a treasure," she said to her husband, bestowing a tender kiss on him. Holl reddened, beaming. "And now let us see what our other kindhearted friends have given."

"Uh," Keith said, flushing red while Maura circled around the box he offered with anticipation. "Since you have a working windmill for electricity, I thought this might come in handy. It's used, but I had it tuned up before I brought it down. I coated the wheel with urethane so you wouldn't get metal burns." He had prepared his speech ahead of time but they seemed to him silly and stilted now. "Um…don't lose the traditional skills you have just because technology makes it easier to perform your tasks."

"Vell put," said the Master, nodding, "and very true. I didn't think you had it in you, Meester Doyle."

"Uh, thanks. Just tear it, Maura," Keith suggested, watching the bride run her hands along the side looking for gaps in the cellophane taped seams. "The suspense is getting painful."

"As you wish." Maura shredded the paper and tossed it aside. Together, she and Holl pried open the cardboard box. "It's a sewing machine," she said. With a good deal of assistance, she drew it out of its protective nest. "A fine one." The name was embossed on the black enamel of the steel body below the cam dials. At Holl's urging she flipped up the lid on top and read the small chart. "Look at all the stitches it will do!"

"Machine doings, huh!" Dierdre sneered. She was the oldest of the old women, a contemporary of Curran, and a clan leader in her own right. "It takes all the soul straight out of the work, so it does. That'll never make anything worth keeping."

"Oh, come, gran," Candlepat admonished her, with a cocky tilt to her head. "Do you truly enjoy hemming sheets and seaming curtains? I don't. The machine will leave your hands free for the fine work, which *is* worth keeping."

"That may be qvite true," Rose said, with a thoughtful expression. Though a Conservative, she was suspected of having Progressive leanings, and in any case trusted Keith Doyle absolutely. She and a few of the needlecraft workers examined the old Singer with pleasure.

"It'll come in most useful, you'll see," Tiron said. "Next year there'll be cloth from the backs of those sheep outside. The first of the looms will be ready by year's end."

Diane blew her nose as Maura undid the paper on the next present and lifted the esoteric-looking machine inside to her lap.

"It's a blender," Diane said, and burst into sputtering tears. Through her sobs, she explained. "I always give blenders for wedding presents. It does all kinds of things. You can return it if you've already got one, or you can exchange it for something else you'd like better. The receipt's in the bottom. Oh, I'm so happy for you!"

"There's never a thought of returning it. We're pleased to be part of your tradition," Holl accepted gravely, "as you are a part of ours. We will use it with joy in the generosity of the donor."

"It's not that big a deal," Diane said, sniffling, but she was pleased.

"The last one's a surprise," Keith said, handing over the cloth-wrapped bundle. "The Niall sent you something from the Old Country."

"Why did he not send it through me, then?" Tiron burst out, disappointed. "And me just lately departed from his domain?"

"You're illegal, remember?" Keith pointed out quickly. "No one is supposed to know you're here."

Tiron nodded, stroking his chin. "I'd forgotten. Ah, but forced anonymity is hard."

Holl pulled the ribbon off the cloth package, and it spilled open over Maura's lap, wave after wave of foamy lace escaping in folds down her knees to the floor. Laughing, the two of them knelt to gather it up. Holl threw a swag of it around his bride's shoulders, where it lay gleaming like joined snowflakes. She beamed and kissed him.

The others exclaimed over the fineness of the work. "How beautiful. Best I've ever seen. Probably very old, feel the texture and the quality. "

"That wasn't finished in a day, nor from any hard, iron machine," said Dierdre smugly.

"No, from a small bone shuttle," scolded one of the other oldsters. "This is the work of years and many hands."

"The card says, 'with best regards and a thousand blessings,'" Orchadia said. "Well, that's very fine of them."

That was the last of the presents. Rose, Calla, and the other ladies serving circulated with wooden cups, followed by their husbands with kegs of wine. They poured libations into larger goblets for their Big guests, who were touched by the special effort.

"The toast to the wedded couple," Dennet said, stilling Dunn's hand before he could drink. The newest student grinned, sharing a smile with Holl's father.

"Sorry. Guess I'm just a little too eager to wish them well."

The Master raised his hands for silence. "I haf vun more announcement before anyvun becomes too merry to comprehend," the Elf Master said. "In three days, please, I vould like from each of my senior students an essay of four pages on the subject of the psychological impact of the Industrial Refolution on those already liffing in the great population centers of Europe at the time. That is all."

Keith, Dunn, and Diane groaned. As the Big students scrambled for paper and pen to write down the assignments, Teri Knox and Lee Eisley exchanged relieved glances.

"Master, I miss you, but I sure am glad I don't have to do the homework any more!" Lee said fervently. He raised his cup in salute to the little professor, who regarded him with austere complacence over the rims of his glasses.

Holding Maura firmly by the hand, Holl turned to Keith with his glass high.

"As the one who's most responsible for helping to facilitate the day's events, Keith Doyle, will you make the first toast?" Holl asked.

Keith flushed. "It'd be an honor." Thinking hard to come up with a toast that wouldn't be too long or too maudlin, he cleared his throat. The room stilled, and all his friends looked at him. He smiled.

"To my friends, Holl and Maura, I wish every happiness," Keith said, raising up his wooden cup. "Today is the first day of the rest of your lives. Make the best of it."

"That's lovely," Diane whispered, squeezing his ribs.

"Very profound," said Pat Morgan, dryly, eyebrows raised over the brim of his glass. "You ought to write greeting cards, Doyle."

"I like it," Holl said, decidedly, touching his wine cup to his bride's. "To today, and everyday hereafter."

Chapter Two

A year and a day later, Keith went calling on Holl.

From the basket of his conveyance, he leaned out and addressed the crowd gathered on the pavement around in the middle of the Midwestern University experimental farm. The handful of students, variously dressed in lab coats or filthy jeans, watched him with interest and thinly-disguised amusement. The ground crew, two men in blue jeans, jackets, goggles, and gloves, walked the balloon at shoulder height, as if carrying a sedan chair, to the designated launch point.

"To the Scarecrow, by virtue of his enormous brain," Keith said, gesturing grandly, "to the Tin Woodsman, by virtue of his Heart…" The rattan basket tipped slightly as he leaned over the side, and he stepped back in alarm.

"What are you doing?" demanded the other man in the balloon basket, turning away from the gas jet he was adjusting. Frank Winslow's vintage WWI flyer's helmet was jammed down over his head, pushing out the goggles standing on his forehead that made him look like he had four round and glassy blue eyes instead of two. "Are you weird, or something?"

"Nope," Keith replied cheerfully, turning away from his audience. "Just always wanted to do that." Deprived of their entertainment, many of them left. A few continued to gawk at the balloon. "Anything I can help with?"

"Nope. Just sit tight and stay out of the way. Let 'er go!" The lanky pilot waved to his crew, and they loosed the balloon and stepped back.

The Skyship Iris was an ovoid rainbow as it rose over the buildings of Midwestern University. Keith clung fast to the edge of the waist-high basket until he discovered that the motion was far less than he had expected, milder even than the college library's geriatric elevator. He felt almost as if the ground dropped away and to the side from underneath them, leaving him hovering in place. The remaining spectators dwindled in size until they resembled grains of rice in the midst of a vast plate of salad.

A ringing sound went off just behind Keith's back as the balloon gained altitude. There was a loud click, followed by the sound of Frank's recorded voice. "Hi. This is Skyship Iris. I'm tied up right now, so could you leave a message at the sound of the tone, and I'll get back to you as soon as I can. Bye." BWEEP!

"Good takeoff, Frank," said the voice of Randall Murphy, one of Winslow's ground crew. "See you at the other end." CLICK!

"You got a phone in this?" Keith asked, wide-eyed as the pilot, now with hands free, ran the tape back to the beginning.

"Sure," Frank said, leaning back against the frame that supported the twin burners. He looked like a skinny stevedore, a full head taller than Keith, and his grin popped out the corners of his narrow jaw. "Gotta keep in touch. Can't just land a balloon next to a phone booth. You figure you have to be self-sufficient in piloting one of these babies. There's a lot of zen involved." He grinned again, showing broad white teeth. "Modern technology don't hurt, either. I figured out a new valve that makes my tanks last for six hours apiece. Walkie-talkie batteries don't hold a charge that long. Cell phone's easier."

"Great!" Keith exclaimed.

Frank had also brought along a sophisticated-looking but lightweight cooler. "For champagne," he explained. "Traditional." Slung by a loop at the basket's lip was a crank-powered AM/FM radio.

In spite of its high-tech accoutrements, the balloon basket resembled a relic of a past century. It was made of woven rattan with a padded bumper and curved base of leather, a fragile-seeming craft in comparison with the metal-and-plastic jets and small aircraft Keith was used to seeing.

As expected, the air was colder the higher they went. Keith shrugged into his thin jacket, zipping it hastily up to his chin, and wrapped his arms around his ribs. The pilot grinned at him and fastened down the flaps of his aerialist's helmet.

"Need a blanket? There's one under the cooler."

"N—no, thanks," Keith said. In a few moments, he was acclimated, and his muscles relaxed. He nodded to Frank.

"Fine and dandy," Frank said. "Enjoy the ride!" The pilot perched on the basket's edge with his long legs up on the other side, and shifted his close-fitting helmet rearwards to reveal his forehead. "Ahhh."

Keith, less daring, stayed by the metal frame and gazed at the scenery. It was still a long way down. Frank was completely at home in the air. Nothing seemed to phaze him, not even floating around in a craft as fragile as an eggshell. In just a short time, Keith himself had relaxed, and was enjoying the sensation of effortless floating. He leaned back and looked around.

The day was fine and clear. For some this might have been a mere pleasure trip. For Keith, it was business. Emptying his mind of fear, excitement, and any extraneous thoughts that might interfere with his concentration, Keith closed his eyes. Somewhere out there, he was certain, were air sprites, Little People of the air. He tried to visualize what he thought would be out there in the sky. Did they look like dragons? Pixies? Airplanes? In such a formless environment, would they be able to take any shape they chose? He let his mind drift to catch the trail of any elusive magical creature that might happen by within range.

Notwithstanding the occasional strong-smelling fume from feed lots they passed over, the air tasted cleaner up there than it did nearer the ground. Keith reasoned that if he were a creature of the air, he wouldn't hang out so close to the ground, not with the whole sky to range. Holl and the Elf Master had scoffed at his theory, but they'd never checked, had they? The only one of the Little Folk to attain any altitude had been Holl, on his flights with Keith to and from Europe, but he'd been too preoccupied to sense anything outside his own concerns. Tiron, as a stowaway on that same flight, had been bent double in a suitcase, and would have remembered nothing but the difficulties he'd had in breathing and finding some measure of comfort among Keith's dirty clothes and souvenirs of Scotland and Ireland.

Still, even if there had been any air sprites around when the two of them had been traveling, they'd have fled screaming from the jet, which Keith felt was too noisy to get close to the sensitive creatures he pictured. He wanted not only to sense the air sprites, but to see them. To do that, he needed to achieve altitude, but in a quiet, non-disruptive fashion. Barring finding wings of his own somewhere, there had to be some conveyance that approximated skyhooks. Gliders were unpowered, and therefore silent, but uncontrollable and too dangerous for an amateur. Helicopters set up too much of a racket. None of the craft with which he was familiar simply allowed him to hang in the air and listen.

When Frank Winslow, a competition balloonist, came to speak at Midwestern, Keith felt a lightbulb go on over his head. The balloon was the perfect vehicle to test out his theories. It was almost completely silent, flew slowly and smoothly, hovering in the very wind currents sprites might live in. Keith was in a fever for the rest of the lecture, wondering how he would convince Winslow to go along with him. After the pilot's talk, Keith took him to a quiet corner of the Student Common Room and laid out his plan.

Upon hearing Keith's theories of mythological beings, Winslow made it clear he thought Keith was nuts, but decided he liked his company and wouldn't mind indulging him to test out his ideas. Frank was perfecting the Skyship Iris for a round-the-world race. It cost nothing extra to have an extra body in the basket while he ran distances he would have covered anyway: he'd probably have a passenger along during his long-distance runs. All he asked for was a portion of his propane costs, like sharing gas money. Keith thought that was more than fair. The flat plains of Illinois were as good a place as any to practice sea-level skimming techniques, pretending the land was the sea.

As Keith opened up his senses, he felt disappointed. Both outer and inner sight told him that the sky was empty. The odd bird intruded its neutral presence on his mental radar. He ignored it, feeling further out.

Something flared suddenly into his consciousness. Off in the distance to the north, he sensed tantalizing hints of a *presence*, a strong one. Tamping down his delight, he concentrated all his thought in following them, projecting as hard as he could thoughts that he was harmless and friendly.

The wave of his mental touch broke over the thing he sensed, and it scattered abruptly into countless alarmed fragments and vanished, losing power and definition as it dissipated, like the sparks from an exploding firecracker. It receded ever further into nonexistence as if it could feel his pursuit. In a moment, there was nothing on which he could put a mental finger. Dismayed, Keith was left wondering if he had just imagined the contact. He sighed, planting his elbow on the edge of the basket and his chin on his hand. Another time. He sent his thoughts around, seeking other magical realities.

There were no more in the air. Below and ahead, the concentrated presence of the Little Folk at Hollow Tree Farm was the strongest magical thing he knew. Anything else seemed unreal and insubstantial, as far as magical traces went. As he got more practice at inner sensing, all the natural things around him acquired a more genuine aura of reality than he had ever known before. A few things just felt more real than others.

"Do you think there's anything out there?" Keith asks Winslow.

"All the time," Frank said. "Not sentient magical beings—well, not *secular* ones, anyway. Got my own ideas about the sky, Gods and elementals and stuff like that. Almost holy." He turned a suspicious eye toward Keith. "You don't want to hear it."

"Sure I do," Keith said. "I'm looking for any kind of clues I can find."

"Well..." Winslow began to explain haltingly, in his usual laconic style. Soon, he warmed to his subject and began babbling like a brook, defensively hurling forth ideas as if he expected Keith to refute them, talking about gods and forces of nature and sentient spirits. Keith pulled a tattered spiral notebook out of his pocket and began to take notes. Frank's personal cosmology was as interesting as anything he'd read in mythology books. Keith guessed that he was the first person Winslow had ever opened up to about his ideas. There was something useful in being known as the weirdest person on the block: it made other people feel that maybe they weren't quite so off the wall when all they were was sensitive or creative.

The sky above them was blue and daubed here and there with cottony white clouds. In the distance, Keith saw birds doing aerial acrobatics, and wondered if Little Folk of the sky would sport like that. Below them, the flat, checkered, green expanse of Illinois farm-land stretched out to every horizon. Like a piece on a game board, the miniature shadow of the balloon skimmed from square to square. Winslow pulled the ring on the gas jet for more altitude. The crosscurrent swept them slightly more northeast than north.

"You sure you can find this farm?" Winslow shouted above the roar of the flame. "I mean, most times I put down where they've got landmarks."

"I can find it," Keith said, confidently, then felt a twinge of worry. What if his inner radar suddenly ceased to operate? Tensely, he closed his eyes for a second, then tuned in, throwing his sense outward toward Holl and his friends. There they were, just where they'd been a minute ago. Keith let his shoulders sag with relief.

"You feel sick, Keith?"

"Nope," Keith assured him, opening his eyes. "Just feeling the basket sway."

"Won't fall," Frank promised him. "Never has yet. Want a brew? Or some champagne? Traditional." The pilot popped open the cooler at his feet and took out a frosted can. Keith shook his head. "Won't be through again for a couple weeks. I'm on my way to Florida after today. There's a race over the Everglades."

"Sounds great!" Keith said. "I want to stay in touch with you, if you don't mind. I'd like to go up again when you get back."

"Oh, yeah, air sprites," Winslow said, with a grin. He jerked on the heat jet tether. The flames roared. "Well, any time I'm in the area, it's okay with me. You've got the number. Heading for South America in November, joining a rally over the Andes. Wind's too strong for ballooning around here after then."

Keith pointed out the roof of Hollow Tree Farm. Frank nodded, and started the Iris descending slowly.

Like a beacon, the presence of the Little Folk shone through strongly from one of the homesteads ahead. From above, Hollow Tree Farm looked exactly like all the other farms on the road. It was only Keith's inner sense that made him signal to Winslow to put down in the right meadow. Feeling a little tired by the effort, he turned off his second sight. Immediately, the auras around everything faded to a nearly invisible glow.

The Iris lowered gently onto the grass between the barn and a field of standing crops. She curtseyed as Keith's weight left the gently swaying gondola. Immediately Winslow started to feed heat to the envelope.

"See you in a couple of hours," Frank called, his voice diminishing as the balloon rose. "Truck'll come and pick you up here!"

Keith waved, and walked off the meadow into the cornfield. The rainbow globe vanished behind the canopy of green leaves.

Corn stood over six feet high in the field behind the house, concealing the individual cottages he knew were standing there. The Little Folk had come up with an excellent system of camouflage. During the growing season, the cottages were hidden by the tall stalks of grain, since each of the little houses stood no higher than the wooden playhouse Keith and his siblings had in their back yard while they were growing up. When the corn was cut, all you could see from the road was the woods behind the settlement.

Even in the wintertime the houses defied detection. Their outer walls were dark wood, carved into strandlike patterns and stained to blend in with the County Forest Preserve that stood behind them. Only someone with superior depth perception who knew what to look for could perceive the miniature village, and that only if they could see through the aversion charm the Little Folk had placed on each structure. Keith fairly admitted he couldn't do it. He relied instead on the white pebbled paths that led through the cornstalks from one doorstep to another until he could make out each home by its shadow.

Despite the protective coloration, each home was very different. Most of the eight that were fully built were occupied by members of Holl's age group, the Progressives, who had quickly shed the fears of the last four decades and taken off to live in the open air, away from the larger community in the farmhouse itself. As was their thrifty custom, the Folk had used scrap wood of every size as well as whole boards to build, binding the conglomeration with skill and magic. Glass windows, pieced together like stained glass, were backed by small, beautifully woven curtains that Keith guessed had been rags they'd unraveled and blended together again. Little details gave away clues to the identity of the occupants of each house. Marm, one of Holl's—and Keith's—best friends, had carved an ornamented trellis-work surrounded by the figures of animals on the wall that faced away from the road. This season, the trellis was covered by climbing green grapevines. Marm's wife, Ranna, was a celebrated wine-maker.

Without knowing Holl's personal taste, or Maura's skill with a garden, Keith would still have picked out the sixth cottage as theirs. Neat as hospital corners, the little borders around the edges of the tiny house glowed with beauty. Garnet tea roses, proportionately accurate for the Little Folk, grew closest to the house, bracketing the dark walls with spots of rich color. Autumn flowers were just coming into bloom. Hummocks of blue asters dotted the dark beds. Most particularly, on either side of the doorposts grew a handful of white bellflowers, a token and a tribute to Holl's difficult journey overseas to win his lady's hand. Keith grinned as he rapped on the roof's edge with his knuckles.

Inside, he heard hubbub, and Holl, his cheeks red, peered out the curtained window.

"It's you, then," Holl said, pulling the door open. "Miss here won't take her sleep. I've been walking her up and down for an hour. I think she knows there was company coming." Without shifting the bundle in his arms he rolled his shoulders to ease them. "Will you take her so I can stretch a bit?"

"Boy, she's grown, hasn't she?" Keith said, accepting his 'niece' in his two hands. The baby, still hairless and toothless, looked like any baby he'd ever seen, except that her eyes were already turning green to match her mother's, and no Big baby ever sprouted those ornately-whorled ears. The points were just a little softer than an adult's, the way a kitten's ears were rounder than a cat's. Asrai recognized Keith and cooed at him before her attention wandered off again after the next pretty shadow. He cradled her on one elbow and felt around in his pocket.

"Asrai?" he said softly. "Hey, baldy, I'm talking to you."

The baby's cloudy eyes wandered up to his face, and focused just for a second. With surprising speed, her tiny fist shot up, and grabbed. She pulled down, trying to get her captured handful into her mouth.

"Aaagh!" Keith breathed, trying not to yell. He put his hand up to get between the baby and his cheek. "Holl, help. She's got my whiskers." Keith's whiskers, a magical Christmas present from the Little Folk some three years before, were tangible but invisible to the average eye.

Holl sprang forward to undo Asrai's fist, and picked the invisible strands by touch one by one from between her fingers. "There, there. Well, there's no doubt now she's got the second sight, is there?"

"You sound pleased," Keith said, rubbing the sore place where his offended vibrissae were rooted. "Why didn't you tell me she'd grab?"

"My apologies. She's always taking handfuls of her mother's hair," Holl explained, a little embarrassed, "but yours was too short to catch. I didn't think of the whiskers. We don't know what she can see, if you follow. We're new at being parents. Any fresh discovery is as if it's the first time it's ever happened in the world. Is it all right?"

"No problem," Keith said. "I guess they can't be pulled out, can they?" He glanced down at the baby, who wasn't at all upset to have her new discovery taken away from her. He put his hand back into his pocket. "Hey, kid, you know I brought you something for yourself."

The baby's eyes fixed on his hand as he waved a blue rubber ring at her. "Look. Teething toy."

"It's a little soon for that, Keith Doyle," Holl protested.

"Nope, my mom said teething always starts before you expect it." Keith fitted the tiny fingers around the ring. They barely closed on the other side. Asrai was so small she looked more like a baby doll than a baby. "Hmm. That was the smallest one I could find."

"She'll grow," Holl said, gruff with pride. The child immediately drew the vanilla-scented ring to her face and put her mouth to the edge. Her little pink tongue explored the bumps on the blue rubber surface, and she looked surprised.

Holl watched her adoringly. Keith glanced up. In contrast to the flowerpetal complexion of his daughter, Holl's face seemed for the first time to be creased and tired. Keith was concerned for his friend, but he made light of it.

"Fatherhood's made an older man of you, Holl."

"And it has," Holl said with a sigh. "For no reason at all the babe wakes in the night and cries. She isn't hungry, and she isn't wet, but she cries. It's amazing to me how loud she can get. I'm glad it's only Marm next door to us. He never minds a thing when he sleeps, and Ranna can ignore everything, but the wailing keeps *us* wide awake."

"Trouble," Keith said, shaking his head. His eyes danced with mischief. "What do your folk say when they're fed up with their kids? 'I wish the humans would come and take you away?'"

Holl favored him with a sour expression. "Very funny, Keith Doyle. May I offer you a snack? You've come a long way."

Keith looked around the interior of the cottage. The floor, covered with smooth tiles of wood, was well swept. There wasn't much in the way of furniture, except for a pair of chairs, a large table and a small one, and bookshelves built cunningly into the walls. Holl caught the sense of his gaze.

"Oh, the food's in the larder under a hatch in the floor. It's not too big, just enough for a pat of butter and a drop of milk, or what have you," Holl said, rising heavily to his feet. "There might be a heel of bread as well."

With concern, Keith watched him go. Holl looked genuinely tired. Keith's mother had said that the first six months after a birth were the hardest. At least Holl and Maura were in the back stretch, now that Asrai had hit the three-month mark. He couldn't believe that this tiny baby who just barely overlapped his hands could yell so loudly.

"Less insulation to hold down the sound, huh, punkin?" he asked her. The baby, wisely asleep with the ring clutched to her cheek, said nothing.

Keith knew better than to trust Holl's assertion that there was no more food on hand than drops and heels. The Little Folk might eat less in proportion, but they liked plenty of good things to eat as much as their Big cousins. Holl returned with a handsomely carved wooden tray bearing a tall pitcher whose foaming, white contents slopped gently from side to side, and a basket of rolls with a good chunk of primrose-yellow butter on a small dish in the center.

"Keva's doing," Holl explained, at Keith's question. "They all knew you were coming for a visit, and she insisted on leaving these to break our fast."

Keith's own particular mug, a long-ago present from the Little Folk, was here on a framed shelf beside those belonging to Holl and Maura. He accepted milk and a handful of rolls. "What, no beer?" he asked, impishly.

"Not when I'm on nursery duty, if you please," Holl said, grimacing. "Whew! It was a long night last night down here. A good thing we're out as we are in the middle of the sky. Under the library, she'd have shouted the stacks down. They'd have thought there was a banshee trapped in the steam tunnels! Maura and I share duties. It's my shift with the babe. She's inside the big house helping prepare the lunch before class."

"She's not having to cut short her education because of the baby, is she?" Keith asked.

"Oh, no, don't you fear it," Holl said easily. "You don't know the benefits of communal living. When there's not an adult with time to help us care for the little one, Dola or some of the other medium sized children help out in between. She'll be here soon, and glad to see you, I won't doubt."

Keith smiled. Dola was Tay's daughter, a sweet, blond child who had a strangling crush on him. She'd accepted Diane's preeminence with Keith only under protest, and had often expressed herself willing to step in as a substitute should Diane be unable to continue as Keith's girlfriend. Dola had a special talent of forming illusions on a length of thin cloth. Keith decided that as a babysitter, that wasn't a half bad knack to have.

"So this is a different thing for you," Holl said, pouring a mugful for himself. "You're not in a class, but you're still earning a grade?"

"It's called an internship," Keith explained. "I'm working in the Chicago office of Perkins Delaney Queen, the advertising agency. They're shuffling me and three other students around the departments until I find the one that will take me for the rest of the semester. I was interested in the business office at first, and then there was research, but I'm having more fun in the design department. If they like me, they'll let me stay on for the spring term, and maybe there'll be a job opening after graduation."

"I am sure you are well liked," Holl said, the corner of his mouth going up in a wry smile. "You have a way of worming yourself into good regard."

"I hope I can make it." Keith sighed. "But it's a tough business. I miss college. I called Pat to see how it's going, and he said it's been a lot quieter without me." He pulled a face, and Holl laughed.

"You don't live on the premises?"

"Heck, no," Keith said, shaking his head. "It's an office building."

"Don't act as if I ought to know that," Holl admonished him. "We lived in an office building."

Keith shrugged. "Well, usually people don't," he said. "I'm back in my old room at home. I miss living with Pat Morgan. We got along really well, all things considered. My brother Jeff resents like hell having me back. He had our whole room to himself for three years, and now he's got to deal with having me crowding him for an entire year, if not for good. Jeff's done everything but draw a line down the middle of the room to mark his territory. I'm glad we don't have a sink in the corner, like we did in the dorm. I'd end up with half the basin and one tap. If the soap's on the wrong side, forget it. Laser beam time." Keith's finger drilled an imaginary hole into his chest. Holl tilted his head to one side.

"Not literally, I hope. It sounds as if it's nearly time for you to have a nest of your own, Keith Doyle," Holl said, nodding. "If you chose, you know you'd always be welcome here, permanently, or whenever you dropped in from above." Holl pointed toward the ceiling.

Keith smiled, genuinely pleased and touched. "That'd be great, but it depends on what I'll be doing after graduation. It's a real temptation. You've sure done a lot with the property. It's shaped up incredibly since last summer. I may take you up on your offer so I can live in a country manor with all the amenities instead of a dinky apartment."

Holl scowled. "Your 'dinky' accomodations might have more to offer you. It is not easy being homeowners. Everything constantly needs repairs. The water continues bad. We allowed a sample to concentrate of the stinking mess we were filtering out, and matched it to the seepage from Gilbreth Feed and Fertilizer Company."

"What, that place across town?" Keith asked. "How's their run-off getting over here?"

"We've written to ask how it's possible that we're getting pollutants from their factory," Holl said. "But there's no doubt it's theirs. Tay and Olanda went over there one night to compare."

"They're dumping," Keith said, frowning darkly. "I wish I could be here to help handle it. Complain. If they don't respond to you, you can write private letters threatening them with the Environmental Protection Agency."

"Oh, we're sending appropriate letters to the editor, and having a fine extended argument with the owner of the company on the side. But let us put the gloomy matters away. The Master would like to see you, if you please."

Keith felt a momentary surge of guilt at the thought of being called before the formidable little teacher. He was up to date on his mail-in essays; what could the Master want him for? "He would?"

Holl must have guessed his thoughts, because he laughed heartily. "A visit, you impossible infant! You're not behind in any assignments from him, unless it's to show your face and be welcomed more often than you are. As soon as Dola comes to look after the babe, we'll go up to the barn."

A shy tapping at the door heralded Dola's arrival. The elf child, now twelve, was on the threshold of young womanhood. Slim and blond, with her elegant ears poking out from the shining tresses of her hair, she would have made a good model for the flower fairies in the books Keith's mother had read to him as a child. In the hot weather, she wore only a knee-length green shift that softly outlined her body. Keith surreptitiously took note of the subtle changes in her figure, but she noticed. Comfortable though she was with Holl, Dola was self-conscious around him.

"How do I look, then?" she demanded boldly, then blushed at her own forwardness.

"All you need is lacy wings," Keith said, gravely. The compliment pleased Dola. She beamed, the long dimples in her cheeks throwing her high cheekbones and pointed chin into relief. Keith reached out and tweaked a lock of her hair. Dodging away coyly, she pirouetted lightly on her toes, coming to rest before Holl, who gently placed the baby in her arms.

"Dola's been the most zealous caretaker we could ask," Holl said, over the girl's head. "She practically attended Maura at the birth. She'll only share responsibilities with Ludmilla, my babe's unofficial grandmother, and that not often." Dola's chin stuck out defiantly to show that even that sharing was unwilling. She clasped the baby close to her. Asrai, half asleep, roused enough to coo at her babysitter. Dola bent to kiss her on the forehead.

"Well," Keith said, watching with delight, "even the best babysitters need a day off. They deserve a little spoiling of their own."

"I wouldn't mind *that* now and again," Dola agreed. She kicked off her socklike shoes and sat down in Holl's chair.

"I'll see what we can arrange," Keith promised. "Some weekend, okay?"

"Oh, yes! Okay!" Dola said, much gratified.

"We'll be at the barn, if there's any need for us," Holl said.

"There'll be no need," Dola assured him. She began rocking. On her lap, the child's eyes drifted closed, and her breathing slowed. Keith waved at them through the window, and followed Holl down the pebbled path toward the outbuildings.

Chapter Three

"So what do you do in the meantime?" Holl asked over his shoulder, as he stumped down the narrow, sloping path toward the dull-red, painted barn. "I can't imagine you with only one activity to siphon off all your energies."

"Oh, pursuing my old interests," Keith said casually. "Remember my theory? Air sprites?"

Holl sighed. "And how could I not?"

"The guy who flew me here is training for an around-the-world balloon marathon. He said he'd take me up whenever he's around," Keith said, ignoring his friend's humorous expression. "If there's anyone to be found in the upper atmosphere, I'll find them."

"If anyone will," Holl agreed, "you will."

From the outside, it looked like any barn Keith might have passed on the county highways. Inside, it had been transformed into a combination school, workshop, and living quarters. Little Folk hurried around like so many of Santa's elves, carrying from here to there wooden handcrafts in varying stages of completion.

The old barn had been converted nearly as much as the house had. Between the rafters its high ceiling was lined with the same fuzzy rows of light that had illuminated the Little Folks' home beneath Gillington Library. The tiniest children dashed in and out of the old stalls, where their elders worked, each on his or her own particular task. The building still smelled pleasantly of hay, though its concrete floor was swept clean. Added to that scent was the spicy blended aroma of fresh sawdust, oil, and paint. Under a window with its shutters thrown fully back to let in the morning's light, Enoch threw them a salute with his wood plane, then went back to smoothing the board he had propped on two saw horses. Keith thought it looked like he was building a new door. When Enoch upended his work on the sawhorses, Keith noticed that the door was constructed, as usual for the Little Folks' woodcrafts, of assorted scrap culled from other projects. They wasted nothing, lending the dignity of utility to even the most hopeless leftovers, even bits of rubber or cloth scrap. Some of the wooden jewelry he'd been selling to the boutiques on behalf of Hollow Tree Industries featured beads laminated with ancient bits of calico and gingham. They had a neat antique-y look that went well with the natural luster of wood. Ms. Voordman, their most faithful customer, had been pleased by the hit the necklaces had made.

It was the proudest accomplishment of his life that he had been able to be of service to the Little Folk in helping them to get on their feet. He wasn't vain enough to think that he'd been responsible for their success, but if he hadn't come along and helped to find them a home, they might have been discovered. It frightened him to think of his friends swept helplessly away to one of those secret government facilities that the tabloids liked to crow about, for potentially-fatal testing or whatever it was they did there. Or that they might have ended up homeless after the library's destruction. A chilling picture crept into his mind of the Folk scattered along the roadway, terrified and starving, ducking into the nearly bare fields during the cold Illinois winters whenever cars passed to escape notice. The dream passed, and Keith laughed, only a little uncomfortably. The day was a warm September afternoon, and this house and barn, though it was in his name, belonged most definitely to them.

He was willing only to take credit for facilitating matters. Kudos for their overwhelming success belonged strictly to them. Their skills had been passed down for centuries and honed with love, and they learned quickly what else they needed to know.

He was warmed by the fact of their existence and their regard for him. He treasured their friendship. It gave him great satisfaction to glance into their lives, as much as they'd let him. It pleased him down to his bones that they existed at all. Sometimes he felt like he was protecting an endangered species.

As Holl and Keith approached, a handful of children sprang off their benches, and ran toward them, shouting. They had interrupted the junior alphabet class. The Master in shirtsleeves, standing before a chalkboard on an easel, peered over his glasses disapprovingly until his gaze came to rest on Keith. He nodded austerely. Keith shot him an apologetic smile and a 'what can I do?' expression.

"You came from the sky," Borget cried. He was nine, a pudgy-cheeked imp with bronze curls. "Didn't you? You flew in the rainbow balloon! We saw you."

"I sure did," Keith said, crouching down to Borget's level, where he was surrounded by the crowd of children. The boy immediately turned on his smaller companions.

"I told you he came from the sky," he said, with an air of one-upmanship. "I told you!"

"Can we try it?" Moira asked. She had striking dark blue eyes in that contrasted richly with her magnolia-blossom skin. "Mother might say yes since it's you."

Keith thought of Moira's mother, an arch-ultra-Conservative, and privately doubted the girl's optimism. "I'll ask," he promised.

"Will you take us to the amusement park?" Anet begged. She had flaming carrot-colored hair and brilliant green eyes. "I read an article about the great wooden roller coaster. I would love to ride it! The writer said the slope was a hundred and sixty feet at a 55° incline!"

"Uh," Keith said, picturing a park full of Little People. He thought quickly. "Well, you know, coasters like that have a sign that say you can't ride if you're under this tall," he swung an arm out to one side at about the level of his chest. "See? Even Holl couldn't get on. The safety harnesses wouldn't hold him because they're made for really big people, and they're made of steel. You could get hurt."

"Aw," Anet said, sadly. "Is there nothing in the rest of the world made for children our size?"

"Not a lot," Keith admitted. "But you have a lot of advantages Big kids don't. None of them have magic lanterns and toys that run by themselves without batteries."

Since those were things the Little children saw every day, it was small consolation. With difficulty, he extracted himself and went to meet his former teacher.

"You are doing vell enough on your assignments," the Master acknowledged, when Keith asked about the subject troubling him, "though you might be spending more thought on them."

"I've been busy," Keith said, shamefacedly. Neither time nor distance had dimmed the small, redhaired professor's ability to make Keith feel like a little child called on the carpet. Whenever he was fixed by a bright blue eye behind the gold frame of the Master's spectacles, he felt like digging his toe through the floor with his tongue caught in the corner of his mouth while he thought up an excuse why his homework wasn't done. "I'll do better on the next one. But what are you doing here? It's Tuesday. Aren't you teaching?"

"I do no longer go in every day to the classroom," the Master said, laying down his pointer. "It is too much of an imposition on my kind volunteers. I vould rather they make only one trip to come here to me, vhere there is less difficulty and," an ironic glint flashed in the glass lenses, "less chance of a charge of illicit entry. Gradually but vith many regrets, ve leaf Gillington Library behind for gut. It is a wrench to many of us, but much safer."

"You stand less a chance of being detected if you don't keep going in and out," Keith said, nodding.

"It is true. Ve are already imposing enough upon our good friends that they must supply the book needs of such a large group as we," the Master said, smiling slightly. "Diane's good friend Dunn has shown much talent for extracting efen restricted volumes for our perusal."

"Well, he works in the library," Keith pointed out.

"He maintains a legitimate entree for us," the Master said. "And though, like you, he professes to owe us a debt of gratitude for his instruction, the debt is many times repaid by his services as our," the sapphire eyes glinted again, "bookvagon." Keith susupected that the term was Dunn's.

The Master stopped, as if a thought had come to him, and rummaged in his pocket. "One of the benefits of staying in vun place and hafing vun's own mailing address is to be able to maintain personal correspondence vith professional colleagues. I haf had a letter from Professor Parker," he said, extending a much-creased envelope to Keith.

"Hey, great!" Keith said, running an eye down the page. The archaeologist was traveling in the United States with exhibits from his dig in the Hebrides. He invited the Master, in his guise as the noted researcher, Dr. Friedrich Alfheim, to come and visit the display when it came to the Field Museum in Chicago. "Well, you ought to go. Are you interested? I'll come and get you. He'd really enjoy seeing you."

"And I him," the Master said. "He has a fine mind." From the Master, that was the height of compliment. Keith retained considerable respect for Professor Parker. It took brains and imagination to see a thriving civilization in burned-off stumps and buried heaps of animal bones. "If it is possible to go, I vould be grateful for the opportunity."

"Consider it done!" Keith said, cheerfully. He sketched a bow to the Master. Holl, rolling his eyes skyward, nudged him in the kidneys with an elbow.

"Come, then," he said. "We can't interrupt the class forever, for all the children would like it, and there're others waiting to see you." Marcy Collier was among them. Keith greeted her as she came over from the sawyer's table, where Enoch was working over a mitre box with a hand saw.

"So how's the romance going?" Keith asked, playfully.

"All right," Marcy said, sighing. "I tried to talk to my mother about Enoch. You know what she said? 'Tell me again, Marcy. I want to hear it from your own lips. Your fiance is an *elf*, and he makes *toys*. Have you told your father yet?'"

Keith laughed, but immediately composed his face to rueful. "Gee, I'm sorry."

Marcy gave him a tiny smile. "Yeah, it's funny. I just don't know how I'll get past that."

"Not to mention your fiance's family connection with the supernatural," Keith said, glancing quickly over his shoulder to make sure none of the Folk were listening to him. To them, all the wonders that they worked were strictly natural. "I know! We'll fix you up with a big biker guy who spits on furniture. Tattoos that say 'I love torture' and 'Blow up the world, starting with...what suburb do you live in?'" Keith drew an imaginary picture on the air.

"You should be in advertising, Keith," Marcy said, shaking her head.

"I'm working on it," Keith said cheerfully.

"And there you are, Keith Doyle!" Tiron called to him from the corner. The Irish elf came over to drag him back to the corner. "Behold," he said, gesturing at the loom, his pride and joy. "And now do you think it was worth the time and trouble to bring me to America." He handed Keith a length of cloth. The fabric was like the beautiful Scottish tweeds he had seen overseas, but this had a life and a magic which reflected the nature of its weavers.

"It's fantastic," he said. Holl, hanging back out of Tiron's way, nodded his approval, too.

"Keith Doyle, there you are!" Catra called, waving a handful of papers at him from a purpose-built carrel against the shadiest wall. "Come and see!"

"I'm in demand today," Keith said.

As nearly as possible, the Archivist had recreated her favorite perch from Gillington Library. From somewhere, the Little Folk had come up with shining walnut rails that surrounded a neat little area filled with polished wood bookshelves and drawers. The only untidiness in the office was the top of Catra's desk. It was scattered with daily newspapers, letters, scraps of paper, books, and scrapbooks. One vast specimen nearly the height of the elf woman was open across the top of it all. They had caught her in the act of pasting a clipping onto one of the pages.

"Here, read it, do," she said, offering Keith a letter she snatched half-hidden from underneath the big book's spine. "Here's the latest sally we've composed to do public battle against the polluters."

Grinning, Keith took the letter. "So you're really writing letters to the editor. How's it going?"

Catra's eyes gleamed. "We're doing well enough, to be sure. We have joined the lobbyists for cleaner environment. Now that we're part of a community, however covertly, we want to aid in improving it."

Keith knew about some of their good works. Over the last year, they had been using their talents to fix things around town, repairing pipes and ductwork so leakage lessened, just like they had in the library.

On half of the table, her sister Candlepat was paying the farm's bills. Using her talent, she was lifting Keith's signature from a sheet filled with examples that he had provided for them up onto a blank check. That way he didn't have to be present every time the Little Folk needed to endorse a check. There were also two examples of "For Deposit Only, Hollow Tree Industries, account 2X-3B-3485" in his script.

"Nice," Keith complimented her. "Couldn't tell the difference myself. You're not thinking of taking up a life of crime, I hope?"

The blond girl pursed her lips playfully. "Catra wanted to use these to sign the letters to the editor as well," she explained, "but Holl said he'd rather not have you have to explain words you hadn't written. I write the text out myself. Tell me why, Keith Doyle, that the letters on a keyboard do not go in the order of the alphabet?"

"I'm not sure," Keith said. "I bet Catra can find out faster than I can."

"Oh, she! She's all taken up in this environment issue," the girl pouted. "She's nearly no time for anything else."

"Okay. I'll look it up for you myself," Keith said, placatingly. "What's the latest?"

"I'm sure it's around," Catra said, when consulted. "It was read aloud with great glee at breakfast time."

They tracked down the text of the letter to Marm, who had spread out blueprints and tools over it, spotting the stationery by a characteristic corner. Holl yanked it free.

"There you are." The letter suggested that Gilbreth had no real regard for future generations, since it wouldn't take care to evolve a waste-disposal program that could solve today's problems today.

"Wow," Keith said. "Inflammatory. That ought to curl someone's hair."

"We're not doing it for tonsorial reasons, Keith Doyle. There's a higher purpose to it as well. If the land is to remain habitable for long, all this must be brought out into the open and resolved as to what is to be done with waste, and whether the process justifies the end product. At present, I do not think you trust your leaders, nor do I think you can. We all read newspapers. The special interests whose matters are taken before yours remind me of Orwell's Animal Farm, in which some animals are more equal than others."

"Quiet," Keith said, "or the Master will hear you. You don't think becoming a father makes you exempt from those surprise essays."

"Would that it did, at least for a time," Holl sighed. "The little one spat up across my geology text two nights back. I cannot think what the university bookstore will assume has happened when we return it quietly to their stock."

Keith laughed. "Ever been in a frat house? Considering what else happens to those books, baby drool won't stand out much. This mudslinging in print will stand out a lot more."

Holl nodded. "That's good to know. We're grateful for the loans, authorized or not, and try to be good stewards for that which we borrow. It's different, doing all this at long distance. We're relying heavily upon the good will of the Master's Big students. So far, they've been most helpful."

"I'm sorry I'm not here to help," says Keith. "You sure you don't miss me?"

"Haven't we had enough excitement in the last year?" Holl asked. Keith raised his hands in helpless agreement.

"Can Hollow Tree Industries manage without me?"

"What do you think? Our work gets done. Deliveries go out. Our income matches well with our expenses. Our goods continue popular. I've a new line of jewelry that your Ms. Voordman wants to see offered to the department stores. We're surviving. Why do you ask?" Holl inquired.

"Well," Keith said, lamely, "I like to feel needed."

"Then feel needed, you widdy, but go ahead and have your job. I'm sure it'll be more interesting than hanging about watching me change diapers."

"Oh, no," Keith said. "That'd be very interesting. In fact, I ought to make a complete photo record. That way, you'll remember this time of her life long after she's grown up and has boyfriends."

Holl gaped at him openmouthed, knocked speechless. Keith was delighted.

"Quoth the Maven, nevermore," Keith said, with glee.

"Will you let me worry about one year at a time without raising the spectre of times to come?" Holl demanded, when he had recovered his voice. "Isn't it enough…"

Holl's reply was cut off by staccato tooting. The Little Folk looked around curiously for its source. Keith stood up hastily.

"Thanks for the hospitality, Holl. I've got to go. That's my ride!"

Chapter Four

The next morning, Mona Gilbreth opened to the editorial page of the Central Illinois Farmer with a mixture of dread and disgust. The ongoing battle between environmental interests and business— her business—had become an embarrassment. She hadn't even known there *were* environmentalists in Sullivan before the paper-borne tirade had begun, about a year back. It had started with a letter about dumping of industrial waste in the local watershed, and gone on from there to veiled and then not so veiled suggestions of guilt. Customers were asking pointed questions about whether the allegations against Gilbreth concerning dumping and toxic waste were true. This wasn't national politics, where the querists were reporters she'd never see again who could be put off with a press release from one of her assistants. She was forced to make expensive changes in her business practices, though she could hardly spare it from her campaign. She had won the nomination for Representative, but it would take careful management and a lot of fundraising to see her all the way through the November election. There was a chronic shortage of donations for the smaller candidacies. None of the big sponsors seemed to be interested in getting behind a single Democrat from Central Illinois. Mona Gilbreth yearned for the day when her political dreams would be realized, she would be elected to her House seat in Washington, and she could shake off the stinking dust of her father's business and her home town. After she left, she could disavow any knowledge of how the business was being run.

At first she wondered if her political opponent was behind the mudslinging. Nastier people were beginning to call them Kill-breath Feed. It was hard to get a stereotype out of people's mind once it was set. Small towns had long memories, she thought, remembering her grammar school nickname of 'Treetop.' Once a year, someone from her year at Sullivan High School was sure to bring that up again. It wasn't her fault she grew taller than anyone else in fifth grade, finishing up at a quarter inch short of six feet before her thirteenth birthday. It was enough to make any sane person take to the top of a church steeple with an M-16.

"Has anyone in the plant been talking to anyone from Hollow Tree Farm?" Mona asked her manager, Jake Williamson.

"You know us," Williamson assured her, leaning back with his thumbs in his hip pockets. The khaki overalls that was the company uniform looked like a prison guard's on his bulky, well-muscled body. Mona was comfortable with him because he was one of the few people at the plant who was taller than she was. "We don't talk to strangers."

"Then how are they so sure the stuff's coming from here?" Mona wondered, folding over the page and creasing it with her fingernail.

"It is, isn't it?" Williamson asked, showing his teeth in amusement.

She ignored him. "These results couldn't have come from an EPA analysis, because we'd have been notified, and that would mean reporters all over the place. Are they following our trucks?"

"Couldn't be. Some of them county routes are as flat as an ironing board. We'd have seen anybody. What's wrong? This H. Doyle write another letter full of insults to the editor?"

Without looking up, Mona nodded. She crumpled the edge with her fingertips, began to tear scraps of paper loose and scoot them around the desktop. She hated keeping up the discussion in public. Always protesting that Gilbreth was innocent of any wrongdoing, that the management was interested and involved in environmental issues. All the petitions were signed and the national convention was over, but she still needed the grassroots support to keep her campaign alive. She just wanted to win the election so she could go to Washington and stop worrying about her constituents. It would have been easier if there were two of her, one to pound the campaign trail and tell lies to voters, and the other to stay here and crack nitrogen.

The election was timely, so that was where she turned her attention. In the meantime, the business was running badly without her continuous intervention. She wished again her father hadn't died. His timing was so inconvenient. The last thing she needed was to be involved with a business whose waste products pushed so many buttons among her constituency. There were loud supporters on both sides of the issue, pro-farm and pro-environment, and sometimes they were the same people, but silence was better than noisy debate any time.

She ran her finger down the page to the end of the letter. There was the signature Mona had been dreading: H. Doyle. The gist of the letter above it was typical and predictable. Unnatural growths of algae had been observed in artesian ponds and marshwater, suggesting that phosphates and other organics had been dumped in the sensitive headwaters, giving rise to explosive and unwanted growth. H. Doyle was angry about the pollution of the groundwater, suggesting that if organic pollutants were disposed of with so much secrecy, might not PCBs and dioxins have been dumped as well? Didn't the name Times Beach render any reaction?

Mona ground her teeth. It did. It was true, Gilbreth Feed and Fertilizer had dumped a lot of its waste on abandoned property. Money was the problem. If for no other reason than to keep her nose clean for the inspection of her political foes, she would cheerfully have paid for proper dumping sites and disposal. As it was, the Gilbreth Company couldn't afford it and still take care of payroll, advertising, and all the other expenses it took to run a company. H. Doyle of Hollow Tree was exacerbating her troubles by humiliating her in public. Mona could feel her temper rising, getting her dander up, as her old grandmother used to say.

"We've got a load of stuff, and the bills aren't paid yet," Williamson said, almost as if he could read her mind. "Got to get rid of it. There's no more room in the tanks, and Browning-Ferris won't make a pickup until we pay."

"Empty the tanks into our trucks. There's a dumping site I want you to use," Ms. Gilbreth said, without looking up from the Op-ed page.

Dola appeared at the door of Holl and Maura's cottage. "*There now,*" she said, disapprovingly, drowning out the unhappy cries. Holl turned toward her, his face full of undisguised relief, his arms full of wet, bare-bottomed baby. "You can hear her nearly all the way to the barn!"

"Bless you, lass, can you do something with her? She's soaked through, I've got a full day of tasks to finish, and I can't put her down!"

The girl's hands were on her hips, and the expression on her face was an echo of her great-grandmother Keva's. "She's all to pieces, and you're no help, are you?" she asked. She took the wailing baby in her arms, and whispered a little song to her. Asrai, recognizing Dola's voice, stopped crying and gurgled. Holl, amused, stood back from the powder-strewn changing table, and let the girl take charge.

"Well, you know me, don't you?" Dola asked, her tone softening as she laid the child down. With deft hands, she cleaned up the spilled powder, swabbed Asrai clean with a moist cloth from the bowl on the table's edge, and dried her. She straightened out a fresh diaper, the loose edges smoothing into a snug fit around Asrai's waist as if it had always been thus. "It's easy to see you need me," Dola said, picking Asrai up against her shoulder and regarding Holl fiercely over the infant's head as she wrestled Asrai into a loose, lightweight smock of fading red-flowered cloth.

"We rely upon you absolutely," Holl told her gravely, with a little bow. "I've promised to help Tiron and Enoch repair the big loom today, and there's a handful of other things that need looking into. Maura has promised that if the weaving turns out well, she'll make you a new winter coat with the first lengths on her sewing machine. Tiron and the Master agree you deserve it."

Dola seemed placated by Holl's adult regard of her. Her small chin relaxed, and she smiled up at him. "It's no worry to me. I'll take care of her as long as I'm needed. Only, Mama wanted me to help with the vegetables for dinner."

"One of us will be back here long before that," Holl promised. He checked his toolbox to be sure his good working tools were inside, and picked it up. "She's just been fed, so she won't need feeding for a while. You grant us a few hours of needed respite every day, and we're not forgetting that. We're grateful to you, Dola. If you get tired, find us in the house or the barn," he said from the door. "There's sweet cake in the cupboard."

Acknowledging his last statement with a bare nod, Dola was already seated comfortably with the baby beside the unlit fireplace, making pictures in the light for Asrai's amusement. Holl smiled at his daughter's happy coo and glided away between the cornstalks.

It was not as satisfactory as it might have been to have such important employment, Dola found herself thinking as the baby dozed on her knee. It was a fine day, what she could see of it. The sun was warm and golden. Anyone could tell the corn crop was a fine, thick one. Her mother, who had a way with green and growing things, was well pleased. Dola herself was glad that their first real summer's planting would feed them easily during the winter to come, but it did block out the scenery so completely. How hard it was to think of the winter, months and months away, new woven coat or no! It was boring to stare out at the crops, and she had not brought a book along. The only reading matter she could find in the cottage were on the bedside shelves, and those did not interest her. Holl favored technical manuals of Big Folk science, and Maura's stack had novels, but in foreign languages. There was not even tidying up to be done to keep her mind occupied. A pity Asrai's screaming made her unwelcome in the general household. She might have been kin, but their clan-leader Curran had a minimal tolerance for noise. It came of spending too many years in enforced silence.

"You'd think we were a lot of Trapped Monks! Well, he didn't say we might not go elsewhere, did he?" she said out loud. "Just to be back before time to make supper."

On a hook next to the baby's cot was a sling woven like a fisherman's net. Made for full grown Folk like Maura or Holl, it was too big for Dola when she first tried it on. She tied the top fold in a square knot. It stood upon her thin shoulder like a fist, but the carrier now lay correctly with its bulge upon her hip. Dola fitted the sleeping baby into the sling and arranged her so that her head was supported by the upward curve of cloth against Dola's side. It felt sufficiently secure. Dola tucked her illusion cloth into her tunic pocket, and they went outside into the sun.

The rhythmic disturbance of moving from one place to another woke the baby to dreaming wonder. Dola caught sight of her gentle blue-green eyes wandering from one bright spot to another in the gardens. For a moment, she was afraid the baby might start crying. Asrai started when a crow burst like black cannonfire from between two stalks of corn, and Dola held her breath, but Asrai laughed out loud. Dola explained to her very carefully what it was she was seeing.

"Maybe you'll remember some of this when you're grown," Dola said, thoughtfully. "I wonder just how much it is babies can understand."

Birds sang and swooped overhead in the bright sky. Dola followed their song out of the cornfield and into the meadow behind it. She hopped across the narrow cut of the stream, and followed the curve of the earth uphill. There was a good spot just over the crest of the gentle rise that was always sheltered from the wind, like the palm of a cupped hand. The two of them were completely alone here. The great farm house and barn were hidden away behind a stand of trees as the cottages were concealed among the corn. No habitation, for Big or Small Folk lay within sight. All around the edge of the meadow was a curtain of trees. Most of it belonged to the Forest Preserve, owned by the state, so Keith Doyle explained to them. It meant that never would a house be built there. The Folks' privacy would remain absolute as long as they lived in this place. That knowledge gave her a feeling of hitherto unimaginable freedom. It was glorious.

She sank into the tall, cool grass and spread out a soft blanket for Asrai to lie upon, face up. The infant, her face protected from the sun by an overhanging dock leaf, inspected the nearby weeds and pulled a handful of plant stems toward her toothless mouth. Dola glanced at them to make certain none of them were harmful or poisonous, then let her taste them. She looked around at the splendor of the day.

Only a few feathered clouds streaked the sky, far above her. It would be bitterly cold when night fell. Aylmer, who read the weather better than anyone else, said rain wouldn't fall for several days. Dola was glad. She'd give all she had for more golden days like this. The privilege of sitting out in the sun seemed an unimaginable gift. She shut her eyes and breathed in the heady scent of growing corn, grass, flowers, trees, and listened to the quiet whisper of the stream.

How life had changed. Before last year, she had never seen an open field. Now she and her people owned this fine stretch of land—owned it safe and secure, thanks to Keith Doyle. Dola sighed. If only he were not quite so Big, nor so old. She was his favorite among her people, she knew, but if they were more on a level, he would act less like a kindly uncle toward her and more like a—what? A boyfriend? Dola felt her cheeks burn. Such things were beginning to intrude themselves on her consciousness as stealthily as the growing changes in her body. Her mother smiled indulgently at her when they had little, private discussions. Why were her own feelings always in such a turmoil these days?

She knew the time had come to turn her back on childhood, but it was such a long, long path to becoming a woman. One day, she'd have a babe of her own. For the meanwhile, it was good practice for her to care for one like Asrai, who was so good.

The baby, fistful of hay stuffed into her mouth, was watching her.

"Well, what are you staring at, then?" she asked, her voice caressing and indulgent. For a moment, Dola heard the echo of her own mother asking the same thing. Perhaps she was further along the path than she thought. Would it really be so hard a journey? "Little one, look at this!"

Dola spread out the vision cloth between her two hands. The scrap of cotton was growing ragged after many years' washing and folding. Now that the loom was assembled, she might have a new cloth woven to her taste. She wanted a piece of white percale, just like the soft, old sheets Keith Doyle had once given the Folk. Or perhaps she would have a brocade, with a white on white pattern and a looser weave to let the dreams through. In the end, it wouldn't matter what it was, or how it was made, so long as the cloth fit between her two hands.

The scant, thready weave disappeared in the heart of the vision she imagined. White was the sum of all colors, the Master had told her, so she was merely separating out each from the others when she made her illusions. It was a talent, he explained, like the ability to paint. Practice would give her more scope for her visions.

Asrai only seemed to see bright colors, so the image of flowers and horses Dola created was exaggeratedly brilliant. A hot, red blossom, then one of deep violet, and one each of sun-yellow and orange-yellow spun in the center of the cloth, surrounded by green leaves and small royal blue blooms. The baby's eyes flitted from one image to another, her damp, rosebud mouth tilting up in the corners. Dola made a shocking pink horse dash from one edge of the cloth to the other, scattering the flowers, eliciting a shriek from her enchanted audience. The horse's image grew in the center of the cloth until only its head was visible, its huge, long-lashed eyes blinking soulfully at Asrai.

"I saw that pony on the television when we lived beneath the library, before you were born," Dola said, delighted. "Perhaps by the time you're grown, we'll have a horse like that here on the farm."

The horse shrank and began to run across and back on the white field of cloth. Asrai's wide eyes followed every passage. Orange and sea-blue horses followed the pink one onto the insubstantial track, legs floating in rhythmic sequence like the beating of a heart. When the baby kicked her small legs and gurgled happily, Dola brought all three horses back onto the cloth and made them race around in a circle. She gave them wings, and they began to glide. Asrai let out a happy shriek.

Movement among the trees at the edge of the Folks' land distracted Dola. Concentration broken, she let the veil fall to her lap. Deprived of her entertainment, Asrai exclaimed a note of protest.

"Hush, little one!" Dola whispered suddenly, putting a gentle hand on the baby's chest. She peered down the hill into the trees.

She couldn't discern shapes through the thick stands of pines, but a metallic boom told her it couldn't be animals crashing about back there. Big Folk did sometimes drive up and down in the roads of the Forest Preserve, but the predominant sounds were almost always engines running. This was different. The baby cooed again, demanding attention.

"Be silent, little one," Dola begged Asrai, and gathered her into her lap.

A big brown truck with a cylindrical tank backed out of the forest and onto the land at the top of the meadow, just beyond the Hollow Tree property line, not far from the head of the marsh waters. Dola stared at it as a Big man climbed out of the passenger seat. He walked around to the back and opened a pipe that began to dribble dark liquid underneath the body of the truck. Dola sat frozen, clutching the baby in her arms. Suddenly, she realized she was visible to him. Her eyes and the eyes of the man met.

Chapter Five

Grant Pilton squinted up at the hilltop and put a hand over his eyes to shield them from the light.

"There's a kid up there, watching us," he called to Jake Williamson. "A little girl."

"What?" Williamson climbed down from the truck cab. "Ms. Gilbreth's not gonna like that. She don't want witnesses. Where is she?" Pilton pointed. "Right up there."

Williamson squinted. The little girl up there looked about five or six years old. "Maybe she don't know what she's seeing. Let's talk to her."

They walked toward her. The little girl sat frozen in place, her wide blue eyes fixed on them like those of a deer caught in the headlights of an oncoming car. They noticed that she was clutching something to her chest. It writhed, and she spoke to it, too low for them to hear her.

"She's got her baby brother or sister with her," Williamson said. "Let's just go up and make friends, and I'll give her a buck or something to go back in the house."

Suddenly, the child sprang to her feet, and ran up the side of the hill.

"There she goes!" Pilton exclaimed. The two men broke into a run, jumping over the shallow stream and charging up the slope.

"Why are we chasing her?" Williamson asked suddenly, stopping on his heels.

Pilton paused only for a heartbeat. "Well, we don't want her to think we're child molesters. She knows somethin's wrong now. We gotta catch up with her."

"We don't want her to get the sheriff out here," Williamson agreed. The thought went through both their minds at once that it would be a bad idea to have anyone investigating their presence in the forest preserve at this time, for whatever reason. Williamson poured on the speed, and outdistanced his companion.

With their long strides, they crested the hill in no time. The girl was just a few lengths ahead of them, the soft soles of her green-shod feet flashing down the hill. Pilton shouted, "Hey!"

The running girl looked back at him over her shoulder. All at once, she dropped to her knees. Suddenly, for no really good reason Pilton could detect, she vanished from sight.

"Where'd she go?" he yelled. Williamson dashed to where the girl had last been visible.

So far as he could tell, Williamson was reaching for a handful of empty air, but he came up with the little girl's upper arm clasped in his big fist. She reappeared as if a curtain was being drawn away from her, then Pilton could see there was a white scarf or something like it on the ground around her feet. The little girl wrenched her arm free to support the bundle in her other arm, and Williamson took hold of her long blond hair instead.

"Right here, you idiot. Can't you see her?"

"I can now, but she was invisible before," Pilton insisted. "How'd she do that?"

"She wasn't invisible," Williamson said, his voice scornful. "She's wearing green, and you've got the sun in your eyes."

"No, she's magic," Pilton said. "She disappeared, like in a trick."

"You're just blind, that's your problem."

"What do you want of me?" the girl demanded, clutching the baby protectively to her chest.

Pilton and Williamson inspected their prisoners. The girl stood about three feet high, with long, silky blond hair that was now tangled and festooned with pieces of weed. She wasn't as young as they'd first suspected. The summing look with which she fixed them wasn't just that of a hyperintelligent six-year-old. She had an old, old look in her eyes. If she hadn't been so small of stature, Pilton would have thought she was just on the early side of teenage.

"Why did you run away?" Jake asked her.

"Well, you were chasing me," she said, her chin stuck out. She looked as though she might cry, and Pilton felt sorry for her. "Let me go. I want to go home."

"What do you want to do, Jake?" he asked, staring at the child. She was a pretty little thing, and scared to pieces.

"No names," Williamson snapped back, looking alarmed.

"Let her go, huh?"

"Shut up! I got to think!" The harshness of his voice alarmed the girl, who tried to take a step away. Williamson tightened his hold on her hair, and she whimpered. The baby, catching her alarm, burst out crying.

"My God, that kid has lungs!" Pilton said, taken aback by the sheer volume of noise the minute baby produced.

"Quiet! Shut it up!" Williamson thundered over the shrieking.

"I can't!" she said, stamping her foot. Tears began to track down her cheeks. "You frightened her!"

"Shut her up or I'll wallop you! Dammit, I can't think with all this screaming going on. Put her in the truck," Williamson said.

The girl's eyes went big, and she attempted to struggle free. Her efforts had no more effect than if she had been held by a stone statue. With a gesture of impatience, Williamson thrust her toward Pilton, who wrapped his hand around her upper arm and steered her over the hilltop toward the tanker. Her bones felt as small as a bird's. He sneaked a glance sideways at her. Through the tresses of her hair, the tip of her left ear peeked out. It was pointed, like a cat's. The girl caught him looking, and tossed her head back. The ear was hidden again, but Pilton was certain he'd seen what he'd seen. She bent her head over the baby, talking in a low, soothing voice. The infant's shrill cries abated about a yard from the truck, and settled into low, frightened sobbing. Her little nose was red.

Pilton relaxed as soon as the noise stopped. It had to be a very new baby. Both of his kids had sounded like that for the first few months of life.

"We've caught a fairy woman," he told Williamson, when they'd stowed the girl and baby in the truck cab. The seats were so deep that only the heads of the two children were visible over the side. Both faces were streaky with tears and huge-eyed with terror.

"Don't talk crazy," Williamson said, turning his back on them. "She's a midget, like those Munchkins in the Wizard of Oz movie."

"I think there's something weird about her," Pilton insisted. The girl stared at them through the truck window, her expression half defiance, half mute appeal.

"Dammit!" Williamson swore, pounding his fist on the tank wall. Pilton saw the girl jump, and her jaw set. "We can't just trust her to keep her mouth shut, not when we've scared the heck out of her like that. We better take her back and let Ms. Gilbreth figure out what to do with her."

Dola was frightened. She wanted to get out of this evil-smelling vehicle and away, but there was so much metal around her that the very air burned. The Big Folk had bundled her in here, without so much a thought for her feelings as they'd give to a package. She curled in on herself, wishing the world would go away. The only thing preventing her from becoming a little knot of acute self pity and fear was her concern for the baby.

Thankfully, Asrai had stopped crying the moment the truck door slammed shut on them, or she'd have deafened Dola completely. It must be the presence of all that cold metal that shocked her silent. This was the first time in her young life that she'd been in a hostile environment. Dola liked it no more than Asrai, but she knew such things existed, and was better prepared.

"I'm with you, little one," she whispered. "I'll protect you, I swear it." Though how she was to accomplish her vow, she had no idea.

Who could these men be? They were dressed identically in button-up coveralls of a drab color and sturdy construction. The outfit looked better on the bigger man. The other one was so skinny that only his shoulders filled out the contours of his uniform. They seemed to be disagreeing on what to do. Meanwhile the hose running from the tank was spewing foul-smelling liquid onto the ground near the source of her drinking water. The elders needed to be told at once, so they could contain the contamination.

Both the cab doors opened at once. Dola put the baby across her shoulder and prepared to climb down, but the two men got in, one on either side of them, leaving no room for her to pass. By the set of their jaws, there was no room for argument, either. She was a prisoner.

What's going to become of us? she thought despairingly.

Without a word, the big one called Jake started up the big engine. The skinny one with hair the soft brown color of river clay kept glancing at her sideways. Jake, driving, didn't look at them once, but Dola could tell he was acutely aware of them. She peeked up at him through her hair, trying to study his face. He didn't look a bad man, but he was scared, too.

"I tell you, this must be a fairy woman and her baby," the skinny one said, talking over her head, when the truck had passed out of the Forest Preserve and onto the main road.

"C'mon, you idiot," said Jake, "there's no such thing as fairies."

"Well, what do you call her?" Skinny poked at Dola's ear.

She was shocked. Incarceration was one thing, but personal assaults were another. Dola turned her head and bit him on the hand. He yelled, and she recoiled, spitting out the taste of his skin.

"Ugh, do you never wash your hands?" she asked boldly. "And it's not my baby, it's my cousins' baby. You'd better let us go home, or they'll be upset."

It was the wrong thing to say. All of a sudden, both men grew quiet. They didn't say another word to her. She looked from one to another, hoping for some sign of kindness or mercy. Dola felt a cold wash of terror roll down the middle of her back. These weren't Keith Doyle and his harmless Big friends whom she knew and trusted. They were strangers, who might mean to do her harm. She might never see home again.

Dola tightened her arms around the baby and stared out the big windshield at the road, trying to memorize the sights they passed. She had to be brave, for Asrai.

In the early twilight, Maura peered into the door of her cottage. It was silent within, and none of the lanterns had been lit. She found the one closest to the doorway and blew on the pointed cotton wick mounted in the scrolled wooden candle between the carved screens. The cotton began to blaze with its bright, unconsuming fire.

There was no sound. "Dola? Where are you, child?"

Maura checked the infant's cot. It was empty, and cool to the touch. Perhaps both girl and baby were asleep in the master bed. She smiled. That would explain why Dola hadn't reported for kitchen duty. The day had tired them both out. Maura put on the rest of the lights in the small cottage.

"Dola?" she said, her voice gently chiding, leaning into her bedroom. "Lass, it's nearly dinnertime." She was astonished that Asrai wasn't awake already. Maura was more than ready to feed the baby, and their physical alarms seemed to go off at the same time.

The cottage was empty. Well, no harm. Perhaps Dola was in the barn, or their paths had crossed, each seeking the other. Maura turned back to the house and began to seek baby and babysitter.

They were not to be found in either place. By full darkness, Maura was beside herself with worry. She had covered nearly all the farm property, calling. The girls weren't in the fields, nor the workshop, nor visiting other children in the clan rooms of the main house. Maura had knocked on the door of all the cottages to ask her neighbors if the girls were with them. No one had seen either child for hours.

"Where can she be?" she asked Holl. "I've been listening for them, but I can't hear them."

"I am sure they are here somewhere," Holl said, trying to be reassuring. He knew Dola to be responsible. Wherever they were, he was certain that they were safe. "Probably Dola's become interested in some small project, or reading a book, and she has lost track of the time."

Maura favored him with a look full of exasperation. She crossed her arms gingerly over her chest. "But *Asrai* would not forget. She must be very hungry. A babe's stomach can only hold enough food for two or three hours. We ought to be able to hear her crying by now."

"Aye, that we should," said Ranna, not unkindly. "If we could train the babe to rise at dawn we wouldn't need a rooster."

"Dola wouldn't have wandered away," Shelogh said, reasonably. "That child is responsible."

The thought, so far kept at bay, arose inexorably in their minds, that Dola and Asrai were gone from the Farm itself. At once, the elder Folk began to suggest alternatives to the unthinkable.

"Could vun of our Big friends have come to visit and taken them away?" Rose suggested. "The good Ludmilla has said often that she vould like to treat Dola for the good work she does in caring for your babe."

"She might have walked into town," Marcy suggested, crouching down beside the Little Folk. She had just returned from class at Midwestern, and was concerned when the situation had been explained to her. "With all the Big People going home over these roads at this hour, she's probably hiding out. And I'm sure she's sorry. Holding onto an unhappy baby when you've missed feeding time is its own punishment."

"Or it might be they've gone on a wee adventure," Marm said, his foolish, bearded face concerned but smiling. "It's a long way back to the Library, but she knows how to get there. Perhaps she ran out of books to read!"

Immediately, Holl wanted to dismiss Marm's idea as foolish, but who knew what ran through the minds of almost-teenaged

children? It was true. All of them did know the way back to their
old home. The distance was too great to walk, but there were buses
that traveled through the county road intersection only one mile away.
If it were the case, she'd have arrived at the Midwestern campus
within the last twenty minutes.

"But it is dark now," the Master reasoned. "She will have taken
shelter somewhere for the night. Dola has learned basic survival. All
vill be vell."

"But Asrai needs to feed," Maura exclaimed. "What will they
do?"

"Peace, daughter," the Master said, patting her hand. "Undoubtedly she has found that her adventure has placed her too far away at
a critical point. Ve vill telephone to Ludmilla and see if she has seen
them. Our good friend will aid her in dealing with an infant who has
missed a meal. Our needs are similar though our sizes differ. It is too
late to bring her here before she is fed, but no doubt some Big Folk
equivalent vill be made to suffice."

The suggestion made good sense, and served to calm Maura
and Siobhan somewhat. Concentrating on eluding detection by either mother, Holl extended a wisp of sense, feeling outward for his
daughter.

"They'll be with her, won't they?" Maura asked, bravely, looking
up at Holl for support.

"Aye," he said, distracted. If she'd seen him concentrating, she'd
know what he'd been trying to do, and worry all the more. "They
won't leave her."

"It is I who speak, old friend," the Master said into the telephone
receiver. All the Folk who could fit into the farmhouse kitchen
were crowded around. "It vould be very good to see you at the
veekend, should you care to visit. No, I call for another purpose.
Two of our children have gone wandering. Have they come to
you? My daughter's child, and young Dola, her caretaker." Holl
watched with dismay as the small muscles in the Master's cheek
tightened. He was disappointed. "Vill you keep watch for them,
and summon us vhen they appear? I thank you." He cradled the
phone and shook his head.

"The Library," said Siobhan desperately.

"Do you want me to go?" Marcy asked.

"It vould take too long," the Master said. "I will ask one who is closer by." He put in another call. Everyone held their breath while the Master counted the rings until the receiver was picked up. "Mees Londen, I haf a favor to ask of you."

Holl was waiting by the telephone when it rang, half an hour later. "Nothing," Diane said. "I went through the whole village with a lantern. I checked every house, and every level of the library stacks. They aren't there. I left a note on the wall with my phone number if Dola goes down there. She'll call you or me when she arrives."

"Thank you," Holl said.

"Dunn and Barry are going over the rest of the campus on foot. They'll call you direct if they find her." Diane's voice was hesitant. "I'm sure they're all right. Probably they're just lost. Can I do anything else to help?"

"You are doing a great deal. Just keep your eyes open for them," Holl said.

"Please keep me posted," Diane begged. "I'd better go. She might be trying to call you."

"That's right," Holl said, and hastily hung up. He waited, hoping that the telephone would ring as soon as he put down the receiver. He stood ready with his hand on the handset to snatch it up, waiting for the bell. His eyes met Maura's. Her lips quivered slightly, then tears overspilled her lashes and streamed down her cheeks. Holl opened his arms. She moved close and put her head on his shoulder, closing her arms tightly against his back. Throat tight, he clasped her to his chest, his lips touching her hair. He was glad for the feeling of being enfolded. The close contact gave him a sense of security which he sorely needed.

No time for subtlety. He let his mind clear to do a full finding. His sense tripped lightly out, touching all the places on the farm that Dola liked to frequent. It met the edges of the property, feeling gently along the forest paths, and into the small pockets of air under the greater tree roots that the children liked to hide in when they played their games. His sense ranged further and further afield, touching the minds of Big Folk drivers in their cars, the metal of which burned him slightly with a freezing hot touch. Dola and his baby were nowhere nearby. He knew in his heart that they lived, but he didn't know where. Enoch burst into the kitchen. Holl, his concentration broken again, turned to his brother-in-law.

"We've been out in the field. Strange Big Folk were there today," Enoch said, his distaste evident. His face was drawn and angry. He ran a dirty hand through his tousled black hair. "Their footprints and Dola's overlap. Bracey did a sniffing, and he says there was a scuffle, and she left with them in a truck. He can't figure out who they are. They drove through a puddle of that muck that those fertilizer people have been dumping on our land."

"My baby's been taken away by the Big Ones!" Siobhan burst into hysterical tears. Tay gathered her into his arms, and sympathetic friends surrounded her.

"Hush, woman," Tay said hoarsely. "Screeching won't bring them back. The girl will come back if she can. All we can do is continue to look."

Siobhan's panic was nothing compared to the agony Maura suddenly experienced as she realized her baby was gone. She began to cry, silently, with more force until she was gasping uncontrollably. Her father stepped forward and clapped a hard hand over her mouth and nose.

"Calm. Gain control. Your next breath vill be a calm one. Concentrate." Over his hand, her eyes cleared, and she nodded. Her mother put an arm around her shoulder, and more friends and relatives gathered close to lend their comfort.

"We must call Keith Doyle," Holl said, holding Maura close. Both their faces were pale and drawn. "He'll know what to do."

The Master nodded assent. Catra snatched up the phone and began to dial.

Chapter Six

"'All rise,'" Paul Meier said, and snickered. He turned to squint at Keith, his thin, curved nose wrinkling with good humor. "Great stuff, Keith. Pithy, and a neat play on words. The client might actually want to use it. I love the concept illo, too." He held up the white rectangle of pasteboard to study. It showed a courtroom scene. There were no human beings in the illustration. All the participants in the trial were baked goods. The jury was twelve muffins in a two-row pan, and in the witness box was an angel cake with a piece of black veil on its top and a hanky folded into the front curve at one side. In the presiding seat surrounded by satin bunting was a yellow, black, and red packet labeled "Judge Yeast." The caption, which Meier underlined again with a fingernail, was "All rise."

"Angel food cakes don't use yeast," Sean Lopez pointed out, disdainfully. His black brows lowered together over his pugnaciously snubbed nose.

"So what?" Meier said, cheerfully. He grinned, white teeth brilliant against his olive skin. "She's only a witness. It makes a great image, Sean, and it makes you remember the product. If the client wants to change the angel food cake for a loaf of challah, he will. They always want to change something. We often leave something in deliberately for them to pull out."

"You go to all the trouble to put in something you know the client will want to kill?" asked Dorothy Carver, tapping one smooth, walnut-hued cheek with the charcoal pencil she held between her elegantly manicured fingers.

"Whatever works," Meier said. "You have to understand what you're dealing with here, kids. It's not an easy business. This is Hollywood East. There's a lot of ad firms out there, and a finite amount of money. We're here to make sure the most money possible falls into our pockets—that is to say PDQ Advertising's pockets. The way we do that is not just through clever ad campaigns, but by making the client feel more special here than anywhere else."

"You mean make him feel like he's our only client?" suggested Brendan Martwick. Keith studied the pen he was rolling between his fingers. Brendan was one world-class brown-noser. He and Brendan had already decided they didn't like each other. Keith believed in group efforts, and Martwick believed wholeheartedly in all for one and every man for himself. He was a snooty north-sider. If he had ever broken down and called Keith 'common' or 'vulgar,' Keith wouldn't have been surprised. He sounded like a barely-updated character out of a Victorian novel, and dressed like a Polo manne-quin. Whatever young and wealthy J. Bennett Throgmorton-Snipe III was doing taking an ill-paid internship when he could have lounged at a desk in Daddy's stock brokerage, Keith couldn't guess. Maybe someone told him advertising was easy. It wasn't.

"You've got it," Meier agreed. "Our time is flexible, as far as they're concerned, because they're paying. You've got to psych out their likes and dislikes, and avoid the buzzwords and shibboleths of their particular industry or product. Not easy sometimes, which is why we have a research department that I think rivals the FBI's." Keith and the others nodded, grinning. The creative director's de-partment was the second department the interns had been assigned to for orientation. Research had been the first. Keith had been im-pressed by the resources the ad company had at its fingertips.

"Will we really get our names on the presentation?" Keith asked, tapping the matte. "Dorothy did the artwork and lettering."

"Yeah? Nice job, Dorothy," Meier said, flashing a half grin at her. "I'll have to check out the client's feelings on having internship students working on his campaign—y'know, if inexperienced kids came up with this hot slogan and ad, why is he paying PDQ the big bucks for professional creative teams? I'll get back to you. No promises, now."

Keith and Dorothy nodded, and exchanged a quick glance. No matter if they got credit for the idea or not, this would be like really working for an ad agency. No experience was wasted, as Meier was fond of saying, but Keith would have been upset if Dorothy's care-ful penwork had gone unrecognized. She was really good. All he had done was blab out his idea, and she put it on paper—really brought the images to life.

A pity they couldn't form a firm alliance. She was less con-cerned about him getting equal credit than he was on her behalf. The way the internship program was set up, the students were frequently pitted against one another, striving for the best assignments and the few advantages that would put them before the eyes of PDQ's management to secure the single job offer at the end of the term

PDQ promised each new crop of interns. Each of the current students were approximately equal in their qualifications. After fighting their way through four interviews and a written essay detailing why they'd be of value to PDQ's program, there were no obvious standouts left among them. Chosen from among eight hundred applicants, half from state universities, half from private schools, each had some personal business background plus artistic or creative talent, as well as high grade point average, personality, and majors in business. They had had to self-promote themselves so fiercely it had become part of their everyday behavior. Keith was disappointed that even after each had secured one of the coveted spots they couldn't seem to put aside the competition. Even he had to fight down suspicious feelings, and he didn't like it.

Keith recognized there was nothing personal in the imposed animosity, but after studying the way things worked at PDQ, he saw how small, core groups of individuals could consistently come up with good, marketable ideas if they weren't in constant fear of being zetzed by the other people in the department. Everyone's ego was on the line all the time. It would have been a more realistic experience if they'd been treated like a creative team.

He shifted his copy of *In Search of Excellence* further underneath his notebook where it couldn't be noticed and decided to can his ideas on cooperation for the time being. The competition would never end. PDQ's policy was to take the best student in any year and offer her or him a position in the company. That plum represented a five to ten year leap in one's career. Instead of having to shine year after year in small companies, it would be possible to come straight to one of the majors.

PDQ would be a terrific job to have. Keith already knew he loved dreaming up campaigns, making up slogans that tickled people but had the heart of the product represented in a few words. If he got the job, so much the better for him, but his usual cooperative soul might cheat him out of it by making him push to have PDQ hire Dorothy or one of the others instead. Sean Lopez was the most jumpy of the group. He was nearing the end of his MBA program, and was actively seeking a position to slide into after graduation in June. Brendan already acted as if the job would be his by right. Maybe attitude would be a factor in the management's eventual choice, but it was sure a pain in the neck for the duration.

As a supervisor, Meier was the best possible choice. He'd gotten his job from a good review during an internship just like theirs, and was actively on their side, a fact that made him different from 85% of the other people working in advertising in general. He warned them about the competitive angle, the cutthroat techniques, the downright theft of ideas and the destruction of careers. He kept bringing in phrases like 'dog eat dog,' and 'every man for himself.' Maybe it was the mark of a good ad campaigner to think in clichés. Keith respected the hard work he put in, maintaining his own job while shepherding and acting as father-confessor to the four interns.

At the very beginning, Meier had read them a lecture. "I don't care where you're from, what kind of background you've got, who your daddy knows. This is another world. Nothing's real here; we make our own reality. If it looks like someone's ripping you off, it's nothing personal. The only job we have is to impress the client first, then all of that client's customers with the sheer fabulousness of that client's product or service. If somebody has to use your ideas to do it, he probably will. Someone might actually come up with an idea that sounds exactly like yours. It's possible; there's only so many ideas out there. There's plenty of ego-tripping here. Ignore it. There's a lot of politically incorrect 'isms.' Ignore them. Do your job, and don't get lost in the office politics. Like I said, in the end none of it's real. It doesn't affect you after you go home.

"This is the most rotten business in the world. You can't trust anyone. No one gives you credit for your work or your ideas. Your suggestions get ignored, then you get blamed when things are screwed up because no one paid attention to your recommendations. Everything costs money. You work late hours for months on a project that's canceled without notice. And the client is never happy with anything you do. Other than that, it's a great job. I want you to know that."

Brendan was still muttering about Judge Yeast. Meier shuffled a handful of papers on the table, and cleared his throat. Martwick instantly turned a respectful and attentive face toward him. Keith resisted the urge to kick him under the table.

"Okay," Meier said. "I'm going to throw out some product names and concepts. Some of them are real, some aren't. Each of you take a few. I want some creative thinking about these by tomorrow. No need to knock yourself out on the artwork yet, Dorothy," he nodded at the young woman, "unless that's the way you think best. We'll brainstorm on all of them over the next few days. Not every one will come up a winner, so I don't want anybody shooting themselves if they don't get the next Clio. We need all the grist we can get, and out of that we may get some goodies. Got that?"

"Yessir," Sean muttered, flipping open his notebook.

"Ready," Keith said. Meier shot him a look full of humor. Keith grinned back. He felt that he and Meier had 'clicked,' getting along instantly from day one, but he understood that there could be no favoritism shown. Still, win or lose, Keith promised himself he'd look Meier up for lunch after the internship was over. They could be good friends.

Meier showed them stat sheets and photographs of a new luxury car, details about a new breakfast cereal, a new soft drink, ground plans for a themed amusement park currently under construction, "and just for the hell of it, I'm throwing in some ordinary, everyday items: flower pots, potatoes, uh, brown paper bags, and carrots. Let's see if you can give me some new thoughts on them, too. Pick one."

"Potatoes," Keith said, quickly.

"Oh, I'll take carrots," Dorothy said. "They're healthy!"

"Brown paper bags," Sean said.

"That leaves flower pots," Brendan said, with an eternally world-weary air. "I can handle it."

"I'm sure you can," Meier said without expression, jotting down names next to the categories. "Okay, folks, that's all. See you tomorrow. Don't forget to clean up in here, okay?"

"Why potatoes?" Sean asked Keith on the way out after they'd taken their coffee cups back to the employee dining room. "Why'd you look so excited about that?"

"Inspiration," Keith said, grinning, tapping the side of his skull with a forefinger. "You know how much vitamin C there is in your average potato? You could start your day with a big helping of potatoes with C. Sunrise Spuds," he said, painting an imaginary banner on the sky. "They're not just for dinner any more."

Sean laughed. "You're nuts."

"The trouble with you," Keith said, "is that you have to learn to let your hair down more."

"The trouble with you," Brendan said disdainfully, picking up his briefcase, "is that your hair is already hanging around your knees."

Keith gave him a big smile as he slipped into the only space left in a crowded elevator, and watched Brendan's annoyed expression narrow and vanish between the closing doors.

Keith made the commuter trip home drumming on the seat between his knees, smiling at passersby who met his eyes. He drove home from the station with all the windows of his old, dark blue Mustang wide open to let the wind cool him down while inspiration cooked. If the competitiveness didn't kill them first, there were opportunities galore for creativity and experimentation at PDQ. While Keith's tensed muscles wound down, his brain was spinning on product ideas. Maybe some of them were way out, but that was half the fun.

In a way, being an intern was better than working for the company, because they could play around with suggestions, without the possibility of being fired untimely if the ideas turned out to be clunkers or money pits. Keith had purposely let the others pass on some of the silly-sounding names so he could have them. He let Brendan take Rad Sportswear in exchange for Appalachi-Cola. None of the others wanted a soft drink with such a weird name, and they couldn't understand why Keith's eyes gleamed at the sound of it. He could picture more scope for Appalachi-Cola. It suggested wonderful images to him.

"As refreshing as a Florida vacation," he murmured to himself, peering out over the steering wheel at the usual afternoon backup. Sounded good to him. Chicago in September was steamy and hot without the promise of white sand beaches to relieve the gasping atmospheric inversion. On a legal pad splayed out on the passenger seat, Keith swerved through the lanes of traffic making notes. Who knew? Maybe one of his ideas would be a winner, and he'd have the joy of seeing a campaign designed around it.

Through the kitchen curtains, he could see his mother taking something out of the refrigerator. He grinned. With an audibly gusty sigh, he threw open the door. His mother turned, wide-eyed, as he staggered in, wrenching his tie loose from his throat with a haggard hand and plopped down in a chair, limbs splayed limply.

"Very dramatic," his mother said ironically, applauding. "You win the Academy Award for best performance by an actor getting home from work. Please don't leave your briefcase in the door, honey." She hooked up the slim leather case with one finger and extended it to him.

"Sorry, Mom," Keith said, springing up like a Jack-in-the-box for a kiss on the cheek. His mother eyed him.

"In spite of the Sarah Bernhardt routine, you do look tired," Mrs. Doyle said, handing over the case. "Have a good day?"

"Great!" Keith said, enthusiastically. "No more orientation. We're working on formulating ad campaigns for new products. This department's a lot more interesting than Research. We can really use our imaginations. Our supervisor, Paul Meier, said this is just what a real creative team does during 'ideation.' I like Paul. He's trying to treat us like regular employees while still leaving us room to make mistakes."

"Too bad all life experiences aren't so forgiving," Mrs. Doyle said, glancing down the hall opposite. It led to the family bedrooms. Keith caught the meaning of her expression, and pulled a longsuffering expression.

"Jeff's home, huh?"

"Yup. Dinner in half an hour, sweetie," Mrs. Doyle said. "You can make the salad after you change."

The battle of the day was fought, but the battle of the evening was just beginning. Keith felt that he got more tired out in four hours arguing with his younger brother than he did in the ten hours of commuting and working downtown.

The younger Doyle was on the floor of their shared room with his back against the bed. After a short glance upward to make sure it wasn't anyone important who entered, he returned his attention to the small electronic game propped on his hunched knees. Jeffrey Doyle had almost a movie star's good looks. He had much the same shaped jaw as Keith, but it had more squared bone, a little more muscle. His hair was red, too, but deeper, with bronze in it, and his eyes had decided on an olivine green, instead of changeable hazel like Keith's. His skin never freckled; it wouldn't dare. He tanned smoothly in the earliest spring sun. In him, the Doyle intensity fueled his emotions. He never forgave a slight, and Keith returning home to stay in the room he had staked out as his own was a personal affront.

"There's a message for you," Jeff said tersely.

It was almost the most civil pronouncement Keith had heard in a month. "Thanks. Where is it?"

Without looking up, Jeff gestured toward Keith's bed.

On the pillow was a scrap of paper torn from the corner of a junk mail flyer. In the corner under the paste-on address label was a scrawl in Jeff's seismic handwriting. Keith scanned it. "Catra called? When? 'Check the front page of the paper'?" he read. "What's that mean?"

Jeff raised resentful eyes to him. "Couldn't tell. She had a weird way of talking. She said something valuable was stolen. Your strange friends." He went back to his game, glowering at the miniature screen.

"Today's paper?" Keith asked.

"She didn't say," Jeff said shortly, and ignored any further questions Keith asked. His audience was at an end. Keith would have to find out for himself.

"Mysterious," he said, hurrying out of the room to find the daily paper. For one of the Folk to telephone long distance meant that something was very wrong.

It had already been consigned to the recycling bin. He pulled section one from the heap and straightened it out. At first he didn't see anything that related to the Little Folk, until he noticed the boxed reference in the upper left hand corner under the daily weather report.

"Archaeological display at Field Museum!" Keith breathed. He felt his invisible whiskers twitch. Surely that was what Catra meant him to read. He flipped through the pages to the main body of the article. There, as the Elf Master had predicted, was the display of Bronze Age artifacts brought to the United States by Professor Parker. The photograph that accompanied the article showed the comb Keith himself had unearthed in Scotland.

"It must have been stolen," Keith said to himself. So that was the problem. You just couldn't have a magic comb bouncing around the city. He picked up the phone and dialed Hollow Tree Farm. The line was busy.

Never mind. He'd go to the Field Museum and investigate for himself. Keith snatched the family membership card from its niche in the desk where his parents kept it, and hopped into the Mustang. The traffic outbound from the heart of the city was thick, but inbound, he had reasonably clear sailing.

The museum's ornamented portico had shadows across it already as the daylight dwindled. Keith shot up the flight of shallow steps to the grand entrance.

"Good evening," Keith said to the woman behind the marble counter just inside the doors. "I'm a friend of Professor Parker." The woman gave him a noncommittal smile, as if uncertain of the significance of his statement. "The English archaeologist who's visiting with the Bronze Age stuff from the Hebrides? Is he here?" The woman still looked blank. Keith glanced confidentially from side to side and leaned closer. "The short one?"

"Oh, yes!" the woman exclaimed, her face lightening, then looking a little self-conscious.

"I'd like to see him, if that's possible."

"Sorry. He's busy this evening."

"How do you know that when a second ago you didn't know who he was?" Keith asked, plastering a foolish grin on his face to soften the question.

Flushing, the woman countered with another question. "Did you want to visit the museum this evening, sir?"

"Uh, yeah." Keith plunged a finger and a thumb into his shirt pocket for the membership card.

The woman beamed to acknowledge a museum supporter. The young man might be strange, but he was a patron. "Thank you, sir. Would you like a map?"

"Will it help me find the professor?" Keith asked, full of innocence, as he took the pamphlet.

"I can't help you with that, sir," the woman explained patiently. Their voices had gotten louder, catching an echo from the polished walls. A security guard on watch near the entrance started forward, hand on radio, but she waved him back. "I can direct you to the Bronze Age exhibit. Second floor."

Using the map, Keith had no trouble finding Parker's display on the upstairs gallery, sandwiched between another small visiting exhibit and the museum's huge Oriental collection. Four or five showcases were dedicated to the finds, which combined the discoveries of two or three groups of archaeologists working in the same region of the Hebridean northwest. Keith felt a surge of pride when he found the case that contained the round clay bottle and the string of amber trading beads that he and his Scottish friend Matthew had unearthed together a little over a year ago. Moreover, their names were typed on the little identification tag pinned in front of it. Parker was generous in giving credit. Keith was delighted. He wished that someone he knew was there, so he could show them his name.

Most of the artifacts were of the shard and fragment variety, with carefully-made mockups of how the pieces were assumed to have looked when they were in use. Once again, Keith was impressed by the way the scientists had extrapolated the shape of the whole items from formless fragments found out of context in three thousand years worth of dirt. Previously discovered examples were used as templates, but it took a good eye to tell the difference between the potential fracture zones of the neck of a jar from its similarly-formed pedestal. Bone pins, small toys, glass beads and the like were all that remained fully intact after the passing millenia.

Keith surveyed the display. Each of these pieces was as ordinary as it looked. None of them aroused that tingle of second sight, calling to him the way the wood-and-bone comb had. Catra's elliptical message had been correct. The comb was not where it belonged. In the next to last case, he saw the little pinned label designating where the comb belonged. A little bar labeled "REMOVED" lay in most of the empty spots where artifacts had been taken out, but none marked this particular absence. His invisible whiskers sprang erect in alarm.

He dropped to his knees in front of the case, his nose almost pressed into the glass. The possibility of the truth hadn't concerned him so long as it was likely there had been a mistake. Keith felt a lead weight drop into the pit of his stomach. He stared into the heart of the case, hoping for a clue. Did someone else latch on to the fact that there was something extraordinary about that one piece, and steal it? The Little Folk would want to avoid letting wander loose any artifact that could be traced back to them. It was safe with Parker. Keith knew he had to find it and get it back here where it belonged. He suddenly felt someone's eyes upon him, and looked around.

A uniformed security guard stood against a pillar, peering obliquely at him, clearly wondering why a young man in suspenders was getting so upset about Bronze Age antiques. It was the same guard who had been near the front door. Keith gave him a huge, mindless smile. The guard scowled, and looked away.

Keith sighed. It was going to be harder to investigate the comb's disappearance with a tail following him all over the museum. Nonchalantly, Keith backed away from the case and stared up at the large map suspended above it, showing the locations in Scotland where the various artifacts had been found. A light sound came from behind him, as if the guard had shifted a foot on the polished floor.

Without haste, though his nerves were going bonkers, Keith sidled away from the Parker display, and ambled toward the nearest stairwell.

Was there any way to trace the comb, using its previous presence in the case as a thread? Keith threw a mental glance over his shoulder, hoping the guard wouldn't notice. The case didn't emit any perceptible energies pointing one way or the other. There wasn't enough magical oomph in the comb to have left a trail. As a psychic detective, he was on his own.

Keith started walking down the stairs. The guard sauntered behind him, the radio on his hip emitting whispering sibilants. Keith looked up and smiled at the man, whose brows drew together in a scowl. He guessed that it hadn't been too smart to draw attention to himself at the museum entrance. Now the staff was suspicious. How could he get rid of his tail?

In the main floor of the museum were the famous dinosaurs, a tyrannosaurus rex standing triumphant over the prone body of its prey. Keith stopped at the well-worn handrail and stared up at its toothy jaws. The guard paused about twenty feet away, arms folded and wearing a carefully neutral expression on his face that made him look no less threatening than the giant dinosaur. Keith studied paleontology, wondering what to do.

There hadn't been a news report on the radio about the theft of the comb from the museum, so either the loss hadn't been discovered yet, or the museum staff was covering up. He wondered how the elves had gotten the word so quickly. Maybe Professor Parker himself had called the Master with the news.

It was likely to be an inside job, Keith reasoned. Those cases couldn't be opened easily by an outsider without keys, and to judge by the persistence of the security staff around suspicious visitors, without being observed. If the comb remained on the premises, maybe he could find it. It gave off a recognizable auric energy that

Keith had detected shortly after he'd found it. That process of investigation, as Holl and Enoch had been at pains to instruct him, took concentration. Keith stared up into the flat eye socket of the tyrannosaurus, and looked past it, focusing his own inner eye.

Suddenly, he was surrounded by ghost-lights, as ordinarily-unseen energies pulsed at him, beckoning him toward a myriad of glass cases visible in the large chambers that led off from all sides of the main hall. More energies thrummed at him through the floors from upstairs and downstairs.

Oh, great, Keith thought, overwhelmed, looking around at the sudden display. He didn't know where to turn first. This place is *full* of magic artifacts.

Well, where better to hide a needle than in a haystack full of needles? If the thief knew the special property of the comb, he wouldn't bother to remove it from the premises. Keith went from one source of energy to another, hoping that one of them belonged to the missing comb. Most of the Hopi kachinas glimmered at him in their case, creating a tremendous mass presence that was the most powerful thing for yards. A few of the Inuit household goods shone brightly against the dimness of the hall where they were displayed. Keith hurried through the aisles, eliminating one false lead after another. After the thirtieth false alarm on the ground floor drew him to yet another Native American display, he made a mental note to research those mystical traditions one day and learn more about the source of their talents.

None of the artifacts he inspected had the correct mental feel, so he was able to slowly fine-tune what he was looking for. The Indian items had their own strong identity, and it didn't match the sensation he had had from handling the comb. Gradually, he began to feel that what he wanted was not on this floor at all, but somewhere below.

A loudspeaker interrupted his thoughts with a pleasant chime, followed by a woman's voice that echoed through the big chamber, drowning out the identityless roar of human voices and footsteps. "The museum will be closing in twenty minutes."

Keith looked around him. A few of the other patrons left what they were doing and headed toward the main entrance or toward the gift shop. No one was paying attention to him. At long last, the guard who'd been tailing him had gotten bored with the seemingly-aimless tour of the Native American rooms, and abandoned him. Hands in pockets, Keith strolled along the inner wall of the museum toward a down staircase.

Maybe before technology humankind knew more about the mystical side of life, but the industrial revolution had changed things. He'd read about a theory that suggested that people stopped believing in fairies after machines were invented that spun thread or made shoes, because those tasks were no longer such hard work. Keith knew better. Humanity was just ignoring its closest neighbors. He smiled, a little smugly.

His new skill made the world look subtly different to him. His expanded perception gave him insights into other cultures in ways he never dreamed of. He was grateful to his little friends for making it possible. Running errands like this was one of the very minor ways he had to show thanks.

The Egyptian rooms were an unexpected ordeal. Definitely the ancient kingdom had a handle on the unseen energies. Ever since he was a kid, the Field Museum displays of mummies and sarcophagi had given him a feeling of exciting and incomprehensible danger, like the chilling sensation aroused by hearing really good ghost stories around campfires, and now he knew why. Every mummy in the glass cases had a creepingly terrifying pseudopod of light coming from it that reached out to him, questing snakelike to investigate him, and as he shrank back from its touch, fell away. It seemed as if each mummy was looking for someone, someone particular—maybe the people who had defiled the tombs where they had once been buried—but was not interested in anyone else.

The keen thrill of terror made him shiver, wondering if he was in for the same kind of retribution for snooping through the remains of the Celtic villagers in Scotland. No, there'd been no sensation of evil or anger there. The priests and embalmers of Egypt had deliberately put a malign influence that reached out long after the body was inert matter, to revenge the departed Pharaohs on the despoilers of their graves.

Lessons in countering the Little Folks' talent for misdirection brought his attention obliquely to an unmarked steel door at the end of the corridor at the opposite end of the hall from the exhibits. It had been painted the same color as the walls to make it unobtrusive. From the musty smell wafting gently underneath it, Keith guessed that the corridor beyond probably led to the archives and storage rooms.

The pulse he was following grew stronger and stronger the closer he got. He was more and more convinced that it was the Scottish comb he was tracing. It *was* still in the museum.

No security guards were in sight, but it wouldn't hurt to use a little misdirection of his own. After a moment of concentration, he observed happily that none of the museum visitors looked directly at him any more. Under cover of a large crowd heading for the stairs, Keith slipped in the door, and closed it gently behind him.

He'd never been 'behind the scenes' in the museum before. It made him feel a little uneasy as if now he'd see the fakery and animatronics that made the place run. Everything remained blessedly if not refreshingly real. The storage rooms at the end of the corridor reminded him strongly of the library stacks at college. They consisted of numbered shelves along narrow aisles, but instead of holding books they held antiquities of every description, smelling of spice, dust, and time. There wasn't much light, but it was sufficient to navigate by, and besides, he wouldn't need to see the comb with his normal vision to find it.

Echoing eerily down the clay-scented corridor came the voice of the public address system. "The museum is now closed. Will you please make your way immediately to the exits. Thank you for visiting the Field Museum." That was it. Keith was now on the premises illicitly. He hoped he could get to the comb and get out of the building without causing a fuss.

The sensation that he was being watched by someone smiling made him turn slowly around to see who was there. He jumped in surprise. The empty eyeholes of a mask from the South Pacific stared at him blankly, the shards of polished shell, jade, and bone set into its face gleaming softly like milky jewels.

Hand on his chest, Keith leaned against the shelf opposite while his heart stopped pounding basso staccato.

"Whew," he whispered.

As it had been in the outer museum, there were plenty of artifacts that provided their own illumination. Keith was able to pass most of them by without even looking at them.

The feeling that the comb was very near persisted. On the other side of the second huge room of shelves were several small doors. Offices, Keith guessed.

A yawn erupted suddenly. He stifled it with difficulty. Using his second sight so much was making him tired. He hoped his energy would last until he solved his mystery and got out of the museum. He wasn't so nimble at making excuses when his wits were fuddled.

The first few offices were dark. Each was small, crammed full in every available corner and on every flat surface with books, papers, small artifacts, stones, and assorted impedimenta. A quick glance into each was enough to tell Keith that what he sought wasn't there. Besides, the yearning cry of the Scottish artifact was still up ahead.

The tingly glow summoned him to the last room on the left. It was larger than the other offices, with an extra door standing ajar in the right hand wall. Beyond the door, Keith could hear someone with an English accent and pedantic cadence lecturing. Good. If everyone was occupied, no one would notice him while he investigated.

To his great relief, the comb was in the glass case across from the inner door. The moment he came around the corner he was washed with a sensation of relief and comfort like meeting an old friend. Whatever had been the purpose of its magical enhancement in the Bronze Age, it gave off a soothing radiation that calmed its possessor or anyone else in close proximity. Not a bad survival trait for something so fragile.

Keith stood back to think, eying the case. It was in plain sight, with no attempt to disguise it or its contents, so there was no question that the comb was down here deliberately, with the blessing and knowledge of the museum. He wondered why the Little Folk were concerned about it.

Maybe their real reason for sending him was feedback from the artifact next to the comb, which was putting out a louder and more insistent signal. It was a thumb-sized, baked clay figurine, made to be strung on a necklace, shaped like a stylized human child except for—Keith had to lean down closely to make certain—the pointed ears.

"Oh, my God," Keith breathed. He wondered who else was aware of the charm's special characteristics, and what conclusions they'd drawn from it. He wasn't sure why the Folk were worried that they might be at risk for discovery from the display of a Bronze age clay fetish in Chicago. Maybe it was something that belonged to them that got lost. Well, if that was the case, he was going to make sure they got it back. But how to 'liberate' it? He hunkered down in front of the glass door to see if there were alarm wires or anything that would go off when he opened it. He put his hands flat against one of the panes and started to slide it slowly leftward.

Suddenly, the voices behind him got louder, and the door at his back was flung open. Keith turned around, blinking with terror at the knees of a group of people mostly wearing gray suits or neutral skirts; all except for the one at their head, an adult human male who was at eye level with Keith. Professor Parker, researcher and lecturer, was a dwarf.

"As I live and breathe, Keith Doyle!" exclaimed Parker, coming forward with his sailor's gait. He extended a cordial hand to Keith. "How very nice to see you! This *is* an unexpected pleasure."

"Professor," Keith said weakly, putting out his own hand.

Parker shook it vigorously. "Well, well, well, what have you been doing with yourself?"

"Oh," Keith replied, smiling up at the small researcher's companions. They didn't seem as pleased to see him as Parker was. He glanced back. His handprints were clearly visible on the front of the display case. "Uh, hot air ballooning. Things like that."

Parker's face lit up with childlike delight. "Really? Very different from the last time I saw you, young man. Above the ground is undoubtedly better for you than below it, eh?" Parker chuckled heartily. Keith joined in, sounding like a sick engine valve.

"Well, Keith Doyle, what a businesslike dash you cut!" The small professor looked him up and down. Keith was suddenly acutely aware of the fashionable short haircut he wore, and that he hadn't changed out of the white button-down shirt with the fatuous patterned suspenders holding up his trousers he'd worn to the office that day. The outfit looked silly next to the conservative autumn-weight gray suits on all the men in the room. Suddenly aware also that there were a lot of them, and some austerely dressed women, too. Though Parker was happy to see him, he'd obviously interrupted a presentation of some kind.

"Uh, thanks."

"And how is my good friend Professor Alfheim? Although it is not uncommon for people our size to have children *your* size, you're not really his son, are you?" Parker asked conspiratorially.

"No, sir," Keith admitted, a little shamefacedly, remembering the subterfuge the Master had employed to have an excuse others would accept why he was helping Keith. "But we are distantly related. There was a good reason why he said so, really."

"Ah." Parker nodded. "I rather thought so. There is a fairly strong resemblance. And how is your cousin Holl?"

"Married," Keith said, with a grin. "And…"

"What? Surely not. He's just a boy. Must be about sixteen by now, what?"

Keith backpedaled furiously, clamping his mouth closed on the phrase 'and they have a baby girl.' "I mean as good as married. He's got a girlfriend, Maura. They're really serious about each other."

He dug into his back pocket for his wallet and pulled out a picture he'd taken of the two of them at the wedding supper wearing their flower wreaths. Keith was certain those hid the points of their ears, but there wasn't time to check before Parker seized the picture and admired it.

"Very pretty. Very pretty. What interesting clothes. Lovely embroidery. Almost medieval. Could it be some kind of Renaissance Festival?"

"Uh, kind of," Keith said weakly.

"What a lot of varied interests you American youths have. I hope you haven't lost interest in the study of past cultures. I thought you showed a lot of promise. Young Matthew is doing very well, by the way. Came to admire your addition to the display, did you? With your contributions in?"

"Well, yeah," Keith said, struggling to turn the conversation his way. He pointed at the case behind him. "You know, Dr. Alfheim would really like to see that little figure. That's really unusual. That kind of thing is really his specialty. Really." He was suddenly aware of how silly he sounded, and swallowed. Parker didn't appear to notice.

"Forgive me, Professor," one of the curators interrupted. "But may we get on with the lecture?"

"Oh, yes, forgive me. Forget my own head, that's what I'll do," Parker said, apologetically, smacking a hand to the side of his head. "Ladies and gentlemen, this is the young man who discovered the comb, by the way. He was one of my assistants that summer. And what a fruitful summer it was, I must add."

"So we are finding out," the curator said, pointedly. Parker took the cue a trifle sheepishly, and returned his attention to Keith.

"It was very nice seeing you, Keith. Please give my best to Dr. Alfheim. I hope to see him some time soon. Perhaps we can all have a little time together then. I would be delighted to show him the clay pendant and give him all the details of its discovery. Oh, and you, too," he added.

It was a dismissal. Keith had no choice but to accede. He stood up, feeling awkward to be taller than the professor. Parker didn't appear to notice. "Uh, I'll tell him."

Keith took another glance at the glass case. The small clay figure continued its insistent psychic wail, so insistent that it made him wonder if he could use the elves' invisibility-avoidance technique to divert everyone's attention away while he took it out, but with another glance at the curator, Keith saw that his chances of staying in that room would only have been increased if he was in another glass case, preferably stuffed and mounted.

"Um, could I stay and hear the lecture?" he asked, hopefully.

Chapter Seven

The same security guard who'd been following him around was summoned to escort Keith out of the building. Keith thought that the guard was enjoying himself just a little too much, hustling him by the back of the neck and one arm through the echoingly empty chambers to the front door. With a thrust reminiscent of a garbage collector shooting a barrelful of trash into the back of his truck, the guard shoved Keith out into the warm autumn night.

Keith stumbled on the uneven threshold and rolled down a handful of stairs before he came to a halt on a landing. He rose to his feet and brushed himself off as the heavy bronze doors boomed shut above him.

At least, Keith consoled his bruised dignity, the comb was safe. He spent the walk to his car and the long drive home thinking up one plot after another for getting the little clay charm out of the museum without being detected. He had to let the Little Folk know that the original treasure was okay, and that the distress call they must have sensed was coming from something entirely new.

Although it was very late when he telephoned the farm, the other end was picked up on the first ring.

"Hello?" Catra's voice said, anxiously hollow.

"Hi, it's Keith. Mission accomplished. The mystery is solved. You've got nothing to worry about," he said, and it was on the tip of his tongue to tell her about the little female clay figurine when she interrupted him.

"Wonderful! Then you mean she's with you? Oh, I'm so glad, you cannot imagine. How did she get there? Why didn't you call us at once when she turned up?"

"You knew about it? Yeah, Parker had it himself," Keith said, remembering his embarrassment at blundering into the austere classroom in the museum basement. "He was using it for a lecture. I interrupted his presentation to the other researchers at the museum. He says 'hi' to the Master. If he wants to come up and see the exhibit, I can take him up this weekend. I'm free." Catra's words suddenly penetrated his consciousness, and he paused to let the outpouring of relief, unusual for the coolheaded Archivist, catch up with him. He blinked. "Who?" he demanded. "Which she? Who's supposed to have turned up?"

"Dola," Catra said pleadingly. "She's gone missing, and Holl's babe with her."

"What?" Keith yelped. Jeff and Keith's youngest sister turned their heads away from the television to stare at him. He lowered his voice at once. "When did it happen? And how?"

Catra sounded ready to burst into tears. The words poured out in a tumult. "Dola was caring for the babe until dinner time. She didn't turn up to do her chores, and she wasn't in the cottage when Maura went back looking for them. Holl and Maura are half mad with fear," Catra said, finally getting the sense that she and Keith had been talking at cross-purposes but were on the same wavelength at last. She explained what had happened, and what action the Folk had taken so far. "Tay's ready to call up the Wild Hunt!"

Keith was horrified. "Oh, my God, no! Did you call Ludmilla?"

"The first thing we thought of," Catra said, "and we've called upon Diane, who telephoned all the other Big Folk. With the evening's delay while we were waiting to hear from you, there would have been plenty of time for Dola to reach the Midwestern campus..." Her voice trailed off, leaving the phrase "if she was able," unspoken but understood between them. "All know the way to Ludmilla's apartment."

"I'm sure sorry I didn't understand," Keith said. "I should have waited until your line was clear to find out what your message meant, 'look on the front page of the newspaper.'"

"No harm done, Keith Doyle," Catra said. "No further harm done, that is. It's my fault. I was so upset I forgot you'd be looking at another paper. Our local had a story about a kidnapped child."

"Look, I'll get down there right away—No, I can't," he said, tearing at his hair despairingly. "I've got to go to work. What can I do?"

"Stay there, for now. You must not toss aside your responsibilities. There are plenty of us here. Tell us what to do."

"Why do you think she's been kidnapped?" he asked.

Catra explained quickly about the Big Folk footprints, and the marks of truck tires.

"Okay," Keith said, thinking quickly. "If someone grabbed her, there'll be a ransom demand. That'll mean a call or a note. They'll probably tell you they don't want interference from the cops, but you can't call the police anyway." The idea passed through his mind of all the pictures of lost kids on the back of milk cartons, and the horrible things he had heard that sometimes happened to them. He'd seen too many true-life crime programs on television. Not to his little pet, Dola, and Holl's baby—it just couldn't happen.

Catra had a practical nature, and she read more newspapers than most of her Folk. She must have guessed what was going through his mind. "Aye," she agreed, speaking carefully. He knew then that there were people in the room around her. "We'll have a watch put on the telephone to wait for a call and trace its source when it comes."

"Good," Keith said. "Gather up all the clues you can as to who might have taken her away. You want all the, er, *forensic* evidence you can find. The Farm is pretty well sheltered. Whoever did it was there on purpose."

"I'd thought of that," Catra said grimly. "And we're not certain as to why. In the meantime, should we search?"

"You bet," Keith said. "If you can do it without being observed."

"It's what we're best at, Keith Doyle, going unobserved. We'll do anything not to endanger the children."

"Let me know what's going on," he said. Keith hung up and sat staring at the phone. For once, he was at a loss for what to do, and realized there was nothing immediate he *could* do. The real world had no business impinging on his friends. For a moment, he wished he'd never discovered them underneath the college library. It was better for them when they were safely mythological. He felt helpless, and he hated feeling helpless.

He picked up the receiver and dialed Diane's number. If he couldn't be there in person, he could at least help coordinate the search.

Mona Gilbreth glared at her employees. Pilton looked, as usual, slightly bemused. He was concentrating hard on keeping his eyes fixed on hers, as if enlightenment could be found through direct eye contact. Jake studied the floor. He seemed embarrassed. Mona didn't care about his feelings. She was so angry she didn't know what to yell about first.

"You two have really dumped me in it this time. Why did you bring those kids back here? What do I want with two little kids? I told you to dump that truck and get back here for the next load. Now their folks will be on the lookout for us. You've involved this company in a felony, and for what?"

"She was watching us dump the tankload in that sumphole," Williamson said defensively. "We couldn't tell what she'd seen, or how much she understood. She ran away, and we ran after her, and it just snowballed."

"Let me tell you about snowballs," Mona said angrily, poking a finger close to his eye. His gaze shifted nervously back and forth between her sharp red nail and her face. "What do you think this is going to do to my political career? Can you see the headline? 'Local business owner kidnaps two local children in waste dumping scandal'? How can we return them, just like that, and tell the parents, oh, it was just a mistake?"

"I dunno, Ma'am."

"This girl's uncanny," Pilton said, drawing his two superiors' attention away from their quarrel. "There's something strange about her. I think she's a fairy or something like that."

"She ain't no fairy," Williamson said, rolling his eyes. "Got no wings, Grant."

"Well, she's real small, and what about them ears?" Pilton wanted to know.

Williamson tried to explain. "It's a mutation, like those people in Spain who have ten fingers."

Pilton checked. "*I* got ten fingers."

"On each hand!"

Pilton was fascinated and delighted. "Weird!"

"If we've finished with the natural history lesson?" Mona asked, with heavy sarcasm. "You keep an eye on her while I think what to do. Where are they?"

"I shut them in one of the offices in the back. It's only got a grille vent for a window. She can't get out that way."

Dola stared as the door slammed shut behind them. There was only one source of air and light in the room, and it was high and small. If she'd had only herself to think of, she'd have been through the frame and out, running for the nearest patch of green no matter how much skin it cost her. Beyond the room's edge, though, she could sense nothing but a sort of organic horror. The miasma tainted the intangible world as well as the purely physical. If her mind could wrinkle its nose, it would have. The comfortable sense of her family and people was hidden far behind the awful curtain. She was in the midst of an industrial complex of huge metal cylinders and bolted-together pipes all emitting hollow and sinister noises.

Asrai whimpered softly in the cold room. It had been a hard time and a frightening ride for the infant for all the child had ridden in a car once before. She was hungry. Dola knew that she had reached the end of her minute patience, and would be giving forth with a fierce and terrible yell at any time. Mother was nowhere nearby, and she doubted these two big men would let them go merely to fulfill the needs of a three-months infant.

As she had feared, the storm soon broke. Asrai started sobbing, catching her breath in short gasps. When Dola picked her up over her shoulder, Asrai let out with one of her famous banshee yells and began to shriek. Dola jogged her gently, talking in a smooth mur-mur, and hoped that one day her ear would cease ringing.

"Come on, then, it isn't so bad," Dola crooned. "You'll dine soon, I promise you, if I have to cut my own veins for you. Calm, little one, please." She noticed an edge of panic in her own voice, and sought to calm herself. "Easy, Asrai. I love you. None will hurt you."

The door opened.

"Well, and not before time," Dola said. She glared at the men who regarded her from the doorway. They glanced impassively back. She held the baby up. "Her mother will be worried about her. We must go back."

Disturbed, Asrai's mournful mutterings grew louder. Her small face and the tips of her ears began to redden. The two men looked at each other and exchanged regretful glances, but when they turned back to her, had once more lost all expression. Dola's temper flared.

"Can't you see she's frightened and hungry?" she asked them. "Take us home! She's got to be fed. A mite like this has little time."

That worried them. They must never have thought a baby could starve to death in the arms of someone caring for her. Skinny looked uncomfortable.

"We can't," he said. "The boss lady said we have to keep you here."

Dola stood up and stamped her foot. The movement startled the baby, who whimpered louder. To those who knew Asrai, it was a warning signal.

"Then get her food, if you won't let her back to her mother!" As if on cue, Asrai let out another siren wail. Both of the men jumped, just as if they were some of the Folk who had no children of their own. In unison, they turned and fled into the echoing hallway, but maintaining enough presence of mind, Dola regretted, to shut and lock the door behind them.

The wait for milk was endless. Dola had to use every trick she had ever learned to distract Asrai from the growing void in her small stomach. Her throat was dry from singing endless nursery rhymes and chanting the nonsense verses that babies didn't understand but loved because of the cadences. She joggled Asrai on her shoulder, and walked around the room, trying to amuse her by showing her Big Person things: the huge, oversized desk, the filing cabinet, the tall locker with its handle as high off the ground as Dola's head, the small washroom with toilet and sink and mirror. All those things were made with a great deal of metal in or about them, and served to make them both more uncomfortable. Dola winced as Asrai continued to shriek. The noise gathered itself in the tons of cold steel around them, and made it sing a high, frightening note that only made things worse.

She boosted herself up into the room's only chair, a petal-shaped extrusion of orange plastic with four tall spindly legs too high to let her feet touch the floor. Its cup-shaped bottom made it difficult to get leverage to rock the baby, but she managed a back and forth motion that soothed Asrai from her screaming rage into unhappy hiccups. By the time the Big Folk arrived with feeding supplies, Dola felt completely worn out, but at least Asrai was quiet.

Jake watched her from the door. She glanced at him distrustfully. The thin man came closer, and handed her a tall can, a plastic bottle, and rubber nipples which would have been good for feeding the cow. Dola held up the can to him.

"What is this?"

He seemed surprised she asked. "Formula. It's a substitute for mother's milk."

Dola tested the temperature of the can against her cheek. "I can't feed her this. It's cold."

The two men conferred and the skinny one left. He came back with a device Dola recognized as a coffee maker. There had been one in the staff room in the Library.

She watched closely as Skinny poured water into the screened top, and waited for it to dribble out into the glass carafe. Skinny broke open the top of the can with an attachment on his pocket knife, and filled the bottle partway, then put it in the steaming jug of water. While it was heating, Dola dealt with the delivery system. The bottle's capacity would have fed the child for days, but the nipple simply wouldn't fit into her small mouth. It would have to be adjusted.

Dola, shaking her head at the thoughtlessness of Big Folk, began to think about the lessons she'd been learning lately with others of her age group: how to enhance and move *with* the substance of what one sought to alter. She measured it. The broad end needed to remain intact so that it would fit between the plastic collar and the bottle top. In her hand she squeezed the rubber bulb, willing it smaller and smaller. Skinny shook his head when he realized what she was doing.

"Hey, that won't help. When you let go it'll just bounce back to its normal shape."

"No, it won't," Dola said. She opened her hand, and the altered nipple lay there, elongated to the shape of a stubby pencil.

"You must be strong," the man said, impressed.

"A trick my father taught me," Dola said, offhand. Let the Big Person think it was strength. He already suspected something of the truth about her. The less he knew for certain the better. The other man didn't believe what he saw, and that was all to the good. She did not want them thinking there was something uncanny about Hollow Tree Farm that bore closer investigation.

A dab of formula on the wrist, and she knew that it was drinking temperature. Fishing the bottle out of the coffeepot, she assembled the bottle and offered it to the weeping child. Asrai refused it. She looked at the men and at Dola and sobbed weakly. Dola was furious.

"Well, you're scaring her!" she said fiercely. "Go off, then. I'm not going anywhere. Do you think we can sneak through keyholes?"

They went. Dola had figured out what was wrong, and wanted privacy in which to resolve the problem. This was the first meal of her life Asrai was not to receive from her mother.

Glancing over her shoulder at the door to make certain the men weren't peeking in, Dola took the old gauze square out of her pocket and put it over her head. Willing it with her strongest thoughts, she caused Maura's face to superimpose over hers. Illusions were easy. The next part was hard. She used the enhancement to make her voice like Maura's as well.

"Hush, now, little love," she whispered. The baby stopped crying, alert, and looked up at Dola's face in surprise. "Well, are you hungry?" She put her arm behind Asrai's back and helped her reach for the artificial nipple. She held the bottle close to her chest to simulate the placement of Maura's breast. Asrai latched onto it eagerly and began to suck. She made a little face and put out her tongue, rejecting it.

"Oh, come," Dola/Maura forced a chuckle, though she was worried through that the unnatural mock-milk might do the child harm. "That's no way to act. Feed, little one, then you shall sleep."

Mollified, the baby began to suckle, desperately at first, then slowing down. She drank half the bottle of formula, an incredible amount. Dola was relieved to watch the heavy-lidded eyes droop halfway, then close entirely.

"Oh, a blessing, a blessing," Dola whispered, wiping the milky lips and kissing the child on the head through her veil.

The door opened behind her. Dola had just enough time to snatch the translucent cloth from her face before her captors could see.

"You're good with her," Skinny said in a very quiet, respectful tone.

Dola straightened her shoulders with some pride. "And so I should be, having helped with her care since her birth."

"I've got two kids of my own," Skinny offered.

"And what would you think, if someone carried one of them off as you have done," Dola said, her eyes filling with tears. She was too proud to let them hear her voice quaver, but she was a child too.

"I brung you something else," Skinny said. The boxes he set down on the desk next to her were decorated with pictures of a plump, golden haired baby, and were marked 'disposable diapers.'

"If she's had a bottle, you'll want this next."

"Well! Logic!" Dola exclaimed, gratefully. She raised an eyebrow at the man. "Thank you," she said, bobbing her head. Skinny seemed embarrassed but pleased.

He pulled a wadded pad out of the first box. They both saw immediately it was too big; it would have fit Dola herself. Skinny took a pad from the second box. It was about twice too big, but Dola could cut it in half lengthwise with the scissors from her chatelaine.

There was another box, made of thick blue plastic. "Cleaning cloths." Skinny pried open the half-lid and showed her one. It stank of some Big Person chemical antiseptic that made Dola cough.

"It's not a cloth, it's some kind of paper," she said, after a close look. "What a dreadful wasteful people you are, first diapers meant to be thrown away, then cloths that aren't really cloth."

The man shook his head, crouching beside her. "I suppose you're one of those green people," he said, amused.

"No, we're not," Dola said, with spirit. "That's a myth."

Skinny paused, as if about to deliver himself of a difficult query. "Do you grant wishes or something?"

"And what if I did?" Dola asked. "Would I do anything for those who've imprisoned me against my will, and endangered my charge?"

"I'll make things nice for you," the skinny man said. He rose and left the room.

Mona sat at her desk with her head in her hands, going over alternate wording for the apology she was going to have to make to those children's parents.

"I'm so sorry we accidentally kidnapped your daughter," she recited bitterly, practicing the sound of it. She shook her head. It wasn't going to be easy no matter how she phrased it. She was embarrassed. When every single instance of public exposure counted, this was going to be a huge demerit. Except for their problems with waste disposal, she had done all the right things to keep the public on her side. She had been responsible for beginning a town-wide recycling program for plastics. All the Gilbreth office stationery was made of recycled paper. Even the wooden desk in her office was made of wood from a replanted forest. That girl and baby were innocent bystanders, snatched up by her employees in the midst of an illegal act. Could she apologize to the parents and ask them not to inquire into what her men were doing there on their property?

Mona felt her ire rousing. Yes, that was right. This girl came from Hollow Tree Farm. They were already trying to ruin her reputation in the community. Instead of ashamed, she was getting angry.

"Miz Gilbreth," Pilton inquired, tapping on the door. "Are we gonna take the kids back?"

Mona looked up at him sharply. "Grant, go back and ask that girl if she's any relation to H. Doyle."

"Yes, ma'am," he said, backing out of the office obediently.

Pilton was back in a moment, looking more bemused than usual. "Miz Gilbreth, she says he's her uncle."

"My God!" she cried, throwing her head back. "I can't eat crow to him! It's the end of my career!"

Headlines danced before her eyes, worse than the ones she'd imagined before. She had to think. The party national committee must never, never get to hear of this incident. Maybe she could negotiate with the man. If the Doyles agreed it was all a mistake, and would promise not to press charges, she could still get out of this with a whole skin and an intact political career.

"Well, we can't have her going back to him and saying we maltreated her," Mona said, half to herself. "We just can't let her go yet."

Pilton looked pleased. "I was just gonna ask you, ma'am, it's kind of cold in that office. If she's going to stay a while I thought I'd go home and bring her my daughter's sleeping bag. Would that be okay with you?"

"Give them anything they want," Mona snapped.

Pilton grunted under the weight of the cardboard carton he was carrying. He shifted it to rest between his hip and the wall as he reached into his pocket for the key to the office, kicked open the door, and backed into the room.

The little girl was just where she'd been sitting when he'd left.

"I got some nice things for you," he said. She looked up at him with dull eyes. The baby was sleeping on her lap. It was a cute little thing; had the same kind of ears the girl did. He wondered if Jake was right, and the shape was just a mutation like her size. Maybe their folks had been drinking the water that was tainted with the runoff from the factory. Pilton himself had seen what too much of that nitrogen feed could do to plants: just think what effect it might have on animals and people. And maybe he was right, and they'd captured a real live fairy girl.

"Here's a sleeping bag for you. It's my daughter's, but she won't need it back right away. It's just been washed, so it smells really good." He held up the quilted bag. Dola glanced at it, put her nose in the air and turned away again.

"Got a few toys for you and the baby. Couple of books and magazines," he showed her colorful digest-sized periodicals. Dola tried not to look interested even though she'd never seen those titles before. "I brought you a portable TV, too. The reception's okay. Here's a TV guide. You want to try it out?"

Dola was very interested in trying the television, and in wrapping herself up in the warm-looking coverlet, but she didn't want to seem too eager to accept his offerings. She hadn't missed the query about her relation to Holl. It couldn't be mere accident that the very people who were ruining their water supply were the same ones who had kidnapped her in their haste. They must be very uneasy. Skinny wanted so badly to make friends, but did she dare to appear vulnerable? He and the other man were responsible for bringing her here against her will. She had the sudden urge to make him pay dearly for her incarceration.

"All right," she said, hopping down from the chair. The seat was warm where her bottom had rested, so she set Asrai down there. Skinny plugged the set in and unrolled a long wire from the top to the metal window frame, where he hooked it in place.

"Got no antenna," he said. Dola watched carefully as he switched it on. A small dot appeared in the center of the screen, unfolding outward toward the boundaries until the picture could be distinguished. The sound warmed up just as slowly. She disliked the electronic hum behind the music and voices. Dola clapped her hands over her ears as the squeal grew louder and began to eat into her consciousness. On the chair, Asrai began to mutter and squirm in her sleep.

"For the love of nature, turn it off!" Dola exclaimed. Skinny jumped for the controls and switched the set off. "Take it away. It's so noisy I'd never enjoy a minute of it with all the terrible squeals and hums it makes."

"I thought you'd like it," he said, hurt. "Look, here's a program guide, and everything." He put the magazine down on the desk and pushed it toward her. "My kids like the cartoons in the morning."

"I don't watch cartoons," Dola said haughtily.

Skinny nodded knowingly, evidently remembering that she was something special. "I guess you don't," he said. He unplugged the set. "I'll take it home."

"No, leave it," Dola said, suddenly curious what Big children's entertainment was like. Hollow Tree had no television, and the sets at the library were not attached to antenna. All she had ever seen on them were educational tapes.

"Can I get you something to eat?" Skinny asked.

Dola assessed the empty feeling in her stomach and judged that her pride wouldn't hold out against a night of abstinence. "Yes," she said. She thought longingly of a treat that was forbidden at home by her Conservative relatives, and impetuously burst out, "Pizza!"

"Sure," Skinny said, and started out the door.

"And it can't be just any pizza," she said, imperiously leveling a finger at him. "It must be in a proper box!"

"Gotcha," he said, shrugging into his coat.

Dola sat by herself watching the television when she heard the man coming back. Hastily, she switched it off, but was privately glad to do so. The evening news was scary. She was glad to be rid of it. No wonder the elders didn't let Keith Doyle bring them a television to keep! It was almost enough to make one fear living in the world.

Skinny's footsteps came all the way to the door, and stopped while keys jingled and entered the lock.

"Here you go!" he said, putting a large, flat box down on the table. "I brought you some soda, too."

Dola approached the box and gazed at it avidly. She only got pizza if Keith Doyle or one of their other Big friends was visiting. Great-gran Keva disliked it because the toppings hid the beauties of her prized bread, and most of the other elders hated it because it was so messy. Dola, like her friends Borget and Moira, loved it, and not just because Keith Doyle did, although that added to its attraction. The label attached to the box gave her pause at first. She sniffed carefully at the huge pizza, and tasted a bite with even greater care. She tried a larger bite of pizza, taking in a small, round slice of a green vegetable. It was very hot, but there was no doubt that it was fresh.

"Why is it called garbage pizza when all the ingredients are un-spoiled?" she asked.

Skinny grinned, still watching her with open curiosity. "That's because they just dump tons of stuff on top of it. It's good. You like cola or lemon-lime?" He proffered two bottles with the tops twisted off.

Dola sampled from one, then the other. Both contained fizzy drinks, the kind the Big Folk liked. She made a face. If this was the ale that custom demanded be served alongside pizza, she'd drink it, but it was a punishment in itself—gassy and without substance.

"I'd rather have juice," she said, and eyed Skinny to see if he'd obey her.

He did. He went away and came back with orange juice, then went away again for freshly squeezed juice when Dola complained about the canned variety. She accorded him imperial nods instead of voicing her thanks, but he didn't seem to find her behavior out of the ordinary, since he thought she was some kind of supernatu-ral being.

The pizza was very good, but Dola felt a little guilty enjoying it so much. She was being indulged more thoroughly because she was kidnapped than on the most sumptuous birthday she had ever had. It was turning out to be one of the best things that could have happened to her. She refused to think of what might happen to her hereafter, but her mother would be so glad to see her come home she'd surely forgive.

By now there were few other noises in the great buildings around them. Occasionally she heard the slow footsteps of a heavy man passed by under the window. It was beginning to impinge upon Dola that unless she could cudgel her wits into coming up with a plan she was going to have to sleep in this room, that she couldn't leave. One of her cousins was wise about locks, and could undo anything Big Folk could do up, but Dola's particular talent was for illusion. She could make the door seem to vanish, but such a vision wasn't good enough to allow her to pass into the hallway beyond.

She was getting sleepy, and wagered that Skinny's wits were becoming muddled with exhaustion, too. Perhaps now was the time to try and make her escape. It was worth a try to see if he could be persuaded by the avoidance charm to miss seeing her, at least until she could sneak past him and away.

Concentrating on the TV program book, she willed the space around its surface to become slick so that all glances would slide immediately off toward something else. When she was having trouble keeping her eyes on it herself, she turned to Skinny.

"Where has that TV book gone?" she asked pleasantly, dandling the baby in her lap.

Skinny looked at the top of the desk, missing the book completely, and cast around. "Well, it was just right here," he said. "I'll find it for you. Maybe it just slid off the desk." He started searching around, even picking up the sleeping bag and shaking it out. He picked up the pizza box and looked underneath, almost touching it when he put the box down. Dola nearly laughed. Slowly, surreptitiously, she started applying the technique to herself and Asrai.

Skinny, eager to please, was all but turning the office inside out in search of the book.

"Well, I know it was here a minute ago," he said, then turned around just as Dola sealed off the enhancement around herself. "Hey, little girl, where'd you go? Hey! This isn't funny. Don't hide on me. Come out this minute!"

Now he was actively searching the room. Dola had to keep dodging around to keep him from touching her. If once he made physical contact no amount of sight-avoidance would work to preserve the illusion.

A key jingled in the lock. Her opportunity was nearly there. Dola gathered herself for the dash. The door opened, and Jake stood in the doorway, a gun in his hand.

"What are you making all that noise for?" he demanded.

Skinny turned around, arms flailing and eyes wild. "She's gone! She just disappeared again, like she did this afternoon. She got away!"

"Crap. The door's been closed the whole time, right? Then she has to be in here somewhere." Jake said. Dola crept up by him, waiting for him to move into the room to help Skinny search. He cocked the gun and held it up by his head. She stopped, aghast.

"Okay, kid," he said, looking around at the empty air. "You come out right now or I'll start blasting everything in this room. You hear me? You show your face right *now* or you're gonna have a bullet your gut!"

Swallowing, Dola went back by the tall locker and removed the avoidance charm. She stepped out, holding the baby protectively with her arms covering as much of her little back as she could. Incredibly, Asrai had slept through all the shouting.

"There," Jake said, "you see? She's still here. And she'd better still be here in the morning," he thundered threateningly down on her. "You got me?" Timidly, Dola nodded. "Good. Come on, Grant. You better get home. Your wife called looking for you."

"Right. Good night, little girl," Skinny said, with a friendly smile for her.

The door boomed shut and locked tight. Dola stood staring at it for a moment, feeling more lonely and scared than ever.

Chapter Eight

Keith spent the next day worrying and wondering about Dola and
Asrai, so much that he didn't hear what Paul Meier was telling him
until the second time through.

"I said, Judge Yeast likes your idea. They're crazy about it, in
fact," Meier said, gleefully. "The clients don't mind that you're an
amateur. They said you gotta get your creative people from somewhere—they don't drop out of the clouds, you know. So your names
are on the layout."

Keith let the realization dawn with a sort of incredulous joy. A
whoop wound its way up from the deepest part of his insides, until
it burst out in a deafening crow of triumph. "Yahoo!" Dorothy
beamed, and the end of her pencil danced a happy rhythm.

"What did they like so much?" Brendan asked. He looked
miffed, but was trying to pretend it didn't matter. "I thought it
was stupid."

"Anthropomorphism," Paul replied, pronouncing each syllable
with satisfied emphasis. "The client thought it brought to mind the
Pillsbury Dough Boy and the Parkay margarine tubs all in one. No
other yeast uses a character, and yet yeast is *the* ingredient in breads
that makes it all happen. What with the growing surge in home baking, this is a big deal. They liked the connotation that the package's a
real judge, not just named for the Judge Company. It suggests that
it's a wise choice for bakers. They want to see a whole campaign
based on it."

"Great!" Keith said, his eyes aglow.

"Glad to hear you're happy about it," Meier said, with a sar-
donic tilt to his head. "Now here comes the work. You and Dorothy get to work on ideation. I want some more suggestions. You're
now working parallel with the pro team. I expect you to come up
with more good stuff than they do. Show me some ideas tomorrow." Dorothy perked up and nodded vigorously at Keith.

"Uh, Paul," Keith said, circling around the table and taking the
supervisor aside confidentially, "could I maybe spend tomorrow doing some field research on say, one of PDQ's downstate clients? I've
just got to get down to the Midwestern campus. It's an emergency."

"Problem with your girlfriend?" Meier asked, suddenly skeptical.

"No!" Keith exclaimed, and lowered his voice to a whisper. "It's something else. It's really important, Paul. I wouldn't ask for any other reason. Would it be impossible to wait the brainstorm session just one day?"

Meier sighed, but lifted his shoulders helplessly. "Kid, this is a tough biz. All right. One day. Down by Midwestern, huh? You can go talk to Gilbreth Feed and Fertilizer, get a feel for what they're up to. They'll like that. We don't usually pay house calls."

"Gilbreth? In Flyspeck?"

"You know them?"

"Sure do," Keith said, with emphasis. Meier gave him a curious look.

"Good. I'll give you a letter of introduction. You can go and get a feel for what they're up to. Ask questions. Look around. Maybe it'll give you some ideas for their account."

Keith already had an idea of what Gilbreth was up to, namely polluting on a large scale and hiding their tracks, but he agreed to visit the factory. An in-depth visit might provide him with some good dirt for the Folk to use in their next letter to the editor.

He smiled at Paul. "I promise I'll take a really close look at everything that's going on at Gilbreth."

Late that night, the telephone on the kitchen wall rang at Hollow Tree. The circle of Folk gathered around it glanced sidelong at one another, rolling the whites of their eyes like frightened horses. Even Holl hesitated, wondering what to do. Marcy looked at all of them, then snatched up the handset.

"Hello?" she said. She turned to Holl, and with a significant look handed him the receiver. The other Folk tensed.

"Hello?" he said. "Yes, this is…Mr. Doyle."

The voice at the other end was male, deep and gravelly. "The girl and the baby are safe. They're healthy—I mean okay."

Holl's eyes narrowed, and the others drew closer around him. He signaled wildly with one arm for them to attempt the trace. The circle drew closer, and joined hands. Some of them closed their eyes; others stared fixedly at Holl and the telephone. Marcy stood outside the circle wringing her hands anxiously.

"I see," Holl said, trying to keep his voice from cracking. "Am I to assume that since you've not brought them to the telephone that there is a problem?"

"It was a mistake," the man said, after a brief hesitation. "We don't want any repercussions. We want a guarantee from you."

Holl's voice sharpened. "How can I know enough to give you a guarantee, or if my daughter is safe? Who are you? Hello? Hello?" The other end clicked loudly in his ear. He spun, wild-eyed. "Did you get a sense of the caller?"

"No' enough," Curran said, sadly, letting go the hands on either side of him. "Only he's as scared as you."

"What did you do that for?" Mona demanded, staring at her employee. They were sitting very close together behind her desk. The telephone receiver had been cradled with a bang.

"The baby's his daughter!" Jake exclaimed.

Mona bit her fingers to keep from yelling. "Not H. Doyle!" she whimpered, her teeth clenching her knuckle. "Not the man who has been single-handedly ruining my business and my political career! Oh, no!" She passed her hands anxiously over her face and dropped her fingertips to the desk, where they drummed almost with a life of their own. "Now, what do I do?"

Jake stared at the wall, a curious expression growing on his face. "Maybe you can make a good thing out of this," he said.

"A good thing?" she asked, bitterly. "What if I just turn in the two of you and ask for arraignment as an accessory?"

"You know we're in this together," the foreman said, shaking his head patiently at her raving. "You could work the situation to your advantage."

"What?" Mona asked, ashamed of herself. She realized that they were partners in crime no matter how this one incident ended. Mona was glad Jake didn't respond to her threat. She had a lot more to lose than he did. "Extortion? Money?"

"Well, a *donation*, maybe." Jake's stress on the word was careful. "He doesn't know about the dumping, not for sure. You could get him to lay off criticizing you in the papers until after the election."

"He doesn't have to know who we are," Mona said quickly.

"He'll find out. The kid knows. She wasn't blindfolded on the way here. You can ask for immunity from prosecution, and tell him to knock off writing to the papers."

"Well, maybe," Mona said, uncertainly, "but after the kids go back home all bets are off."

"Then get money," Jake said, reasonably.

Mona hesitantly dangled the pen over the pad. She certainly could use it for the campaign and to pay for legitimate dump sites until her receivables picked up again. "Okay. Our demands. One, money. Two, immunity from prosecution. Three, no more letters to the editor. In exchange, the children will be returned safely."

"Give him a couple of days to stew about it, and we'll call back," Jake said. He grinned menacingly. "Just like in business. A little pressure, and back off a while to let him decide. He'll cooperate."

"Not a trace," Diane said to Keith when he picked her up at her apartment near the college early the next morning. "I've been back to the library every day, hoping the kids would show up. Not a sound. Nothing. My footprints are the only ones in the dust down there."

She leaned into the car toward the driver's side, and Keith gave her a quick kiss.

"This wasn't the way I wanted to spend my days off down here with you," he said, helping her slide in, "but what else could I do?"

"Nothing," Diane agreed, settling herself in under his right arm as he pulled away from the curb. "It's horrible, and I'm glad you're here. I know the others feel that way, too."

The main room of the farmhouse was crowded. All the Folk, both Big and Little, chatted together in low murmurs until Keith and Diane appeared. They greeted the two students solemnly, and invited them to sit down in the center with the elders. Dunn and Marcy perched on small chairs among the throng of elves. Ludmilla was there on the old sofa between Lee Eisley and Maura. The young elf woman seemed to be at the center of a carefully made up support group. Maura looked not only tired, but haunted. Her usually pink complexion was drained to dull white. She was trying to be brave, but everything reminded her of her missing infant. All her actions were jerky, uncoordinated, and she was constantly on the edge of tears. Catra had admitted over the phone to Keith that some of the others had been laying charms on Maura in the evenings to make her sleep, or she'd wander around at all hours looking for her baby.

Keith was shocked to see how worn out Holl was. As the successor-apparent to the leadership of the village, everyone looked to him for strength and direction, and he could tell Holl was about out of both. It had only been two days since the disappearance.

"We had a call late last night," Holl said. "It was of too short a duration to get any idea from where it came, or who the speaker was, but the children live and are well. Still, the call did not serve to inform us how we may redeem Dola and Asrai, nor why they took them away in the first place."

"This incident has affected us profoundly," the Master said. "In all the years past ve haf nefer had a crime committed against vun of our number. Vittingly or unvittingly, those who abducted the children haf intruded upon our peace."

"My poor little ones," Ludmilla said. The old woman held Maura's hand and patted it.

"We feel vulnerable," Candlepat said, glancing nervously around for agreement. Many of the others nodded their heads. "Much more so than when we lived in secret."

"We risked discovery then, but only when we set foot outside our fastness," Curran said, narrowing his eyes at Keith as if he had personally carried away the children.

"In a way I feel sort of responsible," Keith said. "If I hadn't butted into your lives, you wouldn't be in any trouble."

"You provided us with the means to find a new home," Holl said.

"Yeah, but not until I endangered the old one in the first place."

"Ve could not haf remained in the old place for long," Aylmer said, coming to Keith's rescue. "Ve are better off than effer ve vere. And ve are glad of your friendship."

"Do not take more upon yourself than you deserf," the Master said, closing the subject with an austere stare over the tops of his gold glasses. "You did not perpetrate this crime. Now it must be solfed."

"What can we do?" Maura asked, speaking for the first time. Her voice was thin and seemed to come from a long way off.

"This is impossible," Lee said, his brows drawn. He ticked off his points on his long fingers. "You can't call the police or the FBI.

Advertising in the papers is out. You can't get a phone tap because that takes a court order. It would be great if we could use one of those crime-busting TV shows, but they'd laugh us off their hotlines if we told them we were looking for a couple of missing el—uh, Little Folk." He spread out his long hands. "Where do we start?"

"Can't you do fortune telling or something?" Diane asked hopefully. Curran glared, and started to stand up.

"That's nae the way our talents work," Dierdre said, carefully patient. She grabbed Curran's wrist and pulled him down again.

Holl shook his head. "The others call me the Maven, but I'm a novice at searching for the missing," he said, with a bitter laugh. "We're simply unused to being so far apart. I am the only one of us who has been separated any distance from the rest of us, and I was under my own power. I'm too close to the problem. I've no idea how to proceed."

Keith's eyebrows went up. "Maybe I do. Never mind trying to find the kidnappers. You remember teaching me how to see where the Folk were from Scotland," he said. "It was neat, Diane. In my mind's eye, I could see just a little light in the horizon, like a radar blip. Can you sense just one of your people like that, Holl?"

"It would be a very weak trace," Holl said, his eyebrows ascending, "but I can try it."

The others, especially the Big Folk, looked skeptical. "We've already searched the surrounding countryside in that fashion, Keith Doyle," Enoch said. "We found nothing."

Keith felt impatient at the quitter attitude everyone was displaying. "Well, turn your radar out further. Holl saw you from half a world away. The girls couldn't be farther away than that. Pour on whatever power it takes!"

"We're not machines," Tiron grumbled. "I'm as far from my folk as Holl was from his last year, and I couldn't tell if there's one or fifty back along at home."

"Ve haf no proof that the children are still vithin the immediate area!" Aylmer broke in.

"It's worth the attempt," Holl chided them. Keith gave him an encouraging nod. "Lend me your strength, friends." Tentatively, Maura stretched out her hand to her husband. Around the room, others joined hands, or touched in some way, until all the Little Folk were making physical contact. The Big Folk, tentatively, sheepishly, joined hands and reached out to the others. Holl shut his eyes to concentrate. He was silent for a long time. "I see nothing so far—no! There's something. To the west of here."

"Is it Dola and Asrai?" Keith asked.

Holl shook his head. "It's so small and faraway I'm getting no detail at all, just that there is one of us or someone like us off in that direction. It *feels* right. It's very hard, searching the distance for a pinpoint, instead of aiming in the direction I know it to be, as I did for the village from overseas."

"It *is* her!" Maura cried. "It's my babe."

"You cannot be sure," the Master said gently, "but I think there is something there vorth investigating."

Try as he might, Keith could get no sense of what Holl and the others were doing, beyond the slight perception of mental concentration. Now was not the time to ask for additional lessons in magic; he was going to have to trust the pros.

"Okay, what if we try out that way? Now that we have a general direction to work toward, what if you and me, and some of the others drive around until we can triangulate in on the girls' position."

There were mutters of "Progressive!" and "Big Folk talk," but Holl smiled wryly.

"Military tactic?" he asked.

"Could work," Keith said, raising his hands palm up as if offering the idea.

The Master looked around at the faces of his family and friends. Many of them were bemused, and Tiron and some of the elders looked doubtful, but in some of them the light of hope was shining. "In the absence of other suggestions, Keith Doyle, your motion is carried."

Holl leaned over the rear seat of Keith's Mustang, prepared to dive underneath the folded tarpaulin beside him if any other driver should get close enough to the car to see him clearly. Hope had given him back a little of the elasticity of his normal nature. Keith kept an eye on him through the rearview mirror, prepared to stop instantly if Holl got a solid vector. Walls of tall, green corn and wheat on either side of the road prevented them from getting more than occasional views of the farm buildings.

"Drive slower," Holl said.

Keith eased off the gas, and glanced at the knot of farm buildings to their left. "You still seeing their blip in the same place?"

"I *was* sure," Holl said, shaking his head and sinking back into the rear seat. "It was very strong for a moment. Perhaps more over that way." He pointed westward.

Diane was navigating their progress on a map of the state. She drew her pencil upward on the sheet. "We're half a mile from the next county road. You can turn left there."

Keith glanced around for other traffic as he slowed down for the intersection. They'd been on the road for hours, and had still not pinned down the girls' location within a hundred square miles. Every time Holl was certain he was on the correct tangent to find them, something interfered with his mental fix, and he'd lose it.

Somewhere out on the roads, three other cars, each containing one of the Little Folk and volunteer Big Folk drivers, were doing the same thing. As soon as Keith's suggestion was taken, Marcy and Enoch had immediately offered their services. Dunn and Marm volunteered at once, and went off together in Dunn's little green Volvo. Lee had taken Tay in his car. Ludmilla, though she had driven in from Midwestern by herself, remained behind with Maura and Siobhan.

"How will we know who is who?" Marm had asked, reasonably, while they were coordinating their plans.

"You won't," Diane had said, "but if you find a fifth body out there broadcasting whatever it is you're looking for, then you've found her."

"Besides," Keith had added, "the chances are that their trace won't be moving, and all of us will. If things go right, we'll converge on the place where the girls are hidden."

"That's sense," Enoch had said, nodding. "Let's go."

"Meet at Aunt Sally's diner at three," Keith had said, naming a family-style restaurant that was one of his favorite hangouts, on a county road north of Midwestern University.

Except for confirming the existence of Holl's 'blip,' the day's search was largely unfruitful. No one had much appetite for the enormous meals Aunt Sally's served. The baseball cap Holl wore to disguise his ears drooped low over his forehead as he picked at half of a turkey sandwich. Tay was exhausted, and sat with his head tilted backward, staring at the ceiling, ignoring the plate of fries he had ordered. Marm ate with the single-minded determination of a man who didn't know when he'd next get a meal. Both Tay and Marm must have put some kind of illusion on themselves, Keith decided, since they seemed to be bare-chinned now, but had had beards when they'd left the farm. No sense in attracting attention they didn't need. The lack of hirsute adornment made Tay look even younger than one of the Folk usually did. The waitress had brought all four elves crayons and placemats with black-and-white line drawings of farm animals to color.

"You'd think there's some kind of interference," Marcy complained as Enoch doodled on the picture of a cow with a red crayon. "We had a strong impulse to go eastward, for about three seconds, then it was gone."

"At least we've eliminated part of the state," Dunn said, pursing his lips. He filched fries off Tay's plate and dunked them in ketchup on Keith's. "It's still not going to be easy to pin down."

"Even if we're right, and if the trace we've all been following is Dola and Asrai," Keith said, remembering his lengthy tramp through the Field Museum. "You know, there could be other beings out there."

"I'm sure this has the right sense to it," Holl declared strongly, but with more force than confidence. "I ought to know my own child's emanations."

"There's hope," Marm said. "The mystery trace is within this area." He spread out the driving map, and pointed to a square much smudged with pencil marks. "They're in here. They are." He offered a smile around the table. Keith couldn't help but return it.

"That's still a lot of square miles," Lee said, whistling.

"At least we know they're still in the county," Diane said. "We can cut that down in no time."

"Not today," said Enoch unexpectedly. The black-haired elf turned up a face that was woeful, but pinched-looking and pale around the mouth, with smudges of purple starting under the eyes. "I'm tired enough that any moment I'll start finding squirrels instead. I've only so much strength. I'd give up my last heartbeat to find my sister's child, but I can't guarantee accuracy from here on in. I need rest."

Reluctantly, one by one the other Little Folk admitted to the same weakness. "Our strength's not an inexhaustible well," Holl said, sadly. "All the influence you can raise from an object, or a person, is that which is inherent in it."

"Then we need fresh scouts," Keith said, resignedly. "Tiron said he'd help. I can go on driving until I drop."

"I can, too," said Lee. "All I have to do to get tomorrow off is to call in and tell 'em I'm onto a story. I've never lied to them before, but this is in a good cause."

"I appreciate all your help," Holl said, relieved. In spite of his exhaustion he looked better than he had in the morning.

"I, too," Tay added. "We'd not be able to cover this much physical distance as we have in a summer, let alone an afternoon."

"We'll go back to the Farm and ask for more volunteers," Keith said, raising his hand to wave at the waitress for the check.

At the Farm, there was a telephone message waiting for Keith.

"It was your father," Catra explained. "He says he'd had a call," she looked at the wall clock, "an hour and a half ago now that Ms. Mona Gilbreth will see you this afternoon, and also that Frank is looking for you at Midwestern tonight. Your friend is a poet," Catra said, a wry half-smile lighting up her solemn face. "All the message he left for you was, 'cool, still sky.' A pretty image."

Keith looked shocked at himself for forgetting. He smacked himself in the head. "The ad firm! But I can't go," he said.

"But you must," the Master said at once.

"I can't," Keith insisted. "I ought to be here to help. I can call Frank. I'll beg off from seeing Ms. Gilbreth. It was only an excuse to get down here. Paul won't be too mad."

"You cannot be here all the time. We did get along before you met us. It is time you learned to delegate, young man," the Master said, not unkindly. He shook a finger up toward Keith's face. His straight-backed stance still made him no taller than Keith's middle shirt button. "You haf responsibilities of your own, Meester Doyle. Gif ofer to us. Mees Londen, Mees Collier and these others vill stay and assist. Tell us what should be done, and ve vill do it."

Keith looked at Holl and the others. He knew they counted on him. He thought of baby Asrai and Dola, out there somewhere, scared and maybe in danger. He met the Master's eyes, and read there that the old elf knew the realities of the situation as well as he did himself. He knew what he was asking Keith to do.

Keith's shoulders slumped in resignation. "That's the hardest lesson you've ever given me," he said.

"I hope it is the only vun of its kind you must learn," the Master said, with a sad smile. Keith recalled suddenly that Asrai was his granddaughter.

"I'm sorry," Keith said lamely.

The Master waved away his apology and nodded toward the door. "Nefer mind. Ve vill find them. Go. Perhaps you vill discofer information of interest to us."

Chapter Nine

"Ms. Gilbreth is expecting me," Keith told the plain, cheerful girl sitting behind the combination reception/telephone switchboard desk. The young woman picked up the receiver and punched two numbers.

"Representative from PDQ is here to see you, Ms. Gilbreth," she said, smiling up at Keith. She nodded, replaced the handset, and gave him a coy glance. "If you'll just wait a minute, then you can go back."

Keith thanked her and stepped back to examine the walls of the reception area. Framed photographs of green cropfields hung against walls paneled in cheap brown wood. If he'd owned this place, he wouldn't have spent much money on expensive furnishings, either. The whole place exuded a choking, clinging miasma that had to go home on everyone's clothes, and in every piece of mail sent from the office. Could that be useful in any way? Direct mail advertising to the discerning farmer? he thought with some amusement. The employees he saw were dressed in tan coveralls about the same color as the smell. He wondered how long it took to get used to it. Dust tickled his nose, and he sneezed. Surreptitiously, he took out a handkerchief and wiped the taste of airborne fertilizer off his tongue.

"You can go back now," the receptionist called out. "Second door on the right."

Keith thanked her. The gray-painted hallway had the same threatening anonymity as the corridors in the Death Star. No pictures interrupted the dullness of these walls. Did the proprietor match the unprepossessing aspect of her factory? He expected her to be funereal in aspect, or maybe hearty, like the stereotypical pictures of a farmwife.

Mona Gilbreth fit neither of his preconceptions. She was very tall, a few inches taller than Keith himself, and dressed in a neat and fashionable skirt suit that would have fit right in on Michigan Avenue. With her frizzy hair dyed a uniform rusty brown and her large teeth which, though straight, gave her the appearance of a slight overbite, she was not very pretty, but determinedly attractive. Her makeup was very skillfully applied, playing up her better features, and her hair was firmly coifed away from her face, to give her an open, approachable look. She gave him a strong, cordial handclasp that reminded him she was running for political office.

"How do you do," Ms. Gilbreth greeted him. "So you're from PDQ, Mr...?"

"Keith Doyle," he said, with a friendly smile.

She gave him a sharp glance. "Doyle? You don't have any relatives down here, do you?"

"No, Ma'am," Keith lied. "I'm from up near Chicago." He pulled Paul's letter out from his back pocket and unfolded it. She took it from him and read through it.

Ms. Gilbreth breathed a perceptible sigh of relief. Keith was secretly amused. He could almost hear her mental processes churning as she dismissed the suspicion that he was connected with those pesky Doyles at Hollow Tree Farm who'd been writing all those destructive letters to the editor. "So how can I help you, Keith?" she asked.

"I'm a college student working as an intern under Paul Meier at PDQ," he explained. "He wants us to learn everything we can about the ad business, and research is part of our job. I had to come down to, er, get an assignment from one of my other teachers, and Paul suggested I drop in on you and familiarize myself with your company. To bring your ad campaign right up to the minute," he added helpfully.

Mona smiled. "That's very good of Mr. Meier. I'd be delighted to give you all the information you want. The most important thing I want you to stress right now is my candidacy for state representative. I hope he's continuing along the lines we set out the last time I was up there."

"You bet," Keith said. "I'm sure you'll be impressed with what they're doing when you come up next. Say, while we're talking, would you mind showing me around? I've never been in a place like this before."

"I'd be delighted," Mona repeated, a little taken aback. After a moment's thought, she decided the request was reasonable. "Will you excuse me just a moment?"

Keith gave her a friendly grin as she sidestepped around the desk and out the door. He was pleased. There he sat, right in the enemy camp; the dirt that he would uncover would humiliate her all the more when it hit print. She hadn't stopped dumping on the Forest Preserve and Hollow Tree land, so as far as he was concerned she had another zinger coming. He'd just have to keep his eyes open for any other offenses Kill-breath Gilbreth was getting away with.

With a glance over her shoulder to make certain Keith wasn't following her, Mona hurried up to the front office. "Page Pilton," she told the receptionist. The girl picked up her handset and dialed.

Grant appeared, stupid and willing, in his dusty coveralls. "Yes'm?"

She took him aside. As yet neither the receptionist nor any of the office staff knew about their two detainees in the back office. It was a secret between her, Pilton and Williamson. Until she could figure out how to get rid of them, she couldn't risk having to explain their presence to outsiders. "We've got a visitor on the premises. I'm going to take him on a tour. Go keep that child quiet. I don't want her making a noise and attracting attention. Got it?"

"Yes'm," Grant said again, and headed at once down the corridor toward the office where the children were confined.

He unlocked the door and let himself in quietly. The little girl was sitting in her accustomed perch on the orange chair, reading aloud to the baby from a children's magazine. Without a TV or radio in the room, Grant guessed it was as much to hear a human voice as anything else. They made such a cute picture, like a toddler reading to her doll.

Both pairs of eyes glanced up at him from the colorfully illustrated page when he entered. The girl had been very quiet since the night Jake Williamson had threatened to shoot up the room. Whenever Jake went in there with him, she shrank back, holding the infant protectively in her arms, keeping real still. She was a lot more calm around Grant, which he hoped meant she liked him better. He'd sure done his best to make things nice for her.

Pilton's wife had accepted the excuse that there were a couple of kids visiting from out of town, and allowed him to bring over spare blankets and toys. He'd replaced the single flour-sack towel in the bathroom with a couple of Disney character towels. After the little blond girl had rejected the TV, he brought a radio and a night-light instead.

He knew it wasn't right to keep these kids here away from their folks, but he accepted Ms. Gilbreth's reasoning that they had to bring them back at the right time, to minimize the trouble the company was in for taking them. It was mostly his fault they were here in the first place, so he accepted his employer's excuse.

The blond child continued to stare at him. He sat down crosslegged on the floor and stared back. The child pursed her lips disapprovingly, probably in unconscious echoes of a similar gesture one of her parents or grandparents used.

"Hey," he said, grinning at her, "go on reading, huh?"

Mona took Keith Doyle around the factory complex, pointing out the tanks and piping systems that carried individual products. Each system was painted a different color, giving it an orderly appearance in spite of the tangle of conduit, catwalks, and s-bend pipe that snaked overhead. She was grateful that he didn't ask about waste, then became suspicious that he was leading her on. "You don't ask me anything about environmental impact, young man. Don't you have any interest in that?"

"I do," Keith said, disarmingly, "but I'm not a scientist. I only know what I read in the papers. Besides, I'm here to get the scoop on *you*. I'm working for your hired gun, remember?"

"Oh, yes," Mona said. "Well, remember, I'm campaigning on a 'Preserve Our Environment' platform." She swung a hand up in a graceful gesture to encompass the vast, sea-green tank beside her. "This is one of the most modernized systems for liquid and powder transport in the world. I want other potential polluters to look to me for leadership in preserving—"

"But I'd like to know more about how your business runs," Keith was saying. "More of how you do things right here. Your voters will want to look at the way you operate, your sense of fairness, your history, to give them confidence in how you'll do things in Washington."

The last thing Mona wanted to do was expose her business practices to this nosy youth, but it wasn't good policy to offend anyone with access to the media, especially media she was paying for.

"Oh, but that's so boring," she said, smiling determinedly at him. "Wouldn't you rather hear about the political issues? You see," she said, straightening the shoulder pads on her jacket then touching a wave of her stiff hair with a coy hand, "I want to show an honest image of myself to the voters of Illinois."

Keith nodded politely. "Could I have some literature about Gilbreth Feed? Didn't I hear that the firm was founded by your grandfather?"

"Why, yes," Mona said, flattered. "You've certainly done your research, young man. There are some flyers in one of these offices. Let's see."

She led him up the hallway toward the comptroller's office, where she seemed to recall there was a supply of public relations literature. As they passed close to the office where Pilton and the children were, Mona trembled. If the baby let out one of its rebel yells now it was all up with her. With the room set up as an improvised nursery, there'd be no way of disguising her motives for keeping them there as a benevolent or temporary gesture of any kind. She steeled herself not to look at the door at the end of the hall, so as not to draw attention to it, and ushered Keith into the accounting office.

Dola finished the story and went on to the next one in the magazine. Her voice automatically laid stress upon strings of prose and quoted dialogue in humorous voices without her having to think about it too much—no problem, since she no longer was drawing images in the air to go along with the narrative. The arrival of Skinny meant to Dola that there was something going on in the building that the boss-lady didn't want her to disturb. Dola was more than a little afraid of the boss-lady. The Big woman was formidable in appearance and so very tall. Dola felt intimidated by her size.

Holding her breath, she listened as keenly as she could. There were voices in the corridor, but so faint that they were indistinguishable. One of them belonged to an adult male. Dola was convinced that there was some reason that the Big Folk didn't want her to be seen or heard by the possessors of those voices. Perhaps it was a police officer, who would wonder what a child was doing at a factory. If she could get his attention, maybe he would take her and Asrai home.

Dola glanced at the skinny man. He watched her as if he expected her to perform some other wonder, like the disappearance she had attempted on the hilltop two days before. She was impatient with him and desperate to get out of the room. In spite of the daft way he talked her jailer was too big and too canny to be tricked into letting her slip by him. She needed a distraction—something dangerous, so he'd have to remove them from there to save their lives.

Skinny got up on his knees beside her to coo at the baby. Asrai stared at him, her round, milky green eyes wandering across the big face without recognition but luckily without fear. So long as he was occupied, Dola had time to come up with a really terrifying illusion. A spider. One at least a foot across, climbing up the wall behind him, but further away from the door than they were. That way he'd *have* to get them out. The footsteps were coming closer to the door. They couldn't be more than a few yards away. Her chance was at hand.

She shaped the sending in her mind's eye, seeing it form from eight irregular points on the pocked wall, solidifying in the center into grotesque head and abdomen portions of black and shiny bronze, with hair the length and thickness of cat's whiskers sticking out of the joints of the legs and covering the base of the body near the spinnerets. She admired her work, and glanced down at Grant, timing the moment. If she managed to scare the baby when she screamed, Asrai would lend her lung power to hers, and they'd be free in no time.

Letting her eyes go wide with feigned fear, she started to take in a huge breath, readying a really loud outcry.

Her gasp alarmed Pilton, who looked up. Guessing what she was about to do, he fell forward onto one knee and clapped his hand over her mouth. Quickly he looked around to make sure no one was coming into the room, and saw the spider. Dola made it hiss, spreading its palps and front legs menacingly. With the greatest presence of mind, Pilton let Dola go and put himself between the children and the horrifying arachnid on the wall.

"Look at that sucker!" he cried. "Stay back, little lady. It might jump." The spider assumed a karate stance, waiting for its foe to approach. Getting no closer, Pilton leaned over toward the table, picked up a magazine, and threw it at the spider. Dola had no choice but to imagine it falling to the ground and scuttling into a corner. Grant followed it and smashed it into a pulp with his big boot. "Whew! I haven't seen a spider that big since I was in the Everglades. It's dead. You aren't scared, are you?"

"I'm all right," Dola said, in a very small voice. She sank back, thwarted and a little tired from the expending of energy. The illusion, hidden from view, faded into nothingness. It's a pity I can't like him, she thought, because he's brave.

To her dismay, she heard the footsteps receding in the hallway. She'd missed her chance at freedom once more. Pilton resumed his perch next to Asrai, and was babbling nonsense words at her in a silly falsetto.

"No, the big bad thing's all gone," he said, making the baby gurgle. "Yes, it is. It wasn't gonna hurt you, no. I wouldn't let it do that. No, I wouldn't."

Dola tried to lose herself in the baby's happy murmurs, because she herself was close to frustrated tears. I want to go home, she thought sadly. I wish someone was here to comfort me.

Mona saw Keith off from the front door with relief so great she worried that it might show.

"See you on Monday, ma'am," the young man called. He waved. Mona waved back.

"It'll be a pleasure," Mona assured him. As soon as he was gone, she plopped down on one of the chairs in reception and rubbed her feet. She was exhausted but happy. The youth had led her all over the factory, sticking his nose into all the departments, but he had asked a lot of intelligent questions. She knew about the job PDQ offered its most successful intern. With the kind of initiative he showed, she wouldn't be averse to recommending that very polite young man for the position, if he promised never to come back to the factory.

She went down the hall and tapped on the door at the end.

"He's gone," Mona said. "Thank God. Come on out of there and get back to work."

"Yes'm," Grant said, and looked back at the child. "I'll come back later and bring you some dinner, okay?"

"All right," the girl said very quietly. They closed the door on her.

Dola was doubly depressed to hear the locks clicking shut. By the Boss-lady's tone, she guessed she'd missed a very important chance at escape. She and Asrai were left alone again in their prison. Who knew how long it would be before she had another opportunity. And what did these Big Folk have in mind for her and Asrai? The man called Jake and the Boss-lady treated them like a pair of inconvenient parcels. Would they dispose of them the same way? She was glad neither of them spent much time with her. If they began to suspect, like Skinny did, that there was something strange about her, she and Asrai would never be free to go home again. Catra had passed around many articles from journals and magazines talking about what scientists did to alien-seeming artifacts and remains. She shivered, and covered up Asrai, who was sleeping again on her lap.

Pulling in by a wayside phone booth, Keith called the Farm to offer his help for the evening. He didn't feel much like ballooning, and Frank didn't really need him. He volunteered to forego his lesson and come back. The Master thanked him for his concern, but said the others had elected to call off the search for the night.

"Go to your lesson," the Master added. "You haf vorked hard today, aiding us in our search. Let it be. Ve vill continue tomorrow, and velcome you back at the veekend. As I told you, you cannot continue to take all responsibility for us upon your shoulders."

What the little teacher said was true, but it made Keith feel unwanted and unneeded. He could have helped more. Discontented, he turned south and headed toward Midwestern.

Keith was too late to help inflate the great bag. The rainbow of Skyship Iris was already rising like a multicolored sun beyond the trees on the campus. One of Frank's crew waved him over as he hopped out of his car, and pulled him over to help walk the balloon to its launch point.

His heart wasn't really in it, but he pulled against the light wind, his back and arms straining against the thin fabric of his shirt. He couldn't stop thinking about Dola and the baby. He had the same feeling his friends had, that the girls were off in a northeasterly direction, but the trace was too vague to pin down. You'd think that a small, isolated target like a pair of elven children would be easy to locate, but other things kept getting in the way of a direct connection, as if they were anchored too tenuously in reality to be easily detected. Maura was handling things incredibly well, but he could tell she wasn't going to last too long if the baby wasn't found soon. He suspected some of the others were doing subtle enchantments on her to keep her from going over the edge.

"Hop in," Frank said, peering at him through his flight goggles. "Didn't think you were going to make it."

With the help of Murphy and the other ground crew, Keith clambered over the leather-bound edge of the basket and dropped in. The Iris curtseyed a little. Acknowledging Frank's hand signal to stay out of the way, he sat on the floor and watched while the pilot reached for the burner controls. The flames shot high into the balloon. Smoothly, the Skyship Iris rose into the air.

He was so busy moping over the lip of the gondola, the balloon had risen above the trees before he'd even noticed it. Frank nudged him in the back with a foot.

"What's wrong?" the pilot shouted over the roar of the burner. They rose further into the sky and caught an eastbound breeze.

Keith strained to stare out over the northern horizon toward where Hollow Tree Farm lay unseen in the distance. "Some of my friends are in trouble."

"What?"

"Some of my friends are in trouble!"

"Sorry," Frank said, in his telegraphlike style. "Beautiful day. Hang on, cheer up."

The suggestion began to take effect. It was not in Keith Emerson Doyle to remain depressed for long. The day was beautiful and warm. There was less than an hour of daylight left, and the shadows were growing dramatically long over the landscape, adding depth to its beauty. Keith felt the taut worry in his chest unlock and unfold until he breathed normally again. He let go a tremendous sigh.

Then he started worrying again. What if the children were in serious danger? He thought of Dola as he had last seen her, cute as a button, trying hard to be a grownup but still full of childish spunk. He stared at the ground far below. Dola could be in any one of those houses or among the crops in the fields that stretched endlessly out into the distance. He wished that he could just call out to her, wherever she was, so she would know that they were looking for her, and not to despair. Clumsily aping Holl's magical radar, his mind reached out, sought, touched nothing and kept going, leaving him feeling lost. He wondered if he had missed sensing Dola, and went over and over the same angle. No wonder Holl was pooped. Poor Dola, poor little pet! He remembered seeing her from far above, how she looked with her golden hair reflecting the morning sun as she bent over the baby in her lap.

Keith shook his head to clear it. He was imagining things. Dola had never been outside in the meadow when he'd arrived by balloon.

"Uh, Keith," Frank said, nudging him again. "Co—co—, uh." He seemed unable to finish his sentence.

"Hmmm?" Keith inquired, glancing up, and froze.

"Company," Frank choked out at last.

Keith found himself gazing into a pair of round, sky blue eyes, but they weren't Frank's. In fact, the body they were attached to was hovering under its own power outside of the basket. Keith's own eyes widened until he thought they might pop out.

The creature floating beside the Iris was about a foot high, the cloudy blue-white of shadows in glacial snow. Below the translucent torso its substance thinned down to pale, insubstantial streamers barely solid enough to see. It had delicate, attenuated wings like a great bird, and its face was like that of an owl, but where Keith would have expected to see a beak there was nothing at all, a blank plane, as if the artist had neglected to finish roughing in the rest of a watercolor portrait done in blue-whites and pearl grays. Thin, filmy arms ended in two long, delicate feathers instead of fingers. It tilted its inverted-wedge of a head at Keith. The image of Dola in his mind looked upward and smiled. The being nodded, waving its long fingers.

"So it was your memory I was seeing," Keith said, awed. "What *are* you?"

The light creature recoiled from his outrush of breath. He repeated his question, more quietly, and was rewarded when the being swam closer to him, bobbing in the eddies of the wind.

A vision intruded itself into his sight, an enforced daydream. Keith saw the same creature, with dozens more like it in all sizes from tiny to elephantine, swirling around and playing in the wind high above the face of the earth.

"I'm a jerk," he laughed. "You're *yourselves*. I'd call you air sprites. Is that all right?"

The vision filled with warm, rosy light. "I guess that means yes, huh?" Keith asked, delighted.

Frank must have been seeing the same visions, because he gulped and clutched the hot air release of the balloon with both hands. He stared, unable to take his eyes off the strange visitor.

"Keith, we ought to go down," the pilot said, carefully so as not to offend, but awed and frightened.

"We don't have to," the young man said, in a quiet, caressing voice. It pleased his companion more than his first attempts had, and calmed the pilot a little. "It's harmless. Aren't you?" he asked the floating creature. "Say hello to Frank."

The huge blue eyes turned toward the balloonist, and the vision of a sunrise appeared in their minds.

"Uh…sunrise to you," Frank said, waving a feeble hand.

Keith 'translated' by thinking as hard as he could about sunrises. His unmuffled broadcast was so forceful that the air sprite was propelled backward again. It bobbed up, its large eyes reproachful.

"Sorry," Keith said, sheepishly. "I'll try to think softly. This is new to me."

The intelligent eyes focused on him. They were so clear he could see individual rings of muscle constricting within the irises. He was aware of an expression of humor that fleetingly changed to one of sympathy.

Keith had a vision of a small girl sitting washed in sunlight on top of a green hill.

"That's Dola," he said, and the vision faded. "We're trying to find her. You mean you think you've seen her?"

Images of many little girls flicked before Keith's mind's eye, large, small, black, white, Hispanic, Oriental, alone, or with other humans or animals, on hillsides, beaches, in fields, jungle clearings, in the backyards of houses.

"No, you were right the first time, the first one you were thinking at me. She's the one." Keith tried to picture her.

The sprite picked up on his efforts right away. The image of Dola reappeared and limned in more details, so that Keith could see the scuffed shoes, her bare knees stained with grass, the hammocklike shoulder harness in which she carried Asrai. "That's her. You really have seen her! Yahoo!" he shouted. Alarmed, the sprite dropped away and beneath the edge of the basket, its tail whipping out of sight. Keith leaned over the edge, careless of his own safety. Frank dove forward to catch the back of his belt. "Where? Where is she?" Keith demanded.

The sprite returned to its former altitude, and the pilot yanked Keith firmly back into the gondola. Stumbling backward, he bumped against the control panel. The sprite circled around until it was hovering beside his head. Keith concentrated on the newest sending. *I will ask the others,* it sent, showing itself flitting from one to another of the many like itself. Each cocked its head, filling the air with more images that overlapped, as if they shared their thoughts freely. The sun appeared at the edge of the dream and traveled rapidly across the sky, and the sprite fixed its eyes on Keith's.

"It could take time, I know," Keith said, "but it's important. She was kidnapped, and that baby with her."

"That's the trouble they're in?" Frank asked, his mouth agape. "Man, *say* so! I'd help."

"We can use all the help we can get," Keith said, and thought rapidly. "I think we're on to something with our new friend here. It says it'll go looking for her. If it finds anything, I'll need you to bring me up to talk with it again. Maybe when the others remember where they've seen her last they can lead us to her." He tried to imagine the sprite hovering in front of the balloon, looking over its wing joint at them as it flew along. The sprite's visions took on the rosy hue again. Keith smiled. "Great!"

"Any day the wind's not too strong," Frank promised, somewhat distracted. It was still staring at the sprite.

"Thanks," Keith said sincerely. He turned to the sprite. "Listen, well, look," he amended, noting the creature's lack of visible ears, "let me know when you've located her, okay? Or the closest to when your people remember seeing her last under the sky."

The sprite sent a vision of Dola in her green tunic with the baby on her lap, then of itself. *I recall seeing her last before the bad smell came, and I rose out and away from it.*

"The bad smell?" Keith asked, puzzled.

In the image, the air turned the sickly green he had always associated with tornado weather. The sprite blinked its eyes at him, and the vision changed again to the crowd of sprites. *I will ask the others.*

Frank checked the gauge on the tanks and tapped Keith on the shoulder. "We're going down now," the pilot said. He leaned over the side, looking for a good place to land. When he spotted an open field nearby, he started landing procedures, cell phone on one shoulder to tell the chase crew where to find them.

The sprite circled, staying beside them as the balloon made its way toward the ground, exchanging visions with Keith, but the

further down they went, the little creature began to be horribly
compressed and distorted. The hands blunted into crablike claws,
and the wings stretched out into infinity then shrank to the size of
a cherub's. It blinked regretful eyes at Keith.

I cannot go into the heavy air, it sent woefully.

"Go!" Keith exclaimed. "The last thing in the world I want is
for you to get hurt. I'll see you up here the next time I can."

The filmy being shot upward with alacrity, vanishing among the
streaks of cloud in the evening sky. Keith had a faint vision, the visual
equivalent of shouting from a long distance away, of a sunset. He
exchanged a quick glance with Frank.

"Their way of saying goodbye, I guess," he said with a grin. The
pilot looked shaken. "What's the matter?"

"That…that thing was real!"

"The sky's a big place," Keith said, shrugging. "I bet the beings
you're sure exist are out there, too."

"That's what worries me. Never thought I'd run into any in
person," Frank said, the whites of his eyes showing all around his
irises, magnified by his thick glasses. "All supernatural beings can't be
so friendly."

"Nope, they're not," Keith assured him, running a tongue
around the fillings in his back teeth, "but the nasty ones usually like
to be left alone."

As soon as he got back to Midwestern, Keith ran to the nearest
phone to tell Holl about the air sprites. He was full of plans.

"It made pictures in my mind," he raved, waving one arm up
and down. The woman waiting in line to use the phone booth stared
dumbfounded at him, then walked hastily away to find another
booth. "It's seen Dola and Asrai. It promised to help us find them."

"And how do you know that?" Holl asked. "Is the language of
the air English, too?

"No, they talk through telepathy. It made pictures in my mind,
and it understood what I thought at it. It'll help us. As soon as it finds
them it'll contact me."

"One of your pipe dreams, is it?" Holl asked, drearily.

"Uh-uh! Frank saw it, too."

"I know you want to help, Keith Doyle, but mythical sprites
seeing all is a little too much for me when my troubles are all too
real. Forgive me. You've been a great help to us, and I'm not

ungrateful. I'm merely tired. I'd best clear the line, to be ready in case the kidnappers call again. We'll await you on Saturday."

Keith was disappointed, but he reasoned, as he hung up the phone, that Holl hadn't been there, hadn't seen. He'd prove it, as soon as the sprites came through. If it didn't, they were no worse off than before. It was funny, he thought, that his excitement in finding out about Dola almost made him forget that he had achieved his aim of finding the air sprites. It was a great, important discovery.

In spite of his concern for the missing children, he couldn't help strutting a little as he walked across the campus back to his car. He was probably the first human being to make contact with the ethereal creatures. As soon as this terrible business was cleared up, he vowed to find out everything he could about this new race of hitherto mythological creatures. *Doyle's Compendium of Magical Species* began to write itself in his mind.

"Okay," the hoarse voice said over the phone when Catra picked it up, "We've got three demands."

Catra put her hand over the receiver and relayed the message to Holl. "What shall we do?" she asked.

Holl steeled himself. "Keith Doyle said never to give in to a kidnapper, but we can't risk annoying them. Hear his requirements, but promise nothing."

"Go ahead," Catra said into the receiver. Her hands trembled.

"Here's what we want: money, immunity from prosecution, and one other condition we'll let you know about later, when we deliver the children."

"We have very little. How much money do you want?" she asked.

"Twenty thousand dollars in small bills. Unmarked. No explosives, no dye packets."

"Aye," Catra said, noting the specifics down on a piece of paper. Her companions crowded around to read what she was writing. "Now," she said boldly, "we've a condition of our own. We want to hear the children's voices. Hello?" She turned a frightened face to the others. "He hung up."

Chapter Ten

Meier cleared his throat and rustled his pages of notes. Keith gave him a brief glance and turned from staring out the window to staring at his fingertips then back out the window as if he was looking for something hovering just outside the twentieth floor.

"Today," Meier said, "I'm going to show you a few products that are so new that they haven't even got names yet. The client wants a snappy presentation for her product, and we've got diddly on 'em as yet. I'm showing you these raw, so you see what we have to start with. It's not pretty." The others chuckled.

Meier threw onto the table five small clear packets. "There you go. Becky Sarter grows and dries organic fruits. Dried apricots, dried sultanas, dried berries and cherries, mixed dried fruit. No added sugar or preservatives. Cellophane packaging. Upscale. No name. Demographics of her target market are male and female ages 25 to 45, income level upwards of thirty grand a year, college educated or better. Go for it."

Three of the four interns picked up the packets, turned them over in their hands, searching for inspiration.

"What's a sultana?" Sean asked, feeling the substance of a dried apricot through the wrapper. It was flabby and flexible, like a fleshy orange ear. He wrinkled his nose.

"One of the names for golden raisins," Dorothy said, holding up that package. "Doesn't it sound more elegant?"

"Paul, how about Oh, Gee Snacks?" Brendan suggested, then spelled it. "Stands for the OG abbreviation of 'organic'?"

"Maybe," Paul Meier said. "It's kind of cutesy. Run with it. Gimme some thoughts on a campaign." But Brendan had shot his bolt. He grinned and shrugged.

"Ug-*ly*," Sean said. "You weren't kidding about not pretty. How about 'Ugly fruit, beautiful vitamins'?"

"I approve of the product," Dorothy said. "Environmentally sound packaging, no pesticides. You can compost cellophane, you know. Becky Sarter? How's 'Sarter your day with good nutrition'?"

Everyone groaned.

"Nothing there to hang onto, really, Dorothy. Half a pun is NOT better than none. But you have a lot of basic knowledge there about the product. That's good. But we need a *name*. How about you, Keith?" Meier asked. "Keith? Earth to Keith." He rapped on Keith's notebook with his knuckles.

Keith came back from his musings with a start. "Uh, sorry. What?"

"Let's hear it. What can you do with Sarter organic dried fruits."

"Would the client get all bent up about changing the spelling of his name?"

"Her name, and I don't know. Why?"

"You can't ask a client to change his name!" Brendan exclaimed.

"Why not? They've done it themselves. I read that Chef Boy-ar-dee is really a man named Boiardi." Keith spelled it.

"So what have you got in mind?"

"How about spelling it Sartre, like the philosopher?" Keith asked, mentally thanking the Elf Master for the intensive course in philosophy the last semester of his junior year. "He's the one who said, I think, therefore I am. I think."

"Descartes said that," Brendan said in disgust.

"Okay, so what?" Keith snatched up a pen and drew a bag, splaying the letters out across the top. *Sartre Sultanas. The Raisin d'Etre.*

"It means, the reason for being—I mean, the *raisin* for being."

"Not another pun!" Brendan exclaimed.

Meier stared at it for a second, a tiny grin growing in the corner of his mouth.

"That's funny. It's sly. Not bad for someone who's been staring out the window all day. It might appeal to the environmentally conscious intellectuals who buy organic stuff." He picked up Keith's caricature, drummed on it with the cap end of his pen.

"Hey, we're not supposed to be pandering to intellectuals," Brendan protested.

Meier raised an eyebrow. "We pander, as you call it, to the people most likely to buy the product. The readers who don't get it will buy the product because it's something they perceive a need for. Those who get it will like it more because it's an in-joke aimed at them. That's not all bad, because although the market is small, the availability of the product is limited, too. Says here in the research that there's less than ten thousand pounds of organic dried raspberries available each of the last four years. Even if it increases drastically, that's still nowhere near the amount of good old-fashioned, non-organic black raisins being sold every day."

"You could have pictures in the ads of famous philosophers eating the product," Dorothy suggested.

"Except for Albert Einstein, who the hell is going to know what a philosopher looks like?" Sean said, looking bored.

"'Yum! Much tastier than hemlock,' says Socrates," Brendan snickered.

"Why not?" asked Meier. "Come on, this is what brainstorming is all about. You may not get the best ideas right away, but they'll come if you feel relaxed about what you're doing. Keith here may have looked like he was catatonic, but his mind was racing along."

"You're right about him looking catatonic," Sean said.

Keith made a goodnatured face at him, too preoccupied to think of a retort. He'd been a million miles away, thinking of Dola and baby Asrai.

Meier still looked thoughtful. "Keith, I'm going to take this to the committee." The others looked dismayed. "Come on, guys, it couldn't hurt. The pros have flunked out on this one. We've gotten a lot of self-righteous claptrap about wholesomeness, a couple of environmental fire-eaters offering obscure suggestions, some overly cute b.s., and a lot of blank stares. The four of you have done better on Sarter Fruit in less time than anyone else to date. This could spark the right inspiration in someone's mind. If they don't want Sartre, the raisin d'etre." He chuckled.

Brendan regarded Keith with a look of pure hatred. Keith smiled innocently at him, fanning the fury still higher. If you can't join 'em, he thought, annoy 'em. Keith turned to Meier. "Same understanding as before," he said.

Meier nodded. "I appreciate your trust, kid. I won't take advantage of you. If they'll take it with your name on it, it'll be there."

The door to the little conference room swung open, and a man leaned in. He was tall and slender, with dark, well-coifed hair that had just the faintest suggestion of gray at the tips of the sideburns, and a health-club tan. He glanced at the young folk, and his face lit up. He turned to Meier.

"Paul! Here you are. I've been looking for you."

Meier made the introductions.

"Doug Constance, one of our creative directors," Meier said, sweeping a hand around the table. "Doug, this is Dorothy Scott, Brendan Martwick, Keith Doyle, and Sean Lopez. My latest crop of interns."

"I know! That's why I came in," Constance said, grinning at them.

The four students favored the newcomer with big, hopeful smiles.

"What can we do for you, Doug?" Meier asked.

"Well, we've got a new client we're pitching coming in this afternoon," Constance said. "I thought one of your interns might like a chance to see how it's done, maybe throw in a few suggestions, be right in from the beginning. What do you think?"

Keith sat up straighter. It would be a great opportunity to show his stuff. He could see that all three of the others had the same thought. Without waving his hand and yelling, "Me! Me!" it was difficult to make himself stand out from the group. He concentrated on looking bright, alert, and he hoped, creative. He smiled at the account executive, trying to meet his eyes.

But Constance's eye lit on Dorothy and her ubiquitous sketchbook. "There she is. How about her? Paul, we'd like to borrow this very talented young lady for the afternoon. We'd appreciate her input on Natural-Look Hair Products, and maybe she could do some sketches for layouts. She'd enjoy it, wouldn't you, Dorothy? Could you lend her to us, Paul?"

Paul looked at Dorothy, whose eyes were glistening beacons. "Sure, if you want. Go ahead, honey."

Dorothy rose with alacrity, her sketchbook clutched to her chest, and headed out of the room. Constance held the door open for her, then shut it behind them, with a final wink at Meier. "See you later!"

Disappointed, Keith spared himself one uncharitable thought as he sank back into his chair, that Dorothy would undoubtedly use this opportunity to promote her chances at getting the PDQ job. Maybe he'd have done the same under similar circumstances, but he wasn't so sure.

"Now, knock it off," Meier said, breaking into his thoughts. "I can see what you three are thinking. *No* decision has been made yet on who's going to be picked for the job—if anyone—and you've still got to earn a grade out of this term, so give me your attention. Got it?"

The three young men eyed each other. "Yes, Paul," Keith said. The other two murmured their agreement.

"Sorry, Paul," said Sean, cocking his head sheepishly to one side.

"Good," Meier said firmly, spreading out a sheaf of photographs from a folder. "Now, I've got another product I want your best thoughts on. It's one of my new accounts. Listen up. I'm going to give you these to chew over, then I've got a couple of meetings of my own."

"Come on, Doyle, I know what bifurcated means, and you know what bifurcated means, but the average jerk on the streets is going to think it's something dirty." Brendan shook his head at the ad copy Keith had scribbled on a mock layout.

"Hey, sex sells," Sean said, laughing.

"It's got nothing to do with sex, and I think it sounds dumb. Just like everything he comes up with." Brendan threw an annoyed gesture toward Keith who turned his hands palm upward in appeal.

"No, look, it'd make great copy. It's supposed to be obscure, then you come to the tagline, which would read," Keith held up his yellow pad and declaimed, "'But instead of wading through our grandiose verbiage, why not come and see how our tire sails through water.'"

"'Too wordy for anyone except the New Yorker," Brendan said, drumming his fingertips. Keith shrugged, and started drawing lines through his copy.

"When you're right, you're right," he conceded. Brendan looked surprised to have Keith agree with him, then sat back smugly. He put his heels on the table.

Meier opened the door. Brendan immediately swept his feet off and sat up straight. Teacher's pet, Keith thought in annoyance.

"Nice to see little birds in their nests agreeing for a change!" Meier said cheerfully. "Dororthy not back yet?"

"Nope," the three young men said in unison.

"Okay," Meier said. He flopped into his chair and sighed deeply. "What a day! Okay. What's Dunbar PLC's new centrally-grooved aqua-handler tire going to be called?"

"The Brain," said Sean.

"The English Channel," said Keith and Brendan together.

"No consensus, eh?" Meier asked. "Typical. You sound like you work for an ad agency. All right, Sean, why 'The Brain'?"

Sean turned his photograph of the product and his rough sketches toward the instructor. "Because it looks like a brain, or the top of it does, if you see it straight on. I wrote, "Your car is five times as smart when you add four Brains to the one behind the wheel.""

"That's not bad," Meier said, nodding. "Doesn't hurt to flatter the customers."

"I looked at the *bottom* of the tire where it hits the pavement," Brendan said, "and to me it looked like the rear end of the girl on the beach in the Bahamas tourist commercials, but you don't see *me* suggesting we call it The Tush."

"Why The English Channel, then?"

"Because nothing handles water like the English Channel," Keith tossed off patly. "Dunbar's an English company."

"Americans like things that are English," Brendan added. "It makes you think of people swimming the Channel, which is a real accomplishment. We're riding on that," he finished, cocking a distrustful eye toward his erstwhile partner.

"Har, har," Keith said, obediently.

"True, true," Meier agreed. He glanced at the clock, which showed 5:15. "Okay, you wanna leave me all of this stuff, and I'll look it over tonight? I'll give you my thoughts on it tomorrow, and you can let me know if you want me to propose your ideas or not. Good work, gentlemen."

Keith rose and gathered up his belongings. He realized guiltily that he hadn't thought about Dola's plight in hours. Still, there was nothing he could do for at least another twelve hours, and there was the chance that he could get a call any time that Holl and the others had found the kidnappers and managed to pull off a rescue without him. The important thing was that the children were alive and well.

He carried his coffee cup down the hall and into the employee lounge to wash it out. Only one light was on in the long, narrow room, over the sink at the far end. The flat-napped carpet swallowed up his footsteps, so that the only sounds were his breathing and the water running as he rinsed out his mug. Until he heard the sob.

"Who's there?" he asked gently into the gloom. He made out a shape at the table next to the window, and thought he recognized the outline. "Dorothy, is that you over there?" There was no answer. He turned off the water and put the cup down.

His eyes became quickly used to the gloom as he went to sit by her. Her makeup was smudged, leaving matte streaks on her skin, and she looked miserable. He scooted his chair close to hers.

"You were gone all afternoon. How'd it go?" he asked.

"Horrible!" Dorothy burst out, and her voice caught as she struggled not to cry. He could see that she was not only unhappy, but very angry. "Do you know what that big sell was all about? What they wanted me at that presentation for? A token! Natural-Look's president is an African-American woman. PDQ doesn't have any creative directors who're both female and African-American, so they pretended they needed me there to help with the presentation. I just sat there and nodded the whole time. They listened to my ideas once in a while when I managed to speak up, but you could tell they weren't really paying any attention. It was all phony! For looks! So *she* would think they were politically correct. She thought I was a staff artist. They never told her I was just an intern. I hate this place."

"Whoa," Keith said. "Meier warned us that this business was tough and that practically everyone's a rat."

"I'm just here as a token," Dorothy said, her eyes burning with tears. She scrabbled in her purse with one hand. Keith handed her his own handkerchief. After a second's hesitation, she took it and dabbed at her eyes and nose.

"Nope, you are not here as a token. You've got talent," Keith said firmly. "Come on, how many interviews did you go through to get in here? Same number I did. And you had to have the grades and the background even to be considered, right? After they offer you the job at the end of the year—"

"Hah!" Dorothy said, bitterly.

Keith waggled a finger at her. "Don't interrupt me when I'm complimenting you—You can start making changes here. You can move up to where clients are asking for you."

"You just don't know what it's like." Dorothy turned her head to stare out the window at the dusk. Lights were coming on all over the city, little pinpoints of red, amber, and white.

Keith thought about it for a moment, and gave a half-grin. "You'd be surprised," he said. "Most of my best friends—"

"If you say they're black, I'm going to kill you," Dorothy snapped.

"Nope, only some of my friends are black. I was *going* to say most of them are elves," Keith said. Dorothy gestured disbelief, but the tension began to melt out of her face. "You know, being the only Big Person in the crowd makes it difficult for me, sometimes, especially when they speak their own language, but we have a great time learning from each other. I don't share their common background, so of course I feel left out a lot."

"Yeah, sure," she said, but she was diverted from her rage. "You're strange, Keith."

"My stock in trade," he said, grinning.

At that moment Meier appeared, silhouetted in the hall door. "What's the matter, kids?" He came to sit down at their table, shoulders hunched forward over his folded hands. "Come on, tell Papa."

Dorothy turned to stare out of the window, leaving Keith to explain what happened to her. The lines of Meier's face deepened, and his lips pressed into a thin line.

"I'll take care of this," he said. His voice was calm, but the suppressed power in it told Keith how angry he was. "Dammit, they're supposed to keep their damned games off you students."

"Why, so you can grab our ideas for yourself? So you can use us yourself?" Dorothy snapped.

Meier turned his surprisingly calm eyes on her. "Dorothy. Ms. Scott. I always tell you when I'm taking your ideas, and when I'm not, and I tell you why. I am working for your best interests, although you might not believe me right now. You want the magic of seeing your ideas used by the clients? If not, tell me. I won't propose any of yours. I told you there's resistance to using unpaid interns' suggestions. You agreed to that at the beginning of this session. You want to take it back, you can. It doesn't make any difference to me. I've got my own ideas, and I get plenty from the rest of my creative staff. I don't need yours. I was doing you a favor. There's no reason for you to have to put anything else on the line. You can go on just learning from me about this business, and participating in the class. It won't affect your grade, because it really just doesn't matter to me. You can believe that or not. It's up to you."

Dorothy's eyes fell. "I'm sorry, Paul," she said meekly. "I didn't mean that. I just feel used. Dirty."

Meier nodded kindly, and slid into a chair. "I apologize, too, Dorothy. I work with these yotzes every day, but sometimes they even fool me. Like today. It's my fault I let Doug get away with using you. And I do put your names on the proposals when I can, but you've got to understand how delicate the balance is we've got to maintain. We can't let the client feel at any time that we're incompetent. Okay, let's look at it from another angle. You were in on the initial meeting between a client and a creative team—a crucial moment in the relationship. Did you get anything out of that?"

Dorothy looked at him in surprise. Even the puffiness around her eyes was beginning to recede. "Well, yes, I felt them measuring out what she wanted. It wasn't easy. She had an image in her mind, and nothing we proposed seemed to match it. That was tough. She wasn't good at seeing the potential in rough sketches. She needs to see finished mockups."

"Good assessment. They work out how much she can spend?"

"Uh huh. I guess it wasn't much. She has to aim straight at her demographics without a lot left for general advertising, so it's up to us to figure out where her customers are and how to reach them. After being in research, I know how much it costs to put up certain kinds of ads, so I could see just what she could get for her money."

Meier nodded encouragingly. "And how far creativity, both in the ads and in the placement of those ads, can make that money go. Not easy, but you could begin to understand how we begin to form a campaign. You see? No experience is ever wasted, is it? You feel better?"

Dorothy gave him a look of gratitude. "Yes."

"Great," Meier said. He glanced at his watch. The shiny face picked up a few of the red and white points reflected in from the window. "Okay, I've gotta get out of here, kids. See you tomorrow." He rose, chucking a friendly fist into Keith's shoulder, and strode out.

"I like him," Keith said, watching the door swing shut.

"I do, too," Dorothy said. "And I like you. It was nice of you to come and sit down with me. How come you want to help me, when we're competing for the same spot? We can't both win, you know."

"Oh, I'll get along if I don't get the job," Keith said reassuringly. "I'm not a type-A personality. There'll be other opportunities for both of us, lots of them. Listen, want to grab a bite to eat? I just missed my train home, so I might as well have dinner down here."

"Sure," Dorothy said. The luster was back in her cheeks, and she smiled at him. "Let me clean up first. I must be a mess!"

The Chicago Loop empties out swiftly at the end of the workday. Most of the places the interns were accustomed to going for lunch were already closed. Keith and Dorothy found themselves on the uppermost floor of a shopping center, looking out the window at the city. Ribbons of red lights marked the outbound traffic on the expressways. The river, snaking between high-rises and the Merchandise Mart glistened with the colors of sunset reflected from the sky. On the horizon, tiny planes to the west and southwest appeared in the sky, rocketing along an upward vector: the evening flights at O'Hare and Midway airports. The sulphur yellow of sodium vapor lights made an eerie graph pattern of the streets to the north of the Loop. Keith and Dorothy watched in companionable silence until their meals arrived.

"Paul was right," Dorothy admitted. After she had eaten a few bites of food, she was restored to her usual competent self. "This internship is doing me good, and I like it a lot more than I thought I would."

"Me, too," Keith said. "Before, I sort of thought ads wrote themselves. I mean I wasn't aware of the mechanism that creates commercials and print ads. Now I go around making up slogans and layouts for everything I see. Baloney Billboards," he sketched across the sky, "For the biggest ideas around. Or the watch ad I thought up that no one will ever use."

"Oh?" Dorothy asked encouragingly, amused.

"Yup. Shows a giant watch with its band fastened around the Tower of Pisa. Slogan: if you have the inclination you might as well—"

"...Have the time," Dorothy finished with him. Her laugh, a deep, throaty gurgle, was pretty. Keith beamed at her. "I should have seen that one coming. I know what you mean," she said. "I"m doing it, too. I love it. I draw storyboards and magazine ads. I've got sketchbooks full of the weirdest stuff." She turned serious for a moment. "I really want this job, Keith. It would mean getting right into the big-time business, without starting out in Podunkville."

"Great," Keith said, without a trace of jealousy. "And when I graduate, you can hire me."

"I could use a good copywriter," she said, mock-critically assessing him.

"Why, with your brains and my looks," he said, with a self-deprecating grin, "we'll go places. You could have a great career." He could picture her in an executive office putting people like Doug Constance into line. He could picture her holding Asrai, being hustled along by two large men—no, that was Dola being pushed, the baby clasped to her chest. Keith shook his head to clear it. He looked up.

Outside of the window behind Dorothy's head, a knot of air sprites whisked and hovered. One of them flew forward, showing that the memory belonged to it. Insistent, the image replayed itself in his head. Dola and the baby, being escorted from a big tank truck into a brick and paneled building by two men, roughly sketched out in twilight. He struggled to continue the conversation, but knew immediately he was mouthing gibberish. Dorothy gave him a strange look. He smiled and asked her a question about art, but he wasn't sure exactly what. The sprites flew in irregular patterns, aping his agitation and excitement. They'd found her! They knew where the children were!

"Something wrong?" Dorothy asked. His face had gone pasty, then reddened until it was nearly the color of his hair.

"I just remembered something," Keith said, pushing back his chair and standing up. He grabbed the check. He hoped Dorothy wouldn't turn around and see what he had been staring at. "I'd better get out of here. I'm sorry. I just remembered something. See you Monday!"

With his jacket flung over his arm, he dashed out of the restaurant, stopping only to slap down the bill with some money at the register. Bemused, Dorothy picked up her fork and went back to her meal, neglected since the two of them started building castles in the air. She shrugged. At least he'd been a gentleman about it. Since he had to run off, he had treated, but she was still puzzled why he'd left in such a hurry.

"Well, was it my breath?" she asked herself. The skyline was pretty tonight. When she finished eating, she was going to make a sketch of it.

Outside the window, four air sprites streaked away from the building and parted, taking off in four different directions, their filmy tails fluttering farewell, their thoughts full of sunsets.

Chapter Eleven

"I ain't happy about this, and I don't care who knows it," Pilton said moodily. He sat in the orange chair, elbows propped on his knees, and stared at the ground. "I'm not supposed to have to work Saturdays. I ain't on this shift."

"Nor do I want to be here," Dola said, without looking up. "If we weren't you wouldn't have to." She was diapering Asrai, who had decided to throw a fit of the wiggles. The infant would not stay in the middle of the clean pad, but as soon as her small bottom touched the cold desktop she let out a wail of protest. Dola took Asrai's ankles between her fingers and plumped her firmly down, and fastened the tapes before she could move again.

"I know." Pilton sighed. "But Boss-lady won't let you go yet."

"*Why?*" Dola demanded. With a flourish, she swaddled the baby in her blanket and sat down on the floor on her borrowed sleeping bag. Asrai was now willing to take formula from the bottle without the subterfuge of illusionary disguise, for which Dola was grateful. She took the warmed bottle out of the coffeemaker carafe, tested it, and offered the nipple to Asrai, who accepted it avidly.

"Dunno. Don't ask me any more. I can't tell you."

"You'll be here Sunday as well," Dola said warningly.

"Dammit to hell," Pilton swore, throwing up his hands. "Well, I can't do anything about it now. Hey, I brought you some egg salad sandwiches for lunch. Got some carrot sticks, and a slice of cake."

Dola nodded. She hunched over Asrai. The baby suckled, making happy noises deep in her throat. "I'm bored!" Dola announced. "At home I'd have games and toys, and tasks to do, and there'd be all my friends."

Pilton sat up. "Well, what do you want to do?"

The elf girl could stand it no longer. The imprisonment, the discomfort, the annoyance of not being able to wash her clothes nor having any clean ones to change into, the lumpy sleeping bag that smelled as if it had been wet in a hundred times and washed in orange juice—the stupidity of her jailers. She burst into tears. "I want to go home."

Pilton dropped to his knees next to her. "Oh, come on, little girl, don't cry. Please. I'll do just about anything to keep you from feeling sad."

"She wants what?" Mona Gilbreth demanded. "Craft supplies? No. Simply no. I'm not running a nursery. Tell her if she doesn't knock it off I'm shutting both of them in an empty tank."

"I can't do that, ma'am," Pilton said, shocked. "What would her folks say?"

Mona went white. H. Doyle again. "All right. But don't get too elaborate. I'm getting rid of her as soon as I can." She opened her desk drawer and took out the petty cash box. Resenting every last penny, she counted out ten dollars.

"Any more than this is on you," she said. "I didn't want them here, and I don't want to subsidize their entertainment."

Accepting the money happily, Pilton went off to find embroidery floss and the fixings that went with it for the little girl. He was evolving a kind of superstition in his own mind that he'd have good luck if he could make the fairy child happy. In spite of what Ms. Gilbreth and Jake said, he knew she was magical. He'd seen. If he won her good will and got her to put a blessing on him, he'd be a lucky man for the rest of his life. Maybe she would invite him back to the land of fairies.

When he thought of it, it seemed strange that there were fairies right here in Illinois, when this had been Indian country for ten thousand years less the last two hundred. Never mind. That wasn't the kind of question you asked fairy people if you wanted to stay on their good side.

Tay eyed the Skyship Iris with clear distaste. It was only with an effort he brought himself to get out of the car with Holl and Keith to walk towards the seven-story ovoid.

"It isn't natural," he complained to Keith. "I don't feel safe about this floating around with a big silk handkerchief over my head. It'll spring a hole and run off with us, and we'll be shooting around the sky helpless while it deflates. Are you sure there's no other way?"

"Not if you want to be with us for the search," Keith said, patiently. "The sprites can't come down to our level, so if we want their help we have to go up where they are. C'mon, it'll be fun." At his particular request the Iris's crew had helped set up the balloon, then backed off, accepting his explanation that he wanted to do some complicated photography, and needed the field clear of all other bodies. All it would take to launch the balloon was hitting the release on a series of clamps holding the ropes through steel pegged loops hammered into the ground. The crew waved from the cab of the chase truck. Keith signaled back, holding up his camera. The engine of the truck revved and the headlamps flashed, showing that Murphy and the others were ready to follow when the balloon lifted. Tay hung back. "You want to stay behind, that's okay. We'll go."

"No! I'd best come." Tay folded his arms firmly and tried not to look nervous.

"These your friends?" Frank asked, smiling down widely at Keith's diminutive companions. "Hi, kids," he said, then did a double-take. He stared fullfaced at the two elves with a kind of fascinated horror. "What *are* they?" he demanded of Keith. "Those ears!" The blond male he might have been able to explain away as a kid playing masquerade, but the silvery-haired fellow wore a beard that had to be his own.

Keith blinked at the pilot innocently. "Didn't I tell you the air sprites weren't the first supernatural beings I've met?"

"Supernatural?" Frank's voice squeaked on the last few syllables. Keith grinned.

"Pay no attention to this big fool. We're no more supernatural than he," Holl said, with an exasperated glance at Keith. He stepped forward and offered the shaken pilot his hand. "My name is Holl. This is Tay. It's our children you're helping us to find, and I promise you we appreciate it greatly."

Frank closed his own large hand around Holl's small fingers with the delicacy of someone handling breakable china. "How'd you do, uh...Shouldn't the Air Force or whoever's in charge of extraterrestrials know about them?" he asked Keith over Holl's head. The two elves looked alarmed, and Keith spoke quickly.

"Hey, they're not extraterrestrials, and it's their lives if they want to stay out of sight, Frank," Keith said. "I know you can keep a secret so they said I could tell you. If they don't want anyone else to know about them, wouldn't you say that was their choice?"

"Uh, you're right. Sorry," he said, glancing down at Holl, apology and wonder mixed on his face.

"No harm done," Holl said, with a smile. "Shall we go?"

Keith helped the two elves climb over the edge and into the basket. The Iris, tugging against a light wind, was eager to be off. When Frank nodded, Keith hit the release for the cables, and just to add verisimilitude for the chase truck, started snapping pictures.

The ascent was effortless, the finest Keith had yet experienced. The only sensation was the slight vibration the burners caused in the framework attached to the basket. Fascinated, Holl and Tay watched the ground fall away.

"Like watching a scene on the television," Tay said, with interest. "Zooming back to show the distance...uh, is that a house?" He pointed at the red roof of a distant barn. "A real house?"

"Yup," Keith said, following his finger. "We're about six hundred feet up already. Good cruising altitude."

"Six hundred feet!" Tay squeaked, staggering away from the edge. "I thought we'd be lifting thirty or forty feet to clear the trees!" He sat down in the bottom of the basket with his head between his knees and began to moan. Holl made a wry face.

"Leave him be," he suggested. "We live close to the ground," he explained to Frank, who was looking concerned. "We barely so much as climb trees."

Keith kept an eye on the altimeter as the balloon continued to rise. The Iris swept into a northeast wind and began to sail in the direction Holl said the girls' trace lay. He peered into the distance, hoping to spot landmarks.

"Well, where are they?" Frank asked, when they reached five thousand feet. He glanced around eagerly. "In this temperature I can go to fifteen thousand if need be."

"Please don't," Tay begged from the floor of the basket.

Keith grinned at the pilot. "I thought you didn't want to meet any more supernatural beings," he teased.

Frank squared his skinny shoulders. "Guess if they're up here, I ought to know."

"If it wasn't all your imagination in the first place," Holl said to Keith.

"Both of us saw it, right, Frank?" Keith said. The pilot nodded. "They'll be here, honest."

"I don't care if flying dragons appear," Tay said, miserably hunched among their feet, "so long as they're willing to help me find my daughter."

The dream vision of a sunrise interrupted the conversation. Holl stared at Keith. "What's wrong with my mind?" he asked.

"It's them," Keith said, and began looking around for his new acquaintance. The blue-white tails of the sprite looped swiftly past them around the balloon basket, until the delicate figure was level with them beyond the sheet cables.

"There it is!" Keith said, pointing. "Holl, Tay, look."

Tay glanced up briefly at the milk-colored creature, who blinked amiably at him, and went back to groaning with his head held in his hands. "Such things belong up here," Tay said. "All I wish is to get down to the ground where I belong."

Holl held his breath. He and the sprite stared at one another for a moment, and the young elf broke the silence with a sigh. He cocked his head at Keith. "Well, I owe you an apology, widdy. If anyone could find an imaginary being in the stratosphere, it would have to be you."

The sprite, detecting that Keith was being teased, retaliated on his behalf with a clear image of Maura pushing Holl into the stream. In the vision, the elf landed on his rump in the mossy water. Keith laughed, and Holl shook his head.

"Oh, very well, then, friend, I submit," Holl said, good-naturedly. "You know all and see all. It really is too bad that your amazing discovery must take second place in importance to the rescue of our children, Keith Doyle, but you have my humble admiration."

"Thanks," Keith grinned. "I'll spare you the 'I told you so,' and we can hold the scientific discussion later." He brought up his camera and showed it to the sprite. "Can I take your picture?" he asked. "I'd sure like to show some other people that I met you."

Take? Please do not take from our substance. The mental picture of a diminished sprite, looking woeful, appeared.

"Um, it doesn't actually take anything from your substance," Keith explained hurriedly. "It's only a reflection of you in my camera lens which hits a kind of light-reactive paper. Harmless. I promise."

Timidly, the airborne creature inspected the camera, and its mental vista turned rose-colored. *All right.* It backed up, whipping its tail like a rudder.

"It'll make a noise," Keith warned, focusing the lens.

All right. The sprite held itself still, but showed its agitation in the way its extremities flapped as if caught in a light breeze. Keith pushed the shutter release, refocused, and took a second exposure. *That didn't hurt at all,* the sprite sent to him in surprise.

As if its approval was a signal, another and another winged being joined them, until the air was filled with sprites all signaling their image of sunrise to greet their fellows and the party in the balloon. Keith was busy taking pictures, asking the sprites to pose in groups, or to fly alongside one of the Folk to give him a scale of measure. Few were the same size as Keith's original acquaintance. Some were tiny enough to fly up his camera lens if it had been hollow. One, of which they could see only a wingjoint or an eye in the shimmering, cloudlike mass, was nearly the size of the balloon. It looked like a friendly hurricane coming close to take a look. Most of the winged beings ranged in size somewhere in between. Frank goggled, but he kept control of his craft through sheer will power. Holl looked around and around him in wonder.

"The Master will be glad of those snapshots," he said, with a sigh. "I hope we'll get to know these good folk better later on. How shall we begin this search, then? Will one guide us the way?"

There was a hasty conference among the air sprites from which Keith got the fallout of images changing and shifting. Most of the diaphanous beings swept away with a swift daydream of sunsets left behind as farewell. The party was left with Keith's friend, a larger one who pushed itself forward importantly, and a few of the smaller creatures.

Following the sprite's direction, Frank steered the Iris into a northward current.

"Full tanks, nice day, cool weather, last a long time," the pilot said, nodding.

"Then we will begin," Holl said.

Keith felt on the edge of his mind when the two elves pooled together their strength and began the search for the children. Their sense spread out like a sensitive layer on the sky that could feel all the topography of the land below it, except that it sought mental touches, not physical. He connected with it a little, but couldn't follow it far. That kind of command of talent took years of practice, and a lot more magical oomph than he had. After a while Tay rubbed his eyes.

"It's the same trouble as before," Holl said. "There is something in the way that lifts and lowers between us like a heavy curtain. I sense them only part of the time, but this wispy friend of yours is indeed going toward the scent." He smiled at the hovering sprite, who made a rosy glow at him. The little ones danced around it like fireflies. The larger apparition narrowed its large pupils and twisted in the wind to point forward.

"Make sure you tell me when you want to land," Frank said. "No second chances here. No box wind. Can't turn around."

"If we can," Holl said. "It depends greatly on what our friends tell us."

The large sprite stayed ahead of the balloon, glancing over its shoulder to make eye contact with Keith or Frank. The gesture was for their benefit: Keith could tell it was able to see them in its mind's eye. When the winds wouldn't go where it led, the sprite hovered patiently, waiting for the shift in direction it wanted. It always knew, and made the image of a weather vane turning for Frank, so the pilot would be ready. The original sprite stayed back with the balloon, hovering companionably near Frank.

He showed his big teeth. "My new best friends," he said, manipulating the cords to raise or lower the balloon. "You'll stay around?"

The sprite, its eyes alight, showed the Iris surrounded by itself and many others. Holl grabbed for Keith's arm.

"The trace is very strong ahead," Holl said. "No, I've lost it. I can't believe it winked out just like that." He looked at Tay hopefully, but the silver-haired elf shook his head.

"The interference is like clouds rolling in between us," Tay said.

"Or smoke?" suggested Keith.

Beneath them, the green cropfields had given way to a huge industrial center. Bare earth stained by greasy overflow supported corrugated tanks and pipelines. Trucks ran among them, and minute workers in khaki coveralls hooked up pipelines to the tank trailers. In the midst of the factory campus was a broad, flat group of buildings: warehouses and the office center. At the same time the sprite broadcast the yellow-green sky image of warning, the occupants of the balloon were hit by a wave of stench that surrounded and stifled them.

"Ugh, horrors!" exclaimed Tay.

"That's Gilbreth Fertilizer down there," Keith said, coughing. "Look at all that leakage from the tanks. I bet there's half a dozen health violations right there. I didn't see those when I was there. I think the owner steered me away on purpose." He leaned over the edge and started taking pictures.

"What a smell!" Tay complained. "The very stink makes you itch."

"I know," Keith replied, from behind his viewfinder. "I kept sneezing the whole time."

Holl's expression changed from revulsion to enlightenment. "They're down there," he cried, grabbing Frank's elbow.

"The children?" Keith blinked. "At Gilbreth?"

"Yes! I felt them, just for a minute, safe and well. That chemical soup is what is blocking natural sense. Go back!"

"Can't!" Frank said, regretfully. "We can't change the wind."

The larger sprite whipped around the balloon, showing its agitation in snapshot images forced into their minds. The picture of the little girl forced to walk between two men repeated over and over. Frank waved a hand around his eyes, trying to clear his vision.

"Stop that!" Keith ordered. "We can't think." The pictures stopped at once. The guide drew back, hovering tentatively just beyond the basket's edge, apology in its large eyes. They were passing over the buildings now. Shortly, they'd be beyond the property's edge.

Keith got a sudden inspiration. "Drop her!" he cried.

Frank, mentally weighing safety against the rescue of the children, nodded sharply once and yanked the parachute release. They heard the outrush of air, and saw a burst of sunlight up inside the dome as the great rainbow bag irised open on top. Swiftly, the balloon dropped toward the earth. Whipping its tail skyward, the sprite reversed and followed them downward head first. Keith gritted his teeth as the earth rushed toward them. Wind whistled in his ears.

"Ah, no!" Tay groaned, falling to his knees on the padding at the bottom of the basket. "I'll never leave solid ground again."

The balloon pilot slowed their descent as soon as he hit calm air closer to the ground. The craft jerked slightly, but all four men were well braced.

"Distraction's only good a short time," Frank said tersely. "Leave it to me. Truck's been tracking us. Take it home. Got it?"

"Got it," Keith said, crouching, ready for the impact of landing. Holl copied his posture, and clutched the edge of the basket with both hands.

The sprite shot upward and away, leaving behind a final image of Holl holding Asrai and Tay with his arms around Dola.

"I think that means good luck," Keith said. He saw men on the ground running toward the descending balloon. "Get down!"

He and the two elves ducked further below the edge of the rattan basket and held on. Frank landed the balloon with a hard thump. The gondola bounced and began to scoot along the ground, slowing as air rushed out of the balloon. When the deflating bag started to billow over them, he hissed, "Go!"

Keith slipped over the rear side and helped the elves climb out. They ran, crouched low, under cover of the Iris, toward the industrial buildings, as the men closed in on Frank, shouting for explanations.

"What are you doing here?" one man in guard uniform demanded.

"Hey, it's beautiful!" another cried. "Do you need help, fellah?"

Frank held up his cell phone. "It's okay! Chase car be here in a minute. Give a guy a hand?" He punched in the number of his truck's mobile phone.

The three ran around the corner of one of the brown brick buildings, avoiding the windows, and crouched out of sight of the crowd gathering around Frank and the balloon.

"Where to?" Keith whispered.

"I don't know," Holl said. "I've lost the trace again, but they must be in one of these buildings. The square footage is finite. We'll split up."

"I wish I'd been paying more attention to the floor plan when I was here," Keith said, glancing behind him. Their haven was surrounded by walls on three sides: a dead end. "I never dreamed they'd be *here*. I could've freed them days ago!"

"Never mind," Holl said. "Use your eyes and ears!"

Across the grounds, Frank was instructing an enthusiastic volunteer force in how to drag down the nylon canvas and lay it flat. Little breezes caught inside the lip of the bag made it billow upward. Laughing, the men grabbed for the fluttering edges and tried to make them stay on the ground. They called to others who came out of doors to come and help.

"He's keeping them busy," Holl said. "Go, then!"

Still hunched over, Holl slipped off to the left, signaling to Tay and Keith to go another way. Nodding, Tay went to the right. Keith followed him for a short time, then detoured down a narrow passage between two of the brick buildings.

Chapter Twelve

In her prison at one end of the main building, Dola heard the commotion. She dragged the plastic chair to the window and stood on it to see what was occurring. In the narrow areaway outside, men were running and calling to one another. It didn't seem to be a disaster, such as a fire, for they seemed happy and excited. Something good, then, but unexpected. She pressed her cheek against the glass to see. Out of the corner of her eye she could see bright colors bobbing and billowing where there was normally the marshy brown of the clay soil that underlay this place. While she watched, the colorful mass sagged and flattened out. She couldn't guess what it was.

In her arms, Asrai stirred, suddenly aroused. Dola herself felt a mental touch, a nudge. Nothing physical intruded upon them: it was a push upon her aura, such as her mother might make, to check upon her well-being when she thought Dola to be asleep. This familiar touch was not her mother's but her father's! He had to be close by. The evilness of this place prevented her from being able to feel things far off. She sensed it getting closer. Dola became very excited, knowing she was about to be saved, then was overwhelmingly frightened. His presence here meant Tay was risking himself for her, risking discovery and capture. He hadn't been here before. He couldn't know that these terrible men and woman were intelligent, and would block any attempt he made to free her. She might have to free herself in the meantime, and be ready to run away with him when he came. She cast around desperately for something heavy enough to break the glass.

Asrai wriggled and started to fuss. Dola pleaded with her. "Oh, not now, little one! For the love of all, please, please don't cry now!"

She willed the baby to hold in the shriek she could feel growing inside her like bread rising. A yell would bring Jake or Skinny on the hop, and she didn't want them near. Dola herself felt like screaming in frustration. Oh, if she never had to see them again, or spend another night in this smelly, cold room! Rescue was near. She could feel it.

At the end of the passageway opposite to where all the men were running, Dola spotted a figure running, crouching, then running again, as if to avoid notice. When a knot of workers came around the corner, the figure threw itself among the dumpsters and burrowed behind the trash bags to avoid notice. It emerged again, moments after they passed, and resumed its furtive movement. Dola peered at it. Instead of the slim, muscular figure with silver hair, the intruder was unexpectedly tall and lanky, with hair the color of autumn maple leaves. Keith Doyle! Keith had come to rescue her. Dola saw that she could just get through the window if she broke it out. She had one chance at freedom, and all the odds lay in the element of surprise. First, she had to delay the guard that would surely come when she started breaking the glass. She jumped off the chair and put the baby down in a hastily-arrayed nest of disposable diapers. Grabbing up her sleeping bag, Dola used the heavy cloth as a pad to shield her hands from the metal of the desk as she pushed it as far as she could toward the office door. Its feet groaned a protest that echoed up the corridor. Dola knew it would attract attention. Better to make double sure she had time to escape.

Using as much concentration as she dared, she enhanced the cohesion of one part of the metal door frame for the other, willing them to stick together no matter what happened. She doubted it would hold together long on true metal, but it might earn her precious seconds. She grabbed Asrai in one arm, and picked up the body of the coffee maker in the other. Hefting it, she judged where the one strike she had would do the most good.

Dola sprang up onto the chair. Almost across from her now, Keith stared around at the darkened windows of the nearly empty office wing, searching. She wound up and smashed the coffeemaker's metal base into the window. The pane shattered outward, spraying fragments from a hole only the size of her head. Dola began beating on the remaining shards of glass, hammering them into powder.

"Keith Doyle!" she screamed.

He turned and saw her in the tiny window, waving the plastic appliance through the hole. Her hand was bleeding and her face was pale, but she was alive and healthy.

"Dola!"

"Oh, hurry," she begged. She glanced hurriedly over her shoulder. There was shouting and pounding in the room behind her. She dropped the plastic thing, an automatic coffeemaker, and held a bundle out to him. He rushed to take it from her.

"Hey, you!" a man's voice yelled. A tall, lanky man dressed like the others in khaki coveralls but carrying a brown paper shopping bag, ran down the narrow passage toward Keith. "Who are you? What are you doing here?" He dropped the bag on the ground and made straight for him.

Keith reached for Dola, but jumped back when the man came at him. He tried to dodge around, and was cut off by a feint from his opponent. Dola pulled back, watching in alarm as Skinny took a swing at his head. Keith ducked, avoiding one punch, but taking the next squarely in the ribs. The breath was knocked out of him with a grunt, and he tripped backwards. Dola cringed, holding the swaddled Asrai up out of the way of the fighters. On the ground, Keith kicked at his opponent's shins, making him dance backward. He scrambled back to his feet.

Suddenly, in the shadow of the trash cans, Tay was there. He saw his daughter, and beamed. He signaled encouragement to her, and Dola felt the warmth of her parent's presence, something she had missed for days. It filled her heart, giving her hope. Holl was nearby, too. She could feel his sense but not see him.

"Open this damned door!"

Behind her, Jake was trying to get in, and had discovered the block she had set in the frame. By the muffled double-thump sound, he and another person were throwing themselves against it to break it in. It was not a strong door; they'd be through it in a moment.

"Hurry!" she called.

Skinny had Keith Doyle in a wrestling hold, with one arm across his throat, and was slowly putting on pressure. The young man's face had gone red. He was not doing well at freeing himself. Skinny easily evaded his weakening kicks and backwards-aimed punches. The factory worker shifted and increased the choke hold. Keith gasped and clawed at the other man's arm, trying to pry it loose.

In his hiding place, Tay flung his hands outward, throwing some kind of cantrip at Skinny.

"Kick free!" he shouted to Keith Doyle. "It'll be all right!" Keith nodded weakly, fought for a deep breath, and dropped limp. Skinny, puzzled, bent his head over Keith's shoulder to see what was wrong.

Behind Dola, the door splintered. Jake's meaty arm reached through and felt at the handle, encountered the top of the desk. There was a lot of swearing in the hallway, and Dola heard the Boss-lady's voice.

"Break it down!" the woman shouted.

With a tremendous heave, Keith shifted all his weight forward to get his feet back on the ground. Caught off guard, Skinny bent with him. Keith lifted one heel and brought it solidly down on his attacker's instep, then when Skinny's grip relaxed a fraction, stepped to one side and attempted to throw him over his hip. He struggled unsuccessfully for a moment, looking confused.

"He's fixed in place," Tay hissed. "Get away, then!"

Keith's face lit up as he realized his advantage. Making a knot of his hands, he shot one elbow backward into Skinny's stomach. The factory man doubled up for a moment, and lost his grip on Keith. The student danced away, and Skinny grabbed for him. With wildly flailing hands, Skinny toppled over forward, and hung there at a ridiculous 45-degree angle. His feet were fixed to the ground. Keith danced in, ready to paste Skinny another punch in the mouth, but Tay called out to him.

"It won't hold long in this mess. Hurry!"

Avoiding the man's grasp with an agility that would have done credit to a gymnast, Keith dashed to the window and put up an arm to help Dola out. She thrust the bundled-up infant into his hands and prepared to scramble out after it.

The door of the room burst apart, and Jake, carrying an axe, half-crawled, half-scrambled over the desk. Dola glanced back, and in so doing lost her advantage of surprise. She was partway out the casement when Jake grabbed her by the neck of her tunic and hauled her back.

"Go!" she cried to the others, almost sobbing in frustration. "Run!"

Keith gave her a startled glance, noticed the other faces in the window, and took to his heels, clutching Asrai. Tay and Holl were right behind him.

"It's that Doyle boy!" the boss-woman shrieked. "I knew he was tied up with that H. Doyle! He lied to me! How did they get in here? Where was security?" she demanded. "They should have stopped them at the gates." Jake shook his head, his lips pressed together.

She dropped to her knees beside Dola. "Look, she's bleeding." The angry brusqueness of her voice didn't mask the compassion underlying it, but it was small comfort to Dola. "Get some bandages. Move it!" The woman clenched Dola's shoulder and shook her gently, holding back from hurting her but evidently frustrated. "I hope you realize you've just made things more complicated. Thanks a lot."

"I'll not apologize," Dola said, tears running down her face. She was too frustrated to feel brave. "I'd do it again, too." I wish them well away, she thought.

Keith and the others pounded into the driveway just as the red pickup truck rolled onto the factory grounds. One handed, Keith scrabbled at the door handle, yanked it open, and threw himself inside. Tay and Holl all but jumped through the window after him into the truck cab. Together, they pulled the door to. The men in the back of the truck stared at them, and one pounded on the window for attention.

"What's going on?" Murphy asked, recoiling from contact with Keith's flailing elbows.

"Turn around," Keith panted. "Drive us out of here."

Across the field, Frank, free for a moment from expostulating with guards and factory workers as they squeezed the colorful envelope into a sausage and tucked it into its storage bag, gestured at them violently, *away*. Murphy didn't wait for further explanation. With his chin rammed into his shoulder, he spun the pickup backward in a wide arc, spraying gravel, and gunned the engine. The truck roared out of the compound.

"Who the hell was that?" one of the guards asked Frank.

"Hey, man, if you saw something this big floating around on the ground, you'd think there was a circus here, too. Happens all the time," Frank said, nonchalantly. "People come to look, just look. Ought to come up for a flight some time. Reasonable rates." He reached underneath the control panel for a handful of flyers and handed them to the bemused guard.

Strangers were trying to take his fairy child away! Frantic, Pilton pulled at his trapped feet. The man who had broken the office window somehow put a whammy on him while he reached in and took away the baby while Pilton's grabs for him fell yards short. Fortunately Jake and Ms. Gilbreth stopped the fairy child before she could climb out, too. It would have broken his luck.

He had to get the baby back. Yelling for help, he swung himself into a standing position, tugging at first one boot, then the other to pull loose. No one paid any attention to him. Suddenly, he toppled over, his arms windmilling wildly, and fell with a thud to the dirt. His feet had been freed suddenly from their unexplained adhesion to the ground. Not stopping to wonder how or why, he scrambled up and ran yelling after the man and two boys. He saw them leap into the red truck.

"Hey, you guys!" he shouted at the crowd gathered around the balloonist and his gear. "Stop them!" He was just in time to see the truck disappear down the road in a cloud of dust. His shoulders drooped. Half his luck was gone.

He started walking back toward the building as Ms. Gilbreth and Jake came out of it. The boss-lady's face was drained white, and she looked mad enough to spit nails.

"They're gone," Pilton said unnecessarily.

The truck hurtled down the country road. Keith clasped the bundle closely. It was wriggling, but silent. As soon as he was sure they were out of danger, he relaxed a little, but kept an eye on the rear view mirror for anyone in pursuit.

"It's a shame we couldn't get Dola out of there," Tay said, slamming his small fist against the side window. His pulse had started to slow down after the lightning raid on the factory complex.

"She's okay, though," Keith said.

"Aye, that's comfort," Tay agreed, slewing his gaze moodily around toward Keith. "What have you got there?"

Keith turned to Holl, whose eyes were shining when he realized they had not come away empty handed. "It's yours, I think," he said. He extended the bundle in his hands to Holl.

"Asrai," Holl said, hardly daring to believe it. "That brave, heroic girl saw her chance and used it to free one of them, at least." He took the small armful from Keith, and tenderly raised the fold of blanket over his daughter's face.

"Waaaaaaaaaaaaaaaaaahh!" The moment she was exposed, Asrai let out a tremendous wail of protest. It packed such force and volume that it knocked the three men backward in the truck seat.

"My God!" exclaimed the driver, putting a finger in his right ear and wiggling it to restore his hearing. "What lungs that kid has!"

"Like taking the cork out of a bottle," Keith said, with respect. Asrai took another deep breath and broke into sobs, all but vibrating the truck's metal panels with each outburst. "Wow. She was saving that all up. Probably for days."

Holl looked shaken. "It's good to have her back again, and normal," he said, though he sounded doubtful. He lifted his hands out from underneath her one by one. "And she's wet."

Keith started laughing, half from relief and half from the expression on Holl's face. The others joined in, Holl reluctantly at first, then with greater heart.

"I feel better," Tay said, heaving a deep sigh and settling back in the seat. "Dola's well, and shrewd as ever. Her mother won't be best pleased we missed bringing her home as well."

"We'll get her out," Keith promised. "Soon."

"To think she was so close to home as this," Holl marveled, dandling the baby until she stopped crying. "I can't wait to see Maura's face."

Maura vacillated between joy, relief and tears when her daughter was restored to her. She wept, but gladly, tears glistening in the corners of her smile. All the Little Folk were gathered in the main room of the house, crowding around her, Tay, Holl, and Keith, clucking over the baby or the handful of photographs Keith was passing around.

"You're a hero," Maura told Keith gratefully, clasping Asrai in her arms. The baby was all coos and gurgles now that she was reunited with her mother. Maura refused to turn her loose even to let her be held by adoring aunties and uncles.

"I only get a small part of the credit," Keith insisted. "It was Frank's balloon and his driver that got us in and out of there, and I wouldn't have been able to grab her at all if Tay hadn't glued that security man in place when he did."

"We all did our part," Tay said, grinning as Maura leaned across the chuckling baby in her arms and kissed him on the cheek. "We're all heroes."

"And we owe a lot to our new friends," Keith finished.

"A marvel," the Elf Master said, turning the instant photographs over and over again. "To think we haf nefer suspected their existence. Although since you say they cannot descend to our stratum, nor we easily to theirs it vill be difficult to establish close relations."

"They have a way of making themselves heard," Keith assured him. "I'm going back up as soon as I can to learn more about them."

"We ought to have a celebration," announced Dunn.

"No," Maura said, moving to Siobhan and putting an arm around her waist. "Not until we are all together again."

"Oh, that girl," Siobhan said, dabbing at the corner of her eye with the edge of her apron. "She'll be thinking it's all an adventure, I am sure."

"It's her Progressive upbringing," Keva, Tay's grandmother and Holl's elder sister, said, glaring.

"And there they werre, in the center o' that polluter's home?" Curran demanded, his eyes almost glowing with anger. "That wooman has much ta answer fer."

But first, Mona Gilbreth's representative had something to say for himself. The telephone call came almost on the heels of the triumphant return of the rescue party. The man on the other end of the line was angry.

"We were willing to cooperate and do this peacefully," he snarled. "Now you've ruined it."

Holl had answered the call. "How? By bringing home an infant who was too young to be away from her mother in the first in-stance?" he asked. "You were doing her more harm by not giving her back right away. We'd have forgiven."

The bass voice nearly leaped out of the phone. Holl held the receiver a distance from his ear. "Yeah?" the man growled irritably. "Well, you don't make the schedule around here. I do. Since you can't be trusted not to play tricks we'll do things my way when I'm good and ready." The bang as the other end was hung up resounded from the kitchen walls.

"They can't keep us from getting Dola back," Keith said, slam-ming his fist into his open hand. "We know where she is now."

The Master shook his head. "If someone found something I sought to conceal, I vould move it as soon as I could. This call vas evidently their vay of informing us that vas vhat they are doing."

"Oh," Keith said. "Otherwise they would have said 'we give up, come and get her'?"

"An ofersimplification, but essentially correct," the Master granted, leaning back in his lecturer pose with his belly stuck out. "Her location is vun of their trump cards in order to force us to do as they wish. Vun of ours is that she must do nothing more to antagonize us, or be reported to the authorities. It is much easier to hold on to a stolen child than to clean up spilled liquid. But still it is a standoff."

"Ve ought to haf left a spy," Aylmer said. "He could haf said vhere they take her."

"We don't have to," Keith said, grin widening until it threatened to consume his ears. "We know how to trace her now. And we've got friends in high places." He pointed upward.

When darkness came, Mona oversaw the packing of all Dola's borrowed goods into Jake's pickup truck. There were more things to go: food supplies, and gear for a live-in guard. She intended Pilton to keep an eye on Dola until things were settled with Uncle H. Doyle. They couldn't keep her in the office any more, not when her adversary had the organization to pull off successful, lightning-fast and virtually undetectable incursions as he had. She wondered if he had had commando training, or something like it.

They'd never find the child where Mona was sending her now. Mona had other things she needed to do, and would be relieved to have her unwanted charge out of her back pocket. With almost a week wasted, her campaign was suffering. Her campaign manager had called to complain she wasn't giving him enough opportunities for public appearances. How could she leave, when at any moment someone might discover two kidnapped children incarcerated in an unused office of her factory? What she was doing now, she thought, she should have done at once a week before.

As before, the two men escorted the child to the cab, put her in the front seat, and sat on either side to box her in. Dola glanced up at them distastefully. Williamson turned on the engine and revved it a couple of times to help warm it up. Mona stepped up and leaned in the window.

"You know where to go," Mona said, making the question a statement.

Jake nodded silently, staring straight ahead with his hands on the wheel. Skinny stared at the Boss-lady. Neither of them looked at Dola. She felt like an inanimate parcel once again. She thought of kicking up a fuss and rebelling just to get the attention a living being deserved, then looked around her at the three solemn faces. Better not.

"Make sure you're not followed. And take care she doesn't learn the route in," the Boss-lady said enigmatically. "I don't want any more surprise raids." She turned away. Dola wrinkled her forehead, trying to puzzle out what the Big woman meant. It became evident when Jake took a handkerchief out of his pocket and folded it diagonally. They were going to blindfold her so she couldn't see where they were driving. As if she could have told her relatives where to look. As if she had needed to, if the Big Folk had only known.

The cloth between his hands came toward her, an awful parody of Dola's vision-making ritual, and she shrank away, revolted.

"C'mere, dammit!" he growled.

Skinny seized her from behind, pinioning her arms. She twisted her head wildly, refusing to give in. Swiftly, Jake shot out a hand and caught her by the jaw, pinching in her cheeks with one gigantic thumb and forefinger. He brought his big face close to hers.

"You knock it off, or I'll tie you to the bumper. Got it?"

Terrified, Dola froze. Making no further resistance, she let him tie the cloth around her eyes, which he did swiftly and efficiently. Pilton let her go, then she felt a heavy strap drop across and tighten in her lap. The truck started to move forward. She sat, meekly quiescent, her face burning where the cloth rubbed.

She wondered what horrors awaited her at the next stop. Were they going to lock her into a tank, as Skinny reported the Boss-lady had threatened? Or worse, were they taking her to some Big Folk fastness from which she would never emerge? Tay had found her once. She hoped he could locate her wherever she was going, and carry her off home.

Dola wondered how her father and Holl had located her at all in the smelly factory. She had felt nothing outside the confines of the cold office building. It must be something that Keith Doyle had done. He had so nearly gotten her out of there! She almost ached with the knowledge that she could have been free, if she had been just seconds quicker in climbing out of the window.

The road changed from smooth to rough. Dola was jostled and thrown against the restraint of her seatbelt, unable to guard against the acute turns she couldn't see coming. Jake swore under his breath.

After an interminable and bumpy drive, the truck swerved sharply to the left and stopped. Someone lifted her down and set her on the ground next to the warm-smelling truck. Her blindfold was removed. Smoothing down her mussed hair, Dola looked around her. It smelled green and wet around her, a relief after the week she had spent in the confines of the dusty factory. They were deep in the woods, far away from any other lights than moon and stars. In the almost-full darkness, a black shadow loomed upward before her, one with an angular, peaked top: a house. The walls were made of rough-hewn logs, chinked with grey material that picked up what little light the quarter moon provided. Jake stepped under the eaves and became a bulky shadow as he fumbled with the key in the door. It opened, creaking, and he reached in to switch on the lights. He motioned Dola inside. She felt Skinny's hand in the middle of her back, urging her forward. She went.

Dola could tell that Skinny was uncomfortable in these surroundings, but she was delighted by them. The place, though it was musty, had an honest scent to it, of wood, stone, water, and growing things. She walked around, touching things. A huge tile and flagstone fireplace was built into the center of one wall, which bulged out above the mantle to show the girth of the chimney. Over the hearth itself she saw a heavy hook meant for holding a pot, and an iron door in the chimney in which lay a shelf for baking bread. There was no other stove, so this was where the little house's intimates cooked their meals. Her supposition was borne out by the fact that a small refrigerator in the base cabinet of a Welsh dresser was plugged into the wall next to the hearthstone. Iron pans and pots, and a few lighter ones made of aluminum were inside the upper cabinet alongside an array of mismatched plates, cups, and utensils. Dola hoped she would be allowed to cook. Since moving to the farm, cooking over open flame without worrying about the library cleaning staff calling the fire department over the smoke had been great fun for all those culinarily inclined. The novelty had not yet worn off.

Leading off from the main room were three doors. Beyond the nearest was a bathroom not unlike the one attached to the office in which she had been living, but with a rusty, white-enameled bathtub to one side. The other two doors swung open into bedrooms. Between them, a queer little hatch concealed the broom cupboard, containing cleaning supplies, broom, mop, dustpan, and pail. She ran a finger across the top of the hatch. It came up black with dust.

If the next day was fine, Dola resolved to clean out the house and freshen it up. The cabinet also featured a horizontal bar, presumably for hanging up clothes, the fusebox, and a couple of painted wheels the size of her hand. Jake shouldered past her and turned both wheels clockwise, then went into the bathroom and the small sink alcove next to the Welsh dresser, where he turned all the taps on full. Tortured groaning and juddering sounds came from beneath the floor, and rusty water gushed into the basins.

The furniture in the main room consisted of an elderly couch with scratchy tweed covering; two battered end tables bearing lamps; a deep, padded armchair as old, she was sure, as the Master; a rug made of an endless, multicolored spiral; and two spindly-backed wooden chairs. It was all ancient but solid. Dola examined it with the experienced eye of a craftworker's daughter. The furniture had been so well made that with a change of upholstery it would be good for another lifetime. The rug just needed a thorough cleaning.

Jake and Skinny watched her explore for a while, then went out to get her things. Jake put a heavy box of foodstuffs down beside the fireplace. Skinny threw her sleeping bag into one of the rooms, and more bedding into the other. He had evidently been assigned to stay with her. To judge by his wordless mutters and sour glances, he was unhappy about it.

On his next trip in, he dumped the carton containing her borrowed books and magazines next to the end table. Jake, carrying the last load, nodded briefly to Skinny. He pulled a shotgun out of the box, broke it to check the load, snapped it together and handed it over to the thin man.

"I'll be back to check on you tomorrow," Jake said, pointedly not looking at Dola. Skinny nodded back. Jake walked out the door, closing it firmly behind him.

Dola looked uncomfortably at the gun. She'd never been so close to one in her life. It was chilling. The thing, meant only to take lives, had no aura except the cold radiation of steel. She wondered suddenly if she was ever intended to go home again. Was Jake leaving so he didn't witness her murder? Holding her breath warily, she watched the man study the gun.

As soon as the sounds of the departing truck died away, Skinny chucked the shotgun into a corner of the couch, and Dola breathed again.

"No television, no telephone, no video games, nothing, and the store's ten miles away," Skinny complained, dropping into the armchair. Dust flew out of the cushions. He coughed. "Ain't that the pits?"

"I'll miss none of those things," Dola said truthfully. "What is this place?"

"Hunting cabin, belonged to Ms. Gilbreth's father," Skinny said, offhandedly. "She comes here herself sometimes. Dead shot with a deer rifle." He looked around, discontented. "Got nothing but the bare bones here. I don't like sleeping in strange places. Too many creepy noises."

"Oh, I like it," Dola said, looking around herself and assessing the possibilities of the place, too curious to be haughty. "It's nice here. No humming things."

"Brr," Pilton said. The water was now running clear. He shut off the taps. A wind, autumn-cool, swept in under the door, across his feet, and set up a whirlwind in a cloud of dust on the floor. "No insulation, neither. I like a place that has things all set up for comfort, not a lonely cabin out in the middle of nowhere." Rustling and squeaking erupted outside. Skinny spun on his heel. "What's that?" he hissed.

Sitting on the hearthrug, Dola listened, her sensitive hearing picking up more detail than he could distinguish. The rustling became the movement of wings, the squeaking the voices of animals. "There are birds nesting in the eaves." She pointed. "Up on that side."

"Right," Skinny said at once. "I knew that. Nothing to worry about, right?" His voice went up half an octave on the last word.

"It's nice here," Dola said, in a soothing voice. Listen to me, she thought. I'll be telling him stories next.

"Uh-huh. You ought to get ready for bed, you know." Skinny walked into the room he'd designated as hers. She followed and watched him flatten out the sleeping bag on the bare, striped mattress, and plump up the thin pillow. He rummaged in the brown paper bags until he found the nightlight, and plugged it into the wall next to the bed. Its soft yellow glow warmed the honey maple floor. "That'll do you."

"It will," Dola said, watching him. She smiled slightly, feeling the calm night beyond the cabin walls raising her spirits. "But you can take the nightlight away. I won't need it in such natural surroundings." He bent to pull the unit out and headed for the door. Dola called out after him. "And thank you," she said.

It was the first time she had said it to him, and Pilton was charmed. "No problem," he said. He paused, as if he was going to say something, then seemed to change his mind. "You and I're gonna get along just fine here. G'night."

"Good night," Dola said. An owl hooted beyond the walls. Skinny went white around the eyes, then caught himself, and threw her a sheepish grin. He shut the door behind him.

In the middle of the night, Dola got up to go to the bathroom. When she passed Skinny's room, the glow of the nightlight shone out from underneath his door.

Chapter Thirteen

Mona Gilbreth, in full power suit, strode into the PDQ offices with her head high. It felt as if the beams of the brilliant Chicago sun were shining just for her. People had paused on the street when they saw her, standing back just a little in awe, the way they would in the presence of a celebrity. She was *known*, and it made her feel wonderful.

The taping at the television station had gone very well. The television interviewer was deferential, and stood strongly behind all female candidates no matter what their affiliations. The fact that she was a native daughter of Illinois made him stress the fact that his state was sending more women to Washington this year than any other state. Her campaign manager was delighted with the tape, which could raise her standing in the polls still higher. Her rating was already at an all-time high. Not bad for a campaign run strictly on the cheap. The station had given her a high-quality copy of the interview. There were a few sound bites in it that would make good ads.

Donations were still not pouring in, the curse of all smaller candidates in a tough economic year. Her manager had hinted that she should throw in more personal money to cover the bills that were piling up. She pretended not to understand, and he let the subject drop, saying that the creditors would undoubtedly wait until after the election, especially if it was successful. Mona knew he had hopes of becoming her aide in Washington—and why not? He was a good organizer, great with people. He could get blood out of a stone, which it sounded like he was having to. He was definitely earning his place on her staff.

The telephone call from Jake the night before reported that the child was giving no trouble, for which Mona was grateful. She was going to have to let the girl go sooner or later, but not until she elicited a promise from H. Doyle to let her alone in his turn. She sighed. Money would be nice, too. All that could be dealt with when she went home.

Paul Meier met her in the gray marble lobby, and escorted her personally up to the conference room. Mona looked down her nose at the hawk-faced man, granted him a gracious smile. In the elevator, he complimented her on her suit, her hair, and her shoes, picking with unerring instinct the three items in which she had taken the most professional pride that morning. No question, he was good at his job. Whether or not the performance was put on, it still made her relax and feel expansive.

"We want to show you the spread of where your campaign ads are being placed," Paul said, walking beside her. "I've got a complete timetable, stations, programs, the works. We'd like to do more, but we've done the best we can with the budget."

Another hint for money. Mona, groaning inwardly, carefully put him off. "For now, let's do what we can with what's already on the table," she said, smiling sweetly. "Maybe around election time I'll authorize more."

"Maybe," Paul said practically, "but then you're competing for air time with the big boys and girls. No offense, but this is a presidential election year, too. Early name recognition can save you big bucks later. You don't want to be just one of the names in the pack."

"I'm depending on you to make me stand out," Mona said, confidently, and passed through the door he held open. She stopped in midstep, staring in shock.

Keith, rising as the guest arrived, stared back. Mona Gilbreth stood in the doorway gaping at him like a rabbit caught in a car's headlights. He probably looked as surprised as she did. Mentally, he cudgeled himself for forgetting that when he interviewed her she *had* said something about coming in this Monday. He'd even mentioned it himself when he left Gilbreth. He felt like an idiot. She wouldn't see him as an ally any more, not after the last time she'd seen him, staring at her through a broken factory window stealing back an elf baby.

On the tip of his tongue was a demand that she tell him where Dola was, and why she had kidnapped the children in the first place, but he quashed the impulse at once. He needed urgently to get her aside to talk.

"My latest crop of interns," Paul was saying, swinging a hand toward them. The supervisor pulled out the chair at the head of the table for his guest. She remained standing, so he moved away from her side to the foot. "Four of the brightest young minds ever to set foot in PDQ. I'd like to keep them on deck during our discussion, if you don't mind. Dorothy Scott, Brendan Martwick, Sean Lopez, and Keith Doyle." Each of the students nodded in turn.

"How do you do?" Ms. Gilbreth said, her voice weak at first but quickly recovered. "So you're Paul's next creative team?"

"They've been reviewing your accounts, Ms. Gilbreth," Paul said. "They've been eager to meet you. The rest of your team will be here in a moment. We're planning to cover both of your campaigns this morning, the political and the commercial. We shouldn't waste an opportunity while you're up here in our neck of the woods. Can I offer you coffee? Pastries?"

"Why, yes," Mona said. She was careful not to look back at Keith. "That would be lovely."

"I'll go," Keith volunteered at once. Paul nodded at him, and he shot out the door toward the cafeteria.

Thankful that Keith had removed himself, Mona took a few deep breaths. She knew he was connected not only with Hollow Tree Farm but with PDQ. Why had seeing him struck her so hard? She ordered her pounding heart to slow down. The boy was not likely to blurt out in the middle of a meeting that she had kidnapped his young cousin, or whatever relation the girl was to him, and that she'd demanded money for her safe return. Or was he? Mona couldn't guess how he had figured out the child was concealed there. Was he working with the police? Had there been a tap on the phone line? Perhaps he had observed some trace of the children while he was visiting the factory, and arranged for the raid three days later. The thought made her uncomfortable. She realized that Paul and the young people were staring at her. She shook off the uneasy sensation, and with the air of a practiced stumper, Mona set about getting to know the other students.

It was more for practice than anything else, since none of the young people lived in her constituency. Dorothy sat at the table glancing up at her, and going back to her sketch pad, drawing something. Mona watched for a moment as Dorothy swept long, undefined lines onto the paper that suddenly took on the appearance of a handsome minimalist portrait, and began to add detail. Mona met her eyes and smiled. The black woman smiled back, and opened her lips tentatively, as if she was about to speak, but nothing came out. Mona smiled again, nodding. Abandoning

Dorothy for more interesting prospects, Mona moved on to the two other young men, who were still on their feet beside their chairs.

"It's such a pleasure to meet you, Ms. Gilbreth," Brendan Martwick said, enveloping her hand in both of his and pumping it once as he looked deeply into her eyes. His own were a compellingly intense blue, something she always found attractive. "I've been studying your product line, and I think we have something new to say about fertilizer."

There was a muffled snicker from the girl at the table, and Mona turned her back on her more firmly. She resented anyone making fun of her product. It was hard enough to be taken seriously by the people who actually bought it. "I'm looking forward to it."

"Sean Lopez," the other youth introduced himself. His handshake was jerky and awkward, but his smile was more brilliant even than Martwick's. She was struck by how handsome he was, like a young Tyrone Power. "My grandfather is a wheat farmer outside of Springfield. He uses your products."

"I'm very happy to hear that," Mona said. "I'd like to hear more, but will you just excuse me a moment?" She parted from her two admirers and took Meier aside. "That boy. Keith Doyle."

Meier's forehead wrinkled. "Something wrong with him? I know you met him last week."

"If you don't mind, Paul, I don't want him in here with us."

"Eh?" Paul asked, puzzled. "Keith is very creative. He's a fine student, and has a real knack for ideation. He could be a real boon to this session."

"He looks...well," Mona struggled for an excuse, "like he might...vote Republican, if you know what I mean."

"You're the boss," Meier said, with a shrug.

Brendan Martwick came over to show her a handful of oversized art cards. She glimpsed the black-framed storyboard format on at least one of them. "Ms. Gilbreth, while we're waiting, perhaps we can show you some of the ideas we've been working on."

Meier, allowing Brendan a chance to prove himself, backed off a short distance. Mona smiled at Brendan as he turned over each card and looked up, seeking her approval. She liked the attentive attitude of this young man, and his dashing blue eyes.

"I know it's irregular to have input from college interns, but consider," Brendan said persuasively, "just consider the image of associating yourself with America the Beautiful. 'O Beautiful for spacious skies, for amber waves of grain,' your image appears, and then music under the ad copy, then the plug, 'Gilbreth Feed and Fertilizer, for a healthy future.' Wholesome, environmental, and appealing to patriotism, too. Can you picture it?"

Mona experienced a sense of exaltation. "Yes!" she said. "That's good! That's exactly the image I want. Did you come up with that? What a talented young man you are."

Brendan glanced back at the table to see if any of the others could overhear him. "Thank you, ma'am," he said, begging the question of whose idea it had been. "I thought you'd like it."

"Oh, I do. I like the idea of associating Gilbreth Feed with America the Beautiful." Mona looked at him, and wondered if she could consider him an ally. "In fact, I'd say you have a future in this business."

"I hope so," Brendan said sincerely. "PDQ is giving me a chance to prove myself. I hope I can."

"I've been a client for a long time," Mona informed him. "I know how the program works. Have you any idea whether you're being favored for the job offer?"

Brendan glanced over his shoulder at the young woman at the table, then at the door. Mona guessed that either Dorothy Scott or the young Doyle stood ahead of him. "As much as anyone," he answered at last.

"Well, the word of a client does have some weight around here," Mona said. "If I liked your work I could insist that you be the one given the job."

Brendan smiled, giving her that intense stare. "I'd be glad to put in extra time to please such an attractive client, ma'am."

"I'm sure you'd enjoy the work," Mona said. "That young man who left…"

"Keith?" Brendan asked. He glanced over his shoulder again to make sure no one had heard the surprised exclamation.

"Yes, Keith. You think he's a little ahead of you in the running?"

"Well, I wouldn't say that," Brendan demurred.

"If you helped me, I could see him removed entirely from the race."

"With pleasure," Brendan said, in a low voice, but never losing his edge of smooth persuasiveness. "He hasn't got his mind on his job right now, and I have no idea why. You know," he added conversationally, "there's no place for a scatterbrain in this business. The more on the ball we are, the better it is for you, our client."

Mona let Brendan babble on. Reminded of the child shut up in her summer cabin, Keith's 'niece', Mona felt a twinge of guilt but pushed it down again. She was here to help create a presence for her product and herself, but mostly herself, and to protect herself from Keith and his cronies at Hollow Tree Farm. The campaign was too important to let even worried environmentalists cause her grief. And money was becoming more scarce.

"I want this ad campaign to increase business," Mona insisted out loud, for the benefit of Paul and the others. "I'll be in favor of whatever it takes to raise my receivables."

"How's the bottom line been?" a man asked, coming into the room, and shaking hands with Mona. She remembered that his name was Larry Solanson, and he was her account executive. He'd clearly heard her last statement. "Will you be able to increase your budget slightly this season?" he asked. "The prices for all kinds of ads are going up, and television commercials are going off the scale. In an election year we have to compete for production house time. We could get better saturation of your voter spread with, say, $15,000 more in the kitty."

Mona's heart sank. Not more talk about money, not when she was worrying about whether she was going to be hauled away to jail in the next half hour. Young Doyle had been gone a long time. Was he getting the police? Her worry must have shown on her face.

"Ssst, sst, sst," Paul said, with a concerned glance at her. He made damping down gestures. "Tact, Benjamin." Solanson smiled his apology for being tactless. He pulled out Mona's chair for her.

"Sorry," he said diplomatically. "I always want to do more. I forget not everyone shares my enthusiasm."

The door burst open, and Keith came in, a cardboard tray laden with small cakes and coffee cups balanced between his hands. There was a solid metal coffeepot hooked over his wrist. Gingerly, he set the bottom of the pot down on the table and worked his arm free without jostling the cups. "Sorry for the delay. We were out of doughnuts, so I ran down to the bakery." He started to approach Mona to offer her some, but Paul gestured to him to put the pastries on the table and to sit down. Keith complied promptly, and plunked into the only empty chair at the table, which lay at the far end from Mona. She was relieved that he hadn't come back with police, but he'd attempted to get close to her, and that worried her.

"Very nice. Everyone help themselves. All right," Paul said, after a woman and another man had arrived and taken their places at the table. "We're all here. Mona Gilbreth, you know Suzy Lovett, our staff artist, and Jacob Fish, who's on your creative team." Mona nodded to them, and Meier beamed. "Ms. Gilbreth, it's getting crowded in here. Would it be all right with you to keep one of my students around? Teach them how it's done? They'll understand if you need your space."

It was a tactful lie. There was still plenty of room, but he was giving her an out to avoid having Keith present. The interns looked dejected but resigned.

"Well, I don't mind one. A single observer won't crowd things too much," Mona said, and the students brightened, each hoping to be chosen. "After all, voters are voters." She smiled at them, her gaze lingering longest on Martwick, who gave her an enthusiastic grin and nod. Meier didn't miss the silent exchange.

"Okay, Brendan, you stay." Keith goggled, and raised his hand. "Nope. Room for only one. Everyone else, I've got assignments for you, too. Dorothy, you go help Ken Raito in Art with the prelim sketches on that first Judge Yeast layout. Sean, they're doing studio shots for Dunbar Tyres. I meant to tell you, they loved 'the Brain.' They want to talk to you." Meier nodded to Lopez, who looked suddenly jubilant, setting his big, dark eyes glowing. "Keith, Becky Sarter's going to be here pretty soon for a meeting. She especially requested you be in on the meeting. Go and wait in the lobby for her, will you?"

"Sure, Paul," the redhaired youth said, rising. He smiled at the table. The other two young people rose and followed him out. Mona let out a breath of pure relief when the door closed behind them.

Keith trotted down the hall toward the lobby, his head whirling. There was no point in lingering if Mona Gilbreth didn't want him there, but he wished he had some way of changing her mind. He had sensed conspiracy when Paul suddenly sent the other interns away. Well, she had no reason to welcome his presence. He knew too much, and she didn't know what he was planning to do with his knowledge. Keith wasn't sure if he would trust himself, if he was in Ms. Gilbreth's position. He was capable of embarrassing her, or worse.

All the way to the bakery and back, he had been trying to think how to approach her about Dola. He felt a little ashamed of himself for his subterfuge of going in to the Gilbreth factory to get information on hidden scandals, but more ashamed that he had missed the most important thing there, the children, until the sprites led him back. Now that he knew Gilbreth's secret, and she knew he knew, she was afraid of him. He didn't blame her, but he had to make her see reason. If she would let him act as an intermediary, maybe he could get her to release Dola in exchange for some consideration from the elves. She had let some man do the talking for her over the phone. The terms she had demanded through him were outrageous. Some middle ground had to be reached, and soon. It was a good thing the baby had been returned to her mother. He'd seen how the elves were aroused when one of their own was threatened, and feared that delays on her part would only provoke a more serious response from them. Dola, if she wasn't in any real danger, could take care of herself pretty well. As her mother had said, it was possible the girl was finding her captivity to be merely an adventure and an inconvenience, not life-threatening. He'd had a call from Frank, saying that the air sprites had gotten on to him while he was giving rides in the Skyship Iris. He'd gotten images that showed they'd found Dola's new hiding place. It had been too rough to balloon since, so the sprites were keeping an eye on her until he could get someone from the farm up there with him to track down the location.

"I guess this is what they meant in the song "Someone to watch over me," Keith had said impishly. Even if her family didn't know where she was, she remained safe and well.

He wondered if the woman had any idea of the truth about Dola and her folk, and if she planned to expose them to the world. Keith swallowed. The thought of having to hide ninety elves while he found them a new, safer haven, while being under observation himself, would be really tough.

Passing the receptionist's desk and noticing the interoffice mail on the ledge, Keith thought of sending a message in a courier

envelope in to Ms. Gilbreth during the meeting, asking to rendezvous later. She'd probably show it to Paul, who would misunder-
stand, which would get Keith bounced out of the program.
The team was planning to talk to Gilbreth until 12:30, when they
would take her to lunch. Keith saw that window as his last opportunity to take her aside before she went away again. In the meantime,
Paul had given him an assignment, and he didn't want to do anything
else that would jeopardize his internship.

He had fun with Becky Sarter, who dressed in sloppy sweats but
had a sharp mind and a cheerful disposition, a refreshing change
from the business-suited executives who came to PDQ to be amused
by their willing servants in the creative department. Becky, as she
asked them both to call her, had no unreasonable expectations, and
got a visible kick out of humor and genuine creativity. The executive
on her account sat back and listened most of the time, stopping her
to interject current market data that she didn't have, and making
Keith go back to analyze the ads he had designed for the demo-
graphic range. They talked about limited markets and the frequen-
cies of the ads needed to approach each of them. Keith learned a
lot, and came back to the conference room in a good mood. As he
reached for the handle, the door was flung open, and Mona Gilbreth
emerged. She met his eyes with the same panicked startlement, then
turned away and headed down the hall, Meier and Brendan Martwick
loping behind her like puppies.
I think the 'amber waves of grain' approach is very good,"
Ms. Gilbreth was saying. "Very clever of you to use it for the
company ads, and then my November campaign spots. The tape
brought together all the images I cherish about my company.
Very good."
"They'll associate your good business values and integrity with
your run for the House," Brendan said, almost gushing. "It's a natural. America the Beautiful, and Mona Gilbreth." Mona glowed, and
Brendan looked very pleased with himself.
"Hey, that was my slogan," Keith said, standing in the doorway.
"It could mean real percentage points in the polls," the tall blond
man walking with them said warmly. None of them appeared to
hear Keith. Heralded by its bell, the elevator arrived, and all of them
piled into the car behind Ms. Gilbreth. The door slid shut.

"Brown-nosers," Keith muttered, giving up and turning back to the conference room.

"Don't you be talking down on brown noses," Dorothy said, pointing her own nose at the ceiling, with a disapproving eye on Keith.

"I'm sorry," he said, sighing. He slumped into a chair. "I didn't mean the kind you can smell with. I mean the kind Brendan has that's always stuck up someone's rear end." He glanced significantly toward the door, and Dorothy shook her head, smiling slyly.

She put down her pencil, and got up to close the door after looking down the hall to either side. Keith watched her, curious.

"I don't want anyone to hear this," she said, coming back and sitting down close to Keith. "You've got trouble coming. That Gilbreth woman has something against you. I saw her conspiring with Brendan. He's up to something. What did you do to that woman?"

"It's nothing personal, honest," Keith said. "Purely... environmental."

"Uh-huh. You watch out for Brendan, you hear me?" the young woman warned. "He's a rat at heart, and now he's just been given a free-lance job to do what he'd like best, which is to bounce his competition out of this program." Keith nodded.

"Thanks, Dorothy, I'll be ready. I owe you."

"No way. We're partners," She gave him a thumbs up. "Judge Yeast, remember? And when are we going to work on that big ad spread that Paul wants us to come up with?"

Keith grinned. "How about now?"

"Good! I've got some ideas that beat your old ones hollow. What do you think of that?" Dorothy said, challenging him with her pencil raised like a rapier.

"Bring 'em on," Keith said with delight. "We'll see about that."

Refreshed from a good meeting, Keith felt his creative juices flowing. In no time, they had the beginnings of another good layout roughed out. Keith watched over her shoulder, and started to snicker at her final drawing.

"What's the matter with you?" she asked.

"If you put a loaf of French bread in that position with that slogan, they won't be able to air this commercial before nine P.M. on weeknights," Keith said, composing his face with difficulty. Dorothy looked from him to her sketch, and laughed sheepishly.

"I just don't think in those terms," she said, her cheeks glowing. She swatted his hand with her art gum eraser. "All right, Einstein, what other kind of bread be right for 'Getting off lightly'?"

"Brioches, maybe, or a regular loaf with a big round dome on the top. We'll make it bounce lightly across the screen, instead of lifting off at an angle."

When Brendan returned to the conference room, he had an angelic smile on his face. Keith and Dorothy glanced up at him, then went back to their work. He came around the table and sat down across from them.

"Nice. Have good meetings?" he asked them.

"Hot," Dorothy said. "They love me in Art."

"I was thinking about you during mine, Brendan," Keith said, deliberately taunting. "We were talking about desiccated prunes."

The other young man flushed. "You were all over our discussion, too, Keith. The subject was fertilizer."

"Oh, yeah," Keith said, nodding knowingly, one red brow in the air. "The kind that feeds amber waves of grain."

"Hey," Brendan said, alarmed at the covert accusation of plagiarism, "we're supposed to be a team, right? Weren't you the one pushing for creative fission?"

"What's that about fission?" Sean asked, coming in and dropping into the chair at the end of the table. His notebook had loose pages hanging out at angles. He looked exhausted but happy.

"Keith's fishin' for a compliment," Dorothy said, with a wink. "Gilbreth liked one of his lines. Brendan sold it to her."

"Hey, pretty good, you two," Sean said encouragingly. "This is what the business should be like, huh?"

Paul appeared in the door and clapped his hands together like thunder. "Well, boys and girls, it's been a hell of a day, hasn't it? You've all done very well, and I'm proud of you. I'm gonna let you go early so I can go home and collapse, too. All right? Let's clean up, and free up the room."

While the others gathered their papers and cups from the table, Dorothy showed Paul the layout she and Keith had worked up.

"Good," he said, nodding. "Consistent. Marketable. Keeps the same idea in mind. As long as you make the punch line short, people will remember it." He handed it back with an encouraging smile. "Send it over to Bob, and let's see what he thinks, all right?"

"Sure, Paul," Dorothy said, then added shyly, "I think I'm getting the hang of this."

"I know you are," Paul said. "Good job. Send it over. I'm sure Bob will think the same as I do."

Keith slewed a glance over at Brendan. "No problem, Paul. I'll put it in interoffice mail at the desk."

Keith was lucidly aware of Brendan's eyes on his back as he picked up his drawings and layouts. They followed him to the file cabinet where each of them had a drawer for keeping things in the office. Paul had the master key, but the drawers were left open most of the day for easy access. Keith figured Brendan would strike at that first. He wasn't worried. There was little about physical practical jokes he didn't know, having had dozens played upon him in the dorm. He stuffed his notebook and papers into the drawer at the usual haphazard angles. Under cover of the rest, he crumpled one of them into a ball at the bottom of the drawer, putting his will into it, giving the fibers more strength, and *enhancing* the shape of the piece of paper, square and flat. Leaving the crushed paper concealed, he hastily slid the drawer shut.

"'Night, Paul. 'Night, Dorothy. I'll drop this at the desk for Bob." Keith left the room with a cheery farewell wave to the others, and whistled a little tune as he walked down the hall to the elevator.

He wished he could be there to enjoy the results when Brendan pulled the drawer open.

Chapter Fourteen

Though he was impatient to know how the search was going, Keith waited until he got home that evening before calling the farm. Calla, Holl's mother, picked up the phone.

"They've moved her far away," Calla said, in answer to Keith's question, "but your friends are on the trail. The Big One and the Small Ones of the Air have sniffed out a hiding place they think to be hers."

"That's great!" Keith exclaimed.

"Aye. Holl and my great-grandson have gone out with them to see if the sighting was a true one."

"I can't believe Tay got back into a balloon on purpose," Keith said, laughing out loud. His brother and sister, watching television at the other end of the room, glanced back to see what was so funny, and went back to their program.

"Believe," Calla said, answering his chuckle with one of her own. "Love conquers even the greatest of fears. And did it not, he would still never dare to show the white feather. The Master has gone with them."

"You're kidding!"

She gave her warm laugh again. "No indeed. I wish I were a bird in the sky, to see what it is like."

"There'd be a flock of us up there," Keith said. "Keep me posted. I want to hear the moment they bring Dola home. And I've got to hear all about the Master in a balloon."

"I promise you, Keith Doyle," Calla said. "You shall."

"Your laconic discourse does nothing to enhance understanding," the Master said, disapprovingly. "Please try to use complete sentences. Ve haf plenty of time until the wind calms down and your craft may lift."

Frank took a deep breath and tried again to explain. Holl, leaning up against the balloon basket with his pipe between his teeth, exchanged sympathetic glances with Tay, and pushed the bill of his Cubs cap down over his eyes to hide his expression. Shaking his head, Tay copied his gesture. "Keith's air sprites came this morning while I was giving rides. Scared hell out of my passengers. They zoomed around like fireflies."

"The passengers?" the Master asked, peering at him over his glasses. For all that his inquisitor, fedora hat and all, came up no higher than his middle shirt button, Frank Winslow seemed to be thoroughly intimidated.

"N-no, the air sprites. They made pictures at me."

"Their means of communication, Master," Holl put in. "They can project images into your mind's eye."

"I see."

"Pretty but confusing," Winslow added. "Two pictures over and over again, one of that little blond girl in the dark in front of a—a striped house, and another where she was walking on a leash."

"Around her neck? Like a dog?" Tay asked, his face darkening.

Frank thought about it. "No, like a toddler." He sketched a body harness on his own frame with his hands.

"That gifs me a gut picture of her situation," the Master said. "And they vill help us to find the house mit stripes?"

The balloon pilot made an impatient gesture at the sky. "Yeah, if this wind ever dies down." The nearby treetops were leaning slightly to the northeast, and their uppermost twigs, whistling and crackling, swayed in an impatient dance.

At a small helium tank in the rear of the pickup truck, Frank filled a rubber balloon, tied it off, and let it go. It sped upward and out of sight into the eastern sky. There were already streaks of color at the horizon, reminding them that night was little more than an hour away. Frank watched it carefully, and shook his head. Holl tapped out his pipe and put it away.

"Pity we can't whistle down the wind, as Keith Doyle is always suggesting we can," Holl said, with a twinkle in his eye. Frank looked at him. "Oh, you've not been listening to his stories, have you?" Holl asked. "Do you think I can stick my fingers in my mouth like this," he put thumb and forefinger in his mouth and blew a piercing blast, "and the wind will die down as I will it to?"

At that moment, the treetops on the perimeter of the field straightened up and the swaying came to a standstill, their slight noise dying away. Frank turned to look at Holl, who returned his stare indignantly.

"Coincidence," he said. "Oh, come now, it was about to happen."

"Circus stunt," Murphy scoffed. "I saw the trees on the west calming down half a second before he did it."

"Uh-*huh*," Frank said, his eyes still on Holl. The other elves looked amused. He swallowed hard. "We better get moving, then." He and Murphy moved to pull the bag containing the balloon out of the truck bed.

"How may ve help you?" the Master asked.

Following the instructions of the humans, the Little Folk helped spread out the Iris's balloon, and helped raise its mouth to face the fan while Murphy and Frank fastened the steel loops of the cables to the burner assembly. Swiftly, the great rainbow filled out. Tay, the Master, and Holl helped hold it in place until the fan was replaced by the burners, and the balloon rose off the ground of its own accord.

"Sure are strong for midgets," Murphy offered a grudging compliment. Tay grinned.

"You should run away and join us at the circus," he shouted over the burners. "We've a place for giants like you."

Frank climbed into the basket and Murphy helped flip it upright. "Hop in!" Frank yelled. "She's ready to go!"

Tay and Holl hopped over the edge, and held out their hands to the Master. Murphy held on to the woven belt threaded through the basket, keeping it down until the little man was aboard.

Murphy let go, and the Skyship Iris once again performed her magic, as the earth dropped effortlessly and soundlessly away beneath them, and the trees came forward to meet them.

"Murphy thought you were from the circus," Frank said as soon as they were aloft. "How come he didn't know what you are?"

"People see vhat they believe they see," the Master said. "He believes us to be vun thing, so for him that is vhat ve are. You see us as another thing, but efen you do not truly know."

"You must not be very much help at home," Dola complained to Skinny. He had spent nearly the whole of the first day and half the second reading magazines flat on his back on the old couch while Dola had cleaned around him. She decided she was not going to do all the work and leave him to sit about like an invalid.

"It's just gonna get dirty again," Skinny said, glancing around him. He pointed at the bottom of the door, which hung a thumb's breadth too high in its frame. "The wind comes right through here."

"Well, I can't live waiting for the dust to settle. Will you not help?"

Skinny seemed surprised she'd asked. "I thought you brownie things got all bent out of shape if anyone helped you with the housework," he said.

Dola put her hands on her hips. "I've told you, I'm a natural creature, not a fantastic thing like a brownie."

"Uh-huh, sure." Skinny went back to his magazine.

"Ugh!" Dola exclaimed, throwing up her hands. "I can't take the time to explain things over and over to you."

"Why not?" Skinny abruptly let loose of all the resentment he had saved up. His face turned red, and he waved his arms, advancing on her in fury. "We got nothing *but* time! All my days off, and I've gotta stay nights here, too! And then I'm stuck with a gal who yells more than my wife does. Go ahead, tell me again!"

Dola, big-eyed, dropped her broom and shrank back from Skinny. It was this new side of him Jake appealed to when he handed over the shotgun. She was reminded all over again that Big Folk were dangerous, and though he seemed as much a playful buffoon as Keith Doyle, Skinny was a stranger. She withdrew a half-step at a time toward her sleeping room, wondering if the iron lock on the door was enough to hold him off while she spelled the wood closed.

Skinny's fearsome mood ended as quickly as it had begun when he realized he'd frightened her. He extended a hand to her. "I'm sorry, little girl. I didn't mean to blow up at you. It...this is all wrong, I know it."

Dola nodded, not touching him, not prepared to trust him again so soon. She fought to regain her former confidence, but it sounded in her own ears like bravado. "All right, then," she said, looking up at him. "We're both shut up against our will. We will make the best of it, shall we?"

Skinny nodded slowly. He looked sidelong at her as if asking permission, then went back to the couch and picked up his magazine. She didn't protest. He sat down. Dola picked up the broom and went back to sweeping dust out of the corners. It was less trouble to work alone than to set off the Big One's unchancy temper, but she still resented his laziness.

Once the floor was reasonably clean, Dola sat down on the hearth rug with a frayed pillow slip taken from the store of tattered bed linens in the bedroom dresser. It was useless, having been washed and used until it was threadbare as gauze. It would do to make light strips of the kind the Folk used at home, to supplement the sad light bulbs in the elderly lamps. She cut a small slit in the hem with her belt knife, gathered the edges in both hands, and tore.

Skinny's head popped up again. "What are you doing with that?" He leaned over the back of the couch and yanked the cloth out of her hands.

"Making a cleaning rag," Dola said reasonably. "This place is a terrible mess. Won't your Boss-lady be pleased if it's in better order next time she comes?"

"I guess." Skinny tossed it back at her. "All right. I'm being jumpy. You just scared heck out of me."

As long as he left her alone, she used the quiet time to concentrate on finding her folk in the great distance. The ride, two nights before, had taken so many twists and curves that she was all disoriented. Her mind swept slowly in a great arc, seeking and touching, until she found them. Strong as a beacon, the reassuring presence of the Folk reached out to her and gave her confidence. She wondered what it was that had stood between her and them before, and if they could see her now.

Now that she had a vector to follow, she might start out any time to finding her way away from this place, but only the birds and cartographers knew what stood in the way between here and home. She'd bide her time until she knew more about the land in between. All the necessities were here for her comfort. The moment she was ready, she'd vanish. There wasn't enough metal in these walls to harm her. They were only wood, and felt so weak in some spots that she could kick through with her bare foot. When she meant to escape, it would be no trouble.

In the depths of the old couch, Dola heard the rustle and sigh, as Skinny finished his magazine and put it down. She addressed him, pitching her voice so it was impossible for him to ignore her.

"Do you know why it is the Boss-lady is keeping me here? I am sure she doesn't want me."

"Dunno," Skinny said. "I think it has something to do with Ms. Gilbreth running for election." He clapped his hand over his mouth.

"Oh, I already know her name," Dola said easily. "I know a lot about her. But why would anyone vote for her?"

"Well, 'cause she's for all the right things. Education. The environment. Farmer's rights."

"But it is only sensible to be for these things," Dola said. "Isn't her opponent in favor of them, too?"

"No," Skinny said, then added by way of amendment, "well, he says he is, but he's lying."

"And how do you know that Boss-lady is not also lying?"

That flustered him. "'Cause I work for her. I know she's for those things. She says so all the time."

"Saying is not doing," Dola said, thinking of the nasty smelling sludge that came out of the truck that took her away from Hollow Tree Farm. It was the same that the water-workers were complaining had to be cleaned out of the aquifer. It was proof that Gilbreth employees were the ones dumping, if only she could go home to tell the Master. "It does sound as if there is not much to choose between the candidates."

"You don't know about politics," Skinny said, but he didn't sound sure, either. He fell silent, staring at the window. Dola followed his eyes.

"It's a fine day. What about taking a walk in the woods?"

"No way," Pilton said, uneasily. "You'd just jump into a tree somewhere, and I'd never find you."

"Oh, would you stop?" Dola asked, exasperated. "I live neither in trees nor in little burrows under rocks. Walking's all I wish. Fresh air, and maybe some herbs for the cooking. We must eat, and I'd rather it be flavored with something other than the dusty preparations in those boxes," she shrugged toward the food supplies. "Unless you plan to cook."

"Uh-uh. I'm not so good at cooking. Usually my wife cooks."

"Never fear," Dola told him. "I will continue to make the meals. In exchange, you wash the dishes."

He eyed her. "Who's getting the short end of that deal, huh?"

"You needn't eat your own cooking. Isn't that worth a little trouble?" Dola asked.

Skinny stood up and stretched. "Oh, all right. It's better than being cooped up in here all day."

Dola went to the door to wait. Instead of following her, Skinny started looking around. His eye lit on the length of twine used to hold the food box shut. He lifted it, and yanked it between his hands to test its strength.

"And what is that for?" Dola asked, warily.

"For you," Skinny said. "I can't trust you. Jake and the Boss-lady will be down my throat if I let you get away. Hold your arms out from your sides."

Patiently, Dola held up her arms and stood while Skinny tied a loop of rope around her waist. He took the free end in one hand and unlocked the door.

"*Now* we'll go."

It was well worth the inconvenience to get away from the musty-smelling cabin and into the fresh air. As soon as she was out from under the roof, she felt outward with all her strength for a sense of her family, hoping that her father and Holl would be able to trace her there.

She sensed nothing. Instead, she returned her attention to the world around her. The forest, rich with the rain that had fallen over-night, smelled green and healthy. Dola inhaled breath after breath, enjoying the fresh air.

Skinny stumped along behind her on the narrow dirt path, tugging on her tether from time to time as if to keep her in check. After one annoyed glance over her shoulder to show him what she thought of such treatment, he stopped pulling back so hard. She needed her balance to keep from tripping over roots that rose up suddenly on the way. Her guess that it was a deer path was con-firmed when she spotted the narrow double-slotted hoofprints in the rain-softened earth.

And now to the question of herbs. The men had brought enough food with them to feed the village for two days. She had cooked something out of a box the night before, after choosing which one smelled the least antiquated. All the Big Folk packaged goods seemed as if they were years old. Nothing could make generic macaroni and cheese or dehydrated beans and sauce *delicious*. If she added some-thing fresh, it at least might make them palatable. She spotted a handful of wild mustard growing in the midst of a rough patch of ground. She started toward it, thoughts of cooked greens and spice making her mouth water. She was jerked back harshly, and uttered a wordless protest.

"Where are you going?" Skinny demanded, as she straightened up with the help of a tree branch.

"Only to pick herbs," she said. "Look there."

"Weeds?" he asked scornfully.

"No, food! Look about you! Tender young dandelion greens, a few late fiddlehead ferns, a few early mushrooms here and there. It's a cornucopia of good things to eat, all fresh and all free."

"Well," Pilton thought about it, "if you want to eat them, I guess you can. Maybe your diet's different than mine."

"Healthier, I'm sure," Dola said, ironically. With Skinny in close attendance holding her leash tightly, she picked a huge elephant-ear leaf and began to fill it with young plants. She dropped to her knees beside the lushest bed of plants and began to tell them over. The quick-growing mustard was in all three stages: green, flowering, and past gone to seed. Some was even young enough to yield the tender greens that were the tastiest. Judging Skinny's appetite to be three times' hers, she picked enough to feed them both.

None of the oldest mustard plants had any seed left. All the pods were dried to brown husks and split open. Well, that wouldn't stop the cooks at home who wanted mustard to cook with, and she had the skills to follow their example. She glanced behind her to see what Skinny was doing. He looked down at her from time to time, but he was bored, and was paying little attention to what she was doing. All the better, she thought.

With a little smile, she put two fingers on either side of the nearest blossom and pulled at it, *enhancing* the growth process. Behind the blossom, which began to wilt, the seed pod lengthened into a tube of green as long as her finger and as thick as a pencil lead. It filled out slowly. The petals dropped off, leaving the pistil, and the pod began to turn golden, then sere. She moved on to the next one, until she had plenty of ripe seed, and uprooted the weed into her makeshift basket. Her attentions had aged the plant before its time, but she took care to drop a pod's-worth of seed where the roots had been, to start the next generation of plants growing. No sense in robbing the forest that had been so generous to her.

"What's all that?" he asked.

Dola described everything in the leaf-basket.

"My mama makes good greens," Pilton said, hopefully. Maybe this walk wasn't the wild-goose chase it first seemed.

"So does mine." Dola felt a pang as she thought of Siobhan and Tay.

"Come on, let's go back," Pilton said, with an impatient tug at her leash. Dola straightened up, her treasures in her hands.

Skinny seemed much more cheerful on the way back to the cabin. He even filled a pan with water so she could soak the sand out of the greens. Dola turned them over, yanked out the tough inner veins, and went looking through the foodstuffs to find things to cook with.

Many of the supplies were packet mixes, which claimed to be complete meals. Dola read them all, and discarded anything that had more than three ingredients she couldn't recognize. Soon, there was an aluminum Dutch oven swinging from the pot hook filled with a savory, bubbling mixture smelling delightfully of mustard seed, wild chives, and wild marjoram. There was a can of bacon in the box, a traditional American addition to greens. She handed the package to Pilton to open. Using a hooked attachment in his pocket knife, he ratcheted the lid off. Recalling as much as she could from the recipe, Dola fried a chunk of bacon until there was a film of grease in the bottom of the pan, then added the greens to wilt.

"You oughta use the cast iron pot," Pilton said.

"I don't like those," she said, eyeing the iron stoveware uneasily.

"Well, aluminum causes Alzheimer's disease, you know?"

"This is lighter," Dola said sharply, not wanting to talk about her Folks' sensitivity to iron. "If you cook, you may cook in what you please."

"Well, all right," Skinny said, and went back to his magazines. Dola was glad to have the peace and quiet to think.

It was satisfying to be in such a good place. The logs were well-aged hardwoods, providing a steady, hot flame. Swiftly, she tended the fire under the pot, and mixed a simple dough to make flattened breads on the pot lid while the meal was cooking.

"You're good at that, you know?" Pilton asked suddenly from behind her. He was impressed by the little girl's adaptation to her surroundings, and her knowledge of woodcraft and housekeeping. Whoever taught the little fairy woman how to do it all ought to be proud of their pupil.

She nodded politely at his compliment, and went back to tending the cooking.

It was a pity he'd had to go and have a temper tantrum like that earlier, because the girl had shied away from him ever since. She had ever reason to be aloof, because she was a prisoner. He wished she would like him, because she was really something different. He wondered when he could get her to grant a wish for him.

Not far above three hundred feet, a couple of air sprites swooped in upon the Skyship Iris, circling and circling it, their tails whipping past their eyes at amazing speed. Holl saw the traditional image of sunrise in his mind, and tried to picture a slightly different one in response. They seemed to be happy with his efforts, for they slowed down and stared, the pupils of their huge eyes widening joyfully at him.

"Sunrise is their greeting," he explained to the Master, "and sunset their farewell."

"So Meester Doyle has told me," the Master said tersely. He had said little during the ascent. Holl wondered if he was as nervous as Tay, who had retired to his usual spot on the floor of the basket. Likely not: he seemed to have no difficulty looking down at the ground, but that could be because he was forcing himself. It was also impossible to tell if he was enjoying the flight.

The Master, knowing in advance from Keith Doyle what to expect, was able to communicate immediately in the sprites' pictorial style without needing to verbalize at the same time. Holl knew that there was a conversation going on between them only because he could see the sprites' reply to the Master's queries. He was asking about their origins, their numbers, and what they subsisted on. The images were colorful, but confused, as if they didn't understand why he was asking those questions.

"They seem to haf very limited intelligence," the Master said at last. "Each does not haf much on its own. I belief they haf more of a hive consciousness, like bees."

The sprites protested at once, showing a beehive from which sprites swarmed out and in, that burst apart into individual clouds.

"They say no," Holl translated. In their typically feisty and mischievous response to a challenge, the sprites' next image was one of the Master in the basket of the balloon, smiling broadly and looking around him with wonder in his eyes. Even though the situation was serious, and he didn't show any outward signs of enjoyment, the Master had apparently found there was much to take pleasure in. Holl smiled. "They also say you are having a good time."

The Master peered disapprovingly over his glasses at the nearest sprite. The creature's pupils swelled, giving it an innocent, puppylike expression. It gazed back.

"It's no use," Tay laughed. "They can read your thoughts."

"Then let them see these," the Master said, his brow furrowing. The creatures of the air soared up and back in agitation, then revealed the images Frank had told them about: Dola in front of a log cabin chinked with concrete, and Dola walking on a rope lead before a tall man with brown hair.

"They vill now lead us to her," he said, folding his arms with an air of finality. The sprites swirled away from the basket and took their places ahead of the balloon.

Night was falling. Dola scraped the last of the food out the door onto a pile Skinny had designated for edible garbage. She took the pots back inside and washed them out, then banked the cookfire so it would keep them warm until bedtime. She was getting bored with her imprisonment. Skinny was not worth talking to. There were no friends to play with, no lessons, no books to read, no music, and, she sighed, no Asrai. She felt it was time to formulate her escape.

Skinny was her chief obstacle, but she felt she could get around him, with care. He'd been so suggestible while she was incarcerated in the office. If they hadn't been interrupted by Jake, she and Asrai would have been long gone.

It wasn't too late to prepare the ground again. Besides, Dola chided herself, she ought to practice her lessons. Just because she was from home didn't mean she could be allowed to go rusty. Dola quivered to think what the Master would say if she was saved, and had neglected her education. She glanced up. Skinny was in the bathroom. He always lay at one end of the couch, reading by the light of the lamp over his head, with his feet up on the other armrest. She studied the other lamp. Both had woven cloth shades that reached almost all the way to their earthenware bases. She got up to touch one. The illusions almost leaped from her fingers to the rough fabric. It would hold pictures well. She made a face appear to grin conspiratorially with her.

Normally she had had to hold on to a cloth to keep the illusion alive. She yanked her hands back from the shade, seeing how long the face would remain without contact. She was able to count to sixty before the illusion faded. That was a good long time, she told herself. But how to extend the effect? More concentration might be the answer, lending a little of her will to the tooth of the cloth. The face laughed at her for twice sixty and longer. Dola was jubilant. She made the whole thing seem to vanish. All that remained visible was the toelike shape of the protruding base and the tip of the brass bulb holder on top.

She heard water running, and fled back to her seat on the hearth rug. Skinny emerged, wiping his hands on his pants legs. She looked up innocently at him. He flopped down on the couch and picked up his magazine.

"Where'd the lamp go?" he asked.

"I've not taken it away," Dola said, turning a page in her book. "It's a big heavy thing. I'd not lift it."

"But it's gone." Skinny said, pointing. The earthenware base, much the same color as the table on which it sat, blended in against its surroundings.

"No, it is right there," she insisted. With a sigh for the obtuseness of Big Folk, she rose and went over to the lamp. At the same time that she turned it on, she dropped the illusion. "There. You see? But we don't need it; it is not dark out yet." She turned it off. Skinny gave it an uneasy glance. He picked up his magazine.

Dola left a fading charm on the lampshade, so that it vanished slowly away again. Over the edge of his periodical, Skinny checked again, and jumped.

"You stop that!" he demanded. Dola raised her hands.

"I've done nothing," she said, but she was secretly pleased.

During the next few hours, Dola played with the shadows in the room, practicing making faces appear amidst the hanging curtains and long arms of darkness reach forth from the sides of the chimney. The thin man kept looking up from the page he seemed to have read a dozen times, becoming more and more nervous. The shadows looming about the fireplace grasped for him, and withdrew into the dancing of the firelight.

"I dunno what's going on in here," he said.

"All houses have an aura, did you know?" Dola said, matter-of-factly. "A personality of their own. It may be that this one doesn't like you, holding an innocent child prisoner as you are."

He looked around suspiciously, refusing to acknowledge that he more than half believed her. "It ain't as if I'm hurting you," he said, projecting his voice to the corners of the room. "Besides, you aren't an innocent child. Well, you aren't an ordinary one anyhow."

"Then beware, lest my presence stir up the household spirits to haunt you," Dola said, in the sepulchral voice she used for telling ghost stories to the smaller village children. Skinny blanched.

A light breeze came in under the door and whistled in the chimney. Dola played with the shadows, making pictures on the floor in the firelight. Left to themselves, they crept across the rag rug, spiraled up the leg of the couch like snakes, and waited for the human to notice them. Catching a peripheral glimpse of his stalkers, Skinny's head jerked first one way, then the other. He whimpered. The shadows melted. Dola saw the whites of his eyes all the way around his irises and decided it was time to stop teasing him. He was really frightened. Maybe one more vision, but something harmless and colorful, as she might make for the baby. In the fabric of the rug, she began to craft her illusion.

"I don't want the house to hate me," Skinny said. "Ms. Gilbreth would be real sore if I let you go. But maybe I'd do it anyway, if you do some real magic for me."

"What do you want, a chest of jewels?" she asked, with heavy sarcasm.

"Can you do that?" he asked, surprised, then greedy. Dola was disgusted.

"No! We can barely cover the mortgage payment of a month. Of all the foolish questions. I'm an ordinary girl. All the things I do are ordinary."

"I know better," the man said, leaning back with his arms folded over his chest. "I saw you vanish the other day, and you know it. Do some big magic for me."

She started to stir the influence she was drawing from the rag rug. No illusion was beyond her power, but what if he wanted to touch what she conjured up? It was all very well, having him promise to set her free, but she couldn't pay his price. Maybe she should use the last vision to scare him again. A dragon! No, a rainbow. Dola thought of her father, and Holl, and the Master, out looking for her, standing in a wicker basket high in the air, suspended underneath a rainbow. Keith Doyle had visited more than once in such a conveyance. She attempted to thrust the vision away, putting it down as an unlikely fantasy. Besides, rainbows weren't scary.

At the same time, she felt that someone was looking at her. Something white bobbed past the window of the cabin. Dola bent her head and glanced sideways to watch it. Pictures appeared in her mind, of Tay smiling, Holl falling in a river, Keith Doyle with his camera. She tilted her head further, and saw kindly blue eyes looking in at her through the glass. The face itself made her gasp. It was featureless, the blue-white of cirrus clouds. The head and body were grotesquely distorted, and kept changing shape as she watched. She had no idea what kind of being it was, only that it was friendly and intelligent. It was trying to tell her that her folk were seeking her.

Behind it, far away in the sky, she saw a colorful dome shape, the same thing she'd seen the day Keith and her father had rescued Asrai. All at once she realized it was the great balloon that belonged to Keith Doyle's friend. Taking the bobbing creature's appearance as an omen of good fortune, she decided it was time to escape. The white thing would serve as a proper distraction.

"I can't fetch money for you, but I can make visible the spirit of the house so you can atone. Look there!" She pointed out the window. The white shape floated past again, its body stretching and reforming. "See!"

"A ghost!" Pilton yelled. "This place is haunted!"

Dola leaped to her feet. While he was frozen, Dola meant to make a dash for the door and let herself out. Skinny cut her off in his dive for the shotgun. He pushed her down into the shadow of a chair. She realized too late what Skinny was doing.

"Go away!" she cried to the creature. But the man, rolling over like a commando, drew a bead, aimed, and fired.

The crash of the glass pane blowing out of the window was drowned out by Dola's scream. The white creature, caught in a shape with a grossly inflated head and puny, wasted body and wings, seemed to explode soundlessly. It spread out across the sky, becoming more and more misshapen until it dissipated like oil on the surface of a pond. Before it vanished. Dola saw an image in her mind of the kindly eyes going wide in fear and pain. She sank to the floor where she crouched, rocking, tears racing down her cheeks.

"It was a live thing! You've killed a lively, intelligent creature," Dola wept. "I can't sense it any more. It's gone."

Skinny gawked at the shards of glass hanging in the window frame, went over to look down, around, then up. "No, you made it up. There ain't no body out there. I bet there's nothing in the house, either," he accused her. "You're trying to make me feel bad because you're stuck here with me. It was just an illusion, wasn't it?" He didn't sound convinced, and he was getting worried, watching her cry. "You did the magic."

"I didn't, I didn't," Dola insisted. "It was real. It came to look after me, and now it's dead."

The small sprite fluttering about the balloon cables gave them the picture it received: Dola sitting on the floor of a small building with something white in her hands. Then, abruptly, the air creature became agitated, zooming back and forth like a hysterical firefly.

"What ails this being?" the Master asked. "All it shows us is empty sky." The tiny sprites flying alongside swirled together like dust-storms and broke apart, their huge eyes wide with fear.

"It's gone," Frank said, his voice rough and dry. "They don't know where. What happened?"

"Frightened by something into fleeing out of range?" Tay guessed.

Holl watched the terrified antics of the remaining sprites and shook his head. What he felt from them chilled his heart. "Farther away than that," he said. "They communicate over great distances. It probably can't find its friend because its friend isn't there to find any longer. Something terrible has happened."

All four of them fell silent for a long time. The Little Folk were upset because the missing sprite had assumed great personal risk to go into the lower atmosphere to help them find Dola. Whatever had befallen it was partly their fault. Frank's eyes and nose were red with suppressed grief and anger. Holl guessed that the sprites were to him a representation of a kind of benevolent force of the skies. They meant something more to the pilot than just new acquaintances. Holl was very sorry for him.

Turning his face away from the Little Folk, Frank flicked a careless finger at the gauge. It showed that the propane tanks were nearly empty. "Going down," he pronounced shortly.

Almost automatically, he searched out a safe place to land the balloon, and dialed the number for the chase truck, directing it to the

Applied Mythology

right field. The other sprites surrounding the balloon flew in mournful circles until the Iris dropped below their safe limit, and went away.

Pilton took Jake aside on the porch that evening when he came by to check on them. He told the whole story of the afternoon: herbs, disappearing furniture and all, ending with the story of the ghost and the child's bursting into hysterics.

"This ain't right," he said over and over. "We can't just keep her here forever. The spirits are mad at us. Something awful's gonna happen if we don't let her go home."

"Take it easy, Grant," Jake said. "You saw a wood pigeon or a lost lake gull, not a ghost."

"If I shot a gull, then where is it?" Pilton demanded. "You shoot something dead, there's a body. I know I killed it. You gotta send this kid home, Jake." He was shaken. Jake couldn't understand. He didn't see the thing fly apart into a million pieces, and he didn't have to sit with the fairy woman as she cried her eyes out over something that died but didn't bleed.

"She won't talk to me no more," Grant added. "And she locked herself in her room. She's been there for hours."

Jake went away and came back to keep watch with him while the Boss-lady drove up to meet them.

Mona came out of the cottage, feeling as if she'd just gone twenty rounds in the ring with the heavyweight champion. It had taken all her skill at persuasion to talk her way into the barricaded bedroom to speak to the child, who stared at her sullenly and gave only single-syllable replies to her questions.

"You scared the hell out of me with your phone call, Grant," Mona said, shutting the door quietly. "She's all right. You don't understand how important she is to us. She is our only guarantee of H. Doyle's good behavior. He's got too much on us. You've got to keep her from getting hurt. You're not to scare her any more. You're not even to talk loud. Understand?"

"Yes, Ms. Gilbreth," Pilton said, apologetically.

Mona leaned against the cabin wall. "I don't like this. The whole situation is escalating. I feel threatened, and I don't know what to do. Since her people have proof that it's us, why haven't they called in the police?"

"Probably afraid the kid'll wind up dead," Jake said, a silhouette standing just out of the cabin light. Mona stared at him, shocked, then realized he was right. That would be what *she'd* think.

"They can't call the police," Pilton corrected them scornfully. "They're fairies. As far as the police are concerned, they don't exist."

"No," Jake said, thoughtfully, "but maybe the place is full of illegals. There's a company running from that location, called Hollow Tree Industries. Makes woodcrafts for gift stores. Isolated— perfect place for illegals to hide out. I checked on the census. The place is owned by Keith Doyle."

Mona exclaimed wordlessly.

Williamson continued. "But there's no one else. No voters registered, no driver's licenses at that address, nothing. Just Keith Doyle."

"Course not," Pilton said scornfully, though the others were ignoring him. "No one believes they exist. 'Cept me, of course."

"So neither of us want the cops involved," Mona says thoughtfully. "I didn't think anyone could be so squeaky clean. That evens things out a little. But they *know* it's us. That's the part that worries me. They gave up a little too easily. I want to know what they're up to."

Chapter Fifteen

"At least we know now that she is safe," Siobhan said, shaking her head. She had joined the vigil in the kitchen that evening, sitting up through the next morning, waiting for more communication from their Big Folk helpers or the kidnappers. They had called Keith Doyle to tell him about the disappearance of the air sprite. Their friend was devastated, but was as helpless as they to do anything. Holl begged him not to cut another day out of his work schedule, but to work on their behalf from where he was. Keith swore that was what he would do. Diane had phoned in a few minutes later, saying she had talked to Keith. She volunteered to take the next trip up with Frank Winslow as a proxy for Keith. The Little Folk were not certain when they would hear again from the pilot. After the balloon landed, he had packed up his craft, driven them home, and driven away again, all in complete and bitter silence. His grief was deeper than any of theirs.

The sun had been up for an hour, and still no call. Siobhan was beyond tears, and into a kind of exhausted resignation. "A pity the little one could not tell you where to find her."

"It may have tried," Holl said, gently, "but its fellows were too upset at its disappearance—I dare not call it death, for we don't know—to tell us of its last sendings. The area where it flew is forested and hilly. We could explore it, but we would have to do so on foot. Our bumbling around would likely alert Dola's guardians."

"If this was our Library," Curran said, peevishly, "we'd hae no trouble at a'. We knew every nook of th' place. This big world belongs to Big People, and has noothing to do wi' us."

"Our hands remain tied," the Master said.

"I'd shut the gates on the lot of them in a twinklin'," Curran finished. "We can do f'r oursel', have done and still can."

"Now, father, you know ve may not do that," Rose said, taking his arm. "Ve haf taken on responsibilities, and those ve may not lay down." The crotchety old elf seemed ready to continue the argument when the telephone rang.

Catra jumped up to take the call. She picked up the receiver to listen. Turning to the others, she put her hand over the mouthpiece and nodded her head. Holl strode over and took the handset from her.

"Hello?" the man's voice said.

"Put on your mistress," Holl said. "I will not talk to you any longer. We know you're not alone."

Ignoring the look of desperation on his employer's face, Jake extended the phone to Mona. She was shaking too much at first to take it and had to hold the receiver in both hands to keep from dropping it on the desktop. Jake leaned in close to listen.

"What do you want?" Mona whispered.

The hated voice of H. Doyle spoke. "Give us your final condition so that we can have our child back again."

"Is this being taped?" Mona asked.

"You'd not believe me if I said no, so does it matter? Tell me your condition."

"I want you to stop pestering me in the paper," Mona said, her voice growing stronger as she felt herself getting heated. "No more letters. No more complaints. You're ruining my campaign, my business—my whole life. I never want to see or hear from Hollow Tree as long as I live. Leave me alone!"

"I see," the voice said. "I must consider this. I will call you back." There was a click on the line, and a dial tone.

"He hung up on me," Mona said, aggrieved.

"It's a stupid woman," Tay's wife declared, bitterly. "All we have to do was make a promise we would bother her no more, and she would give back our girl."

"I dinna believe it," Keva said. "Nor should ye."

"It vould not be enough now," the Master said. "The grievance does not end vith us. She has been responsible for damaging the land vith her poisons. She vould still be liable for her crimes against nature. She must stop. If for no other reason than those, we could claim injury from her. It is our land upon vhich she has been pouring out the trucks full of vaste, and the harm is done. There has been no promise from her that she vould nefer again commit the same deed. She vill haf her punishment, and it vill be appropriate. As in the Mikado, let the punishment fit the crime. Keith Doyle has said not to antagonize, but not to gif in. I agree mit his suggestion." There was a protest. He signed to the others to be silent. Out of respect, they sat down to listen. The Master continued.

"Let us appear to be cooperating for the moment. When the time comes, we will have our vengeance. She has commanded us under threat to refrain from criticizing her. It is a small thing. Ve shall appear to do as she asks. In the meantime, let us undermine her. Others vill seem to write the diatribes. Ve vill influence those mit whom ve come in contact."

Holl's lips smiled, but his eyes were hard. Tay, beside him, nodded. "Good thinking, Master."

Holl dialed the number for Gilbreth Farm and Feed. The sweet voice of the receptionist answered, and offered to transfer the call. The other end was snatched up on first ring.

"We promise we will make no more direct attacks upon you."

"Good," Mona Gilbreth said. Holl thought she sounded relieved.

"What about the girl?"

Gilbreth paused. "I'm too busy today. I'll be in touch with you later." She cradled the phone hastily, but didn't bang it down.

"She retains overt control," the Master said, nodding, "but the real power is still ours. Now ve vill make her nervous. In time, she may gif up Dola mitout asking us to fulfill her demands."

Following the Master's instructions, Catra and Marcy sat down over the human woman's personal computer and composed a handbill about clean environment and honesty in government. Marcy supervised the printing out of a hundred or so copies and handed them over to the Little Folk who enhanced the sense of reasonability of the text.

"It vill haf the underlying effect of making the reader question the potential polluter in their midst," the Master explained. "The seeds vill be planted. Efery day she delays returning Dola to us, the effect vill be stronger."

At Midwestern University, the administration and the Voters of the Future Program had set up a platform for the local candidates to use. Both Mona and the incumbent seeking reelection to the House seat she wanted were going to be allowed equal opportunity to address the students and faculty. On the advice of her campaign manager and some of her volunteer workers who were of college age, Mona had altered her speech, leaving out references to farm subsidies and retirement benefits, in favor of the environment, education, and rights for the disabled. Her workers, visible in their pressed-foam skimmer hats with rose-colored bands, worked the crowd, handing out buttons and balloons. The campaign staff for the other side countered, handing out blue impedimenta to those who wouldn't take "Gilbreth for Congresswoman" literature.

Her adversary, an older man with grizzled hair and distinguished white sideburns, whose once athletic shoulders were slipping gradually into his midsection, approached her and offered her a firm handshake. She returned it with a dignified nod.

"Ladies first?" he suggested, gesturing at the podium.

"Oh, no," Mona countered, with an artful smile. "Please go ahead, Congressman. *Seniority* ought to count for something."

She hadn't actually said, 'Age before beauty,' but the Congressman couldn't have missed the inference, and she didn't want him to. The heavy folds of fat under his chin shook with annoyance, but he bowed to her and mounted the steps of the platform. His force of bodyguards and volunteers separated from her bodyguards and volunteers, and arrayed themselves around the stage. The Congressman cleared his throat into the microphone, and the crowd quieted down.

His speech was predictable, enumerating his successes over the years on behalf of his district. Mona yawned, covering up with her hand but still visibly enough to be seen by half the attending student population. A couple of her campaign workers grinned openly. At length, the incumbent descended, and disappeared into a circle of voters and reporters shouting questions at him.

Mona waited to be introduced by her campaign manager, then took the podium as if it was the dais of her throne.

"Ladies and gentlemen, we've heard from the distinguished gentleman from Washington. I now present to you the Environmental Candidate, Ms. Mona Gilbreth!"

There was applause, and some scattered cheers. Mona smiled down on her audience. She found that to be effective, the formula that the younger the listeners, the shorter the speech always worked best, even if it meant the other candidate having more 'air time' than she had. 'Leave them wanting more,' she thought. People in the audience showed real interest as she outlined her specific causes and enumerated what she would do to support them once she took office. There were a blond girl and a black man with a bunch of children, handing out flyers at the perimeter of the crowd. There must be some kind of protest going on. But then, this was a college campus. There was always a protest going on somewhere. It couldn't have anything to do with her. She gave her audience about five minutes less than the Congressman had, then came down to shake hands and kiss a few babies, so to speak.

As her opponent had, Mona was mobbed as she got off the platform. "Ms. Gilbreth!" one young man called out. He rushed up and pumped her hand to the accompaniment of the flashing and clicking of cameras. "I'm glad you're a woman candidate. I'm voting for you."

"Thank you," Mona said, smiling for the reporters. "I'm going to Washington for *you*." The student drew away, beaming. Another took his place.

More followed with similar comments and well-wishes. She shook hands with all of them, posed for pictures, with her campaign manager standing about ten feet away, beaming at her. The session was going very well. This was not the group from which she could expect much in the way of donations, but enough of them were residents of the district that if she earned their respect and kept it, they'd continue to send her back to Washington for the next generation to come.

A few of the students asked earnest, complicated questions, and she fielded them with the answers that were becoming so pat in her mind they were almost sound bites.

A short, heavyset young woman came forward clutching a flyer. "Ms. Gilbreth, I'd like to know if in your business you follow the safe procedure in getting rid of toxic waste. Are you using licensed haulers and disposal systems?"

"Why, yes," Mona said, the smile freezing on her face. Thankfully, her noncommittal answer was at the ready. "As you know, the Environmental Protection Agency has approved very specific and stringent processes for disposing of toxic waste. My technicians have all of them at their fingertips."

"What's in the waste you dump?" a young man asked. He was thin, with red hair. Mona looked sharply at him, thinking it was Keith Doyle. When she saw he was a stranger, she relaxed and smiled.

"Mostly nitrogen-based by-products. A complete list of the chemicals is available from my office. Thank you." She turned ostentatiously to the next querist. The young man retired, obviously dissatisfied, but he was crowded away from her by well-wishers and other people who wanted to talk to her or just shake hands. As the crowd began to thin away, her campaign manager came over to stand beside her. There were scattered flyers on the ground. He picked one up and began to read it while Mona dealt with more questions and some unwelcome comments, and posed for just a few more pictures. Mona glanced over at her manager. His face seemed almost to change visibly while he read. Tucking the paper into his jacket pocket without seeming to think about it, he sidled up to her.

"You are following environmentally safe waste procedures, aren't you?" he whispered, in a brief lull between questions.

She got exasperated with him. Maybe his post on her staff wasn't so secure after all. "Of course I am," she hissed.

The crowd dissipated at last, and she stalked off the student common to the waiting limousine. Her campaign manager trailed behind in her wake, wondering what he'd just done wrong.

Nine-year-old Borget arrived in the barn panting. "Master, there's a police car in the drive!" he cried. "Rose wants to know what to do!"

The Master set his pointer tip down on the floor. "It has begun. She moves against us using the techniques of harassment. If ve do not show the face she expects, she vill expose us."

Catra and Candlepat stood up from behind the archives desk. "Should we flee?" Candlepat asked. "We can hide in the cornfields."

"A mass exodus should not be necessary." The Master turned to Marcy, who stood with Enoch at the sawyer's table. He made her a little bow. "Mees Collier, may I ask a favor?"

The county officer leaned on the bell again. Nice house, set in pretty lands, but kind of isolated among all those trees. He peered through the gauzy curtains hanging behind the glass panel in the door at the big, wood-paneled room. Empty. He had no idea what the Gilbreth woman wanted him to investigate. She handed the sheriff a line about illegal aliens running a factory out of this place. There was one car in the driveway. It had a city sticker for one of the Chicago suburbs, but that didn't really suggest a flood of immigrant workers. Well, one more ring, then he'd go around the house to the barn, see if anyone was home out there. He pushed the buzzer, and leaned up against the glass with his hand shading his eyes. "No one here, dispatch. No, wait a minute. Here comes somebody."

A pretty girl with very pale skin and black hair came running out of one of the doors leading off the big, wood-paneled room. She pulled the front door open.

"Can I help you?" she asked, smoothing a wisp of moist hair off her face.

"Sheriff's police, ma'am. Is there a Mr. Doyle here?" He checked his notes. "The owner of this place, Mr. Keith Doyle?"

"He's not here right now," Marcy said, trying to stay calm. "He's working in Chicago this semester. Is there something I can do for you?"

"Who are you, miss?" the officer asked.

"My name's Marcy Collier," she said. "I, uh, live with Keith." She could almost sense Enoch glowering at her from his hiding place, and felt her cheeks burn. The officer probably thought she was embarrassed because of the irregularity of the arrangement, not because she was lying.

"Well, Miss Collier, you've got to answer to your own conscience for that. I understand there's a business run off this farm?"

"Why, yes, but that's not illegal, is it?" Marcy asked.

"No, ma'am. This property is zoned for certain commercial operations. Are you involved in this business?"

Marcy could hear whispering from the Folk conferring in the kitchen. Maura was there, too, with Asrai. She prayed the baby wouldn't cry. It would be impossible to ignore Asrai's air-raid siren voice, and she didn't want the officer thinking she was concealing an illegitimate baby, as well. If the rumor got back to her parents, she was dead. "Only peripherally. I help out sometimes with packing boxes and things. Keith and I go to the same college. The workshop is a cooperative. We have lots of friends who come in and use the tools. Um." Greatly daring, she added, "Would you like to see it?"

"I'd like that just fine," the officer said, still serious. He holstered his radio in a square pouch on his belt. She escorted him in through the great room and into the kitchen. The red barn was visible through the window at the far end of the room.

Marcy picked up a hastily discarded dishrag one of the Little Folk had dropped on their flight from the house. She tossed it casually onto the drainboard. She hoped he thought she had been interrupted doing dishes when he rang. The officer seemed to be looking at everything in the room, counting the stacks of small benches and kindergarten-sized chairs.

"There's just one phone line here, isn't there?" the officer asked, pausing in the middle of the room.

"That's right," Marcy said. "Right there." She pointed, then held open the back door, wishing he'd follow her out. He glanced at the waist-level wall phone and did a double-take.

"What's it doing down there?"

She tried to think of an excuse and wondered what Keith would say. "Oh, my aunt's in a wheelchair," Marcy said, at last, swallowing. "She can't reach it if it's at eye level for us."

"She visit a lot?" the officer said, squinting at her.

"Oh, yes."

"Any other extensions in the house?"

"Well, no," Marcy said. "I mean, why? There's just two of us. The workshop is this way."

The September grass was too dry to take footprints, so there was no traces from the Little Folk who had fled for cover in the barn or the fields beyond it. Out of the corner of her eye, she spotted Enoch slip out of the house behind them. He was keeping watch on her, in case the officer became unfriendly. She smiled affectionately, then hid the expression, not wanting to explain herself to her visitor.

The barn almost echoed, so devoid it was of living things. Even the cat who'd been asleep on the Archivist's desk was gone. Lonely dust filmed the usually shining power tools and tables. Marcy, used to the small signs after more than a year of living among the Little Folk, knew that all the signs of disuse were illusionary, and that there were many pairs of eyes watching.

There must have been more than adequate time to empty the workshop. Most of the supplies were put away on the shelves and in the open-faced cabinets. The Master had even had time to erase the equations on his chalkboard before concealing himself. The pointer lay casually placed across the easel tray.

"Nice, huh?" the sheriff asked, going around the room. He ran a finger through the sawdust on the floor next to the drill press. His were the only footprints marring the scattered wood shavings. "What do they make here?"

"Oh, Christmas ornaments, cooky cutters, necklaces," Marcy said. She showed him the elaborate chain of wooden beads and stones she was wearing. Enoch had given it to her for her birthday. The officer seemed impressed.

"Pretty good. I like the design," he said, nodding. "Creative. My wife'd like it." He picked up one of the small lanterns that stood on a worktable, waiting to have the filigree screens dropped into the slotted sides before the small roof and ring was fixed on. He put it down and lifted the power drill. "You make some of this stuff, too?"

"Goodness, no!" Marcy exclaimed, her voice squeaking a little. She aimed a hand at the power tools. "I don't know how to use these things. I'm just an Arts and Sciences major. I hardly do anything practical."

There was a nearly-inaudible, high-pitched giggle in the loft. Marcy almost gasped. She wondered if the policeman could hear the breathing and low whispers, or if she was just being too sensitive. He looked at the numbers of chairs and benches set out in rows before the Master's easel.

"Everything's so small," he said, jokingly. "Are you sure you're not violating the child labor laws?"

"Oh, no!" Marcy said, horrified. "We—we have a lot of children who come in for demonstrations. You know," she said, reaching back in her memory for something Keith had once said, "Junior Achievement?"

The officer nodded. "Oh, yeah, belonged to one of them myself when I was twelve," he said, fondly. "Well, okay. Sorry to bother you, miss. I can find my own way back to my car."

He tipped a small salute to the young woman and climbed the slight slope up toward the house. Ms. G. just had a bee in her bonnet, he thought. She was probably looking for another cause to back for her campaign, and decided to pick on what sounded like a hippie commune workshop smack in the middle of her constituency. Turned out to be nothing, and he'd tell her so. Her daddy had been a big man in the county when he was alive. His daughter ought to just tend to her business before she tried to take his place. By all accounts the fertilizer factory was suffering from neglect. He wasn't planning to vote for her anyhow. His wife said something about women's liberation, but he just classed

Mona Gilbreth in with all the other politicians he'd ever seen. The county officer climbed back into the car and lifted the radio to report in. Politicians were all alike. You couldn't trust a one of them.

Not long after the officer disappeared around the corner of the house, Rose appeared at the back door and waved a dish towel. All clear. Marcy sank down onto one of the benches with her shoulders slumped, and just breathed.

Enoch emerged from beneath the workbench and came over to sit beside her. He seized her hand and kissed it fiercely.

"I don't even like to hear you say things like that," he said.

"I'm sorry," Marcy said, helplessly. "That was all I could think of."

"Never mind," Enoch said, the scowl softening to a tender smile. He moved closer and put an arm around her. "It was...expedient. Do you feel all right?" Marcy nodded.

The Master seemed to appear out of thin air. He patted her on the shoulder.

"Vell done, Mees Collier. The first attack has been repulsed. Our own counterattack goes on, to continue a military metaphor. There vill be more sallies by our foe, of that I am certain. Ve vill be ready."

"Keith Doyle?" the secretary said into the microphone of her headset. She checked the office clipboard and reached for a pad of pink forms. "I'm sorry, he's not in right now. May I take a message?"

"No, wait!" Brendan, passing by the desk in the reception hall, jumped in front of the secretary and signaled until he got her attention. "I'll take it."

"Hold, please." The woman pushed a few buttons that transferred the call to the phone on the desk.

Brendan picked up the receiver. "Hello?"

"Keith?" a woman's voice asked. The tinny quality of the sound told Brendan it was long distance.

"No, sorry. I just work with him. I'll be seeing him this afternoon. Can I give him a message?"

"No, I guess I can call back. Do you know when he'll be in?"

"Uh, no," Brendan said. "He's off with another one of our co-workers, Dorothy. They could be a while, you know what I mean?" He gave the phrase all the lascivious glee he could muster.

"No, I do not know what you mean," the woman said, with asperity. Brendan was delighted.

"Well, you know, they call 'em 'nooners' but they can last longer than the noon hour—oops," Brendan interrupted himself and continued in a horrified whisper. "Is this his girlfriend? It's nothing. I'm gossiping. Rumors can be so malicious. Forget I said anything. Sorry. I'll tell him you called. Bye." He hung up the phone and sauntered away from the desk. The receptionist barely spared him a glance as he went by.

Only a few moments later, Keith and Dorothy, their arms full of paper bags from the bakery, came in together through the glass doors. They were laughing at some private joke. Keith held the door open by leaning against it as Dorothy passed through. Every time she glanced up at him, he wiggled his eyebrows, and she burst into a fresh attack of giggles.

"Hey, Keith," Brendan said, coming over and helping himself to a jelly doughnut from one of the bags. "Your girlfriend called."

"Hey, thanks, Brendan," Keith said.

"Don't mention it." Brendan smiled.

It was only late afternoon when Mona returned to the plant, but she felt as if she had been out hiking forever. It had been a tiring and irritating day. Her feet nearly sighed with relief when they sank into the meager padding under the carpet in the reception area.

"Ms. Gilbreth," the receptionist said as she passed by going toward her office to put her legs up. The girl held out a stack of pink slips. "I've got a whole bunch of messages for you. Here's your mail, too. Oh, and there's a couple of men around here somewhere. They said they were from the EPA."

"The EPA?" Mona asked, her heart sinking as she thought of the dumping she had authorized in forest preserves all over the county, and not only in the one behind Hollow Tree Farm. Had someone spilled the beans? "As in Environmental Protection Agency?"

"Yes'm. They showed me their badges, so I called Mr. Williamson. I guess he took them around."

"Thank you," Mona said, hobbling down the gray hallway. She stuffed the handful of messages into her purse. "Could you find me some coffee, Beryl? A whole pot."

"Sure, ma'am," the receptionist called after her.

All the whistle stops after her early morning speech at Midwestern had been horrible reruns of the first. People Mona had never met before came up to complain to her about her policy of waste disposal and ask pointed questions concerning her support of openland greenways. Siccing the EPA on her factory was the crowning insult. She wondered if there had been time to shovel dirt over the leaks in the number eight tank, or to take the suppurating truckloads of overdue waste off the grounds.

Jake arrived at the same time as the coffee. Mona, her shoes discarded under the table, poured her mug a quarter full, swirled it around to cool it a little, gulped it down, and refilled the mug to the lip.

"All right," she said, settling down behind her desk with a sigh. "What's this about the EPA?"

The foreman shook his head. "It's nothing, ma'am. They got a call from some indignant female claiming Gilbreth is full of violations. She was such a pest the inspectors promised to look into it right away. I cooled it with them. They'll come back for a spot check next week, after we've had a chance to clean up."

"My God, if we can find the money between now and then. What lit a fire under them?" Mona asked, feeling personally put upon. "Normally it takes months to set up an investigation."

Jake shrugged. "Who knows? Who cares? They're gone."

She started to turn over each of the messages. "What's going on here?" she asked, astonished. "These are all complaints about the plant. Air pollution, air pollution, runoff, the smell, dumping, runoff, the smell—was there a letter in the paper yesterday that I missed? The day before?"

"No, ma'am, I've been keeping an eye on things. There's been nothing from *them* for the last week, since you've had the kids." He let his words trail off and raised his eyebrows significantly.

"Small mercy," she said, but she didn't feel consoled. The letters, some of which had been delivered by hand, were full of the same kinds of complaints she'd been fielding all day long. One letter was printed in a juvenile hand and full of exclamation points and underlining. "Even kids think I'm the incarnation of Satan. How could that be? I'm running on a pro-environment package. What set these people off?"

"How about the guy you're running against?" Jake asked.

"Not a chance," Mona waved a hand. "He hasn't got the imagination to stir up this kind of hate mail. Who are all these people who are complaining?"

Jake glanced at the phone. "You know who to ask."

"They wouldn't dare!" Mona said. But she was worried. D-Day for the election was getting closer and closer. Any questions about her integrity now would make it harder for her to continue, especially when money remained so scarce. The rest of her mail was bills. Some of them—*most* of them—said "Second Notice" or "Final Notice." She couldn't hold the creditors off forever, and she didn't dare kite checks, not with the last House banking scandal still fresh in everyone's memory. She had to get money somewhere, not only to cover convention expenses, but also haulage fees, or she was ruined. Under the circumstances, any hope of borrowing cash discreetly from the election funds was out of the question. So was dumping any more waste on Hollow Tree Farm, dearly as she would have loved to. Nobody deserved it more. "I've got to stay clean."

"Maybe, but if it was me, I'd let the kid go, take the money and run." Jake had a disconcerting trick of reading her mind when she was thinking about money.

"I can't," she said, taking another healthy swig of coffee. It was still too hot, and she gasped out, "Everyone's watching me too closely right now."

"Here's the sheriff's report," Jake said, taking an envelope out of his pocket. "There's nothing out of the ordinary at that farm. No one was there but a girl who says she's Doyle's live-in. She said she's a student at Midwestern. That checks. She couldn't have had a baby in the spring, and she's not old enough to be the mother of the kid at the cabin unless she started in grade school. You also got a call from your little pal at PDQ. Keith Doyle reported for work this morning right on time. Except for an hour for lunch he's been there every minute."

"So Keith Doyle and H. Doyle aren't the same person," Mona said. "Who is it that's answering that phone?"

Chapter Sixteen

The morning papers were also full of eloquent letters complaining about Gilbreth Feed and Fertilizer. None of them was signed H. Doyle, but they voiced similar questions and concerns. Some were written to provoke the most severe reactions in their readers. The Folk felt their flyer had met with wonderful success, and it was only a matter of time before responses appeared in print, provoking an outcry from the ostensibly wounded party.

Holl was clutching the editorial section in one hand and drinking his morning tea when the telephone rang. He put the cup down to pick up the handset.

"Back off!" Mona Gilbreth's voice blasted from the receiver. Holl held the handset at nearly arm's length to save his ears. The echo bounded off the kitchen walls. "You promised no more letters to the press. You know what I could do if you're trying to thwart me. The girl's all right, and she'll remain all right, but get off my back!"

"It was not I," Holl said, drawing the mouthpiece close enough to speak. "I gave you my word, and I am keeping it. Not one of those letters was written by me."

He thrust it away, wincing, when she began to shout again. All the Little Folk in the room could hear her next demand perfectly. "What about the rest of the people who work at Hollow Tree Industries? Did they write them?"

"I swear that no one who works for Hollow Tree sent a single letter to the editor," Holl said carefully. "Call any of the people who signed the letters. Would I endanger my own flesh and blood?"

"If you're smart you won't," Gilbreth snarled.

"You can't keep her forever," Holl reminded her. There was a very long pause.

"If you don't back off and leave me alone," the woman at the other end said in a careful, deliberate voice, "I will tell the National Informer that your little girl is really a pixie, and you'll never get her back. She'll spend the rest of her life in freak shows or laboratories."

"No!" Holl exclaimed involuntarily. He stared up at the others, knowing that they had heard every word.

Tay looked shocked. Holl knew his face only echoed his nephew's expression of horror. It was the nightmare that had haunted them from the time they set foot onto the Midwestern campus more than four decades ago: freak shows, experiments, the end of privacy and integrity. The last year and a half in comparative safety on their own lands only made the force of Gilbreth's threat that much more terrifying. Such an outcome had to be prevented at any cost. Tay backed away from the phone and began to converse in low voices with the others. There were startled exclamations, and Siobhan began to cry. Maura broke away from the crowd and came to him, twisting at the ring on her finger. She offered it to him in both hands. Holl looked from the winking blue stone to his lifemate's eyes, and she gave him a helpless but brave smile. Regretfully, he nodded. It was the only really valuable thing they owned. A love token to redeem a loved one seemed only right.

"No," he repeated into the phone, in a quieter voice. "We'll send you a token of our good faith to prove that we will stand by your conditions."

"All right," Gilbreth said. "I'll wait for it."

Mona sat with her hand on the phone for a moment, feeling strangely triumphant.

"Inspiration?" Jake wanted to know.

"No," Mona said, tiredly. "I got the idea from Grant. He's still going on about those deformed ears the girl has—he thinks it means that she's the will o' the wisp or Tinkerbell. Sounds like they've heard something like it before. It got one hell of a strong response, didn't it?"

"Sure did." Jake stretched back in his chair with his hands behind his head. "I wonder what this token'll be like."

"They must be illegal aliens," Mona said, looking thoughtful. "That H. Doyle has got to be an illegal, or else why would they stay so cagey even while I'm threatening to give his niece away to the circus? That has got to be why they're always hiding. Hmm. His name sounds Irish."

"So what?" Jake asked. "So does Gilbreth."

"Yes, but I was born here. I bet he wasn't, him or his family. Maybe I can get them deported," she said, picking up a pencil and tapping it against her teeth. The thought made her happy. "After he pays the ransom and I give him back his kid."

"How could she know?" Tay asked, wringing his hands.

"I don't know if she does," Holl said. "It could have been a shot in the dark. In any case, we've stooped to bribery to insure Dola's safety. Keith Doyle will not be pleased, nor will the Master, but what else could we do?" He held up the ring and drew his small carving knife from the sheath on his belt. "I swear I'll replace this with something as good or better one day," he said to Maura.

"Never mind," she replied, shaking her head ruefully. "If it will save Dola from the Big Folk you could take my finger with it."

With a deft motion, Holl prized the sapphire from the setting and handed the ring back to Maura. "We'll mail this stone today. She must soon set a time and place for the exchange of ransom. We'll be ready for it when the time comes."

Wednesday morning, Paul Meier had assigned his interns to work together on a series of ads for a regional cleaning service, but inspiration was not coming easily. "Come To Dust" should have provoked something clever out of the students, and Paul was showing his disappointment. He was particularly unhappy with his star 'ideator.' Keith's mind seemed to be everywhere except right there with him in the conference room.

"Come on," Meier urged them. "It's Shakespeare. Shakespeare?" He leaned over his cup half-full of dilute coffee and congealing non-dairy creamer, and appealed to the four interns. Dorothy was deep in her inner world, making little sketches of faces and fashion designs. Sean was earnest but empty. Brendan was bored, and didn't care who knew. Meier slammed his hands down on the table and rose behind it. "All right. Give it a rest. Someone go read Cymbeline and meet me back here after lunch." He headed for the door, and Sean and Brendan trailed listlessly behind him.

The bang of the door closing behind them seemed to have aroused Keith out of his reverie. He looked around for the others, and ended up meeting Dorothy's gaze.

"Cymbeline?" Dorothy asked.

"Shakespeare play," he said, forcing a worried grin. "What about it?"

"'Come to dust' is a quote from Shakespeare," she said patiently. "That's the name of our product line here. Got no images for the ads. That's what we've been doing all morning. Where's your brain, the moon?"

"Maybe," Keith said apologetically. He picked up the data sheet PDQ had received from the parent company. "Uh, it's a clever line, like it was meant to mean something about cleaning. You have any idea what Cymbeline is about?" Dorothy shook her head. "Me, neither. Well, how about young men and women in Midsummer Night's Dream costumes pirouetting around a living room dusting and vacuuming?"

"Yes, why not? I can do that." Dorothy said. The lines flew out from under her pencil. With a few deft touches, she created lively figures in floating draperies wielding feather dusters and mops.

"Cute," Keith said, watching her enviously. "I wish I could do that."

"All it takes is practice," Dorothy said, self-deprecatingly. "I bet you'd be good."

"My, my, what have we here?" Brendan asked, coming in and looking over Dorothy's shoulder. "Very nice."

"Good enough to steal?" Keith asked. Dorothy's eyes widened, but she said nothing.

"Temper, Keith," Brendan said, wagging a finger at him. "See you after lunch."

"What's he done?" Dorothy asked as their *bête noire* disappeared out the door again.

"Nothing much," Keith mumbled. "Forget it."

"Well, why don't you tell Paul about it?"

"I don't want to bring him into it," Keith said. "It's personal."

"Uh-huh," Dorothy said. "Everything gets personal with Mr. Smug out there. Sorry I asked. Want to get something to eat?"

"I'm not really hungry."

"Hey, come and watch me eat, then," she said.

"Sure," Keith said, forcing a modicum of good humor into his voice. With an effort, he stood up and followed her. His legs and arms, as well as his brain, seemed to have been encased in lead. Nothing was moving today.

"Keith?" the secretary called, as they appeared in the reception hall.

"Yes?"

"Telephone call for you. I can put it through to the conference room if you don't want to take it out here."

Keith hoped it was Diane. "I'll take it back there. Thanks." He shrugged regret at Dorothy. "Sorry. It's important."

"Win some, lose some," she said. "See you later."

Keith dashed back to the room and punched the blinking light on the telephone. "Hello?"

"Keith Doyle?"

"Holl? What's wrong?" Keith suddenly had a mental picture of the elves besieged, and remembered what he was supposed to have been doing before he became so preoccupied.

"Nothing more, be reassured. We've had an interesting conversation with the woman, and I wanted to bring you up to date." Holl repeated the exchange he had had that morning with Mona Gilbreth, and what they planned to do.

"You shouldn't send her anything, Holl," Keith said, pacing up and down in the empty conference room. "She's kidnapped your baby, killed a being we hardly knew anything about, and she's still refusing to say when she'll let your other kid come home. You'll have her on your back forever if she can get you to start paying blackmail because you think she knows you're elves."

"We're not," Holl said firmly, "and it ends the moment we have Dola back," Holl promised.

"Well, yeah, she's what's important," Keith agreed. "What are you sending to Kill-breath as this token?"

"The stone from Maura's ring," Holl said. "It's a small thing, truly."

"Oh, Holl," Keith said, sympathetically, then suddenly stopped pacing. "Oh, God, where are you going to get anything like that for the rest of the ransom?"

"We will not. The rest need not resemble the first offering. We will substitute something appropriate."

"You keeping up with orders? Is there anything coming in?"

"Now that we have come to terms with shock, loss, and violation, we are functioning. All is well on that end."

"Well, you can't miss the house payment," Keith said practically, walking around and around the conference table and playing out the phone cord between his fingers as he thought. "We'll find a way to raise it." He wished once again they could call in some kind of authority. It would solve the problem long before it got to the ransom stage. He started to plan out loud a lightning raid on the gift shops in the Midwestern area to collect orders, but none of it really added up to the amount Gilbreth's henchman had demanded. "I don't think even Ms. Voordman would have an order that would amount to more than a fortieth..." Holl stopped him in midsentence.

"We'll manage," the elf said in a soothing tone. "The solution needn't be thought of in this same minute."

Keith stopped pacing and leaned his head against a wall. "Sorry. I'm under pressure. One of my fellow interns is making a total pest of himself. He follows me all over the place. He poured coffee on one of my layouts. It took forever to reproduce." Holl murmured sympathy. "Thanks, but that's not the worst of it. He fielded a call from Diane and told her I was out with Dorothy, one of the other interns. We were only having lunch, but he made it sound like we were having a quickie affair. Now Diane's not speaking to me. I called her back, and she kept hanging up on me. He convinced her that within one month out of her sight I've turned into a Casanova with my coworkers. I wish I had something to rub his face in, say wet concrete studded with live scorpions. I haven't been able to concentrate on anything all day long. Dorothy warned me Gilbreth had sicced him on me, but I never imagined he'd stoop to sabotaging my love life."

Holl sounded sympathetic but amused. "You sound as if you're under siege in that great fastness where you work. All will be resolved in time."

"Yeah," Keith said. "I know. We just have to live through it. There are more important things to worry about, like Dola."

"Aye. But for pity's sake, Keith Doyle, if you want to assuage Diane's concerns, why do you not declare yourself to her?"

"Aw, come on, Holl...Gotta go," Keith said suddenly, hearing the doorknob turning and seeing an unwelcome face appear. "Brendan's coming," he whispered in a breath that only an elf would be able to hear.

"Ready for the next round, Keith?" Martwick asked brightly, slapping his briefcase on the tabletop.

"Looking forward to it, Brendan," Keith said, hanging up the phone. Sean came in and put his jacket into the closet.

"Have a good lunch?" he asked them. They glared at each other and smiled at him.

Dorothy came in with Paul Meier. "So where is it, Keith?" Paul asked, slapping his hands together and rubbing them. "Dorothy tells me you got something together on "Come To Dust" just before lunch time. Let's see."

Keith sifted through the papers on the tabletop, growing more frantic as he reached successive layers without seeing the sketch.

"What's the matter?" Meier asked.

"The sketch isn't here," Keith said.

"Did you take it somewhere?" Dorothy asked.

"No. I was only out of the room for a minute," Keith said. "I've been in here on the phone almost the whole time." He looked at Brendan, who raised his hands innocently.

"I didn't see it. I left before you guys, remember?"

It didn't mean he hadn't come back. Keith opened his mouth, planning to deliver a sour retort when Paul interrupted him.

"Well, come on, kids. If it's a good idea, I want to see it. If the sketch is missing, do another one."

Keith turned appealing eyes toward Dorothy. The artist hated to do things over again, but she reproduced the drawing with admirable skill, and showed it to Paul. He nodded over it and stroked his chin.

"Kind of predictable, but I bet the client had an idea like that anyway. I don't know why they didn't just suggest it when we first met with them. Not bad."

"I'd rather you said it stunk than you thought it was *predictable*," Keith said, feeling discontented.

"That's the attitude you want for advertising," Paul said, approvingly. "All or nothing. Well, work on it if you're not happy. Look, it's better than nothing. Okay, everyone, we'll give it a rest. Here's your missions for this afternoon."

Keith hardly listened as he was assigned to go run coffee and doughnuts for the Appalachi-Cola account vice president. He hated to be thought of as mediocre, and was now completely annoyed with the world. Brendan was just the biggest part of what was wrong with it all. Keith thought with dismay how much he had come to dislike Brendan over the space of only a few days. The smug youth had been a minor annoyance in the first weeks of their internship, but he was now a downright pain in the ass. He heard Paul call on Brendan.

"…You're going to work with Larry Solanson on the Gilbreth campaign," the supervisor said. "She likes you. Larry likes you. It's a good situation." Brendan looked even more self-satisfied than usual, and patted his leather-sided notebook. "Good. We'll meet back here at the end of the day to count noses." He held up his coffee cup for a sip and noticed it was empty.

"I'll get you some," Brendan offered, keeping up with his new role as fair-haired boy. He took Meier's cup over to the side table. While his back was turned and the others were watching him perform the small task of pouring coffee, Keith tipped up the cover of the notebook with a pencil, and read some of the notes jotted down about Gilbreth on the top page under the heading "Pamphlet."

I didn't know she was a Rhodes scholar, Keith thought with interest.

"Say, Paul," he asked, as Brendan came back with the coffee, "is PDQ responsible if we disseminate false information?"

Meier's black brows drew down over his long nose. "Sometimes. Why?"

"No reason, Paul," Keith said, rising from the table to get his notes. "Thanks."

He was fairly sure the jottings he had done on the Appalachi-Cola account the week before were in the back of his file drawer. As he opened it, he checked the charm-alarms on his files. One of them had been triggered.

Carefully, making sure no one else was watching him, he flicked the file folders forward with the edge of a storyboard card, and felt his way to the violated envelope. Nothing had been taken out; in fact there was something there that shouldn't have been: Dorothy's first sketch for "Come To Dust."

"I should have known," he muttered.

Keith asked the secretary in reception for an outgoing telephone line, and called the Chicago Public Library from the remote phone. "Reference information hot line? Yeah. Is there some kind of list of Rhodes scholars?" he asked, being careful to keep his voice down. "Uh huh. Could you check a name for me?" Messengers, agency employees, and clients passed around him while he waited, all immersed in their own business. Keith smiled at the ones who met his eyes. "Uh huh, that's great. Yeah, thanks."

He walked away from the phone whistling.

Mona couldn't understand how her nemesis could avoid detection so neatly. H. Doyle was *always* there when she called, but never there when anyone else visited. The police hadn't seen a trace of him on the first or subsequent visits. The phone company representative reported seeing only the one young woman. When she left for the afternoon, no one answered the door, and no signs of life were apparent either in the barn or the house. The INS officer went over within minutes after Mona hung up after speaking with H. Doyle, but he was already gone and no one on the surveillance team had seen him leave. The line check confirmed there was only one line into the house, and only one phone inside, and that one was at half-height on the kitchen wall. She wondered if, as the young woman's comments had suggested, that he might be in a wheelchair, but no wheelchair-bound person could move so fast when the investigators dropped by. And he wasn't Keith Doyle, because Brendan Martwick reported that Keith was in Chicago at work at the times she called. There was something very weird going on at Hollow Tree Farm.

In the meantime, the harassment continued. Mona got more carping phone calls and letters of complaint, and suffered confrontations in the street and at rallies. She called up the farm and accused H. Doyle, who gave her his word that he wasn't responsible. He continued to push for a meeting date to have the girl returned to him.

Mona was waiting to see the 'token' he promised before she would make any commitment. She wasn't about to sell out cheaply, not with accounts receivable barely covering the in-plant expenses. Gilbreth Feed was pushed to its credit limits. She put off paying some bills to cover the haulage account to please the EPA inspectors on their return visit, and used charm on her other creditors so they would wait a little longer for their money. They were not pleased, but her promise that they would receive the very next available funds ensured they'd keep supplies and services running satisfactorily.

The EPA surprise inspection had set off another firecracker. Mona, returning from more campaigning Wednesday afternoon, found an urgent message from the office of the Democratic National Committee waiting for her. With her heart hammering in her throat, she dialed the number and asked for Jack Harriman, the assistant to the state chairman.

"Mona!" the hearty voice greeted her. "Glad to hear from you. So glad you called back."

"Jack," she said, equally heartily. "To what do I owe this pleasure?"

"Well, lady, it's like this. There's a rumor floating around up here that you're having a few problems with EPA standards—some overspill from your tanks?"

"Well, perhaps a little—it's fertilizer, of course," Mona replied, in the sweetest voice she could muster. "There are nothing but farm fields on all sides of the plant. It doesn't hurt corn to feed it more fixed nitrogen, especially in this season. You ought to come down and see for yourself. Very green."

"Uh, no, thanks, lady," Jack said. "I'm an urban cowboy, myself. What we want to know is, if there was a chemical spill, why didn't you report it to the EPA or the county yourself? That's the kind of flak we're getting up here."

Mona swallowed. "I'm sorry you're being harassed, Jack. It happens to me all the time."

"That's not good in this kind of messy election year," the assistant said. Mona could sense the veil coming off the threat. "We're too vulnerable. If it goes on, it could turn into a media circus. Your viability comes into question, Mona. The party might have to pull back on endorsing you. Out of pure survival instinct."

"What?" Mona cried. "But we're almost there! It's September. What about my position in the community? My platform?"

"We can't go on calling you the Environmental Candidate if you're…misleading us all about your environmental standards," Jack said reasonably. "I'll be frank with you, lady. If the Committee—not to include myself in that group, but we've all got to kowtow to them—starts to feel you're an embarrassment, they're going to cut their losses and run with the candidates they think can go the distance." He sounded apologetic. "We've got to keep the Democratic majority in the House. Unless you've got something substantial to add to the Committee?"

Mona knew what that meant. The higher-ups were taking her public humiliation as a chance to ask for a donation. Her perceived wealth as a property and business owner was once again working against her. Only she knew how bare the cupboard was, but she had little choice. They were forcing her to cough up or concede.

"Of course," she said, keeping her voice level. "I'll have something substantial to funnel towards the party very soon."

Jack offered effusive thanks, and hung up. Mona cradled the phone feeling flustered and angry. She was certain that the continued annoyances—culminating in a threat to discontinue her dearly-won candidacy—could be laid at the feet of Hollow Tree Farm and the Doyles, in spite of their promises. She knew there was no way to prove her suspicion. They kept saying they would never do anything to jeopardize the safety of the child. It was hard to argue with that kind of logic, but equally hard to disagree with the gut feeling she had about them.

The blond child was still staying holed up in the cabin bedroom, emerging only for the necessities. Williamson reported that Grant Pilton was upset because she had been doing the cooking, and now he had to rely on his own meager skills. The child was becoming more of a nuisance with every day that passed. Mona resolved to get rid of her as soon as she had a good, financial reason to do so.

Chapter Seventeen

A little discreet questioning by Keith around the office on Thursday gleaned the information that publishing false data was regarded as the advertising industry's equivalent of insider trading: it was okay as long as the perpetrator didn't get caught. Keith fully intended that Brendan would get caught.

The vice president in charge of Mona Gilbreth's accounts was very pleased with Brendan, a fact that the young man announced to anyone who would listen, or anyone who didn't move away too quickly. He dropped first names with alacrity, something Keith and Dorothy, at least, found funny.

Keith thought the V.P. would have been happy with anybody willing to do all the gruntwork on a project but leave most of the credit for him. He was trusting Brendan to do everything right, so he hadn't been checking on what was going into those press releases that he approved. Brendan bragged at length about his new connection with the vice president when he returned to the conference room at the end of the day. Keith, sitting next to him, rolled his eyes toward heaven as the paean of self praise went on and on. Sean, across from Keith, grinned.

"So you think it's all in the bag for you, huh, Brendan?" Sean asked, uneasily. In spite of the fact that the creative team for Dunbar professed undying love for Sean's ideas, Dunbar was kicking up a fuss at the PDQ administration. Sean was afraid that if Dunbar went shopping for another agency PDQ would consider it his fault and drop him from the program. He'd been nervous all week. "The job and all?"

"Surely, my man, surely," Brendan said, delivering a loving pat to a sheet of paper sitting on top of his notebook. "Larry loves my touch with a press release." He rose. "'Scuse me."

He left the room, leaving the press release temporarily unguarded. Keith couldn't resist temptation like that.

"Immortal words," he said, spreading a clean sheet of paper on top of Brendan's draft. "Rest in peace." He signed the cross over it. Sean laughed and went back to his tire ads.

Staring hard enough at the paper to burn holes in it with his eyes, Keith willed the blank sheet to take on an image of the print below.

As Brendan returned to the room, Keith snatched back his sheet of paper, curious why no print had appeared. He glanced at the back, then wondered what part of Catra's instructions he had gotten wrong. The copy had been reproduced in perfect mirror image on the side that had touched the original.

He secreted the page in his notebook and carried it into the hall to peruse. Backwards or forwards, the release made interesting reading. Brendan had decided, either on his own or after prompting by Mona Gilbreth, to pad her credentials to make her sound much more impressive a candidate than she was. Keith intended that Brendan would get caught with his factual pants down, but not right away. He didn't want to jeopardize Dola's life by retaliating against Gilbreth's student stooge. Once Dola was safe, all bets for Brendan's future sanity, career, or peace of mind were off. Brendan was going to pay for making trouble between him and Diane. It was especially irritating when there was no time to go down to Midwestern in person to straighten things out. Keith was delighted Brendan himself had provided him with the proof that he was indulging in unapproved business practices. As long as Keith kept his eyes open for attacks by Brendan and kept a step and a half ahead, he could wait until the correct opportunity came along to help Brendan get what he deserved.

Thankfully, there was nothing else going on down at the farm to which he needed to give his attention. At least at present, Gilbreth was holding the line on letting Dola go. The harassment of the Folk on the farm made Keith furious, but they assured him they were handling it.

Ground searches by the Little Folk with Big Folk drivers had been curtailed because all the college students had classes. He wasn't forgetting, as Diane had accused him hurtfully over the phone, that other people had their own responsibilities. He winced at the memory of her angry voice. Brendan had a lot to answer for.

It had been too windy downstate to fly, grounding the balloon surveillance team, and besides, Frank Winslow hadn't exactly been in the mood since the air sprite popped out. Keith couldn't blame him. He knew the way he would feel if anything serious did happen to one of the elves. All in all, there was no way to find Dola until Gilbreth was ready to give her up. That meant Keith could only worry until the weekend when he could go down to supervise the hunt himself and make up with Diane.

Keith stuffed the paper into his notebook and went back in to join the others. Where one indiscretion lay, there would undoubtedly be more. He suspected that Brendan was also pushing the envelope on the budget for the Gilbreth double account. He had seen an order for "Amber Waves Of Grain" posters sitting on the secretary's desk in the foyer. There was an additional request appended in Brendan's handwriting for a hundred single-sheets. Chances were good that neither Paul nor Solanson had authorized them. Keith saved up the fact to tell Paul when he needed ammunition. It was a chance to get back at both of them. Gilbreth had enlisted Brendan to make life tough for him, and he intended to return the favor with interest.

Maybe if he could get a hold of the single-sheets when they arrived, he could infuse them with a sense of revulsion. He'd laughed out loud when the Master had told him about Diane, Dunn, and the enhanced flyers at Gilbreth's rallies. It was too good an idea not to repeat. Just to make certain, he took a copy of the print order.

The weekend was only two days away. Keith wondered how he could hold on only forty-eight hours more. Saturday morning, wind, rain, or shine, he was going down to Hollow Tree Farm. He was determined that they would get Dola back that day, or bust.

Mona Gilbreth received her mail with trepidation. On top, her receptionist had placed the increasing stack of overdue bills and dunning memos from her creditors. The very sight of them depressed her. More letters, she noted with dismay. Unable to stomach answering even one more, she tossed them unopened into the waste basket. There was one more item, a small box.

"What's this?" she asked.

"I don't know, ma'am," the receptionist said. "It was in the mailbag."

Mona turned over the small cardboard carton, and nearly dropped it. On the back, the return address was Hollow Tree Farm. She took the pile of mail and the tiny box and hurried with them into her office, and locked the door.

Inside the box was a round blue jewel. Mona picked it up and let it rest in her palm, admiring the lights that shone through it onto her skin. The sapphire looked almost *too* perfect, but it had an aura of genuineness that impressed her into deep and silent respect.

The jeweler, an old friend of the family, came at her request to have a look at the stone. After making a careful examination of it, first through his half-spectacles, then through a loupe and a small microscope that he carried in a case, he looked up at her over the half-rim frames.

"You're right, Mona dear. It's real, and worth a pot of money. It's an antique cut, absolutely flawless. *Perfect.* I haven't seen anything like this outside of a museum, even the Smithsonian. May I ask where you got it?"

"It's a family heirloom," Mona said. "I just inherited it." She held up the box it arrived in, but carefully kept the address out of sight.

"Wonderful," he said, shaking his head.

"Could you sell it for me?"

"Without any trouble, dear. You leave it to me. Shall I take it with me now?" As she had, he seemed to be reluctant to put it down.

"Um…what's it worth?"

For answer, the jeweler took a pad of paper and pen, and wrote a number on it. He pushed it towards her. "Not a penny less than that, and maybe more."

Mona gazed at the figure. For the first time in two weeks she started to think that things were looking up. The jeweler packed the sapphire into a padded, plastic pillbox, and placed it carefully into the box with the microscope.

"I'll call you. If nothing else, *I'll* buy the stone from you. As an investment. I'll call you by the end of the day."

"Thank you!" Mona remembered to say as the old man left.

She picked up the phone and dialed out. As soon as the other end was answered, she said, "That's quite an interesting package I received today. I wouldn't mind hearing there was more where that one came from."

"There is," H. Doyle said. "We'll give you two pounds of the same if you return our child." Two pounds of fabulous jewels, each stone worth a fortune! Mona was elated. She must have punched exactly the right button to make these people squirm. "When can we meet?"

"Wait a minute," Mona said. "It has to be exactly the right place. I'm not going to let you bully me into someplace I feel vulnerable. I want the least exposure possible. I'll be in touch with you," she said.

Without waiting for H. Doyle to protest, she briskly slapped down the phone and strode out of the room, pausing long enough to grab her purse.

"Hold all my calls," she said to the receptionist on her way out the door. "I'm going shopping!"

Dorothy came into the conference room, looking panicstricken. Brendan smiled up at her, but her gaze went past him and lit upon Keith.

"Hey, I thought you sent the storyboard for "Getting off lightly" over to Bob," she said accusingly. "I just met him in the hall. He says he's been waiting three days for it."

"I did send it," Keith said, his mouth dropping open. "I put it in interoffice mail on Monday."

"Well, it didn't get there," Dorothy said warningly. "I'm not going to do it all over again."

"It'll be okay," Keith said. "I'll go and explain to the team what happened."

"They won't be happy," Dorothy said, following him out the door.

Brendan was delighted. It was the first trick he had played on Keith that had really paid off. He'd had the most incredible run of bad luck trying to set Keith up. File drawers Keith used wouldn't open to anyone else's touch. Some wouldn't close after Brendan pried them open. Sprays of paper exploded out of pigeonholes and notebooks without any visible mechanism propelling them. He was dying to ask Keith how the trick worked, but he didn't dare. Keith would want to know, and reasonably, too, what Brendan was doing in his files.

The weird thing was that Keith always seemed to know what stuff had been messed with. Brendan didn't know how he did that, either. Maybe there were spycams in the ceiling? He checked the room's corners, looking for surveillance equipment. It wouldn't surprise him if he did find them. There was no trust whatsoever in this place; he ought to know.

He gloated, wondering just what Keith was planning to say to the creative director about the missing storyboard, which only he, Brendan, knew was floating in the Chicago River under the Michigan Avenue bridge.

"What are we going to say to them?" Dorothy demanded, as they strode down to the media coordinator's office.

"Nothing but 'I'm sorry this is late,'" Keith told her. "We have to stop here, first." Keith pushed open a door, and held it for her to pass through in front of him.

"Research?" Dorothy asked, recognizing the department.

"Mrs. Bell, hi there!" Keith said. "How's my favorite investigator?"

"Can the crap, sonny," Mrs. Bell said. She was a short, plump woman with a cigarette perpetually stuck in the corner of her mouth. Her desk was the only untidy spot in the room. She was legendary for her organization, and Dorothy had learned to revere her in the short time the interns had spent in her department. "What do you want?"

"Can I have my file?" Keith asked, bowing on one knee to the research librarian.

The woman reached into a deep drawer and pulled out a brown cardboard portfolio. She brushed cigarette ash off its surface. "Taking it with you?"

"Nope," Keith said, untying it and fishing through its contents. Over his arm, Dorothy could see dozens of storyboards and sketches. "What is this?" she asked.

"Security," Keith said. "Since my stuff started disappearing, and getting sent to the wrong offices, or getting things spilled on them, I've been making color xeroxes of everything and hiding them down here. That way I never lose any more work. There we go." He pulled out a copy of the Judge Yeast layout and handed it to her. Deftly, he retied the folder and returned it to Mrs. Bell. "Come on," he said cheerfully. "The team won't wait forever."

Brendan slipped into Paul Meier's office in the afternoon. Paul glanced up from his work. "Hi, Brendan. All done with the Gilbreth campaign?"

"Coffee break," Brendan said, managing to make it sound amusing and beneath his notice.

The subtlety was not lost on Meier. He raised an eyebrow. "So what can I do for you? Sit down." He gestured at a couple of chairs against the wall.

Brendan squatted down on a chair and pulled it up to Meier's desk with a hand between his knees. "Paul, I wanted to bring something up. I feel kind of delicate about saying anything."

"Well, that's a first," Meier said dryly.

"What?"

"Nothing. What is it?"

Brendan settled his other hand next to the first and leaned on them, swaying forward confidentially. "Well, in the last week or so, something seems to have been bugging Keith. Oh, he's here, most of the time," Brendan said, laying slight stress on the last phrase, "but his *mind* isn't here."

"I noticed, but he seems to be doing the work," Paul said. "What's the problem?"

"Part of our grade is based on attendance, right? Well, he's been taking days off. The rest of us all come every day. It isn't right, when we're expected to show up. Take last Wednesday. He wasn't here because he had to run downstate because of a personal matter. You sent him to see Ms. Gilbreth. When she came in on Monday, she wouldn't talk to him. What do you think he must have done?"

"I can't imagine. So what are you suggesting? That he shouldn't get the same grade as you because he's got poor attendance and he enrages the clients?"

"If he's upsetting clients, should he even be in the program?" Brendan asked delicately. "If his personal life affects the way he treats clients?"

Paul tilted his head back and looked down his long nose at Brendan. "You raise some interesting points, Brendan. You think maybe I should talk to Keith?" he asked, his voice expressionless. "Find out if he made an ass of himself downstate?"

"Oh, yes," Brendan said, then added hastily, "but I'd appreciate it if you wouldn't mention me, okay? I'm just trying to keep the program running at its best."

"I'm sure you are," Paul said, standing up. "Thanks for coming to me."

Brendan left the office at a quick trot. He was halfway down the hall before he gave vent to his joy. Ms. Gilbreth was going to be so pleased with him. The job was absolutely his, in the bag, signed, sealed and delivered. He bent, fist clenched, into a convulsive gesture of glee. "Yes!"

The executives and employees passing him by in the corridor shot half-curious looks at him, and kept going.

Meier caught up with Keith, as the redheaded student was carrying a veiled storyboard from a conference room down to the art department.

"How's it going, Keith?" Meier asked, falling into step beside him.

"Great," Keith said. He was cheerful. "The vice president for the Dunbar account just pitched 'The Brain,' and the client loves it."

"That's not your slogan," Meier said. "It's Sean's."

"Nope, but Sean is part of our group," Keith explained. "Every time one of us succeeds, there's less resistance among the account executives for listening to student-generated ideas."

"Don't be so sure." Meier shook his head. "Remember the delicate balance between someone being overjoyed at getting ideas he didn't pay for and someone preserving his job. But I'm glad you're an optimist. Keith, it's come to my attention that you and Ms. Gilbreth didn't exactly hit it off. Now, she's not PDQ's biggest client, but she's important to us. We don't want to lose her. Is there something going on between you that I don't know about?"

"Nothing to do with me, Paul," Keith said, picking his words carefully. "It turns out she knows one of my cousins. They don't get along. They have...different views."

"On politics?"

"Yeah, among other things. They've had a couple of run-ins recently, and I'm just catching the flak."

Meier was mollified but not fully convinced. "Well, all right, but get some work done, huh? I've got another new product that needs some hot ideas, and you're my idea man. Fairy Footwear, kids' wear from America's Shoe. Fantasy stuff for little girls on up to teenagers, but orthopedically correct."

"Hmmm," Keith said. "'The most comfortable thing on two feet'? 'The lightest thing on two feet'?"

"Keep going," Meier said, pushing the door of the art department open for him. "I think you're on to something there. By the way, are you and Brendan having problems? I caught him stuffing papers into your file drawer Tuesday morning. He said they all fell out."

"Fairy Footwear," Keith mused, sitting in the students' borrowed conference room with a pen and legal pad. He tapped his upper lip. "What do fairies and shoes have in common?" He started doodling. "Shoemakers? No way. Little girls aren't interested in making shoes. Dancing?"

Dorothy came in. "Hey, sketching is my act."

Keith grinned up at her. "Sorry."

"What's that?" Dorothy asked, pointing a red-tipped finger at his drawing.

"They're dancers," he said. Keith hastily covered up an illusion of a real dancer he had cast on the edge of the pad to give him the pose he wanted, and let her look at the rough sketch. By their postures, his stick figures seemed to be afflicted by fleas, nervous tics, or live fish down their shorts. They were ranged in a circle around a hemispherical lump covered with jagged lines that were meant to indicate grass and flowers. Dorothy shook her head and clicked her tongue at them. Keith flushed.

"Come on, I know drawing isn't my long suit. I'm working on something for Fairy Footwear. This is a fairy ring," he said. He started to explain about fairy mounds, rings, and the associations in olden times people had with certain kinds of geological and biological features. In a few minutes, his explanation had developed into a full-scale lecture.

Dorothy found herself getting interested, and settled in at the table with her elbows propped up. "You know a lot about this legendary stuff, don't you?"

"My life's work," Keith threw off lightly. "I'm a research mythologist when I'm not coming up with hit slogans and ad layouts." He drew stick figures of creatures with wings. Without intending to, he started filling in the features of the air sprites, then changed his mind. Sprites didn't have feet to wear shoes on. "The old storytellers used to say that fairies danced in these rings, and where they stepped, things like mushrooms grew up. They're really caused by the natural outward progression of a multi-generation fungus colony."

Dorothy wrinkled her nose. "Ugh. I didn't need to know that." His hand had slipped away from the edge of the pad. She grabbed his fingers and moved them to see what was under them.

"How come you draw your roughs in stick figures when you can do drawings like that?" she asked, pointing to the beautifully realized image of a dancer.

Keith hastily covered the illusion again, and scrubbed at it with the eraser to make it look like he was wiping it out as he dispelled it. "I think better in stick figures, I guess," he said. "The fancy stuff takes too long."

Dorothy flung back the cover of her sketch pad. "So you're thinking of fairies dancing, huh? What do your fairies look like? Besides white, I mean. That much I can guess."

Keith thought about what fairies did look like. He thought of the last time he had seen Dola, and had a sudden, overpowering inspiration.

"You know, I know a little girl who would be perfect for a commercial like this," he said. "Dancing in the moonlight, with little wings on her shoulders. She looks like one of the, uh," he searched his memory for the name of the artist, "Kate Greenaway watercolors of fairies."

"Oh, I know those. I know the style. Describe her," Dorothy said, her pencil poised. "Sounds like you've got an idea. You tell me, and I'll draw it. You're not gonna get the executive excited about a lot of stick figures."

Keith pictured Dola as best he could. "Well, she's about three feet tall, with long blond hair. Her eyes are blue. Her nose is little, and tilts up at the tip, yeah," he said, watching Dorothy draw. "Like that. And she has a pointed chin, but it's not a sharp point, more like a little ball. Her face is thin in the jaw, but it gets wide over her cheekbones, and there's a shadow underneath them that goes up to meet the line of her ears."

"Which are pointed, right?"

"Yeah," Keith said surprised.

Dorothy sighed. "I should have guessed."

At length, Dorothy had a gorgeous representation of one small winged girl dancing in a moonlit glade, holding hands with other beings whose features were only suggested by shadows.

"That is absolutely fabulous," Keith said. He stood up. "It gives me all sorts of great ideas. I've got to go tell Paul." He tore the drawing from the pad and made for the door. "Thank you!" he called over his shoulder.

"No problem," Dorothy said, shaking her head.

"It's pretty," Paul said, after listening to Keith's enthusiastic ravings about the drawing, "but really, I don't quite see it."

"A spokeswoman," Keith said. "A...a mascot for Fairy Footwear. They could have the Fairy Footwear Fairy. Kids would learn to recognize her, like grown women look for Paulina Porizkova or Cindy Crawford. We could have a whole search to find The Fairy Footwear Fairy. Statewide!"

"Well, yeah," Paul said, starting to look more interested. "Yes, good. You need more realization for this. Why don't you get Dorothy to do a whole storyboard for you. You've got to really sell this to the customer. I think it's great, but I'm only the V.P. I don't buy campaigns *for* the customer."

"Okay," Keith said, rolling the drawing into a tube. "Tomorrow I'll have something that'll knock their eyes out!"

"It'll get the ball rolling," Keith expostulated into the phone, waving one hand in the air as he paced up and back in the family kitchen. "If I can get PDQ to cooperate, they'll have a casting call to find the right little girl to fill Fairy Shoes. That'll be Dola. It'll be a way for us to get Ms. Gilbreth to bring Dola up here to Chicago."

"All very well to speculate," Holl said, trying to get Keith to calm down, "but how do you convince them to spend the time and money seeking all the way down here for their model?"

"The illustration in the ad is going to look just like her," Keith said. "By the time I get through with them, they won't be satisfied with any other model. They'll want her. All we need to do is get the brass to agree to put out a casting call right away. As Paul said, I've got to sell it to them, and I don't think any old storyboard will do the job. But if we can get Gilbreth to bring her up here, pow! We've got her!"

"The best of luck to you, Keith Doyle," Holl said. "We'll be ready to go whenever you say."

Making sure Jeff wasn't in the house, Keith pushed both beds in their room as far against the walls as they would go. In the space, he set up a card table and draped it with a white sheet. Using Dorothy's illustration as a model, Keith started to work on his sample commercial.

"If you can see an illusion," he reasoned out loud, "you can film an illusion."

From a locked suitcase hidden under his bed, he unearthed a wooden 'magic lantern' given to him by the Little Folk. Its particular virtue was that it was able to record about a minute's worth of sight and sound of anything it was pointed at. He peered at it, and blew dust off its gauze 'screen.' It hadn't been used in a couple of years. He tested it, making faces into the screen, then directed it to play back. His face, shrunk down to an inch across, confronted him, grimacing horribly. Keith grinned, and began to construct his illusion.

On a cassette tape recorder, he excerpted about a minute of the celestina and flute portion of the Dance of the Sugar Plum Fairies, and played it over and over, listening to the rhythm. In the center of the table, he raised an image of the fairy mound he had seen in Scotland.

It was easier to draw an illusory ring above it and affix more illusions to it, carousel style, than to try and make independent figures dance in a circle. He didn't think it was necessary to really define the others with more detail than cartoons of fairies, but the figure of Dola had to be absolutely exact. He dug out photographs he had of her, and even played back the videotape of Holl's wedding to make sure he got the image right. The child had been wearing a wreath in her hair that day. Keith fashioned his Dola wearing the simple green tunic he'd last seen her in, and the flower circlet. With an indulgent hand, he added lacy wings, and made her smile. It was almost as if she was really there. He wished he could touch her.

"We'll spring you, I promise," Keith told the simulacrum.

From Paul's product photos, he added shoes to Dola's feet of an incredible lime green with purple, pink, and teal accents. Maybe it was because the combination of colors blunted the senses, but they looked good against the green grass of the mound.

"Now, come on. Let's dance."

It was exhausting work getting the figures to move and caper the way he wanted them to. He was grateful the magic lantern worked by itself. He felt it was very appropriate, using illusions to help free Dola, whose special talent was making illusions.

On the twentieth try, he got the movements to correspond to the beat of the music, and was looking forward to calling it a wrap when Jeff barged in.

Keith looked up in horror. The little figures froze in place. Keith fought to hold on to his concentration. There was no way he'd be able to conjure them back the way he wanted them before morning, but he cursed his brother's timing.

"Hi," he said weakly.

Jeff stared down at the table. "What's this?" he asked.

"Computer holographs," Keith said, desperately. "You know. Puppet figures, entered into computer memory banks. Then we shoot them through a special split lens, and when you project it, it makes a holographic image. See? Pretty good?"

"Bull," Jeff pronounced. "There's no computer, no projector, and I don't see any strings." He shook his head, showing the first respect he had had for Keith since they were kids, and it was tainted with a modicum of fear. "Is it...magic?"

Keith said nothing. Jeff dropped down on the bed across from him.

"There's been weird stuff going on with you ever since you went away to college, and Mom and Dad won't talk about it," Jeff said, warily. "You aren't in one of those *cults*, are you?"

"No. Honest to God," Keith said. "I swear. All natural. One hundred percent organic."

"Well," Jeff said after a long pause, "then can I watch?"

Chapter Eighteen

The 'holograph' session went on a lot longer than Keith had originally envisioned. Having broken the ice, Jeff demanded further demonstrations. He wanted to know everything about magic, the Little Folk, and all of Keith's studies, and kept him talking almost to dawn. He weaseled a loan of some of Keith's most precious books on mythology, but the upshot was that by morning, they were friends again.

"I don't get it," Keith told his father privately after breakfast. "I thought he'd be scared into freaking out, but instead he spent the night asking questions."

"What's so strange about that?" Mr. Doyle asked, his grin a twin of his elder son's. He patted Keith on the back. "He is a Doyle, after all."

In the conference room that morning, Keith ran the commercial for Paul and the others. Hiding the magic lantern against the back of the videotape recorder under the television, he pretended to roll a tape cassette. The interns and their supervisor watched spellbound, and broke into loud applause at the end.

"Again!" Paul called from the head of the table. "Run it again! This is absolutely amazing. You did this in one night?"

"Yup," Keith said. "You know you only gave me the assignment yesterday."

"Colossal! God, you must be exhausted."

"Computer animation?" Sean asked.

"Something like that," Keith admitted.

"The setup must have cost a fortune," Brendan said in a sour voice. He was jealous of the admiration Keith was getting.

No one paid attention to him. "This is just great," Paul said, watching the circle of cartoon fairies whisking the figure of Dola around and around to the tinkling music. The closeups cut in, first of Dola's twinkling feet, clad in the gaudy sneakers, followed by one of her glowing face. The America's Shoe logo appeared over the next long shot. "You know, this is close enough to pro quality that they might just air it like it is."

"Oh, no! Uh, they can't!" Keith said, frantic.

"Why not?"

Keith swallowed. If they did take his perfect images, where was the need for searching for the right performer that would thereby rescue a little girl who'd been kidnapped? But he couldn't say that. "Uh, I'm not union," he choked out. It was lame, but effective. Paul snapped his fingers.

"Damn, you're right. That would skunk us for sure with the networks. Come on. We'll take it to Scott in America's Shoe right now. This is brilliant! He's got to see it. He'll wet his pants."

The media director for the America's Shoe account, a man with a broad and silky mustache, agreed that Keith's commercial was everything that the shoe company was looking for.

"It's got legs, pardon the pun," the director said, with an apologetic grin. "Just like this it could run—*last* a long time. *Years.* Search for the Fairy Footwear girl? We'll have to. A great idea. Good publicity, too. I'll put it up to the company this afternoon. You've saved me a ton of work, making a sample ad to show. The idea is always to leave as little to the client's imagination as possible, and this more than does the job. We could have a cattle call by the end of this week. The search for the Footwear Fairy." He drew a banner in the air.

"The end of this week?" Keith asked excitedly. "Tomorrow?"

"Sure, why not?" Scott said, showing his teeth under his mustache. "Things happen fast in the advertising business. Hot stuff, Paul. They'll love us. We've only had the product two days, and we're already in production. This could be worth a million."

"They might not take it," Paul said.

"Oh, they'll take it," Scott said.

His prediction was correct. By afternoon, Keith was asked to join the meeting with the representatives from America's Shoe. He showed the ad over and over again to the growing delight of the executives.

"God, it's perfect," said the director of public relations, a slender and balding man in his forties. "I *hated* the name when the designers came up with it, but you've made me love it. I'm behind you a hundred percent."

"It's a go," the finance director said. "I cannot believe how fast you came through, Paul, Scott. Absolutely cannot believe it." He chuckled.

"Brilliant," said the vice president from America's Shoe. She beamed at all of them. "I knew we were right to hire PDQ."

Keith sat beside the video ensemble, happy as a clam who had just won the Irish Sweepstakes. At the end of the meeting he reclaimed his magic lantern and stuck it into his briefcase. The executives drifted out toward the lobby, escorted by Paul, still talking about market share, frequency, and the search for just the right model.

"Uh, Scott?" he said, "can I take the press release down to the P.R. department?"

"Take it down?" Scott said. "You can write it, if you want, Keith." He looked at his watch. "If you get your butt in gear and turn it in in the next half hour, we'll make the Saturday morning papers with time to spare." He sighed. "Even short notice like this will mean we'll be mobbed," he said sadly. "Every stage mother in the city will have her kid here before we open in the morning."

"How about statewide?" Keith suggested. "You only want to do this once, right?"

"You *are* a glutton for punishment. Sure. Statewide. Alert the troops. You'd better take the rest of the day off after you turn out the P.R. release. You'll need your strength tomorrow."

"Me?"

"Sure, kid. It's your idea," the director said. "You get to suffer the consequences along with the rest of us."

"Great!" Keith exclaimed.

Elated, he ran up to use a typewriter in one of the copywriter's offices. The words for the press release ran out easily under his fingers, and in no time, he had a notice of the correct length in the correct format ready to be signed off. He included a frame from his mockup commercial to illustrate the report.

Paul gave the text his approval. "A little flowery, but so what? It's your first time. Get out of here, and I'll see you in the morning. You look shot to pieces. Get some sleep. I'm sending the others home as soon as they finish today's assignments."

"Thanks, Paul!" Keith said.

On the way out, he took a small package addressed to Paul out of his file drawer. He thought of leaving it in Paul's mailbox, but elected not to, in case things didn't go as he hoped Saturday. Better to make sure, instead of jinxing the procedures ahead of time by being too cocky; he decided he'd rather wait and see.

Saturday morning, Jake Williamson and Mona Gilbreth paid a visit to Pilton at the cottage in the woods. Jake gave Pilton the daily paper and a carton of fresh milk, while Mona talked her way into the back room to see how her bankroll—she stopped herself in mid-thought, her *guest* was doing.

The girl looked at her sullenly from the corner of the room, her cheeks sunken and unhealthy looking. It seemed that she had been in that position for days. She only had Grant's word that she'd even set foot out of the room.

"Are you sure she's eating?" Mona demanded, coming out of the bedroom. Behind her, the door lock snapped shut. The child must have flown to latch it as soon as she was out again.

"Yes'm, peanut butter and jelly sandwiches," Pilton confirmed, glancing up from the gossip column. "She eats about one a day. She never talks to me any more, even though I said I'm sorry."

"You've got to stop apologizing for shooting her imaginary friend," Jake told him severely.

"It wasn't imaginary, Jake," Grant insisted. "I saw it too! And I thought maybe she'd be my lucky charm."

"Well, she's certainly been mine," Mona said. Her jeweler friend had come through with a buyer for the antique sapphire, and the enormous sum was being transferred directly to her account. She had called each one of her creditors to say that the bills were being paid in full. She hadn't felt so wonderful in ages. Taking care of the outstanding invoices hadn't left a lot for the Democrats, but the ransom the child's folks had promised to pay would take care of that. She was just waiting for the right moment, the right place, to claim it.

"Well, you see, ma'am?" Grant said. He read through the gossip column, and came to a framed notice at the end. "Hey. Look at this," he said, holding it up for the others to read. "We can win this contest. We got us a *real* fairy."

"Aw, shut up, Grant," Jake said, impatiently.

Mona took the page away from him and read it carefully. Light dawned on her face.

"No, he's right," she told her foreman. "That's a good idea, and I don't think it was accidental. See? This contest is being run by PDQ. That Doyle boy must have set it up so we can exchange the kid for the cash quietly with H. Doyle where no one will notice. It's today. We can make it to Chicago if we start out right away. Her folks can have her back, if they have the money, and good riddance to her."

Pilton was aghast. "You mean take her there, but not enter her? That's crazy. Look at this ad—it's almost a ringer for her."

The fairy in the illustration *was* almost a perfect image of the little girl. Jake and Mona exchanged glances. Both of them knew it was deliberate, beckoning to them. The next move was theirs.

"You're right, Grant," Jake said, placatingly. "We couldn't lose with this little girl. We'll take her up there and enter her in this contest. If we're really lucky, we'll come home with the big prize."

Pilton's grin popped the sides of his jaw. "Yeah!"

"Get the girl ready," Mona said. "I'll be back in fifteen minutes."

"All right," Mona said into the phone. She had gone out to find a roadside booth and dialed Hollow Tree's number. "We saw the ad. This is it. We'll meet you there. You bring the ransom. I'll bring the girl. We'll exchange, er, packages, and get it over with. Yes, there. No police or press or any funny stuff."

"The ransom will be there," H. Doyle promised.

By ten A.M., the hall outside of the PDQ media director's office resembled back stage of a winter performance of the Nutcracker Suite, sharing a dressing room with a production of the Wizard of Oz. Hundreds of little girls in some suggestion of gauzy costume, accompanied by their mothers, a few with their fathers, and a few in the company of agents stood or sat against the walls of the corridor. A couple, in undisguised ballet garb, did stretches with hands on chairbacks for stability. Most of them were wearing makeup. A handful had gigantic, commercial rubber pixie ears stuck on, which gave the tinier girls an aspect of having three heads.

The parents all had portfolios in their laps or against their knees, notebook-sized up to leather zip cases that would hold theatrical posters flat. Keith, Dorothy, Sean, and Brendan had been given stacks of applications and a quick lesson in how to process the talent through to the media director.

"Just be polite and keep them happy while they're waiting," Scott said. "They'll be on good behavior right up until the time I turn them down for the part. Every one of them knows there's only one winner in this game, and they want to be it."

"I know you'll be fine," Paul said. "If there's a real problem you can't handle, come and get me." He added his blessings, and disappeared with Scott and the America's Shoe executives into the inner sanctum.

Keith threaded his way between the shrill-voiced children, fielded the questions for a couple who wanted to know where the bathroom was, and helped a woman in charge of an entire Brownie troop in Halloween princess costumes fill out her application forms, all the time searching the faces for the ones he knew. Holl, Tay, Enoch, and the Master were coming up with Marcy. Dunn was already there, sitting close enough to an African-American child and her father to seem as if he was with them. Lee, interviewing a simpering mother and her precocious child, winked at Keith over their heads. He was there to do a human-interest story on the shoot for his newspaper, and run interference where and if needed.

A couple of the creative staff and the receptionist had come in to help out, too. The only stranger was Scott's assistant, a thin, intense young woman with pixie-cut brown hair and huge glasses that dominated her small face. She flashed lightning-quick smiles at everyone, and kept the queue moving smoothly with charm and the implied threat of expulsion.

Diane had arrived by herself. She had taken charge of a clipboard, listened silently as Keith explained how to fill out applications, and was running completed forms up the end of the hall to the media director's office in no time. No one questioned her assured, confident presence. Each of the executives in the audition room thought she belonged to a different one of them. She ushered a set of Japanese twins, aged about eight, into the office, sweeping right by Keith without seeming to see that he was there. She passed him again, her eyes focused straight forward. He tried to stop her and talk to her, but she shook his hand off her arm without looking at him.

From the time she had arrived, she had refused to speak with Keith. Whenever he had tried to talk about anything but Dola or the auditions, she had tuned him out and kept walking or started a conversation with one of the others from Midwestern. Frustrated and upset, Keith watched her go by.

Dorothy came up to him after seeing the performance repeated more than once. "You look like one of Little Bo Peep's lost sheep. What's wrong with her?" she asked, in an undertone. "I thought she was your girlfriend."

"Brendan," Keith said, his face red. "He told her you and I were, well, having a thing, and she won't believe it's not true. Well, we have had dinner together a couple of times. I didn't deny that. I wouldn't. But she took it all wrong. You know how persuasive Brendan is."

"Yeah. He wants to be in advertising," Dorothy said, wryly. "Hang loose."

Diane, with cool efficiency, helped one of the newcoming children fill out her application, and atttached the portfolio photograph to the back with a plastic paperclip.

"Just sit here for a moment, and we'll call you," she said. She favored the little girl and her parent with a polite smile, and moved on to the next one. Dorothy moved in on her, and paying no attention to her protests, pushed her up the hall and into the empty lunchroom. Diane tried to break free, but Dorothy kept her arm in a solid grip.

"You and I have got to talk," Dorothy said. She planted her back against the door, blocking Diane's attempts to pull it open.

Diane retreated a few feet, tossed her head back and stared down her nose in mock hauteur. "You're extremely pretty. I can see why Keith's attracted to you. Let me go. I'm leaving." She made as if to force her way past, but retreated before actually laying hands on the other young woman.

Dorothy sighed and put hands on hips. "Listen, honey, I've got a man of my own. I don't need yours, and believe me, that man is *all* yours. You know it, too, or you wouldn't be here right now helping him. Why make life tougher for him than you need to?" The blond girl was staring at her as if Dorothy was speaking a language that she could just barely understand, but enlightenment was dawning. "You poor child," Dorothy said, with sincere sympathy, "I can tell you're so much in love with him that you'd believe any stupid thing you heard about him, right?"

"Yes," Diane said, in a whimper. "You're absolutely right."

Dorothy shook her head. "Tch, tch, tch. Don't you know he's shown your picture to everybody in this building? He talks about you nonstop. I've known about you from Day One. You've got to consider the source, you know. You go ahead and tidy up, then come out again. That place is Crazyville out there. We need you. You're being a big help."

Kindness from one she thought was a rival was too much for Diane. Her eyes filled up with tears, and she fumbled in her pocket for a tissue. Dorothy walked over to the sink and yanked a couple of paper towels off the roll.

"You know, your boyfriend sat and listened to me cry in this very room not too long ago," Dorothy said, handing them to her. "What goes around, comes around." She slipped out of the room and left Diane alone.

Feeling as if she had misunderstood everyone horribly, Diane sat and snuffled miserably until the paper towels grew soggy in her hands. Poor Keith, with so much on his mind, and she had refused to listen to him when he was telling her the truth.

She felt her way blindly out of the lunchroom and found the nearest lavatory. Staring at her redeyed reflection in the mirror, she resolved to go tell Keith she had been wrong. After dousing her face in cold water, she went out to find him.

Keith spotted Marcy standing on her tiptoes at the end of the hall. She waved at him, then lowered her hand. He nodded, to let her know he understood. The Little Folk were in the building. He glanced around to find Holl, and came face to face with Diane. He goggled at her.

"Diane, I..."

"I need to talk to you," she said. Her eyes were red.

"This way," he said, taking her by the hand. He led her toward the conference room, afraid to let go in case she changed her mind about talking to him.

On a Saturday, that part of the hallway was deserted. None of the children, eager to cooperate and act like professionals, had defied the arrow sign in the foyer and gone down to investigate the opposite corridor. Keith started to reach for the handle of the conference room. Diane suddenly pulled back against his grasp.

"I don't want to go in there," she said.

As suddenly, Keith felt he didn't either. It took him a moment to recognize the force of an avoidance charm. The Master and the other Little Folk must be inside. Keith pushed at the substance of the charm. He braced himself against the curtain of repulsion, pushing through by main force of will.

"I don't want to go in there," Diane repeated, trying to pull away.

"Yes. You. Do," Keith gritted out, and they were through. He shoved the door closed behind him, and the two of them were suddenly face to face with the four elves. Politely, the Little Folk drew back to the extreme end of the room, to give the couple privacy.

Keith reddened. "Excuse us," he said. He dragged Diane across the conference chamber to the closet, pulled open the door, pushed her inside before him, and closed the door. The only light was a thread that peeked in past the doorjamb. It drew a glimmering line down one side of Diane's face, illuminating a tear drifting onto her cheek from her lashes. Keith pulled his handkerchief out of his pocket and dabbed at it. She took the small cloth from him and clutched it between her hands.

"Everyone's pushing me around today," she said, miserably.

Keith waited for her to blow her nose.

"Now," he said in a low voice. "I'm sorry you misunderstood what was happening up here. I tried to explain, really. I'm sorry you were upset with me. It wasn't my fault."

"I know," Diane said. She snuffled. "I hung up on you. I'm sorry, too, but I was so hurt thinking you could go off with anyone else. I've been under such a strain, worrying about the children, and then there was that poor air sprite getting killed, and I had a Chemistry exam I thought I blew, and then *he* said you were in bed with somebody else, and well," she finished in a burst of woe, "I *missed* you down there and it hurt thinking you didn't miss me as much."

"But I love *you*," Keith said, genuinely surprised, "and someday I want to marry you, when we're both out of school and I can explain to your parents why it wouldn't be a detriment to have me in the family."

Abandoning the handkerchief, Diane laughed. She threw her arms around him and squeezed him in a rib-cracking hug. Keith took the opportunity to express the devotion that had been building up for the past weeks of separation, kissing her with increasing ardor.

"Oh, Keith, my parents already like you," Diane said, managing to get a few syllables out between kisses. "And I love you, too."

"Ah!" the Maven said, clear across the room from the closet. His sharp hearing had picked up every word of the whispered conversation. He settled back in his chair with his hands behind his head. "*Finally*." The Master, Enoch, and Tay added their indulgent smiles.

"But Mommy!" a shrill voice announced from the hallway, "that girl butted right in front of me!"

The child's voice was clearly audible in the closet. Keith and Diane broke apart and looked at each other, feeling guilty.

"Dola," they said together. They fled out of the conference room and into the hall to separate the two ten year olds, who were circling each other like prizefighters. The parents, each behind their own child, clutched applications and portfolios like cut and patch kits. One girl, round-faced and freckled, confronted the other, smaller and slimmer, but with a long, hollow-cheeked face.

"She pushed in ahead of me first!"

"Ladies, please!" Keith said. "Hey, both of you look absolutely pixielike, don't you think so, Miss Londen?"

"Oh, yes!" Diane exclaimed, not knowing exactly where Keith was going, but following valiantly.

"There's hardly any way to choose between you," he said, in a confidential whisper, hunkering down on his heels beside them and holding both girls' hands, "so we're going to turn you over to Mr. Martwick, who's going to take you right inside for your interview. All right?"

The girls glared at one another, but both recognized the benefits of getting in ahead of the rest of the crowd, even in a joint audition, so they nodded. The horsefaced child beamed determinedly, and turned back to her mother to have her rouge reapplied.

As soon as they were ready, Keith marched both children over to Brendan, who was just emerging from the office at the end of the hall. "Mr. Martwick, in the interest of fairness, both of these amazingly fairylike youngsters have got to be taken in to see our media director *next,* don't you agree?"

Brendan, uncertainly, grinned at the girls and yanked Keith aside. "What's going on, Keith? Relatives of yours? One of them's Gloria

Swanson reincarnate and the other one's the Pillsbury Dough Girl. They haven't got a chance."

"They were fighting," Keith said under his breath. "If you want to keep it from becoming a mob in here, get them in and out as fast as you can. Picture it: five hundred little girls all screaming and crying…"

"Say no more," Brendan said, blanching at the mere idea. He took the girls' hands and escorted them into the office. "Right this way, please." The parents followed, bestowing smug glances on the other mothers who were still waiting. The door closed behind them.

"Whew!" Diane breathed. Dorothy came up behind them, and winked at Keith.

"Nice work. Nice work on Brendan, too."

"Thanks for straightening things out for us, Dorothy," Keith said.

"I'm so sorry for thinking there was something wrong," Diane said, her cheeks reddening.

"Hey, no charge," Dorothy said. She floated away from them to take on the next group arriving in the building.

Taking a moment for a breather, Keith went back to the conference room to check in with the Little Folk. They knew now to expect him, so the spell's substance pushed back before him like a curtain.

The elves sitting around the boardroom table grinned up at him as he came in. He realized that they must have heard his whole conversation with Diane. Feeling foolish, he ignored their expressions. Business was business.

"I'm glad you got here," he said. "Now we're ready. You sure she said she'll be here?"

"I do. I think she'll be as glad of it as we are," Holl said.

"The situation has passed beyond her management," the Master said, regally upright at the head of the table. "She must resolf it, for she cannot continue to lif vith it for any measurable period of time."

"Good," Keith said. He retrieved his packet of papers from a spell-jammed file drawer where he'd placed it early that morning. "As soon as she turns Dola over to us, I'm giving this to Paul Meier."

"What is it?" Enoch asked.

Keith grinned wickedly. "The rope to hang friend Brendan up by his ankles."

"Oh, give it to me," Enoch said, holding out a hand. His dark eyes glowed like embers. "I'd be pleased to help any of that woman's collaborators to hang by any parts that would give them the most pain, after all she's done to us. I'll make sure Paul Meier does not read it until the correct moment."

Keith was alarmed. "Don't put any compulsions on him, okay? He's a good guy."

"I was not," the elf said, slightly affronted. There was a flash of the old, sullen Enoch Blackhair of the days before he fell in love with Marcy. "It will be on the papers. Your friend will find them irresistible when the woman has passed in and out of the building once."

Keith breathed relief. "That'll be perfect." Another wail erupted in the hallway. "Oops, gotta go!"

"I'm scared," Diane told Keith on one of her increasingly frequent passes by. "What if they don't come?"

"They'll come," Keith said, exuding a confidence he didn't feel. He glanced around to see if any of the other interns were looking, leaned over and gave her a quick peck on the cheek. She smiled. Things were back to normal between them—or better. Keith was relieved.

"Hey, Keith," Brendan called to him, coming out of the office. "They want coffee in there. You want to get some?"

"What's the problem?" Keith asked, closing the distance. "Forget how to boil water?"

"Hey, they need me in there," Brendan said. He decided not to argue with Keith. Looking around, he found another potential sucker. "Hey, Sean, you want to get some coffee for the media director? Two with one sugar, one with cream and no sugar. And maybe you could see if there's some doughnuts."

"Sure, Brendan," Lopez said, always willing to help. He strode off toward the lunchroom.

Keith let Brendan go back into the inner sanctum. He didn't dare leave the corridor again, out of concern that Mona Gilbreth would come while he was away, and he preferred that Brendan wasn't in the way. He passed, and smiled at, a little blond girl wearing a belted tunic, soft shoes, and a Peter Pan hat. Her shining hair hung down over her knees in braids tied with big bows of ribbon at the ends, and she had huge rouge spots over her sharp, high cheek-bones. Her elf ears looked pretty good, very realistic. He got three steps beyond her and did a full double take and turned around on his heel for a full stare. It was Candlepat. She came up and shyly tugged on his shirttail, and he stooped down to speak to her.

"I'll never forgive you for not knowing me," she said mischievously, "but look around you."

Two benches away, her sister Catra sat, dressed in an oversized tent of gauze and crepe, looking very fairy-like but too sophisticated for this kind of thing. Rose's granddaughter, Delana, with her massed tresses of red, drew eyes to the far end of the corridor from the media director's office. With a little more careful scrutiny, Keith made out Pat Morgan, wearing a false mustache, pretending to be the girl's father. Why not? he thought, realizing that he had asked Pat for advice on casting calls, but forgotten in his haste to ask for his help.

"Lee brought us," Candlepat said, as if reading his mind. "All of us wanted to help bring Dola home, but the ones who look too old," she preened, knowing she herself looked like an advertisement for the fountain of youth, "stay home and await our success."

Keith, looking around him and realizing how much of the cavalry was behind him, laughed. The stage, as far as it was ever going to be set, was set.

One by one, the line snaked forward. Some emerged from the Media office with tears in their eyes, others hopeful but bemused. The parents were invariably indignant that they had to wait so long, and scornful that their precious infants were being rejected.

The child professionals, used to lengthy casting calls, were incredibly well-behaved during the ordeal. No one acted out by running up and down the hall, but a few took out their boredom and frustration on the other children, rivals for the single part to be had. Keith wasn't quite in time to save the child who pulled Candepat's long, golden braids. The girl spent the next several minutes chasing an imaginary bee that buzzed around her head. No one but Keith and the other Little Folk could see the enhanced dust mote. The girl was near tears before Keith came up behind Candlepat and gave her a meaningful poke in the shoulderblade. Her response was to turn huge, innocent, blue eyes upward to him, but the bee vanished immediately.

"C'mon," he said. "I've got to watch the door. I can't keep an eye on you all the time."

"I do wish you would," she said, with a hopeful expression, not missing a chance to vamp him. Keith grinned.

"Go away, little girl, you bother me," he said, in his best W.C. Fields voice.

More children came in as the line moved up to make room for them.

Dola did not really understand where they were taking her when they rousted her out of the little room in the cottage. For a change, she was not made to ride in the bumpy truck, but instead in a plush-padded automobile seat with Skinny beside her.

They had been driving for hours. Dola was worried, because she was moving ever farther away from the comforting trace of her people. Boss-lady spared her only the briefest glances over the back of the front seat. Jake didn't talk to her. And Dola could not understand what Skinny was talking about with his ravings of a contest to find a real shoe fairy.

Her last word on the subject was "I do not make shoes." Since then, she sat with her arms folded across her chest, ignoring Skinny's attempts to make conversation.

The scenery they were driving through was very different than anything she had seen outside of television. She could see for a long way ahead of her. The city was taking over the landscape, brown and gray superseding green. Gigantic buildings thrust up out of the ground, getting more and more imposing as the car approached them.

Inside, she was feeling terrified and small, but she kept a cool exterior, as if she visited Chicago every day of her life. She had listened to the low exchanges between Jake and Mona Gilbreth, but none of it had made her any wiser as to her coming fate. Would she be left alone in this cold city?

The car turned onto a street entirely lined with skyscrapers, veered sharply around a corner, and plunged down into the darkness of a curved ramp. At the bottom of this terrifying ride was nothing more than a parking lot, but strangely secreted underground. Dola was made to alight from the car and walk between Jake and Skinny. She felt like a military prisoner marching between guards.

The only noise in the corridor they walked was their foot-steps and breathing. They passed briefly up onto the surface of the city street, up a flight of three stairs, and into a building fronted with gray glass panels and gray glass doors. Jake pushed one of these open.

Massed voices of countless, shrill-voiced children all talking at once struck her ears like the clash of cymbals. The Big Folk hustled Dola through one more door, and she stood at the end of an infor-mal line consisting of a hundred little girls and a hundred mothers and fathers. In the midst of the crowd, she saw Keith Doyle.

She wanted to scream out to him to get his attention, to get her away from her captors. Jake saw her take a deep breath and jammed his huge hand over her face. "You keep quiet until we tell you to talk." Keith disappeared, and Dola's heart sank.

The four of them pushed forward through the crowd. Dola tried to struggle loose to run and find Keith. Skinny kept a firm grasp on her arm and tugged her back into line. One father, whom they all but pushed out of the way, looked at her and up at the men. "Listen, guys," he said, "if she doesn't want to audition, don't make her. Sheesh."

"She could get lost in here if she gets loose," Mona said. "Hang on tight."

Pilton looked around in disdain. "She's ten times prettier than any of these kids." He pointed. "Look at that one, with the flat face. She doesn't have a chance. None of them do."

"Shut up, Grant," Jake said, wearily. "We're not here to really enter this beauty contest. We're here to give her back to her folks."

"No?" Pilton was disappointed. "You *know* she'd win in a sec-ond. Why don't we wait and see what the judges say, then give her back. I want to win the reward." He looked down at Dola and beamed. "She couldn't make me a chest of jewels, so I guess she just attracted luck for us."

Keith popped his head in the conference room door. Tay, by the window, was pacing up and down. The Master sat at the head of the room, his eyes fixed on nothing. Enoch kept looking around, sighing impatiently. Holl was at the table with a large bag between his hands. They all looked up at Keith.

"They're here," he said.

Holl tied up the bag, but not before Keith got a look at the contents. He was dumbstruck.

"My God, where did you get all those jewels?"

"Go on," Holl said, urgently. "Hurry."

The two men kept Dola at one end of the room. She looked up at Diane, who hurried over to hand both of them forms and pencils. The blond woman smiled down on her, but her expression showed she thought Dola was a stranger. Not comprehending, the child felt more lost and alone than she had. Skinny let go to fill in his sheet of paper, but Jake kept his grip.

Thankfully, Keith reappeared. The Boss-lady bustled up to him, and her voice was still audible to Dola half a room away.

"Well?"

"Ms. Gilbreth, what a pleasure to see you!" Keith said out loud, turning from side to side to see if he could attract anyone's attention. None of the parents or children in the room had any time for anyone else's concerns.

Mona turned pale.

"Shh," she begged him, covering the side of her face with one hand. "No names, *please*! I'm ready to make the exchange."

Keith looked back over her shoulder at Dola, and winked. "How do I know that you'll let her go when we give you the ran—the package?"

"Don't be a fool! This has all gone on too long. Now, come on. Give me...what I asked for."

Keith peered sideways and nodded. A boy with blond hair came out of an alcove where he had been waiting, concealed. He showed her a bag. He hefted it, and it shifted with a sound like clattering dice.

Mona's eyes widened with greed. "Good!" She reached for it. The boy drew back.

"We want the girl released first," Keith explained.

"No!" Mona said. "I want to be out of here first. I don't want anyone to associate me with you or anything else. And I'm holding you to your word—no persecution in the press, now or ever!"

"Sure," Keith said, ostentatiously raising his hands to shoulder level. "Whatever you want." Seeing his signal, Lee advanced upon her with his notebook in hand, camera slung over arm, his dark face earnest.

"Ms. Gilbreth? Ms. Mona Gilbreth! I'm Lee Eisley with the Indiana Daily Star. Can I have a word with you?"

"You lied!" Mona shrieked at Keith. "You promised no press!"

"I've got nothing to do with him," Keith said, giving Lee a puzzled look. "He's here covering the human-interest story."

She spun on her heel, and drew a sharp vector with a red fingernail toward the door. The big muscle-man grabbed Dola and started to hustle her outside. The Master and the others flew out of their hiding places.

"Hey," said one mother, watching them run past, "they're not auditioning boys, too, are they?"

With a sweet, regretful smile, Candlepat abandoned her interview with the casting director's assistant and ran toward the others, rolling up her sleeves. The assistant ran after her.

"Wait!" she cried.

Brendan, emerging from the media director's office, ran up to Keith. "Wasn't that Ms. Gilbreth?"

"Uh, no!" Keith said, not wanting Brendan in the middle of things. "Hey, there's Paul in the doorway. I think he's looking for you."

"He is?" Brendan turned around. The door had drifted shut. "I'd better get in there."

Keith waded through the dozens of children wondering what was going on and out into the foyer, where a peculiar kind of fight was going on.

The skinny man who'd beaten up on him at Gilbreth's factory was under attack by Holl, Candlepat, and Enoch. Marcy and Diane were flailing at the bigger man with their clipboards, while Tay wound up a handful of air and flung it straight into the man's solar plexus.

"That's for being greedy!" he cried. "And that! That's for keeping my girl."

Battered and groaning, the big man doubled over in pain.

"What'd you do to him?" Keith demanded in a frantic whisper.

"Gripes," Tay said, in satisfaction. "He'll be no use the rest of today, tonight, and as long as it'll hold."

"That," Holl said, gumming together Pilton's back teeth, fingers and toes, "is for the air sprite, and for Frank Winslow whose heart you broke."

The skinny man promptly fell over onto the floor and tried to help himself up, with his hands glued together into flippers.

Mona saw that she was getting the worst of the disagreement. Children, little children, were beating up her two bodyguards. It was time to get out. No more easy cooperation, she vowed, hustling the child toward the doors. She would take the girl to the backwoods of Montana and chain her up with mountain lions, and move her from place to place so those lying Doyles would never find her again. She dodged past the two black men. The darkhaired girl tried to get in her way. Like a linebacker with the ball, Mona held on to Dola and made for the gray glass doors.

"She's getting away!" Candlepat shrilled.

"No!" Keith yelled.

He grabbed Holl's shoulder and threw an illusion with all his strength and will on the nearest gray glass panel. A door handle shimmered into existence, and the handles on the doors seemed to vanish.

Mona grabbed for the sole visible doorknob and threw herself against the door to get it open. Nothing happened. She hammered on the panel, wondering if it was stuck. In the momentary delay, the small woman with the big glasses advanced upon her and threw herself almost into Mona's arms.

The others were closing in around the three of them. Mona was cornered.

"She's perfect!" the casting assistant cried, dropping to her knees beside the little girl. "How could you *think* of leaving before we saw this absolutely enchanting child? I think that Walter would love to see you. Wouldn't you like to stay for an interview, Miss?" she asked the blond child.

The little girl looked to Keith Doyle for guidance, who nodded violently. The little girl nodded violently, too.

"Oh, yes!" she said. "Wouldn't that be nice, Ms. Gilbreth?"

"Ms. Gilbreth, how about an interview?" Lee said, raising his camera, and focusing for a picture.

"Take it and go, Ms. Gilbreth," said a low voice behind her. She felt something shoved into her fist.

Wide-eyed, Mona recognized the voice of H. Doyle, and looked down at the childsized being behind her. The family resemblance was there, including the strangely deformed ears. But he was so small...Her mind refused to accept any more conflicting data. He pushed open one of the real doors for her. Panic stricken and overwhelmed, she clutched the bag and shot out of the room. As soon as they could, the two men followed her.

The casting assistant took charge of Dola and led her back into the main hall, chatting in enthusiastic tones about her coming audition.

"You look so real, as if you were a real fairy," the young woman told her.

Diane whispered in Keith's ear. "Do you know, she's been zinged, and she doesn't even know it?" He caught her sly grin and returned it.

As they returned to the hall, Keith watched as slowly, inexorably, Paul Meier reached for the packet of papers left on a chair and started to read them. Enoch's spell was effective, and right on target. Brendan came up to confront Keith.

"That *was* Ms. Gilbreth I saw!" Brendan said. "I'd better go to her. She'll think I didn't notice she was here."

"She just left, Brendan," Keith said, shaking his head.

"Well, I'll catch her. Be back in a moment." He started to follow her, but Paul Meier came up behind him and took his arm in a firm grip.

"Brendan, can I talk to you? It's about these pamphlets you wrote up on the Gilbreth campaign. I didn't know she was president of Greenpeace. And this stuff about her Ph.D. in chemistry—don't you know anything about ethics? Or research? Do you know what putting out false information does to PDQ's reputation? I want to have a little word with you in the conference room. Do you have a moment?"

Blanching, Brendan let himself be led away.

Still talking, the casting assistant came up to Keith. "Was Dola here with Ms. Gilbreth? Who's her guardian?"

Tay started forward, but Keith pushed in front of him. "I am. I'm her...cousin."

The young woman beamed. "Keeping it all in the family, eh? Well, come on. Scott has got to see this girl." She went on at length about how perfect Dola would be for the layout, and how perfect the makeup job was that someone had done on her. Keith Doyle agreed with everything she said.

"And the Tinkerbell outfit, just adorable," the assistant gushed, escorting them past the crowd and into the office.

"This old thing?" Dola said, astonished. "I've been wearing it for two weeks!"

"Well, it's got such authenticity, doesn't it?"

Scott, by contrast, had only one sentence to say to Dola.

"Do you want the job?"

Dola, having gone from incarceration in a lonely cabin to having the world make a fuss over her, was delighted to agree to anything Keith Doyle was so happy about. "Oh, yes! But what is it?"

"Great," said the tall man with the mustache. "Shooting begins Monday. You come here. Contracts. Here. We want you to sign right away. You have an agent?"

"No. Do I need one?" Dola asked, looking up at Keith, who glanced it over.

"Between you and me, Scott," Keith said, "is this an honest contract?"

"It's okay," Scott said. "It's fair. Standard form. How about it?"

"It's okay," Keith said, handing a pen to Dola. In careful, Palmer penmanship, Dola signed 'Dola Doyle' on the line.

"Pretty name," Scott said, accepting the document. "Eupipinous."

"I think you mean 'euphonious'," Dola corrected him gently.

"Hey, smart little kid."

"It runs in the family," Dola said, with a sly upward glance at Keith. He put his arm around her shoulders and squeezed.

"Well, the part's filled," Scott said, leaning back in his chair and smoothing his mustache, "although I think the artist had someone particular in mind all along, didn't you, Keith?'

"Well, yes," Keith admitted.

"That's all right. It worked out perfectly. You've got just one more dirty job to do."

"What's that?" Keith asked.

"You've got to tell all those kids out there to go home."

Chapter Nineteen

When the hall was cleared out, Keith took Dola back to the conference room, where all of the allies, Big and Little, were waiting. Marcy and Diane set up a cheer as soon as Dola appeared.

As soon as she saw Tay, Dola ran across the room and jumped into her father's arms to give him a big hug and kiss. She all but danced from person to person, giving them enthusiastic embraces. Even the Master unbent when she hopped up to kiss him on the cheek.

"I want a bath, and I want to eat something that tastes like food," Dola said, reaching Keith and Holl at the end of the line, "and oh, how is Asrai?"

"She misses you," Holl said gravely. "You'll see her soon."

"Thank you," Dola said. "And thank you, Keith Doyle." She tried to jump up into his arms. He caught her up and swung her in a circle. Diane spun Keith around and hugged Dola at the same time, making an affectionate sandwich out of the little girl.

"I'm *so* glad to see you safe," Diane said, fiercely. "Are you all right?"

"Oh, yes, I'm fine. Skinny was kind to me. I almost liked him, up until the time he shot the ghost—oh, Keith Doyle!" Dola cried. "I've remembered what I was going to tell you! When I was in the house in the woods, we were visited by a creature. I've never seen one like it. It looked like a ghost, and it made pictures in my head. It was friendly. I think it was looking for me. And then the skinny man shot it! There is another kind of being, not like us or like you, but intelligent! I grieved when it was killed, but I guessed that where one existed, there must be more. You must go looking for them, right away!"

Keith exchanged solemn glances with the Master and Holl. "I think I know who you're talking about."

"You know? You've seen it?"

"Yup."

"Can that not wait?" the Master said. "Ve must leaf here before they close up the building."

"Right. Sorry, Master," Keith said. "Congrats, everyone. Are you all going home now?"

"Certainly not," Catra said.

"No, indeed," said her sister. "Lee has promised to take us to the amusement park. I think we well deserve the treat, and no old Conservatives to say no—uh, er, unless you disapprove, Master?" she amended humbly, noticing the village headman's half-lidded gaze upon her and suddenly remembering they were not as devoid of authority figures as she thought.

The Master lifted the corner of his mouth, which for him was a mark of great good humor. "No, in fact I agree. You deserf a reward. It is Big Folk culture, but vun afternoon vill not spoil you. Go."

Delighted and grateful, they started talking about the wonders they were going to see. "I hear there is also a shopping center near by!" Candlepat exclaimed excitedly.

"Oh, yes," Marcy said, drawn into the conversation. "Right across the street. It's *enormous.*"

"Oh, no," Lee said. "I'm not going to take a bunch of women all around no shopping mall."

"Me, neither," Dunn said, shaking his head. "The park. That's it. Okay?"

The young women surrendered with disappointed nods. "All right. We agree," Catra said, a little dejected. "The park it is." The party, consisting of everyone but Holl, the Master, Tay, Dola, Diane and Keith, divided itself into carloads, and prepared to go.

Keith reached into a pocket. "Wait!" he called. "It's on me." He took money out of his pocket and handed it to Lee. "Have a good time."

"We'll see," Lee said, with a wink and a grin. He shepherded the others out the door.

"Do you want me to take you home now?" Keith asked the Master. Tay and Dola, who had been talking together a mile a minute and heard nothing, glanced up at the mention of home. "Dola's been away a long time. I know everyone will want to see she's okay."

"Not at all," the Master said, wagging a finger at Keith. "A telephone call vill do for now. You haf promised me to take me to see Professor Parker and his display. I hold you to it. I vish to go. And also this brave child deserfs indulgence after her ordeal. You shall take her somewhere special aftervards."

"With pleasure," Keith said, bowing him out of the room. "I never mind spoiling Dola. Your chariot awaits. You old softy," he muttered under his breath.

The Master glanced back at him, clearly having heard every syllable, a frosty look through the glasses, which quickly changed to an amused twinkle.

A thought struck Keith as they were leaving PDQ.

"Holl," he said, taking the elf aside, "you don't have $20,000. Where did you get all those jewels you gave Mona Gilbreth?"

"We gave her what she expected to see," Holl said, reaching into a pocket. He handed Keith a faceted ruby an inch across. Keith handled it with awe.

"My God, that's beautiful! Did you find a mine or something?"

"Oh, no," Holl said. "We found a box in the pantry." He put one in his mouth and chewed it. It broke apart into fragments, then melted away. Keith watched, thunderstruck. "They're made of Jell-O. Remember? We had some at our wedding. Maura reminded me."

Leaving her assistants to deal with their peculiar and sudden ailments, Mona hurried to keep her appointment at the national party headquarters. Jack Harriman met her at the door.

"I've got something really special to show you," she said, brandishing the bag. "Call everyone. They have to see, too."

With such a tantalizing mystery at hand, all activity in the central office came to a swift halt. Telephones rang unattended, as Mona Gilbreth prepared to unveil her great secret. Even the state party chairman was present in the crowd around a table in the middle of the big office.

"Okay, lady," Jack said, giving her a big smile. "We're ready. Lay it on us!"

Quivering with anticipation, Mona held out the bag of jewels. It was worth far more than the twenty grand she had demanded from H. Doyle. With this treasure trove, she would reinstate herself as the Environmental Candidate. It would rocket her in popularity among the party. She could sponsor committees. People would look up to her. She could almost feel the chair in her Washington office under her tailbone.

"Here's my donation to the Democratic Party for this election year!" With a flick of her wrist, she sent the jewels scattering across a tabletop.

There were gasps and cries of wonder. People picked up the gems and played with them, tried them on their fingers. In the strong lights overhead, the blues, greens, and reds glimmered like a fantastic stained glass window.

"It's a fortune," the state chairman said, seizing Mona's hand and shaking it. "What a windfall! Thank you, Ms. Gilbreth—or should we say, Congresswoman?"

Mona beamed. "Just Mona, please," she said. *Noblesse oblige*, she thought, enjoying the adulation.

"Hey, what's the matter with this one?" one of the volunteers said. She held out an emerald. Some thing was wrong with one of the facets. It looked as if it was chipped, but when the young woman flicked it with her fingernail, it quivered.

All around her, the same thing was happening to all of the other gems. Gradually, they became sticky and started to melt. People drifted away from Mona's side, leaving the lumps of colored goo on the table. After a short time, there was nothing left but brightly colored puddles. Mona looked up at Jack and the state chairman.

"I'm afraid," Jack said, with regret, "this isn't going to earn you any election year goody accounts, lady."

The chairman walked away from the table and stalked back to his office. "Tell her to get out of here, Jack," he said. The door slammed behind him. Mona stood staring at the puddles of goop.

"If you're smart," Jack said, raising his shoulders apologetically, "you'll give as the reason for your concession that you're too busy keeping your business environmentally sound. People will buy that." He patted her on the shoulder. "Good luck, lady."

Mona tottered toward the door, wondering desperately if the first stone she had received would have turned to goo as well. If so, she was ruined, forever. She glanced back at party headquarters, already back to business as usual. No one paid attention to her. Unhappily, she slipped out of the door.

The guard at the Field Museum recognized Keith on sight. He was ready to pitch him out the door at once, until Professor Parker came barreling out of the office to meet his guests.

"Dr. Alfheim, how wonderful to see you!" The little professor's kind face was beaming. "I am so delighted to see you all. And who is this delightful child?"

"My sister, Dola," Holl said, at once. "We're in town to have a tour."

"And this youngster?" Parker asked. "A friend of yours?"

Tay started forward to protest that he was not a child, and that Dola was his daughter. Keith waved madly behind Parker's back to shut Tay up. Holl had to use a charm on him speedily that locked together his jaws so he couldn't talk.

Through gritted teeth Tay grumbled. "You didn't have to do that. I'll play along. I thought he was one of us."

"In the search for the truth, yes," Holl whispered to him as they followed the small professor into the heart of the museum, "but there's a divergence in our family trees a good deal farther back than between you and me."

"Yes, my tenure here has been very interesting," Parker said, talking rapidly to the Master, "very interesting indeed. A pity you didn't see my lecture, but I'll be happy to lend you the notes."

"I vould be fery grateful to haf them," the Master replied.

"What did you do to that guard?" Diane asked Keith as they trailed behind the Master and his friend. She noticed that the uniformed man was still behind them at a distance.

"Nothing," Keith said. His face was red to the ears.

As they made their way down through the main floor, the elves began to twitch uncomfortably because of the many magical presences in the museum, but were visibly discomfited when they got to the basement. Dola stuck her fingers in her ears and kept them there. Parker escorted them to his little cubbyhole and excused himself.

"I think my notes are in the secretary's desk. I will be right back."

"It's the charm on the left," Keith said, unnecessarily, as the Master and the other Little Folk crowded around the glass case to see. "What is it?"

"Most interesting," the Master said. "It is a charm for finding—a location beacon. It is designed as a toy for children, as you see. It may be sewn to the clothes, or carried in the hand like a doll. This one might haf been used as either, as you may see by the loop. It sends out a compelling signal to let you know where the child is, especially if the child is lost or too small to call out for help by itself. After many centuries, the signal has simply become louder and louder when no one answered."

"Oh," Keith said, and paused thoughtfully. "That would have shortened up our hunt for Dola by a whole lot. How come your kids don't have them?"

"Vhy?" the Master asked, rhetorically. "They haf not been able to go out of eye's distance in decades. This is the first time ve haf had room to range, when any could get lost."

"I'm making one for Asrai the moment we get home," Holl vowed. He noted the design, began to figure out the mechanics of the spell that made it work.

"And I one for Dola," Tay said. He smiled down at Dola.

"Interesting," the Master said, turning away from the case.

"Well, don't you want to get it out of there?" Keith asked in an undertone, worried. "Anyone who can hear it, *you* know...I'm sure I'm not the only one."

"No. You are surely not the only one. But all you haf to do is turn it off." Master laid hand over top of case, closed his eyes, concentrated. Gradually, the low, blood-chilling wail for attention died away and stopped. Keith could feel his ears uncurling. Holl and Tay similarly relaxed, and Dola took her fingers out of her ears.

"That's only the worst of the unheard noises," Holl said, epigrammatically. "We must get out of here."

"I do agree," the Master said. "The ambience of this place is becoming most painful. But I do not vish to cut short my fisit vith my friend."

Parker returned at that moment with a bundle of papers, which he handed to the Master. "Wonderful thing, the high-speed photocopy machine," he said, smiling. "Americans have so many marvelous machines. Here are copies of all my data from the dig. I'd appreciate your feedback, having seen the site. For example, read this..."

"Yes, indeed," the Master said, hastily. "Perhaps not now."

"Professor Parker," Keith interrupted. "You're a stranger in these parts, too. I'm taking Dr. Alfheim around on a tour of the city. You want to come along?"

"Well, bless me, I think I'm free this afternoon. Why not? I'd be delighted. I'd love to get out of here for a while."

"Moved and seconded," Holl said, with relief.

"Oh, Keith Doyle," Dola asked in a hushed whisper as they left the museum. He had to lean close to hear her, and she pulled his ear down to her mouth. "You promised to show me—you know—how to find the ghostly beings."

Keith exchanged glances with Diane and Holl. "Okay. I think I know just exactly where to look."

"You do?" Diane asked, skeptically.

"Sure I do," Keith said, cheerfully. "Come on." He gave one hand to Dola, and the other to Diane. The two of them skipped alongside him down the steps.

"...So the man goes all over Europe with his camera," Keith said, pantomiming taking pictures in every direction, "shooting hundreds of rolls of film." He stood in the corner of the observation deck on the 95th floor of the John Hancock Center, telling jokes out loud and translating them simultaneously into mental images for both halves of his appreciative audience. Inside were Holl, Tay, Diane, and Dola, watching with fascination as the other half of his listeners gathered outside the window. Dola pressed herself against the glass, exchanging winks and blinks with the friendly 'ghosts', no longer distorted by the pressures of heavy atmosphere. More and more of them gathered as his story progressed.

The Master, together with Professor Parker, sat talking together on chairs against inner building walls, discussing archaeology, and paying no attention to the entertainment.

"...The man takes pictures of everything he sees—everything! Children, scenery, interesting garbage cans, cats, you name it. He has to get a separate suitcase for all of his film. The customs agents ask him if he bought stock in a foreign branch of Kodak. When he gets home, his best friend calls him up and asks, so, did you have a good time?

"'I can't tell,' the man said.'" Keith visualized his tourist shrugging. "'The pictures haven't come back yet!'"

Dola laughed delightedly, and the sprites outside the window showed their approval by swooping to and fro in a complicated knotlike dance like happy Japanese kites.

Keith chuckled. "You're my kind of audience. Oh, and have you heard the one about the man who went door to door selling mud packs...."

"Keith Doyle," Holl said, tapping him in the right kidney, "your audience is growing beyond my ability to fend off the attentions of the crowd around us."

Keith looked up, aware for the first time how the crowd of air sprites had grown, and how numerous the Big Folk tourists were becoming. "Ooops, sorry," he said sheepishly. "That's the end of the show, folks. Hey, look, the balloon racers are getting closer."

"Which one's Frank's?" Diane asked. Keith pointed to the Skyship Iris, well back among the pack, but moving towards them in a frisky air current.

"Oh, it's so pretty!" Dola said.

The flock of sprites broke up, most of them flying up into the clouds, where they instantly blended in and disappeared. One came close to the window, winked at Dola, and fled out over the lake toward the balloons. She stared after it, starry-eyed.

"They're so nice," she said, turning her face upward to Tay. "Father, I wonder if we might build a tower on the farm so I can visit with them."

"We'll see what your mother says," Tay said, diplomatically, putting an arm across his daughter's shoulders.

The Master came up to join the group admiring the cluster of colorful balloons. Only a few of the sprites remained, including Keith's first friend, who hovered at eye level.

"The Professor had to leaf us. I am fery interested in our new friends here," the Master said, looking up at the sprites with interest. "I vould know more about them."

"Well, to me, the most important thing is you know you're not the only ones out there, I mean right here," Keith said, pointing this way and that. "One day, there ought to be a mass conclave of all the little folk in the world, so you can all get to know each other."

The air sprites responded to this idea with a mindnumbing display of creatures of all shapes and descriptions.

"You mean these all exist?" Keith said. "Yeah, if I can get them all interested, we could have one fabulous party."

"You organize it," the Master said, after a disbelieving stare at Keith, "and ve vill come."

"You bet," Keith said, dreamily. "Maybe we can even find the real *bodachs* of Jura." An idea struck him. "Say, Master, I wanted to ask. After seeing how the advertising business works, are you sure you don't want me to make up an ad campaign for Hollow Tree Industries? It'd be a prizewinner."

"No, thank you," the Master said, fixing him with a disapproving stare calculated to drive the idea right out of his mind. "After vhat I haf seen I belief ve vould much rather be a vord-of-mouth success."

Epilogue:

"I have this incredible compulsion to go shopping," Diane said, looking up at the great screen. "I don't know why."

Keith plastered innocent fingertips to his chest. "Don't look at me. Must be something in the air."

He smoothed the front of his rented tuxedo and looked around at the crowd. It was easy to tell who at the Clio Award banquet was in the business, and who were guests. The advertisers were paying no attention to the commercials being shown on the big screen over the dais, and the visitors couldn't keep their eyes off it. Too bad, when there were so many more interesting things to look at.

Diane, for example. She looked absolutely incredible in her drop-dead evening gown of black satin and lace, with a cluster of pink-tipped ivory roses clipped to the bosom. Beside her was Dorothy and her boyfriend, Jerome, who had medium brown skin, but startling green-hazel eyes that picked up lights from his date's metallic lamé gown that was green one way you looked at it, and pewter-black the other. Dorothy looked drop-dead gorgeous, too. She was celebrating getting the offer from PDQ. Her selection, she pointed out, was partly due to Doug Constance, suffering an attack of conscience, throwing his weight behind her.

"I'm happy for you," Keith said, raising his glass to her. "I really am."

"Even though you didn't get it?" Dorothy asked. "We were neck and neck there."

"It really doesn't matter to me," Keith promised. "It never did. And I'm planning to get my Master's degree, so I couldn't come to work right away anyhow."

"He means it," Diane said.

"If you ever come on the market, I may take you up on your application as a copywriter," Dorothy said. "No one at PDQ's as crazy as you. You hear from Sean?"

"Yup." Keith said. Dunbar Tyres had, as he feared, picked up and moved to a rival agency, but on their recommendation, the new agency had hired Sean on the strength of 'The Brain.' "It's too bad about the shift, but I'm glad he got credit."

"Okay," Meier said, "but you and Brendan get credit, too, because Goodling Tyres UK like The English Channel, so nothing's wasted. You'll be seeing the commercials over the winter. I'll call and tell him, but I'm not so sure he'll be glad to hear my voice."

"Where is he?" Diane asked.

"Oh, he went back to Daddy's stockbroker firm," Meier said, with a wink. "We didn't charge him for the extra billing for Gilbreth, although we could have. Accounting is working it out with her. Her account has been...er, temporarily downsized. She'll be on her feet again one day. Still, PDQ got the best of the deal." He leaned over and patted Dorothy's hand. "We got this talented young lady on our staff, and someday she's gonna knock 'em dead."

"Maybe you'll hire me next year, huh?" Keith asked, playfully.

"I may be forced into it," Paul said.

"Why?" Keith asked. "Because of working with Dorothy?"

Paul shook his head, his usual wry smile on his face. "No, but you never know."

There were network cameras set up all over the room, gathering what Paul described as 'pick-up shots.' Keith concentrated on eating neatly to avoid looking like a slob when the camera panned their table. The technicians running the equipment became more energetic, and started passing hand signals to each other.

"It's starting," Paul said, turning around in his chair.

A tall man with gleaming white teeth stood up behind the podium and raised his hand. Everyone stopped talking to listen to him. He made a short speech and went straight to the nominations. Another man in evening wear handed award after award to a gowned woman, who passed them to the happy recipients. Speeches of thanks were short and frequently witty. Keith enjoyed the spectacle.

"...Winner of the honorable mention, Judge Yeast, 'All Rise', Perkins Delaney Queen," the master of ceremonies said. Bob, the account executive, accepted the statuette as the big screen showed the Judge Yeast commercial.

"I'm proud of the two of you," Paul said, leaning over the table. "First crack out of the box," he said when Bob sat down, "and you got an honorable mention. You can hope for better in the future."

"I hope so," Keith said.

"Count on it," said Paul.

The account executive was effusive. "This young lady," he said, framing Dorothy with his hands, "This brilliant young woman had the vision. The client was crazy about it, and you can always tell when a team really loves their product." Dorothy and Keith exchanged glowing glances. Diane squeezed Keith's arm, sharing their triumph.

"I hope that means a raise, Bob," Dorothy said, slyly.

"Praise is free," Paul said, shaking his head. "You gotta do better than an honorable mention for a raise."

The M.C. went on with his presentations. Paul stopped the conversation at the table with a wave of his hand as the America's Shoe commercial featuring Dola appeared over the M.C.'s head.

Keith admired the way the production team had taken his idea and run with it. In the aired commercial, Dola sat in a field of tall grass with a wreath of flowers on her head until the music began. The whole thing had been shot with a soft focus filter. She sprang up and ran lightly down a path of short-cropped grass, to join an animated circle of dancers on a fairy mound. The camera followed the motions of her feet, then cut to the delight on her face.

"What a cute little girl she was," Dorothy whispered. "You were right. She was absolutely perfect for the campaign. Relative of yours?"

"Sort of a cousin," Keith whispered back. "She loved acting. I think we've created a monster."

Dorothy shook her head. "She's going to break hearts when she grows up, you know."

He exchanged wry glances with Diane. "She nearly broke mine already."

Diane leaned over to whisper to him. "I forgot to tell you, Holl says the water is pure again."

"Great!" Keith whispered back.

"Shh!" Paul hissed.

The announcer's voice interrupted him. "And the award goes to America's Shoe, Fairy Footwear, Paul Meier, Scott Milliard, Dorothy Scott, and Keith Doyle."

"Go on, go get it," Keith urged Paul.

"Nope, you do it," Paul said, the half smile becoming a full grin. "You deserve it. Here's to this one and many more." He raised his glass.

"Huh?" Keith said.

"Accepting this award," the M.C. said, "will be Keith Doyle."

Keith looked at Paul, who winked. "You knew about it."

"I set it up! Everything's on purpose in advertising, kid. I told you. Now, go. Enjoy."

Flushed, Keith made his way to the podium, shook hands with the M.C. and the award presenter, and accepted the small statuette. He leaned over the mike and cleared his throat. The room became silent. Diane held up her hands and blew him a kiss.

Keith smiled at the audience and looked into the lens of the television camera. I sure hope this is being televised downstate, he thought.

"I don't have a prepared speech, so I'd just like to thank my team, Paul Meier, Scott Milliard, Dorothy Scott, Sean Lopez…and," his eyes twinkled mischievously, "all the Little People who made this possible. Thank you."

Author Biography

Jody Lynn Nye lists her main career activity as "spoiling cats." She lives northwest of Chicago with two of the above and her husband, author, packager and game designer Bill Fawcett. Nye was born in Chicago, and except for brief forays to summer camp and college has always lived in the area. She was graduated from Maine Township High School East and Loyola University of Chicago, where she majored in Communications and English, and was an active member of the theater groups, the student radio stations, and the speech team (original comedy and oratorical declamation). She has three younger brothers: a pediatric neurologist, an electronics trouble-shooter, and a CPA. Her mother is a nurse and an artist, and her father owns his own accounting firm.

Before breaking away to write full time, Jody worked at a variety of jobs: file clerk, book-keeper at a small publishing house, freelance journalist and photographer, accounting assistant, and costume maker.

From 1981 to 1985, she was on the technical operations staff of a local Chicago television station, WFBN (WGBO), serving the last year as Technical Operations Manager. During her time at WFBN, she was part of the engineering team that built the station, acted as Technical Director during live sports broadcasts, and worked to produce in-house spots and public service announcements. She also wrote mystery game materials free-lance for Mayfair Games.

Since 1985 she has published 20 books and over 50 short stories. Among the novels Jody has written are her epic fantasy series, *The Dreamland*, beginning with *Waking In Dreamland*, four contemporary humorous fantasies, *Mythology 101, Mythology Abroad, Higher Mythology, The Magic Touch*, and two science fiction novels, *Taylor's Ark* and *Medicine Show*. Jody also wrote

The Dragonlover's Guide to Pern, a non-fiction-style guide to the world of internationally best-selling author Anne McCaffrey's popular world. She has also collaborated with Anne McCaffrey on four science fiction novels, *The Death of Sleep, Crisis On Doona, Treaty At Doona* and *The Ship Who Won*. She also wrote a solo sequel to *The Ship Who Won* entitled *The Ship Errant*. Jody co-authored the *Visual Guide to Xanth* with best-selling fantasy author Piers Anthony, and edited an anthology of humorous stories about mothers in science fiction, fantasy, myth and legend, entitled *Don't Forget Your Spacesuit, Dear!*, "a science fiction book you can actually give to your mom."

Her newest book is *The Grand Tour* (August 2000), third in the Dreamland series. Also in the works, a contemporary fantasy co-authored with Robert Lynn Asprin, *License Invoked*, and a fourth in the Mythology series, *Advanced Mythology*.

Over the last fifteen years, Jody has taught in numerous writing workshops and participated on hundreds of panels covering the subjects of writing and being published at science-fiction conventions. She has also spoken in schools and libraries around the north and northwest suburbs.

When not occupied in petting cats or writing fiction, Jody reads, travels, does calligraphy, bakes, or gardens.

Jody Lynn Nye
A bibliography of her work as of August 2000

Books:
The Dragonlover's Guide to Pern, Del Rey (1989; trade paper 1992; 2nd ed. 1996)
Visual Guide to Xanth (co-authored w/Piers Anthony), Avon (1989)
Mythology 101, Warner Books (1990)
The Death of Sleep (co-authored w/Anne McCaffrey), Baen (1990)
Mythology Abroad, Warner Books (1991)
Crisis on Doona (co-authored w/Anne McCaffrey), Ace Books (1992)
Higher Mythology, Warner Books (1993)
Taylor's Ark, Ace Books (1993)
The Ship Who Won (co-authored with Anne McCaffrey), Baen Books (1994)
Medicine Show (Taylor's Ark II), Ace Books (1994)
Treaty at Doona (co-authored w/Anne McCaffrey), Ace Books (1994)
The Magic Touch, Warner Books (June 1996)
Don't Forget Your Spacesuit, Dear; editor, Baen Books (July 1996)
The Ship Errant (The Ship Who Won II), Baen Books (December 1996)
Waking in Dreamland (Dreamland I), Baen Books (May 1998)
School of Light (Dreamland II), Baen Books (June 1999)
The Grand Tour (Dreamland III), Baen Books (Aug 2000)
Applied Mythology (Omnibus of books 1,2,3), Meisha Merlin Pub., Inc (Aug 2000)

Short stories in anthologies:
The Fleet, "Bolthole," Ace Books (1988)
The Fleet II: Counterattack, "Lab Rats," Ace Books (1988)
The Fleet III: Breakthrough, "Crossing the Line," Ace Books (1989)
The Fleet IV: Sworn Allies, "Full Circle," Ace Books (1990)
The Fleet V: Total War "Change Partners and Dance," Ace Books (1990)
The Fleet VI: Crisis, "The Mosquito," Ace Books (1991)
The War Years I: Far Stars War, "Volunteers," NAL (1990)
The War Years II: Siege of Arista, "Unreality," NAL (1991)
The War Years III: Jupiter War, "Gold-digging," NAL (1991)
The Crafters, "The Seeing Stone," Ace Books (1991)
The Crafters II: Blessings & Curses, "Miss Crafter's School For Girls," Ace (1992)
Halflings, Hobbits, Wee Folk and Warrows; "Moon Shadows," Warner Books (1991)
Alternate Presidents, "The Father of His Country," TOR Books (1992)

Space Cats, "Well Worth the Money," Baen Books (1992)

Battlestation, "Star Light," Ace Books (1992)

Battlestation II, "Shooting Star," Ace Books (1993)

The Gods of War, "Order in Heaven," Baen Books (1992)

More Whatdunits, "Way Out" (co-authored with Bill Fawcett), TOR Books (1993)

Quest to Riverworld, "If the King Like Not the Comedy," Warner Books (1993)

Alien Pregnant By Elvis!, "Psychic Bats 1000 for Accuracy," DAW Books (1994)

Dragon's Eye, "The Stuff of Legends," Baen Books (1994)

Deals With The Devil, "The Party of the First Part," DAW Books (1994)

Elric, Tales of the White Wolf, "The White Child," White Wolf (1994)

Superheroes, "Theme Music Man," Ace/Berkley (1995)

Excalibur, "Sword Practice", Warner Aspect (1995)

Chicks in Chainmail, "The Growling", Baen Books (Sept 1995)

The Day The Magic Stopped, "Flicker", Baen Books (Oct 1995)

Fantastic Alice, "Muchness", Ace Books (December 1995)

Dante's Disciples, "The Bridge on the River Styx", White Wolf (1996)

Lammas Night, "Sunflower", Baen Books (February 1996)

Otherwere, "What? And Give Up Show Business?", Ace Books (1996)

Future Net, "Souvenirs and Photographs", DAW Books (1996)

Many Faces of Fantasy (WFC Book), "Sidhe Who Must Be Obeyed", (10/1996)

Space Opera, "Calling Them Home", DAW Books (1996)

Elf Fantastic, "The Dancing Ring", DAW Books (1997)

First Contact, "Take Me to Your Leader", DAW Books (1997)

Acorna, "Pony Girl", BIG Entertainment (1997)

Zodiac Fantastic, "The Billion-Year Boys' Club", DAW Books (1997)

Wizard Fantastic, "Bird Bones", DAW Books (1997)

Urban Nightmares, "The Bicycle Messenger From Hell", Baen Books (1997)

Did You Say 'Chicks'?, "The Old Fire", Baen Books (1998)

Alternate Generals, "Queen of the Amazons", Baen Books (1998)

The Quintessential World of Darkness, "The Muse", Harper Collins (1998)

Mob Magic, "Power Corrupts", DAW Books (1998)

Tails From the Pet Shop, "A Cat's Chance", 11th Hour Productions (1999)

Twice Upon a Time, "Spinning A Yarn", DAW Books (1999)

Chicks and Chained Males, "Don't Break the Chain!", Baen Books (1999)

Stardates, "The Stars in Their Courses", Dreams-Unlimited.com (Dec 1999)

Flights of Fantasy, "Eagle's Eye", DAW Books (Jan 2000)

Perchance to Dream, "The Piper", DAW Books (2000)

Daughter of Dangerous Dames, "Riddle of the Sphinx", 11th Hour (May 2000)

Such a Pretty Face, "Casting Against Type", Meisha Merlin Publ. (June 2000)

Game materials:
Ellery Queen Mystery Magazine Game, Mayfair Games (1986)
Nick Velvet Casebook (EQMM Game), Mayfair Games (1987)
Dragonharper (Crossroads game/book), TOR Books (1987)
Encyclopedia of Xanth (Crossroads game/book), TOR Books (1987)
Dragonfire (Crossroads game/book), TOR Books (1988)
Ghost of a Chance (Crossroads game/book), TOR Books (1988)
Shattered Light computer game (mystery quests), Simon & Schuster (1999)

Teleplays:
Dinosaucers (animated TV series) "Toy-ranosaurus Store Wars" script, DIC

Articles:
"Dungeon Etiquette" article, The Dragon #130, TSR (1988)
It Seemed Like a Good Idea at the Time, various articles, Avon Books (2000)

Works still to be published:
100 Crafty Little Cat Crimes, "Land Rush", Barnes & Noble (2000)
Dracula's London, "Everything to Order", Ace Books (2000)
Warrior Fantastic, "Conscript", DAW Books (2000)
Murder Most Romantic, "Night Hawks", Cumberland House (2000)
Guardian Angels, "Desperation Gulch", Cumberland House (2000)
Oceans of Space, "Pyrats", DAW Books (2001)
Xena, Warrior Princess, "As Fate Would Have It"
License Invoked (co-authored with Robert L. Asprin), Baen Books (2001)
Advanced Mythology (Mythology IV), Meisha Merlin Pub., Inc. (Aug 2001)
The Lady and The Tiger (Taylor's Ark III), Ace Books (2002)

Don Maitz

The work of Don Maitz is quite literally fantastic. For some twenty years, he has created paintings containing elements of fantasy, exaggerated fact, and imaginative fiction. His work began appearing from New York City based book publishers and continues to evolve in that market. He has received wide exposure as the original artist of the Captain Morgan Spiced Rum pirate character that appears on bottles, billboards, and magazines through national advertising campaigns. Joseph Seagrams & Sons, National Geographic Society, Kodak, Bell Telephone, Bantam Doubleday Dell, Warner Books, Ballantine Del Rey, Penguin USA, and Harper Collins Publishers are some of his clients. His work has been produced for the limited edition print market with images released by Mill Pond Press, and a poster with the Greenwich Workshop.

He has illustrated books and stories by such authors as; Isaac Asimov, Ray Bradbury, C. J. Cherryh, L. Sprague De Camp, Raymond Feist, Eric Lustbader, Stephen King, his wife, author/artist Janny Wurts, and Roger Zelazny.

His works are internationally recognized and acclaimed. He has twice been presented the world science fiction's premier accolade, the Hugo award in the Best Artist category. Also, a special Hugo award for Best Artwork in 1989. He has earned a Howard award from the World Fantasy Convention, a Silver Medal of Excellence and Certificate of Merit from the Society of Illustrators in New York City where his work has been included in four of their prestigious annual exhibitions. He has received ten Chesley awards from his peers in the Association of Science Fiction and Fantasy Artists. His paintings have been featured in exhibitions at NASA's 25th Anniversary presentation in Cleveland, Ohio, the New Britain Museum of American Art, at the Park Avenue Atrium, and the Hayden Planetarium in New York City. They were also featured at two separate shows at the Delaware and the Canton Art Museums, the Discovery Museum in Bridgeport, CT, and in the Orlando Science Center, Florida. His works are included in the permanent collections of the Delaware Art Museum and the New Britain Museum of American Art.

Born in Bristol, Connecticut, Don grew up in the adjacent town of Plainville where he proceeded through the school system. Existing in the mundane environment this town suggests, an active imagination was a Godsend. Drawing became an adventurous escape. School art classes, an art correspondence course, and evening figure drawing classes at the University of Hartford led to enrollment at the Paier School of Art from 1971-75. He graduated top of the class, receiving instruction from Ken Davies—one of America's foremost still life and trompe l'oeil painters, Rudolf Zallinger—Pulitzer prize winning muralist and Time Life Books illustrator, Leonard E. Fisher—Pulitzer prize winning fine artist, book illustrator and author, and Deane Keller—portrait and figure painter affiliated with Yale University. These are just a few of the talented and actively working professors that provided instruction. Four of his professors authored and published art instruction books.

Don Maitz's work has enhanced various published formats including: books, magazines, cards, a record album, posters, limited edition prints, puzzles, and computer screen saver programs. Two art books collections of his color paintings have been published. They are *First Maitz* and *Dreamquests*, both are now sold out. He illustrated a signed, limited edition of Stephen King's novel, *Desperation*. Best selling screensaver software entitled *Magical Encounters* and *Magical Encounters II* compile a variety of his work with the works of his talented wife Janny Wurts.

Don Maitz spent the 1985 school year as guest instructor of illustration, drawing, and multi-media at the Ringling School of Art and Design in Florida. Some time later, he married Janny Wurts and together they moved their combined studio and residence to Florida.

Come check out our web site for details on these Meisha Merlin authors!

Kevin J. Anderson
Robin Wayne Bailey
Edo van Belkom
Janet Berliner
Storm Constantine
Diane Duane
Sylvia Engdahl
Jim Grimsley
George Guthridge
Keith Hartman
Beth Hilgartner
P. C. Hodgell
Tanya Huff
Janet Kagan
Caitlin R. Kiernan

Lee Killough
George R. R. Martin
Lee Martindale
Jack McDevitt
Sharon Lee & Steve Miller
James A. Moore
Adam Niswander
Andre Norton
Jody Lynn Nye
Selina Rosen
Kristine Kathryn Rusch
Michael Scott
S. P. Somtow
Allen Steele
Mark Tiedeman
Freda Warrington

http://www.MeishaMerlin.com